season of lies + crimes of truth

# truth
# and
# lies

based on

New York Times & USA Today Bestselling Author

# PEPPER WINTERS

crown of lies + throne of truth

# truth
# and
# lies

*boxed set*

*New York Times* & *USA Today* Bestselling Author

# PEPPER WINTERS

# crown of lies

**Truth & Lies Boxed Set Edition**
**Includes: Crown of Lies**
**Throne of Truth**
**Copyright © 2017-2018 Pepper Winters**
**Published by Pepper Winters**

**Published:** Pepper Winters 2017: **pepperwinters@gmail.com**
**Cover Design:** by Cover it! Designs
**Editing by**: Editing-4-Indies (Jenny Sims)

# Dedication

This book is dedicated to all those eagle-eye readers who will most likely notice I'm an English-born writer who uses words with pesky S's (tantalise), double L's (travelled), and the occasional extra U (favourite). I've done my best (and enlisted help) to catch the English in this American book, but to any New Yorkers who spy a few…all I can say is, I tried. I now have a love-hate relationship with Z's, learned a boot is a trunk and a lounge is a living room, and just how magical one language can be with two correct ways of writing.

Happy reading!

# Prologue

*IN EVERY GIRL'S life, there is betrayal.*

*Betrayal from loved ones, unknown ones, and from the ones we choose to make our own. However, where there's deceit, there's trust, too. And sometimes, those two things camouflage themselves to mimic the other.*

*That was what he did.*

*The man who first stole my body and then stole my heart was the ultimate magician with lies.*

*I think a part of me always knew what he kept hidden. I always suspected and maybe that was why I fell for him despite his deceit.*

*But then his fibs fell apart.*

*And it was up to me to decide if I wanted to give him*
*trust*
*or*
*betrayal.*

# Chapter One

"YOU CAN'T BRING your daughter to work on a weekend, Joe."

"Says who?"

Steve crossed his arms, doing his best to come across as strict but failing. "Says you."

I hugged my frilly dress-covered chest, my head bouncing like a volley-ball between Dad and the man who helped run his company. My back tensed, waiting for their voices to climb and anger to emerge, but their elderly faces remained happy.

Ever since Mom died four years ago, I'd become susceptible to outbursts of emotion. I hated when Dad raised his voice or someone had a fight in public.

Dad looped his arm around my tiny shoulders, hugging my body to his. "When did I say I couldn't bring my darling daughter to work on a Saturday, Steve?"

Steve winked at me, his dark blond hair trim with his mustache bushy. "When you wrote the rule book for your company, *Joe*. There was fine print."

I knew they were joking—playing a game I couldn't figure out. I'd been to the office every day of the week, including Saturdays and Sundays. But because they expected me to buy into their little drama, I did.

I allowed myself to act younger than I felt, even though I was still a child and shouldn't grasp age and maturity just yet.

Mom's death and my induction into the workforce from a tender age had given me two ideals to follow: adulthood and adolescence. A lot of the time, I was treated and responded like an adult, but today, I didn't mind acting younger because I *wanted* to be younger for a change.

I wanted to be allowed to cry because today had become a massive disappointment and if I was a kid, I could let my hurt show. If I was an adult, I had to suck it up and pretend I was fine with it.

My sadness originated from something so stupid. I shouldn't care—especially seeing as I knew better. But Dad had let me down on a silly birthday tradition, and I didn't know how to tell him I was sad without coming across as a pouting kid who didn't value everything she already had.

"Rule book?" I piped up, glancing at Dad. "You wrote a rule book like school has? Is it as stuffy and strict on silly things like sock length and uniform?" I wrinkled my nose at Steve's crumpled shirt and creased trousers. "If you did, how come you're not dressed the same?"

Dad wore pressed slacks, gray vest, and a blazer with navy piping on the sleeves. Every cuff and pleat were military in perfection.

He looked nothing like the other suited men in his high-rise building, especially Steve in his shirt-wrinkled glory.

But that wasn't new.

Dad had been immaculate every day of his life since I could remember. Even in the photos of him holding me as a new-born at the hospital, he'd been in a three-piece suit with a chrysanthemum (Mom's favorite flower) in the lapel.

Steve chuckled. "Your school has a uniform, Elle?"

He knew this. He'd seen me here after school in my despised splendor.

I nodded. "I hate it. It's scratchy and gross."

"But you look so adorable in it, Bell Button." Dad hugged me closer. Secretly, I loved his cuddles (especially because we only had each other now) but outwardly, I had a twelve-year-old reputation to maintain.

Still playing their game, I sing-songed, "Daa-ad. You said you wouldn't use that name."

He cringed dramatically. "Whoops. I forgot." He tapped his temple. "I'm an old man, Elle. I can't remember everything."

I nudged him with my shoulder. "Just like you forgot you wrote a rule book saying no daughters allowed on weekends."

"Exactly." He beamed.

"And how you forgot my birthday?"

*Whoops.*

I didn't mean to say that, but I'd bottled it up all morning. I did my best to joke, but my hurt refused to hide. He'd never forgotten before. He'd always woken me up with a silly gift and then done whatever I wanted for the afternoon.

Not the case today.

I'd turned twelve, and there'd been no cake or candles—not even a birthday hug.

Instead, he'd cooked me toast, told me to dress smart, then dragged me to work with him. He took me to the office often, but I'd hoped today would've been a trip to Central Park together, or at the very least, lunch at my favorite Thai restaurant.

*Is fun no longer allowed?*

Now I was older, did I have to earn an income like he'd kept telling me? That it was time to put the meager few years at school into practice?

*I thought he was joking.*

Then again, he was joking with this whole role-play. My heart skipped, doing its best to understand what was going on.

Steve gasped. "You forgot your own daughter's birthday?" He tutted, shaking his head. "Shame on you, Joe."

"Watch it. I can still fire you." Dad's face contorted as he struggled not to smile. He gave up, allowing a broad grin to spread. "That's the reason why I broke the rules and brought my daughter to work on Saturday."

I froze, unable to stop the happiness fizzing into being.

*Wait...does that mean he didn't forget?*

"What...to make her slave away?" Steve's eyes rounded. "Could've waited until she was thirteen, at least." He winked at me. "Let her see the world before shackling her to this place."

"She'll have plenty of time for that." He hugged me close, marching forward, pulling me with him. "Come along, Bell Button."

I rolled my eyes. "Again with the Bell Button."

"Deal with it." He chuckled, his graying hair catching the neon lights as we strolled down the wide hallway. The view of downtown Manhattan sparkled in the windows. Sitting regal on the forty-seventh floor, the offices of the CEO and top managers of Belle Elle never failed to impress and terrify me.

Dad owned this building along with a few others. He was loaded, according to the girls' gossip at school. However, only I knew how much time and energy he put into his company and was very proud of him. But also scared what he would expect from me now I was older.

For years, things had been changing. My childhood had ended two months after Mom died, revealing how different both our lives would be from then on. No more fairy-tale stories or bedtime read alongs.

No more *Aladdin* or *Beauty and the Beast*.

No more make-believe.

Instead, Dad read me ledgers and showed me catalogs of new season apparel for the company. He gave me homework on how to navigate our website and taught me how to decide if buying a dress at two dollars was good sense if we sold it for nineteen. To work out rent, taxes, employee salaries, and other overheads to see if that dress would make any profit (turned out it was only twenty cents after expenses and too low to make a sustainable profit).

I'd lived and breathed this place since I was so young. And now, it seemed it even controlled my birthday.

Dad stopped at his office and held the entry wide for me to scoot through. I continued to his desk while he closed the door. I loved his desk. It reminded me of an ancient tree that'd been outside our brownstone for years until it was cut down.

Throwing myself into his comfy leather chair, I spun around, kicking his drawers to increase my inertia on the second spin.

"Elle." Dad blurred as I spun again. He wasn't mad. His face split into a smile as he chuckled. "You'll make yourself sick."

I planted my hands on his desk, coming to an abrupt stop. "No, I won't. Those ballet lessons helped with my balance, remember?"

He nodded. "I do. You were a lovely swan in the Swan Princess."

I smiled, forgiving him for forgetting my birthday because really, spending time with him was all I needed. Here or there, it didn't matter as long as he and I were a we. "You need me to try some of the kid's clothes today?" I reclined in his chair. "Help design the window display from a girl's point of view?" I'd learned how to do all that, and I was good.

The company—Belle Elle—had been in my father's lineage for longer than I could comprehend. One of my great, great, too many great grandfathers had called his little shop Belle Elle after his wife, Elizabeth Eleanor, whose nickname was Belle Elle. I knew that because multiple case studies on my ancestry and newspaper articles existed. It was yet another element of my homework: to learn as much about our legacy as I could because in this world—where the US didn't have a royal family—we were classified in some circles as blue bloods.

Long standing citizens of an empire that'd been here since

colonization. Slowly growing bigger and delivering more products from basic coats and hats for men and parasols and shawls for women, to full wardrobes, housewares, entertainment, and jewelry for any age.

Belle Elle was the largest retail chain in the US and Canada, and someday, it would be mine.

To a twelve-year-old girl who had fun playing dress-up with child-size mannequins once the customers had been kicked out, helped staff arrange new window displays, and could take costume jewelry home occasionally because her dad could write off a necklace or two, I was excited at the thought of this being mine. But to the woman slowly evolving—the one groomed on an hourly basis for such a future—was afraid.

Would I have what it took to control such a place?

Was it what I wanted to do with my life?

"I didn't forget your birthday." Dad linked his hands in front of his vest. "But you already knew that because you're my daughter and the brightest girl in the world."

I smiled, dropping my head in embarrassment. His praise never failed to warm and comfort me. I wouldn't tell him I'd worried to begin with.

*I truly thought you forgot.*

He continued, "Today is a very special day and not just because you were born." He plucked a piece of lint off his blazer, looking every inch a powerful CEO rather than the loving father I knew.

No matter where we were going, he always wore a suit. He made me adhere to the same strict wardrobe of pressed blouses, dresses, and smart trousers. I didn't, nor had I ever, owned a pair of jeans.

Perhaps today that would be my present.

I sat quietly, politely, waiting for him to continue.

"I brought you to work to give you two presents."

*Phew, he truly didn't forget.*

I tried to hide my eagerness. I knew how to camouflage my true feelings. I might be a child, but I was born an heiress and had been taught to act unaffected in every situation—good or bad.

"Look to your right."

I obeyed, reaching out to touch the black binder that always rested there. Dad would bring it home with important documents inside then take it back to the office with yet more vital paperwork. I was never allowed to touch it unless he was around—and only then to bring it to him.

I hesitated as my fingers ghosted over the soft leather.

He smiled. "Go on, you can open it."

I pulled it toward me and cracked it wide. There, like all the other times, were white, crisp pages scarred with multiple black lines of adult jargon.

"What does it say at the top?" He popped his middle blazer button and perched on the side of the desk. His long frame towered over me but not in a bad way; more like a willow tree where I liked to curl up and nap in Central Park on the rare days Dad did nothing.

"Last Will and Testament of Joseph Mark Charlston." My eyes raced to his. "Dad…you're not—"

He reached out and patted my hand. "No, Bell Button. Not yet. But one can never be too careful. Up until last week, my Will and Testament left the running of our family's company to Steve until you came of age. However, I never felt comfortable bequeathing such responsibility to someone outside the Charlston family."

I gnawed on my lip. "What do you mean?"

He pulled a pen from the small gold holder on his desk. "It means I've had it revised. I have no plans to leave this world early, so don't worry about that. And you, my dear, are beyond intelligent for your age, so I know you'll take all of this in your stride. Your education about our processes, factories, and employee structure will be accelerated, and when you're ready, you'll become CEO, and I'll step down."

My mouth fell open. That sounded hard. When would I have time to go to school and make friends other than the staff in the makeup department where I hung out when he worked late?

But how could I say no? I was all he had. He was all I had. We had to stick together.

My heart lurched, needing confirmation he wasn't going to leave me, despite his assurances. "You're not dying, though?"

He shook his head. "Never, if I had my way. This isn't meant to scare you, Elle, but to show you how proud I am of you. I won't deny that it will be so rewarding to hand over this legacy sooner rather than later, knowing with all my heart you will take it to even greater heights than I ever could." He passed me the pen. "Initial each page and sign."

I'd signed enough contracts even at my young age to know how to do it. Stocks that he'd put in my name; a house he'd purchased in some state I'd never heard of—even a limited edition painting that came from an auction house in England.

Bending over the paperwork, I curled my fingers tight around the pen, ignoring the sudden shakes. This was no different from all those other documents, yet it was so much more. This was my life. This was more than growing up and celebrating a birthday. This was every day, every moment, every final say that would manipulate me until I was Dad's age. I didn't have the luxury of figuring out if I wanted to be a doctor or an astronomer. I'd never go to the Olympics as a swimmer (even though my instructor said I was more rock than dolphin). I'd never be anything more than Noelle Charlston, heiress of Belle Elle.

My heart beat with a strange squeeze as I placed the pen on the paper.

"Oh, wait a sec." Dad pressed the intercom to connect him to his receptionist. "Margaret, can you come in, please?"

Immediately, a pretty, middle-aged redhead entered and came forward. Weekends were no different from weekdays in this company. "Yes, Mr. Charlston?"

"I need you to act as a witness."

"Sure." She smiled at me but didn't say anything as I flipped through the seventeen pages and initialed each, then took a deep breath and signed my name. The moment I'd finished, Dad grinned and spun the deed to Margaret. "Your turn. Sign in the witness box, please."

I passed her the pen.

She took it. "Thank you, Elle."

My nickname (not Bell Button—which remained a mystery on how it came about. Dad said it was something to do with how much I loved buttons when I was little, and bell rhymed with Elle) reminded me how I'd been named in a roundabout way for the first wife of our company. The woman who'd created an empire beside her husband until he'd died of pneumonia, and she ruled on her own for forty more years. Elizabeth Eleanor—the original Belle Elle.

Scrawling her signature, Margaret passed the contract back to my father.

He signed in the last box with utmost concentration and an air of relief.

"Is that all, Mr. Charlston?" Margaret asked.

"Yes, thank you." Dad nodded.

She gave me a small wave, before retreating to her adjoining office, leaving Dad and me alone once again.

He looked up from signing, his older eyes meeting mine. His face fell. "What is it? What's wrong?"

I shrugged, doing my best to seem carefree and not think about how big of a throne I had to fill. "Nothing's wrong."

He frowned. "You look...afraid."

*I am.*

*I'm afraid of a world where you're gone, and I'm in charge.*

*I'm afraid of not being the daughter you think I am.*

But he could never know that. This was my duty. My birthright. No matter my age or experience, I knew enough to know my existence was always destined for Belle Elle.

I smiled. "I'm not. This is just my face."

He chuckled. "All right, 'just your face.' Seeing as giving you our legacy for your birthday—ensuring you'll forever have wealth and stability—isn't a present to get excited about, look under my desk."

Happy butterflies replaced the fearful moths in my belly. "You mean...there's more?"

His eyes twinkled with fatherly love. "Of course, there's more. Now look."

I scooted the chair back and glanced between my dangling legs. Tucked against the back was a box tied with a big purple and silver ribbon.

The fear of responsibility and the weird obligation of having my life already mapped out for me vanished. I bounced in the chair. "You got me a present!"

He bent over and kissed the top of my head. "You're my entire world, Elle. I'd never forget the day you came into my life. And I would never dream of making you sign stuffy documents without giving you something fun for your birthday."

"Thank you so much!" I beamed, impatience to open my present stampeding through me.

"You don't know what it is yet."

"I don't care. I love it already." My eyes latched onto the box, desperate to see what it was.

He took pity on me. "Go on, open it."

I didn't need a second invitation.

Plopping off the chair, I crawled on all fours beneath his huge desk and tore eagerly at the ribbon. It fell away, pooling on the carpet. Cracking the lid, I peered inside.

The gloom beneath the desk made it hard to see, but then a

tiny gray face appeared.

"Oh!" Full body shakes quaked through me as excitement and adoration exploded. "Oh! *Oh!*" I reached into the box and pulled out the cutest ball of fluff I'd ever seen. Falling onto my butt, I cuddled the kitten close. "You got me a cat?"

Dad appeared, pushing his chair away and ducking to my level. "I did."

"But you said I couldn't have any pets. That we were too busy."

"Well, I changed my mind." He turned serious. "I know the responsibility I'm putting on you, Elle. I know all of this is hard to figure out when you're barely starting life. And I'm sorry you don't have the freedom some of your friends do. I've been strict with you, but you're such a good girl. I thought I'd better give you something you actually wanted for a change."

I cuddled the kitten harder. It didn't squirm away or try to swat me like the cat in the pet store did when I snuck in on my own one day while Dad was distracted. This one purred and nudged its head beneath my chin.

Tears sprung to my eyes. Love billowed and overflowed. Somehow, I loved this little bundle as much as I loved my dad, and we'd only just met.

Gratefulness quickly overshadowed the love, and I placed the kitten on its feet, crawled as fast as I could toward Dad, and barreled into his arms.

"Thank you." I kissed his rough cheek. "Thank you!"

He laughed. Wrapping me in a tight embrace, he smelled so comfortingly of lavender soap. The same soap Mom used to make and stank up the house with while cooking a new batch.

"Thank you so much. I love him."

The kitten padded toward us and mountain climbed onto our joint lap.

Dad shook his head. "It's a girl. She's twelve weeks old just like you're twelve years old." He unwound his arms as I plucked the little kitten and buried my face in her sweet smelling gray fur.

"What are you going to call her?"

I frowned, taking the question seriously. "Silver?"

"Silver?"

I kissed her head. "Her fur looks like silver."

Dad chuckled. "Well, it's a perfect name."

"No, wait. Sage."

"Sage?"

"I want to call her Sage."

He didn't need to know I remembered most of the herbs and aromatherapy oils Mom used to make lotions and soaps. Sage was the last herb she'd given me a lesson on, and the leaves had a silver fuzz over them. Whenever I thought of that day, Mom felt closer and not so far away in Heaven.

I nodded firmly with my decision. "Yes, her name is Sage."

He gathered me close again, kissing the top of my head. "Whatever you decide, I hope she looks after you, like you'll look after her."

I rubbed my nose against the kitten's cold, wet one, shivering against the weird sensation. "She will. She's going to come to work with me every day." I hunched, cradling my new best-friend. "Is that okay? Can she come to work with me?"

Dad's face fell again. What he said was true. He was strict with me, but he was strict with himself, too. He missed Mom just as much as I did. Did he think I wouldn't love him as much now I had a pet?

I reached up and touched his sandpaper cheek. "I love you."

Light returned to his gray eyes. He hugged me tight on his lap, our little trio squishing into one entity for a second. "I love you, too, Elle. And you don't have to ask if you can bring Sage to work. She's yours. As long as she's not on the shop floor, you can take her to the offices and do whatever you want."

I sighed in happiness as Sage navigated the cliff-top created by our legs. "You're the best dad ever."

His smile faded, the joy of the moment lost as he shook his head. "I'm not, Elle. I know I can never replace your mother and I know I'm asking so much of you to pick up the mantle of this company so young, but I love you more than anything, and I'm so grateful to have you in my life."

His words were heavy for a twelve-year-old. And they remained heavy even years later.

That birthday was ingrained into my memories for two big reasons.

One, I would never be lonely again thanks to Sage being in my world.

And two, Dad knew what he was sentencing me to and did it anyway.

I thought Belle Elle already owned me.

I was wrong.

# Chapter Two

<u>**SEVEN YEARS LATER**</u>

WHO KNEW TURNING nineteen would be such a sad day?

I sniffed back a stupid tear as I inputted end-of-the-month financial figures into the spread-sheet to prepare for the M.M.M.—also known as the Monday Morning Meeting.

I'd been at the office since seven thirty—just as I had every morning since I left high school at sixteen. I'd left because I'd learned all the generic life hacks the teachers had in their arsenals and didn't have the time, or the need, to go to university before my birthright gobbled me up entirely.

Belle Elle was my university, and I'd been attending nights and on weekends my entire life. As far as my knowledge and skills went, I was capable of running this company even before I hit twenty.

My father had made sure of it.

I was no longer a lonely little girl craving the freedom of her peers. But a resigned young woman who carried the livelihoods of thousands of staff upon her shoulders. It was up to me to ensure Belle Elle ran smoothly and made a profit to fill the pay packets and make sure employment continued.

My hard work and long hours were rewarded with positive yields and exciting business expansions. I earned satisfaction from new contracts and cheaper production costs. I'd never been to a party or acted out because work began too early to stay up late.

I lived and breathed merchandise and balance sheets.

*And I'm fine with that.*

I knew no other life. I had no right to feel so trapped. I had an amazing father, an incredible future, and everything I could ever want. I'd been given so much, but the price of such power and greatness was the removal of so many things I'd never enjoyed.

I'd never had friends because who wanted to hang around a geek who didn't know how to play? I'd never walked around the city on my own because the world was far too dangerous. I'd never gotten into trouble or done anything reckless. My days were surrounded by bodyguards, drivers, and managers.

The girls I knew from school only pretended to like me when I gave them discounts on dresses and shoes. In fact, the week before junior prom, I'd suddenly become the most popular girl in school, only to hear them whispering in the changing rooms at Belle Elle about how much they were saving thanks to lying to my face about friendship and the discount I'd given them.

And the boys were afraid of me because I spoke like an adult and crunched real-time spread-sheets in math rather than solved the basic algebra equation on the whiteboard.

I was never alone but forever lonely.

If it weren't for Sage, I'd probably have run away by now. But I couldn't leave her, and I *definitely* couldn't leave my father.

They needed me.

*Everyone* needed me.

Thinking of the little fluff ball made her appear. The sleek, pretty cat hopped up onto my desk, deliberately knocking over the old Tic-Tac holder full of paperclips. She swatted it again for good measure.

Instantly, the stress of the day and ache in my back from hunching over a desk for too long receded. "Hello to you, too."

She meowed, her cute gray face scrunching up as if she disapproved of me working past dark once again.

Ever since Dad gave her to me, she'd never left my side. The only time she wasn't with me was while I was at school, but seeing as that was over a few years ago, she was now my silent silver shadow. She traveled on my neck like a living scarf and trotted after me when I hosted meetings with men three times my age—who tried to trip me up and belittle me at the start of my reign. They soon learned I might be young, but I knew this company better than any of them.

Belle Elle was my mother, my best-friend, and boyfriend.

It was my world.

Taking off the black framed reading glasses I'd taken to wearing after staring at a laptop for hours at a time, I scooped Sage up by her middle and dragged her onto my lap.

She purred loudly as she head-butted my chest. I kissed the back of her neck, nuzzling into her. Her fur was as soft as spun moonlight; her purr the only thing that made me shed the constant feeling of anxiety and despondency.

"You know how I feel, right?"

She purred louder.

"Am I a horrible person for feeling trapped?"

She pulled a face.

"I do everything that's asked of me. I take over more and more elements of the company with no refusal. I love my father with every bone in my body. I've dedicated my life to making him proud. I have self-worth, wealth, and the knowledge that I'll never have to ask for anything." I pressed my face deeper into her fur, doing my best to stem the unwanted self-pity. "So why do I feel so lost, Sage? Why can't I shed the idea so much more is out there besides work?"

She meowed, jumping from my arms to my desk and walking across my keyboard to scatter qwerty keystrokes in boxes where only numbers belonged. I tried to get mad, to yell at her because she'd just caused another ten minutes' worth of work to delete her tampering and ensure the numbers I'd inputted were still correct.

But I couldn't.

Because work was my life, and life was my work. I had nowhere to be, no one to see—nothing demanded anything of me but Belle Elle.

"Maybe that's my problem?"

Sage flicked her tail.

"Maybe I need to forget about work for a change and do something completely different." Standing, I moved toward the floor-to-ceiling glass windows and looked upon New York below. Twinkling lights, cars, and pedestrians appeared and disappeared beneath streetlights like different bugs—some large, some small—but all of them moving with purpose.

What would it be like to be down there with them? To wear jeans (gasp) and eat food from a street vendor (oh, no)? To be on my own, rather than watched by a driver and bodyguard.

*Don't I deserve to know what else is out there before I give up everything?*

Today, I'd turned nineteen.

I was old enough to have sex but not old enough to drink. I was old enough to run a billion-dollar company but not old enough to wander alone in a city promising such adventure.

My fingers flew to my neck, clutching the beautiful sapphire star necklace my father had presented me with this morning. We'd both been pressed for time but he'd sent the cook away, and together, we'd whisked up buttermilk batter and created a mismatch of blueberry pancakes before he gave me my gift.

It'd been a wonderful morning, and I'd treasured his company, the pancakes, and my necklace, but I couldn't help feeling like something was missing.

Mom was missing, of course.

But something else.

*Someone* else…a friend on two legs instead of four.

After an hour together, Dad and I had headed to work and lost ourselves in the cogs of such a demanding mistress.

I didn't know if he was still in his office working late, just like he would never know if I snuck out and pretended to be a girl from a different life for the night.

*Wait…what?*

The idea came out of nowhere. The betrayal and willingness to sneak behind my father's back was a horrid, terrible concept. Yet…so enticingly exciting.

*You could do it…just for one night.*

*Do what?*

The five points of the sapphire star bit into my fingers as I glanced at the congested street below again.

*Be one of them.*

*Do what they do.*

*Go where they go.*

*Be free.*

My heart bashed my ribs as the idea slowly manifested into potential.

Tomorrow was yet another day belonging to Belle Elle. But tonight? Tonight was my nineteenth birthday, and I'd yet to give myself a gift.

Could I do it?

Could I be brave enough to leave my world and everything I knew in order to sample what I could never have?

Could I seek something I didn't know how to find?

Sage wrapped herself around my ankle, head butting me with approval. Or at least, I'd take it as approval because suddenly, I couldn't imagine *not* doing it.

The prison gates I'd lived behind all my life creaked with rust and whined with disapproval, slowly hinging wide. I had a few short hours before the clock struck twelve and the enchantment of my birthday would vanish.

*It's now or never.*

Tonight, I would give into my urges and taste freedom for the first time.

And tomorrow, I would stop these childish regrets and fully embrace my crown as the Belle Elle empress.

# Chapter Three

MY FIRST STOP was the shop floor of Belle Elle.

Being our flagship location, the merchandise section took up multiple levels of the skyscraper. We sold everything from top-of-the-line technology to baby toys and everything in-between, and I knew every nook and cranny. I'd spent the majority of my life helping design displays and solving stock issues.

But not tonight.

Tonight, I wasn't there on business.

Taking the elevator down from the offices, I swiped my keycard and entered my passcode to prevent the alarms going off. The store had shut to the public an hour ago, and the hushed world of cotton and silk welcomed me.

I clipped in red high heels past pantsuits and high-fashion attire straight to the teenagers department. Ever since I'd signed Dad's Last Will and Testament—and even before that—I'd dressed like a woman. I'd never dressed in a garment with a popular quote or profanity like the kids at my school. I'd never worn anything valued at less than four hundred dollars.

That was about to change.

Browsing the racks of diamante encrusted jeans and off-the-shoulder tops, I found myself critiquing the display and position of the mannequins rather than shopping for an outfit.

*Stop it.*

*You're a customer right now, not the boss.*

Forcing myself to exhale and loosen my shoulders from stress, I stopped beside a table with discounted denim. I grasped the pair neatly folded on top and shook it. The baby-blue washed jeans had a skinny leg and silver embroidery on the pockets.

I did my best not to recall the cost of bulk buying these from Taiwan. How I'd placed the order at the start of last year to be out for this season. How, even on sale, we were still making money because that was how businesses worked. Price high and then slowly discount until no more remained in stock, our margins slowly narrowing but still profitable.

*Ugh, stop it.*

*You're not an heiress tonight. You're just Elle. A nineteen-year-old about to break all the rules and go out.*

What would my driver, David, say when I didn't call him in a few hours to take me home? What would Dad say if I had so much fun tonight and I didn't return home until daybreak?

*Does it matter?*

*You have to do this for yourself.*

*You're an adult.*

Clutching those thoughts, I stole the pair of jeans, pilfered an off-the-shoulder cream and black top from the rack beside it, scooped up a black lace scarf from the new arrival podium, and traded the clothing department for the shoe emporium.

If I was going to walk around New York until midnight, I had to wear comfy shoes.

My blood-red heels would have to go.

Eyeing up a rack of recently ordered sneakers, I decided on a pair of white ones with rose gold piping—something I would never be allowed to wear as the figurehead of a billion-dollar company.

I'd worn heels every day of my life since I could remember. The only difference was they were lower when I was a child, and now, they were soaring, sharp stilettos.

Taking my new wardrobe into one of the changing rooms, I once again found myself assessing the locks on the doors and the wobble in the mirror from the second-rate glass. No flaws should exist in any aspect of our sales experience.

I made a note to have all the mirrors replaced next time we overhauled this department.

Slipping from my pencil skirt and black blouse, I rolled down my stockings and frowned at my underwear-clad form. The black bra offered support to my generous B-cups, but would the straps look hookerish peeking out from the off-the-shoulder top?

I had no experience dressing like this, even though I'd gone to countless runway shows and hand selected the latest fashions.

*Suck it up and stop procrastinating.*

Tugging the tight jeans on, I slipped the top over my head and secured the lacy scarf around my throat. I made sure it hung loosely so as not to cover the blue star glittering on my skin.

*Ugh, no.*

I yanked the scarf off again and draped it over the door.

It wasn't needed.

I touched the sapphire star. This would kill my father if he knew how unhappy I was after he'd given me everything. I could never explain the emptiness inside when I was so blessed on the outside. And I could never admit that I'd heard him discussing my love life with Steve the other day. Wondering if now was the time to parade me in front of New York's finest bachelors in order to find a willing right-hand partner to run Belle Elle.

I shuddered as I traded my stilettos for the white sneakers. The thought of giving my life to a company that'd always been there was one thing. The idea of sharing my life with a man who would never understand me was appalling.

A meow sounded, followed by the streak of silver fur as Sage appeared under the changing room door.

I scowled. "What are you doing down here?"

I ought to regret teaching her to jump up and swat the buttons on the elevator. She was like Houdini with her ability to chase me down anywhere in the building, no matter if I'd kept her in my office or taken her to a meeting.

"You know you're not allowed on the shop floor."

She flicked her tail and leaped onto the small stool where I'd placed my pencil skirt. She meowed again then licked her paw.

"You also know you can't come with me tonight, right?"

Her head wrenched up as if I'd uttered some terrible curse.

She spread her claws and licked between them, daring me to say such blasphemy again.

I ignored her display of feline annoyance, pushing her off my uniform. "You heard me, Sage. Don't pretend otherwise." Bundling the clothes up, I took one last look in the mirror and decided I looked sufficiently teenagerish. I sure looked nothing like the head honcho of Belle Elle.

"Good." I nodded, fluffing up my blonde hair that cascaded down my back to my waist. Dad constantly moaned for me to have it cut, but it was my one rebellion. The length wasn't practical, and most of the time, I just let it air dry into messy waves. The only part of the perfect rule-abiding CEO that was wild.

Heading back to the shop floor, I grabbed a shopping bag from beneath one of the many cashier stations and tucked my expensive clothes inside. Once folded neatly, I tucked the glossy bag into the cupboard beneath the till where manila folders rested with daily tasks and checklists.

Two more things and then I would be ready to go.

*I need a coat in case it gets cold and some cash.*

I hadn't brought my handbag down from my office. Not that it would've made a difference if I had.

I had no cash. If I needed something, my assistant bought it for me. I only had a credit card for emergencies (not that I'd ever used it), and my I.D badge to access restricted parts of the building.

Sage joined me from the changing room and prowled down the aisle, dragging my attention to a small table with funky purses on display. Seeing as I'd stolen jeans, a top, and a pair of shoes already, I supposed taking a purse wouldn't matter.

And hell, while I was at it, I might as well take some spending money, seeing as there wouldn't be anyone to buy me anything tonight.

Using the universal key attached to my lanyard and badge, I unlocked the cash register and looked at the float. There were no big bills, only regimented change ready for a new day of transactions. The rest of the day's takings would already be counted, bound, and in our vault, ready for a bank run.

*No matter.*

Three hundred dollars in twenty-dollar bills would be fine.

Taking the wad, I wrote a quick note on a Post-it: *Noelle Charlston borrowed $300 in petty cash. Please contact her assistant, Fleur Hemmings, on extension #4456 to reimburse for morning business.*

I placed it where the bills had been (so no one would get into trouble for missing money), closed the till, and headed toward the purse display. Selecting one with a graffiti skull on a black background, I tucked the cash inside. The loneliness and strange lostness inside me slowly trickled away, blossoming into fear and excitement.

I flashed the skull wallet at Sage. "See, I can be a rebel if I want to."

She licked her lips, her whiskers quivering.

Stepping around her, I beelined for the final thing on my list.

I'd never worn anything less than thousand dollar cashmere coats. However, tonight I would wear...

I tapped my fingers, deliberating the jacket choice.

*Tonight, I'll wear a patent leather black bomber with a price tag of*

*$19.99.*

Pulling it off the hanger, I fondled the cheap material. I'd always wanted to wear something like this. As I slipped it on, two emotions skittered: terror and the sudden desire to return all the clothes to where they belonged, and eager frustration to begin my exploration of the Big Apple.

I was afraid.

I was excited.

I was so sick of being sheltered and only being good at one thing.

*It's time for that to change.*

"Happy birthday to me." I tucked the wallet into my bomber jacket pocket, scooped Sage from the floor and rubbed her nose with mine. "I love you, but you can't come."

Her little face pouted.

"Don't look at me like that. I won't be gone long."

She meowed sadly.

My heart squeezed, but I steeled myself against her guilt trip and headed toward the elevators. Walking was so much easier and comfier in sneakers than heels. *No wonder people choose them over fashion.*

"I'm sorry, Sage, but it's only one night." Holding her firm with one hand, I pressed the button to summon two elevators.

One to go up and one to go down.

The up one came first, and I plopped her into it. Giving her a smile, I pressed my office level on the top floor. "Go back. Curl up in your basket. You won't even notice I'm gone."

She meowed again as the doors slowly closed.

I whispered, "Don't look at me like that. It hurts too much."

I hugged myself the moment she'd gone, feeling utterly alone and terrified.

*Why am I doing this?*

I should forget it and just go home.

But then the down elevator pinged and waited for me to be brave and commit to one night away from Belle Elle.

Hesitantly, fearfully, I stepped into it and prepared to become someone else.

Someone free.

# Chapter Four

EVERYTHING seemed different.

*Everything is different.*

The air tasted richer. The traffic sounded louder. The temperature felt cooler. Even the sensation of cheap vinyl around my shoulders and cushy sneakers on my feet was different.

Nineteen years and this was the first time I'd been introduced to the world without finery or rules keeping me barricaded from living.

I inhaled deep, coughing a little as a taxi spewed exhaust. The burn in my throat was so foreign to the filtered air of the Belle Elle building that I grinned rather than grimaced.

The purse with its cash whispered to be spent, and my identification badge remained hidden in my pocket, reminding me who I was and how irresponsible I was being.

I had no phone for Dad to contact me. No method of communication or way of calling for help if I got lost or into trouble.

I was willing to put myself at risk just to live a little; to taste a different life to the one I'd been given.

I couldn't lie and say it wasn't exhilarating, but it was also absolutely *terrifying.*

Those first few steps away from Belle Elle physically hurt. The ache in my chest at disappointing my father hollowed me out until even my excitement at doing something new couldn't fill.

A few times, I second-guessed myself and almost turned around. I stopped, spun, and looked back at the huge hulking building where the shopping mega store was run.

But then I reminded myself if I didn't do this, I would never know what it was like to be normal. So I sucked it up, turned back around, and put one sneakered foot in front of the other, slowly entering the empire of downtown New York.

Strangers bumped into me, tourists asked me to take their photograph, and street vendors yelled about their wares directly into my face.

The sensory overload slowly eroded my shame for sneaking out and forced me to pay attention to every minor thing.

For hours, I walked.

I stared.

I breathed.

I let life take me wherever it wanted for a change. I had no idea where I was going or how to get back, but I let my feet get me lost because I had money to catch a taxi home. I knew my address—I wasn't that sheltered. I could afford to go wherever I wanted, and at the end of my adventures hop in a cab and return with a new depth to my existence. And a secret I would happily harbor forever.

At some point, I must've done a block and looped back on myself, so instead of turning left when I arrived at Times Square, I turned right and continued letting the city show me what I'd been missing.

Flashing billboards tried to convince me I needed the latest Jeep and Hummer. Hollywood stars and starlets glowed in LED wonder with snippets of upcoming movies. *Madame Tussauds* promised wonders forever encapsulated in wax, and *Ripley's Believe It or Not!* beckoned me to see things not common in everyday life.

Walking past a souvenir shop, a bunch of clocks held up by mini Statues of Liberty showed I'd wandered for a while.

Ten p.m.

By now, if I'd stuck to my routine, I would be at home, fresh from a quick treadmill-run and shower. I would answer a few last-minute emails and crawl into bed to read the latest romance before my eyes closed and the e-reader bopped me on the head.

Not tonight.

Tonight, strangers smiled or yelled—depending if they wanted me to do something for them or get out of the way. I either moved too fast or too slow, unable to fall into the rhythm of the mismatched crowd I'd adopted. My jacket overheated me from walking and being cramped into streets with sweaty people made me claustrophobic. My feet were flat, and my tummy was empty.

But nothing could detract from how freeing and awe-inspiring every experience was.

Turning another corner, I spotted a food truck promising the best Mexican this side of the border. Hadn't one of my bucket list items been to eat from a street vendor?

*It might make you sick.*

Yes, it might. But food poisoning would be yet another adventure I'd long been denied. Pulling the purse from my pocket, I joined the queue and waited my turn. As I shuffled to the front, I craned my neck to look at the guy leering down in a grease-spotted apron.

"What can I getcha?" He chewed a piece of gum, fingers twirling his pencil in impatience.

I narrowed my eyes at the menu behind him. "Um, what do you recommend?"

He scoffed. "Recommend? Lady, do I look like I have time to shoot the shit with you?" He pointed at the crowd behind me with his pencil. "Hurry up. I got paying people to feed."

I opened my wallet and pulled out a twenty. "I'll just have something chicken." I handed him the money. "Oh, and not hot. I don't like spice."

"Got it." He snorted. "Chicken and bland. Boring order for a boring girl."

I tensed. "Excuse me?"

He looked me up and down. "Beat it, princess. Your order will be ready in five minutes. Pick-up is at the window down the truck." He tossed me a dirty ten-dollar bill. "Here's your change."

I curled my fingers around the money, annoyance and hurt making equal acid tracks inside me. I'd never been talked to that way. No one dared.

The fact he'd called me boring, when I completely agreed with him, pissed me off even more. I wadded up the money and threw it at him. "Know what? Add a beef something or other to that order, too. And make it extra spicy."

I walked off toward the collection window before he could insult me anymore.

# Chapter Five

THE BEEF WAS a bad idea.

After collecting my dinner, I strolled toward Times Square where a few tables and chairs had been placed for milling pedestrians. The table was filthy, the chair rickety, but I'd never eaten with such vibrancy as my entertainment before.

The tinfoil wrapped burrito steamed with flavor as I opened it and inhaled. Determined to prove the greasy man wrong, I took a bite of the beef, chewed, and grinned.

*It's not so bad.*

Then the heat began.

My tongue shrivelled up.

The Mexican food kicked me hard. Quicker and hotter until my grin switched to a gasp, wheezing in spicy agony.

*Water!*

*Oh, my God, I need water.*

My eyes streamed with tears as I grabbed both burritos, left my commandeered table, and bolted toward the convenience store blinking with billboards of ice-cold water and cola bottles.

Charging inside, I yanked open a glass-fronted fridge, grabbed a water, and tore off the cap. I downed it in three seconds. And *still,* the fire burned my tongue and lips.

Gasping, I grabbed a chocolate milk.

Struggling with the cap, I finally got it open and took a few greedy sips. The full-fat milk helped temper some of the hateful rage. I exhaled a sigh of relief.

"I hope you're going to pay for that." A shop girl with pink hair raised an eyebrow.

Wiping my lips with the back of my hand (something I would never do in my real world), I nodded and collected another water bottle while somehow hugging my mostly-untouched burritos.

"Yes, sorry. The spice caught me unaware."

She grinned. "Oh shit, did you piss off Pete?"

"Pete?" I placed the two water bottles (one full, one empty) and the half-drunk chocolate milk onto the conveyer belt.

The shopkeeper passed them over the scanner, ringing up the sale. "Yeah, the guy who owns the Mexican street meat." She giggled. "He makes a mean taco, but man, he's cruel on the hot sauce."

I ran my tongue over my still stinging lips. "I kind of asked for it." Shrugging, I smiled. "I don't get out much. I wasn't aware not to antagonize food sellers."

She bagged my purchases. "Yep, everyone knows that. Especially not to piss off the street kings."

I dug into my wallet and pulled out a twenty. She took it, opened the register, then passed me my change. The fact she spoke to me with no tension or concern made me relax.

I was so used to talking to women from a boss-employee relationship. No one joked in my presence or told me what to do in case I fired them. And those who did try to befriend me only did so for a promotion or raise.

I could taste fakery like a rotten apple.

We shared another smile before awkwardness crept in. I didn't know how to end a friendly conversation or even when to leave after buying something.

The girl saved me from standing there like an idiot. "Well, you have a good night. And don't piss off any more people, you hear?"

I nodded. "Got it. Thanks for your help."

"No sweat." She gave me a small wave before disappearing from the till to finish stocking a shelf with chips.

Making sure I had both burritos and my valuable liquids to get me through the fire-breathing dragon of Pete's revenge, I left the shop and re-entered the manic world of shoppers and tourists.

I ducked and jived through the crowd, intending to sit back down and try the blander chicken burrito, only to find my table and chair had been nabbed by a family with three young children who blinked glassy-eyed with tiredness in the glow of the bright neon lights.

All the other tables were occupied.

*Oh, well.*

*I don't mind. I can walk and eat.*

Laughter caught my ears. I glanced at a table two down from

where I stood, where four teenage girls sat. My lips twitched to share in their joke as I looked at what they were laughing at. Horror slammed into me instead.

They sneered and giggled at an elderly homeless man picking up aluminum cans in a trash bag.

I ached for him and the hopelessness of his situation. He was fully aware of the jokes and whispers, doing his best to ignore the girls as he chased a can caught in a puff of wind.

I'd been on the opposite end of homelessness all my life. I'd been born into a role that would ensure I'd never know the pain of cold and hunger. I'd been given so much, and what had I done? I'd run away for the night like an unappreciative teenager.

*What was I thinking?*

Embarrassment coated my insides. I couldn't look at the clothes I'd taken from Belle Elle or the food I'd bought with money grabbed from the till. Things I had every right to use but somehow felt like I'd stolen and broken my father's trust.

The girls continued to laugh as a can rolled out of the man's trash bag through a tear in the bottom.

I wanted to slap them for their immaturity and lack of empathy. I wanted to forget I'd ever thought I wanted to be a typical girl rather than who I truly was: a capable young woman who would never stand by while another was ridiculed.

Marching toward the homeless man who knocked on fifty (Dad's age) with a scruffy gray beard and holey beanie, I stopped and picked up the can. "Here you go."

He froze.

The way he watched with trepidation and suspicion lacerated my heart. His entire body waited for abuse, fearing what other misfortune I'd bring into his life.

"It's okay." I urged him to take the dinged-up can.

He did, reluctantly.

Once he'd tucked the can into his bag, I looked at the gauntness in his face and the way he licked his lips at my burritos.

My own hunger vanished.

"Here." I pushed the plastic bag containing the water and chocolate milk, followed by the burritos, into his arms. "You have them. I've only taken one bite. I'm not contagious, I promise."

His mouth fell open as he cradled the icy drinks and hot food.

Awkwardness fell and tears I didn't understand itched my spine. The look in his eyes was full of shock and utter gratefulness.

He quickly stuffed the food into the baggy pockets of his

jacket and swigged the half-empty chocolate milk until it was gone. Wiping his lips with the back of his hand, he murmured, "Thank you."

I smiled. "You're welcome."

I knew it was time to leave. But I couldn't walk away—not yet.

Pulling my wallet out, I took the twenties, minus eighty dollars for me (as emergency funds to get home), and placed them into his hand. "Please, have this as well. Eat and have a night in a hotel somewhere."

He curled his fingers tightly around the money. "I don't know what to say."

"Don't say anything." I stepped away. "Have a good night. And I'm sorry for those girls laughing at you. That's terribly rude. We're not all like that."

He blinked as if coming out of a fugue.

"Goodbye." I walked away feeling better and happier than I had in…well, forever.

# Chapter Six

ELEVEN P.M. AND the novelty of walking around a bustling city had begun to wear.

I didn't want to spend any more money on food—just in case a taxi cost over eighty. I had no idea how much transportation would be to get home.

My feet ached from all the miles I'd traveled. My back hurt from not being used to standing. And the crowd steadily became less polite and more disorderly as the night grew later.

The jostling of limbs and pushiness made me nervous, and thoughts of returning to a quiet bedroom where I knew who I was and how to play by the rules enticed me.

Stepping from the curb, I shot across the road (narrowly missing a speeding car), and stood on the corner where a pile of rubbish had gathered from passing pedestrians and shop-fronts ready for collection.

I looked up and down the road, hoping to see the yellow glint of a cab. I hated that only a few hours into my bid for freedom, I already wanted to go home. I truly was a boring girl like the food vendor had said.

But at least I'd explored on my own.

*I know now I'm not missing anything.*

*I can put my childish whims behind me and agree the grass is not greener on the other side.*

I stood for a few minutes, waiting for a ride but nothing came. Deciding to change my position, I joined the crowds again and carried on a little further. Once the congestion thinned out, I stood in front of a small alley and resumed my search.

Left, right, look and hope.

I stayed in place so I could raise my arm quickly the moment I spotted a cab.

The world faded around me as I focused on waiting for a ride. The allure of soft sheets and quiet rooms helped delete the chaos I'd been a part of for a few short hours.

I didn't notice the two men at first.

Perhaps I was too naïve or blind, but I didn't expect a hand to lash around my elbow on both sides—two men crowding me between them.

My heart leaped into my throat, gagging me from screaming.

My eyes popped with disbelief as they jerked me backward into the alley.

*No!*

I didn't comprehend what was happening.

*Let me go!*

I'd never been handled with such force before.

Their touch dug like five-finger traps into my arms.

Hurting.

Bruising.

*"Help!"* My heart stuck in my throat, preventing any more than a strangled beg. My uselessness gave them all the time they needed.

With a sinister chuckle, they dragged me deeper into the darkness, away from streetlights and people and taxis.

"Let me go!" I struggled, kicking and flailing. "Help! *Help!* Someone—"

But it was too late.

They pulled me further, laughing louder as my feet skidded uselessly on the grimy ground. In some strange recess of my mind, I noticed how dirty my shoes had become. How black now smeared the pristine white.

"No! *Stop!*" I lost my shock-stupor, giving into fighting terror.

I bent and buckled.

I kicked and squirmed.

But they were too strong.

The street was too far away.

The world was too obsessed to care.

"Let. Me. *Go!*"

"Shut the fuck up." The harsh command was as sharp as a fishhook, digging into my mind with evil.

"What do you want?" I fought harder, winded and so, so worried. "I don't—"

"Told you. Shut the fuck up." They held me tighter, their fingers digging into my flesh like cleavers. "What we want is our business, not yours." One of them laughed.

Three-quarters down the alley, where the sounds of a busy metropolis were muted in favor of rankness from awful smelling trash, they shoved me forward, slamming me against the wall.

The air in my lungs vanished, leaving me empty.

I doubled over in pain as the nodules of my spine crunched against brick. I tried to suck in a breath, my long hair tangling in a mess over my shoulder.

I peered up through the blonde strands, doing my best to formulate an escape. To them, I was an inexperienced little girl who they could rob and hurt with no consequences. I had to prove to them otherwise.

*Even if it's the truth.*

The men chuckled, nudging each other with congratulations.

I didn't wait to see what would happen next. Pushing off from the wall, I sprinted through the small gap and dug for every bit of strength and courage I had. My mouth opened to scream— to scream as loud and as long as I could—but one man grabbed me, slamming me into his chest. The other plastered a metallic smelling palm over my lips, silencing me.

Sandwiched between the two, I understood my dire situation.

The terribly, stupid *bad* situation.

"Where do you think you're going, little bitch?"

Hardness, where there should be no hardness, prodded me in the front and the back. They ground their cocks against me.

I shuddered, understanding right away that whatever they wanted from me wasn't just monetary but physical.

*And I can't do a thing to stop it.*

Tears sprang to my eyes, but I did my best to blink them away. I'd let shock get me into this mess. I wouldn't let pity make it worse.

Their breath turned heavy as they pressed harder into me. Not caring that their heads touched each other in their bid to consume me.

My bones turned to ash as my heart suffocated.

*Please, please don't let them hurt me.*

Being normal was suddenly the most idiotic concept in the world. I would gladly return to Belle Elle and never leave the crystal tower of business for the rest of my life. I would work every hour, of every day until I died if I could just walk away from this untouched.

*Please!*

---

I wriggled in their arms, trying to bare my teeth beneath the guy's palm to bite. He kept my lips firmly glued while his hips thrust against me from behind. His rocking knocked me off balance into his accomplice's sickly embrace. "Know what tonight is, pretty girl?"

*My nineteenth birthday.*

*My stupid attempt at being normal.*

I sucked in a breath, dragging in their scents of corruption and filth.

"It's the night you give us a good fuck then, if you're good, we let you go."

Horror flowed like ice water only to solidify into a glacier as his friend whispered, "We want your money and your jewelry as well as your cunt. Give them up willingly, and this will end much better for you."

He reached down, cupping me between the legs.

I moaned like a feral cat about to be butchered.

"Don't and things will get very, *very* bad." His fingers clenched around my core. "Fucking bad. Got it?"

When I didn't move apart from blinking yet more terrified tears from my vision, he pressed his groin into my belly. "Nod if you get it."

I didn't want to obey.

I wanted to tell them to *die*.

His friend snaked his arm around my middle, clutching me so hard my ribs bent, and the hardness in his pants bruised my spine. "Nod, bitch, then we'll let you go." He thrust again. "But if you scream, we'll beat you fucking bloody, and you'll wake up with nothing. Not even your clothes."

My lungs ached from lack of oxygen; caustic terror burned holes in my veins, drowning me in blood.

The man in front kissed my cheek. "Last time. Nod if you agree to our terms."

What else could I do?

I had no weapons, no experience. The most I could hope to do was delay by obeying until I spied an opportunity to run.

*Please let that opportunity come sooner rather than later.*

It hurt even more than stepping from Belle Elle in shame, but I nodded.

The moment I did, they stepped back. The one in front readjusted his trousers, fisting himself. "Fuck, it makes me hot when they obey."

*They?*

How many women had they done this to?

The world had been a vibrant adventure before. Now, it was a cesspool of criminals.

The man behind me came to my side, hemming me against the wall. They placed themselves strategically to block my exit. The shadows kept most of their features hidden, but one wore a baseball hat with a red logo, and the other dressed in a white jacket with the Adidas logo on the front pocket. They were the same height (about a foot taller than me) and both had dirty teeth as they smiled matching evil grins.

The one who'd been behind me in his Adidas jacket pointed at my neck. "First, let's focus on the jewelry, shall we? Give me that necklace."

I gulped. "What?"

The one in the baseball cap wagged his finger. "No talking. Do what we say, or you're fucked."

I flinched as he once again fisted the hard length visible in his pants. "First, we get what we want, and then you get what *you* want."

*What I want?*

My lips curled in disgust.

*What I want is for you to drop dead in agony.*

His accomplice chuckled. "What you want is a cock, stuck-up bitch. You can't deny it. Well, it's your lucky night. You'll get two soon enough. Now, hand over that fucking necklace."

"Please…" I clamped my hand over the sapphire star that I'd only had since breakfast but already meant so much. "Don't—"

"Breaking all the rules, aren't cha?" A fist came out of nowhere, crashing against my temple.

Bright pain detonated through my skull, forcing me back and sideways against the wall. I couldn't see past flashing lights. I couldn't hear through the ringing in my head. But it didn't stop one of them from grabbing the chain around my neck and yanking hard enough to break. The white-gold sliced into my nape before giving way, making me cry out in pain.

A hand landed on my breast, squeezing hard while a foot kicked my legs open and fingers grabbed between my thighs.

I moaned again, shaking my head to rid the receding punch. "No…stop."

A hand smashed over my mouth. "Shut the fuck up."

My vision slowly came back as Adidas dug his hands into my

jacket and pulled out my purse. He counted the bills while Baseball Cap kept me gagged and pressed half-standing, half-slouching against the wall. "Eighty bucks? Seriously, that's all you have?" His sneer was accompanied by gross breath. "We'll just have to get it out of you in other ways."

Digging his hand into my back jeans pocket, he pulled out my Belle Elle identification card. The flash of my portrait in a crisp black blazer and my blonde hair artfully coiled reminded me how far I'd fallen from my queendom.

If they killed me, my father would never know what happened. There would be no way to I.D my body or any explanation of how I ended up in an alley on my nineteenth birthday and not safe at home with him.

I hated how selfish I'd been.

How *stupid*.

If I survived this, I would never bemoan my life again. I would never take my company for granted. I would live an existence of utter gratefulness.

"Noelle Charlston. Looks like you have a cushy office job." Baseball Cap smirked. "Bet you use that nice ass just for sitting rather than anything else." He leaned into me, pressing his erection against my hip. "Ever been fucked over your desk, office girl? Ever given a boss a blowjob for a promotion?" He thrust hard. "I like the thought of you giving me a blowjob." He nodded at his friend. "Get her on her knees."

I scrunched up my face as I screamed internally.

I'd gone through school without boyfriends of any kind. I'd stolen a single kiss on the dance floor of my high school prom, but it hadn't included tongue. No boys had braved my father to ask me out. I was light years ahead in experience of managing and running a company, but so ill taught when it came to sex.

Blowjob?

No way did I want to do that. I had no idea how. And the idea of sucking on that part of a man made me want to vomit on my dirty sneakers.

But what I wanted no longer mattered.

My knees screamed as they pushed me to the ground.

I daren't look up.

Baseball Cap ducked with me.

Sitting on his haunches, he smirked. "Before we show you ours, you have to show us yours." Before I could argue or move, he ripped off my bomber jacket and tossed it into the darkness behind him. He tore at the off-the-shoulder t-shirt until it hung in tatters, revealing my black bra.

"Let's see what your tits are like."

Everything shut down as his hand moved forward to cup me. I turned inward.

I tried to delete what was about to happen.

Only, he never connected.

A blur in the dark materialized like a phantom.

A man's grunting erupted.

Adidas fell backward, yanked by an unseen force. Baseball Cap whirled around, his fists up, ready to fight. "Who the fuck is there?"

Adidas groaned as a shadow connected with his stomach then with his jaw. I blinked in disbelief as the apparition stepped into the light, revealing another man with a black hoodie over his head.

He didn't introduce himself.

He twirled around and kicked Adidas in the chest, sending him careening to the dirty ground.

The new guy turned and locked eyes on me. Beneath the gloom of his hoodie, his intense gaze tangled me into knots. For a split second, my heart kick-started from fear to relief then sank back into terror.

First, there were two.

Now, there were three.

I wasn't safe.

Even if the newcomer seemed to fight on my side.

Scrambling to my feet, I pulled at the ruined pieces of my top.

The new guy followed my torn clothing, eyeing my bra. His jaw clenched and a low growl echoed in the alley. Whatever had sewn us together for those few seconds snapped.

He launched himself at Baseball Cap.

He tackled the wannabe rapist to the ground, punching him once, twice, three times in the stomach.

They rolled around, legs kicking, arms whirling until the hooded figure swung a well-aimed sucker-punch right into the nose of Baseball Cap.

The man dissolved from hooligan to helpless. His arms and hands came up to shield his face. His mouth bloody and breath ragged. "Fuck, we give, we give. Stop!"

Immediately, the hooded figure clambered to his feet. Wrenching a hand over his face, he grunted. "Second time I've caught you assholes. There won't be a third."

Adidas pushed off the concrete with both hands, climbing unsteadily to his feet. "Fuck you."

The hooded figure stepped forward and, with a quick jab, delivered another punch into Adidas's throat.

"Ah, fu—" He collapsed to his knees, his hands around his neck, gasping like a lunatic. "I—I can't—breathe—"

To my horror, I smiled a little. I had no sympathy for him, but I shouldn't take enjoyment from such violence.

*Should I?*

The hooded man pointed at Adidas squirming on the floor. "That was for being rude." His leg came out again, connecting with the white jacket covering Adidas's ribs. "That's for being a cunt." His face turned toward me, but I couldn't see his features in the dark. Never looking away from me, he threw another punch at Adidas's head. It wasn't at full power, merely a swat—a telling off. "And *that's* for her."

Stepping back, he crossed his arms. "Now, what do you have to say for yourself?"

Adidas still hadn't learned his lesson. He spat blood, glistening black in the night. "Fuck you twice, man. You can't scare us."

The hooded man took a menacing step closer.

Baseball Cap dodged forward, nursing a sore arm. He held up a hand in surrender, some sort of chivalry coming through to protect his asshole friend. "Look, we're done, okay?"

The hooded man glanced at Adidas—the asshole who'd been moments away from stealing my virginity. His voice lashed out like a dark whip, demanding obedience. "And you? Are you done?"

Adidas nodded profusely. "Fine. Sure."

"Good." The hooded man held out his hand. Blood marked his fingers, but I couldn't tell if it was from him or his victims. "Cough it up."

Baseball Cap scrambled backward, shaking his head. "Nah, no way." He patted his pocket with a sick gleam in his gaze. "Nah, man. You take the girl. We'll take the cash."

Hooded Man cocked his head. It was nothing more than an innocent move, but it dripped with threat. "Do you want to die tonight, Gio? Because I can arrange that."

*Gio?*

*He knows their names?*

*How?*

Adidas scoffed. "Do you know who you're fucking talking

to?"

Hooded Man glowered. "I know *exactly* who I'm talking to and wouldn't your fucking father be glad to hear what I have to tell him?" He pulled his hoodie higher over his face, making himself featureless, a black void. "If you don't stop and call these fucking games quit, I'll do worse than beat you."

*What the hell is going on?*

I couldn't decide who was scarier: the two men who'd grabbed me or this savior wrapped in black.

The hooded man's voice was a menacing growl—a mix between gravel and velvet. His body was lithe beneath the oversized hoodie and holey jeans. He looked like a skater-rat—the poster child for rebellion and lawlessness.

He had the air of one of our in-store billboards with a rough and ready skater in a half-pipe selling baggy jeans and chain belts with a spray can in his hand. When I'd approved the marketing, I'd feared it was a little 'rough' for our clean brand for teenagers. Turned out, that banner was tame compared to this man.

Baseball Cap stepped forward. "Hand over the money, Sean."

"Oh, for fuck's sake," Adidas grumbled, reluctantly pulling out my cash. I didn't care about the money, but if the faceless savior wanted to return my property, I wouldn't argue.

Hooded Man held out his hand.

Sean, the Adidas punk, angrily shoved the dollar bills into his grip. The second the cash changed hands, it vanished into the hooded man's jeans like a magic trick.

He turned to me, his face still a dark secret. "Did they steal anything else?" His gaze traveled down my front where I held my torn top together.

I flinched under his inspection, wishing my bra didn't peek out behind my hands, and my bare stomach wasn't so on display. My head pounded from the punch, and the pungent whiffs from the alley didn't help my swirl of nausea.

When I didn't reply, Hooded Man pointed at my destroyed top and discarded jacket on the floor. "Did they? Steal anything else, I mean? They tore your clothes. Do you want me to ruin theirs in return?"

My eyes widened. "Wh—what?"

His head tilted, hearing me speak for the first time. A low chuckle came from the blackness of his hood. "I can make them strip and run home naked if it would make you feel better." He waved at my tattered top. "You don't need to hide. I won't let them hurt you. You're safe with me."

The midnight rasp in his voice negated his promise. He was the safest of the three—for now. But he wasn't safe compared to my father or staff. He was the exact *opposite* of safe.

I swallowed, standing proudly despite my lack of modesty. "I have no desire to see such vermin naked."

Adidas sneered. "You want to see my cock, bitch. Can't deny that shit."

I gave him a look I wished could melt his skin off his bones. "Believe me, I would rather go blind."

Baseball Cap bared his teeth. "That could be arranged."

Hooded Man took a step toward me, putting himself between them and me. "As entertaining as this is, I don't want to commit murder tonight." He glanced at me then at the two men who would've raped and hurt me if he hadn't shown up.

*What am I doing?*

*Antagonizing criminals? All for what? A little dignity after having my self-worth threatened?*

Holding my chin high, I said, "They stole my I.D card for work. I would like that back."

*So they can't break into Belle Elle and I'll have yet more explaining to do.*

Hooded Man turned to Adidas. "You heard her. Give her back the I.D."

Adidas cursed under his breath but pulled out the lanyard with my tag from his pocket. The second it switched hands, it once again joined my vanished cash in a blink.

Hooded Man closed the distance between us, turning to face them as he did. He protected me with his body while confronting them. "That's it. Run along."

Baseball Cap pointed a finger. "We'll get you back."

Hooded Man shrugged. "You keep being scum, and I won't be so nice next time."

"You keep thinking you're untouchable and we'll go out of our way to prove you fucking bleed like the rest of us."

Hooded Man stalked forward, his hands splaying before curling into fists. "We can prove you wrong, right now."

"Fuck you—"

"I prefer women but thanks for asking."

Baseball Cap charged. "I'm gonna kill—"

Adidas grabbed Baseball Cap's arm, stopping him mid-stride. "Come on, man. We've got better things to do."

Baseball Cap fought him, but then a slow smile spread his lips. "Yeah, you know what? We do." He smirked with evil. "*Much* better things." Blowing me a kiss, he said, "Pity we didn't get to have our fun, office girl. Bet you're torn up you didn't get to see what we wanted to give you, huh?"

Hooded Man crossed his arms. "Fuck off—"

He'd fought one battle for me. I wouldn't let him have the credit on this one.

Stepping around him, I let go of my tattered top and stood in my bra-naked glory. The fear. The adrenaline. The *pride*. "You're right that I'm an office girl who has no experience in fighting the likes of you. But you're wrong that I wanted to see your shrivelled-up jerky sticks."

Baseball Cap snarled. "You bitch."

"No, you don't get to call me that. *You're* the bastard. You're delusional and a disgrace, and if you think it makes you more of a man by trying to rape me, I'll do you a favor and cut off that jerky you call a cock and cook it for you." I smiled sweetly. "Along with office duties, I'm not bad in the kitchen, and you and your salami are only fit for frying and feeding to the dog." I held up my hand. "No wait, I wouldn't feed you to my dog, and I don't even *own* a dog."

"Ah, fuck." Hooded Man darted toward me just as Baseball Cap launched himself at my throat.

I stumbled back, only to slam into the arms of Hooded Man who spun me around, shielding me with his body. His fist came up, connecting once again with Baseball Cap's jaw.

"You can't even take shit from a girl without needing to be an asshole?" Hooded Man cracked his knuckles. "She's right. All you have in your pants is dried-up jerky." He swallowed a laugh. "Run along now, before I actually give this girl a knife and watch her fillet you for her frying pan."

Adidas grabbed Baseball Cap for the second or third time— I'd lost count. Together, they backed up. Their eyes black as the alley we stood in.

Baseball Cap raised his finger, pointing at both of us. "You'll fucking pay. Both of you."

Then they turned around and bolted toward the street.

# Chapter Seven

FROM ONE DISASTROUS situation to another.

Silence fell in the alley.

*They're gone.*

*But he's still here.*

My skin prickled with intensity from the hooded figure, standing dangerously lethal and so damn close. I didn't look at him. I didn't want to make eye contact or give him any reason to become the villain after being the knight.

I looked at the ground. "Um, I owe you a thank you."

My naked stomach tingled as he scuffed a pebble and turned to face me. The darkness of his hood masked his features, but I felt his eyes lingering on my bra.

The reckless confidence I'd had when facing down Baseball Cap and Adidas vanished. I snatched the ends of my torn top, pulling them closed. The broken material hid a little but not enough of the black lace or swell of my flesh.

My heart bucked.

Had he chased them off because he was a Good Samaritan or because he wanted what they were about to take? Despite his assurances he wasn't like them...how could I be sure?

"Look, whoever you are. Thank you for saving me. But I must insist you let me go." I spotted the bomber jacket Adidas had torn off me and ducked to pick it up. Holding the black material in front of me like a shield, I said, "Step aside. Let me pass."

The glittering lights of civilization promised safety down the long tunnel of the alley. All I wanted to do was go home.

Home.

A taxi.

*I need money.*

Holding my hand out, I kept my eyes down. "Can I have my

belongings, please?"

"Your belongings?"

His deep voice somehow avoided my ears and echoed deep in my belly instead. I shifted on the spot, a chill from him and the night sky painting me in goosebumps.

He came closer, tipping his chin up. Shadows slunk back as if afraid of him as I clutched bravery and looked up.

Everything about him was cloaked. "I won't bite."

I flinched, doing my best to drink in his face so I could remember it—just in case I had to file a police report.

*Which I don't want to do as my father must never know about this.*

His eyes and forehead remained hidden by his hood, but his lips were in full view. Firm and masculine with just the right amount of stubble that'd turned into a short beard. He was rugged, bordering unkempt.

One hand vanished into his jean's pocket. "Do you mean these?" He fanned the cash and my I.D badge.

I nodded. "Yes, those. Can I have them?"

He counted the bills. "Eighty bucks?"

I tilted my chin. "It's all I need."

Why did I feel like the biggest liar in history? I didn't know what it was like to have only eighty dollars. I had unlimited funds. Just because I didn't shop or had no one to lavish gifts with didn't mean I didn't appreciate the freedom of never having to look at a price tag.

"Need to do what?" He cocked his head, the hoodie still covering his gaze.

"If you must know. To taxi home."

"Ah." He said it like a full stop. As if it made perfect sense to this evening of nonsense.

I wriggled my fingers. "So…can I have it back?"

He ran my lanyard I.D through his fingers. "Let's talk about this first."

"What about it?"

"Your name is Noelle Charlston?"

"What of it?"

"You're named after Christmas."

I huffed. "I'm named after—" *One of the richest founders in retail.* I held my tongue. I didn't need this rescue to turn into a kidnapping for ransom.

"Named after what?" He danced the I.D over his knuckles with a dexterity that made my mouth go dry. A streak of blood marred the laminated photo.

I stepped toward him, despite every neuron wanting to run.

"My name is Elle. Just call me Elle, give me back my things, and let me go."

"I don't think so, Elle. Not yet."

I froze. "Excuse me?"

"You intrigue me."

"So?"

"So, it's not often someone intrigues me."

"Why?"

He moved closer. His body heat was noticeable in the chilly evening. "Because I don't normally take the time to actually talk to people. You're an exception."

I didn't know if I liked being an exception. Did that mean he might do other things that were an exception—like hurt me when he'd normally free me?

Nerves made me shiver. Clamping down on such weakness, my hand lashed out and snatched my I.D card. "There. I've taken back what's mine. You can't get mad. It never belonged to you." My eyes landed on the money. "Give that back, and we'll go our separate ways."

He smiled. His teeth were straight and white in the dark scruff of his beard. "I don't think so, Noelle Charlston."

"Elle."

"Okay, Elle." He took another step, ungluing shadows from around him until only a foot separated us. I sucked in air as his black sneakers crunched on loose gravel and his hands came up.

I stiffened, waiting for him to take what his runaway buddies had tried. Only, his fingers didn't connect with me, they connected with the material of his black hood. Slowly, he pushed it away and let it fall, revealing his face.

My lungs forgot how to work as I drank him in.

Fierce eyebrows gave expression and authority to the intensity of his dark brown eyes. Dark hair bordering on black curled around his cheeks, forehead, and ears, speaking of wildness rather than tamed. His strong nose and refined cheekbones were perfect adornments to the beard bordering his lips.

Hell, those lips.

They were soft and damp and almost kind when everything else about him looked cruel.

I'd been around men in the office, but all of them were either overweight, older, or gay. I'd never been so close to an attractive male similar in age and completely ruthless in violence.

I stepped back, cursing the wobble in my knees. I wanted to put it down to fear, but my stupid heart said otherwise.

I was *attracted* to him.

Here of all places.

Him of all men.

My body found his utterly appealing for the first time in my life, and I had no idea how to deal with that.

What did that say about me?

I'd narrowly avoided being hurt and somehow indulged in an attraction for a man I'd met in the worst circumstances.

*I'm not normal.*

Whatever interest I felt could not be tolerated.

I narrowed my eyes. "What do you want from me?"

He smiled, his mouth once again bewitching me. "Not sure yet."

I pinched myself, trying to get my runaway hormones under control. I wasn't some horny teenager. I was a CEO who almost got molested. So what he was good looking?

*That means nothing!*

*You need to go home.*

*Right now.*

Steeling myself against him—grateful when my heart stayed in a normal *thud-thud* and not the desire-fueled flutter from before—I snapped, "What do you mean?"

He shifted, kicking one leg out for balance. It wasn't anything but an adjustment, but it drew my attention down his body. To how tall he was. How his thigh shaped the dirty denim. How he wore mystery like an expensive new fashion must-have. "I mean, there's something about you."

*There's something about you, too.*

Even the darkness of the alley couldn't detract from three things I noticed right away:

One, he was entirely too handsome (or I'd been far too sheltered to be alone with him).

Two, he had an aura about him that demanded respect that wasn't born but earned.

Three, he was filthy but didn't seem to care as I followed a stain in his hoodie then a scuff then a hole.

He just stood there, allowing my inspection as he repaid the favor. His eyes had fingers, trailing over my skin with gentle feathers, forcing me to catch my breath even though I remained still.

*Oh, my God, get a grip, Elle.*

*Yes, he saved you.*

*Yes, he was brave enough to stop a crime.*

*But that's all there is to it, and all there'll ever be.*

*You are not a silly girl who gets crushes.*

*Time to go.*

Whatever this was meant nothing.

It couldn't.

Things like this didn't happen in real life, and they certainly didn't happen in *my* life.

Just because Dad had stopped reading me fairy-tales long ago didn't mean I needed to fabricate such ridiculousness now.

I forced myself to look at his face. I'd almost forgotten what we discussed, which was idiotic, and crazy, and so unlike me, panic whizzed through my blood, making me curt. "Money. I need it." I held out my hand, hating the wobble. "I want to leave."

"Leave?"

"Yes."

"You can't leave."

"What?" My eyebrows shot upright as my pulse thrummed in my punch-bruised temple. "Of course, I can leave. I *want* to leave. You said you wouldn't hurt me."

He held up his hand, oblivious to his dirty nails and dried blood on his knuckles. "Easy. You can go. I'm not holding you captive—I didn't mean that."

"What *did* you mean?"

He wafted the money, making the bills flop in his fist. "I mean…we need to talk about this money."

My hackles rose. "What about it?"

He ran his tongue over his bottom lip, distracting me. His gaze locked on mine, either aware of the reaction he caused or seeking answers to his own curiosity.

His voice lowered to a murmur. "I saved your life."

"You did." My voice slipped to a whisper, accepting the quietness almost with relief. Tension unwound from my shoulders only to spool tight again as he said, "I think the generous thing to do is offer me your cash."

Half of my brain knew why—he'd given me a service and nothing in life was free. But the other half was so befuddled, so drunk on his beard-covered jaw and kissable lips, I wrinkled my nose. "What for?"

He coughed with a thread of annoyance. "Payment, of course. For saving you. We just agreed that's what I did?"

Another injection of adrenaline flooded my veins. I nodded, wound up and jumpy with the way he watched me. "You're right. You did save me. It's only right you earn a reward." I wouldn't deny him payment—especially when it looked as though his clothes had seen better days. But I also couldn't fight the small terror of how I would get home.

*You walked here.*

*You can walk back.*

Technically, I could. I just couldn't envision walking through the city after what had just happened without jumping at shadows every step.

*I'm not cut out for the outside world.*

I should've stayed in my tower and played with my cat and ran my father's company like I'd been groomed to.

Hooded Man flicked the money with his spare hand. "Great. I accept. Thank you."

"Thank *you* for saving me."

He flashed his teeth. "You're welcome."

Something switched between us, removing the threat of violence, putting us at an impasse.

His shoulders sagged a little. Glancing at the money, his face darkened as if fighting an internal war. Suddenly, he held out the bills. "Here, take it."

"But I just gave it to you. You're right—"

His fingers latched around my wrist, while his other hand slammed the notes into my palm. "I don't want it."

I gasped at the heat of his touch. At the way my skin ignited beneath his. How the crackle of awareness increased a thousand-fold. And then it was gone as he yanked his hands away and backed up.

Dragging his fingers through his black-brown hair, he muttered, "I should go."

Here was my chance to return home without any more mishaps. I could nod and agree and walk out of the alley to summon a chariot to drive me back to my realm.

But his despondency made my fear switch to empathy. Just as I'd fed the homeless man in Times Square, I wanted to help this one, too.

*If he is even homeless.*

For all I knew, he was a masked crusader running around the

city, getting dirty by helping women like me who had no right being out so late alone.

I broached the small space between us. "I truly am grateful."

"I know."

Steeling myself, I leaned forward and stuffed the bills into the front pocket of his hoodie.

Such a bad move.

Inside was warm with the faint grit of crumbs and life-dirt but against the soft material was a hard stomach, breathing fast.

"What the fuck are you doing?" His voice was a spur, kicking my heart into a frenzy.

I yanked my hand from his pocket, leaving the cash inside. "I want you to have the money. In return for a favor."

His face tightened. "I've already done you a favor, remember?"

"I remember." I glanced at his bloody knuckles where a few had swollen and bruised with injury. "Would you let me look at your hands or at least buy you some Tylenol?"

"No."

*Okay…*

"In that case, all I ask in exchange for the money is you to escort me home."

Home?

*What the hell are you doing?*

I couldn't afford to let this vagabond know where I lived. Dad would be mortified. Our furniture and belongings would probably be stolen once he figured out our daily schedule and knew when the house was vacant.

*You're an awful person.*

How could I think such things after he'd saved me?

*Trust.*

I had to trust him, despite outward appearances and circumstances.

*Believe.*

I had to believe in my gut when it said he wasn't to be feared.

I wanted him to have the money over a grouchy cab driver. All he had to do was walk me back.

"You want me to take you home?" His mouth parted. His face remained in shadow, visible but still a mystery. "Are you serious?"

"Yes."

"You want me to know where you live?"

"If you were going to hurt me, you would've done it by now." I opened my arm to incorporate the alley. "We're alone. You already know I'm terrible at escape. Yet you've been a perfect gentleman."

He barked a laugh. "Gentleman? Right." He scrubbed his face, highlighting the dirt on his neck as he looked at the sky. "How do you know I'm not just delaying my attack to put you at ease and make you pliable?"

"Pliable? Who uses the word pliable to discuss hurting women?"

He smirked, lips smiling, eyes not. "Me."

"And who is me?"

He frowned. "What do you mean?"

I put my hands on my hips. "You know my name. What's yours?"

He stumbled back. "You—you want to know my name?"

Was that a bad thing? Had he done something terrible and didn't want anyone to know? "Isn't it normal for strangers to share with another? That's how they stop being strangers."

He coughed, rubbing his nape. "Not where I'm from."

"Where are you from?"

His shock faded, smothered once again with a cocky attitude. His shoulders came up, proud and standoffish. "You're nosy."

I bristled. "Only making conversation."

"Well, don't. Let's just go, shall we?" He looked around the alley. "I hate places like this."

I wanted to ask what sort of places were those, but I didn't dare. Instead, I focused on how I could get home. "Will you walk with me?"

"You think I'll protect you?"

*Well, yes.*

"You did before."

"That was because I don't agree with rape and robbery. Not because I have a hero complex. The minute you're out of this alley, you cease to be my concern."

"Oh." I didn't know why that hurt as much as it did. Straightening my back, I sucked up my fear, preparing to strike out on my own—like I always did. "Okay, then. Well…how much do taxis cost to get to Upper East Side?"

One eyebrow raised. "You live on the Upper East Side and have no idea how much taxis are?" He peered harder. "You don't just work in an office for minimum wage, do you?"

I didn't know why, but I wanted to maintain my identity as a low-income earner. I didn't want to come across as bragging, or worse, rubbing his nose in it. The longer we talked, the more I saw what his clothes hinted at.

He either lived rough or didn't have a home. He wasn't like the homeless man I gave my dinner to—this man didn't smell, and his clothes were cleanish (minus a few stains) even if they were a little holey. But he had that scrapper look about him—a glare in his eyes, speaking of mistrust and hardship.

"Let's agree to keep personal information secret, okay?" I asked. "You don't want to tell me your name. I don't want to tell you anything more." I held up my hand. "Agree to take me home, and we won't ask questions. Deal?"

It took a little while, but he finally slipped his hand into mine and shook.

It took everything I had not to react to the desire crackling from his palm.

He smiled. "Deal."

# Chapter Eight

NEW YORK WAS an exciting city to explore on my own.

But exploring it with another person—someone intensely attractive and utterly unpredictable—was one of the most incredible things I'd ever done.

Ten minutes had passed since leaving the alley and in ten minutes, my pulse had skyrocketed then equalized to a steady thrum of awareness.

Walking beside him shouldn't be such an adventure. He was just a man. This was just a city. But every footfall felt different. Every breath and glance and heartbeat.

We navigated the crowds together, pulling apart and re-joining as the curb became congested then empty. Midnight struck the clock in Times Square, reminding me my birthday was officially over and a new day had begun.

I should be in bed.

I should call Dad to tell him I was okay, just in case he noticed I'd never come home.

Worries layered me, taking away the complex, not-entirely-understood joy of strolling through the city at night with a strange man at my side. I did my best to shove the thoughts away, but they remained like a constant toothache.

"This way." The man stepped off the sidewalk and crossed the road, keeping an eye out for oncoming traffic. "You sure you want to walk?"

"Yes, I'm sure."

"Okay." He stuffed his hands into his jeans pockets, his shoulders bunched around his ears. He couldn't be cold. The air temperature wasn't too bad. Although, I had shrugged into the bomber jacket and zipped it up to my throat to replace the ruined top, so perhaps it was colder than I gave credit for.

A fine layer of sweat decorated my spine from walking at his quick pace.

He didn't dawdle like I had. He moved ahead with long, leggy strides, expecting me to keep up. He didn't glance at me or ask questions. It gave me time to steal glances, whipping away memories of his height, mannerisms, and habits.

Not that I could read him.

His body language remained closed off; his arms tucked tight, jaw clenched firm. The beard hid the bottom half of his face, keeping him partially masked and perplexing.

Each step granted different thoughts: recollections of what'd happened with Adidas and Baseball Cap and what could've been the ruining of my body and mind if they'd succeeded in raping me. Followed by the relief that this cryptic wanderer had been there at the right time and saved me.

How could I ever repay that?

He hadn't just prevented a robbery. He'd stopped me from turning into a different person. He'd provided me with shelter from a crossroads that might've switched my existence from Belle Elle heiress to mentally broken dependant.

*I wouldn't have let it break me.*

But how could I know that? I believed in myself because of Dad's tutelage and support. But I was still young. Nineteen was nothing compared to the years ahead. The years this man had given back to me in a selfless act of protection.

The more we walked, the deeper the debt I had to pay. Shock gave way to realization of how close I'd come to being raped. I could still be in that alley, beaten, bloody, destroyed.

*But I'm not.*

He turned into more than just a stranger; he became my shield. A shield I needed to repay by any means necessary because eighty dollars was *nothing* compared to what he'd done.

My thoughts kept me busy as we did another block, heading past closed stores and an occasional drunk pedestrian. I snuck glances at my companion, growing ever desperate to ask questions and learn pieces about him. To talk to the man who I'd only just met but who'd impacted my life more than anyone.

Did he know how grateful I was?

Did he understand what he'd done by saving me?

If he were homeless, I would help him.

If he were struggling, I would pay him.

A life for a life.

I wouldn't stop until I'd saved his as he'd done mine.

His dark gaze captured me. Turbulent and deep, the pools of ferocity and calculation hid softer emotions underneath. We weaved around thinning foot traffic, linked in some kismet way, moving close and apart, tethered with shared incident.

I hated that I'd already lied to him. That I hadn't told him my real profession and hidden who I was. But I liked him believing I was nothing more than an office worker with a shoe box for a home. I liked him thinking I was normal and not untouchable like all the boys from my school had.

*I like the way he looks at me.*

Like he felt something, too. Something he couldn't understand—something that wasn't sexual or chemical or named. But something tugging us to stay together, to chase whatever it was that bounced from him to me.

I smiled softly, dropping my head as his stare became too intense. The hot blush on my cheeks hinted at my inexperience but also my openness around him. If I didn't feel something, I wouldn't care how he looked at me. If my tummy hadn't turned into a trampoline, my heart double bouncing on my lungs, I wouldn't mind the taut silence slowly growing tighter every second.

My father would be happy I'd found a...friend?

Dad's firm but fair face appeared in my mind.

*Oh, no!*

My hand swooped to my throat to touch the sapphire star he'd given me—the star that made me feel so close to him. The one he'd bought me out of love.

It wasn't there.

My neck was empty.

*They took it!*

*I forgot to tell him to get it back.*

I slammed to a stop, looking over my shoulder as my fingers danced along my naked collarbone. Dad would kill me! He would know I'd been out and mugged because there was no other way I would've let that necklace go.

*Shit.*

"Is everything okay?" He slowed a little, his arms relaxing with hands stuffed in his front hoodie pocket.

"My necklace. They still have it."

He stopped. "What necklace?"

"My birthday present." I sighed heavily, the weight of tears already crushing. "I know a silly necklace won't mean much to you, but it was sentimental."

He spread his legs, once again drawing my attention to how lithe and fast he looked. "You didn't mention it when I asked if they'd taken anything else."

"I know!" I grabbed my hair, twisting it with nerves. "I forgot. It all happened so fast."

"If it meant so much to you, you should've remembered." His tone wasn't condescending or cruel, but his words bit into me like wasps.

I swallowed my sadness, embracing anger. "It was new. He gave it to me this morning."

"And you're sure they took it?"

"Of course, I'm sure." I spun around, yanking my hair off my nape to show the cut left behind from when they'd yanked the chain. "See?"

"I asked for your belongings to be returned." His face hardened as if taking my loss personally. "They returned them."

"I know—"

"Be grateful you didn't have to give up something else other than a birthday trinket." He licked his lips, sullen annoyance bright in his gaze. "By the way, happy birthday." He turned and stalked forward, either expecting me to follow or doing his best to revoke his promise to escort me home.

He was right, of course. A silly gemstone in exchange for avoiding pain? It was a small price to pay. But my God, it hurt to think of my father's gift—my beautiful sapphire star—in the hands of those creeps. Being touched by them, sitting in their grimy pockets, destined to be sold to someone who would never know its origins.

*Dad will hate me.*

Guilt ate at me with sharp silver teeth. My father would understand if I told him the truth about what'd happened—if I was brave enough to admit I'd left without telling anyone. He would forgive me.

But what would this man think of me? He'd rescued me, and instead of being relieved, I'd almost burst into tears because a necklace that was worth a few thousand had been taken.

A life was worth more than a bauble. I wasn't a silly child anymore.

I'd never been a silly child.

*I won't start now.*

Breaking into a jog, I caught up to him and touched his forearm. "I'm sorry. I made it seem like I wasn't grateful. That I was blaming you for not getting it back." I licked my lips. "I'm not. I'm just sad I let them take it, but you're right. It's only a necklace."

He slammed to a stop, his eyes locked on where I touched him. He swallowed hard. "You don't have to explain to me."

"Yes, I do. I owe you. I don't want you to think I'm some sort of princess."

He shifted, his mouth pursing as he looked me up and down. "What birthday?"

I blinked. "What?"

"How old did you turn?"

"Oh, um—" I struggled to tell him. Not because I wanted to keep my private life private but because he was older than I was. He looked mid-twenties with hardness only born from fighting every day of his life. I was soft where he was sharp. I knew how to fight but in boardrooms and on conference calls, not on the streets.

He sighed. "I get it. You don't have to tell me." Pushing away, he continued walking; his jeans scuffed by his dirty sneakers.

"No, wait." I trotted after him. "I want to tell you."

He paused as I returned to his side, comfortable beside him even though I didn't know him. "I turned nineteen."

He laughed, low and short. "Wow, I knew you were young but not *that* young."

"How young did you think?"

His eyes tightened. "Twenty, twenty-one."

"That's not a big difference."

He pushed off again, wedging his hands into his pockets, revealing a habit. "Still a teen."

I didn't let that irritate me. "How old are you?"

A slight chuckle sounded as he pulled his hood back up, hiding his shaggy black-brown hair, adding yet more shadows to his handsome face. "Older than you."

With the hood and the night sky, his face danced on my memory, already fading—as if my eyes hadn't captured his features enough to imprint long-term recollection.

I crossed my arms. "Tell me. I told you."

He glanced at me sideways. "Twenty-five."

"Six years. That's not much."

"It's enough to get some people thrown in jail."

"Some people?"

He tossed his head with a tight roll of his shoulders. "Forget it."

We walked in silence for a moment, my fingers trailing once again to my naked throat. I hated that I'd forgotten about my necklace. That I hadn't taken stock and asked for it back. Did that mean I wasn't worthy of such a gift—if I didn't appreciate it enough to remember?

In a rash decision, I said, "You know, if I had remembered to ask for my necklace, it wouldn't have been mine anymore."

He scowled, waiting for me to continue.

"It would've been yours."

Surprise flickered over his obscured face before finally settling into polite refusal. "No."

"No?"

"Just no."

Prickles raced down my spine. Half of me wanted to force him to accept the imaginary gift. A sapphire could've converted to showers and meals and a roof over his head rather than dangle around my silly little neck.

But he hunched his shoulders—not in a regretful way but more regal, more honorable than I'd ever seen. "I don't need your fucking charity."

His curse cut through our odd conversation.

I couldn't undermine his good deed by forcing him to hypothetically accept something he would never have. But he had to know how much I appreciated his help. "I'll give you more money when we get home, okay? I'll make sure you're compensated—"

"I'm not after your damn money," he snapped. "If I was, I could've done what they did and robbed you where there were no witnesses."

The busy city faded around me. "You wouldn't."

"You don't know me."

"You're right. I don't." I ignored my sudden shiver. "So tell me."

"Tell you what?"

"What do you want? Where are you from? How can I return the favor?"

He bared his teeth. "I want nothing. I'm from nowhere. And you can't return it."

I didn't let his fisted hands or taut body sway me. "Wanting nothing isn't true. And you're from somewhere…but I get if you want to keep it secret. Surely, there's something you need." I waved my arm at the congested pavement. "You're not walking for your health." I pointed at his bloody hands. "Talking about health, you should probably have those looked at." I moved closer, grabbing his wrist without thinking.

He stiffened.

Electricity sprang from him to me and me to him and every which way around us until we stood in a web of sparks from just the simplest touch.

His jaw clenched; his eyes narrowed and dark. Placing his hand over mine on his wrist, he ever so slowly pulled at my fingers until my grip was no more. Dropping my hand from him, he whispered, "There is something."

I shook my head, lost and confused and so scrambled I couldn't follow. He noticed the question in my eyes, answering for me. "There is something I want *from you.*"

"What? What do you want?"

He glanced away as if he hadn't meant to say that. For a second, he looked like he'd bolt into the crowds and vanish. But then he cleared his throat. "Do you trust me?"

"What?"

His chocolate eyes locked on mine again. "Do you trust me?"

"I just met you."

"Doesn't matter. Yes or no."

What should I say? That yes, in some weird way, I *did* trust him. Or no, I wasn't stupid enough to trust someone who beat up two guys and then kept me longer than necessary in an alley.

He glowered, his intensity once again causing goosebumps. "Yes or no. It's not hard."

Slowly, I nodded. "Yes, I trust you."

"Good." He wrapped an arm around my waist and yanked me off the footpath. Without a word, he herded me across the road. Reaching the other side, he let me go but didn't move far away.

Shared body heat hummed between us, growing thicker with things I didn't understand. Things all so new and foreign but desperately wanted. "Where are we going?"

"Central Park."

"What?" I slammed to a halt. "You can't be serious. No one goes in there at this time of night. For safety reasons and for security. It's not open."

He grinned; the streetlight above him painted him in a golden glow, looking part angel, part devil. "I know a way in."

I backed up. "I've changed my mind. Let's just go home."

His face darkened then solidified into determination. "You don't get to do that. You just agreed to trust me." He stepped forward, his chest brushing mine. The cheap material of the bomber jacket rubbed the lace of my bra, making me achingly sensitive. My neck bent to look up at him, drinking in the way his hair ran wild around his face, and his beard masked him, revealing only what he wanted to reveal.

"I'll take you home afterward." His hand came up, brushing aside a wayward blonde strand, his fingers kissing the side of my face.

I jolted but couldn't move away. The concrete had turned into super glue.

Before I could reply, he dropped his touch, grabbed my hand, and dragged me toward the wall of Central Park.

He looked over his shoulder as we patrolled the rock barricade. Hauling himself up, he swung his legs over and dropped into nothing.

I dashed to the wall and looked down.

In the darkness, I barely made out his shape a few feet below.

His head tilted toward me, once again cloaked in the shadows he seemed to rule over, only his hands and face visible as he reached up. "Jump. I'll catch you."

*You'll catch me?*

I wanted to yell, but the occasional late-night dog walker on the other side of the street kept me quiet. This was illegal. I didn't want to get caught. Imagine the publicity if this got out that I'd snuck out on my birthday, almost got molested, gave my dinner to a homeless guy, then gallivanted around the city doing bad things with a total stranger.

*Who the hell am I?*

I should turn around and find my own way home. I should hop in a cab and pay the driver when he dropped me off with the petty cash that was stored in the cloakroom upon arrival at Belle Elle.

I had so many options.

So I had no excuse when I deliberately chose none of them.

I slung my jean-clad legs over the wall, inhaled deep, and let go.

# Chapter Nine

HIS ARMS WERE warm steel.

He caught me in my semi-slide as I plummeted down the rock wall. He didn't manage to catch my entire weight, and my legs jarred as they hit the ground, but he cradled my torso with infinitesimal gentleness.

We stayed like that for far longer than necessary, swaying in each other's embrace, somehow deleting the stranger danger and becoming acquainted instead.

He cleared his throat, moving back.

I shivered as his arms unraveled, leaving me to my own gravity, removing himself from my orbit.

He waited until I had my balance before striding into the gloom. "Now that we're in, keep an eye out for security guards."

Fear multiplied. "Guards? As in guards with guns?"

"Probably. Doesn't everyone in America own a gun?"

I hated that he was right. Even my father had one locked in a case at home. Not that he'd ever used it—that was why we had bodyguards.

The thought of how different our worlds were made me self-conscious. What would he say if I admitted that the building glowing the brightest on the horizon was mine? That I crunched numbers and paid bills on a daily basis valued at more than he'd probably seen in his entire life?

He didn't notice my sudden heavy steps as he slinked through the few bushes and disappeared into the dark.

Following him, I did my best not to imagine monsters in the swaying foliage and remain level-headed. I missed Sage. I missed her whiskers and long, silver tail. I missed normalcy and a place where *I* was in charge and not the universe taking me on a jeopardy-filled odyssey.

But even as homesickness filled part of my heart, freedom filled the other. The longer I was in his company, the more I found the confidence to be the girl who stood up to crooks in nothing but her bra. To speak my mind and chase after a man who did strange things to my stomach.

And above all, not to embarrass myself.

Whoever my guide was, he had an air of aloof confidence that made it vital he saw me as strong not weak if I wanted him to notice me and not just pity me.

We didn't speak as we navigated the bushes. A few lights here and there offered illumination, while the flashlight of a security guard patrolling in the distance made us hug the treeline.

"Where are we going?" I whispered.

"You'll see."

Our sneakers scuffed through brush and twigs, so loud to my ears but no doubt unnoticeable by whoever enforced the laws about breaking into this place.

Popping from the undergrowth, we dashed across a path and entered a grassy field with caged baseball courts under the half moon.

"Come on. Hurry." He held out his hand, guiding me toward the super high chain link fence. "Climb."

"What?" I peered into the star-lit sky. "Are you insane?"

He looked over his shoulder as a branch snapped. "Hurry." Pushing me upward, he didn't give me a choice. His hand landed on my ass, searing his fingerprints into my flesh. A comet somehow fell from the dark velvet above and lodged itself in my chest.

It took every ounce of concentration to climb when all I could think about was his fingers touching me where no other man had before.

He followed me, scaling so much faster with experience. Reaching the top, he slung his body over and just let go. His black-clad body fell with all the grace of a jungle cat.

I didn't have the balls.

I crawled over the top—thankful there was no barbwire—and climbed down a few rungs before finally dropping to the stable ground below. My fingers smarted from gripping the harsh metal.

He showed no sign of being affected at touching me in an intimate place so I didn't either—even though my ass cheek throbbed as if he'd spanked me.

"Won't they see us in here?" I glanced around for security

cameras. I spied one aimed at the home diamond. "Wait." I hissed.

He turned around, his eyebrow arched in question.

"The camera." I cocked my chin at the lens glinting in the starlight.

"It doesn't work."

The way he said it made it sound as if he knew exactly why it didn't work. *So he's a vandal and a vigilante?*

Fighting my nerves, I paced after him until we stood in the center of the field. All around us (outside the chain link) were manicured lawns and sweeping trees to give watchers a spot of shade on hot days.

Once in the middle of the playing field, he fell into a cross-legged position and tugged my hand to join him.

I struggled against his weight for a second but finally gave in and joined him. The moment I was sitting, he pushed my shoulder.

My abs clenched against his pressure, trying to stay upright.

But it was no use.

His eyes locked on mine, adding more authority until I gave up fighting and followed his command. Down and down, until my spine kissed the soft grass.

My heart chugged blood like it was starving.

Untangling his legs, he reclined, slowly slotting his body along mine, stealing my breath, making every cell spring into tiny knife-like blades of sensation.

His gaze landed on my lips, drawing awareness and concentration into overpowering levels. My head swam with the possibility of him kissing me. His gaze hooded, his own thoughts of kissing me coating his face.

I didn't know how I felt about him kissing me. Would I let him? Would I scream?

I hated to admit that I *would* let him. That I'd probably kiss him back. That despite my wariness, I trusted him, and if I was going to do something as reckless as kiss a total stranger under the moon in the middle of Central Park, it would be this nameless man.

*Is this what he meant when he said he wanted something from me?*

Did he think I was easy?

A sure thing?

Even with such awful thoughts in my head, my body didn't buy into the shame.

My chin arched. I licked my lips. The world stood still.

He swayed closer, propping himself up on an elbow to hover

his face over mine.

*Oh God, he's truly going to kiss me.*

My first real kiss.

Something I would remember for the rest of my life, regardless if I remained a spinster to Belle Elle or married a man who would always be second best to my career.

But then…he stopped.

Pulling back, he shook his head and lay back down. "What the fuck am I doing?" Cradling his head in the palm of his hand, he looked up at the moon. For the shortest glimpse, a tortured need glimmered in his gaze then disappeared.

I sucked in a much-needed breath, trying to decide what the hell just happened.

My mouth went dry. My chest full of feathered wings. Jitters took over my motor skills as I replayed the almost-kiss over and over.

A few minutes ticked past.

The grass rustled as he sat up, digging his hand into his hoodie pocket.

Pulling free a wrapped chocolate bar, he glanced at me with a faint glint of possession and indecision.

My stomach growled at the sight of food, reminding me I hadn't eaten since a mouthful of spicy beef burrito. He smirked at my noisy tummy then courteously but reluctantly offered me the chocolate. "Here. You sound hungrier than I am."

My hand came up, accepting his gift. Waiting to make sure I had hold of it, he dropped his arm. He sighed heavily, finding it hard to tear his gaze away from the chocolate and focus on the moon.

His own stomach gurgled quietly as he placed a splayed hand over his waist and pressed down.

Everything inside me hurt. The vulnerability of him in that moment. The generosity of giving up the only food he had, even though he was most likely starving. I worked with people on a daily basis who would rather throw out entire platters of food than donate it to those in need. The news on TV was full of greed and cruelty and rich assholes thinking only of themselves.

And then there was him.

A man I didn't know. A savior I'd only just met. But someone who had a profound effect on me in the hour we'd been together.

He sighed again, swallowing hard as he finally tore his gaze away and looked at the stars.

When was the last time he ate? Where did he get a candy bar? When was the last time he'd eaten anything more substantial than just chocolate?

My hunger turned to indigestion as I did my best to guess his story. His body hunched as his stomach stopped growling. His sneaker-covered feet were thread bear and rubber-worn, speaking of so many miles traveled and no sanctuary found. The silver glint of the moon played on the black of his hoodie, making it seem as if he dressed in liquid mercury.

My hands shook as I opened the candy bar and slowly unwrapped it. His jaw clenched at the noise of the wrapper. The soft rustling of grass hinted he wasn't as relaxed as he appeared. The tension rippling off him was that of a starving wolf wanting to attack its prey but finding restraint...barely.

I couldn't stop staring at him. Couldn't stop my heart from pushing through my ribs to go to him. To demand his name, his background, to know how he had such a power over me.

*What is this...magic...between us?*

Was it like this between any boy and girl? Was the desire to cuddle close and listen as much as the need to curl close and kiss the basis of...*dare I say it*...attraction?

I scoffed.

*Attraction?*

*What do you know about attraction, Elle?*

*You're a closet romantic who knows nothing but spread-sheets and merchandise.*

I was an idiot to believe there was something going on between us—known or unknown, unique or mundane.

The chocolate bar melted a little in my fingers. My tummy churned; I did the only thing I could do. I had to accept his gift now; otherwise, he would know I suspected he was homeless and hungry and would never tolerate my pity.

But I couldn't eat it all because if he *was* homeless, what else would he have? How long would that eighty dollars last him in a city that was so expensive just to survive?

Tearing the chocolate in half, I sat up and placed his half on his knee. "Thank you."

His eyes found mine as his hand latched over the candy. His gaze danced over my face, lips, and hands. His fingers curled almost unconsciously around the chocolate with a feral gleam, just daring me to take it away.

Slowly, he nodded, accepting that I knew things he didn't

want to say and agreed to eat because, if nothing else, there was trust between us.

I gave him some space by looking away.

Taking my time, I nibbled on the chocolate, nougat, and caramel, doing my best to focus on taste rather than my physical awareness of him.

It was impossible.

The entire evening—from the perfumed park, to the dewy grass, to the silent man inhaling half a chocolate bar—seared on my mind like an old-fashioned photograph, developing from blurred to sharp with hasty capture. A memory created by this man, this night, and this sugary confectionery. I would never again walk through Central Park without remembering him or how much he'd shaken up my innocent, boring world.

Taking tiny bites to make the treat last longer, I didn't expect conversation. So when a soft murmur interrupted the silence of the park, I jolted.

"Do you come here often?"

I wanted to giggle. It sounded like a cheesy pick-up line. He didn't crack a smile or soften. He was serious.

I looked at him through the waterfall of blonde hair that'd fallen over my shoulder. He'd already finished his dinner (or was that breakfast or lunch or a midnight snack?) Once again, the shadows of his beard and the silver-light made him seem mystical and not quite real. Too handsome to be real. Too *much* to be real.

I swallowed my nerves and chocolate. "Not as much as I would like."

"Why?"

"Because I work all hours of the day. I rarely get to leave the office."

He shifted his eyes from the open field to the tall buildings in the distance with their glowing windows and adult obligations. Belle Elle was the brightest jewel, mocking me, telling me to come home.

"Do you like it? Being cooped up all day with no freedom?"

I shrugged. "Who truly loves their work?"

He didn't reply.

"I get satisfaction from doing a job well done. I like knowing I've done something worthwhile." I looked down. "So yes, I guess I do enjoy it."

He kept his attention on the buildings, glaring at Belle Elle as if he already knew it owned my life and soul, and that whatever this was, it was nothing compared to contracts and lifetime legacies. "It must be nice to afford expensive things like birthday necklaces."

I licked my fingers free of my final bite of candy. "Do you know much about jewelry?"

He threw me a caustic look. "I'm not completely ignorant. Just because I'm—" He cut himself off, returning to stare at the cityscape. "I know enough."

"I'm not saying you didn't."

"Just drop it."

"For your information, I didn't buy that necklace. It was a gift. I did mention that."

He tensed. "From a boyfriend?"

"Would it bother you if I said yes?"

He laughed harshly. "Why would it bother me?"

I shook my head, my cheeks pinking in embarrassment. I had no idea why I'd asked or why it hurt so much that he'd found my question funny. "No reason."

I couldn't look up. The grass was suddenly incredibly interesting. I plucked a few blades, running them through my fingers.

Out the corner of my eye, I saw him twist slightly, his face hidden. Slowly, his hand came up, his fingers nudging my chin. I didn't want to look at him, but his pressure gave me no choice.

I let him raise my head. Our eyes locked and breathing became a task I could no longer perform.

"Do you trust me?"

I trembled as his fingers slowly unfurled from guiding my head up to linking around my nape.

I couldn't speak.

I managed the smallest nod.

His fingers tightened, pulling my face toward his. I sucked in a shallow breath as his gaze dove deeper into mine and his tongue wetted his lips. "I—I won't hurt you."

His whisper landed on my mouth just before he pulled me hard.

Our lips connected.

I froze.

The scent of grass and strange male hit my nostrils. The wildness of open skies and midnight made me uninhibited and free. My eyes grew heavy, closing of their own accord as he added pressure to the kiss, tilting my head with his grip behind my neck.

I gave up every control without a thought. My spine turned to water. My insides to steam.

He groaned a little, understanding my submission even when I didn't.

Scooting closer, his lips parted. The tip of his tongue darted out to test me. Test to see if I trusted him enough to let him kiss me in an empty park. Trust him enough not to go too far or hurt me.

I answered back in the only language I currently knew. My lips opened, my tongue hesitantly touching his with truth. The explosion of chocolate made me moan under my breath as he licked deep inside my mouth.

He didn't hesitate.

There was no sloppiness or confusion. His hand held me steady, his mouth worked mine, and every part of me flared with drowning, dark desire.

He shifted until his knees nudged mine, his arm wrapping around my waist, deleting the space between us. The awkwardness of sitting on damp grass wrapped in a man I didn't know didn't stop the heat of the kiss from escalating.

Our tongues met and retreated.

Our lips slipped and connected.

With every heartbeat, we increased speed and depth until I lost control of the rest of my body and found my fingers in his long dark hair, tugging the lengths, learning the strands weren't soft like silk but thick and dreadlocked with neglect.

That I was kissing a potentially homeless man didn't stop me from wanting more. Grabbing a fistful of his hair, I pulled him demandingly into me.

He swayed closer then snapped. He pushed me backward, forcing me to lie down. The moment I was horizontal, he lay down beside me. One leg pressed over mine, his thigh deliberately going between my legs. His body weight pinned me down.

I tried to fight, doing my best to hold on to some resemblance of decency, but the moment he lay half on top of me, wedging our bodies together as if this was *exactly* what we were born to do—with his erection against my hip, and his arm around my waist, and his tongue in my mouth, and his touch on my neck...I gave in.

I wasn't afraid.

I wasn't lost.

Not like I was an hour ago when two men pressed their

unwanted pieces of anatomy against me. This man…I *wanted* him to. This man I didn't know but shared an intoxicating connection with.

Lights flashed in my eyes as his tongue dove deeper, dragging another moan from every crevice left inside me. I looped my leg around his, arching my hips, pressing against his hardness, feeling myself swell and heat and melt and *yearn.*

He groaned long and low as our hips fought to get closer. Impatience I'd never felt before suddenly hated denim and zippers and rules.

Nineteen and never been kissed.

I would do it all over again if this was my first true sexual experience. If every firework going off in my eardrums and eyelids was because of him, I would gladly be celibate for the rest of my days to deserve more.

Because of him, I was unhinged and grinding with insanity, giving into madness I'd never understood.

How had my night ended like this?

Where had this spontaneity come from?

This recklessness?

My teeth caught his bottom lip, dragging a slip tide of violence and need from him. He growled into my mouth, nipping and licking exactly like the starving wolf I thought he was.

"Fuck, what—what are you doing to me?" His breathless grunt did things. Glorious, *delicious* things. His voice created knots and bows with my insides. It filled my stomach with whirlwinds; it affected my core until my panties grew as damp as the grass we lay upon.

I loved knowing I affected him the way he affected me. Adored that we were in this craziness together—tripping into whatever rabbit hole we'd found and deciding to kiss and kiss until we splatted against the bottom.

His hands roamed, skating over my sides, keeping to the boundaries of pleasure. I arched, twisting a little to intercept his fingers as they swooped up and found my breast.

We both gasped, stealing oxygen from each other's lungs and sharing a moan-filled shudder. My hands felt empty—I needed to touch something of his. Something I'd never touched before and didn't know how but I wanted to. So. Damn. Much.

Lights appeared again. I was delirious with need but with no experience or knowledge on how to relieve such desire.

I wanted him to do something. Touch something. Remove

this tingling sparkling supernova deep in my belly. But he tore his lips from mine, his head flying upward in a rain of messy hair and smeared chocolate.

"Shit." He pulled away, leaving my body wanting and unsatisfied. "We've got to go. Now!"

The lights were brighter with my eyes open.

It wasn't him.

It was security.

"Hey, you!" A flashlight shone directly on us.

Kissing forgotten, he jumped to his feet and grabbed my hand. He hauled me effortlessly upright and yanked me into a run. "Go!"

I didn't hesitate.

My sneakers dug into the grass, propelling me as fast as I could.

"Stop!" The security guard gave chase, his flashlight bouncing erratically. He skirted the outside of the baseball field but most likely had keys as he jogged breathlessly toward the stands rather than try to out-run us as we bolted for the other side of the fence.

Reaching the chain link, the nameless man I'd just kissed grabbed my hips and boosted me a foot into the air. "Climb. Fast." His voice wasn't out of breath but throbbed with urgency. He rippled with the need to bolt.

I clutched the metal and scurried as fast as I could with my shoes barely fitting into the holes. The fence wobbled as he scaled it faster than I could, swinging over the top and dropping down.

"Come on!" he hissed.

I climbed faster, curling myself over the top.

He paced below, holding his arms out. "Jump. I'll catch you."

"What…*again*?" That he'd already demanded to catch me twice in our short relationship almost made me laugh. Had we formed habits already?

Hysteria at being chased made jumbled emotions run riot. Laughter became nervousness. Attraction became anxiety.

"Do it, Elle." His tone gave no argument.

The security guard had vanished, but it didn't mean he wouldn't pop up any second. Clinging to the other side, I looped my fingers tight.

"I'm here." He braced his legs, waiting.

Giving him one last glance, hoping to God he was a man of his word, I squeezed my eyes and let go.

The fall set my stomach tangling with my throat. I landed

awkwardly like a bride who'd fallen from the altar into her groom's arms.

He grunted, pulling my horizontal form into his embrace. He stumbled but didn't drop me. Our eyes met; a half-smirk hijacked his lips. "Couldn't stay away from me, huh?"

I swatted his shoulder. "You're the one who told me to jump."

His face darkened. "I'm also the one who kissed you."

A flashlight appeared; a garbled shout was closer.

"Shit." He let my legs go, swinging me to vertical. The instant my feet touched the ground, he grabbed my hand and yanked me forward.

We ran.

Air and speed and night-sky.

More flashlights appeared from other ends of the park, dancing with rays of righteousness as back-up guards arrived, chasing us like hounds.

"Oh, my God!" I yelled. "What do we do?"

"Keep running." He pulled me forward, slipping into a faster gear.

I wasn't unfit (thanks to my regular gym sessions) but I couldn't keep up with his pace. My lungs burned. My mouth opened wide, gulping at unhelpful air.

A security guard appeared to our left, bursting from the night-shrouded bushes. Behind him ran four men in uniform.

Police.

*Holy shit.*

*Why are the police involved?*

We hadn't vandalized property or hurt anyone. We'd gone for a stroll and kissed under the moon. What was so wrong with that?

"Fuck!" Nameless squeezed my hand, doing his best to drag me faster. "Come on!"

I shook my head, stumbling, dragging him back. "Ca—can't." Tugging on his grip, I did my best for him to release me. "My legs are cramping. Let me go."

"No." His fingers locked tighter. "I won't let you get arrested because of me."

*Arrested?*

That awful word and terrifying implications gave me a final shot of energy. I ran as fast as I could, for as long as I could. The flashlights slowly lost ground but then sped up to match us.

*It's no use.*

Lactic acid built up and up until I limped rather than ran. He had no choice but to either let me go or slow down. I didn't want him to leave, but I also didn't want him to face a situation he didn't need to.

"Go on." I gasped. "Run. I'll catch up."

He glowered at my lie. "You won't catch up. They'll take you into custody." He punched a sapling as we sprinted past. "Fuck! This is all fucked up!" Sweat glistened on his brow, his black hood streamed behind him. The soft slaps of our shoes on the pavement matched our ragged breathing.

He wasn't afraid of a reprimand. He was livid at being caught. I was sure we weren't the first to jump the wall and find some private time together. He was wrong to think we'd be arrested...surely?

But it was more than that to him. Whatever existence he lived was a dangerous one. I didn't know what he survived, yet here he was, pulling me forward on false energy granted from half a chocolate bar.

I had no right to get him caught. Not when I hindered him while he tried to do the right thing by keeping me safe. For the second time.

*He doesn't even know me, yet he's claimed responsibility for me.*

My heart lurched, doing its best to force out lactic acid and provide life-granting blood to my suffering legs. But I was done. There was nothing left to do but stop and accept the punishment.

"Listen!" I tugged again, planting my feet to create drag. "You go. I'm slowing you down."

"Shut up. Just trust me." He didn't look back or let go. "Run!"

I had money for lawyers if it came down to being arrested. He most likely didn't. I couldn't be responsible for taking his freedom away.

"No! Just let me go!"

Looking over his shoulder, he eyed the police slowly catching up. A decision flashed in his gaze just before his feet changed direction and he hurled me into the bushes off the path.

We crashed into branches and leaves. The world became an evergreen maze. But then he shoved my back against a trunk, wedged his body against mine, and kissed me so damn hard, so crazily thorough, I suffocated from running and kissing and every dangerous passion he poured down my throat.

My hands came up, clutching his hoodie as his tongue tangled with mine, knotting and licking, stealing every last breath I had.

Pulling away, he rested his forehead on mine, a roguish smile replacing his grimace. "I'm not letting you go. I've only just found you." A tenderness glowed in his brown eyes that I'd never seen from another other than family.

My knees trembled. "You don't even know me."

He placed a whisper-kiss on my mouth. "I don't have to know you. I *feel* you." His hand slowly threaded up my side, taking liberties I'd given him in a moment of insanity on a baseball field.

Never looking away, he cupped my breast, running his thumb over my flesh.

I moaned a little, my jaw going slack as desire sprang thick.

He kissed me again, stealing my cry, pressing his hips against mine. "I feel you like this." He squeezed my breast softly. "And I feel you like this." He rocked erotically. "But I feel you most of all with this." His touch climbed from my breast to my heart, pressing down over the rapidly beating muscle. "I don't care that I don't know you. I know enough."

I didn't know what to say.

This couldn't be real.

How had my night gone from alley robbery to bush-filled kisses? How had I transcended from lonely workaholic to falling for a man I'd only just met? A man who lived on the opposite scale of me in every little thing. Wealth and poverty. Safety and danger.

"Come home with me." If I were older with my own apartment, that invitation would've reeked with sex. But I wasn't older and didn't live alone. My need for him to be with me wasn't just about me but him, too. I wanted to protect him, shelter him— to give him a better chance than the world had so far.

He chuckled, brushing his mouth over mine. Deliberately ignoring my demand, he murmured, "You asked me before if I would've been pissed if a boyfriend gave you that necklace."

I stiffened then melted as his tongue licked mine sweetly. "The answer is yes. I would've been fucking pissed."

My face burned. My lips tingled. I couldn't help my stupid grin. "It was my father."

His hand lashed out, dragging my face to his for another messy half-violent, half-tender kiss. I sucked in a breath as the same intoxicating arousal billowed. I bit his bottom lip. He groaned, nipping me back.

"This is crazy." I hugged him close.

"All things worth fighting for are crazy." He kissed my forehead.

"But I don't even know your name—"

And then we were flying.

Something heavy and brutal knocked us sideways, tackling us as a flashlight split through our sanctuary of bushes, showing the silhouette of a hulking security guard as he threw us to the ground.

Twigs sliced through my jacket, pebbles and dirt smeared my hands, and Nameless grunted in agony as another guard landed on top of him.

My shoulder screamed as I rolled incorrectly. The earlier punch to my temple pounded in sympathy, making the park swim.

Curse words and limbs flew as Nameless fought. "Get the fuck off us!"

"Easy, kid." Another guard appeared, grabbing a flailing foot. "It's over. Give it up."

The man who'd landed on me slowly stood up, towering with smug victory on his chubby face. "Can't run, girl. You're surrounded."

I glowered, scooting closer in the dirt to Nameless while he punched and fought.

"Let him go!" I clambered to my knees, whacking the back of some pudgy guy in a high-vis jacket. "Get off him!"

My arms were pinned behind my back.

"Give it a rest." Someone hauled me upright. "Don't assault a security guard, ma'am, unless you want to add that to your misdemeanors tonight?"

I tried to spin. But the man who held me gave no leeway. Yanking me backward, he said to Nameless, "Don't be a hero. You're outnumbered. Stop wasting time."

My eyes connected with the man I'd kissed. He ceased fighting, turning limp rather than scrapping with the security guard. We didn't look away as a police officer stepped forward and ducked to grab his wrists.

With a sharp smile, Nameless swung once, twice, then gave up. A last hoorah rather than an attempt at escape. His head didn't bow as his arms were yanked behind his back like mine, and the sharp click of handcuffs being fastened interrupted the night.

He breathed hard as the police officer jerked him to his feet, not caring half the garden came with him in a tumble of dried leaves and dirt.

The security guard who'd launched on him stood too, limping

a little but with a cruel sneer on his face at winning.

We were marched out of the bushes and made to stand on the pathway where joggers and pram-strollers would walk in a few hours when the sun rose. For now, it was a processing place for illegal canoodling.

My heart thundered as I twisted my wrists in the cold metal imprisoning me. Tearing my gaze from Nameless, I glanced at the police officer lurking close to his captive. "Please, you don't have to arrest us."

Another police officer with graying hair and a heavy artillery belt rubbed his jaw. "See, that's where you're wrong. Trespassing is a serious offense. As is indecent exposure. Plenty of crimes committed tonight."

"Indecent exposure?" I scoffed. "When?"

"Making out in a public place."

"That's not illegal."

"I saw him feeling you up." A security guard with a sweaty face grunted. "Who knows how far you would've gone if I hadn't interrupted. Sex on a baseball field? That's a punishable offense."

My cheeks pinked. I didn't want to discuss anything to do with sex with these idiots. "That's your word against ours. We would never go that far. We're not savages."

"Speak for yourself." Nameless chuckled. "You can argue until you pass out, Elle, but you won't win." He narrowed his gaze with hate at the guards. "I know the law, and the law doesn't give a shit about the truth."

"Watch your mouth, son." The cop with the heavy belt pointed in Nameless's face. "You're already fucked, so I wouldn't be adding any more ammunition to your file if I were you."

File?

*Wait, he has a file?*

Shaking my head, determined not to let questions undermine me, I looked at the officer who seemed to be in charge. "Look, we're sorry. Can we just pay a fine?" I looked at Nameless, suffering such guilt that he'd saved me from being raped, given me one of the best experiences of my life, and now, he would be imprisoned all because I couldn't run fast enough. "Let us go. I promise we'll leave and never come back."

"No can do, little lady." The police officer with his heavy belt whispered to a colleague, nodding to something said on the radio clipped to his lapel.

He smirked at Nameless. "According to reports, you were

seen beating up two men earlier tonight. They said they found you about to rob and rape a young woman, and they tried to stop you. For their troubles, you almost broke one of their cheekbones and cracked a rib or two."

"Bullshit." My kisser bared his teeth. "I was the one trying to prevent *them* from doing that." He cocked his chin at me. "That's the girl they were trying to hurt."

The officers and security guards all raised an eyebrow. "Is this true, ma'am?"

I shrunk a little but nodded. "Yes. He saved me."

"Saved you?" The officer coughed. "Saved you and then brought you to a closed park to do what?"

I swallowed. "I'm very aware of how this looks, but he's right. We met when he saved me. They—they were going to hurt me."

"And *he* would've hurt you if we hadn't appeared."

"No, that's not true."

"You don't know him like we do, miss."

A police officer came over to pat me down while another patted my savior's body. My heart stopped when they found the eighty dollars in his hoodie pocket.

"Didn't rob you, huh?"

"That's mine, fuck face." Nameless fought against the handcuffs.

"Of course, it is," the lead officer said. "How many times do we need to tell you, lying only makes it worse for you?"

I froze.

*How many times?*

How many times had he faced situations like this?

I tried to catch his eye. To apologize. But he kept his glare on the officer who pocketed the eighty dollars. The money that could've bought him a better meal and a roof for a night.

Another person arrived on the scene, his heavy footsteps familiar even before he appeared in the flashlight glow of the security guards. I should've known he would turn up. He had a police scanner and had most likely been looking for me ever since I didn't call for him to drive me home.

My shoulders rolled, wishing I could melt into the concrete and disappear.

He flashed his credentials I knew stated him as ex-marine and in the employ of myself and my father. David Santos, my driver, bodyguard, sometimes personal assistant.

*Shit.*

He threw me a quick glance then focused his intense black gaze on the lead officer. His barrel chest, large arms, and black suit that matched his ebony skin soaked up the night. "I'm here for Ms. Charlston. She's done nothing wrong."

The police officer standing beside me argued, "She's been caught trespassing—"

"Wait." The lead agent stepped forward, shining light onto my bodyguard's identification. He then beamed the flashlight at my face. "What did you say her name was?"

"Charlston. Noelle Charlston." David ground his teeth. "Ring any bells?"

I was grateful he was here, but I didn't want him to fight the battles I'd lost.

"David, it's fine—"

"Be quiet, Ms. Charlston. Let me handle this." He stood taller, his gloved hands clenching. "From Belle Elle?"

The lead officer stiffened. "Wait, Joe's daughter?"

"The one and the same."

The officer paused.

A second later, he ordered, "Release her."

Instantly, the handcuffs were unlocked, and I was pushed forward. I shot to the side of the man who'd saved me, kissed me, and given me the best birthday night out I could've asked for. "What about him?"

An officer laughed. "Oh, he's coming with us."

"But you—you can't. He saved me. He did a good thing. Don't punish him for jumping a fence and enjoying a park."

The officer smirked. "Oh, we're not arresting him because of that."

I couldn't look away from Nameless' face. My lips ached to kiss him again. His eyes roamed over me, full of the same tender affection and almost awestruck attraction from before. I had to be near him until I figured out what this meant. What this was between us.

*They can't take him away.*

"Then why?" I demanded, living in daydreams of taking him home, giving him the guestroom to shower and rest, cooking him blueberry pancakes, and introducing him to Dad in the morning. "He hasn't done anything."

The officer's laughed as if all in on a joke I hadn't heard. "He's done plenty."

"He has multiple outstanding warrants. Tonight is our lucky

night." Jerking Nameless to his side, the lead officer added, "He's going away for a long time."

Nameless merely hung his head, his jaw working with a violent edge.

"You can't do that."

The cop's face drew with annoyance. "I think you'll find we can, Ms. Charlston. Now, if you know what's good for you, you'll go home with your guard here and forget all about this one."

He shook Nameless. "Say goodbye because I doubt you'll be seeing him again."

I moved forward—to do what I didn't know. To kiss him, run away with him—somehow fix this, so it didn't end this way.

He smiled sadly. "Do what he says, Elle. Go home."

"I can't go. Not without you."

"You know the way now. You don't need a guide to walk you."

I shook my head. "That isn't what I meant, and you know it."

He chuckled. "You said it yourself. It was too crazy to be true."

I ached to grab his hand, to hug him, but with so many pairs of judging eyes on us, I froze. That would be one of my biggest regrets in life. That I didn't reach out when he needed me the most. "Please...tell me your name. I'll get a lawyer. We'll fight these stupid claims."

"All right, time's up." An officer marched forward, grabbing Nameless around the elbow and dragging him away.

Tears sprang to my eyes. Uncertainty and fear spiraled at the thought of never seeing him again. "Please! What's your name?"

Nameless stumbled from another shove, his gaze never leaving mine. He looked sad and pissed and lost and resigned. So many emotions all at once. "It was fun while it lasted."

"Tell me!"

But he merely gave me a harsh smile, trying to mask the grief on his face. "I really enjoyed kissing you, Elle."

And then the officer turned him away and marched him into the darkness.

# Chapter Ten

THE DRIVE HOME was one of the hardest things I'd ever lived through.

David didn't say a word; he merely drove with iron concentration and astute silence. He didn't ask questions. He didn't ask for a report from the police. He just escorted me from the park as if I'd come out of Belle Elle like a normal evening after work.

He didn't comment about how I'd been caught with a man. He didn't speak at all apart from to tell me to be careful climbing into the backseat of the Range Rover Sport.

Pulling up to the brownstone where I lived, he cut the engine and jumped out. A moment later, he pulled open the door for me and nodded in the darkness. "Have a good night, Ms. Charlston."

"Thank you, David. You too."

I didn't ask if he'd keep this to himself. My father would know. I wouldn't be able to keep my night-time wanderings a secret. But at least neither of them would know about the alley and how I'd met Nameless.

He nodded again and hopped back into the Range Rover.

I kept my chin high even though my heart sputtered at the thought of what would happen to Nameless. Was he in prison now? Would he go to trial? What sort of warrants did they have?

My questions would have to wait because the second I climbed the steps and entered the home I was raised in, my father grabbed me in a boa constrictor hug.

"Oh, holy hell, Elle. Where the bells have you been?"

I couldn't even rib him for his weird expressions tonight. I squeezed him back, drained and confused, lost and sad. "I'm okay, Dad."

"You ran away!" He pulled back, disappointment and hurt

bright in his eyes. "Why would you do such a thing? And on your birthday, no less."

I shrugged out of his embrace. "I didn't run away." I kicked off my sneakers and padded into the living room where hints of my mother still existed everywhere. From the pristine cream linen couches to the white gauze draped around the window bay. A baby grand piano sat in the corner next to the ornate fireplace while knickknacks from my parents' travels littered side tables and coffee tables in a cluttered but designer way.

My piano lessons flittered into my head as my fingers played an imaginary chord, giving me something to focus on when all I wanted to do was burst into tears.

Dad followed, throwing himself into his overstuffed chair that'd long since compacted and wrinkled from his weight. "Where were you, Elle? You say you didn't run away, but you were found in Central Park. At one a.m! Do you know how dangerous that is?" His eyes cast over me. "And what the hell are you wearing?"

Damn, David had already told him.

I looked at the black bomber I couldn't unzip; otherwise, he'd see my torn top and bruises. My skinny jeans smeared with dirt and chocolate. I was so far removed from the daughter he knew. The daughter who lived in fashion catalogs and had nightmares of Christmas sale stocks being too low. I shouldn't be daydreaming about a man who tasted like candy or a kiss beneath the stars on a baseball field.

Had that really happened?

*Was it real?*

I sighed, knowing I had to grovel before I could ask what would happen to Nameless. "I'm sorry, Dad. I—I wanted to see what the world was like for someone who wasn't an heiress."

He sucked in a breath. "Why?"

"Because I'm nineteen and never explored the city on my own. Because I'm running a billion-dollar company and never been to a party or gossiped with girls or kissed a boy." I looked up, pleading with him to understand. "I wanted to be normal...just for a few hours."

He sighed.

Silence fell as he reclined heavily into his chair. Whatever anger he had blew itself out.

That was my dad.

He rarely exploded, and when he did, it didn't last long. Guilt sat even worse because now his anger had gone, his second-guessing and regret burrowed through me.

I inched to the edge of the couch, getting closer to him. "I was coming back. The man who was arrested was walking me home safely."

"Arrested?" His head snapped up.

"Yes. I think he's homeless and probably has a few crimes of stealing to eat. But tonight, he saved me." I wouldn't go into the details with my father—he didn't need those mental images of me trapped and scared to haunt him, or worse, use them against me if I ever tried to leave on my own again—but I did need to fight for the man who'd fought for me. "He was an utter gentleman, Dad. He was kind and a little rough but overall someone worthy of being given a chance."

I linked my fingers, squeezing tight to overcome my nerves and push ahead. It was a trick I used in the boardroom when firing a department head if they were found embezzling or not doing their job.

I could never show weakness.

*Ever.*

Tonight, I'd shown weakness, and it'd almost gotten me raped and a man locked up.

"We need to help him."

Dad frowned. "Help? How?"

"We need to hire a lawyer—get him good representation, so he isn't incarcerated."

He scowled. "If he committed the crime, it's only fair he suffers the consequences."

"Doesn't he deserve someone to fight on his side, though? I don't know his name but I doubt he has anyone. He saved me. The least I can do is try to do the same."

"You were gallivanting around the city with a man, and you didn't know his name?" He groaned, shaking his head. "What were you thinking?" He stood suddenly, rubbing his face as if in denial. "Elle, you've had a long night. I'm going to bed, and I suggest you do the same. Sage is in your room. I collected her from the office when I went to check on you and found you were gone."

His guilt trip worked. I slotted myself into his weary arms. "I'm so, *so* sorry. I should've told you."

"Yes, you should have." He hugged me, although reluctantly.

*But if I had, you wouldn't have let me go.*

He spoke into my hair, no doubt smelling spicy beef burritos and dangerous alleys.

I was glad my long hair covered the bruise on my temple and whatever other calling cards those thugs had left were hidden beneath my clothes.

"I know this is my fault, keeping you so sheltered and buried under work, but my God, Elle, I never expected you to go chasing after the first boy who showed interest in you. A boy who was *arrested*, for goodness' sake."

I smarted with shame. "It's not like that. He wasn't just any boy. He was—"

When I didn't continue, he sighed sadly. "He was what? A friend? A soul-mate? A teenage crush?" He pinched his nose. "Elle, I will never stand in the way of you finding love. I *want* you to find love. Not a day goes by that I don't wish your mother was still alive to teach you how valuable love can be, but I won't permit you to throw away everything you have with a stupid infatuation over a criminal who doesn't deserve you."

"Dad...don't—"

His eyes dropped to my throat. Pain arrowed through him, followed by rage. "Where is your necklace?"

I jolted.

"Tell me, Elle. The sapphire star I bought you. The one I spent hours deliberating over. The one I bought because the blue matched your eyes and the star symbolized how much you mean to me?" His fists shook. "Where is it?"

I looked at the beige carpet. "I lost it."

The lie turned to paste on my tongue, but it was better than the truth. Better for him to blame me than to think of his gift in the possession of heartless thieves who meant me harm.

"For God's sake, Noelle." He shook his head, tiredness etching his eyes. "Not only were you irresponsible with yourself but with your gift, too. If you planned on using tonight as a demonstration that you were capable of spending some time alone away from the company, consider it a failure." His voice deepened with authority. "Until you can prove you are still the considerate daughter I raised, I don't want you leaving this house without David, do you hear me?"

My tears turned to anger. Heat smoked through me to argue back. To tell him just how suffocated I felt, how lonely, how lost. But I'd already hurt him tonight, and now, he'd hurt me.

We were even.

I smiled tight, hiding everything. We both had more to say but wouldn't verbalize. He was disappointed in me. I was frustrated by him.

It was best to go to bed before we uttered things we couldn't take back.

"Goodnight, Dad." I moved around him and left the living room. "I'm sorry about the necklace."

As I climbed the sweeping staircase to my room on the third floor, my mind returned to the man who tasted like chocolate and had hands that could touch so sweetly but also cause such violence.

I would never forget him.

And tomorrow, I would do what I could to help him.

Because he'd helped me, and in some crazy way, he'd claimed my young, naïve heart.

I would get him free.

No matter how impossible that task would be.

# Chapter Eleven

## THREE YEARS LATER

"DON'T FORGET, YOU have that dinner meeting with your father, Mr. Robson, and his son tonight at the Weeping Willow." Fleur smiled, hoisting another armful of contracts and financial portfolios.

I removed my reading glasses and took the folders from her. The heavy thud as I placed them on my desk ricocheted through me. "Yes, I remember."

*And I want nothing to do with it.*

For the past year, my father had used every business meeting with his right-hand man, Steve Robson, to try to set me up with his son. He thought I couldn't see through his tricks, but the way he kept finding excuses for us to be around each other wasn't subtle.

"Anything else, Ms. Charlston?"

"No, thank you. Please don't put any calls through. I have too much work to finish."

"Of course." Turning in her pretty purple dress, Fleur left my office. Her wardrobe was smart but flirty, reminding me that outside the thick glass windows existed sun and heat and summer.

I hadn't been away from an air-conditioned building for more than a few minutes at a time for months. If I wasn't being driven from office to office, I was in store warehouses or shop-fronts or doing my best to catch up on sleep, that for some reason, had become elusive for the past three years.

Ever since my one night of freedom, sleep had evaded me. Dreams never came. Nightmares visited often. The damn guilt because I wasn't able to help him eroded me day by day.

*You said you wouldn't think about him anymore.*

I said that every morning.

And by every lunchtime, I failed.

The best I'd been able to do was realize how stupidly idealistic I'd been. My dad, bless his heart, had helped show me that it wasn't Nameless who I thought I'd fallen in love with that night but the *idea* of love.

No one could fall for a stranger in a few hours. Especially a girl who'd been attacked and molested and then corralled into breaking and entering a national treasure. My nerves and adrenaline would've heightened every experience, making it so much more than what it was.

I'd read into things. I'd imagined the heat behind the kisses and painted a perfect romance, when really, all there'd been was a dirty boy and a baseball field.

*That's all.*

I recognized myself for what I was.

I was young, fanciful, and Dad was entirely right that work took precedent over a silly infatuation.

He was nothing to me.

Just a man from my past who took my first kiss.

*Got it, stupid heart?*

I sank heavily into my chair. My elbows stabbed into the desk as I rested my head in my hands. Even now, with all my pep talks and conclusions, I still felt guilty for not doing more.

*That's why I think about him.*

Not because I still believed we were meant to be, or the craziness between us was serendipitous, but because I'd failed and left him alone in a prison that no doubt took whatever good was left in him and spat him out cold, cynical, and cruel.

I hadn't lived up to my oath.

A life for a life.

He'd saved me.

*And I haven't saved him.*

For months, I'd tried to track him down. I'd called the police stations, the county jails, even a few lawyers who worked pro bono to see if they'd been given his case.

But nothing.

I had no name and only a vague description—hampered by his beard, the night, and his hoodie.

The picture in my mind was of mystery and infatuation rather than a crystal image helpful for sketch artists or explanations.

It was as if he never existed.

But I knew he did because I still thought about the sapphire star necklace, and every time I snuck a piece of chocolate, Nameless exploded into my mind. I should get over it. It was one night. A nineteen-year-old's stupid crush.

I was more mature now.

Overworked and completely wrung out. Sage was getting older, but she still came with me to the office every day, still purred on my lap when sums and figures made my head spin, and still cuddled with me in bed when loneliness for a life I'd never have overtook me.

Two years ago, when my father had had a heart attack, I gave up my adolescent immaturity and no longer resented my role. The doctors said he would get better, but he should step down from being the boss.

The Last Will and Testament I'd signed came into full effect, and he placed me as the sole controller with the majority share of our stocks and the final say on all decisions.

To say I was scary to men of my own age when I was just an heiress was one thing, but to date now I was a conglomerate commander was utterly impossible.

Dad believed in love.

I didn't.

Not because I didn't want it but because my life's work had stolen that possibility from me. I had to accept that I had no time for romance, no patience for dating, and no prospects at partnership other than business expansion.

I was so lucky compared to most.

*Love is a small price to pay.*

I lived and breathed for my company, and on the rare evenings I had off, Dad was determined to play matchmaker with me and Greg—Steve's son.

It didn't matter that I had no interest in Greg.

I didn't care he was only three years older than I was and held a bachelor's in business from Yale. He was dry and humorless and the exact opposite of Steve, who'd been in my life from the start with his quirky nicknames and jokes when I started running Belle Elle.

He was my uncle in every way apart from blood.

Greg was the unwanted cousin who I wished was related to me so I had a legitimate reason for denying his advances.

Sage nudged my ankles, meowing softly beneath the desk where she hung out in her basket full of blankets and stuffed mice.

"Yeah, yeah. I know he's only looking out for me."

Dad wanted me to marry and find a partner to help run Belle Elle with. He'd met Mom when he was twenty, and it'd been love at first sight. He couldn't understand why I was still so very, very single at twenty-two.

It obviously didn't cross his mind that I was a powerful woman in a still sexist world where men—even if they didn't come out and admit it—were emasculated by a woman with a bigger salary than them.

My thoughts remained tangled as I diligently worked through the reports on our Hong Kong division before Fleur knocked on my office door, wrenching through my concentration.

"It's six p.m. You need to leave in thirty minutes."

"Wow, really? I thought it was two p.m. only five minutes ago."

She giggled, her long brown braid jiggling over her shoulder. "Like you always do when you get in the zone—you lost time." She waltzed in with a dry-cleaners bag covering a black dress.

Placing it on the arm of my rolled leather couch, she said, "I don't know why you don't let me bring you something more fun and vibrant from the shop floor. I have a sneaking suspicion you'd look great in green." She held up her hands to make a frame around my face. "A rich emerald. Or perhaps a deep sapphire like that star you keep sketching when you're on the phone with suppliers."

I waved her away. "Black is fine."

"Black is all you ever wear."

"Black is business and no-nonsense."

"But life isn't." She smiled sadly. "Life is fun and chaos." Backing toward the exit, she added, "You should remember that sometime...." She left before I could fire her—not that I ever would because without her and Sage, I would have no one I could actually talk to who wasn't my father.

I glared at the black dress.

I wouldn't lie and say wearing another color wouldn't be fun, but I didn't have time for fun or shopping or fashion. I did the work so other people could do those things while leaving their money in our cash registers.

Sighing, I rubbed the back of my neck, saved my progress, and closed my laptop.

Sage slunk around my ankles, knowing the routine and that work was over for the day. "We're not going home, I'm afraid."

Her little face pouted, her whiskers drooping from her tiny nose. Picking the silver cat from the floor, I placed her on my desk as I stood to prepare for this sham of a date.

I kissed her soft head. "Don't look at me like that. At least you get to snooze in the car. I actually have to talk to the jerk."

She stuck her tongue out, coughing with a hairball.

"Yes, exactly. I feel like vomiting, too." Heading to the couch to collect the dreaded dress, I murmured, "The sooner this dinner is over, the sooner I can go home and forget."

*And try to dream.*

*Of being nineteen again and kissing a man with no name.*

# Chapter Twelve

THE RESTAURANT WAS packed as usual.

Friday night was the night every high-powered suit liked to be seen at the Weeping Willow. The eatery had opened four years ago, and in that time, it had created a name of fine dining, utmost decadence, and a gin bar with more selections than any other in New York. They prided themselves on expensive, exclusive liquors. And even had a bottle of gin valued at ten thousand dollars a shot.

*Ridiculous.*

"Ah, there you are!" Dad stood as I approached the reserved table at the back. The booth glittered in deep turquoise while a chandelier representing the branches of a willow tree wept over the circular table.

"Hi, Dad." I kissed his cheek, happy to see he had color on his face and a twinkle in his eye. Even though the doctors had told him he had to take it easy, he didn't. He still pulled long hours in his office across the hall from mine. And he stressed himself out by overthinking my future and lack of family if he suddenly died.

He was a lot of things my father but three words to describe him was a cuddly teddy bear. He had a habit of ignoring practicalities in order for happiness to rule.

"You look lovely." He grabbed my hand, forcing me to spin.

The black dress whirled around my kneecaps while the spaghetti straps clung for dear life to my shoulders. The bodice hugged nicely, but overall, it was a simple style in a simple color.

It was one of Belle Elle's biggest sellers—not because of how well it was made but because it was the perfect backdrop to show off accessories. Gauzy scarfs looked great with the spaghetti straps, necklaces earned prime real estate, and even big earrings polished it to runway class rather than high street clone.

Tonight, the only accessorizing I'd attempted was a dark blue shawl and a lick of eye shadow with thicker mascara. My blonde hair hung down to my tailbone. All my energy was spent on the company, not on myself, and I didn't particularly care if it showed.

I swallowed a groan as Greg stood up and kissed both my cheeks. His hand landed on my elbow, slightly clammy and annoyingly clingy. "You look gorgeous, Noelle."

*I hate when he calls me that.*

I hadn't been Noelle for decades.

I was Elle of Belle Elle.

The queen of retail.

I forced a smile. "Thank you. You don't look bad yourself." I nodded in approval at his black slacks and one size too big for him dinner jacket. The lapels were embossed with velvet. On any other man, it would probably look distinguished and sexy. But on him...*kill me now.*

Not that he was ugly—far from it. Greg had great dark blond hair, chiseled features, and a trim physique. What lurked beneath his looks was what turned me off. There was no...connection. No spitfire or chocolate smoke. And sometimes, just sometimes, I sensed a darkness in him that had nothing to do with me constantly turning down his requests for a date.

He had a coldness that made me wary even to be alone with him in public.

Most of the time, I chalked up my over imagination to the slight trauma from being dragged into the alley all those years ago.

I had to stop reading into things and imagining the worst.

I looked around Greg to his father, Steve. "Hiya."

Steve didn't bother unwinding from the booth but blew me an air kiss. His hair had turned white over the years, but his sense of humor never dried up. "You look as pretty as that Barbie doll you used to love before Sage came along."

I rolled my eyes. "Did you just call me a Barbie? In public?"

He shrugged. "Hey, it's not derogatory. Just saying you have a tiny waist, nice boobs, and blonde hair." He ran a hand over his casual gray blazer. "Look at me, I'm the perfect Ken—or at least, I was a few years ago."

I laughed, forcing myself to relax even though Greg still hadn't let go of my arm.

My father saved me by tugging me to his side and pushing me into the booth. I went willingly, trapped between Steve and Dad, facing Greg across the table.

Something rubbed my ankle.

My eyes shot to Greg's green ones. Turned out, I wasn't far enough away to prevent him playing footsies. I kept the same smile I used on assholes in the boardroom plastered to my face, even though I wanted to stab his face with the steak knife.

"So, Elle, you working hard tomorrow?" Greg grinned conspicuously as his foot stomped on my toes. "Want to go see a movie or something?"

The waiter brought our drinks—the joy of being known and regulars at this place. The server placed neat whiskey in front of my father and Steve, a gin and tonic for Greg, and a virgin daiquiri for me.

Just as I'd never been free since the night I met Nameless, I'd never been drunk. Not that liquor didn't appeal to me but the fact that each day I started work before the sun rolled out of its soft cloudy bed, I had no time for a hangover.

One day, a few pieces of the laces keeping me straight and narrow would snap, and then I'd derail and cause untold pain to my father by being stupidly irresponsible. I would drink to excess, sleep with a stranger, and call in sick for a solid week.

But that day was not today.

"I work hard all the time, Greg." I batted my eyelashes sweetly. "I'm afraid I never have time to do things like go to the movies."

"What about a walk?"

"That too."

"Carriage ride through Central Park?"

My smile faltered, remembering the arrest and subsequent disappearance of the man in Central Park. "Definitely too busy for that."

Dad coughed. "Now, Elle. You're making it sound like I'm a slave driver."

I laughed softly. "Not you, Dad. The company."

His face fell, trying to read my reluctance. I wouldn't tell him that most of the time, I used work as my alibi to avoid dates because the only man who asked me out was Greg, and that was only because he thought he knew me because our fathers were old friends.

Not to mention, if he married me, he would get the empire that he'd been raised with thanks to Steve's involvement. I couldn't begrudge his desire to control something that had been such a big part of his life.

But I could prevent it from happening.

Steve laughed, toasting me with his whiskey. "Here's to a workaholic who happens to be so damn good at her job."

I didn't know if I wanted to toast to that, but I did, clinking my glass with his.

The waiter appeared to take our meal order as the menu changed weekly. Before I could glance at the new specials, my father slid from the booth and mumbled he'd be right back. An itch started right in my heart. I rubbed my chest as love for the gray-haired man in his immaculate three-piece suit washed over me.

*Where is he going?*

I knew I'd hurt him with refusing Greg's advances, but I didn't mean to rib him with how much I worked.

That wasn't fair.

Greg interrupted my melancholy by ordering loudly. "I'll have the venison. Rare."

Steve pursed his lips before saying, "Make that two." He placed the heavy flocked menu onto the table, eyeing me expectantly. "You, Elle? I know your father will have the chicken or fish—on account of his heart—but you?"

I quickly scanned the list. I had no appetite, and my thoughts were across the room in the private gin bar to the side where my father had vanished. "I'll have…um, the salmon, please."

"No problem." The waiter took our order, tucked his electronic device that'd most likely already sent our order to the kitchen into his vest pocket, and collected our menus. The moment he left, awkwardness fell on the table.

Steve glanced at me then Greg. "So, you two, what's new in the world of twenty something's?"

I smiled for his sake, not Greg's. "Well, you know my world. You see me every day at the office."

"And you know mine because you see me every day at home." Greg rolled his eyes.

He was twenty-five and still lived at home.

Here, I could be smug and look down my nose. A few months ago, I'd moved out of the brownstone and into my own top-floor apartment only two buildings away from Belle Elle headquarters.

I'd cheated and bought it fully furnished, so some of the furniture wasn't to my taste, but I didn't have time to interior design or visit the stores or even browse our own shop for decorations. It had taken all my courage to move out, especially after Dad's heart attack, but I couldn't be there anymore.

Dad had understood.

He'd supported me and helped me pack and move the meager possessions in my bedroom and a few knickknacks from the living room.

For the first week, Sage had caterwauled at the view, telling me off for removing her from the brownstone where she could sneak into the garden late at night and do whatever it was that cats do. In the new place, she was glass and concrete bound, looking at the clouds rather than rodents.

"How are you enjoying your own place, Elle?" Steve followed my train of thought, surprising me.

I shrugged, smoothing out my napkin over my lap. "It's good. The building has great services with a gym and pool. It even has movie nights and neighbor parties once a month."

*Not that I've been to any of them.*

"That's fantastic." Steve grinned. "Perhaps Greg could come over one day, and you can show him how easy it is to live on your own. Get him out from under my feet."

"Yeah, good one, old man." Greg snickered, sipping his gin and tonic.

I shuddered, doing my best to hide the horror at the thought of having Greg in my apartment. With me. Alone. Of kissing Greg. Of letting him remove my dress and touch me. Of letting him see me naked and sticking his—

*All right, stop right there.*

I no longer lived at home and was one of the few women on the Forbes' richest list. I'd achieved so much, but in reality...in the three years since my first kiss, *nothing* had changed.

I hadn't been kissed since—unless a friendly peck on the cheek from doting father figures counted. I hadn't been naked around anyone, male or female. I still held the curse of not having enough time to lose my virginity.

Most days, I had no libido because I worked such long hours. But some nights, I remembered how it felt to be touched and have a man's tongue in my mouth and how I physically *ached* for something I hadn't understood that night on a baseball field.

And I delivered a release I'd become rather expert at.

"Yes, Elle. I could come over...say next week?" Greg rubbed his shoe against my leg, snagging my pantyhose and no doubt causing a ladder. "I could bring a bottle of wine. We could finally *get to know each other."*

Steve scowled at the heavy reference to sex but didn't interfere. After all, we weren't children anymore. Yes, we had two meddling old men trying to influence our love lives, but I wouldn't give in to this.

Not after everything else.

*Talking of my meddling old man.*

*Where is he?*

The waiter arrived with four plates of delicious smelling food, all artistically arranged on turquoise plates with silver piping.

Inching from the booth, I ignored Greg's question and smiled at Steve. "Excuse me. I'd better go tell my father his dinner is on the table."

"Yes, good idea, Elle." Steve nodded, already picking up his knife and fork to dig in.

Greg narrowed his eyes, giving me a tight grin. "Fine. I'm not going anywhere."

Fighting my shudder, I slithered from the booth. My heels tap-tapped over gray-veined marble as I left the busy restaurant and entered the cozy gin bar. Teak wood hung in noise absorbing panels from the black ceiling. Stools with polished chrome and padded leather lined up neatly by the long bar while clusters of comfy chairs encouraged secrets to be shared and pacts to be made in the dark.

The whiff of alcohol and cigar smoke lingered on every air-eddy. I had no idea how the Weeping Willow got around the non-smoking rule, but small plumes of silver escaped men's lips as I made my way to the bar.

Specially positioned spotlights speared through the bottles on offer. All twenty-two hundred of them—according to the owner who bragged when he'd first opened the place. Alcohol glittered like fireflies, tempting a drinker to keep testing until they found their soul-mate in liquor.

I expected to find Dad nursing another glass of whiskey, staring broodingly into the amber liquid as he sometimes did when I acted out or he couldn't shed the memory of Mom.

That wasn't the case tonight.

I slammed to a stop.

*He's laughing with a complete stranger.*

Dad sat on a bar stool with his feet tucked on the chrome foot-rest, a glass of whiskey (like I predicted) resting in his hands but forgotten. His face was alive, eyes unguarded and crinkled in mirth. I hadn't seen him so animated in years.

It warmed me and worried me in equal measure.

I looked at the man he was with. The guy had his back to me, but the cut of his suit was impeccable; his body toned and slim, his hair dark and thick with lighter highlights that could've been graced by a hairdresser or natural.

From where I stood, a couple shielded me like a living wall, but I was close enough to hear my father say, "Well, that sounds fantastic. You really should meet her."

Fantastic? What was fantastic?

I sucked in a breath as the stranger laughed. "It would be an honor to meet her. I'm sure she's as wonderful as you describe."

*Are they talking about me?*

The couple hiding me moved, leaving me exposed. I should walk forward and introduce myself. I should stop eavesdropping and act professionally. But something about the way my father and this stranger spoke sent my hackles bristling.

Staying behind milling people with an array of alcohol gripped in tight fingers, I slowly inched closer to the two men, straining with every step to hear.

"My daughter is very accomplished." Dad's tone billowed with pride. "But you sound rather successful yourself, so that shouldn't be a problem."

"Problem?" The man took a sip of his drink. "I assure you, I've never had a problem with women before."

Oh, the arrogance dripping from him.

Dad chuckled. "I wasn't saying *she'd* be a problem. More like you shouldn't find her power off-putting if you have success of your own."

*Oh, my God, what is he talking about?*

Where had my father gone? When had he turned into this hearts-and-flowers romantic, trying to match me off to any man who passed his screwed-up interview?

*He's always been like that.*

I hated that that was true.

The stranger nodded. "I can understand how a woman with a high corporate job and wealth can be terrifying to most." He leaned forward. "However, I can assure you, that won't be the case with me."

He spoke as if my father had handed me over to be bedded and wedded.

My teeth ground together as Dad said, "I must admit, I

haven't heard of you before. Are you new to New York?"

The man swirled the liquid in his glass. "Yes. Arrived a few months ago. Unfortunately, my benefactor was not well, and we needed treatment that was only available here as a trial."

"Oh, I'm sorry."

My hands balled as my father gave this total stranger such sympathy. "And you're single then? You're planning on staying in town?"

Holy crap, the embarrassment level just erupted into volcanic proportions.

"I am. Customarily, I don't date. But now my benefactor is on the mend, I can indulge in playing the field."

Indulge? Play the field? My hands curled with indignation. Who *was* this man?

"My daughter isn't a conquest, Mr. Everett. If I do introduce you, you must give me your word you won't use her."

This had gone on long enough. I had to do something. Namely, throw my drink into Mr. Everett's face.

"Believe me. I have no doubt one look at your daughter, and I'll be quite happy to be monogamous until she gets to know me." The man raised his glass again, giving me a side profile glimpse of elegant cheekbones and handsome jaw.

I stiffened. He spoke as if I was a sure thing. That he could make me fall for him just by being alive.

I wanted to kill him.

But then I wanted to kill my father more as he smiled. "I'm sure you'll like Elle. She's beautiful and insanely intelligent."

Mr. Everett chuckled. "I'm fairly sure I can make your daughter like me in return. I have a knack, you see."

"A knack?" My father's face tightened, noting the cocky confidence of this man he was trying to marry his daughter to. "What sort of knack?"

"A knack for women who can't stand the opposite sex. A way of convincing them to give up control and relax for once."

*Holy shit.*

I rarely swore but *holy shit, shit, shit.*

This guy...there were no words for his arrogance.

Dad glanced at his untouched whiskey. "I admit Elle doesn't seem to like the prospects I put in front of her." His face fell. "I only want her to be happy. To have someone to shoulder the burden of her company with. To laugh occasionally with." His voice softened with sadness. "She hasn't laughed in so long. I'm worried about her."

If I weren't so angry, I would've suffocated under a fresh wave of guilt. I moved forward a step, breaking my cover, swirling with mixed emotions.

However, Mr. Everett ensured I'd never feel guilt again as he said, "Introduce me to your daughter, Mr. Charlston, and I promise you I'll make her——"

"Make me do what?" I stomped in my heels, crossing my arms. My heart whirled wild while my breathing threatened to show how annoyed and hurt I was.

I glowered at both men.

My father shrunk, knowing he'd screwed up. But the stranger merely pinned me with piercing eyes and sent a chill down my spine.

He looked arctic and unreadable.

He smelled expensive and impenetrable.

He sounded powerful and untouchable.

My worst nightmare wrapped in perfection.

Tearing my gaze away, I hugged my anger and spat, "You sit here planning my future like you have control over me. What? You think you can make me fall in love with you? Get on my knees for you? Do whatever you tell me to, oh master?" I snorted. "The flat-out disgusting *nerve* of you!"

Mr. Everett rubbed his bottom lip where a droplet of liquor glistened. "If you give me time, I'll prove to you I can make you do all those things…and more."

I spluttered in outright shock. *"Excuse me?"*

My father stood up, putting himself between me and damn Mr. Everett. "I don't think that's quite appropriate conversation for the first introduction, sir."

*"Seriously?"* I eyed my father as if he was a stranger, too. "When is that sort of talk *ever* appropriate? When he's got me cuffed to a damn bed and making me cook him dinner? God, Dad." I threw up my hands, my skin flushing with indignation beneath my black dress. "Wow. Just wow. *Both* of you."

Backing away, I held up my finger when Dad tried to reason with me. "Nope, not going to hear it." I spun on my heel then looked over my shoulder, doing my best to ignore Mr. Everett and the way his gaze slipped over me, lingering on my breasts before latching onto my mouth. "Oh, and, Dad, once you've finished trying to be the world's worst matchmaker, your dinner is on the table."

I stormed off, unable to make the blazing exit I wanted as a crowd of people interrupted my flow, teetering slowly with their arms full of drinks, chatting about things I couldn't care less about.

I wanted out of there.

Something warm and firm tapped me on the shoulder, somehow finding bare flesh beneath the scarf wrapped around me. "Before you leave..."

My heart relocated into my mouth as I whirled around, coming face to face with Mr. Everett.

Up close he was even more stunning.

*Damn him.*

*Curse him.*

His dark eyes were calculating and intelligent, his lips perfectly formed with the barest hint of five o'clock shadow over his jaw and down his throat. His Adam's apple bobbed as he swallowed while the columns of muscle flowing from his neck to his chest, just visible beneath an open-necked silk gray shirt, upset me in ways I didn't understand.

He was pure, one-hundred percent male, and he watched me as if I was a woman who'd already sacrificed herself on his ego temple, and he was about to dine on her soul.

I crossed my arms to hold my insides together, trying to prevent the leaping gazelle my heart had morphed into from splattering at his feet. "What? What do you want?"

His eyes darkened to molasses. "I want—"

Dad sidled over, caution and worry etching his wrinkled kind face. "Now, Elle. Let me introduce you two properly."

"I think Mr. Everett has done all the introducing I need to hear." I tilted my head. "Isn't that right?"

Mr. Everett smiled ever so slightly, looking more sinner than gentleman. "I've only just started, Ms. Charlston."

Dad raised his arm, waving it a little in surrender as my heels ground into the marble, preparing to go to war. "Now, now." Coming to my side, he patted my forearm. "I apologize for talking about you. But you've got the wrong idea. This is—"

"Mr. Everett. I know." I glowered. "I just learned, thanks to you, how he thinks he can turn me into a simpering idiot all because he's deemed me interesting enough to meet." I leaned toward Mr. Everett, not caring I gave him a shot down my cleavage or the way he sniffed at my orchid perfume. "For your information, asshole, I don't like men because of this exact reason. You're either a mamma's boy or think you rule the world." I pointed a finger in his face. "You'll never rule me, so you might as well stop whatever little game you're playing with my father and fuck off."

"Elle!" My father gasped. "What the hell, Bell Button?"

And he used Bell Button.

*Of course, he did.*

My life was officially over. Not only had he tried to set me up with this sexual deviant in the middle of a cigar-clouded gin bar, but now, he gave away childhood nicknames as if they meant nothing.

"Nice, Dad. Real nice," I muttered under my breath.

Mr. Everett noticed, a smug smirk twisting his lips. One look into his eyes and I knew he'd stored away my embarrassing title for ammunition in the future.

*But there will be no future.*

Because in ten seconds, I wanted to be gone and never see him again.

"I'm suddenly not hungry." I narrowed my eyes at my father. "Please give my apologies to Steve and Greg."

"Steve and Greg?" Mr. Everett repeated.

I sneered. "Two more men I refuse to have anything to do with so don't think yourself special."

Dad clutched my elbow. "Now, Elle, don't be hasty. You know how much you love the food here."

"*Loved.* Past tense." I gave a brittle smile. "This place doesn't hold the allure it once did, thanks to recent events." I looked Mr. Everett up and down icily, hoping he'd get frostbite.

Mr. Everett chuckled under his breath. "Are you always this dramatic or is it a product of being given everything you've ever wanted since you were born?"

The bar vanished.

The world quietened.

My heart stopped.

"*What* did you just say?" I leaned forward, swaying so close I had to take a step toward him, so I didn't tumble against his chest.

My father knew how inconsiderate that sentence had been. He moved from ceasefire to full-on battle negotiations. "Elle, before you start." He gulped. "I'm sure Mr. Everett didn't mean it like that."

"Oh, I did." Mr. Everett crossed his arms, somehow holding his glass of clear liquor upright, showing just how close we stood to each other when the sleeve of his shirt brushed the silk of my black dress.

Any higher and he would've touched my breasts.

*Cocky bastard.*

"I meant it exactly the way it sounded."

Red painted my vision. The endlessly long days. The pressure. The lost childhood and servitude. I couldn't let him get away with such a remark. I couldn't stand there and let him *smirk* as if I was a tantrumming adolescent who'd never worked and believed money came from fairy farts.

I inhaled hard to deliver my perfectly poised rebuttal.

Mr. Everett stood patiently, dripping with arrogance. "Well?"

I opened my mouth.

And then...I shut it again.

*He's not worth it.*

*No man is.*

*They're all the same—believing I'm some bauble in my father's empire.*

Some jewel they could commandeer for themselves and take over the company just like they'd take over me.

*No.*

*Never going to happen.*

I would forever be a virgin-bound husk before I ever wasted more breath and temper on a man who would always remain below me.

I moved my arm as Dad tried to squeeze my elbow, asking for discretion and quietness. He knew me. He knew I was borderline Hurricane Noelle. He'd seen me blow up only twice and both were at cocky men who believed their top salaries entitled them to cheat on their wives and not give a shit about their work.

One had cried as he left Belle Elle headquarters. The other had retired with a tarnished reputation.

Dad glanced nervously around the bar, waiting for Armageddon. Instead of giving him a second heart attack, I twisted my elbow, grabbed his wrist, and jerked him sideways. "Come along, Dad. I think this man has poisoned your mind enough."

"Elle, darling—"

"Don't you 'darling' me. Next time you think of setting me up, Dad, stop. I don't want another forced meeting with Greg just because you and Steve can see us playing house. I don't want some pity introduction with men who pass your critique. And I *definitely* don't want to see this one again. Ever." I sneered at Mr. Everett, doing my best to ignore the frustratingly erotic smile on his face.

He raised his glass of clear liquor, taking a sip. His gaze drifted over me with eyes as dark as goodbyes and a jaw so sharp it would slice my finger if I were ever stupid enough to touch it.

"He said you were head-strong. I didn't believe him." Mr. Everett chuckled in a deep rasp. "I've seen evidence for myself, and I have to admit…" He leaned closer in a cloud of expensive, heady aftershave. "I like it." Glancing at my cleavage quickly, his eyes flew back to mine. "Unhand your father, Ms. Charlston, and agree to a date with me."

My jaw fell open.

Did he just ask me out?

After all that?

I kept my face cool and uninterested. "Never in a million years."

"A million is a long time."

"It's also a lot of money if you want to be sued for sexual harassment."

He grinned. "I happen to have excellent legal counsel. You'd never win."

"I don't need to win to tell you to leave me the hell alone."

"Go on a date with me, and I might agree to your command."

"What part of 'leave me alone' didn't you hear? A date would defeat that wish to never see you again."

He smoothed his silky gray shirt. "I decide what to hear and what not to." His eyes narrowed with untold authority. "And I've decided your father is right. You are my type. And I'm yours. It's normal for us to find out what nature intends."

I couldn't.

I just couldn't deal with this insanity.

"We should find out what nature intends, huh?" I reached forward and plucked his still-filled glass from his stupidly perfect fingers. "*This* is what nature intends." I dumped the contents onto his ridiculously sexy swept back hair then leaned in until our noses brushed. "Come near me again, and I'll strike a match to see how well liquor and fire like each other."

Not caring about my father or Steve or Greg or even damn Mr. Everett, I straightened my shoulders and stormed from the restaurant.

# Chapter Thirteen

MY COMPUTER EARNED the brunt of my anger.

The poor keyboard was bruised in places no technology should be bruised.

Ever since the Weeping Willow, I'd been strung so tight, my insides had transformed into something snarling and wild with big teeth. I felt like something lived inside me, ready to leap free.

*Probably been reading too many shapeshifter romances again.*

But still, all night I couldn't relax, and all day I revved with disbelief at Mr. Everett's gall.

Then again, was there anything to be truly upset about? He was an opportunist, and my father had been his victim. No harm done. I'd seen past the ruse and kept my father safe and far away from a scam artist.

*So why can't I dampen the temper raging in my blood?*

*Because he's the only man to get a rise out of me?*

The only one to show me a little of the truth hidden beneath the prim dresses and eloquent politeness of a workaholic?

That I had passion.

Depth.

*Needs?*

*No, that can't be true.*

Men were part of the population I didn't need. Even Belle Elle could survive without the male counterparts. The sales figures for women's fashion were two-hundred times that of the men's department. In fact, I should propose at the next business meeting to cancel all male lines and just pretend the world had done itself a favor and deleted anyone with a penis.

*You're talking gibberish.*

*Thank God that can't happen as you'd miss your father.*

Thinking about my father and the word penis in the same

context was disgusting.

But thinking of Mr. Everett in the same context...

*Still disgusting.*

My hands curled around my pen. This was Dad's fault—the same father dead set on marrying me off before my next birthday.

The clock on my desk said it was almost 5 p.m. I'd lasted the day and used my anger to wipe my to-do list clean. I'd never finished so early before, and I wished I had more tasks to do as there was no way I wanted to go home yet.

Poor Sage fed off my nervous energy, pacing around my office rather than napping in the twilight sunshine. And I was hungry again for the fifth time today—burning through calories faster than I could replace them.

Someone knocked on my door.

I looked up. "Yes?"

"Elle?" Fleur stuck her head in. "Your father wants a word before he retires for the night."

I froze. "Why?"

*Another disastrous date set up?*

Fleur frowned. "Um, not sure. He's family...I guess he just wanted to say goodbye?"

I dropped my pen, dragging a hand through my hair. "Of course, stupid of me. You're right. Send him in."

She gave me a sweet smile, sidestepping enough for my father to enter. His gaze, as always, went to the Chinese wallpaper to my left with cranes and rice paddies. The decoration line had been a trial we'd done in the houseware department four seasons ago, and it'd been a huge hit. I'd used some of the product myself to make sure it had longevity and style.

"How was your day?" he asked, coming around my desk to kiss the top of my head.

"Good." I sighed. "I got everything I needed to done."

"That's great." He grinned, but it didn't reach his eyes. His apology hovered in the space between us, big and marshmallow-like, and entirely obvious to both of us.

"Spit it out, Dad." I closed my laptop and shut my diary. "What's up?"

He blurted. "I'm so sorry about last night, Bell Button. I was wrong. You were right. He was a stuck-up jackass."

I smothered a laugh. "Jackass, I agree with."

His shoulders fell, his slim figure bowing while resting his hip against my glass desk. "I won't do it again, and I promise Steve and I will back down about forcing you and Greg together. I know you're not a fan, and it's wrong of me to interfere." He picked up my fountain pen with turquoise ink—the only frivolous thing I used when everything else was black and white with Belle Elle regulation. "I should let nature take its course and let you find your own true love."

I groaned under my breath. "Don't you start with what nature intends."

Splashing alcohol onto Mr. Everett's head filled my mind—payment for using that same line.

Had he thought about me in the shower while rinsing off? Had he cursed me when dropping his suit in for dry cleaning?

*Serves him right.*

Dad's eyebrow rose, but he wisely didn't comment. The soft lamp on my desk highlighted the threads of silver in his hair like Christmas fairy-lights. "Is there anyone? Anyone at all?"

I stood, grabbing my handbag and swooping down to pluck Sage from her basket. She crawled up my arm and settled like a furry sausage around the back of my neck. "No. No one. And you have to come to terms that there might never be." I patted his shoulder. "I'm happy. I don't need a man to validate my existence."

*Besides, I'm so young still.*

He acted as if I were already slipping down the side of the age-hill of no return.

His eyes grew sad. "If you knew what love felt like, you wouldn't be so sure about that statement, Elle."

"I *do* know what love feels like. From you and Mom and Sage." I moved toward the door, turning off floor lamps that I found gave a homely glow as I went. "Promise me you'll stop meddling, and I'll take you to dinner to make up for last night."

He strode forward, happiness replacing his regret. "On one condition."

I sighed dramatically, reaching up to scratch Sage beneath her chin. "What condition?"

He came forward and rested his hands on my shoulders, not caring when Sage swatted him with her paw. "Just promise me that when a man does come along who makes you fall in love, that you'll give him a chance. That you'll reserve judgment until he's proven he's worth holding on to, and then you'll never let him go."

My heart plummeted to my toes as I smiled brightly, hiding

the internal agony he'd just caused. "I'll amend one piece of that promise and agree. *If* a man comes along. If that miracle happens, I'll give him a chance before I squish him."

What I didn't say was I'd already met that man. That significant person who got under my skin and made me dream.

Only thing was, I hadn't held on tight enough.

And I'd lost him.

# Chapter Fourteen

THREE DAYS LATER, my life had returned to normal.

No more sleepless nights thanks to Mr. Everett—they were sleepless because of my guilt toward Nameless. Mundane mornings on the treadmill flowed into agonizing afternoons with board meetings.

Life was controllable once again.

Fleur continued to help me run the empire while Dad took a few days off at my insistence. His skin had lost some color, and I'd caught him coughing the other day with a rattle I didn't like. If it was the flu, I wanted him safe and warm at home while Marnie, the cook, made him healthy snacks. I didn't want opportunistic germs straining his already strained heart.

Steve helped me host a few conference calls from Beijing and Montreal about our new infant line releasing next month, and work once again tugged me deep into its clutches, erasing any memory of tipping alcohol onto some stranger's head.

Until the third day when I scooped Sage up and headed to the shop floor for a quick walk around. I did random inspections throughout the week—never announced or fore-planned, so employees weren't prepared.

If I had a spare fifteen minutes, I found no better place to stretch my legs than strolling around the racks of new-smelling merchandise, eyeing up displays, spying on staff, and scoring any areas that needed tweaking.

As the elevator carried me from the top floor to the bottom, the mirrored walls showed Sage as she lay over my shoulders, tapping my dangling crystal earring that matched the ivory dress with soft caramel lace. The lacy panel covered my chest and worked in a flower pattern to flare over my hips before reconvening at the hem.

Fleur had added it to my paperwork pile to take home with me last week. I'd thought it was too detailed and feminine for work attire, but when I'd tried it on this morning, I didn't want to take it off. The paleness of it should've washed out my blonde complexion; instead, it made me glow as if I'd just stepped off a plane from Tahiti.

Not that I knew what that was like. The only air travel I did was to factories around the world, and I ended up wearing ear protection and overalls while marching around in heavy boots with a clipboard.

The doors opened with a soft chime, and I strode forward in matching caramel heels, clipping quickly over the anti-slip driftwood-planked floor that our focus groups said calmed them with the gray tones and encouraged spending mentality.

Everything—from the warm beige on the walls, to the deep purple curtains in the changing rooms—was chosen by a color guru who convinced us purple made people believe they were rich because it was the color of royalty and wealth, and beige stole their worries and stress, allowing them to see the treasure trove of merchandise that could all be theirs for the small price ticket tucked demurely inside.

"What department should we investigate first, Sage?" I murmured so as not to attract attention from shoppers.

Not that I could avoid being noticed, seeing as I strode purposely through Belle Elle with a cat wrapped around my shoulders. Luckily, she was of the small variety and not tubby like some cats I'd seen.

I glanced toward the lingerie department where an equal number of awkward men bought gifts for their loves ones while bold women brazenly fingered G-strings and garter belts.

I knew the manager, Kim, would keep her staff in line; the displays were impeccable with its small scaffold of pantyhose, playful kink, and lace. I wouldn't waste my time on areas I didn't need to improve.

Narrowing my eyes, I searched for sloppily folded sale items or imbalanced banners or scruffy shop assistants.

The houseware section was a little messy with its figurines and lamp cords. The women's shoe department needed a memo to tell them to pick up empty boxes from customers pulling them from the shelves. And children's wear would definitely earn a slap on the wrist for a banner promising twenty percent off bibs when a high chair was bought.

That promotion ended two days ago.

However, the area that set my heart racing with chaos was the man's division where five-thousand dollar blazers were tossed over racks, obscuring pressed trousers and faultless shirts. Ties draped over mannequin arms like streamers, and the sock table was a rummaged disaster.

Sage meowed softly, most likely saying in kitty talk for me to calm down before I found the unsuspecting manager and fired him on the spot.

"Where the hell is he and his staff?" Striding forward, my hands curled as yet more disorder revealed itself. A shirt had fallen off its hanger and lay on the floor. The floor! Belts tangled in a viper-nest on the cash register.

*What the hell is going on?*

"Three warnings, my ass," I muttered. "This is grounds for instant dismissal."

I didn't care the men's department hardly ever covered the extravagance it cost to run with its cashmere imported material and on-site tailor from Savile Row. This was Belle Elle, and it had severely let my company down.

"What's the manager's name again?"

Sage snuffled into my neck.

"You're no help."

She meowed.

No matter how many racks I charged down, looking for a victim wearing a Belle Elle nametag and noticeable lavender work shirt, I couldn't find anyone. Not one.

*Where on earth are they?*

There should be at least three to four staff manning this section at all times.

My eyes fell on the brightly lit sign for the changing rooms.

I shouldn't.

Women weren't permitted in there. But surely, the boss was.

Tilting my chin with authority, I marched through the archway and slammed to a stop.

If I thought the shop floor was a disaster, the changing rooms were a catastrophe.

Clothes everywhere!

Thousands of dollars of merchandise on the floor and piles drowning the leather-studded ottomans.

"What is the meaning of this?" I placed my hands on my hips as four men—who I paid a decent hourly wage and should be on the shop floor enticing people to buy—all gathered around something of utter fascination.

Something I couldn't see.

The floor manager swiveled in place, his mouth falling open. "Oh, hello, Ms. Charlston. I'm sorry I didn't see you there."

"You didn't see me because clothes are *everywhere*. It looks like a World War Ten started in here." I motioned to the pyramids of expensive suits just crumbled on the floor as if they were five-dollar t-shirts. "Clean this mess up, immediately. And get your staff at front of house. There're no assistants out there."

"Of course, Ms. Charlston." The manager nodded; his identification tag showed his name was Markus. "Right away." Clicking his fingers, he snapped, "George, Luke, get back out there. Ryan and I can finish with Master Steel."

Instantly, the two younger staff members dropped the shirts looped over their arms onto the already overflowing ottoman and dashed past me with respectful, apologetic smiles.

I didn't watch them go. I couldn't. My gaze glued to the little human I hadn't seen thanks to staff and shirts surrounding him.

"Oh, I'm so sorry; I didn't know I'd interrupted something." I glanced at Markus. "Why didn't you say something?"

"Because you're right, ma'am. We don't need four attendants to dress one child."

I eyed the kid who stood in front of the floor-to-ceiling mirror, swimming in men's trousers and a blazer that came to his knees. I gave him a quick smile, moving closer to Markus. "Why is he in the men's department and not in children's wear? He'll never find anything to fit him."

The boy looked at me in the mirror, not bothering to turn around. "I'm not a kid."

I startled at the sharp staccato of his adolescent voice. The pinched look in his cheeks and wildness in his gaze spoke of a child running out of patience and either close to tears or temper. I hadn't been around many kids, but I guessed he was nine or ten.

"I want a suit. Penn said I could have a suit. Like him. I want to dress like him and Larry."

Sage squirmed on my shoulders, squinting at the boy. Just like me, she wasn't used to bossy children. Not equipped to reply to a sentence I had no way of understanding, I looked back at Markus. "Can you explain?"

Markus grinned at the boy. "Of course. This is Stewart. He prefers Stewie, though, don't you?"

The boy nodded. "Stewie." He poked a finger into his chest. "That's me."

"Okay…" I smiled as if it was a perfectly acceptable name and not a thick-type soup I found utterly unappetizing. "And Stewie wants a suit."

Stewie grinned, showing a gap in his front teeth where a baby tooth had fallen, and an adult one had yet to appear. "Yup. Penn is helping. He said all men have to have at least three suits. One for a wedding, a funeral, and business."

"A funeral?" My heart sank. "Is that where you're going?"

"No." Stewie brushed chestnut hair away from his face, eyeing his rosy cheeks in the mirror and ears that slightly protruded. "But it's better to be prepared. That's what he and Larry always say."

I moved forward, my hand sliding upward to scratch Sage as she hissed at the small creature. "And who are Larry and Penn? Your fathers?" The world was an open society these days. Larry and Penn could be married. Or they could be his uncles or teachers or just friends. Or brothers. Hell, Larry and Penn could be generous kidnappers for all I knew.

Stewie screwed up his nose. "Ha, that's funny." His mirth faded. "Wait…I kinda suppose they are. Now, I mean. I never had a dad before." His angular face brightened. He wasn't chubby like some children of his age were. He had a hard edge about him that couldn't be tamed, even in the ridiculously huge suit with cuffs hanging over his hands like penguin flippers.

I glanced over my shoulder to Markus. "Where are his fathers? Why are you and my staff playing babysitter?"

"Um, he's only here with one gentleman, Ms. Charlston. And he just popped out for a moment. Urgent phone call, I believe." He shuffled. "But he made the mess, not us. He and Stewie tried to find something smaller—smaller belts, socks, ties—an entire wardrobe, you understand. We settled on agreeing that Stewie would pick a suit he liked, and then we'd send it to be tailored to fit him."

My eyes widened. "But that will end up being an entirely new suit. There is no way a tailor can turn a man's thirty-eight into a boy's twelve."

"But isn't that what I'm paying for?" a cool, svelte voice murmured behind me. It throbbed with glamour while somehow bordered curt impatience. "Isn't that what Belle Elle prides itself on? Providing what other stores cannot? Because if it isn't…then my apologies; we'll go somewhere else."

I spun in place, my heart already leaping into a churning sea at his tone.

The moment my eyes locked onto the newcomer's dark brown ones, the past three sleepless nights and long hours caught up with me. Shaking hijacked my arms and not because I'd upset a customer and tarnished a little of what he rightfully said was our motto but because it was him.

*Him!*

"You."

"Yes, me." Mr. Everett smirked. "Nice to see you again."

"What are you doing here?"

He rolled his shoulders, his fingers tightening around his phone. "Same thing as everyone else, I suspect. Putting our money into your pockets."

I crossed my arms. "Yet you leave your son for my staff to babysit. That isn't part of their job description."

"I apologize. It was an urgent call and only lasted a few minutes." He looked past me to the boy swimming in wool and hand stitching. "You okay, Stew? Find something you like?"

Stewie turned and headed toward us, his feet dragging the trouser lengths like clown socks behind him. "Yep. I like this one."

Mr. Everett eyed the soft gray with navy blue pin striping. "Me too. Good choice."

Stewie shrugged out of the blazer and passed it to Markus who stood ever professional, minding his own business.

I couldn't decide if I wanted to run away or shove this miscreant out of my store. Son or no son.

*Wait…he has a son.*

*He's married to a man named Larry and has a son.*

Not only had my father got the story completely wrong at the bar, but Mr. Everett had also fibbed about being interested in me and having a 'knack' with women.

My temper steamed, and before I could censor, I said, "Turns out you're full of lies, Mr. Everett."

His eyes narrowed as a dark cloud settled over his face. "Excuse me?" He opened his arm as Stewie slotted himself against his side, reaching for his phone and swiping in the passcode to pull up Angry Birds.

I stepped back as Sage sank her claws into my neck in warning.

*Good call, kitty.*

---

I let my arms fall, and tension disperse. It meant nothing that he'd lied or that he was gay. Why hadn't I seen it? Of course, he was gay. He was far too well dressed and manicured in every way—trim nails, groomed eyebrows, and thick sorrel hair with the occasional honey highlight. That couldn't be natural.

He wasn't natural.

He was fake.

And I was done.

"I apologize for interrupting your shopping experience. I hope you enjoy the rest of your visit to Belle Elle." Stepping forward, I did my best to avoid his bulk in the narrow hallway with changing rooms on either side.

He wasn't courteous and didn't step aside to let me pass. He just stood there, giving me the choice to squeeze past the small gap or wait and glare into his eyes.

The same eyes that had molten heat and a perpetually pissed expression. He was like sugar and salt, pollen and poison—someone dangerous. Prickles of self-preservation urged me to leave while frissons of curiosity whispered for me to stay.

I didn't like either.

I didn't like him.

Needing to gain control, I looked at Markus. "Please ensure this department is tidy as soon as possible. And ask the tailor to triple check Stewie's measurements so the alterations are perfect first time."

"Yes, Ms. Charlston."

"His name is Master Steel. Not Stewie," Mr. Everett clipped. "Just like I'm Mr. Everett to you and Penn to him and you're Ms. Charlston to everyone and never Noelle."

*What the hell does that mean?*

I stiffened. "Let me pass."

"No."

I sucked in a breath. "Don't ruin a nice afternoon out for your son, Mr. Everett. Your husband would be very sad to receive a phone call saying you'd been arrested for disrupting the peace in my department store."

His body shifted from tense to downright nasty. His hands opened and closed as if he'd like nothing more than to strangle me. His gaze flickered to Sage around my nape then back to my face. He didn't seem surprised I wore a silver cat as an accessory. "You'd like that, wouldn't you?" His lips quirked at the corners. "For your information, I'm not married. And I prefer my dates with tits rather than balls."

I flinched. "Hardly suitable conversation with a child present."

Stewie mumbled with his eyes glued to Angry Birds. "I've heard worse. Believe me."

"Worse?"

What sort of environment did Mr. Everett expose this kid to? Why was he so skinny? Should I get child services to do a 'random' house call?

"If you recall, Ms. Charlston, I asked you to go to dinner with me the other night. Why would I do that if I wasn't interested in women?"

I ignored his question. It didn't matter what his sexual orientation was or his reason for asking me out.

I wasn't interested in either answer. "I'm not sure why you had the need to inform an impartial stranger of your relationship preferences, Mr. Everett, but I can assure you, I don't care in the slightest."

I moved forward, nudging his shoulder with mine, letting Sage's tail flick his throat as I circumnavigated toward the exit. "Now, if you don't mind. I have more pressing things to attend to."

I looked at the little boy. "Goodbye, Master Steel. I hope you like your new suit."

Without a backward glance, I marched as prim and proper as I could, yet some feminine part of me put an extra swagger in my hips. My own body irritated me, wanting to come across as aloof and sexy when really I shouldn't give a damn.

I *didn't* give a damn.

I'd dumped his drink on his head a few days ago, and now I'd told him off while he was spending *his* money in *my* store.

*Oh, well.*

That was all he was good for.

Adding to the bottom line and becoming nothing more than a nuisance on my day's agenda.

"Come on, Sage. Let's go back to the office." I made my way quickly through the racks, noticing the mess had been tamed to its usual regimented glory. The long sweeping walkway linking the departments beckoned; I increased my speed.

Something strong and unbreakable latched around my wrist, yanking me backward.

I tripped in my heels, falling.

I crashed against a very warm, very unmovable, very, *very* toned chest.

Sage meowed, leaping from my shoulders with feline grace and landing on her feet as whoever had the audacity to grab me spun me around and planted two possessive hands on my upper arms. "You don't get to do that again."

I focused on his mouth and how damn close it was. How his aftershave reeked of heavy notes and woodsy musk. How his fingers dug into me like talons.

How dare he touch me like that?

How dare he believe he had the right to leap over bounds of propriety and somehow trap me in the middle of an argument I wasn't even aware existed.

Snatching my arms from his grip, I glowered. "Don't get to do what?"

"Be rude and leave." His glare laced with dynamite. "At least, this time, you don't have access to liquids."

"If I did, I know where I'd pour them."

His temper crackled, igniting a magnetic field between us until invisible lines of energy lashed us together. Confused energy. Misplaced energy. Energy that couldn't possibly spark to the same frequency when I couldn't stand the sight of him.

"You'll never do that to me again."

"I agree." I nodded with a perfect snap. "Because I plan on never seeing you again. Glad we could agree on something for a change."

He rubbed his jaw, looking me up and down. "You said you never wanted to see me again at the restaurant, yet here we are." He looked around the store, noticing what I'd already seen—that we were alone amongst a lake of clothes, hidden by towers of suede jackets and designer jeans.

He stepped closer, backing me up into a rack of limited edition laptop bags for the hard working male. "Did you think about me, Ms. Charlston? Did you think about my offer?" He licked his bottom lip. "Did you think about what we could *do* together?"

The way he emphasized 'do' sent a ripple of frustration through my belly. Frustration born of annoyance and that dreaded awful concoction of lust. The same lust that'd swarmed without warning the night of my nineteenth birthday. The same lust that'd almost made me lose myself to a man I'd only just met.

I'd learned my lesson that night.

I wouldn't forget it now.

In this light, with the shop fluorescents blaring down and the patchwork of clothes around us, Mr. Everett looked nothing like that man in a black hoodie. It'd been dark that night with so many things happening. My memory struggled to cling to truth rather than embellish with myth. I remembered Nameless had black hair matted into dreadlock-curls, a beard, and clothes that'd long since needed a wash. His eyes were a rich brown like devil's cake. His lips masculine and handsome, adding animation to an otherwise guarded face.

If he'd been my savior, then Mr. Everett was my nemesis in his perfected splendor and arrogant attitude.

My wits came back, pushing away the heat in my stomach and the fizz in my heart from confronting this man once again.

I slipped into CEO mode, shutting everything else off. The force-field hissing between us severed as I forced a laugh as brittle and bright as glass. "Wow, I knew you had an ego, but I didn't know it'd taken up residence of your entire body." I tapped my bottom lip with an ivory painted nail. "What question would you like me to answer first?"

He frowned. "What?"

I counted on my fingers. "One, no I didn't think about you because you barely factored on my radar of noticeable things. Two, no I didn't think about your offer because frankly, I forgot about you the moment I walked out of that restaurant. And three, I most certainly did not think about what we could *do* together because that would mean I noticed you, which I didn't. Which, I believe, I just clarified."

Sage wrapped her lithe silver-furred body around my ankles, creating static against my pantyhose. I bent down and scooped her up, careful to keep my eyes away from Mr. Everett's crotch. I wedged her like a teddy bear into my embrace rather than letting her resume her position like a parrot on a pirate's shoulder.

I needed her close. I needed to use her as support so I could get out of there and away from this man without either slapping him or kissing him.

I couldn't understand why my mind flashed with broken things—of violently attacking him, of giving into the unexplainable fury he invoked in me.

The way he watched me, with a languor simmering with bitterness, said if I gave into such stupidity and started something, he'd be the one to end it with me slammed against the wall and his hands up my skirt.

I didn't like him.

I most certainly didn't want him.

*At all.*

He chuckled softly. "Now who's the liar, Ms. Charlston?" He sniffed the air, almost as if he could drag my perfume and truth into his lungs. "You did think about me and you're thinking about what we could *do* right now." He lowered his chin, watching me from shadowed eyes. "Aren't you?"

I clenched my teeth and didn't reply. A haughty sniff would have to do because I didn't trust myself not to curse him to the underworld and call for security.

I never suffered passion as sick as this. Never wanted to cause physical harm to someone I'd only just met.

He was all wrong.

He made my good turn bad.

*Leave.*

*Right now.*

With a glare, I spun around and stalked toward the walkway and freedom.

Only, there he was again, darting around me and planting himself in my trajectory. Wedging his hands in his gray slack pockets, he smirked. "Want to know my answers to those three questions?"

His voice rippled over my mind but his posture turned a simple question into a labyrinth of disbelief. Something about the way he moved—the way his hands sought the sanctuary of his pockets.

It was familiar.

He tore apart my wondering by leaning close, plucking the energy lines still humming between us. "Do you want to know?"

"No."

"Too bad." He had the gall to walk forward, forcing me to either accept his closeness or step back.

I didn't want him touching me, so I backed up.

And then another step.

And another.

Back and back he forced me, all while our eyes never unlocked and no physical touch ensued. He did touch me, though. His gaze set fire to my skin with every second he stared. I cursed the way my stomach clenched as my spine pressed against a cabinet holding t-shirts in every color for any occasion.

He smiled coldly. "Seems you aren't opposed to doing what you're told, after all."

"What?" I squeezed Sage so hard, she sharpened her claws on my wrist.

"I wanted you against a flat hard surface and what do you know...you're against one."

My mouth went dry as his hand came up, looping around the silver pole of the cabinet stand. He didn't hem me in, but he did lean forward until most of his weight pivoted on his arm, his body hovering so damn close.

He made me prickly as a cactus, hot as a rainforest.

And wet.

I couldn't remember the last time someone had puppeteered my body in such a way.

*Well, yes I can remember.*

But at the same time, I didn't want to. Not while I was affected by a man so totally different to that chocolate kisser in my past. It was ridiculous but I felt like I cheated on him—trampling over my oath to help him, ripping up the debt I had to find and save him.

I hadn't lived up to my promise and every second I spent licking my lips, drunk on cheap chemistry, I cheapened what'd happened between us.

The same rush of pleasure I wanted Nameless to take now begged for a new master.

*And I don't even like this man.*

I didn't like myself.

But it didn't matter because my heart understood he was an egotistical asshole and my body deemed him acceptable enough to scratch my lust-itch regardless.

His gaze dropped to my mouth. His voice was soft, coaxing. "One, I did think about you. A lot more than I should probably admit. I thought about forcing you to accept my offer, so at least I could get you behind closed doors. And I most certainly thought about what we could *do* together."

His head erased the distance, his minty breath slipping past my lips and somehow taking up residence in my lungs, suffocating me. "I thought about it in the shower, in bed, fuck, even in my office." His head came down. His nose nuzzled the shell of my ear, disrupting the crystal earring so it tinkled softly.

His other hand came up, a single finger unfurling and tracing an electrical cord down my arm, slipping to my side and boldly pressing against my waist to my hipbone. "You're a stunning woman, Elle Charlston, and your father was right. Whatever man you end up with is a lucky fucking bastard, but I don't think anyone stands a chance."

He looked into my gaze with cold, pitying look. "You have a prison gate around yourself that you're too afraid to unlock and be free."

I *hated* that he understood me when he had no right.

I *despised* the way he'd used the word free when I myself thought that phrase far too often.

And I *loathed* that his body heat stung mine with sensation and my nipples tightened to pain.

I had no resolution to push him away.

His fingertip suddenly left my hipbone and landed on Sage's head. "It's funny that you're carrying your pussy around. Is that an invitation in some strange way?"

I spluttered. "Get your hand off my cat."

He immediately held it up in surrender before once again tracing a fingertip from my shoulder to my wrist.

It took every ounce of training and discipline not to shudder or puddle to the floor. How long had it been since someone had petted me? How long since I'd been touched other than a quick fatherly hug or pat well done?

*Never.*

*That's how long.*

Because even Nameless had never stroked me. He'd grabbed me, kissed me, fondled me, but never stroked.

I squeezed my eyes, doing my best to find normalcy. Grasping the frigidness inside that still remained like a never thawing glacier, I was glad my misplaced yearning couldn't melt it.

I was better than this.

Better than him.

Sidestepping where his arm wasn't latched to the cabinet, I ducked around a rack of hanging slacks and cloaked myself with government. "I think you over-estimate yourself, Mr. Everett. I don't care if you thought about me and I don't appreciate thinking about what you were doing to yourself in the shower."

I grew bolder as he stood there silently, a malevolent glare in his gaze.

Sage had enough of my embrace and crawled back to her spot on my shoulders. With my arms free, I let them hang proud and regal with my back tight and smile plastic. "If you thought you could overpower me, make me weak in the knees, and force me to go on a date with you, you failed yet again. Not only am I even more determined never to see you again, but you just gave away two very significant pieces of information that mean you're not nearly as mysterious as you think you are."

"Oh?" His eyebrow raised, the faintest sign of confusion lurking beneath the heated coal of his irises. "And what exactly is that?"

I grinned condescendingly. "Out of all the department stores in New York, you happen to choose Belle Elle. And out of the three chains we have in the city, you chose the head office. Why is that? Because you thought you might bump into me?" I shook my head. "Pity. I must admit you came at the right time and coincidence decided to shove us together but only to allow me to clarify that no matter what you say or do, my answer will forever remain no—"

"Seeing as you're taking way too much pride in thinking you figured out my shopping habits, let's move on. What's the second thing I've revealed?" His patent leather shoes squeaked as he moved, once again hinting he wasn't as comfortable as he implied.

His uncertainty fed my resolution. I held my chin high. "That you aren't just a man in a suit looking for a quick one-night stand in a bar."

"I'm not?" His face shut down. "How can you tell?"

"Because you have a son. Because you care enough to spend a fortune on something ridiculous because it's based on self-worth, not the wardrobe. And because you and this unknown Larry person obviously have some resemblance of a heart. Otherwise, that kid wouldn't want to have anything to do with you, yet he willingly curled into you to play Angry Birds."

His posture resembled a furious predator. "You're more observant than I gave you credit."

"No, I'm normally this observant." I clipped onto the walkway to freedom as if I was Dorothy on the yellow brick road to the wizard. "You just don't know me."

I strolled away before he could reply.

# Chapter Fifteen

"THIS INVITATION JUST arrived for you." Fleur waltzed into my office the following day in a pink and yellow sundress that somehow flirted the line between work-appropriate and beachwear.

I glanced from my laptop to the flocked envelope she held, hating the way my mind took the interruption and ran swiftly from human resource issues to once again thinking about Mr. Everett.

I'd successfully pushed him away more times than I would admit. I did not need him in my brain anymore. I didn't even know *why* he was in my brain.

We had some weird form of connection, but I wouldn't buy into the bait and I definitely wouldn't be seduced by a man I couldn't stand.

"Who's it from?" I held out my hand as she approached my desk and placed the heavy invite into my awaiting fingers.

"It has a return address. Chloe Mathers, I believe."

"Chloe Mathers?"

*Why do I know that name?*

A memory tantalized me with some long ignored recollection, begging to be caught and tugged.

*Chloe Mathers...*

Fleur smiled and showed no intention of leaving as I spun the envelope in my hands and sliced it open with a letter knife.

I frowned, pulling free a single card with bronze accents on the corners and the standard description of being invited to a get-together.

My mind slammed into remembrance.

"Oh, no," I groaned. "*That* Chloe Mathers."

Fleur planted her hands on my desk, intrigue all over her face. "Who is she? It doesn't sound like you like her."

"It's not that I don't like her. More she doesn't like me." I flipped the invite upside down, trying to see something personal or hint that perhaps she'd sent this to the wrong person.

"She was the most popular girl in school. For a few months of the year, when it came time for school parties or proms, she befriended me. She and her little group of stuck-up witches would ply me with sleepovers—that I didn't want to go to, but my dad made me—and hold a seat for me in class—which I never sat in because they just cheated off my work—all to drag me to Belle Elle and get them discounts on dresses and shoes."

"Children can be such brats."

"Yep." I nodded distractedly, remembering how much I'd hated high school. How every hour I spent in the faculty classrooms and listened to teachers drone on was a waste because, unlike my peers, I didn't get to go home and play outside or hang with sweet boyfriends on the weekends.

Once the bell rang, David picked me up and drove me to Belle Elle where I'd work until well past most other students' bedtimes.

I looked up, nibbling with uncertainty and nerves I thought I'd deleted from being an outcast at school. "Do you think they sent it by mistake? Why would they invite me?"

"What is it?" Fleur plucked the invite from my hold, scanning the details. "It has your name on the top, so it isn't a mistake."

She read out loud, "You're cordially invited to spend the evening reminiscing and sharing life's progress with the girls from St. Hilga's Education this coming Friday at the Palm Politics. Yourself and plus one are invited." She wrinkled her nose. "Ugh, I can hear their contemptuous attitudes just from a generic invitation."

I hung my head, massaging the muscles in my neck. "It's short notice, isn't it? Do they mean this Friday or next?"

She glanced at the envelope, peering at the stamp. "Uh oh, it's tonight. It was sent a week ago. I guess it got lost in the mailroom. It is, after all, addressed to Elle the Ding Dong Belle."

I smothered my face in my hands. "Oh, God, don't remind me of that awful nickname."

"Man, kids are cruel," Fleur muttered.

I didn't untangle myself from my hands, pretending the pink light coming through my fingers could erase my childhood, and I could forget about pranks and nasty little girls.

Fleur straightened some paperwork on my desk, stacking a

pile of folders, and placing a few stray pens into my stainless steel holder. When order had been granted, and my nerves had calmed somewhat—reminding me they couldn't hurt me anymore—that I was in my Belle Elle tower and they were down there in Manhattan somewhere, I looked up and breathed deep.

We were living our lives. Away from each other. It was perfect.

Only Fleur ruined my co-existence by saying, "You know you have to go, right?"

"What?" My mouth hung open. "No way in hell am I going."

"You have to. Not to prove to them how incredibly successful and powerful you are but to prove to yourself."

I scoffed, plucking a pen from the holder and tapping it wildly against my notepad. "I don't need to do anything of the sort."

She planted a hand on her hip, giving me a raised eyebrow and a look that said 'yeah, right.'

I ignored her. "No way. No how." I snatched the invite and stabbed my finger at the plus one. "Besides, I have no one to go with. If I had some drop-dead gorgeous man who could remind me to stand tall and not let them win, then *maybe*. But I don't, and they'll most likely have their man candy with a rug rat or two. And I'm still an outcast like I always was in high school with her cat."

Sage nudged my ankle, yawning with her cute little tongue shaped into a funnel.

"I love you, Sage, but you're hardly 'bring to a party' material."

I'd already unwittingly showed how sad and depressing my personal life was to Mr. Everett by wearing her on my shoulders yesterday.

*No.*

I'd had enough embarrassment in my life already without adding more to it.

Refreshing my laptop screen, I did my best to read forecast numbers and find them riveting.

Fleur shifted. "I really think—"

"No." I kept my eyes glued on the spread-sheet. "Now, if there isn't anything else, I'd appreciate some quiet, so I can get this done."

She sniffed but turned and plodded dramatically to the door. Reaching it, she turned with a spin so fast it kicked out her dress into a tulip flare. "You know what? I'm taking charge of this. You wore that ivory and caramel lace dress because I made it easy for you to do so. This is the same sort of thing. I know you don't like him, but he's handsome and will have your back."

My heart froze into a popsicle.

*She'll call Mr. Everett?*

*How does she know about him?*

*He won't have my back.*

*He'll find some other surface to push me against and terrorize me more.*

I stiffened. "No, Fleur. Whatever you're thinking. Stop it."

"You'll thank me once you've seen yourself in their eyes. When you've felt their awe at how hard you work and their envy at your unlimited bank accounts. And you'll pretend you aren't, but you'll be happy when they flirt with your man and find out he only has eyes for you."

*She's going to do it.*

*She'll call him.*

*She'll deliberately sabotage my desire never to see him again.*

Before I could tell her I had no intention of being fulfilled by jealousy or had any desire to announce to the undeserving witches from high school what my bank account looked like, she was gone.

To ruin my life.

And I couldn't do a thing to stop it.

# Chapter Sixteen

"I'M GOING TO kill my assistant tomorrow."

David raised an eyebrow as I climbed from the backseat of the Range Rover. "Nice of you to inform me. I'll ensure the appropriate lawyers are called."

I gave him a grim smile. "I do not want to be here, David. Do you think—"

He smothered a slight grin. "Ma'am, if you want, I'll drive you right home. But if you don't mind me saying, you look beautiful, and it seems a shame to waste such beauty without having one drink before you go."

I narrowed my eyes. "You're a meddler. Just like she is."

"I'm nothing of the sort. In fact, I'll help with the murder tomorrow if tonight is not a success." He closed the back door and headed toward the driver's seat, leaving me abandoned on the sidewalk about to enter the dragon's playground. "Consider me a willing accomplice. Now, go and have fun, and call me when you're ready to leave."

My emotions were full of poutiness and frustration. I could just tell him I was ready *now*. But I wasn't a four-year-old, and he was right. It would be a waste not to go in for a second— especially after Fleur's wardrobe ministrations.

Not that I approved.

The dress she'd chosen was the most daring, risqué thing I'd ever worn. For a cocktail get-together, she'd gone over the top with a russet-gold silk gown that slinked around my ankles and split up one leg to mid-thigh. The back was non-existent with just enough height to cover my ass but leave my spine exposed, while the front swooped up to my throat in a gathered cowl.

She'd even gone as far to do my hair for me. She'd fishtail braided it, so it sat over my left shoulder and kept my naked back on display.

The entire time she fussed with my hair and makeup, I'd muttered she was fired and to start looking for other employment.

But once she showed me the finished product, shoved me into the car, and told me my date would meet me there, I had to admit a smidgen (a teeny tiny smidgen) of excitement filled me to have a night out with people other than business associates or my father and Steve.

And to be honest, I looked forward to spending an evening looking the way I did while tormenting and verbally sparring with Mr. Everett. It was the thought of him being there to take the spotlight off me from the nasty school girls that moved my unwilling feet into the nightclub where a small section had been roped off for our reunion.

Palm Politics was a strange blend of tropical fronds and the décor of a court of law. One freedom and sunshine. The other prison and shadow. The bar was the podium where the judge would sit and the booths dotted around were a mini oasis in a boardroom of wood and strobe light sentencing.

Goosebumps covered my skin—partly from cold and partly from anxiety at facing these women again—especially in a place such as this. Why couldn't it be a simple bar with no theme or message?

I hated anything to do with law courts and police—it only layered my guilt with more rancid icing at the thought of Nameless.

I'd tried. I'd failed. I hadn't given up but even the weekly phone calls I made to police officers who were kind enough to answer my questions had no news.

If I was a lucky sleeper who enjoyed vibrant dreams, I might've concluded he was merely made up of fantasies and heroism, bound together by imagination magic, and made brilliant by adolescent devotion.

But he had to have been real.

I still had the faintest scar on my nape from where my sapphire star had been ripped away, and I still endured the faintest seduction of chocolate on my lips when I was blessed enough to doze in his dream-company.

Standing in the paddling pool of partiers, I doubled my promise to do more. To track him down, no matter the cost.

*Starting tomorrow.*

*Or tonight if I can leave early.*

---

My minor discomfort at being watched by leering judges and glinting prison bars switched to major annoyance as Greg appeared from the crowd, holding a glass of champagne and a gin and tonic.

My heart instantly tobogganed down a cliff and shot off the edge in denial.

*Oh, God, I'm so stupid.*

Of *course*, Fleur hadn't invited Mr. Everett.

No one knew I'd seen him again, and only my father knew what'd happened at the Weeping Willow.

*She has no clue he exists, so how could I think she'd invite him as my date?*

*I'm an idiot.*

She hadn't ruined my aloofness at refusing Mr. Everett's offer to take me out. But she had sentenced me to endure a terrible evening.

There would be no banter.

No sexy butterflies.

Nothing but obligation to ensure I remained professional—so I didn't hurt Greg, my father, or Steve, and could look everyone in the eye on Monday with no regrets or dismay.

It didn't matter my life would be so much simpler if I just gave into what everyone wanted. But my heart was stubborn and didn't find Greg romance material in the slightest.

"Hi, Elle." Greg passed me the champagne.

I didn't even like champagne. If he cared for me as much as he pretended to, he would've remembered that from all the forced dinners we'd endured with our fathers.

The night suddenly looked a thousand times worse.

I might be a bitch in the boardroom, but I wasn't mean, and Greg had dropped whatever plans he had to be here with me just because Fleur had called him.

I wouldn't be nasty.

But I wouldn't be overly gracious, either.

"Hello, Greg." I sipped the cold bubbles, hiding my grimace. "It's very nice of you to come with me. I hope Fleur didn't interrupt your evening."

He grinned, swiping a hand through his dark blond hair as his overly white teeth caught the strobe light glittering above. "Not at all. When she called, I couldn't believe my luck. Finally, a night out just the two of us." He leaned in with a wink. "Away from the chaperones."

I hid my distaste, forcing a smile. "Exactly."

He slotted himself beside me and, without asking permission, wrapped his arm around my waist. The warmth of his bare forearm tingled my spine and not in a good way. He'd come to this wearing a white t-shirt and black jeans. He looked handsome, of course—he was a good looking guy—but compared to the gown I wore and the finery Fleur had graced me with, I came across as ridiculously overdressed.

My heart plummeted even further off the cliff, splattering on the unforgiving terrain below.

Tonight had slipped from disaster to annihilation. Chloe would never let me live this down if they were all in semi-formal clothing and I appeared dressed like a prom queen.

*Does it matter, though?*

My brain tried to be mature and see the bigger picture. So what Greg wasn't in a suit—it wasn't life or death. So what I might be over-dressed and Chloe might be the same cow I remembered—none of it made any difference to my tomorrow. I would still be me. I would still be as safe and as happy as I was yesterday.

*Be brave, Elle.*

*And then leave with dignity.*

Straightening my shoulders, I stepped out of Greg's embrace but immediately looped my arm through his before his face could fall.

Squeezing his bicep in thanks, I said, "Let's go mingle, shall we?"

\* \* \* \* \*

Two hours I lasted.

Two hours where I was no longer me but a *better* version of me. Noelle was left behind, and Elle used the same techniques from dealing with men twice her age to wield mundane conversation with girls she'd long since forgotten about.

There was potty-training chats with Melanie and fake oohing and ahhing over her one-year-old Facebook pictures. There was biology class reminiscing with Frankie, pretending I felt the same way about our teacher Mr. Bruston, and how sexy his mustache had been.

*Yeah, not at all.*

There were snippets of cattiness from Maria and Sara about who ought to have gone out with Rollo Smith in summer camp, and the requisite fond recalling with Chloe about shopping late at night and running riot through Belle Elle when Dad let us sleep over in the lady's ware department.

She called me Elle the Ding Dong Bell only twice.

But each was like a knife in my side.

I didn't let it show.

I didn't hint at vulnerability or let my guard down.

Greg had no clue how hard this was for me. He merely guffawed at the nickname and plied me with more champagne I didn't want.

Every single conversation I put my all into. I smiled and nodded and listened. My cheeks hurt from fake grinning, my feet ached from standing, and my exposed back became extra sensitive to everything. My skin prickled with minor drafts as people moved behind me, warm patches as people stood close by, and even the tell-tale tingle of people staring at me, itching spots on my shoulder blades as their eyes became fingers and stroked me.

Out of the sixteen people here—eight women and eight men—Greg and I held our own. My dress had started the poshest of them all, but as more people arrived, I'd settled into an array of chiffon and lace, finally accepting that Fleur knew what she was doing.

The dress didn't take away my power. It *gave* me power. And for the first time, I believed in my own self-worth outside of Belle Elle. That I could hold my head high and not be afraid of judgment or wrongdoing. That I was my own person and not just a cog in the conglomerate my family had created. My world was just as good as any others—if not better.

The relief in that gave me a well of kindness to forget that Greg got on my nerves, and I didn't turn away from his touches of affection. I accepted three more glasses of champagne, even though the room grew warm and my skin glowed with bubbly heat.

By hour two, my bladder had done all the retaining of alcohol it could, and I excused myself to find the restroom.

Greg gave me a kiss on the cheek—which I didn't wipe away because the liquor made everything that much more acceptable— and left the roped-off area to make my way through the club.

I guessed the time was ten p.m. or so, but already, the place crawled with bodies and the aura of a good night ahead.

Finding the bathroom, I entered and slammed to a stop as I came face to face with my reflection in a full-length mirror.

*Who the hell is that woman?*

Her braid was a little disheveled with curls free and soft around her face. Her lips were puffy from licking droplets of champagne with remnants of pale pink lipstick. Her smoky eyes rimmed blue that looked far too sated and happy to be real.

I looked...loose.

My limbs moved with a relaxation I never had when sober. My movements less jerky and sedate.

*Being tipsy suits you.*

I rolled my eyes, listing a little to the left as the room swayed.

Being tipsy was a new experience and one I wouldn't often do. The false courage and intoxicating bravado could screw up my careful rules.

Greg suddenly didn't seem so annoying. Chloe wasn't such a bad girl. And the thought of going to work tomorrow was a task I had no intention of fulfilling as long as the beat of a bassy tune worked through my bones.

Wanting to return to the party, I quickly did what I was there to do and washed my hands. Drying my fingers on a paper towel, I ran the remaining dampness over my arms to cool my overheated skin.

I'd come to this club cold, and now, I was burning up.

Something else was burning up, too.

Something that normally only came alive around few very select males. My breasts were heavy, and a tugging sensation deep inside my belly demanded another drink—to let go for once. To stop fighting and let Greg kiss me because he was the only male around who knew what I was and who I had to be. He'd been raised in the same environment.

So what he annoyed me most of the time and didn't seem to truly care about me but only my legacy? He was a man. I was a woman. It was time to do something about my little problem and figure out how to be a sexual creature and not an untouched virgin any longer.

Striding from the bathroom, I walked with purpose, brushing against strangers and enjoying it for once rather than cringing at having no personal space. Up ahead, Greg laughed and touched Chloe's waist, bending to whisper something in her ear. The rest of the group mingled in twos and fours, chatting and drinking.

I knew those people.

I had a life.

I was invited to party with them.

I had freedom, after all.

Only, whatever freedom I thought I had jerked to a stop as a man's arm snaked around my waist, yanking me back. My languidness from champagne meant I folded neatly into his embrace, too slow to fight.

His lips landed on my ear. "If it was coincidence yesterday, it has to be fate today."

I froze.

Whatever tipsiness I suffered tripled as his hands roamed my ribcage, taking liberties he wasn't given, rubbing the soft silk into my skin in ways that should be illegal.

"Hello, Elle." His lips traced from my ear to my throat, nudging my braid to gain better access.

I shivered.

My body melted—not from him but the champagne. It *had* to be the champagne. I wouldn't allow it to be him.

Sucking in a breath, I tore myself from his embrace and swiveled to face him.

He was just as divine. Just as cocky. Just as dangerous.

"Are you stalking me?"

Mr. Everett grinned. "I wouldn't dare."

He stood in a gray suit with the cuffs of his blazer and white shirt pushed half-way up his forearms. How he managed to get the material that high over how muscular his arms were, I didn't know. The strobe light decorated his hair, making it seem light then dark, light then dark. The yin and yang of right and wrong—the glimpse of imperfections that made him eternally frustrating.

"After all, why waste my time when the universe keeps putting you in my path?"

My mouth watered as his gaze locked onto my lips. A black ravenousness filled his eyes that any hot-blooded female understood—virgin or promiscuous.

"I don't believe it's the universe." I blinked, forcing myself to cling broken-nail tight to sanity. "I think it's some sort of game you're playing."

He lowered his jaw, stepping closer until our chests brushed. My nipples tightened embarrassingly hard. Not wearing a bra meant my reaction was noticeable through the burnished gold dress.

He licked his bottom lip, his gaze dropping to my breasts then back to my mouth. "If I *was* playing something, are you intrigued enough to learn the rules?"

"Never."

His lips smiled but his face was toxic. "Little liar."

His hand came up, tucking a wayward curl behind my ear. His fingers captured the diamante chandelier earrings I wore, tugging gently. "I think you are ready to play with me, you just don't want to admit it." He bent his head, breathing into my ear. "I've been patient, but I meant what I said to your father. I can make you do things, Elle. Things you want to do. Things *I* want to do. I particularly liked when you said you'd get on your knees and call me, what was it? Oh, master?"

I jerked back, but with his fingers holding my earring, I daren't move quickly or far.

He bent forward. His tongue licked my lobe just once.

A lightning bolt arched from his tongue to my belly. A crack. A fissure. A deep cavernous ache I needed, *needed* to fill.

"One date," he murmured. "That's all I'm asking."

The champagne switched to more potent alcohol. Had I truly had four glasses? It felt like twelve.

I swam in air. I wobbled in heat. I swayed as his hands locked around my hips, dragging me into him. Surrounded by people yet all alone in our little cosmos, he rocked his erection into my stomach, grinding his teeth with the same angry desire rampaging in my blood.

The room spun. I did my best to keep control. "I don't—I don't even like you."

"I don't like you."

"Then—" He shocked me mute as he kissed my cheek, then rewarded such sweetness with a nasty nip.

"Then what?" he taunted. "Finish, Elle."

My head weighed more than the galaxy. "Then…let me go."

"Can't." The tip of his tongue soothed the pinch of pain from his teeth.

*Can't?*

My mind doggy paddled through syrup.

*Why can't you? Isn't mutual affection the first key to unlocking passions padlock?*

His fingers looped around my throat, full of threat, robust with peril. "Liking each other doesn't matter." His fingers dug tighter into my skin. "What matters is how you feel about this." He glanced around, assessing how public we were, before his hand swooped between us and cupped between my legs.

The world shot to a standstill.

There was no more music. No more club.

I stood in mud so thick, I couldn't move. My only way free was this bastard and he was the one drowning me.

Everything inside me clenched then stretched then multiplied with a thousand screaming *'mores.'*

"Tell me to stop, and I'll stop. Tell me to remove my hand, and I'll remove my hand." His fingers feathered over me, rocking his palm against my clit; his fingers pressing over the tight lace protecting me. "But if you tell me you're all right with this, if you tell me to keep going, then you play by *my* rules. You become mine in every fucking sense."

I shivered as his fingers probed harder. I'd never been touched that way—let alone in a crowded bar.

"I—I don't know." Words were the hardest thing in the world to form. "I don't know what to say."

"I'll help you." His hand vanished. His body separated from mine as he grabbed my wrist and dragged me into the dark hallway of the bathrooms. Marching past the men's and women's, he tucked me against the wall and pressed me hard against it.

The moment I was trapped, he put his full weight on me, grabbed my leg, and hoisted it over his hip.

I gasped as he rocked his erection again, pressing directly where his hand had been only seconds before. "Oh—"

"That's one word." His face flashed with raven desire. "Say a few more. Agree to play with me."

My head wanted to roll back and break away as his mouth fastened against my throat—kissing, biting, sucking. I wanted no more thoughts, no more dos and don'ts. No more reasons why this was wrong and I needed to end it before I forgot everything.

My hands automatically flew to his hair, yanking on the softness, twining my fingers through his thick, healthy strands. The exquisite feel of him jerked me from the moment. For a second, I'd expected dreadlocked curls and chocolate. Of soft beards and urgent moonlight.

My body swelled but my heart shriveled.

Mr. Everett was not Nameless. Yet he was the second man to ever kiss and touch me in such a way—an accolade I didn't know if he deserved.

"Wait—I don't know what you want."

He chuckled into my neck. "I thought it was fucking obvious." He thrust up, his shoes squeaking a little on the hardwood floor as he slammed me into the wall with his pressure. "I want to fuck you, Elle."

My insides puddled at the crudeness. My ears rang for more even while my lips curled in disgust.

"I want to take you, own you, control you." His voice bordered on feral. "I'm not going to lie. I could say I wanted to date and pretend to fall for you. But I won't."

Conversation helped remind me I was human not an animal. I latched onto words. "So...you just want sex?"

"What I want is to kiss you." His head came up, his lips glistening from sucking my throat. "Let me do that, then decide on the rest."

He hypnotized me. He corrupted me.

I breathed fast.

He saw a split-second answer—an answer I wished I could retract—and his mouth descended on mine.

His lips were soft but commanding, tearing through my chastity, spearing his tongue past my teeth.

I moaned as he took a kiss and turned it into something else. He switched it into water and fire and heat and chill. He hoisted me up the wall until the floor no longer existed, just air. Holding me up with his hips jammed against mine, he seared our bodies together.

And then, it was over.

Sharp, sweet, sudden...entirely soul-destroying.

"Say yes."

"Yes?"

"Yes to letting me have you." His voice blistered. "Say yes and you're mine and whatever comes next is my choice, not yours. You'll answer to me. I'll do whatever the hell I want. Sometimes, you'll hate me. Other times, you'll be grateful for my interference. Most of the time, you'll probably want to kill me."

He kissed me again. "But I can promise you if you say yes, fuck I'll make you feel good. I'll give you what you've been looking for. I'll make you free."

The stream of eloquence matched his hard-edged charm. He was pretty. Too pretty. So pretty it masked the ugliness hidden inside. It made me forget that there were more things to seek than just beauty—deeper things. Things he didn't possess.

In that hallway, in his arms, I didn't care.

I hated that I didn't care.

But that was the truth.

He made me shallow.

"Elle?" A voice interrupted our rapid breathing and aching

bodies.

Instantly, Mr. Everett let me fall to my heels, backing away and subtly arranging his blazer over the obvious erection in his slacks. His eyes never left mine, full of promises and menacing intimidation.

I gulped, looking over his shoulder at the man who'd interrupted whatever the hell had happened.

*Greg.*

Smoothing my hair, I stepped forward.

Mr. Everett fell into rhythm with me, crossing his arms like a silent protector and aggressor all in one.

Greg glowered at him. "Who the hell are you?"

Mr. Everett glanced at me with a wicked smirk. That smirk held every sentence he'd uttered. Every command and description. He wanted me. I wanted him. He didn't like me. I didn't like him.

Hatred turned to frenzy.

A perfect drug for danger.

Everett's lips moved; his voice worse than the champagne with intoxication. "Who am I, Elle?"

My blood quivered to finish what he'd started. My brain short-circuited to bypass the fact I wanted him while hating him. If he could knock me so off balance with just a kiss, what could he do to me in bed?

He'd made me selfish as well as shallow.

*But I can't sleep with him.*

Could I?

I didn't like him. I didn't trust him. I definitely didn't believe I could ever fall for him.

*So what?*

*You're old enough to have sex with no strings.*

*He's proven to have a heart somewhere. He has a son.*

*He. Has. A. Son.*

He could have a wife and baggage and so many other mysteries I couldn't hope to solve. Carnal greed could never trump such laws.

Curling my hands, I shook away the fervour he'd dazed me with.

It didn't matter I wanted, needed, craved. It would never happen…if he was with another.

*But he might not be.*

*Are you saying you'd ignore everything else and use him if he's single?*

My nerves returned a thousand fold.

When I didn't reply, Mr. Everett prompted me. "Answer your friend. Tell him who I am to you." He narrowed his eyes. "Are we playing or shall I walk away?"

Such an innocent question loaded with sexual mist and unsatisfied misery.

My fingers fell to my dress, stroking the material, seeking comfort and answers.

"What the fuck is going on, Elle?" Greg marched forward.

I couldn't believe the champagne had made me think I could tolerate him. After being kissed by Mr. Everett and then even remotely entertaining the idea of doing the same with Greg, I couldn't imagine it. It would be like seeing the most spectacular sunset only to be told I had to live in fog the rest of my life.

"One second, Greg." I held up my hand, testing the locks and chains around my sexuality as they quaked under pressure. "Answer one question, Mr. Everett. Then I'll give you an answer."

"Fine." A sly grin decorated his handsome face. "But rest assured if your answer is yes, that's the last time you'll call me Mr. Everett."

"Oh?"

He looked triumphantly at Greg as he bent to whisper in my ear. "You'll be screaming my name as I stick my tongue inside you. You'll be sobbing my name as I make you come over and fucking over."

I stumbled.

His hand grabbed my elbow, a low chuckle on his breath. "That name is Penn. You might as well get used to it if, of course, your answer is what I hope."

"Elle, are you sick?" Greg came forward, his eyes trying to murder Mr. Everett...*I mean Penn.*

I waved him away, flushed and nauseous, entirely too skittish to be hemmed in by another man after flashes of nakedness and dirty sex swarmed my mind.

"Yes, I'm fine." Ignoring Greg and giving all my attention to Penn, I asked, "My question is, are you with the mother of your child?"

Penn didn't reply.

"What?" Greg's eyes widened. "Not only are you cheating on me with this scumbag in a nightclub hallway but he's cheating on a family?" He threw his hands up. "For fuck's sake, Elle, I thought you were better than that. Your father believes you're better than that. *My* father believes you're better than that."

I snarled, hating the disgust in his voice even though I hadn't done anything wrong. Not yet, at least. If that was how those who knew me would look at me, I wanted nothing to do with whatever kinky pleasure Penn offered.

But it was as if Penn knew that.

He brought me close, whispering in my ear again as I kept my eyes locked on Greg. "I'll answer your question, but I'll also answer the other you just thought. First, I'm not married nor have I ever been. I'm as single as you are. I'm as confined as you are. That's all you need to know. Second, you're right to think people will judge you. The moment I've been inside you, people will know. You'll be different. You won't be able to help it. Rumors will start. Friends will change. Future love interests will hate you."

I stiffened, but he pulled me closer. "But I won't let you be subject to those rumors alone. Tell me yes, and I take control. You won't have to make any decisions or take responsibility for what we do. It'll all be on me." His tongue traced the shell of my ear, hidden from Greg thanks to my fishtail braid. "Give me that word, Elle, and I'll show you exactly what I mean."

I stood at the crossroads, staring at Greg and the future my father wanted—the one where I stood side by side with a man who knew Belle Elle the way I did and would help run the business—while a stranger held me and pressed his cock against my hip, blatantly claiming what wasn't his to claim.

One was a long-term choice. The other a short-term adventure.

I'd had enough long-term commitments in my life. I wanted to be different. I wanted a rumor or two because that would mean I was interesting and not predictable.

Greg made my decision ridiculously easy.

He came forward and grabbed my other elbow, pulling me away from Penn. "Elle, I'm willing to overlook whatever you just did with this bastard. You're drunk. I know I should never have given you that champagne. Let me take you home where you belong."

Home.

I no longer wanted to be at home.

I wanted to be lost and crazy and wild.

I yanked my arm from his hold. "I'm sorry, Greg. But I should've told you."

"Tell me what?"

Locking my eyes on Penn's, I whispered, "Yes. My answer is

yes." A little louder, I added, "But it doesn't mean I like you."

"Doesn't mean I like you, either." Penn smiled full of cream and sharpness and calmly wrapped his arm around my shoulders, tucking me close.

Together, we faced Greg.

I didn't know what I expected Penn to do, but it was his turn to be in charge. I was in charge on a minute basis in every aspect of my world. If he wanted to share that control in a few areas, then fine...*be my guest.*

"I must apologize, too." Penn smiled coldly. "We weren't ready to tell people, but I guess now is as good a time as any."

"Tell people what?" Greg's eyes filled with panic, not at knowing he'd lost me but that he'd lost any chance at owning Belle Elle. His true colors revealed.

Relief siphoned through me to be free of whatever takeover he'd planned. To finally see what I'd suspected all along—that I was right to be wary of him, smart to listen to the faint warning bells whenever he was around.

"Tell them that Elle and I...we're together."

I flinched a little as Penn kissed my cheek. Still uncomfortable and aroused and so confused I had no idea if this was what I wanted or not.

*Too late now.*

"Elle is mine. In fact, I'm taking her home right now. My home." He pushed me forward, deliberately forcing Greg to the side so we could pass. "We'll just say our goodbyes to the others."

Greg spluttered something I didn't hear.

I turned to Penn. "What do you mean the others?"

"The reunion you're here with."

*How does he know that?*

It added to all the other questions I had about him. All the ponderings and wonderings and itchy uncertainties he invoked.

Was it coincidence at Belle Elle or manipulation that he'd been there when I'd done my rounds?

Was it luck he was here tonight or careful planning?

Would answers to those questions change what I was about to do with him?

That was one question I didn't want an answer to.

My heart raced, already out of breath with what I'd agreed to participate in. "Let's just go. I'll call them tomorrow with my apologies."

"Oh, silly girl." He laughed. "The moment you said yes all

your choices became void. This is my game now."

# Chapter Seventeen

"YOU MUST BE Chloe."

"I am." The girl who tormented me in high school simpered, tossing her red hair like a high-strung model. Her green dress complemented the tan she said she'd earned from the Caribbean last week. Her gaze sank into Penn as if he were some prize to be won. A prize she'd very much like to taste.

Penn pulled me to his side, feathering his hand up and down my arm. Such a simple touch, but it bruised with claiming and domination.

"I believe you know my partner, Elle." The mastery of his voice and damning sentence locked my spine and made Chloe jolt.

"Wait, partner?" She blinked. "I thought she was with Greg." She glowered at the way Penn found subtle ways of touching me. Her eyes found mine, hot with jealousy.

I'd never seen that grisly emotion on her face before. She believed I was beneath her to ever covert what I had.

*Not tonight, it seems.*

She sniffed. "You got two men now, Ding Dong Bell? A little greedy, don't you think?" Her giggle was forced and fake.

For a moment, I'd been proud to earn her cattiness. Penn was the type of man any woman could appreciate and desire with his crisp suit, unreadable eyes, and aloof handsomeness.

But that damn nickname stole everything, hurtling me back to the school hallways as if I'd never left. I wanted to sink into the ground and never reappear.

I waited for Penn to mock me, just as Greg had. I tensed for him to snicker and roll his eyes at my misfortune. But he stood cold and primitive, a velvet purr falling from his mouth. "That's an unimaginative slur to call a friend, don't you think?"

Chloe fluffed her hair. "Oh, Elle knows it's in affection.

Don't you, Bellie?"

I didn't respond.

Penn did, though. "Unoriginal nicknames are a sign of low intelligence." His snark cut through her tartness with an axe. "And in answer to your condescending question…Elle only has one partner. Me. And believe me, I'm all she'll ever need." His eyes smouldered with decadent chocolate. "I'll make sure of that."

His caresses turned heavy with guarantee. He danced the line of appropriate and wicked, deliberately stepping over it to antagonize those I had no wish to antagonize.

I wasn't petty or prideful.

I wanted to leave.

I opened my mouth to reply, but Penn squeezed me, keeping me silent. His touch was a hot poker controlling me and making me wet in equal measure.

The other girls from school slowly looked up from their conversations, paying attention to the tense standoff while trying to appear uninterested.

They didn't fool Penn or me as he smiled his signature sexy smirk and grabbed my chin. His lips planted on mine in a brutal kiss, marking me, consuming me as his tongue stole my arguments and his power pinched my remaining breath.

He stupefied me.

He bewitched me.

The instant I released the tension in my spine, he let me go—as if he'd deliberately kissed me to keep me out of my head and in my body with him.

"Are you going to tell them the good news, or shall I?" His authoritative tone blended with a dark flirt.

I blinked. "Tell them what?"

I was one step behind.

I couldn't catch up.

I'd never been that way before. I'd always been the boss—always leading. I didn't know if I liked being a follower.

"Tell them you've decided to let me own you."

"Wait, what?" Chloe's mouth hung open. "What does that mean?"

I shook my head, rubbing the sudden goosebumps on my arms. Penn said we were playing a game. Yet I didn't know the rules or what was expected. To verbalize it in such crude terms in front of the bitches from my past wasn't appropriate.

My forehead furrowed.

He answered Chloe before I could. "We met a few days ago, and it was love at first sight." He dragged me close. "It took some convincing but Elle has agreed to give me a chance." He glanced at Chloe, filling his pretty face with ardent satisfaction. "She said yes."

"Yes to what?" Frankie appeared, eyeing Penn from his black shoes to his five o'clock shadow.

"Yes to marrying me."

The world screeched to a halt.

*Wait…what?*

"No, I—" I flinched, trying to tear myself from Penn's embrace.

He held me tighter, his fingers sinking like keys into my arms, turning a lock, keeping me bound to him and useless.

Chloe's mouth hung wider. "Wow, Elle, I never knew—"

"Never knew she was the sexiest woman alive?" Penn snarled with sudden viciousness. "Never knew she was one of the richest women alive? Never knew that she was ten times the fucking woman you'll ever be?"

I stood stunned.

Why did he fight for me?

This was too much. Too fast. Too scary. Too far out of my comfort zone.

Yes to marrying him?

I *never* agreed to that.

I'd agreed to sex.

Stupid, silly, sensual sex.

*And now, it's time to say no.*

I tore myself from his embrace, my body shaking. "Stop. That's not true. Don't spread such lies." I stared helplessly at Chloe whose face had turned snow white. "I'm so sorry. Ignore him. I don't know what's gotten into him. We've only just got together. We're not engaged. He's not—"

"What my fiancée here is trying to say—" Penn interrupted. "Is she's too kind-hearted to rub her success in your face even though you do the same to her. I don't need to hear stories of what it was like to grow up with you. I see her, and I see you, and I understand the shadow you made her exist in. But not anymore."

His teeth flashed as he snarled. "I'm stealing her from you now. From all of you. She's mine. And it's a sad loss that you never figured out what an incredible creature you had under your noses the entire time."

Greg sidled up, hate stares fired at Penn. "You don't know jack, dipshit. Elle and I were raised together. I know her a fuck load better than you ever will."

"You're the blindest of them all." Penn pointed at him. "I don't care how long you've known each other. You fucked up." He laughed low. "You'll never get her back because she'll never be the same once I've had her."

My cheeks turned into flames of hell. I ducked my chin, doing my best to hide. I wanted the club to vanish and Penn to disintegrate into dust.

Words and curses tangled to spew at him, but he pulled me from the crowd, away from cringe-worthy declarations, away from high school trolls and wannabe boyfriends, and through the nightclub to the fresh air outside.

I managed a few gulps of oxygen before he yanked me down the alley between the nightclub and a restaurant and slammed me against the brick wall.

Quicksilver memories of another alley and another man tried to twist my present with my past. Garbled commands, ripped clothing, fists flying in the dark.

Nameless shot bright into my thoughts.

His black hoodie, his closed-off answers, his mind-melting kiss.

And then history had no power as Penn's lips crashed over mine and he replaced my remembered kiss with a savage one.

He kissed me and then he *kissed* me.

Each swipe of his tongue blasted through my decorum, dragging alive the sexual being who'd never been allowed to evolve.

His right hand bunched my dress up my leg. My brain tried to split—to focus on the foot traffic only a few feet away and not on the blistering heat of his fingertips on my inner thigh.

And then nothing else mattered as his touch found my core, pushing against my underwear.

He didn't ask permission.

He didn't pull back to see if I was okay with this.

He merely kissed me and fingered me over the lace.

All I wanted to do was to let go. To trust in the magic he created in my blood and allow him to be as arrogant as he wanted. To take charge.

But I couldn't.

I couldn't let him get away with what he'd said. His lies. His verbal bashing to people I had to converse with.

He was far too brash and daredevil for my world.

His mouth kept working mine, dragging a moan deep from my lungs.

I had a second before I drowned under his powerful wave and lost myself. A second and then I would be gone, and I couldn't blame anyone but myself.

So I bit him.

My teeth sank into his lip, not holding back as I did the only thing I could to slow things down and *breathe*.

He stumbled backward, holding his bottom lip where a bead of blood welled. "Fuck."

My ribcage rose and fell. I sucked in gasps, giving in to the slight hysteria he'd caused. I held up a shaky finger. "Don't touch me."

"Touch you? Fuck, I own you."

My braid caught like Velcro on the bricks behind me as I shook my head. "No. You don't."

His eyes etched with black. "You said yes, remember?"

"Yes to a beneficial sexual relationship. Not to damn marriage!"

"That's what's got you afraid? Marriage?" He chuckled "I have no intention of marrying you."

I frowned. "Then why lie about it?"

"Why not?" He shrugged. "Why do other people have to know exactly what we do and who we are? Why do they have to hear our truth when they're so fucking fake themselves?"

I hated that he had a point.

He placed a hand on the brick wall by my head, his body swaying into mine. If he touched me again, I doubted I'd have the willpower to stop him for a second time. My clit still throbbed from his touch, the echoing bands of release a phantom cry in my veins.

"Stay back."

He lowered his head, a tight smile on his lips. "Fine." Holding his hands up in surrender, he kept his distance but didn't move away. "What will it take for you to let me touch you again?" His voice dropped to sand and sleet. "Because I *really* want to touch you again."

I shivered, doing my best to keep my thoughts focused and not on the molten heat inside. Having him so close didn't help. He'd been gorgeous in the club—dappled in strobes and painted in shadows—but out here; out here where the vague lights of apartments and streetlights didn't dare enter the sanctity of the alley, he was camouflaged in darkness.

His shoulders strained against the stitches of his suit. His forearms ropey and tanned with his cuffs pushed up. His entire body flexed as he waved a hand with feline grace, hiding the throbbing tension between us, pretending he hadn't just fired my libido to the point of excruciation.

"I'm not answering any more of your questions," I hissed. "Who the hell are you? What do you want from me?"

Sighing heavily, his lips pouted, blood smeared a little to make him seem part vampire. "You already know what I want."

"But who *are* you?"

"I'm someone you can be free with."

"I don't know what that means."

"It means you don't need to be afraid of me."

I clasped my hands together, seeking comfort from myself. Fighting with a strange man—even one who'd touched and kissed me—in a deserted alley wasn't exactly encouraged. Once again, Nameless came to mind and I couldn't stop comparing the two men.

Nameless had been the hero.

Penn was the anti-Christ.

One saving, one damning.

I knew which one I preferred.

I stood firm in my heels, locking my limbs from betraying my lie. "I'm not afraid of you."

He cocked his head. "Are you sure about that?"

"I'm not sure about anything anymore."

He ran a hand through his hair, disrupting the strands into a mess. "Isn't that the point?"

"Stop answering everything with a question."

"Fine." He stood tall, his legs spread with dominion. "You said yes to me. I won't let you take that back. But I will try to ease your mind." His face tightened as if this game had higher stakes for him than he let on. "I'll only say this once, so listen carefully. I will lie to others about us. I will paint a picture that isn't true. I will curse and hurt and do whatever I damn well want, but you have my word on one thing."

My voice carried on a hesitant whisper. "What word?"

"That I won't lie to you. What you see from me will be the honest fucking truth. I'll only hurt you if you want me to hurt you, and I'll protect you even while I do it. Give me yourself, let me take control, and I promise you, you'll enjoy it."

My heart only heard the word hurt and envisioned images of him abusing me. "Why would I enjoy you hurting me?"

"The answer to that question will come later. It's a matter of showing not telling."

I paused, sucking in another breath. My world had vanished, and I had no way of returning. Once again I stood at a fork, hidden in a dirty alley. Unlike last time, where I'd had to beg Nameless to help me, Penn had to do all the convincing.

He shifted in the darkness, dragging my attention back to his height, body, and undeniable command. "Tell me your objections."

"My objections?"

"Your objections to letting me fuck you."

My mouth watered but I didn't swallow. I wouldn't show any signs of weakness. "I have too many to list."

"Try me." He crossed his arms.

My eyes wanted to drop to the ground. My fingers wanted to stroke my dress with nerves.

I did neither of those things. I treated him as I would any bossy manager, negotiating our terms for a successful business deal. "I find you arrogant and rude."

*Which makes me wet.*

My nose turned up. "I don't like liars, and I don't like men who think they can use me."

*Even though I'm contemplating giving my virginity to you.*

He rubbed his jaw, his gaze dragging over me as if he could hear my silent answers and focused only on those. "I'm arrogant because I've earned my success the hard way. I'm rude because I have no time for idiots." Stepping forward, he hovered over me, pressing me against the wall with sheer will. "You already know I won't lie to you."

His head crept over my personal boundary, his nose nuzzling my ear. "And I promise you, I'll use you. I'll use you every morning and night. I'll use you on your knees. I'll use you strapped to my bed. But with every use, you'll beg for another. You'll *beg* me, Elle." He bit my earring, tugging it until a sharp bolt of pain appeared. "That's what you should be afraid of. Nothing else."

I pushed him away, taking a greedy step toward the sidewalk.

I wasn't equipped for this. I needed to ease into sex, not be thrown headfirst into debauchery. "I've changed my mind. My answer is no."

Strong fingers wrapped around my wrist, yanking me back. "Like fuck it is." He pressed me against the wall face first. His hands clamped on my hips, pulling me back to meet his as he thrust up.

I moaned, long and low. A noise I'd never made before and had no idea where it'd come from.

"Oh, Elle, you're a little liar yourself." He tightened his hold, grinding into me. "Is that what you want? Seduction? Do you need to be seduced to let me inside you?" He bent over me, his lips landing on my shoulder blade. "Because I can do that. I can coax you, or I can force you. I can give you any fucking fantasy you want."

His voice darkened to nightmares. "You don't have to hide with me. You want it rough—" He looped his hand around my nape, crushing my cheek into the brick as his other hand slid down my body and scooped up my dress, up and up until his fingers found my inner thigh and aggressively cupped my core.

My heart exploded through my ears as intensity I never thought existed came alive beneath his fingers.

But then he switched.

The violent hunger in his touch melted into gentle petting. He pulled me away from the brick, hugging me, supporting me while his tongue licked my neck and his fingers feathered so lightly over my clit. "Or do you want it soft?"

I shuddered in his arms, confused when my body reacted more to anger rather than sweet.

"I'm attracted to you, Elle. I have been since I saw you. I know you want me too because right now, my hands are on your pussy, and you're so fucking wet." With a harsh breath, he pushed aside my panties, running his finger along my bareness.

He hissed in my ear as my hips rocked involuntarily. "There you go. Stop lying to yourself. That's the worst crime. Tell me what you want."

"I still don't like you enough to tell you."

He was utter temptation.

Beyond reasoning and comprehension. But he pissed me off as he chuckled low in my ear, taking pleasure in my undoing as he pressed his finger into me.

I lost the ability to stand. The delicious throaty echo of his laugh sent a coil of desire shooting right into my soul.

I clenched around his finger as he sank deeper.

"Your body likes me enough for your mind and heart."

My nerves heightened to a magnitude I couldn't withstand. His touch. His control. His manipulation—it made him more than human.

I didn't stand a chance.

"Just sex…" I panted as he fingered me.

"If that's what you want."

"Just lust."

"So much fucking lust." His touch seemed to double in size, dragging heat and sharp, sharp need.

A single finger.

It was too much.

It wasn't enough.

But my body, after years of neglect and build-up of countless nights imagining such a thing, surrendered entirely.

Penn sucked in a breath as I allowed my head to fall back over his shoulder, giving him utter control. He held me against his body, his finger never ceasing.

"Is that another yes?" He kissed my throat, biting it as his finger thrust upward. "Tell me it's a fucking yes before I lose my goddamn mind."

I nodded.

And that was it.

Penn Everett vanished, replaced by a hunter. Spinning me around and shoving me against the wall, he kicked my feet open and drove his finger higher.

My mind panicked that he would take me here like this. My first time would be against a dirty wall outside a nightclub, but he proved I was right to trust him. That I could give him power even though I'd never like him. That I would always hate him, purely because he wasn't Nameless and I'd clung to the ridiculous delusion that I'd find him, save him, and find a happily-ever-after.

Penn was the harbinger of truth in that respect.

I'd failed Nameless. I would never find him. It was time to accept that and move on.

Starting with sex.

"I'm going to make you come." Penn breathed into my skin. "And then…you're going home. We'll save my place for another night."

The bands of muscles in my core clenched around his finger as he pressed my clit with his thumb. His free hand grabbed my jaw, holding me prisoner while he kissed me so damn deep.

With his tongue inside my mouth and his finger matching the same pulse, I let it happen.

I didn't hold on.

He didn't drag it out.

I'd always been sensitive—always had a naughty ability to seek pleasure in banal situations. I'd stopped blushing years ago when I crossed my legs in a meeting filled with stuffy businessmen and enjoyed the tingle of desire just from the seam of my underwear. I'd accepted my body and how hotly it ran, simmering sweetly, ready to overflow into climax whenever I wanted.

Penn didn't know that.

He knew nothing about me.

But somehow, my body spoke to his and his touch sought those triggers inside.

His finger arched up, hooking hard.

*Holy...*

My mouth popped wide, shuddering in yeses.

He grinned in triumph, knowing he'd found one button to punish me with but there were countless more.

His kisses turned reckless. His fingers thrusting *right there*.

The recipe turned tentative sparks into fireworks and fireworks into detonations and detonations into a mushroom cloud of pure bliss. The orgasm scurried up my legs, down my spine, and convened in my core to explode in an avalanche of pleasure.

"Oh...*God.*" I sucked in air as I drowned, but he didn't give me time to breathe. He kissed me, sucked on my tongue, and let me ride his hand until the final wave of my release abated.

Slowly, his body peeled away from mine. "Well, that was interesting."

His lips disengaged, leaving me bruised and stinging while he repositioned my underwear and removed his touch, letting my dress slither over my thighs.

Without another word, he pulled me away from the shadows toward the busy pavement, caught the eye of David, my driver, who'd miraculously appeared, and placed me reverently into the Range Rover.

# Chapter Eighteen

THE NEXT DAY, I went to work as if nothing had happened.

As if everything at the Palm Politics was a figment of my imagination.

As if I hadn't come or given Penn any part of myself.

I still hated him.

But my body...*it wants more.*

Fleur handed me my meeting minutes, and I performed my duty in two conference calls like normal.

But *nothing* was normal.

I couldn't stop replaying what had happened. Where the hell did Penn go after he'd taken what he wanted...or was that given? He'd given me an orgasm without expecting one in return. He'd sent me home rather than kidnapped me to his place.

Had he gone home?

Had he found some other stupid woman to fall for his corrupted charm?

I hated that I wondered.

He was nothing more than sex. We'd agreed to that. *I'd* been the one to stipulate it.

*So why does it leave a sour taste in my mouth?*

As the day wore on, I itched to research him. To find out who he was, who Stewie was to him, who the mysterious Larry was. What did he do for work? Where did he live? What had he told my father in the gin bar?

He left me with more questions than Nameless did.

I didn't know how to contact him. I didn't know how to tell anyone what had happened. He'd done exactly what he said and controlled me without trying.

By the time the afternoon rolled around, my heart was ragged from fretting and my insides tight and jumpy. I couldn't stop imagining how I'd next bump into him and what he would make me do.

Would I say yes?

Would I say no?

Would he even give me a choice?

Those two daydreams caused twitchy anxiety to infiltrate my blood.

I stared blankly at my computer screen, dying for a distraction from both work and Penn when Fleur stuck her head into my office. "Um, there's someone here to see you."

Instantly, my body screamed yes. All while my mind bellowed no.

Then rationale took over.

*It can't be.*

How could he gain access to my building? Why didn't he call to tell me he was coming? Security wouldn't just let him up unless I'd cleared his name, which I hadn't.

My libido leaped at the thought of him, but self-preservation flipped into CEO mode. Last night had been terrifying in both good and terrible ways. He had a habit of making me forget myself and spinning lies I couldn't unscramble.

I couldn't have him on my turf. "Tell him I'm too busy. Either take his phone number, and I'll call him when it's convenient, or he'll have to make an appointment off site."

*Take that, Penn.*

"Do you know who it is?" Fleur asked, suspicion bright on her adorable, pixy face. "Why are you acting weird?"

"Weird? I'm not weird."

"I didn't say *you* were weird. I said you're *acting* weird." She fiddled with an orange button on her burnt sunshine dress. "What's his name?"

"Who?"

"The man you're avoiding."

"Who said—"

"Spit it out, Elle."

I chewed a smile. "Penn Everett."

Fleur inched closer, her eyes wide. "Did you meet him last night at the party? Oh, I knew you should've gone." She swooned dramatically. "Did he ask you out? Wait, I thought Greg was your date?"

I pretended to enter a few numbers into my laptop. "I met

him a few days before the party, but yes, we confirmed an arrangement last night."

Fleur jumped up and down like a child. "An arrangement. What sort? A sexual sort? Look at you, you sexy minx. I demand you tell me everything."

"Not until you tell him to leave." I pointed at my door, laughing a little at her antics. "In fact, tell him I'm far too busy for the next four years, and even though my answer is yes, he'd better have the patience of a saint if he wants to see me again."

*Let's see how he gets around that.*

He wanted to play games. Well, I could make up a few rules as we went.

She giggled. "Whatever he did to you last night has done wonders for your sense of humor." Moving toward the door, she grinned. "Finally, you're learning how to have some fun." She saluted me before vanishing out the door. "Leave it to me. Consider instigation with a new love interest in progress."

I groaned under my breath as snippets of male voices sounded in the hallway then were cut off as Fleur closed the door, preventing more eavesdropping.

I probably shouldn't have ordered her to tell Penn to wait four years. What if he took it seriously and left? As much as his personality appalled me, the thought of him leaving before delivering on his promises made me mildly sick.

Hating myself, I pushed away from my desk and tiptoed to the door. Pressing against it, I struggled to follow the conversation on the other side.

"You must be Steve Hobson?"

That voice...it was already so familiar—hardwired to my belly and gasoline for every hidden desire. The sly smoothness; the cocky deepness. It wasn't fair he was handsome and spoke like a rascally poet. He might not be marriage material, but he definitely delivered on fantasy.

Penn wasn't my future, but he could do very well for my present.

Steve's voice flowed through my door. "Yes, I am. I'm Mr. Charlston's oldest friend and colleague. You are?"

Without any hesitation and a lot of smugness, Penn said, "I'm Elle's fiancé."

My knees gave out.

*What?!*

I thought that lie was just for the girls at Palm Politics. He couldn't go spreading such untruth around. My father would hear.

*Oh God, Dad.*

He'd be elated.

And then he'd be crushed when I called it off.

"Ah, yes. My son, Greg, mentioned something about an incident last night," Steve said. "I thought he was exaggerating." The disappointment in his tone crushed me like a little girl.

"I figured he'd mention it." Penn's voice dropped to deadly seriousness. "I'm aware your son has feelings for my wife-to-be, sir, and I only have respect and regret that he didn't deserve her affection. But rest assured, if he gets in my way, I won't tolerate it."

"What does that mean?" Steve snapped.

"It means Elle belongs to you in business. But she belongs to me in everything else." His tone lowered possessively. "We're together now, and no one will interfere. In fact, I'm here to collect her. It's time for her to come home. We have lots of things to *do* tonight."

Even behind the door, the sexual innuendos reeked with promise.

Steve cleared his throat, no doubt wondering when I had the time to hook up with a complete stranger and why Greg wasn't the one taking me home. "I see."

My tummy clenched at how forlorn he sounded.

I liked to think it was purely for wanting me to be happy and believing his son was the right candidate for the job, but some part believed he had ulterior motives. He'd been nothing but loyal to this company, my father, and me, but running a business for so long that wasn't yours must take a toll. Possession was a fundamental human flaw.

"You must excuse me; I'm late for our date." Penn chuckled. "As you know, Elle is strict on time-lines."

Fleur's voice piped up. "I'm afraid, Mr. Everett, Ms. Charlston has said she's busy for the next four years, and you'll have to make an appointment."

"What?" His tone snapped through the door.

A nervous giggle percolated in my chest. Why did I want to piss him off? I'd pay for it later, no doubt.

*Shit, this was a bad idea.*

"Why is Ms. Charlston telling you to make an appointment when you're telling me you're her fiancé?" Steve asked suspiciously.

"No disrespect, sir, but it's none of your business."

Steve replied, "I think you'll find it is. Elle means a great deal to her father and me. She's really stepped into his shoes and taken the company to even greater heights. She's far too successful for her own good, and that means pariahs are out there who see her as an easy target to her vast empire."

*Damn you, Steve.*

Everyone made it sound as if I were some elusive unicorn to be hunted and snared. I wasn't special or unique. I was bland and boring. A workaholic imprisoned since birth.

"I'm not one of those pariahs, believe me," Penn muttered. "However, I can't say the same for your son."

Oh, my God. Did he truly just say that?

"Excuse me?" Steve blurted. "My son and Elle are extremely close. It's only a matter of time before they progress from friends to something more. Whatever you think you have with her is at best a silly fling and at worst a future heartbreak. But mark my words, Greg will be there to pick up the pieces and make sure Elle is happy and protected. I don't for a second believe in this marriage bullshit."

I hated the optimism in his voice along with the vaguely concealed threat for Penn to back away. That somehow Steve, even though he'd watched me turn from child to woman, still believed he controlled me enough to decide who I should share my body and life with.

*I'm surrounded by manipulators.*

"That will never happen," Penn snapped. "After the interesting conversations I've had with Ms. Charlston, I can safely say she isn't remotely interested in your son."

*Oh, no. Please someone stop him.*

"In fact, she distinctly said she didn't want to have a thing to do with him. She wants me. And she has me. Just like I have her. We're engaged."

Steve mumbled something I couldn't hear.

Penn said, "That may be, but perhaps Ms. Charlston should be given the space to decide who she wants in her bed. Currently, that's me, asshole."

*Okay, that's it.*

Wrenching my door open, I barreled into the waiting room. The soft furnishings and potted trees couldn't distract me from my blistering anger toward the two men.

"Once again, I'm shocked stupid." I clamped both hands on

my hips. "Steve, I expected better of you."

Steve had the decency to look down with his face flushed. "Sorry, Elle. I wasn't saying that you and Greg were together but trying to protect your right to decide."

"No, you weren't. You were trying to keep Belle Elle in the family. You and Dad are everything to me, and that's why I won't hold a grudge, but if you try to push me together with Greg again, I'll refuse to speak to you. Do you understand?"

"But Greg really likes you."

"Don't care. Not interested."

Wow, the relief in finally speaking the truth and not worrying about other people's feelings was immense.

"Hello again, Elle. Does this mean you're available for our second date now and not in four years' time?" Penn planted his feet and smirked. "After all, you just admitted you're more interested in me than anyone else."

I turned burning blue eyes on him. "I'm only interested in watching you fall off one of our buildings, Mr. Everett."

He chuckled. "Oh, now. Don't be like that. I just did you a favor. One of many, I might add. You no longer have to deal with Greg." He fiddled with a cufflink. "That was because of me. You owe me."

"I don't owe you anything. I revoke my yes." My nose tipped upward. "It's been amended to a resounding no. Now, go away."

I spun around and marched back into my office, slamming the door in his face. The second I was away from him, I kicked off my heels and bolted into the bathroom. Grabbing the sink, I stared at myself in the mirror. Hot points danced on my cheeks, and wild insanity replaced my calm capableness.

*What was I thinking by saying yes to that man?*

I hated the way he made my blood boil. I couldn't stand the way he spread rumors and none-truths on my behalf. No man since Nameless had earned a reaction from me—either in like or hate. I wasn't ready to fight. I didn't have time to welcome attraction.

"God, this is all a mess."

He was a mistake, and one I had to fix right away before he railroaded my life and ruined everything. If he didn't take my no as gospel, I would call the police to instate a restraining order.

*Perhaps, I should become a nun?* Then I'd never have to worry about sex or marriage.

I could just focus on what I was good at.

Business.

Splashing water on my face, I rubbed at the smudge of mascara and tamed some of the flyaways. Feeling mildly normal, I nodded at my reflection. Agreeing that my work was done for the day and I'd go home, take a bath, and try to forget about Steve, my father, and most of all, damn Penn.

Opening the bathroom door, I jolted as the man I wanted to throw out my window sat smugly on the couch facing my bookshelves of magazines listing our clothes, houseware awards, and charity plaques for our work with selected organizations.

"You again!"

"Me." He looked me up and down. "You got your shirt wet."

I glanced at the sheer white fabric that was now see-through to the dusky pink bra I wore beneath it. I slapped a hand over my chest and stalked toward my desk. My stomp didn't have the same effect in stockinged feet as it would've in heels, but at least I was able to shrug on a cream and black piping jacket and hide a bit of my damp cleavage.

Sage ventured out from under my desk, baring her little fangs at the interloper.

"I thought I told you to leave." Doing my best to get back in control, I snapped, "Besides, it's not a shirt. It's a blouse. If you weren't such a Neanderthal, you'd know that."

"Why would I know that? I'm a guy who wears guy's clothing. I have no interest in women's unless it's on the floor after I've taken them off her."

I glowered. "Fascinating insight into your true character, Mr. Everett." I pointed at my door. "As you weren't invited into my office, I'll kindly ask you to go. For the second time. And while you're at it, retract your lie about our upcoming nuptials."

"You lost the power to tell me to leave the moment you said yes." He never took his eyes off me. "It's too late to change it to a no. However, if you're so incensed, then hear me out and I'll go…for now."

I moved around my desk to stand in front of it and crossed my arms. "Hear what? I'm sure I heard all I needed to. You're an egotistical maniac who I have no interest in doing anything else with."

"Your body told me a different story last night." He chuckled. "And just to clarify, if I wasn't an 'egotistical maniac' as you put it, then you'd consider letting me fuck you…like our original agreement?"

I frowned. "What?"

He stood up, breaching the space between us until he stood only a foot away. My skin prickled as goosebumps erupted under my wet blouse.

Sage hissed, swatting the air with her claws in warning.

Penn took no notice of her. "I'm sorry." His face darkened with sincerity. "I know I didn't have a right to talk about you like a trophy to be won from your father. And I'm sorry for warning Mr. Hobson to keep his son away from you." He smiled tightly. "I would say I did that for your benefit, but really, I did it for me." His eyes fell on my chest. "I don't do well with competition."

"Well, your rules and jealousy are pointless because I have no intention of going to bed with you."

"Lies, Elle. I thought you'd agreed we'd only have truth between us."

His deep, heady aftershave stole up my nose, tying my thoughts into a sinful knot.

I didn't reply as he deleted the remaining space between us.

I leaned back, my butt hitting the edge of my desk and my tummy locking into place.

"You know...I work in an office, too. I know how lonely these job spaces can be." He licked his lips. "I also know how fantasies can spring from nothing." His hand crept forward.

I flinched, expecting him to touch me. However, he placed his palm on the glass table, hemming me in on both sides. "Tell me, Ms. Charlston. Have you ever had sex in here?"

I froze. "Excuse me?"

His gaze hooded. "Has anyone bent you over your desk and fucked you? Stolen your power and used it against you?"

I shivered uncontrollably. My mouth urged to scream for Fleur to help. Was he threatening to take me? Here in my office?

I shoved him.

He stumbled backward, a black look dripping over his features. He shook his head, dispelling the clouds, once again settling into cocky. "I take that as a no."

For a split second, I remembered the words from the assholes who hurt me in the alley. *'Have you ever been fucked over your desk, office girl? Ever given a boss a blowjob for a promotion?'*

It wasn't an unusual concept.

I was sure many people had done just that and had lots of fun doing it. But I never had. And I wouldn't today—not with Penn or anyone else who threatened my safety and position. *Especially* when chilly ice replaced my blood, struggling to separate that night in the alley and today with Penn.

The way he watched me was too close to the guy in the Baseball Cap—too intense, too focused on something he couldn't have but would happily take anyway.

"Leave, Mr. Everett."

"I told you to call me Penn."

I cocked my chin. "Fine. Leave, Penn."

"Not until you agree to dinner with me."

"Never."

"Never is too long to wait." He glowered. "And besides, we've already agreed on the ground rules. You want to fuck me. I want to fuck you. Playing hard to get is only making me want to do that sooner rather than later."

"No."

"No what?"

"No to everything. I told you, I changed my mind."

"Why?"

"Because I said so."

He licked his lips. "Yes, but why? Why change your mind after what happened last night? From what your father said, you work too much, you have no friends, and you severely lack fun in your life."

My heart sank. "He said that?"

"I read between the lines."

"Well read between my lines. N-O. Spells no. I'm too busy to play with you."

"I said I was sorry."

I stiffened, trying to sniff his new game. "Go on."

He shrugged. Even that was sexy, dammit. "I shouldn't have put words into your mouth. It's up to you to decide if you want people to know about us." He looked up beneath his brow. "And the only way you can decide that is if you go on a date with me."

I opened my mouth to argue, but he interrupted—another habit he seemed to have. "Don't answer for yourself right now. Answer for yourself in five years' time. Where do you see yourself? Here in this office doing the exact same thing with the exact same unhappiness?"

*God, I hope not.*

"Or do you want to see if you could have this and more? Work and play? Love and obligation?"

My eyes shot daggers. "You think I could love you?"

"I think you could have fun with me."

"I think otherwise."

He grinned. "That's what this is about. To see if our opinions line up."

"Are you going to leave if I say no again?"

"Nope." He came closer. "I'll just keep showing up at really inconvenient times until you say yes." His aftershave drugged me again. "Choose the easier option, Ms. Charlston. Let me have you. It's the only way forward."

"What will you do to me?"

Instantly, my office thickened with sexual tension.

My breath hitched as his eyes drifted to my mouth.

His voice lowered to scorching charcoal. "Anything I damn well want." His hand cupped my cheek, holding me tight. "I'll strip you, taste you, devour you. I'll eat, lick, and bite you. And only once you're begging will I fuck you."

My body flushed as hot as the sun, as bright as Venus, as untouched as Pluto.

I shoved him away and stalked to the exit. All I wanted to do was dare him to try it. To fight and claw and let him subdue me because, *holy hell*, he made it sound delicious. But the other part— the vanishing part—was afraid of losing herself.

Sex was too powerful.

Sex should be done between two people who liked each other and not a couple with nothing in common.

I cleared my throat and my mind. I clung to common sense. "I suggest you leave before I knee you in places a lady should never knee a man."

He hunted me, bringing with him cyclones full of lust. "If you want to touch that part of me, I would prefer it was with something softer than your knee." He chased me, once again corralling me against a hard surface.

This time the door.

"Your hand would work." He cupped my wrist, slipping his fingers through mine. "Your hand is welcome." His eyes turned jet black with need. "I could come from your hand alone."

I fought my shiver but couldn't stop the goosebumps darting up my arms. His touch was possessive but soft. Strong but coaxing.

His fingers squeezed mine as he swayed closer. "Or if you didn't want to use that part of your anatomy, your mouth would do equally well." He licked his bottom lip. "In fact, I want both."

"Never."

"Never?" He smiled. "Don't lie." His hand crept up my arm to my shoulder, adding pressure until my knees threatened to buckle. "Let's see how soon never is, shall we?" He kissed me sweetly. "I fingered you until you came last night. The least you can do is blow me."

*I like the thought of you giving me a blowjob. Get her on her knees.*

The rapists and alley stole the present, hurtling me back before Nameless had found me. Before he hurt them for hurting me. Before he prevented my life from tumbling into ruin.

Why did Penn cause flashbacks that I'd successfully put behind me?

Why did he awake sharp instincts?

And why were those instincts scrambled between trust and mistrust, unable to see the truth hiding in his lies?

My office returned. The alley disappeared. Penn was still there. His pressure on my shoulder stronger, pestering me to fall into servitude before him.

I breathed hard. "You expect me to wrap my lips around your cock? Here? Now? In my office?"

He nodded. "Absolutely." He fisted my hair without warning, tilting my head to attack my throat with his mouth and teeth. "Here, you're god. Here, you're in charge. It turns me the fuck on knowing you're the one with all the power, yet you're considering getting on your knees to serve me."

It took every ounce of willpower, every brave denial, but I managed to untangle my fingers from his and tear my neck from his kisses. "Too bad for you, you'll have to remain turned on. I have no intention of doing such a thing."

"What are you afraid of?" His eyes narrowed. "You know this is a game. You understand the rules."

"I don't understand any of this."

"The rules are sex. Mutually enjoyed sex. Despite what you think, you like being told what to do." He gathered me close, inhaling my perfume. "Give me two minutes. Two minutes to command you, and if you don't like it, I'll walk away."

My heart beat crazy. "Two minutes?"

He bit his lip, nodding. "You have my word."

"If you break it, I'm turning you into a eunuch with a sharp kick."

He chuckled, stepping back and spreading his thighs. "There are worst things I can imagine than your leg between mine." His eyes were dark as nightmares. "But for now, get on your fucking knees."

*Get her on her knees.*

A similar command had torn me apart. The thought of sucking strange men in an alley grotesque. However, this command turned my chest into a furnace, charring my heart to dust.

I didn't know what happened to my brain.

I didn't understand how hate could be such an aphrodisiac.

But he circumnavigated the CEO. He spoke to some primitive part of me.

I wanted to tell him to leave.

I wanted to prove I had more respect than that.

Yet I sank down the door to my knees.

Sage watched me as if all her respect for me as her human evaporated.

*Damn cat.*

Penn shuddered, looking part monster, part angel. "Shit, you make me hard when you obey." His gaze fell on my breasts. "Now that you're playing, we're going to do a little show and tell."

*Before we show you ours, you have to show us yours.*

The alley.

I was back there again.

Huddled in pain, grasping at dignity.

I stayed silent, doing my best to stay alive while my heart tried to slam through my ribs.

The past and future were merely two dimensions separated from each other by the present. Yet I lived in neither. I existed in the glue bridging them together, somehow allowing three years ago to affect today.

I wanted Nameless to barge into my world and rescue me for the second time.

Penn's hands fell to his belt, pushing aside the tails of his midnight blazer, and undoing the leather slowly. "I'm going to show you what you do to me, Elle. But in return, I want to see you."

*Let's see what your tits are like.*

I gulped.

He morphed into one of those bastards, flickering with Adidas symbols and expensive suits. He never looked away as he pulled the belt, unthreading it and letting it hang in the loops. "Unbutton your shirt."

Forcing myself to shed the memories and focus entirely on him, I latched onto the most idiotic thing I'd ever uttered. "It's a blouse."

"I don't care." His growl echoed through my core. "Unbutton it."

My hands shook but slowly connected with the pearl buttons and hesitantly undid one.

This was now. Penn was now. Nameless was yesterday.

It took more effort than I could afford, but I shut the door on the past and slotted firmly back into the present.

"The next." Penn trembled as he locked his hands on the button of his waistband. The crisp cream shirt and dark jeans he wore made him untouchable yet so normal.

I popped the next button, breathing hard and quick.

He followed, undoing his and pulling on his zipper.

Without waiting for his command, I undid buttons three then four; my eyes locked on his hands as he pulled his zipper down and down.

When my blouse hung undone, and his zipper had nowhere else to go, our eyes met.

Our lips parted; mirrored images of desire.

"Open it." His voice had lost the playful kink from before, slipping straight into serious smut. "Let me see you."

With bravery I didn't know I had, I pushed my blouse away from my breasts, revealing the dusky pink bra.

He groaned, his hand disappearing into his jeans.

My stomach clenched so hard, so deep, I bent over a little in surprise.

His lips twisted. "Do you like that?" He squeezed himself, his thighs tightening beneath the denim. "Do you like knowing I'm this hard all because of you? That I haven't been this hard in years. That all I can think about is sticking this in every place you'll let me."

Oh. My. *God*.

I swam in heat. I drowned in liquid. I was so wet my panties were soaked.

"Pull your bra down, and I'll show you more."

My fingers hooked on the front cups of my bra as his latched around his jeans and levered them a little off his hips. Never looking away, objectifying both of us by only watching our bodies and not our souls, he reached into his tight black boxer-briefs and pulled out his cock.

My core spasmed as I swallowed hard and pulled my bra down, revealing my pebbled nipples and heavy globes of flesh that had long since been neglected.

"Fuck, Elle." His hand grasped his long length. The head glowed with darker flesh, a droplet glistening on top. Veins ran down the sides, bulging with desire—the same desire throbbing in my clit.

All I could see…all I could think about…was sex.

My legs parted a little as my hips became loose and wanting. An emptiness echoed inside me, becoming more and more cavernous the longer I stared at him.

"Do you want this?" he murmured, his face black with lust.

There was no banter or connection. Whatever respect we had for each other was tarnished by the way I stared up with him standing over me with his cock in his hand. It ought to be degrading, but I found a different sort of power on my knees. The way he panted. The way his hips rocked with a subtle sway even he wasn't aware of.

We no longer lived in the real world but sex, sex, sex.

I nodded just once, licking my lips.

"Jesus, Elle." His head fell forward as he squeezed the tip. "Say it out loud. Do you want my cock?"

I didn't care if anyone was outside my door eavesdropping. I didn't care that I should stop this and throw him from my office.

I embraced the river flowing inside me and whispered, "Yes."

"Where? Where do you want it?"

So many places.

So many foreign, wonderful ready-to-be explored places.

But first, the one he wanted. The one he'd hinted at, and the reason I was on my knees. "My mouth."

He groan-growled as he stepped forward. His shoes hit my knees, his height towering over me with his cock speared from his angry fist. "Suck it then."

My breasts ached with pain I'd never experienced.

I sat taller on my knees.

I reached forward.

My fingers so close to claiming him.

But then he stepped back, tucking his erection away, shaking with need and discipline. He didn't do up his belt or zipper, but he flashed a silver watch on his wrist. "Your two minutes are up."

The sexual trance he'd put me into shattered.

I shivered with sudden cold and yanked up my bra in

disgrace. Grabbing the sides of my blouse, I huddled before shooting upright with rage so bright, so brilliant, I wanted to rip him into pieces.

"That's it?" I snarled. "Was that all a stupid game to you? A ploy to show me that you can make me do what you want, after all?" A heavy gathering sat between my legs, throbbing to be touched. Desperate for a release.

"I wanted to be sure there were no lies. You saw how much I want you. I saw how much you want me." He kept his distance, refusing to touch me. "Next time, I won't accept your bullshit."

"Next time?! You think there'll be a next time? This was the only time, and you just humiliated me."

"Yes, well, you almost made me come just by licking your fucking lips."

I opened my mouth to retort, but angry tears crept up my spine. The lust in my blood eroded my self-control. Spinning around, I grabbed the doorknob and yanked. I didn't care his trousers were undone. I didn't care my blouse was open. I wanted him gone. I wanted it now.

His hand slammed against the wood, shoving it back into the frame with a loud smack. His body heat pressed against me, the teeth of his open zipper digging into my pinstripe skirt.

"You think you can leave? I didn't say you could."

"Let me go."

His hands pressed flat against the door, caging me.

Sage meowed loudly, attempting to join my battle to make him leave.

I couldn't think with him so close. I could only feel. And by God, I could feel. *Everything.* His breath on my nape, his chest rising and falling against my spine. And his cock twitching against my ass.

The domination and power of his will were tangible things, suffocating me under his command. Everything outside of him and me ceased to exist. My entire body begged for whatever he would do next even while my mind bellowed at me to scream.

Whatever existed between us was visceral, indescribable, completely imprisoning.

"I'll never let you go. Not until I'm through with you." His lips landed on the top of my shoulder. "Turn around, Elle."

My body shuddered in an overwhelming wave of arousal. I wasn't supposed to like this. I wasn't supposed to get wet under his cruel, commanding tone. His body heated with hunger and demand, dragging urges from deep inside me. Urges I could no longer deny.

I wanted him.

And I didn't know how to handle that.

I refused to turn. Sadness interfered with my desire, scrambling me up inside. "I can't do this with you. I'm not equipped."

His lips caressed my hair. "You can. You're doing it right now."

"But I don't know what comes next. I—I—"

"You do. You know exactly what comes next." His hand splayed over my stomach, pulling me back into his hips. His cock was big, hard, and so hot. "This goes inside you. It makes all that confusion and emptiness vanish."

I spun in his arms.

"How? Nothing has that power."

"Trust me." His fingers latched around my throat, pinning me against the door. He fell forward, wedging his entire length along mine. Aligning his cock to my clit, he thrust.

The action was so crude, so basic in mating, I moaned.

"Wrap your legs around my hips."

Shifting my skirt high so I could spread my legs, I jumped and did exactly what he told me, my body taking control.

He grunted as he caught my weight before crushing me against the door again. "We're both going to come. We're going to do it together. And we're not going to overthink it or ruin it by refusing what our bodies so fucking desperately need, got it?"

I had no other choice.

I nodded.

I didn't know if he meant he planned to take me against my door or if he'd use his fingers or expected my mouth but all questions died like flightless birds the moment he thrust again.

Reaching between us, he pulled down his trousers, freeing himself and wedging his naked cock against my panty-covered pussy.

With my legs around his waist, his hardness lined up perfectly against every inch of me.

"Christ, you're soaked." He looked down. "Soon, I'm going to see every inch of you, Elle, but for now, you owe me an orgasm."

Confusion hit me. So he meant to keep the tiny piece of cotton and lace between us? That we would grind and come but not consummate?

His jaw clenched, his messy hair tumbling over his forehead. His biceps bulged from holding me as he curved into me. "Kiss me." His voice was hoarse.

I gave up my questions and denial and tipped my head up.

He groaned, capturing my mouth with his. His lips were firm and warm. His pressure the perfect accompaniment. His tongue dived inside, tasting me, fighting me with deep licks.

And then, he moved.

Slow and deep, thrusting his long length against my wet panties, grinding into me at exactly the right spot. His hands dropped to my ass, tightening and pinching with each rock, driving me insane.

He didn't attempt to enter me. He remained on the outskirts, keeping cotton as our prison guard, letting temptation be our mistress.

I lost track of everything as his kisses swept me away and his hips kept me anchored to him and only him. I distantly noticed my hands swooped up to capture his face and hair. Tugging and yanking, I directed him to kiss me harder, thrust faster—deepening the connection between us.

He growled into the kiss, his tongue turning into a lashing whip as his body moved faster over mine, igniting electricity and chemistry and fire. The pounding of his heartbeat echoed into me as we clawed and clung, climbing and climbing, desperately seeking the pleasure just out of reach.

"Fuck, I want you." He thrust harder. "I can't stop." Cupping my ass, he angled me in just the right way. My clit spindled with the beginnings of an orgasm.

I pressed tight against him, aware of every hard intoxicating piece of his body.

His face contorted. "Jesus, I'm going to come."

My skin misted with sweat, blistering with sensitivity. Penn's hand slid up my thigh, grabbing me so hard I shivered with a mixture of fear and abandon.

A low rumble vibrated in his chest as his pace increased and I clutched him tight. Our teeth clacked together as our kiss turned sloppy, our bodies turned manic, and the orgasm teasing us erupted into being.

I split in two.

I melted into a puddle.

Wave after wave, I shuddered in his arms, cringing and crying as his cock kept me flying far too high. I was vaguely aware of his head falling back, his fingernails breaking my skin and the shot of stickiness on my inner thigh.

Even sated, my body still strained to get closer, to increase our contact until he was inside me, not just touching me.

I didn't know who shook more—him or me.

Lowering his head, his face blank and eyes dazed from his release, he claimed my mouth again with a thread of violence I hungered for. He drank me as I drank him. We groaned together as he rocked slower this time, highlighting sore extremities, encouraging final tingles to remain.

Then someone knocked on the door.

Shattering our moment.

Reminding us we weren't alone.

# Chapter Nineteen

"ELLE, ARE YOU free for a quick chat?"

I froze in Penn's arms as Dad's voice deleted any sexual heat, slamming me back into a girl who had no right, *none*, to act the way I just did.

"Shit," I hissed under my breath.

The knob turned beside my hip where Penn still wedged me against the door. His eyes narrowed as he grabbed it, preventing it from unlatching.

"Answer him," he growled low. "Tell him to leave."

"Elle? Are you in there?" The knock came again.

My racing heart made it hard to speak. "Yeah, Dad, I am. Just—it's a bad time. Can you come back later?"

A slight pause followed by a huffed, "This is important. I'd rather we have a quick talk now."

Every nightmare had come true.

"Uh, okay. Just—"

Penn stepped back, letting my legs slide from his hips to place me on the floor. The moment I was standing, he let me go, hastily tucking his cock into his jeans and yanking up his belt. He gave me a look so villainous he stole my breath.

"Just give me a minute!" My hands flew to my hips to pull my skirt down, but Penn stopped me with a slight curve in his lips.

His finger smeared something sticky and cool on my inner thigh. His voice didn't break a murmur. "You're about to have a conversation with your father while my cum is drying on your skin." He smiled ruthlessly. "I think it's safe to say you're mine now."

I couldn't talk to him about cum or sex. Not with my father only a few feet away. Shoving him back, I wrenched my skirt down, hastily did up my blouse, and dragged my hands through my wild hair.

Eyeing Penn, who'd tucked in his shirt and buttoned his blazer, I didn't ask if he was ready before jerking the door wide and smiling so fake and big, I was sure I had sex written all over my face. "Dad! How nice to see you."

He flinched, looking me up and down in surprise. "That's quite a welcome, Elle." His gaze slid past me to Penn standing in the middle of my office, a respectful distance away from me. "Ah, so Steve wasn't lying."

Strolling into my office, my father sniffed. "Can someone please explain to me what is going on? I've heard rumors of an engagement?" He turned to me, hurt blazing in his eyes. "Elle?"

*Oh, no.*

I fired harpoons at Penn before striding forward to sit on the couch, needing to get off my feet before my knees gave way. Sage immediately hopped onto my lap, reprimanding me with her beady little gaze. "It's not what you think."

"Not what I think?" Dad strode forward, never taking his attention off Penn. "Wait a minute. I know you."

Penn cleared his throat, holding his hand out in introduction. "We've already met. At the Weeping—"

"Willow, yes. I'm old, but I'm not senile," Dad grumbled, shaking Penn's grip before letting go and marching to my desk where he leaned against the edge with his arms crossed.

Just like that, he stole the position of authority, doing his best to manipulate me even though he probably wasn't aware he'd slipped into parental mode.

All my life, he'd done this. A subtle posture, a minor head tilt. I loved him, and he loved me—and I knew he'd never do anything to hurt me—but he did control me as much with disappointment as he did with affection.

"I wasn't saying you were." Penn straightened his shoulders, his gaze landing on my thigh where beneath my skirt the remnants of his orgasm slicked and coated my legs.

The urge to cringe was strong. I wasn't used to having such things left on my body after doing something not exactly permitted in an office. But there was another urge too…slightly bolder than the first. The urge to demand Penn got on *his* knees for a change and wipe it off.

The image of him bowed before me knotted my insides, even though I knew it would never happen. He was too in control to ever let me boss him.

"Well, someone had better start talking before I call security." Dad narrowed his eyes at me. "You hated this guy a few nights ago, Elle. You threw your drink in his face. What the hell did I miss that he's not only permitted into our building, but I hear from Greg and Steve that you're engaged." He rubbed at his chest. "I'm hurt that I found out that way. I'm even more hurt that my own daughter misled me."

Panic gathered as I worried about his heart. Why was he rubbing his chest? Should I call a doctor? I wanted to mollycoddle him but worried that if I changed the subject to health rather than clarify this massive misunderstanding, I'd be in a lot more trouble.

I gathered my hair over my shoulder, twisting it into a rope. "You don't have any reason to be hurt, Dad. It's all a big mistake."

"What do you mean?"

I stroked Sage's warm fur. "I mean we're not engag—"

"She means we were going to ask your permission, but unfortunately, sir, my possessive nature came out last night when Greg implied I wasn't good enough for your daughter." Penn strode toward me and took the spot beside me on the couch.

Sage stiffened but didn't try to kill him for being so close.

Smoothly, like he'd rehearsed this very moment, he captured my hand, brought it to his lips, and kissed my knuckles. "I'm aware Elle and Mr. Robson's son have been raised together with the understanding of one day marrying, but that is no longer an option."

Dad's mouth hung open. "It isn't? Why?"

Penn gave me a sly smile, dripping with intrigue and falsehoods. "Because, with your blessing, of course, I wish to marry Noelle."

I groaned, hanging my head. "He doesn't mean that, Dad. It's a game—"

Penn silenced me with a quick pinch to my hand. "She isn't fully aware how I feel about her yet. She believes I'm ridiculous to want to marry her when we've only just met, but she isn't an old romantic like we are, is she, sir?" He grinned at my father, baiting him with the tasty hook guaranteed to spark his interest.

Dad snapped it up, bait and sinker. "You believe in love at first sight?"

Penn leaned back into the couch, dragging me with him, imprisoning me with his arm over my shoulders. The move was relaxed, but his body hummed with tension I couldn't decipher.

"Absolutely. The moment you mentioned her at the bar, she sounded like my type of woman." He turned piercing truthless eyes to me. "And the instant I saw her, the moment she gave me a vodka shower, I knew." His free hand nudged my chin with sharp knuckles, guiding my lips to his.

Sage leaped off my lap and tore under my desk.

I tried to pull away.

I had no intention of kissing him with Dad present. But just like all the other times, he gave me no choice. His mouth caressed mine with chaste affection—the perfect recipe of truth and besotted affection to hoodwink my father.

I hated him for that.

I despised the way he lied to my last remaining flesh and blood.

Tearing my lips from his, I tried to stand, to go to my father and explain this was all a big misunderstanding and not to listen to him.

But it was too late.

My father had lost the suspicious glint, his body no longer tight with protection. His heart had flown back to a happier time when he met my mother and fell ass over head at first sight.

His face glowed. "You mean this is real?" He glanced between Penn and me. "This isn't a prank? All that animosity at the start, Elle, you were just overly passionate?" He chuckled. "I remember your mother had that tenacious streak. She'd swat me for no reason on lots of occasions." His voice grew wistful. "I miss that."

"You've got it all wrong. It's not tru—" I started.

"It's very real," Penn murmured. "I've fallen for her, and I've already claimed her. I hope you don't mind."

"Mind?" My father leaped upright, smacking his hands together. "I'm ecstatic. To think Elle finally has a partner to lean on. A man who comes with his own success to ensure hers isn't taken advantage of."

Temper percolated. He spoke as if I were some damsel who needed protection from big bad ogres rather than a very capable businesswoman.

But I couldn't fault him for being so enamored with the idea that I would be as happy as he was with Mom. I just wished it were true. Dad and I very similar but in matters of sensibility versus dream-world, I had no tolerance for make-believe anymore.

I'd trusted that crazy spark with Nameless. I'd begged my

father to help me turn the city upside down and turf out the truth. I'd cried myself to sleep more times than I could remember wishing Dad would be more helpful in finding the one man who made me feel so alive, so myself, so true in every sense.

But he'd refused.

Sure, he'd helped at the start. He'd gone with me to the local prisons and stood beside me while I garbled about hoodies and beards and alley-rescue. But his patience, that normally had no bounds, was tight and short lived.

I'd finally gotten him to admit his reluctance one night when I'd threatened to sell my shares in Belle Elle and step down if he kept road-blocking me to find Nameless.

All it had taken was two sentences to see how stubborn he was. I still remembered it clear as crystal: *"I've indulged you for long enough, Elle. It's time you forgot about that boy and moved on."* His face had lost its jovial love, slipping into sternness. *"He's a criminal. If you think I'd let my company be co-run by someone with a record, you don't know our code of ethics very well."*

And that…well, that had been the end of my quest and the moment of me switching childhood for adulthood. I'd seen something pure in Nameless but my father only saw what society called him.

Even if I had found him, I would never have been allowed to bake him blueberry pancakes or let him sleep safe in the guest room. My father, for all his kindness, actually had a flaw. And it hurt me more than I could ever say.

Sadness crushed me as Dad rushed over and pumped Penn's hand. "Congratulations. I'm so happy for both of you." Tears glistened in his eyes as he dragged me from the couch and bear hugged me. "Bell Button, I'm so—I'm—words can't describe how much this means to me. To know you'll be cherished and adored and no longer be alone when I'm gone."

His arms banded so damn tight, my lungs had no space to expand.

I patted his back, torn in pieces about doing the right thing and telling him right away or letting the lie snowball and end up killing him when the truth came out. I also nursed the three-year hurt that he'd approved Penn just because he came from wealth and success (which I had yet to find out about) and didn't have a record. He was acceptable. Nameless was not.

As much as it would kill me to destroy his sudden elation, I couldn't do it. I couldn't let him believe I'd chosen the dream he had for me. This was Penn's fault, not mine. My father's pain would come from the asshole who thought he could lie to my father and not be reprimanded.

"Dad, can I talk to you. In private?" I shot a glare over my shoulder. "The engagement isn't what you think. Penn and I aren't truly getting married."

"What?" He pulled away, his face falling into ruin. "But I thought—"

"She's being cautious, sir." Penn stood and joined our huddle. "She doesn't believe in love at first sight. She thinks I'm trying to hurt you with lies." He grinned coldly. "What she doesn't understand is a man like me needs assurances before I fully invest myself. I need her agreement on marriage in order to fully open myself and reveal everything I have to offer." He shook his head sadly, completely ignoring me, and continued talking to the hopeless romantic of my father. "I'm sure you understand. After all, you look like a man who has lived with a broken heart for many years." His tone softened, but beneath it lurked glittering steel. "Your daughter has the power to break, not just my heart, but my world. Is it so wrong of me to want her hand in marriage now, so I can be brave enough to show her everything I can?"

I rolled my eyes. "That is a load of utter bull—"

"It makes perfect sense." My father hugged me close. "Elle, I'm so proud of you and how mature you're being about all this. I'm aware you're more cynical than I am when it comes to love but seeing you with him—it makes me so, so happy."

*Only because you believe he's good for Belle Elle. That he's unsullied with gossip or misdoings—unlike another.*

I'd had enough. My temper snapped. "I'm not going to marry him, Dad. Both of you stop this charade right now."

Penn glowered, hiding his glare as my dad laughed. "You say that now." He tapped my cheek like a child. "I know when there is connection and chemistry. And you two have it in spades."

He backed toward the door. "In fact, I'm going to leave you in peace, but you have my blessing. Both of you." He glanced at Penn. "I'm glad we had that chat at the bar. I know a bit about you, Mr. Everett, so you're not a total stranger. However, when you get a chance, how about a round of golf or a beer to patch up any remaining holes in my knowledge? Eventually, I'd love to meet your benefactor and any other family you might have."

"Of course." Penn bowed his head with old-fashioned respect. "At the soonest opportunity." He grabbed my hand, holding me tight. "And please, call me Penn."

What would Dad say when he found out Penn had a son?

What would *I* say when I found out what Penn did for a living and why my father valued his success so highly?

What would any of us say when the truth came out, and this was over?

My father opened my office door, beaming so bright I thought he'd swallowed a star. "All right then, Penn." He chuckled. "Well, Penn, play your cards right, and soon, I'll be calling you son-in-law." Blowing me a kiss, he added, "Welcome to the family, son."

I waved like a robot as he disappeared and closed the door.

He left.

I lost it.

Whirling on Penn, I hissed, "Get out. *Right now.*"

He grabbed my cheeks, yanking my face to his. His lips collided hard and brutal, his tongue lashing mine into submission.

I didn't fall for his seduction this time. Shoving him, I darted around my desk and pressed the intercom to Fleur.

She answered right away as Penn stalked me, coming closer with a shadowed look in his gaze.

"Anything I can get you?" Fleur's voice helped remind me the world hadn't stepped into the twilight zone, and I was still the queen of this establishment.

Sage stood proudly on my desk, giving Penn an evil cat-smile, knowing he was in trouble.

Straightening my shoulders and drawing up every ounce of courage, I snipped. "Yes, call security. My *fiancé* needs help leaving the building."

# Chapter Twenty

I MANAGED TO avoid my husband-to-be for three days.

He called the office.

He somehow got my cellphone number.

He already had my father on his side.

And he'd corrupted my body against me.

But he hadn't succeeded in controlling my mind, and he *definitely* hadn't mastered my heart.

I was weak where he was concerned, I would admit that. And he'd drawn me into his untruths to the point I couldn't look my father in the eye and tell him it was all a big fabrication.

He was too happy. His skin was rosier, his walk bouncier, and his outlook on life chirpier. Fears about his heart and another attack kept me from shattering his happiness.

For now, I'd let him believe Penn and I were together. But once I'd earned what I wanted from him and was no longer a virgin with commitment issues, I would break it off, end the fake engagement, and go on with my life.

Who knew, perhaps I would surprise everyone and accept Greg as my future partner because at least he was normal and predictable. I could have my fling with danger and then appreciate Greg all the more.

Everyone used everyone else. I didn't let guilt eat at me for using Penn—especially when he was the one using me just as much.

"We're here, Ms. Charlston. Would you like me to wait, or do you believe the meeting will last a while?" David twisted in the driver's seat to face me sitting in the back.

My hair hung neatly over my shoulder, my black skirt with cream lace belt and Chinese blossom jacket painted me as the leader of the largest retail chain in the USA.

I clutched the folder on my lap. "The last time I met with this supplier, I didn't leave for four hours."

"I remember." David grinned. "I also recall you texting me apologetically saying you wouldn't be much longer."

I nodded. I was younger then and less adept at offsite meetings and the guilt at leaving David waiting in a car for so long. That was his job—along with other tasks, but I didn't expect him to be bored or uncomfortable.

"If you have errands you'd like to run, feel free. I'll call thirty minutes before it's due to end to give you time to return."

"Are you sure?" His large bulk twisted further in the seat. "If you think it's only going to be a short meeting, I'll wait."

I shook my head. "I'd rather know you were busy than bored."

His ebony skin bounced the streetlight off his forehead as he laughed. "Sure. Well, I'll have my phone, and I'll keep an eye on the time. If I haven't heard from you by ten p.m., I'll head back anyway."

"Okay." Hoisting the files into my arm and grabbing my handbag, I let myself out of the Range Rover and smiled at the doormen who bid me welcome to the Blue Rabbit.

I'd eaten here before. The tapas menu served second-to-none delicacies with delectable samplers. Not that I'd been able to eat very much because last time had been a business meeting, just like tonight.

Most of my social engagements, minus the last-minute high school get-togethers, were with bigwigs from other companies, improving our relationships or building on already established trade agreements.

Stuffing my face with salmon crostini or risotto balls wasn't exactly correct etiquette.

Striding in cream heels, I approached the maître-d. "Hello, I'm looking for the Loveline party?"

"Ah, yes. Right this way." The headwaiter nodded and guided me into the restaurant, around quaint tables and big tables to a large one at the back of the room where it was quieter. Blue velvet drapes hung on the walls while the salt and pepper shakers were in the shape of cute bunnies.

Nearing the table, Jennifer Stark stood up and waited with her hand outstretched. "Hello again, Ms. Charlston."

I shook her hand warmly. "Please, call me Elle."

"Elle then." Letting me go, she sat back down while motioning to the three other diners around the table. "This is Bai, Andrew, and Yumaeko from the merchandising and production departments in Shenzhen."

"Hello." I nodded politely.

Settling into the last remaining seat, I glanced once around the restaurant, afraid that just like the other times I'd been in public, Penn might show up. He seemed to have a knack for finding me.

Jennifer leaped straight into it while two waiters brought water and an array of starters to the table. "As you know, Loveline is an up-and-coming label we're hoping will find a niche market at Belle Elle."

I opened my folder and pulled out my voice recorder. I'd long since stopped trying to take notes. This way Fleur could type up the important points when I headed into the office tomorrow.

"Can you tell me a bit about what Loveline will consist of?"

Jennifer smiled shyly at her co-workers before reaching into her bag and pulling out a pamphlet. She kept it face-down, passing it over the white tablecloth. "The world is much more open about sexuality these days, and we believe capitalizing on this openness is a prime opportunity, especially with more erotic literature and movies in the mainstream market."

I turned the leaflet over and promptly slapped it against my chest, so the young waitress didn't see the giant glittery dildo on the front. "You're proposing sex toys? In a major department store?"

"We're proposing toys for adults in a private room located within the lingerie department, yes."

My cheeks burned.

Up until Penn came into my life, I hadn't had to deal with sex at all. Now, my dreams were saturated in skin and panting. My days consumed with kissing and thrusting. And now, I had to talk about dildos being sold under our brand.

"I'm not so sure that's appropriate."

Jennifer grinned, her red hair tied in a neat bun on the top of her head. "I thought you'd say that, so I brought the latest numbers from Mark Sacs in Australia, who recently introduced the Loveline to their department stores with record-breaking success." She slid another pamphlet toward me, only this time, the numbers and graphs weren't so risqué.

My eyes widened as I glanced at the figures. "Wow, that's

impressive."

"The entire stock of two hundred Seahorses and three hundred Hummingbirds were sold in the first week alone. They've had to reorder three times since introducing, along with a massive bump in sales on lingerie just from add-on purchases." She grinned. "The bottom line talks, Elle."

I looked up. "What exactly is a Seahorse and a Hummingbird?"

Her business partners chuckled as she slid over a small black bag with pink crepe paper sticking from the top. "I thought you might ask. Included are samples from our top sellers including the Tiger Tail, Rattlesnake, and Panda kiss."

"All named after animals?" I tugged the bag and placed it securely in my lap, leaning over the top to keep the contents hidden while I peeked inside.

There in neat, classy see-through teal boxes were an array of dildos, vibrators, and bejeweled plugs.

I closed it, swallowing hard as my fantasies imagined Penn wielding one of those as he fisted his cock in his hand. Jennifer was right. Men and women still played. I was in a long-running game myself and had no doubt others dabbled with toys and apparatus.

Why not capitalize on such an emerging and now acceptable market?

*Dad will have a fit.*

But I was the boss.

And I was curious.

Placing the bag by my ankle, I linked my hands on the table and smiled. "Let's talk."

\* \* \* \* \*

Penn (8:45p.m.): *Three days is too long. I've allowed you to avoid me out of respect. But tonight, you're mine.*

Penn (9:15 p.m.): *I have methods to find you, Elle. I gave you my word I wouldn't lie to you, so believe me when I say I'm tasting you tonight and you'll fucking beg for more.*

Penn (9:35 p.m.): *Seeing as you didn't text back, I've used the GPS on your phone to find your location.*

Penn (9:55 p.m.): *Fuck, you look sexy while you talk business.*

My head shot up, glancing around the restaurant.

I'd felt my phone vibrate a few times during the business meeting but hadn't checked it. I didn't want to be rude and interrupt the flow of figures and forecasts. I'd only taken it out to text David and tell him I was almost done and to bring the car around.

That was until I found multiple texts from Penn.

My heart mimicked the rabbit salt and pepper shakers, hopping around my chest as I searched the last remaining diners. Being a Tuesday meant few people lingered over their meals, needing to head home for another early start tomorrow.

"Everything okay?" Jennifer asked, signing off her credit card bill for the tapas we'd nibbled on throughout the presentation. I'd offered to pay, but she hadn't let me. Not that she would mind, seeing as I'd placed a significant order to be delivered in two months to test the market.

It was sinful buying sex toys to put into a mainstream retail chain, but with a bit of rejigging in the lingerie department, a grotto for adults could be built rather easily with strict rules about entry and all the necessary precautions of unlabeled opaque shopping bags and codes on receipts rather than in-depth details of their purchase.

If I was honest, it was rather exciting.

Just like the complex feelings I had at the thought of Penn watching me.

But after scanning all the tables, there was no sign of him.

"Yes, I'm fine." I looked back at her, slouching in relief and fizzing with disappointment.

*He's not here.*

I didn't know why he caused two polar extremes. I wanted him here. I didn't want him here. Neither was a lie. I literally felt both things at once.

Jennifer pushed her chair in, gathering her materials and smiling as her colleagues stood. "It was a pleasure to meet you again, Elle."

We shook hands. "Likewise."

I closed my folder and ensured I had my little black bag of samplers and my handbag.

Together, we all left the table.

I turned toward the exit.

And there he was.

His elbow leaned on the bar while his ankles crossed elegantly. He held a tumbler to his mouth, his eyes glued to me as if he hadn't been looking anywhere else. As if he *couldn't* look anywhere else.

Half of me wanted to slap him while the other half wanted kiss him until we were kicked from the restaurant for obscene public displays of affection.

I swallowed hard as my feet remembered what to do and followed Jennifer and her partners toward fresh air and my awaiting car ride.

Tipping the rest of his drink down his throat, Penn pushed away from the bar and strolled ever so casually but not casually at all toward the same door I did. He wasn't in a suit this time, but in a black long-sleeve sweater pushed up to his elbows and faded denim jeans. The material wrapping his chest clung to every ridge and muscle, reminding me I'd seen what he hid in his jeans but hadn't seen anything else.

My fingers itched to tear it off him.

To find out if he was as perfect naked as he was dressed.

My heart mangled itself into sexually frustrated pieces as I exited and lost sight of him. Jennifer and her partners said their goodbyes before hopping into a Town Car to return to their hotel.

David jumped out of the awaiting Range Rover and grabbed my belongings. "All good? Ready to go?"

I should say yes. I should leap in the 4WD and demand he peel away like a racecar driver to keep me out of the clutches of Penn Everett. But I dawdled deliberately, raking a hand through my hair and pretending to soak up the balmy night sky.

"I'll take her home."

The smooth, sensual voice wrapped around me from behind as Penn stepped to my side and placed his hand on my lower back.

Three days deleted in a poof of desire.

My anger with him for lying.

My rage at being manipulated...all gone.

He'd made this itch inside me intolerable.

He would have to be the one to fix it.

Penn smiled, leaning forward to capture the little black bag from David's fingers. "We'll take that, too."

My eyes widened as I gulped. "How do you—"

*Know what's in there?*

I stopped midway because the question was useless.

Judging by his texts, he'd been watching me for a while. He would've seen flashes of the product as I fondled a few under the table, testing the rubber dildos and doing what Jennifer suggested to see how lifelike they were.

My cheeks burned as Penn captured my hand. "Elle, please

tell your driver that you're happy to let me take you home and that I'm not kidnapping you or holding you under duress."

I blinked, noticing David's tense shoulders and the way he'd pushed aside his blazer to reveal the hidden holster and handle of his weapon. "It's okay, David. I know him."

"Ma'am?" He didn't take his eyes off Penn. He looked him up and down. "He does look familiar, now that you mention it."

Familiar? Why would he look familiar?

Penn was anything but ordinary and I was fairly sure I'd never bumped into him before. Besides, he himself had told my father he'd only recently returned to New York after being away for a time.

I said politely, "His name is Penn Everett."

Penn amended. "Ms. Charlston's fiancé."

I cringed. Words dangled on my tongue to deny it, but what would be the point? My father already believed, Steve, Greg…what was one more in the scheme of this storybook?

David shifted in place. "I see." He didn't relax, though, which I found mildly disconcerting.

He turned his attention to me.

Years ago, when my father had hired him to protect me, we'd worked on a series of codes I could say if I felt threatened or couldn't speak honestly. If I was being held at gunpoint or being robbed, a simple phrase would send David into military mode.

"Any other orders for the night, ma'am?" He waited, giving me time to speak one of the codes.

*I'm tired and believe I'll take a bubble bath tonight*: code for a kidnapping.

*I'm not feeling well; I might walk instead*: code for a robbery or gun in my side.

I said neither.

The silence dragged on a second too long before Penn tugged on my fingers.

Without hesitation, I moved with him. "No, not tonight, David."

David didn't try to save me again.

# Chapter Twenty-One

TEN MINUTES INTO the walk, my nerves got the better of me.

Squeezing Penn's fingers, I asked, "Where are you taking me?"

"My place."

"Why?"

He chuckled, his face shrouded in darkness. "Why do you think?"

My tummy clenched as his voice lost its decorum and slipped into sin.

"To fuck you, of course." His teeth flashed as he added, "I've waited for as long as I can. You haven't told your father I was lying about our engagement, and you haven't run back to your bodyguard. Therefore, I know you're up for whatever I have planned, and you will not argue." His jaw lowered. "Will you, Bell Button?"

My mouth watered with how wrong but how right that sounded. Fantasies of what could happen tonight unraveled with lightning desire—

*Wait.*

*He called me Bell Button.*

Anger took precedent. "That isn't your nickname to use."

"No?" He raised an eyebrow. "Yet you let—what was her name? Chloe—call you Ding Dong Bell. Do you prefer that?"

My teeth locked together. "I prefer neither. Elle is perfectly acceptable. So use it."

He laughed in a soft sigh. "So defensive."

"Not defensive. Protective."

His head shot up, his eyes sinking into me like barbs. "You feel the need to protect yourself around me?"

"Constantly."

His shadow swallowed me. "Why?"

"Why what?"

"You know what. Answer the question and stop dancing around it." The way he pushed for an answer hinted he had ulterior motives to know why I barricaded myself from him. Why I would never let myself feel more for him than just physical desire.

We'd known each other a week or so. I was woman enough to admit I found him immensely attractive. I was girl enough to admit I liked the idea of instant true love. But I was realistic enough to know that would never happen for a business owner like me.

Besides, he was ruthless in his own success. Webbed in lies and hidden in half-truths, he was not a man to trust with anything breakable—especially my heart.

My body would bruise.

But it would heal.

It didn't stop the fact that Penn wanted something from me.

If it was just sex, then our motives were in line.

But the more I spent in his company, the more I sensed that wasn't his end game.

I narrowed my eyes, trying to see past his arrogant shields and read what he truly meant. But all he revealed was a man supreme in his ability and self-worth. A man as proud and as pompous as a peacock.

*Yet...he has a son.*

How could someone so cold and emotionally unavailable have a child dependent on him? Where was Stewie's mother? Who was Larry? What the hell would happen between us once we'd slept together?

The questions built on top of his in an unstable Jenga tower. One wrong answer and the entire foundation of our so-called relationship would crumble.

Tonight was not the night to let it fall.

Tomorrow it could.

Because by tomorrow, I would've got what I wanted, he would've got what he wanted, and things would go back to the way they were. Penn and his lies would fade from my life before he caused any more damage.

"You ask why, yet I could ask you the same question." I pushed ahead, leaving the glow of a streetlight and stepping into a pool of night. "Why do *you* protect yourself from *me?*"

He slammed to a stop. "I don't."

"You do."

His jaw worked, his hands opening and closing by his sides. "I'm guarded; there's a difference."

"Is there?" I cocked my head. "Funny, I would say protective and guarded were the same thing."

He stormed toward me, grabbing me by the throat and marching me backward until I hit the façade of an apartment building. The brick was hard. He was harder. I was the soft middle that didn't stand a chance. "If you ever try to psychoanalyze me again, you'll be sorry."

I swallowed, forcing fear past the cage of his hand around my neck. Even now, my body hummed beneath his grip. It seemed my cells had embraced the sensation of eroticism and found any grasp appropriate.

"Why would I be sorry?" My voice barely registered audible. "What would you do? Kill me?"

I meant it flippantly, casually. A phrase tossed around far too often and never meant. But instead of either ignoring the cliché dare or admitting he ran much darker than I thought, he smiled with all the sharpness of a butcher's arsenal. "Perhaps."

My heart leaped out of my body, racing to borrow a telephone to call the police. But my insides burned with a different flavor than before. If lust was a color, I'd been bathed in reds and pinks for days. Now I swam in blacks and deep, deep purples, wanting nothing more than to let go and forget who I was and become who I dared never be.

Straining against his fingers, I deliberately strangled myself in his hold. "What are you going to do to me if I accept I'll never know you and admit I don't want to? What will you do when I admit I'm using you like you're using me? Fuck me?"

He never looked away; never reduced the pressure on my throat. "I told you that was my intention."

He constantly had me at a disadvantage. I was sick of it. If I wanted to hold my ground, I had to start acting more myself and not a timid little girl. Gathering my courage, I murmured, "Stop threatening, and get it over with then."

His fingers spasmed. His body weight landed on mine. "Get it over with?"

"Yes. I want you to fuck me then leave me alone."

A slight groan fell from his lips. "You can't say things like that on an empty street."

"Why not? I would've thought empty would be preferable to busy. No one is here to watch."

He shook his head, dark hair dancing over his forehead. "Busy means I'm forced to keep my hands to myself." He yanked me close, dropping his fingers from my neck to my breast while his left arm looped around my waist.

The soft thud of the bag holding the sex toy samples landed on the sidewalk as his hand massaged my flesh, his thumb and finger pinching my nipple. "An empty street means I could turn you around, hoist up your skirt, and sink inside you without being seen."

I shivered.

It sounded so wrong.

It sounded so *good.*

Forcing myself to remain sane, I looked up at the buildings all around us. The faint glow of families and the shadows of activities moved subtly above. "We'd be seen, regardless if we saw them or not."

He followed my gaze, his throat exposed as his head tipped up. His fingers twitched on my breast. "You're right."

His touch fell away as he took a step back. "Pity."

Collecting the bag again, he slipped back into a prowl, dragging me with him.

\* \* \* \* \*

"You live here?"

He nodded as he pulled a key from his pocket.

"As in the whole building?" I looked up at the mini skyscraper with its high sash windows and faded duck-egg blue exterior.

"It needs work, but that's why I bought it." He unlocked the ancient doorknob and pulled me into a foyer with art deco tiles, a square chandelier, and peeling wallpaper. The ceiling soared at least four stories above us with a double width staircase curling up in a spiral to multiple floors.

"Wow."

He let me go, moving toward the wall where the flick of a bronze light switch magically graced the place with illumination. The soft click woke up countless light bulbs, glittering with dust and weathered with time.

"Like I said, a work in progress." Once again, he captured my wrist, carting me up the stairs. He didn't give me a chance to marvel at the original craftsmanship or question how long he'd been the owner.

It was as if the building didn't exist to him. As if the only thing that mattered to him was me.

I didn't speak as we made our way up and up. He didn't stop on floor two or three or four. He kept tugging me higher until we entered floor ten or eleven and unlocked yet another door in the dingy moth-nibbled hallway.

It was like stepping into a different world.

We'd headed through a time capsule and entered a resplendent suite of art deco charm, 1930's decoration, and immaculate presentation.

My mouth fell open as I drifted forward. "This—this is incredible."

"Of course, it is. It's mine." He locked the door behind him then strode through the space. "Just like you." His jaw tightened beneath his five o'clock shadow. "I only own incredible things."

My heart lurched rather than my body.

Was that an odd compliment? A nod that he did care for me beyond physical gratification?

*Don't be absurd. Your heart is wrong. It's on a sabbatical, researching myths on love and finding no solid proof it exists.*

Penn was everything poems and fables promised. If it wasn't for the brooding anger or taut protection he sheltered behind, of course.

If only I could make him swallow a truth serum and tear out answers—reveal just how shallow or deep he ran.

I couldn't take my eyes off him. I expected him to fit in with this space, to feel at home and move freely, yet something didn't sit right. He kicked off his shoes and padded barefoot over polished mosaic wood floors, but something was missing. He wasn't at ease. He moved as if this was as foreign and new to him as it was to me.

*Why is that?*

"How long ago did you move in?" I kicked off my heels, placing them by the kitchen island.

Penn smiled. "You're asking questions?"

"Is that against the rules?"

He paused; something flickered over his face that I couldn't decipher. "Some aren't. Others are."

The crypticness gave me a headache. "So you can't tell me how long you've lived here?"

"You overheard part of what I told your father at the

Weeping Willow. I've moved back to town recently. So if you believe that, then you'll believe that this is a new purchase."

"Why do I need to believe something if it's true?"

He didn't reply.

I pushed with another question. "You said your benefactor was sick. That you returned for him. Is he okay?"

A softness flowed over him—something so unexpected and endearing to see. Whoever his benefactor was, he cared for him a lot more than he would admit. "He's fine now. It was a rare form of blood cancer. They have it under control."

"That's good."

"It is."

The conversation stalled. Awkwardness settled like a third wheel. I felt responsible. Before, our silence had been potent with desire. Now, it hung heavy with confusion.

Why did I care about him, this building, and whoever his mystery benefactor was?

*I'm here for one thing only.*

Same thing as he was.

Taking a deep breath, I marched across the room. His arms opened wide, knowing what I did—that the only way to delete the sudden weirdness between us was to return to the basics.

The place where hate and like didn't matter.

His lips stopped my thoughts. His arms ceased my worry. He let whatever restraint he had left fray and stalked me backward, his mouth never leaving mine, his sheer power corralling me against a sideboard.

His fingers grabbed my jaw as he kissed me hard.

His taste of mint and darkness flooded my senses.

I trembled in his hold.

As quickly as the kiss began, it ended. His fingers stung my oversensitive skin as he tugged me forward, moving stealthily toward a door past the open plan kitchen, living room, and dining. All around, large picture windows allowed the city to entertain us with its electric vibrancies and pedestrians below.

Opening a door, Penn let me go, allowing me to drift forward into his bedroom while he tossed the black bag onto his bed.

I followed it as the silver glitter dildo called the Seahorse bounced out and lay accusingly on the dark gray coverlet.

Penn didn't notice. Or if he did, he didn't glance at it. I doubted he'd notice anything else now I was in his lair. I was his conquest, his trophy. I didn't know why I got the feeling this was more about him than it was about me, but in an odd way, I was glad.

I could take what I wanted without having to worry about emotions getting in the way. I could keep myself protected all while giving him every intimate part of myself.

I shivered as he stalked toward me, crowding me against the wall. He seemed to prefer me locked in place, unable to go anywhere.

He hadn't offered me a drink or something to eat.

He'd brought me here to fuck me.

That was all.

I knew I might be hurt by that later. That for all my bravado and belief I could keep this about sex, I might still over-analyze and read into every moment. But right now...right now all I wanted was him. All I needed was him, and I was prepared to be cold-hearted to do that.

"You're so fucking beautiful, Elle," he murmured, planting one hand on the wall by my head, imprisoning me. The pulse in his neck was visible as his gaze slipped from warm sable to brutal black. His other hand landed on my cheek, his thumb grazing my jaw to the corner of my mouth.

He paused, holding his thumb there. "You don't have a clue what you're doing to me, do you?" He pressed his erection against my belly. "And I'm not going to tell you."

*What? What am I doing to you?*

The way he said it ached with tenderness. For the briefest second, he wasn't some rich tycoon about to strip and devour me but a sweet seducer drowning beneath his own untruths.

That was the problem with being guarded.

People with lies could never make friends. But people with trust could never make enemies.

Both were weak.

I sucked in a breath, parting my lips, allowing him to insert his thumb into my mouth.

The intrusion was sexy and hot, and his skin tasted of salt.

I wanted to ask why he wouldn't tell me. That I wanted to know what crazy power I had over him when I felt so helpless in his presence. But he leaned forward, licking my bottom lip as he held my mouth open with his thumb. "I'm not going to tell you because I'm going to show you."

He leaned against me, chest to chest, hips to hips. He trapped me just as he had in my office and the alley and the street and my department store.

He trapped me, and it dredged up yet more memories of three years ago when a hooded man freed me from robbers and awoke my teenage soul. The differences were startling. One man had unlocked my world. This one did his best to imprison me.

Neither would be successful.

Only I held that power, and it was my prerogative to lend it to another or deny it.

A faint hint of anger and untapped desire siphoned from him to me, yet beneath that, there was something else. Something I hadn't felt from him before.

Softness wrapped in barbwire.

It didn't diminish the intensity of how he watched me, touched me, controlled me with the multiple facets within him. His facial scruff scraped my cheek as he bent his neck and kissed my throat. My eyes slammed closed as his teeth bit my collarbone. His aftershave shot up my nose as his hands landed on my sides, swooping up to rub my nipples with his thumbs.

His lips traced up my neck, kissing but not gently. Nothing about Penn was gentle. It all came from a place of violence mixed with pleasure. The slipperiness of his teeth added a thrilling dimension to his warm mouth, and I moaned as he once again captured my face in his strong, cool fingers and tipped me just the right way.

His lips sealed over mine, sweet to start then vicious. My body slammed against the wall, harder and harder as he tried to consume me, his lips causing bruises that would never heal.

I had no choice but to let go. To give up standing and breathing and thinking.

If I didn't, I'd scream with his possession.

Giving in was the easiest and only option.

Because then I could stop thinking and just *be*. Be a woman, desire...me.

He controlled every minute thing.

He was right when he said he wouldn't lie to me.

The kiss told me things he no doubt wanted to keep hidden. Things like 'this is me, this is who I am. I won't apologize'. And beneath that...beneath those sexy messages of wanting to fuck me was a deeper, darker thread.

A thread that dared me to argue, to probe deeper into who he was, to switch him from passionate stranger to someone I could perhaps call...not a friend, but at least an acquaintance.

His other hand looped around my spine, jerking me from the wall, shoving his fingers down the back of my skirt. He fingered the lace of my G-string and the top of my ass, rocking his erection into my belly.

*I need air. I need sanity.*

But he scooped me into his arms, letting my legs dangle between his as he stalked toward his bed and threw me down, tossing the black bag onto the floor.

His face contorted with lust. "We'll use toys another time. Tonight, I just need you." Grabbing my jacket, he forced me to wriggle free as he removed my arms from the sleeves.

The minute I lay there in my blouse and skirt, he smirked. "I hope you're not too attached to these."

With a furious yank, he ripped my blouse apart. The tiny seashell buttons pinged into all corners of his room while cool air kissed my naked belly, revealing my black lace bra.

He groaned, bending over me to press a kiss on the swell of my breast.

Without thinking, I held his head to my chest, breathing hard, panting quick, running my hands through his hair with affection I didn't necessarily feel.

He reared back, his gaze narrowed and full of rage.

We stared at each other, silently waging, trying to figure out how lines had blurred already. Pulling back to stand by the edge of the bed, Penn left me speechless, breathless, wondering what the hell was happening, and just who he was beneath the surface.

His hands landed on his belt, yanking the leather free and ripping it from the loops.

My skin was needy and demanding. I wanted him close. I wanted him on me. Screw the tiny voice of fear that my first time would hurt.

"Take off your clothes," he growled thickly, his voice no longer entirely human as he shoved his jeans down his legs and stepped out of them.

Sitting up on the bed, I obeyed, shrugging out of my damaged top and reaching behind to unhook and unzip my skirt. The moment it unfastened, I lay back down, shimmying from the material until he grabbed the ends and yanked it the rest of the way.

My garter belt glittered in the low lamps by the window and door. My pantyhose reminded me everyone else knew me as the queen of Belle Elle, yet Penn was the only one to tear me down until I was naked and begging for a single touch.

His gaze latched between my legs where my black G-string matched my bra. He bit his lip, then grabbed my ankles, yanked me down the bed, and pressed himself on top of me. His fist slammed into the mattress with all the frustration and rage he wouldn't admit, making my heart hammer and blood race.

"Fuck, I want to be inside you."

I surrendered to his feral kiss, letting him direct and guide me. His fingers plucked at my garters, undoing my pantyhose until they hung undone around my thighs. He rocked his cock against me— the only things separating us were two pieces of cotton.

Terror tried to interrupt my pleasure—things like birth control and protection and the fact I should tell him it was my first time.

But embarrassment kept my lips shut.

Penn was experienced. He couldn't hide that fact with the way he attacked my mouth and body with confidence born of expertise.

If he'd noticed I was a follower in this and no longer the leader I'd been groomed to be, he didn't care or mention it. I just hoped he'd take charge of the protection issue, and if he entered me too fast, then I would say something but not before.

I clutched at his black top, needing it off. Needing skin on skin.

He listened, tearing his mouth away to reach over his head and pull the second to last piece of clothing off.

My hands flew up of their own accord. I traced his abs and up to his chest. He didn't try to stop me and the luxury, the *privilege* of touching him filled my blood with heated desire.

Staying braced on one arm over me, his fingers looped around my panties and pulled them down. My hand latched onto the other side, keeping it high, protecting my modesty. I didn't know why, but sudden shyness attacked me.

He gritted his teeth. "Let go."

I bit my lip, refusing silently.

"Elle." His growl sliced through my unwillingness.

Closing my eyes briefly, I let go and allowed him to drag the lace down my legs. He slipped them off my ankles and tossed them over his shoulder. Clamping a powerful hand on my inner thigh, he spread my legs. "So fucking beautiful."

I trembled as his stroked upward, running his fingertips along my wetness. "Christ, Elle."

My mouth opened as he pressed a finger slowly inside me.

My breasts ached, and I reached behind me to undo the confines of my bra. He grimaced with agonizing need as I revealed the final part of me. He swallowed hard as my body welcomed his finger, my hips rocking upward to meet him.

"Touch me," he commanded. His finger hooked inside me, dragging a gasp through my lungs. I reached forward blindly, unsure what to do and how hard to grasp.

He tipped forward, giving me access to his boxer-briefs.

With an out of control heartbeat, I pulled aside the tight cotton and inserted my hand into the warm depths.

He shuddered as my fingers latched around him.

"Jesus." He bowed as I squeezed hard, unsure if soft or violent was his undoing.

I copied the pressure he used on me—not being gentle, not giving him time to adjust to being touched.

His finger speared upward, pressing against the sensitive spot inside that turned everything into liquid gold. Grunting a little as I fisted him deeper, he inserted another finger.

The stretch. The burn. His fingernail scraped a little as he didn't give me time to adjust.

I matched his punishment with my own, digging my nails into his shaft, pumping him in the same way he thrust into me.

"Goddammit." His head bowed, his lips wide. "Fuck, that feels good."

His greedy cock leaped in my hands, demanding more. Something hot and sticky coated my fingers as I swooped over the crown and back down again.

He hooked his finger deeper, causing me to writhe on the bed. My voice erupted on a gasp. "Oh, God."

"Finally, you speak."

I shivered, sinking back into myself as he stroked and teased. Words seemed a million miles away in the realm of conversation and humanness. I was somewhere deep inside where only feeling and sensation were permitted. "I wasn't aware you wanted me to."

"I want to know how this is for you." His eyes blazed.

"How?"

His thumb landed on my clit. "Do you like this? Do you need more? Less? Tell me."

I answered back with a squeeze of his cock. "Do *you* like this?"

He groaned. "Do you really need to ask?" His hips thrust into my palm. "I'm practically coming all over your goddamn fingers."

The confession sent lust and desire and giddy, giddy happiness fizzing like fireworks.

My body slowly melted, becoming more inviting, wetter, hotter.

He noticed.

A dark gleam entered his gaze. "I have no intention of fingering you all night, Elle. Just like I don't expect you to jerk me off." His fingers stroked me ruthlessly. "I want to fuck you. I need to be inside this." He hooked his grip, pressing something intimately hardwired to an exquisite button inside my belly.

Another press and I could've climbed up whatever pleasure hill I currently trampled, striding closer toward the summit. But each time he pushed me, he pulled me back a little—making me out of breath and desperate for the top where I could finally rest and be rewarded.

He pulled away, removing his touch, making me empty. "Tell me now if that's going to be a problem." He fisted himself, looking between my legs. "Tell me if you're having second thoughts because once I'm inside you, I won't be able to stop."

Now was my final chance to admit I wasn't ready. That this was too soon. Too fast. Not done by rational women.

But the words weren't there.

The only ones I knew were: "I want this. I want you to fuck me."

His eyes snapped closed as his stomach tightened. "Your wish is my command." Shoving my thighs wider, he pushed his boxer-briefs down his legs and threw them to the floor. Reaching for his discarded jeans on the bed, he pulled out a condom packet and passed it to me.

"I take you're not on the pill."

I took the slippery foil. "No."

"Fine." His jaw gritted as his gaze locked on my shaking hands. "Put it on me then."

I had no intention of telling him I'd never done this before. Ripping the packet, I carefully pulled out the odd smelling latex and pinched the top like I'd been shown in sex education at school.

He didn't say a word as I positioned it over his crown and rolled it down his very impressive length.

He shuddered as my fingers went further than necessary and cupped his balls. His eyes flared wide before I pulled away, unsure if I was allowed to do that or not.

Wedging his hips between mine, he snarled, "Answer me one question."

I was obsessed with the sight of his sheathed erection only inches away from my core.

He grabbed my chin, forcing me to meet his eyes. "Are you a virgin?"

I stiffened. "How—how would you know that?"

"I don't know that. That's why I'm asking."

I licked my lips. "I'm—"

He waited with angry eyes, the tip of his cock nudging against my entrance. "Tell me, Elle. Otherwise, this will be very painful for you." Pushing forward, he entered me just a little.

The discomfort burned, but in a good way; but he had so much more to go. So many ways to rip me apart if I wasn't honest with him.

I dropped my eyes. "This is the first time I've been with a man."

His forehead furrowed. His face replayed a memory I couldn't see. His hips pushed forward again, inch by lazy inch. "I'll go slow."

I tensed. "Okay."

We breathed in the same ragged rhythm as he slipped ever so slowly into my body. When he hit an unbreakable barrier, I clenched with trepidation and pain.

He stopped.

A few dazzling drumbeats of my heart, and I forced myself to relax a little.

He pressed deeper.

His dominion was collected but incomplete. There was nowhere I could look without him being there. No scent I could breathe without it being him.

I couldn't do a thing but allow him to penetrate me in every sense of the word.

Another inch and a sting began—an awful burn that brought tears to my eyes. I turned my head, doing my best to bury my face or bite down on freshly laundered sheets.

"Hurts?"

I nodded, unable to look at him. I was a failure at this.

"I told you I'd protect you even when I was hurting you, remember?" He grunted, dragging my eyes to him. He loomed over me like a demon with muscles etched in shadow, a face chiseled from granite.

I nodded.

"Well, then, this is going to hurt." The flash of lust on his face distracted me then all I knew was pain and pleasure and pain and pleasure and pain, pain, *pain*.

He impaled me swiftly, sharply. No more creeping softly. No more adjusting or seduction.

He fucked me.

He took me.

He consumed me.

# Chapter Twenty-Two

"OPEN YOUR EYES, Elle."

I couldn't, not with the tears trickling down my cheeks. Tears I didn't even understand. I wasn't crying because it hurt—the pain had already faded a little. I wasn't even crying because I'd given this man who I didn't know the final piece of me that no one else had earned.

I cried because in his strange arms, with his delicious body inside mine, I found a smidgen of that freedom I'd tried so long to find.

"Open your eyes," he ordered again, rocking into me.

I obeyed, drinking him in, noticing the small beads of sweat on his brow and the wildness on his face.

I shifted beneath him, my hips adjusting to fit his. My tears dried like salt tracks. "You're huge."

"You're tight."

"It feels…nice, though."

"Nice?" He half-smiled, fighting back the quick flashes of darkness he kept hidden. "Just nice?" He pressed into me. "No other description? No better word for me fucking you?"

"Sore?"

He scowled. "I was thinking of another."

"Hard? Full? Desperate?"

His face eclipsed with shadows. "Desperate?" His voice switched to ragged breath. "Desperate for what? This?" He arched into me, his back bowing, his hips driving into mine with power and precision.

My neck tensed, my skull digging into the bed as my shoulder blades came off the mattress. A wave of pain and a crash of pleasure. It seemed I couldn't enjoy one without enduring the other.

But I'd never experienced anything like it.

I wanted more.

So much more.

But I'd have to wait because bliss like this meant he must've come, and I'd read men couldn't have multiple orgasms like women.

*You haven't come yet.*

It didn't bother me. Tonight had been a simple task to lose my innocence. It rid me of that minor complication, and the next time (if there were a next time), there would be no pain, only pleasure.

My hips moved, kissing the top of my mound to his lower belly. A thank you. A request. A bit of both.

He licked his lips, self-control etching his face. "You want to continue?"

"There's more?" My lips parted as eagerness washed through me. "You didn't...finish?"

He chuckled; it shook his body inside mine. "I won't take offense to that. But if you honestly think I'd just enter you and be satisfied, you need some serious lessons on how I fuck."

He looked down at where we joined, encouraging me to watch, too. He pulled back a little before pushing forward. The pain morphed to pleasure, warming and melting with a fine veil of sharpness.

Embracing the fire feeding on the lust inside me, I placed my hands on the top of his ass where his back clenched beneath my fingers. "More."

He planted his fists into the sheets by my head. "Fine." He slipped from slow to serious, driving into me.

My core clenched around him. A twinge of discomfort tried to steal me away.

Screw the pain.

I wanted this.

All of it.

He groaned long and low, his hips thrust upward, hitting some part of me that shattered into stardust. His hips jack-knifed into mine, as deep and as close as he could go. He let go. He drove again.

Thrust. Thrust. *Thrust.*

Whatever place orgasms lived suddenly swarmed alive like a hive with its ferocious queen. The buzzing flew from my toes to my knees to my spine, from my fingers to my arms to my tongue.

Everything ignited, and I jumped.

I jumped from the tower of Belle Elle. I forgot about my career, my rules, my boundaries.

I deleted myself.

I met Penn in the black debasement and spoke crude consonants and tasted dirty vowels. "I want you to fuck me. I want you to make me scream." I dug my fingernails into his ass, jerking him to me. "Give me what I want." I bowed off the bed, capturing his mouth with mine, taking control all while submitting the remaining power I had. "Fuck me...please."

I should've prepared for the unleashing.

I should've expected what would happen with such an invitation.

But it still took me by surprise. Still thrilled and terrified and teased.

"You fucking asked for it." His smile was pure criminal as his stomach tightened, and he drove into me so hard, so fast, his hips bruised my inner thighs. His mouth latched onto mine, our teeth clacking, our tongues knotting, every last masquerade at being civilized...gone.

He didn't just take me up on my offer.

He doubled my stakes and went for everything he could claim.

He fucked me.

No, that was woefully unjust.

He broke me, fixed me, split me.

His body slammed again and again and *again* into me. His cock sliding in heat and wetness, dragging more from me. The orgasm buzz increased, consuming everything.

His stamina made my legs jelly. Every feminine atom burst with bliss. My hips tried to meet his, but his pace kept me pinned to the bed. With a ragged breath, he slapped a hand over my heart, pressing my lungs, preventing me from gasping, counting my charging heartbeats.

My skin burned with sweat, turning his grip slippery. His fingers slid off me, slamming into the mattress. His arm buckled, wedging his entire weight on me. His hips thrust as if he had no power over his body anymore. As if all he was, all he was meant to do, was possess me until I possessed him in some karmic twist of fate.

I gasped and panted and gulped as sex turned to the most basic of coupling.

He buried his face into the sheets, his back suddenly going ramrod straight, his cock pulsing inside me.

I froze, not knowing what to do.

I knew exactly what I wanted to do.

My fingers turned gentle, caressing his spine. The moment I touched his sweat-misted back, he reared up, baring his teeth. "Don't. I'm just—" His jaw worked. "I'm so fucking close."

"Don't stop."

His face scrunched up with sexual agony. "I don't want to finish yet. I haven't had enough of you."

My cheeks pinked even as triumph blew trumpets in my belly. "Oh."

He bent and kissed me, unapologetic with lust and his desire to come. His eyes remained closed, barring me from reading him or trying to guess if this physical act meant more to him than mutual release.

I couldn't figure him out, and I desperately needed to if I was going to survive whatever he'd done to me.

Because he *had* done something to me.

He'd awakened me, and I could never go back to sleep.

"Fuck, you feel too good." With a feral grunt, he pulled away, withdrawing, and leaving me empty. Sliding down my body, his legs fell off the bed, his knees thudding against the floor.

Before I could ask what was wrong, his hands landed on my inner thighs and pushed my legs apart. His mouth—the same one that'd been kissing me—landed on my core, his tongue pulsing inside me with a different kind of wetness, a more intimate kind of heat.

I bowed off the bed, clutching the sheets in shock. "Oh, my *God.*"

He bit my clit with careful teeth. "You're sore, and I need to fuck you hard. I doubt you'll find a release with me. So...you're going to have one now."

The sheets didn't provide enough traction to grip onto. I grabbed his hair instead.

He cursed something deep and dark. His voice twisted my stomach into bowties. His tongue entered me again. It wasn't enough after the deep penetration of his cock; the shallow claiming left me straining for more.

But then his hands joined in too, pinching my clit as his fingers ran beneath his tongue to press inside me, granting girth and dexterity, pushing me up the cliff of an orgasm I'd bathed in since he turned me from pure to deviant.

Just like in my office, he didn't mess around.

He wanted me to come.

I would come.

My legs tried to close around his head, but he slammed a hand onto my thigh, spreading his saliva and my arousal. Grabbing my wrists, he kept then pinned on my belly while his tongue worked me harder.

The orgasm had colors like a dark rainbow—all blacks and grays and reds and oranges. I felt it gather. I saw it swirl. And when it descended from my bones and ligaments to gather in my womb, it glittered like some magical malicious force.

His tongue was the wand that spent that magic, dragging it from me, forcing it to explode in body-crippling waves.

"Oh, God. Oh, God. Oh, *God*." I climbed the bed, him, the world. I went blind, deaf, mute.

I drowned in every crest.

I hadn't finished coming when he climbed my body, hooked my leg over his hip, and slammed back inside me.

"Yes!" It was a scream. I had no shame. I screamed again as he drove brutally fast and deep. "Yes. Oh, God, *yes*."

The pain…was no more.

The pleasure…was too much.

Thick, hot, welcome and an undeniable primitive need to feel him all the way, deeper, deeper, harder, harder.

His tongue slid over my neck, his teeth settling over my artery like a wolf mounting its mate.

I kissed his shoulder, reveling in the saltiness, the rawness of how two naked people could be.

My fingernails landed on either side of his spine, digging hard.

"Harder," he ordered with a commanding bite. His tone kissed the dregs of my orgasm, rekindling it, fanning it, transforming embers into flames.

The soreness turned to a luscious pulling as he drove faster.

"Fuck, take it. Fucking take it." He reared over me, his elbows locked, his fingers tangled in my hair, keeping my head imprisoned and eyes pinned on his.

The bed creaked as he worked both of us into a slick mess of sweat and pleasure.

I couldn't look away, and in his brown gaze, I found something unbearably carnal, so unfiltered and truthful that my core tightened, begging for another release.

His lips smashed against mine, cutting me off from his thoughts. I lost my mind and gave into the time-honored instinct to rock with him, to accept his control, and allow him to feed and deny me every hunger he summoned.

"Fuck, you feel good. I knew you would." He hit me at an angle that sent the world fracturing with black spots. His expert claiming sent another spindle of need to join those hungry flames.

I was sore and loose and wet and delirious, and I didn't think I could come again. But he had a power over me I couldn't ignore.

A smaller more tentative release found me, ecstasy radiating into my fingertips as I trembled and gathered beneath him.

My eyes remained open as the bands of muscle contracted almost secretly, tiptoeing through my body as if unpermitted.

I came softly, deliciously, wantonly.

His eyes widened. "You came?"

I swallowed as a final clench left me boneless, lost, and entirely drugged with endorphins.

"Fuck, you came. You fucking came with me inside you." His gaze possessed me, and he lost it. Positioning himself higher over me, he grabbed my wrists and slammed them over my head.

And then, he *fucked* me.

"Shit, shit...*shit*." His voice scrambled with breath. Inside me, he grew thicker, heavier, harder, hitting the top of me with every pound.

He was wild, unleashed; his control and lies undone.

His face, normally so handsome and regal, splintered into a broken veneer as he let go.

*"Fuck!"* An animalistic roar fell from his lips, his orgasm tearing up his back and into me.

I let him do what he needed.

I drank in his vulnerability and relished in the fact he let me see him the way not many people would.

He shattered.

He shivered.

He shuddered as the last wave wrung him dry.

Only once long moments had disappeared, and we'd returned from whatever stratosphere he'd catapulted us to, did his fingers unlock from my wrists and trail down my arm to cup my cheek.

With eyes soft and no longer angry about things I couldn't understand, he kissed me.

This kiss was different.

It wasn't a claiming or a thank you.

It was a stripping back; a peeling of the masks we wore.

An acknowledgment that we'd started something that, unfortunately, wouldn't have a happy ending.

# Chapter Twenty-Three

THE LARGE CLOCK hanging in Penn's kitchen said I'd only been at his place one hour and thirty-two minutes, yet the whole world had changed.

Either time sped up without me, or we shot into the future where everything was different.

Where I was different. My body was different. My entire outlook altered.

I ran my hands down my buttoned blazer for the tenth time, smoothing my skirt. I tried to ignore my tangled hair that needed a deep condition and an hour with a brush, and pretended I wasn't bare beneath my clothing.

Once we'd finished and Penn withdrew from me, we'd dressed silently and reconvened in the kitchen. I stuffed my lingerie into the black bag full of sex toys, intending to take both home. However, Penn grabbed the handles and placed the parcel on a cupboard on the way out of his bedroom.

He didn't say a thing.

His body language alone said all of those items were staying here—whether I liked it or not.

He moved barefoot while I clipped in heels. He ducked around the large island and grabbed two glasses from a frosted-glass cupboard. Filling them both with water from a carafe in the fridge, he passed one to me, watching me over the rim as he drank.

He'd slipped into light colored jeans and a black t-shirt, looking every bit the bad boy I should never introduce to my father, let alone go along with his lies that we were engaged.

Nerves multiplied with tiny legs, racing over my shoulders the longer we stared in silence and drank. I wanted to call David to collect me. The longer I stood in Penn's presence, the more he withdrew to the point that any warmth that'd existed between us howled with frost.

I shifted on the spot, placing my half-drunk glass of water on the counter. "I guess—I guess I'll go home now."

He raised an eyebrow and finished his water. Wiping his lips with the back of his hand, he nodded. "Good idea."

I tried to hide my wince, but I wasn't successful. I didn't know why he'd shut me out—then again, he hadn't let me in. He'd invaded my body, but that didn't give me a return pass to rummage around in his soul.

The idea of calling David and waiting for him inside Penn's apartment wasn't appealing. The sooner I was away from the harsh intensity where splinters of whatever we weren't saying stabbed me, the better.

Hugging myself—making sure my broken blouse was tucked tightly into my skirt to prevent gaping open and my blazer was buttoned tight—I nodded as if we'd concluded business and the meeting was over.

Realistically, this was a business contract. He didn't like me. I didn't like him. But the sex had been incredible. I had nothing to compare it to, but if I had to do it all over again and let Penn relieve me of my virginity, I would.

Moving toward the door highlighted how sore I was. The tenderness of my inner thighs, the achiness of my core. The heavy pulling made me want to sit down, not walk down flights of stairs and wait on a cold street for my driver.

But I wasn't welcome anymore.

Penn's glare said as much.

He lied about us being engaged, yet couldn't lie about how much he needed me gone.

I stopped by the exit, keeping my back stiff. "Well, goodnight."

"Goodnight." He'd escorted me to the door as if not trusting me to leave on my own. Reaching around me, he unlocked the door and opened it. He pursed his lips as I stepped over the threshold. He didn't smile or offer a word of kindness or even condolences.

It felt like a break-up even though we were never together.

I shrugged, fighting the urge to fidget. "Um, thank you. I...enjoyed that."

A slight smile warred with an impenetrable glare. "Me too."

Nothing else.

No hug. Or promise to do it again soon. Just two little words that put a full stop—no, an entire page break—between what'd happened in his bedroom and now.

Questions whispered in my ear. *Do you want to see me again? Why did you keep my lingerie and sex toys? Did I feel as good to you as you did to me?*

I silenced each and every one.

Turning my spine to steel, I raised my chin and walked away.

* * * * *

My phone was dead.

Of course, it was.

Tonight had gone from blissful to full of heartache, and I only had myself to blame. Standing outside Penn's building, I took note of how far my apartment was. I figured it was walking distance but didn't know how long it would take. And in heels, after an incredibly long day, and extremely passionate sex, my body was not in the mood to hike through the city.

Another night slipped over this one. A night where I'd willingly stepped from the confines of my company and explored without a phone or back-up plan. Nameless had found me, saved me, and relieved me of some small part of my innocence. Tonight, Penn had claimed me, corrupted me, and stolen the rest.

Both nights had left me with sadness and unease.

I shivered as a gust blew down the street, encouraging me to walk and ponder rather than stand like an idiot kicked out of Penn's home.

Putting one foot in front of the other, I didn't let the tickle of rejection climb up my spine and squat on my shoulders. I kept focused and cool—nothing more than a CEO out for a midnight stroll with a torn blouse and soreness between her legs.

Rather than tramp all the way home (and get lost in the process), I'd walk toward the busier side of town and hail a cab. I would've given away a small fortune for my phone to work so I could call David. A few years ago, I hated being surrounded by staff and not having any freedom. Now, I appreciated having people I trusted. It made my life stream-line, not this messy unknown I currently lived in.

Catching a cab hadn't worked well for me last time. I had an awful feeling something terrible would happen again. Mainly because the similarities about that night with Nameless and tonight with Penn couldn't be ignored.

I let myself think freely about Nameless—without frustration toward my father or guilt. To recall the ease in his company even though we had just met. The trust he demanded even though I knew nothing about him. I felt safe with Nameless, despite the overwhelming teenage attraction scrambling my insides. With Penn, I was terrified for my well-being and personal relationships as he bowled through them with falsehoods.

My father didn't understand that, in some awful way, I'd doomed myself that night. I'd taken an adventure full of danger and kisses and made it far too idealistic. I put Nameless on a pedestal and figured if I couldn't have him, I didn't want anyone— effectively blinding myself to other prospects—other men who I had no doubt would be just as special and probably much better suited for me.

*Just because I don't like Greg doesn't mean I won't like every male in the world.*

And besides, I was still so young. Dad forgot my age most of the time. He saw me as the pillar of his company and his happiness. Because I didn't have a family of my own yet, he believed he'd failed.

Marrying me off wasn't about me but him.

*Why didn't I see it before?*

I slammed to a stop.

Dad was a good parent, but when it came to having everything neat and organized, he overlooked my age, wants, and who I was as an individual. So what if he wanted me to be partnered off?

I didn't. Not yet, at least.

It was time to tell him not to meddle in my life anymore and for me to stop using his heart attack as an excuse to bow to his every command.

Nodding in resolution, I strode off again with renewed vigor. The ache between my legs throbbed, making it hard to concentrate, but for the first time in years, I felt calmer. Like I'd taken control of my future in some small way.

I'd slept with Penn on my own terms. It hadn't ended as nicely as I'd hoped, but I'd used him and enjoyed it. I'd expanded Belle Elle with a line of adult toys. It was risky and tantalizing, but I'd made that decision.

I was in charge of all things.

*I can do this.*

*I can be honest with myself and him.*

Stepping off the sidewalk, I crossed the deserted street, heading toward the glow of the business district ahead.

Unfortunately, New York was bipolar when it came to a woman walking on her own. One moment, it could be the most welcoming host with its tidy streets and beckoning streetlights, and the next, it could switch into a two-faced joker with piles of rubbish and a lone hooded man patrolling toward me beneath a burned streetlight, letting darkness swallow it whole.

I slammed to a stop. My heart left its normal home in my ribs to split into two and drop into my legs.

In an ordinary situation, on a bright sunny day, having a faceless stranger prowl toward me wouldn't be an issue—mainly because I'd have David there. But in this situation? It bothered me. A lot.

Looking behind me, my brain came up with and discounted ideas as quickly as they came.

*Run.*

*Hide.*

*Walk forward.*

*Return to Penn's.*

*He's probably harmless.*

*You're reading into things.*

Regardless of the truth, none of my scattered thoughts were options because the hooded figure looked up, revealing the black void where his face should be. The distance between us vanished step by step. I crossed the street again, hoping I was just in his way and not his target.

The moment my feet touched the other side, the man copied me.

*Shit.*

The crunch of his dirty sneakers echoed in my ears as he came to a standstill a few feet ahead. His fists hung by his side, his long legs encased in black jeans while the dark gray hoodie was covered in red stains that I hoped were from ketchup and not other sinister goo.

I stopped breathing.

Was this the world's cruel joke? That I couldn't be safe on my own at all? That the two times I'd been without my dad, David, or another man, I was victim to anyone who wanted to prey on me?

Was the earth sexist and teaching me I needed a man to survive?

Anger scalded away my fear. "What do you want?"

The man chuckled. "Money."

"I don't have any. I left my purse with my driver."

*Shit, shouldn't have said driver.*

He licked his lips—the only thing visible beneath the cape of the hoodie. "Ah, you're one of those."

"One of what?"

"Rich bitches." He came closer, reeking of unwashed body and dirt. "Gimme your money, and no one gets hurt."

Three years ago, I would've screamed for help and bolted.

Now, I was handicapped in heels and aching from sex. I was older. I'd battled more wars with men in the corporate world. If he wanted money, fine. I would argue that he should go and earn some rather than steal from innocent pedestrians.

"Go away. I'm not interested."

"Not interested?" He cocked his head. "What part of 'gimme your money' sounds like a negotiation?"

I crossed my arms, hoping he wouldn't see my torn blouse beneath. "Doesn't matter. I'm not giving you any."

"Yes, you fucking are." His fists clenched. "Now."

"I'm not lying. I have no money."

He took another step, forcing me to take one back.

His lips turned up in a vindictive smirk. "Jewelry then." Trailing his eyes over me, he noticed my crystal earrings. "Those. Gimme."

Without hesitation, I pulled them from my lobes and handed them over. I wore nothing else. No bracelets or rings. The only necklace I'd loved was my sapphire star that'd been stolen from me in such similar circumstances.

"And the fucking rest." He palmed my thirty-dollar earrings I'd sampled from the Belle Elle costume jewelry rack as if they were the Hope diamond.

I splayed my hands, cursing my shaking. "I told you. I don't have anything else."

"Bullshit."

"I'm telling the truth."

He advanced again. This time, I held my ground even though my heart once again grabbed its rape whistle ready to blow.

"How about I search you? Make sure you're not lying?"

I gritted my teeth. "Touch me, and you die."

He laughed; it bounced off the buildings standing as witnesses to our standoff. "Sure, bitch. What you gonna do? Stab me with your shoe?"

I looked down at my patent silver pumps—the flash of bling to match my earrings. "Thanks for the idea."

Kicking one off, I quickly scooped it up and brandished the metallic spiky heel. "You've taken what I have. Now, get lost."

Pushing back his hood, he bared his teeth. He wasn't ugly, and he wasn't handsome. He was just a thief, hungry and doing bad things. "I don't think so, rich bitch."

Nothing about him was familiar, but he was a lonely man in a hoodie late at night.

My curiosity wouldn't forgive me if I didn't confirm for sure.

My tummy clenched as I went against survival and leaned in. I searched his face. I gave in to the consuming question that'd popped into my head the moment he'd appeared.

*Is it him?*

Was it Nameless?

But hope turned to dust.

*It isn't him.*

This man was older—pushing past thirty. His teeth were black, his skin sallow, his hair lank and thinning. He was skinny and about Nameless's height, but unless he was a really rough-looking older brother, my homeless savior wasn't here.

He charged forward, grabbing my breast with rancid fingers. "Can't pay me, then I might as well hurt you."

"Get your fucking hands off me!" I stumbled back, swinging my shoe, doing my best to connect.

He ducked, grabbing me.

I struck.

Vicious victory warmed me as the sharp heel grazed his temple.

"Fuck!" He reared back, holding the side of his face.

That was all I needed.

Kicking off my other shoe, I turned and transformed into something that could flee. A rabbit, a gazelle, a horse, a bird.

I pushed every ounce of power into my legs and struck off barefoot.

I didn't focus on the pebbles hurting my soles. I didn't scream as I stood on a piece of broken beer bottle. I didn't cry as my insides howled from being used and now forced to gallop.

I just focused on freedom. Like every day of my life.

"Come back here, you bitch. You owe me!" The footfalls of my assailant gave chase, driving me to grab every air molecule, transform every dreg of energy, and turn it into rocket fuel as propulsion.

I careened around the corner, spying Penn's building.

So far.

*I'll make it.*

I skidded on an old newspaper but didn't slow down.

The thief cursed and grumbled, keeping pace with me, slowly catching up.

Headlights appeared in the distance, bright and glowing, warm and welcoming.

I flew off the sidewalk, directly into the car's path.

Instead of slowing down to help, the vehicle sped up as if to run me over and deliver my corpse to the man currently wanting to hurt me.

I waved my arms. "Stop. Help!"

The darkness in the car showed a single driver, their hands clenching the wheel. He drove directly for me. I had a split second to decide what to do—where to run before he struck.

But the collision never happened.

The driver wrenched the steering and drove over the curb, slamming to a stop.

The engine screamed as the front door flung open and a man leaped from the interior. "Get in the fucking car." He pointed at me. "Now!"

It took a second to register.

My ears knew that voice.

My body knew that body.

I'd never been so thankful to see someone. Even if he'd thrown me from his house. Even if he hurt me in ways I wouldn't admit.

Penn threw himself over the hood as the man chasing me skidded to a standstill only an arm's length from grabbing me.

I pressed against the car, my mouth gulping air. My feet burning from sprinting on concrete and debris.

Then my pain was no more as Penn launched himself at the man. "You motherfucker."

Together, they went down.

Penn landed on top of him and didn't give gravity the joy of crunching him into the pavement before his fists rained on his face.

He didn't speak. Just beat him.

The robber did his best to cover his face with his arms, curling up, trying to push Penn off. But he didn't stand a chance.

I counted one, two, three, four, five fists to the jaw before Penn effortlessly pushed off from the man's chest and stood over him.

He cracked his knuckles as if he'd just washed his hands not doused them in some criminal's blood. "Rob again. Try to rape again. And you're fucking dead." With a black shoe, he kicked the man in the ribcage. "Got it?"

The guy looked up, blinking through a rivulet of blood. For a second, his eyes were blank, full of hate and rebellion. Then they focused on Penn's face. On the way he stood so regal and calm, demanding utmost obedience. Recognition popped in vibrant color, and the robber swayed to his feet, wrapping an arm around his kicked chest, and holding his head with the other. "Shit, it's you."

*What?*

I froze, desperate to know what he meant.

Penn stiffened. "Leave. Tonight is your lucky night."

The man nodded, dropping his eyes, forgetting I even existed. Turning in his filthy sneakers, he took off at a stumbling jog.

He ran away with my earrings, just like the men in the alley ran away with my sapphire star.

I'd been saved again, but this time...all I felt was terror not desire.

# Chapter Twenty-Four

"GET IN THE fucking car, Elle." Penn's voice remained low and hushed but rang with steely authority.

*He knew him.*

*He knew Penn.*

*How? Why? What does it mean?*

I blindly grabbed the door handle and cracked it open. Numb, I slid into the passenger seat as he strolled nonchalantly to the driver's side and climbed in.

A few seconds passed after the doors slammed shut, cocooning us in heavy, oppressive silence. His bloody knuckles clenched the steering wheel as if he could throttle it.

My throat had permanently closed with fear and questions. So, so many questions.

How did that man know Penn?

Who *was* Penn?

And why...just why...did he beat up that man with the same effortless grace as the man in the alley that fateful night?

Penn reached across the gear stick, placing his hand on my thigh.

I flinched, yanking my legs to the side.

His fingers dug into my muscle, keeping with me. He breathed hard, squeezed me, and then let me go. Pressing the clutch, he slid the still rumbling engine into gear and drove off the curb and back onto the road.

The bump jostled us, but we didn't speak.

I daren't.

I didn't know what to think.

Part of me wanted to over-analyze everything; to replay the

way he disciplined that guy and try to connect dots that weren't there. My imagination worked over-time, doing its best to believe that perhaps I knew Nameless' identity all along. That maybe, just maybe, he'd been the one to find me after all these years and not me failing to find him.

But one awful flaw sat like a toad in that perfect fantasy. Penn didn't have a gentle bone in his body like Nameless. Nameless was cool and prickly but beneath that armor had been kindness—sweet wrapped up in daggers.

Penn was just the blade, shiny and impenetrable, one dimensional with refracting surfaces to distort my true perception.

The only problem was I couldn't distinguish one punch from another. I was seeing things—making things up—trying to link two very separate incidents into one.

*To do what?*

*Find meaning in why I slept with Penn?*

Validation that I wasn't some romance-broken girl, after all?

"I owe you an apology." His voice barely registered over the hum of the tires on the road.

I tensed, staring out the window. "I owe you thanks."

His head snapped left and right in denial. "No. I kicked you out. I thought your driver would collect you, but then you walked off."

"You were watching me?"

He didn't reply. "You almost got hurt."

"But I didn't."

"If you had...fuck!" He punched the steering wheel, making the horn blare, shattering the sleep in many apartments. "I would've fucking killed him."

"I wouldn't have asked you to."

He glowered. "I wouldn't have done it for you."

"So you would've taken a life purely because you wanted to and not to somehow avenge me?"

"I would've killed him because he touched what wasn't his to touch."

My heart beat wild. "So you protected me, not because I shared your bed and gave up a significant part of me, but because in your twisted ideals, I'm a possession that only you can touch?"

His jaw worked as he drove fast through residential streets. "Yes."

"Not because you feel anything for me?"

"No."

"Anything at all."

"Nothing."

"But the sex was good."

"Yes."

"Do you want to see me again?" I hated that I had to ask; that I cared about the answer. He'd turned into a bastard who terrified me. He'd hurt that thief with such ease.

But with him emotionally withdrawn and icy, it helped remind me what we had was purely physical. I didn't like him. Not in the slightest. I didn't even feel some resemblance of gratitude-induced affection from him rescuing me. He turned everything that could be good and exciting into bad and unwanted.

But I'd tasted what sex could be like. And I wanted more. I wanted to be selfish for *me*. So, for now, I'd accept his asshole persona and ignore my questions.

"I don't know." His confession wasn't what I expected.

"You don't know if you want to sleep with me again?"

He half-smirked. "We didn't sleep together, Elle. We fucked."

"Thanks for the clarification." I huffed, crossing my arms. "Forgive me; do you want to fuck me again?"

His fingers latched tighter around the wheel, the leather creaking. For a moment, his head shook with a silent no. Then a cocky smirk stole the truth with yet another lie. "Yes, I want to fuck you again."

*Why the hesitation?*

*Why say we are engaged if he only intended to sleep with me once?*

*Why the cold shoulder and strict boundaries?*

*Why, why, why?*

"Good." I sat prim, reveling how the ache in my womb turned liquid again. "Me too." Testing my innocent mouth with erotic commands, I added, "I liked fucking you. I want more."

His gaze shot from the road to mine. "More?"

I swallowed, fighting back my embarrassment. "I want your uh…cock. I want you inside me again."

He groaned and focused on the road, the speed we traveled far too fast. "Fuck you for saying that."

"*Excuse* me?"

"You heard me."

I had no come-back for being cursed at.

How rude.

*What an ass!*

I sat silent, stewing as the neighborhood switched to one I

knew and my penthouse on top of the white sparkling building up ahead beckoned me home.

Home.

Where Sage would be waiting and Penn could fuck off with his secrets, curses, and lies.

Pulling to a stop, he turned off the car and climbed out.

I didn't wait for him to get my door. Cracking it open, I jumped out only to wince and hobble as the cuts from running tormented me.

"Fuck, look at your feet." Before I could reply, he scooped me into his arms and carried me toward my building.

The doorman nodded and opened the large entryway without showing any signs of shock. Penn left his black Mercedes coupe parked haphazardly on the street and marched me through the foyer of my building.

"Everything okay, Ms. Charlston?" Danny, the night manager, called. His lined face worried beneath the navy cap of his uniform. He eyed Penn with wariness.

Preventing me from yelling for help or for Danny to call security, Penn growled, "I'm taking my fiancée to her apartment. She's fine."

I squirmed in his arms. "You are not my fiancé. Stop telling everyone that." Waving at Danny, doing my best to keep up appearances rather than panic the neighborhood, I said, "Everything's fine. Sorry for the odd entry."

Danny waved back, frowning and unsure but polite enough not to intrude.

The moment we left the foyer and entered the bank of elevators, I hissed, "Put me down." I pushed at Penn's chest. "I can walk."

"Your feet are bleeding."

"I don't care. I want you gone."

He looked down, his brown eyes bordering oak-black. "That wasn't what you said a few moments ago."

"That was before you told me to fuck off."

"I didn't tell you to fuck off. I said fuck you. There's a difference."

"There's no difference."

He punched the elevator button and strode into it as the doors opened instantly. "Press your floor."

I did so then froze as the doors whispered shut, imprisoning us. "Wait, how the hell do you know where I live?"

"I researched."

"You stalked, you mean."

Once again, he didn't reply. The ride upward was awkward and strange and loaded with every foreign sensation imaginable. I hated him holding me, but I liked his protection at the same time. I hated the way he took control but liked his need to make sure I was safe.

*Ugh, I just hate him.*

*I don't like any of the other stuff.*

The elevator stopped, and Penn stepped off, pausing in the middle of the fancy wide hallway. Two doors—left and right. Two penthouses taking up one-half of the entire floor each.

He glanced at me. "Which one?"

I crossed my arms—or the best I could while reclining in his embrace. "Don't you already know?"

His gaze tangled with mine, deliberating to show me a truth or lie.

He chose the truth.

Striding toward the left door—the correct door—he waited while I inputted the nine-digit code rather than a simple key then leaned on the door handle to enter.

I made a mental note to change the sequence tomorrow, seeing as his eagle eyes had watched the nine digits with quick intelligence.

His attention swooped over my foyer where a chandelier hung from the ceiling in crystal glitter before pooling onto the floor with a glass table imprisoning it. For a statement piece, it had oodles of wow factor.

A loud meow sounded just before a silver streak charged from the white couch facing the floor-to-ceiling windows directly for Penn. Sage latched onto his leg, no doubt sinking her claws into his calf.

I laughed softly. "Seems I'm not the only one who doesn't like you."

"The feeling is mutual, I assure you." Wincing, he stalked forward—with Sage still clinging to his leg—entering my sleek kitchen, where every cupboard looked like a high gloss wall with no handles or appliances in sight—all hidden or magically designed to keep such necessities of life a mystery.

Placing me on the white bench top, he grabbed Sage, ripped her off his jeans, and plonked her down beside me. She swatted him, hissing, but immediately leaped into my lap and purred, stretching to lick my chin with her sandpaper tongue.

"You did well." I scratched her neck. "Thanks for protecting me."

Penn snorted, turning to locate the sink. He wouldn't find it. It was hidden beneath a large slab of bench top that revealed the tap and bowl with a press of a button by my orchid plant.

He searched for two seconds then stalked off, leaving me gaping after him.

*Where the hell is he going?*

A few moments later, he returned with a white towel from the guest powder room and a bowl that had contained blue marbles for decoration now filled with tepid water.

Without a word, he dropped to his knees and grabbed my foot.

I froze, speechless as he wet the towel then slowly, carefully, with all the tenderness in the world washed my feet, running the towel so, so gently over the lacerations from the beer bottle I'd run over.

I sucked in a gasp, my breath wobbly as he cleaned the towel and the water turned pink with my blood.

There was nothing else in that moment.

No questions. No lies. No lust.

Just him giving himself in ways I never imagined he would.

My heart stopped thudding, settling for the slightest tiptoe as if afraid one wrong move or noise would shatter this strange new existence.

His hands were swift but sure, soft but serious. He didn't tickle me while he felt my instep to make sure no debris remained, and he didn't take advantage when my legs spread with instinct as he rubbed my ankle with his thumb.

He tended to me, and once I was tended to, he stood, placed the bowl onto the counter, then grabbed my face in his warm hands.

He stared into my eyes, barriers in place, curtains protecting his true thoughts. He didn't speak, but he leaned forward and his lips claimed mine in the most sensual kiss I'd ever been given.

His tongue was velvet. His mouth cashmere.

I swooned into him, utterly seduced and unbound.

There was magic in this kiss, a spell promising secrets, a connection to sever all other connections.

And then, it was over.

As silently as he'd washed my feet, he turned around and

walked out of my apartment.
    Just like that.

# Chapter Twenty-Five

A FEW DAYS passed.

I didn't contact him.

He didn't contact me.

It was as if he never existed.

If it weren't for the fading cuts and bruises on my feet, I would've struggled to believe the night at his place even happened.

My mind was a broken record—even work couldn't distract me.

All I could think about was Penn washing my feet, Penn hitting that guy, Penn sliding inside me.

He'd shown two totally different sides of himself, and I couldn't unscramble what it meant. I'd hoped having some time to myself would deliver decisions on what to do. To make up my mind to forget about him or chase the answers slowly turning me hollow.

Spread-sheets and conferences calls didn't help, and the lack of contact did the opposite of what I wanted. My heart grew fonder (just like that stupid saying). My idiotic mind sketched him in a kinder light than the one he'd shown. I second-guessed his pretension and conceit, making up stories that would explain his sudden switch to guardian and medic all in one.

Just like my unpaid debt to Nameless, I had one toward Penn now. I owed him thanks at the very least for ensuring I returned home safe and my injuries were disinfected.

When he finally *did* text me, I no longer wanted him to fall off the face of the planet but was grateful to hear from him.

Penn (08:47a.m.): *How are your feet?*
Elle (08:52 a.m.): *Fine. I never said thanks for taking care of me.*
Penn (09:00 a.m.): *Are you saying it now?*

Elle (09:03 a.m.): *Maybe.*
Penn (09:06 a.m.): *Are you sore?*
Elle (09:08 a.m.): *My feet?*
Penn (09:08 a.m.): *No. The other part I touched that night.*

Sex between us exploded into my senses: sight, sound, taste, feel—I wasn't in my office but back in his bed. I had no intention of letting him know how much I wanted a second round.

Elle (09:09 a.m.): *Oh yes, that's right. I'd forgotten about that.*
Pen (09:10 a.m.): *Do you want me to refresh your memory?*
Elle (09:11 a.m.): *Perhaps you should.*
Penn (09:12 a.m.): *I want to fuck you again.*
Elle (09:14 a.m.): *So do it.*
Penn (09:17 a.m.): *Fair warning, I won't go so easy on you next time.*

I choked a little.

I'd played fairly easy to catch, and the thought of tangling in bed together sounded far too tempting. But if I let him into my body again, I might not be able to keep my feelings out of it. Damn him for washing my feet and showing me he could care. How could I keep my heart frosty if he'd thawed a little?

The answer was I couldn't.

We'd slept together. We'd had three days apart. It was a good time to end this charade before everyone he'd lied to got hurt. I'd thanked him. I could move on.

Elle (09:20 a.m.): *I've changed my mind.*
Penn (09:23 a.m.): *What the fuck does that mean?*
Elle (09:27 a.m.): *It means the sex was amazing, but it doesn't change the fact you lied to my father. You made him think he can relax knowing I'm going to be taken care of—his words, not mine. I can't let him believe we're truly together. He has heart issues. I enjoyed the other night but don't expect anything more. Let's end this now before it gets complicated.*

No text came back.

My phone vibrated alive in my hand.

*Penn calling…*

"Oh, shit." Huddling over my desk, I deliberated whether I should ignore the call. Problem was he knew I was around because I'd responded to his texts.

Sucking in a breath, I pressed accept. "Hello."

"Don't hello me, Elle."

"Okay…"

"Don't okay me, either. Especially in that tone." His voice dripped with sex, pooling directly into my core.

"Well, if you're not going to let me speak, why the hell did you call me?"

"I'll tell you why. Because I found your last message ridiculous."

I held my tongue, waiting for him to continue.

"It so happens I've spoken to your father."

"What?"

"And he approves of us."

"He'll approve of anyone with a penis and a pulse."

*As long as it's not Nameless or someone with a criminal record.*

"Thanks for that stab at my self-worth," he purred. "Nevertheless, I have a lunch date with him today. If you say you're sorry and admit you want me to make you come again, I might let you join us."

I couldn't do this.

"Hold up. You *might* let me come on a date with my *own* father?" I rolled my eyes, glowering at Sage as she pranced over my desk. "I can't hear you because your ego is so inflated."

"I think you mean my cock. My cock is inflated thinking about fucking you again." His voice dropped from crude to cool. "I'm meeting your father at the Tropics in three hours. Come or don't. Your choice."

He hung up.

I had a good mind to call him back and screech that I wasn't some possession to be played or a toy to be tormented. But someone knocked on my door. "Elle?"

*Oh no, this day just keeps getting worse.*

"Yes, Greg, you can come in."

He strode in with all the arrogant airs of a playboy dressed in a baby blue polo and pressed jeans. His dark blond hair was tussled in just the right way to hint he was always this good looking with no effort, when I happened to know—from many childhood get-togethers—that he took *hours* in the bathroom manscaping.

Yet another reason why I could never be with Greg. He valued his appearance more than any other thing in his life…including whatever woman he ended up with as his wife.

"Hi, Elle." He perched on the edge of my desk, his butt

nudging aside paperclips and scattering pens. "Whatcha doing today?"

Sage gave him a kitty-glower and leaped off the glass to return to her nest of blankets by my feet.

I forced myself not to roll my eyes. "The usual. Running my family's company. You?"

"Just had the weekly brief with my old man. Logistics is boring compared to all the number-juggling you guys get to do up here."

When Greg left school, Steve and my father had worked out a position for him to fill. A position that wouldn't affect Belle Elle's reputation or bottom line if he lost interest or screwed up. Being the head of the logistics department ought to be a full-time, full-on occupation, but his executive assistant was far too good at her job, and Greg took that as an opportunity to play retired.

"It's not fun." I smiled huge and bright. "Believe me."

*And you're not allowed to fiddle with things you know nothing about and don't give two craps over.*

He plucked my turquoise ink fountain pen and spun it in his fingers. "Want to go to dinner with me tonight? Hanging at the Palm Politics with those girls from your school was fun." He flashed me a grin. "I enjoyed it. And I know our fathers did. They're so happy we got together on our own accord and not at a family dinner."

Unable to help myself, I grabbed the pen from his fingers and placed it back on the desk. "Sorry, Greg, I'm busy. Maybe next time."

"Next time what?" His eyes narrowed, that edge of darkness revealing itself. "Next week, you mean? Next month? When, Elle? I'm not going to wait around for you forever, you know."

The faintest clanging of warning bells began. His smile remained, but the harsh malice he managed to hide so well glimmered.

I sat taller. My will to be cordial faded under the need to kick him in the balls and show him that he might've seen me in tutus and crying over bullies, but he didn't know me now. I wouldn't put up with his passive-aggressive behavior—certainly not in my office.

"I never asked you to wait, Greg. In fact, I distinctly remember telling you I only want to be friends."

He scoffed, once again snatching my pen, daring me to steal it back as he clenched it hard in his fist. "See, that's the thing with you, Elle. You send mixed messages."

I rubbed the anger prickling my arms. "Don't confuse your own meddling for my approval."

He leaned forward, bringing spite and jealousy whiffing into my nose. "I don't meddle. You want me. Everyone fucking knows that."

I pursed my lips, hating the way my heart scampered when I wanted to remain angry.

It would be so easy to do what Penn did and lie. To say I was with him now. Engaged. But I wouldn't do that because I didn't need Penn to fight my battles for me. Besides, Penn had told him point blank that I was his now, yet Greg tried to claim me anyway.

I went with a roundabout lie. A dressed-up little fib. "You're mistaken. I'm with someone."

"Bullshit. Go out with me. One date. What's so bad about me that you won't even *eat* with me?" His annoyance shimmered like a bloodthirsty guillotine ready to fall. "Stop being such a bitch."

The gentle clanging of bells turned into an orchestra of caution. I *hated* him looming over me, perched on my desk. I stood, pushing my chair back, and crossing my arms. "Call me a bitch again, and I'll have you fired."

He slapped his thigh. "God, you're adorable when you act all CEO."

I ignored that.

Reaching for the only thing—the only person—who popped into my head, I snapped, "Are you expecting me to cheat on, Penn?"

He guffawed. "Cheat? Come on, Elle. I know it's all a scam. You've known the guy two minutes. I've known you for twenty-two years. He doesn't stand a chance." He leaned forward, smelling clean and soap-like compared to Penn's mysterious deep aftershave. "You're having a fling. Shit, I've had them too. You think I mind if you fuck him?"

I bared my teeth, holding my ground. "You should if you're as in love with me as you claim."

His smile was toxic. "Love? Who said anything about love? I said we're meant to be together. We're compatible. Our families own Belle Elle, and we work side by side. I'm not afraid of some bullshit asshole who thinks he can steal what's mine by sticking his dick in you."

Every nerve ending wanted to bolt out the door. My eyes shot to the intercom button where Fleur could bring reinforcements.

Alone with him in my office was worse than alone on a street with a thief.

*I can't let him get away with this idiocy. Such treason.*

Rebuttals came swift, forming fast on the typewriter of my mind, slipping into orderly fashion to school him. I'd had enough practice with bastards like him.

*You don't intimidate me, asshole.*

Greg continued, loving the sound of his own threat. "You've had your fling, Elle. But I'm the one you're meant to be with. I'm the one who has our fathers' blessings, and I'm the one who deserves Belle Elle, not him or some other schmuck who thinks they can steal what's mine—"

My patience snapped.

I left prim and proper and embraced fire and ferocity.

Grabbing his baby blue polo in my fist, I yanked him off my desk. He stumbled to his feet, shock making him pliable.

"Listen to me, Greg, and listen good." My voice was a hiss. "You will never and have never owned Belle Elle. Belle Elle is *mine*. You work here. You. Are. My. Employee. If you think I would *ever* marry someone like you—someone pompous and self-centered and nasty—then all the years together haven't taught you a thing. I *rule* you, Greg, so get the fuck out of my office, get back to logistics, do your goddamn job, and if you ever try to threaten me again, I'll call the police." I shoved him away from me. "Am I perfectly clear?"

For a second, the world teetered. Two scenarios lived side by side.

One, me bleeding on the floor from Greg's punch, my skirt ripped, and his hands where they should never be.

And two, him backing down and finally conceding defeat.

I was stupid not to recognize the war brewing between us. To let Steve and my father make it seem like a harmless flirtation while Greg had already kicked me from my office and plastered his name over the plaque on the door.

He'd been counting my money and power since he left diapers.

"This is the end of whatever this is, got it?" I held my head high and pointed at the door. Sage meowed loudly in support. "Leave. Now. I won't ask again."

Slowly, a sly smile slithered over his lips. He no longer looked preppy but provoked and already planning retaliation. "I see you're not a little girl any longer, Elle." He swayed forward. "I like it."

"Get out!"

He chuckled and strode to the door, leaving me gobsmacked that he'd obeyed.

Opening it, he turned and blew me a kiss. "Just so you know, your little speech was cute, but I know you don't mean it. You're as much a liar as that asshole you're fucking." He wiggled his fingers condescendingly in goodbye. "I'll visit you next week, Elle—give you some time to cool down."

His eyes turned to ice. "However, the next time I come for you; next time I ask politely for you to join me on a date, you're going to say yes, Noelle. Just watch."

# Chapter Twenty-Six

"ELLE! WHAT A pleasant surprise." My father stood from the neatly dressed table with a toucan bird arrangement and multi-colored water glasses stark against the white table-cloth. Even the cutlery had splashes of color in the form of engraved parrot feathers on the handles. The restaurant wasn't called the Tropics for nothing.

"Hi, Dad." I accepted his cheek-kiss, smoothing down my light gray dress with black and pink panels on the sides. The skirt was tight, just like the bodice, making self-consciousness tangle with the anxious residue of dealing with Greg.

He wouldn't back down—I saw that now.

I'd done my best to be productive after he'd left, but my instincts wouldn't stop ringing those damn awful alarm bells, and my mind ran in a panic trying to find a solution.

I'd told Greg I would fire him, but without cause, he could sue. Not to mention the mess it would cause between Dad and Steve.

They were best-friends. Such good friends, I honestly didn't know whose side Dad would pick if I told him I wanted Greg dealt with and gone.

I sucked in a breath, trying to calm down. The stupid couture dress restricted my ribs from expanding. Once again, I'd been dressed in something against my will.

When I'd told Fleur to hold my afternoon meetings because I had to go monitor a lunch between my father and Penn, she shot down to the retail floor and returned with this dress, a lace scarf made from bohemian wool (whatever that was), and single stud diamond earrings.

My hair she left loose but added a few curls while the rest she straightened. It hung even longer than normal down my back.

"What are you doing here?" My father smiled, pulling out a chair and inviting me to sit. "Not that I don't want you here, of course."

I knew Dad would arrive fifteen minutes before Penn. He was forever punctual—to meetings or lunch dates, even the theater productions my school forced me to participate in when I was a child.

Penn would be on time, I had no doubt. But I would use these few precious minutes alone with Dad to my advantage. First, I would deal with Penn, and then I would deal with Greg.

Not wasting any time, I grabbed the yellow and green napkin and spread it over my lap. "We need to talk, Dad. Quickly before Penn shows up."

His eyebrow rose. "How did you know he's my lunch companion?"

"Because he told me. He mentioned I could join, so I'm not gate crashing without an invitation."

His face melted with romance. "Ah, young love. He can't stand to spend even a few hours away from you."

*Yes, that's why he's avoided me for three days.*

I avoided telling him that, along with all the other secrets I suddenly seemed to have from my father.

*Is that what lust and love do? Does it segment off a person's life from shareable to private?*

I'd been so open about my entire world before Penn came along. Now, I struggled for subjects that were appropriate.

Taking a sip of the water already sparkling in rainbow glasses, I blurted, "Penn and I aren't really engaged—just like I've been telling you from the beginning."

Dad froze. "What?"

"He lied to you. I have no idea what he intends to do or say today, but I wanted to tell you...none of it is true. If he starts telling you I'm pregnant or that we're eloping to Cuba or I'm moving in with him...don't believe a word of it. Okay?"

His face turned white. He reached for his water.

Fear for his heart tried to gag me, to steal back what I'd said and tell him it was all a misunderstanding; that I was the one lying. Only, he shocked me by asking, "*Could* you be pregnant?" His eyes filled with wisdom he didn't often let me see. For a man so successful in business, he embraced his kooky nature and whimsical fancy so much, he made me forget how intelligent he was—how no deal—good or bad—went through without his scrutiny. "Why would he lie about you being pregnant if there is no truth to you being together?"

My lips glued tight. I had no answer to that.

He lowered his voice, glancing at the other diners in the quaint restaurant that served healthy salads and light lunches. The ceiling had been painted with a rainforest canopy. The windows adorned with artwork of dangling spider monkeys while the occasional python dripped from a light fixture. "Be honest now, Bell Button."

I shook my head. "I'm—no. We're not together."

"But you have been."

"We're not engaged. That's all you need to know."

"Not yet, anyway. I admit it was a bit quick, and I was going to address his intentions today and get to know him a little better, but you can't deny you're interested in him and he's interested in you. It's all over you, Elle."

I didn't like the sound of that.

*What's all over me?*

The tension from dealing with Greg, or the apprehension from dealing with Penn?

I missed uncomplicated. I missed being alone without males messing things up.

Brushing aside that nasty revelation, I leaned forward. "If I ask you to do something for me...would you?"

He answered with no hesitation. "Anything. You know that." He placed his hand over mine on my napkin. "Name it."

"Hire a private investigator."

"What?"

"Research Penn Everett."

"Why?" His eyes narrowed. "Has he hurt you? Did something happen?" He looked me up and down as if he could see bruises and misdoings and was ready to shoot the guy in a wild west duel.

"No, but something doesn't sit right. Something happened the other night. It made me think about the man I mentioned when I was arrested in Central Park."

His body language shut down.

He removed his touch, sitting taller in his chair. "I thought we agreed that that nonsense was over. You did your best to find that boy. I shuttled you around law courts and police stations with nothing more than a vague description. I was patient, Elle. I went along with your desire to track him down, but we didn't find him. I thought you'd let that go."

*I only let you think that. I'm still looking. Still hoping.*

"I had—I mean, I have. But I would like someone to look into Penn's background. Where he's from, who his parents are, what does he do? Does he have a criminal record, for goodness' sake? Is that too much to ask?"

"It's not too much to ask." That sexy, silky commanding tone slipped down the back of my neck. "In fact, if you do exactly that—ask—I'll gladly fill in those blanks without hiring someone to tell you."

"Ah, Mr. Everett. I mean, Penn." My father stood, extending his hand in welcome. "Pleasure to see you again."

I remained straight-backed in my chair, not apologizing for what Penn had overheard even when I wanted nothing more than to huddle in shame.

Penn shook Dad's hand then turned his endless dark gaze on me. "Go ahead, Elle. I invited you here so you could ask questions. That we might have a conversation rather than base our connection on purely physical."

I blanched, glancing at Dad. Penn just admitted we had a sexual relationship.

My father crinkled his nose a little before clearing his throat and offering Penn to take the seat next to me. "Yes, conversation can be very worthwhile. I think it's a great idea." He glared in my direction. His stare said it all: *you want to know something? Now is the time…so ask.*

# Chapter Twenty-Seven

MY QUESTIONS SAT heavier and heavier with every second that ticked past.

This sham of a lunch date had been going on for forty minutes in which time a waitress in a bright orange uniform had taken our orders: Dad had a Vietnamese pork salad, Penn had a Thai beef noodle, and I had a mango fish salsa.

The artfully presented meals had been delivered, and as we ate, Penn and my father shared tidbits of golfing handicaps, best courses around America, what Penn planned to do with his benefactor now he was feeling better, and every other boring nonsense non-important topic they could cover.

Not once did he mention Stewart—his son.

Not a peep about Larry—his friend/brother/father/secret lover.

Not a whisper on the past he refused to share.

By the time I'd finished eating, my stomach churned, and anger simmered so hot, I couldn't damper it no matter how much water I drank.

Greg had ignited my temper. Penn just added rocket fuel.

Dad noticed I was strung up. He didn't make it easier on me by trying to link me into conversations with open-ended suggestions like, "Elle used to come with me on the odd time I went fishing. Do you like to fish, Penn? Perhaps you two could spend some time together away from the city?"

Penn pushed away his empty plate, cradling a glass of water. He hadn't ordered any alcohol as if he didn't want his mind to be affected in any way. "I don't like to fish. But I'm open to spending time with Elle in other ways." He licked his bottom lip free from a water droplet. "In fact, we could go away next weekend, if you'd like? I have to visit a friend out of the city."

I crossed my utensils, pushing away the rest of my lunch. It was now or never. "What friend?"

Dad glanced at me, hearing my sharp tone. He didn't reprimand, though. Settling into his chair, he gave Penn and me the space to discuss everything we'd left unsaid.

Penn placed his glass on the table, narrowing his eyes.

This was the start of the battle.

*Bring it on.*

"Do you really want to know the truth, Elle?"

"Yes."

"Sometimes lies are easier."

"Truth is the only thing I want."

"Fine." He ran a hand through his hair, disrupting the dark shine, encouraging wayward highlights to glimmer. "My friend is in Fishkill Correctional Facility. I visit him when time permits."

"Prison?" I frowned. "Wait, isn't that a place for mentally disturbed?"

"Insane people?" Penn shook his head. "It used to be. Not anymore. Now it's a medium security."

Dad leaned forward, finishing off his pork salad with a grimace. The glow of Penn's company and rosy hope for a happy future was marred by the mention of a prison.

I chewed a smile.

Dad asked, "What did your friend do?"

Penn cleared his throat—not in an embarrassed way but more of a 'how much to reveal' pause. "He's a thief."

*A thief.*

The punches from the other night.

The way Penn didn't hesitate to cause bodily harm.

There'd been two in that alley three years ago. Two men who'd tried to rob and rape me. Was it possible Penn was one of them? Or was he Nameless? A cold-hearted version of the hero with no remaining empathy? Or was he someone completely different and I'd made all the clues up in my head?

I needed to focus, but after dealing with Greg, I struggled to see Penn as much as a threat as I did before. He was a nuisance with his story-telling, but he wasn't malicious like Greg had revealed.

I couldn't decide what question to ask, so I skipped to another just as important. "Does your son live with you?"

Penn scowled, his body tensing against the subject change. "Why do you think he's my son?"

I scrunched my napkin. Was he about to lie again? "I saw you at Belle Elle. He spoke about you and Larry as father figures."

"Father figures," he repeated noncommittally.

"What does that even mean?" My temper spiked. "You are, or you're not."

"I am, and I'm not."

I crossed my arms, doing my best not to overflow with annoyance. "That isn't even an answer."

Dad jumped in. "What you're saying is he's adopted?"

Penn smiled, granting him respect but not me. "On the way to being adopted, yes."

"On the way?" I sniped.

"Yes, the paperwork has been filed. We're awaiting the good news."

"We?"

"Larry and I."

"So you *are* gay?"

Penn looked at me condescendingly as if I just didn't get it. "No, Elle. I'm not gay." Taking another sip of water, his eyes darkened over the rim. "I thought we clarified that the other night when you came to my home asking me to help you with a small matter."

Dad locked his gaze on me. "A small matter? Is everything okay, Elle?"

I fought the heat blooming on my cheeks. "Yes." My teeth locked together, making it hard to reply. "Fine. Penn is just being troublesome."

"*I'm* being troublesome?" He pointed at himself, shaking his head. "I think you'll find I'm being nothing but cooperative."

"If you were being cooperative, you would tell me who you truly are, where you came from, who Larry is, who Stewie belongs to, and what the hell your friend is doing in Fishkill." I breathed hard, not caring my father watched me as if I was about to snap. I'd already snapped once today, and I bounced on the tightrope to break again. "Tell me the truth, Penn—if that is even your name. Then perhaps we'll see how cooperative I can be."

Silence cloaked the table. My outburst rang in my ears.

Penn didn't move.

Dad shifted in his seat, but I remained locked in a vision battle with the man who'd taken my virginity, kicked me out, then rescued me.

I didn't want to admit it, but beneath my hate and dislike and mistrust and wariness was the fluttering of feelings. When he'd washed my feet...I'd softened. When he'd pressed inside me, I'd caved. I didn't want to acknowledge it, but he'd affected me more than just physically.

And I hated that more than anything.

*This isn't worth it.*

I had a business to run. Greg to deal with. Distractions such as this were a waste of my time.

Standing, I threw my napkin on my dirty plate and sniffed. "You know what? I no longer care. It was a pleasure getting to know you, Mr. Everett, but I don't want to see you again."

Turning to my father, I added, "We're not engaged, Dad, nor have we ever been, trust me. I slept with him—you might as well know that, seeing as he's implied it in every innuendo he could. Do I feel good about that? No. Do I regret it? Yes. Am I pissed he lied to you about our engagement? More than anything. Now, if you'll excuse me, I'm returning to the office where I'm in control and don't have to put up with men like him—" I pointed a finger at Penn's carefully schooled expression.

I didn't wait for my father's reply. Or for Penn's rebuttal.

As I stalked past tables full of laughing diners, I crushed my heart for flying so fast. I'd done nothing but run away from that man since we'd met.

I disguised it with bluster and bravery, but really, I was terrified of him.

Petrified of the way he made me feel beneath my dislike.

Scared of the way my instincts nudged me harder and harder to look past the man and see someone I thought I'd never find.

But most of all, I was disappointed in myself.

Because for the first time, I'd been the one to lie.

Everything I'd said to my father, every word I'd growled about Penn—wasn't true.

I felt good about sleeping with him.

I didn't regret a thing.

And yes, I was annoyed about his lies, but I was more interested in the snippets of truth behind them.

It didn't matter now.

I had other fights to win.

*It's over.*

# Chapter Twenty-Eight

CENTRAL PARK HAD two faces.

The sinful one it showed in silver moonlight with hooded nameless men, and the innocent one where sunshine dappled green grass and children squealed in the distance.

It'd been so long since I'd strolled through the lush greenery.

Three years too long.

*Nameless...*

He was in the trees and the breeze.

He was all around me but never there.

My heels clipped on the sidewalk, keeping me locked in the fury vortex of the restaurant. Needing to calm my heart rate, I slipped off the pretty pink (but crippling) shoes and switched pavement for turf.

The springy softness gave simplicity to the complication my life had become over the past few weeks.

The Tropics restaurant was nestled in a prime position on the border of the park. I had intended to call David immediately to collect me, but then the sunshine promised to calm me before book-keeping and running staff added a different kind of stress.

I would walk for a bit, soak up some vitamin D, and then call David to return to Belle Elle and deal with the pile of worry I'd left there. I'd cuddle Sage, work until my eyes were too sore, then return home and lock every single door against the world.

I hadn't gone far—a few minutes at most when footsteps sounded behind me. Firm and faultless, masculine and moving fast.

My back tingled as I strode into a faster pace.

If it was who I thought it was, I didn't want to talk to him.

Pacing quicker didn't help.

Angry fingers looped around my elbow, yanking me

backward. "You don't get to leave, Elle. Not like that." His eyes were brighter in the sun—more aged port than oak whiskey. A few lines etched around his mouth as if he struggled just as much as I did.

Which didn't make any sense, as he'd been the one messing me around since the beginning. He was the one who'd caused Greg to explode with jealousy and threaten me. He was at fault in all of this.

I jerked my arm back, breaking his hold. He only let me go because a woman with a stroller narrowed her eyes as she went past. "Stop following me." I fell into another barefoot stride, cursing him when he matched my rhythm, joining me on the grass, his black shoes glinting in the sun.

I hated that in his graphite suit with ice blue shirt, he came across as priceless and sharp as a diamond. There were no mistakes in his veneer. No hesitation—as if he held all the clues.

*Which he does.*

"You ask questions, yet didn't stick around to hear the answers."

I snorted. "As if you'd tell me the truth."

His fingers looped with mine, pulling me back gently this time.

I gasped as he ran his thumb over my knuckles. His face softened. His shoulders fell. Somehow, he switched the fight between us into a white flag. The urge to push and push—to crack his façade—paused, willing to accept him in that moment. Mask and all.

He half-smiled, a mixture of reluctance and tolerance. "Try me. Ask again."

I blinked as the sun blinded me, dancing off his hair, hiding his face for a second, so he stood there with no features or belonging to a name.

He could've been anyone.

He could've been Nameless.

He could've been one of the men who mugged me.

*He's a stranger I let inside me.*

I shuddered at a how irresponsible I'd been. How I'd let myself be glamoured by his fancy games and pretty face. How I'd let lust take ordinary brain cells and transform them into flirtatious floozies.

*I don't like him.*

*I don't like him.*

*I don't.*

The sun sparkled, burning my lies even as I forced them to be true.

Tiredness suddenly blanketed me, heavy and thick, stifling and oppressive. There was only one answer I needed to make all the other questions obsolete. Just one. The biggest one of all. "You want me to ask? Fine, I'll ask." I inhaled deep and jumped in. "Where you were on the 19th of June three years ago?"

Nothing happened.

No trumpets, no choir, no streamers at winning the magical prize for asking the right question.

There was no flinch or shock or outright denial.

The date when I'd met Nameless, when I'd kissed him in this very park, meant absolutely nothing to Penn.

His body remained relaxed, his head cocked curiously to the side. "What?"

I wanted to tell him to forget it.

That all my silly sleuthing and ponderings were wrong.

I had my answer.

But now I'd ripped off that particular bandage, I couldn't stop. I had to let it out before it crippled me. "It was my nineteenth birthday. I ran away from Belle Elle for one night alone. I walked, I explored, I was hurt by two men. A third saved me." I sucked in a breath as emotions that should've subdued and faded by now swelled. "He brought me here. To Central Park. We kissed." I moved closer.

He stepped back, his face hardening with things I couldn't decipher.

"We ate chocolate. We *felt* something—"

"Penn, there you are. You're sooner than I expected."

A man appeared from the passing crowd, holding a remote control airplane with Stewie by his side. The kid clutched a controller as if dying to activate the plane and send it soaring rather than leave it trapped in the older man's grip.

Penn exhaled hard, his face etched with things I desperately wanted to understand. His posture had somehow lost its sedate softness, mimicking a granite statue. His mouth a tight line. His fists curled rocks.

Tearing his gaze away from mine, he visibly struggled to smile. He shoved his hands into his pockets in a mixture of defiance and self-protection—just like another I'd known once upon a time. "Hi, Larry."

I jolted.

Larry.

*So this is Larry.*

My habit of studying people who were either in business or in some way advantageous to me came back. I guessed Larry was in his mid-sixties with salt and pepper hair, stocky build, and intelligence brimming behind black framed glasses. He looked at Penn with utmost fondness and pride.

Penn took a step back from me.

Invisible ropes snapped, untethering us with painful ricochets.

My previous confession vanished as if it'd never been, destined never to be clarified or denied.

Clearing his throat, Penn regrouped and performed social niceties. "Larry, this is Noelle Charlston. Elle, this is Larry Barns. My benefactor."

Two answers in one.

Larry and I nodded, extending hands to shake. His grip was warm from holding the airplane, his fingers gruff but kind. "Pleasure. I've heard a lot about you."

My eyes widened as I flicked a quick glance to Penn. When, how, and why would Penn discuss this sorry excuse of a relationship? Why would he talk to another yet never talk to me?

*Because you're just a girl in his bed. This man shares his life and secrets.*

I'd never been a jealous person, but I suddenly understood the green acrimony knowing Penn would never let me in like Larry. That I was wasting my time—time I'd stupidly spent when I'd promised myself my heart was impartial to whatever Penn conjured.

Jumping in before Penn could, I said, "Happy to meet you, too. I've heard your name in passing." A small part of me wanted to hurt Penn; to ruin whatever tales he'd told this man about me. "I must clarify a few things upfront. I'm not engaged to Penn and have no intention of ever doing so."

Larry chuckled. "Oh, I know you're not engaged."

I took a step back. "Ah, well, I'm glad. I wasn't aware what rendition of lies Penn had told you."

Penn had the decency to flinch. "I might not have ethics as pure as you, but I don't lie to Larry. Ever."

They shared a look that weighed with countless years, trials, and confidentiality.

The intimacy made me uncomfortable. Not because they were lovers, like I'd thought, but because they were father and son in every sense of the word. It didn't matter they had different last names and most likely blood—family was created not born.

My eyes fell to the boy still hankering after his remote control airplane. His hair tousled in the wind, his eyes bright and happy.

Stewie was part of that family. Soon—according to Penn— he'd be legally part of it if it were true about an adoption. But that didn't help unscramble my other questions. If Penn was adopting Stewie, did that mean he knew Stewie's mother and felt obligated? Perhaps, Larry was the one adopting and not Penn? Would that make Stewie his brother?

What titles did each have in this weird family dynamic? My head hurt trying to figure it out.

Stewie tucked the controller under his arm, reaching for the airplane in Larry's hold. "If you guys are gonna stand around talking, I'm gonna fly Bumble Bee." In typical boy fashion, he hadn't acknowledged me or noticed the heavy tension between the adults.

I took a deep breath, ignoring the men and focusing on the boy. "Your plane is called Bumble Bee?"

Stewie nodded. "Yup." He pointed at the tail where a hand painted bee in its black and yellow glory glowed.

"Wow, very cool. Bet it hovers really well."

"Nah, it soars." Stewie grinned. Today, he wasn't in the suit Penn had had tailored for him. Instead, he wore jeans and a green t-shirt with the slogan, *I don't think outside the box. I never got in it.*

His innocence tugged at a piece of me. I envied him a little. Envied him for being a part of Penn's life—knowing him in a way I didn't and probably never would. Even if we did give our connection a chance, how could I ever be sure what he told me was the truth?

Larry asked, "Did you have a good lunch together?"

I raised an eyebrow at Penn, letting him answer that. He muttered, "It ended sooner than it should've."

I nodded at his reply. "It did. But for valid reasons."

Larry rubbed his jaw, brushing gray bristles from not shaving this morning. "Ah, I see." He smiled. "Well, I have no doubt Penn will make up for it, Elle. You don't mind if I call you Elle, do you?"

I shook my head. "No, it's fine."

"Come on...can I fly?" Stewie shuffled on the spot, eyeing the open grass just down the path.

Larry chuckled. "Yes, yes, impatient one. Let's go."

Stewie whooped and shot off, carrying the massive plane like he would an oversize puppy with his arms wrapped tight.

"You're welcome to come and watch," Larry invited, motioning for me to join him.

My first instinct was to shake my head and back away. "Oh, no, that's all right."

But Penn stepped closer, his eyes dazzling in the sun. "Come."

He blinded me. Dumbfounded me. Did he always look so resplendent, so persuading? Or was it the warmth of the sunshine and the fact my body heated with now familiar need? I no longer had skin but a map of desire that needed to be touched. "I don't know—"

"You want answers, but you're too afraid to chase them." He stepped back, withdrawing his overpowering intensity for me to go with them. "I thought you knew how to fight harder than that."

His voice deepened on the word fight.

My ears twitched.

Was he admitting to something?

Or was it me merely reading into things again?

"Come on, Elle. Ten minutes. What's the harm?" Larry grinned. "I'd be honored to enjoy your company a little longer."

My willpower fizzled.

I found myself nodding. "Okay."

# Chapter Twenty-Nine

STEWIE WAS RIGHT.

Bumble Bee did soar, climbing past the treeline into the cerulean blue horizon.

"He's done that a few times." I squinted upward, my hand shielding my eyes from the glare.

"He has. It was his birthday present a few months ago. Every chance he gets, he practices." Larry clapped as Stewie executed a perfect swan dive and recovery. "He's obsessive about things he wants. Doesn't let it go until he's perfected whatever it is he's chasing."

Penn stood on the other side of Larry, closed off to me, using the excuse to watch Stewie's aerobatics to avoid looking at me.

Stewie ran forward as the plane caught a gust of air and wobbled mid-flight. He didn't look where he was going and tripped over a twig in the middle of the field.

"Oh, no!" I slapped a hand to my mouth as Stewie toppled forward.

Penn charged.

With speed not quite human, he scooped Stewie mid-fall and swept him around in a circle using his inertia before placing him on his feet.

Stewie laughed, high-fived him, and continued flying his plane as if nothing had happened.

Yet *everything* had happened.

To me, at least.

In that microsecond when Penn caught Stewie, all shields were down. He was younger, older, kinder, crueler, innocent, and guilty all at once. I saw hints of what I daren't believe was possible. My heart took over and hammered with hope.

Each thud was a question.

*What if?*
*What if?*
*What if?*
What if Penn was Nameless?

What if Larry had somehow found him, saved him from prison, and done what I'd failed to do?

What if he'd come back for me?

But if that was true, why was he so mean? Why so closed off and impenetrable? We'd felt something that night. Something real if only so fleeting. Why punish me?

*Would you listen to yourself?*

*You're making up stories that have no earthly way of being true.*

*You're worse than Disney with your ideals of true love against any odds.*

*This is reality, Elle!*

Larry interrupted my inner scalding. "Penn said you have questions that he hasn't answered yet."

I startled. "He admitted to that?"

"Of course. We're open about most things."

"That's an honorable thing." I knitted my fingers together. "He told me you'd come to New York for treatment. Judging by how well you look, I think it worked."

Larry ran a hand over his bristle-covered jaw. "I hate that I had to lean on him so much." His smile was sad. "Nothing has more power than seeing someone you care about sick or grieving." He shrugged the sudden dysphoria away. "But you're right. The treatment worked. Thank goodness. I wasn't prepared to leave just yet. I have too many things to do before I go."

"Things?"

"People and things." He smiled secretively. "My work, and now Penn's, is never done."

My brain dried up. I had no reply. I didn't know what he meant or how to ask for clarification.

"Penn mentioned he'd taken you to the new building he just bought. What did you think?" Larry prompted with a new but just as aggravating subject.

"What did I think?"

"All that space. It's exciting, isn't it?"

"Space to do what?"

Larry winked. "He'll tell you. It's not my secret to ruin." He looked at me pointedly. "I see you struggling. If my suggestion means anything—which I know is asking a lot, seeing as you don't know me—but if you want to know him, give him a chance. It isn't what you think. And you'll need an open mind to accept. But we're all a little corrupt, doing our best to fit into a world that's broken but still demands perfection."

"What—what do you mean by that?"

"I mean thieves can become saints. Saints can become thieves. Most of us deserve a second chance."

Penn looked up at that moment, his dark gaze targeting mine. He half-smiled, his hands loose by his sides, his body straight but not as stiff as before. Without thinking, he placed his palm on Stewie's shoulder as he bumped into him, racing below Bumble Bee not looking where his feet were going.

That simple caress—so expected and wanted was enough to crack my already fractured shell.

Penn's hair was no longer shiny with sunlight but covered with a black baseball cap. Either Stewie had given it to him, or he'd had it hidden in a pocket. Either way, it shielded his eyes, and I saw another scenario I didn't want to see.

Penn could easily be no one. He could be someone. He could be pain or happiness or heartbreak.

That was the problem.

How was I supposed to fall for a liar?

Blindly?

Trustingly?

Not at all?

I needed time.

I needed space.

*I need to think.*

"It was lovely to meet you, Larry." I tore my gaze from Penn's and smiled at the older gentleman. "I've got to go."

I left before Penn could change my mind for the second time.

# Chapter Thirty

SAGE CURLED UP on my lap as I sipped a glass of sparkling apple juice and stared at some TV program I hadn't paid attention to for the past two hours.

Ever since leaving Central Park, I'd been in a fog I couldn't shake.

I'd returned to work but had been absolutely hopeless. Steve had found me heading into my office and asked how Greg and I were. He acted as if he didn't know his son had threatened me, and I didn't want to flippantly tell him in a Belle Elle hallway. I scheduled a meeting with him next time he was free to discuss a leash for his wild heathen of a son.

Dad hadn't returned to the office after the restaurant, Fleur answered my urgent emails on my behalf, and for the first time since I had my appendix out two and half years ago, I claimed health reasons and headed home to do my best to get my head on straight.

Greg worried me.

Dad concerned me.

Steve annoyed me.

And Penn…Penn claimed my thoughts in my home as much as he had in the park or at my office.

My heart had a box with three different puzzles mixed up inside. The pieces were tangled, their edges able to fit together to form an incorrect Frankenstein of three scenes, but unless the three puzzles were separated, none of them were true.

Puzzle one: Penn was nobody but a successful businessman who was bored and liked to lie.

Puzzle two: Penn was Nameless and treating me with contempt because…?

Puzzle three: *I have no idea what's puzzle three.*

"What am I doing, Sage?" I cuddled her close, drawing comfort from her warmth and familiarity. "I've slept with the guy once, and I suddenly can't stop thinking about him? Is that normal behavior? No wonder love is frowned upon. It's a workaholic's nightmare."

She purred, not even bothering to open her eyes and answer me.

A knock reverberated through my apartment. For a second, I thought it was the TV, but then it came again from behind me.

The door.

*Someone is at my front door.*

The only people who ever visited (make that person) was Dad.

*No one else.*

*Don't let it be him. Please.*

The knock came again.

And again a few seconds later.

"This isn't fair," I breathed into Sage's fur as I scooped her into my arms and climbed off the couch. Every step I took toward the front door sent my heart chugging a proverbial wine bottle until I wobbled with fake intoxication.

Looking through the peephole, Penn stood smart in different clothes than this afternoon's lunch date. He'd put on light-colored jeans and a white long sleeve t-shirt that sent my libido melting.

"I don't have anything to say to you." I hoped he could hear me through the door. "Please, go away."

"I'm not leaving. Open up." He held up a brown paper bag with a gold embossed logo on the side. "I've brought dessert."

*Dessert?*

It was ten p.m. on a week-day. Most normal people had finished eating by now and were winding down for bed.

Shifting Sage into one arm, I reluctantly opened the door. "Bribing me with sugar won't work."

"Are you sure about that?" He smirked. "You opened the door, didn't you?"

I scowled as he stepped over the threshold uninvited. "Only to tell you face to face to go away."

"Tell me after we've had a sugar fix."

I grumbled under my breath and shut the door. Following him into my kitchen, I took pity on him this time and motioned toward the sheer wall where a simple push opened the cupboard holding the cutlery.

He found the utensils, grabbed two spoons, then skirted around me and headed toward the couch. Dropping his weight into the comfy white leather, he placed the brown paper bag on the glass coffee table and pulled out two containers of chocolate mousse.

The emblem of the bakery was from the Gilded Cocoa. A high market delicatessen that served the best pastries and confectionery in New York.

Fine, I would admit. He had good taste.

Sage decided she'd had enough attention and leaped from my arms. Landing on four dainty feet, she took off into my bedroom where no doubt she would claim my pillow like she did every night, telling me in no uncertain terms that my bed was actually hers.

"Are you going to have one of these, or are you going to make me a diabetic?" Penn glanced over his shoulder, eyeing my black maxi dress.

I'd made the mistake of showering when I got home—hoping it would relax me—then dressing in my comfiest piece of clothing.

With no underwear.

I didn't want to eat mousse with Penn in my apartment with no underwear on.

"Sit, Elle. For fuck's sake."

"Don't swear." I shuffled around the couch and took a stiff seat beside him.

"Don't tell me what to do."

"Don't turn up uninvited to my apartment."

"Don't fucking ask questions you're not prepared to hear the answers to."

We breathed hard, fists clenched, fire glowing in our veins.

Reaching for the chocolate, Penn shoved a glass container into my hand and jabbed a spoon into the other. "Eat. Then if my company is so goddamn repulsive, I'll leave."

"I don't even want dessert."

"Christ, you test me." Shifting closer, he stole the spoon he'd only just given me, scooped up a decadent sized mouthful of chocolate, and pressed it against my lips. "Take it."

I pressed my mouth together. The scent of rich cocoa and cream made my taste buds tingle, but I wasn't refusing the sweet— I was refusing him for reasons I could no longer truly remember.

He smeared the chocolate over my lips, painting me with edible lipstick. "Open, Elle." He couldn't tear his eyes away, his chest rising and falling the more he teased me with the dessert. "Open, just once."

His voice throbbed with sudden need.

I reacted to his lust, inhaling quickly, opening just enough for him to slip the spoon into my mouth. The moment the cold metal hit my tongue, and the richness of chocolate mousse sang on my taste buds, I moaned a little.

His jaw clenched as he withdrew the utensil, leaving the morsel behind for me to suck. I didn't chew. I let it dissolve and infiltrate my blood with a rush of sweet, sweet sugar.

"Again." His voice no longer resembled a man but a beast aching for sex. My nipples hardened beneath my dress as I obeyed without question this time.

The heat in the living room increased by a thousand degrees. He scorched me with every move, stare, and command.

Lust wasn't just a word; it was an axe that cut all chains of propriety. It was the gun that shot common-sense dead. Lust was a kidnapper and killer all in one.

Gathering more chocolate, he sucked the spoon clean, his tongue flashing out to make sure he caught every last drop. The fact he shared my spoon, *licked* my spoon did crazy things to my tummy.

Another scoop of chocolate.

This time, he inched closer, placing the container on the coffee table and grabbing my nape with his free hand. Holding me steady, he pressed the mousse to my mouth, breathing hard.

I opened for him.

He placed the dessert on my tongue.

I sucked the sweetness off.

He withdrew the spoon.

He didn't give me a chance to swallow.

His fingers tightened around my neck, jerking me forward. I tumbled into him, my mouth opening in surprise, his lips smashing against mine with violence.

His tongue met mine, the chocolate thick and cloying and rife with memories of another chocolate kiss.

Nameless.

I'd been fighting for so long. Too long. I carried guilt too heavy. I wallowed in shame too great. Kissing Penn while my heart remained in the past with another chocolate kisser unraveled me.

The long day.

The angst, the worry, the unknown.

I snapped.

Throwing myself into his arms, I intensified the kiss until our teeth smashed and violence was the theme not desire.

He fought back, letting himself go.

His hands tore at my dress, finding the straps on my shoulders and shoving them down to imprison my arms while freeing my breasts.

Shoving me backward, he instantly smothered me with his body. "You want this? You want to fucking do this?"

I nodded, unhinged. "Yes, fuck me. Don't hold back."

"Jesus, I can't. I can't hold back anymore."

It was messy, sugar riddled, and full of things we needed to say, but we had no time or rationality left to talk.

Shoving my dress up, he found I wasn't wearing underwear.

He lost the last shred of decency. "Fuck, Elle. Just—fuck." He crushed me, his mouth suffocating mine, his taste becoming that of chocolate and sin. His fingers found my wetness. His body convulsed as he jammed his erection into my thigh.

I didn't wait for instructions.

Grabbing his belt, I undid the loops, unzipped his fly, and sank my hand into his tight boxer-briefs to grasp his hot length.

His back turned rigid as he pressed into my palm.

Two fingers speared into me, filling me fast and hard.

I cried out.

He silenced me with yet another dangerous kiss.

His thumb landed on my clit, rubbing me in circles while his fingers rocked against my G-spot.

Everything locked tight. The quivering need built and built. The desire to snap my legs closed made me squirm beneath him.

"Condom. Back pocket," he snarled, working me hard.

Somehow, I managed to slip my hand into his jeans and find the condom. I shattered between living in the brewing orgasm and forcing myself to remain sane enough to wrap him in latex so he could fuck me.

The thought of him replacing his fingers and just how incredibly good it would feel was the only thing that kept me coherent enough to rip open the packet, roll down the slippery protection, and sheath him.

He nipped my neck, shoving my hand away and wedging himself between my legs.

"You don't get to run from this. Not again." He thrust.

He didn't line up or take me gently.

One moment, we were two people.

The next, we were one.

My body screamed as he split me in half.

Then sobbed as the orgasm he'd conjured turned into something with serrated blades for teeth and sharp, sharp bliss.

"Look at me." He drove into me again. "Look at me if you're going to come."

The tightening hurried inside me. His hips pumped into mine, our clothing forgotten in our rush to join.

My gaze locked with his, imprisoned for eternity by the fierce triumph, the epic guilt, the tangled lies he webbed.

I was no longer a shy virgin. I was no longer a meek woman. I was past any shame I might endure by letting go and living entirely in this moment. "Fuck me. *Please.*"

"Come. Then I will."

How had he completely possessed me? How was it he'd claimed me so I would do anything he asked, be anything he wanted?"

Pleasure built into a supernova, roaring, pulsing, demanding to pulverize into stars.

He thrust again, anger painting his face. "Give in, Elle. You're mine." His hips kept punishing, adding punctuation to his eroticism. "You know it. I fucking know it. So let me fucking claim you."

I closed my eyes. I couldn't look at him. I couldn't let him see that I wanted to let go. That all my life of business wheeling and dealing was nothing compared to what this felt like. But I didn't trust him. And trust was too big a problem to ignore.

I could never just listen and not question. I'd never be able to fully let go, open up, and stop searching for his secrets.

But that conclusion could be shared after.

Right now, I would obey because it meant we'd both find mutual happiness if only for a few orgasmic seconds.

Then...I would show him the door.

For good.

His hips drove into me. "Stop thinking. Let me inside you."

I took it figuratively, opening my legs wider.

His primal growl echoed in my chest as I gave into him. I went supple, submitting entirely. He angled himself higher, somehow swooping upright, hoisting me into his arms while still filling me deep.

Sitting on his knees on the couch, he cradled me in his arms while my legs draped either side of him. His fingers became white-knuckled as they locked around my hips, keeping me wedged as far down his cock as he could.

His head fell forward as he watched us fucking. Slowing, his cock pulsed inside me, dragging out the pleasure to agonizing joy.

"Oh, God, yes…like that." My body turned limp as I focused completely inward. He supported me as he did it again, slowly learning me as I learned him, trading our dictionaries, our thesauruses, making sense of this new language we'd developed.

"Please, Penn," I whimpered as the billowing orgasm became a physical entity. It was part human, part wind, part ocean. It needed somewhere to go, someone to explode for.

"Fuck, I love it when you beg." His lips latched onto mine. We kissed hungrily. We kissed savagely. "Do it again."

I didn't hesitate. "Please. Please make me come. I *need* to come."

His grip bruised me as he thrust up, sending my breasts bouncing.

My thoughts scattered, my nerve endings trembled, my entire body clenched. "I'm so close. God, please…"

"Come, Elle. Fucking come."

My breathing stopped.

The world turned sparkly and gray.

I couldn't hold off anymore.

My brain turned to sounds rather than words.

My body turned to liquid rather than bones.

I came.

I came and came as Penn fucked me as ruthlessly and as thoroughly as any hot-blooded lover.

The moment I finished, he looked down, shoving aside the bunched material of my dress, hypnotized by his cock driving into me. "Fuck, yes. This—this is truth right here, Elle."

His hand roamed to my breast, clutching my flesh with passion bordering on pain.

Grabbing my hair, he drove into me harder, harder. His roar added gasoline, and I plummeted stronger and faster than ever before. My back bowed as he pulled my hair with a vicious yank.

"Shit, take it. Take me. Take everything." His words scrambled with grunts as he chased me off the cliff.

His orgasm quaked his body, his forehead smashing against my shoulder as he emptied himself.

He didn't look up for a long moment. His breathing ragged

and lost.

I stroked his hair, calming him even though I needed calming myself.

Time lost all meaning as we slowly returned to earth and disengaged.

I couldn't look him in the eye as he pulled off the used condom and placed it in the brown paper bag the mousse had come from.

Standing, he tucked himself away and did up his trousers, followed by fastening his belt. Once presentable, he raked a hand through his hair.

"Tomorrow night."

I looked up, smoothing my dress, still shivering from orgasm aftershocks. "What?"

"If you have any plans, cancel them." He strode around the couch, pausing in the middle of my apartment. "You're coming with me. Dress in silver. I'll pick you up at Belle Elle at seven."

He left me alone with the chocolate mousse and my crazy conclusions.

# Chapter Thirty-One

ALL DAY I'D struggled between working and reminiscing about sex.

I was sore again, entirely focused on Penn every time I moved, and my body clenched from being used. He'd consumed me and utterly confused me.

Why chocolate?

Why *kiss* me with chocolate?

I hated that I now had two experiences with dessert and kissing.

The two memories did their best to mingle, to convince me that Penn was Nameless and Nameless was Penn.

I didn't have a picture of Penn, and Google had nothing on him—no company profile, no Facebook account. I wanted to stare into his face and force my brain to recall Nameless. To delete the scruffy beard and dark dreadlocks—to see if there was *any* chance (no matter how small) that the distinguished cocky businessman currently seducing me was that ragamuffin from my past.

\* \* \* \* \*

By the afternoon, I was semi back to normal. There were no erotic texts from Penn, no pop-ins from Greg, and the back-to-back meetings with Japan wholesalers and a new supplier of handbags in Beijing meant I could remain focused on things I knew, rather than things I didn't.

Around noon, Dad brought me a chicken Caesar salad and kissed my forehead like I was still his twelve-year-old protégée. He stared at me as if he was awed and a little afraid. "Two things. If you still want me to hire a private investigator, I will—for your peace of mind."

"Thank you." I patted his hand, grateful but not as gung-ho as I thought I'd be about snooping into Penn's background.

"And two," Dad continued. "Greg cornered me this morning."

My heart picked up a sword while my voice remained nonchalant. "Oh?"

"He said you guys have agreed to go to dinner tonight."

I exhaled with frustration. "I did nothing of the sort." Deciding now would be a good time to tell him how wary I'd become of Greg, I added, "He's not as suave and sophisticated as you think, Dad." I fought my shiver. "He said some pretty nasty things to me yesterday. I wasn't comfortable."

Dad's eyes became snipers. "He did?" He rubbed his jaw. "I must admit I thought it was low of you to date Penn yet see Greg on the side. I should've known you'd never do such a thing."

"The male race could die out, and I *still* wouldn't entertain the idea of Greg being dateable."

He sighed. "I'm beginning to see that. I'm sorry I pushed you into something you're not happy about."

"It's fine. But would you do me a favor and have my back next time he tries to do anything?"

Dad nodded fiercely. "Absolutely. I'll have a word with Steve that you're with Penn now, and even if you weren't, you guys are old enough to set yourself up without meddling old matchmakers who don't have a clue what they're doing."

The heavy weight I'd been carrying for years slowly chipped off my shoulders, becoming manageable instead of mountainous. "Thank you."

"Don't mention it. I just want you to be happy. That's all I've ever wanted, Bell Button."

He stood and headed for the door. He smiled sadly. "I know you want answers about who Penn is before you give him a chance, but if I've learned anything, it's that love is the biggest truth there is." He shrugged. "All the rest—the questions and worries—it's all just noise."

He closed the door before I could reply, leaving me to my lunch.

* * * * *

By the time six p.m. rolled around, my back ached from spending the afternoon hunched over my laptop, and my eyes hurt even after wearing my glasses.

Fleur barged into my office with yet another dress wrapped in a clear protective bag. "Time to get ready, remember?"

I tugged my glasses down my nose, pinching the bridge.

"Huh? I thought I was finished for the day."

"You are. You have that seven p.m. thing with your fiancé, remember?"

I groaned. "Ugh, don't call him my fiancé."

"He is, though, right?" Her face slipped with doubt. I wanted to be the one to fill her with truth, but I was tired and cranky, and I'd had enough for the day. I decided to take the more diplomatic approach and ignore her question.

Vague memories of Penn's invite—or command—about me joining him tonight came back. I'd stupidly mentioned it to Fleur when I'd arrived this morning.

I stood up, nerves joining my blood to stream around my heart. I didn't want to go. I was mentally exhausted.

Draping the dress over the couch, she placed a Belle Elle shopping bag beside it. "Inside are some heels, hair accessories, and a shawl. I also took the liberties of bringing up some lingerie for you too."

I rolled my eyes. "You know way too much about me. I don't know if I'm comfortable with you knowing my bra size."

She waved it away. "You know all your secrets are mine to keep." Marching to the door, she added, "Give me a call if you need help with your makeup and hair. I'm just finishing the spring catalog mock-up before heading home. Jack is taking me out to Mexican, and I can't be late."

It wasn't the first time she'd mentioned her boyfriend or life outside of Belle Elle, but for some reason, tonight it hit home. She had a life. She had someone to share it with. Was it so wrong of me to sample that? What made Penn Everett such a bad choice? And was he bad or was it all in my head? Why was I trying to twist him into another? Nameless was gone.

*It's time I grew up and gave him a chance.*

"Thank you for the dress."

"No problem." She smiled and disappeared.

Striding to the couch, I unzipped the bag, pulled out the softest silver gown I'd ever seen, and headed into my private bathroom to shower and prepare.

\* \* \* \* \*

Penn (06:55 p.m.): *I'm downstairs. I won't come up because if I do, I'll fuck you in your office and then we'll be late. Come down.*

I slammed my phone down—partly because of the sudden shakes at seeing him again and partly because of his rudeness.

Staring at myself in the mirror, I second-guessed keeping my hair loose even though I'd secured it to the side with a clip in the shape of a crescent moon decorated with mirrored mosaics.

Fleur had once again chosen a stunning dress. The silver and white lingerie beneath the dress added secrecy to my outfit that I may or may not show Penn. The thick satin gown covered my body with sleeves draping like wings down my arms with the off-the-shoulder style. The length came to mid-calf with acres of material ready to flare out at the slightest movement.

I looked as if I'd stepped into the moon and come out wearing its metallic essence.

Penn (07:00 p.m.): *You're late.*

My teeth ground together as I scooped my phone into the little silver beaded bag and left my bathroom. Sage looked up from her spot on the couch, meowing softly. I padded over to her where my heels were. I kissed the top of her head. "I'm going to miss you, but you can't come."

She pouted as if to say there'd been multiple events she wasn't invited to these past few weeks.

Scratching her under the chin, I promised, "Dad will come and pick you up. You can spend the night at the brownstone and explore the garden rather than be stuck in the top floor apartment. How about that?"

She gently bit my finger in grudging agreement.

"See you later, kitty." Stepping from my office, I locked my door and double-checked I had what I needed. I'd done my own makeup and was pleased when one of the janitors did a double take at my smoky eyes and nude glossed lips.

*I'm late, am I?*

I'd show him I wouldn't simper and apologize. I was worth waiting for.

Taking the elevator down, I spotted the black limousine before I saw him.

Penn stood with his arms crossed and back reclining against the luxury vehicle. He didn't move as I swiped my keycard to exit the locked sliding doors, and my heels clipped elegantly across the sidewalk.

Belle Elle glittered behind me with window displays, rich red awnings, and the biggest sign on the block blazing our brand and promise.

Penn pressed his lips together the closer I got, his body stiffening. He didn't reach out and touch me. He merely stepped sideways, opened the car door, and inclined his head for me to hop in.

Keeping eye contact with him, I obeyed, ensuring I gathered up the dress and climbed in demurely. However, some inner minx decided to rise to his challenge and fight fire with fire.

I opened my legs a little, flashing him a quick glance of the white garter belt holding up sheer pantyhose and the silver lace hiding the place only he'd touched.

He slammed the door so hard the limousine rattled.

Nervousness climbed up my spine, waiting for him to walk to the other side and climb in. I jumped as he wrenched it open, claimed the seat beside me, then punched the intercom to the driver hidden behind a black wall. "To the Pemberly."

"Yes, sir," the driver said as the car moved into motion with a swan-like glide. Downtown moved past tinted windows while traffic noise and city smells invaded the interior through the open sky roof.

Still, Penn didn't look at me.

His hands fisted. His jaw clenched so tight, the muscles in his throat looked as if they'd shatter.

I didn't know what to do. Had he had a bad day? Was he that pissed at me for being late?

Not that I was late. *He* was early.

If he wanted to stew and not talk to me, then fine. I could do the same. Placing my handbag on the seat between us, I settled into the leather and glared out the window.

A second went past.

Barely a second.

Before my handbag went slamming to the floor as Penn swiped it away.

"What on earth—"

His lips bruised mine, his hands grabbing my waist, dragging me unceremoniously across the backseat and into his lap.

He attacked me in every sense of the word.

We were so close.

But it wasn't enough.

Pushing off his chest, I swiveled from damsel in distress in his arms to opening my legs, pushing my dress up my thighs, and straddling him.

His growl echoed so long and deep, I became instantly wet.

"Christ, Elle." He stole my mouth again, his hands coming up to capture my face, his fingers tight against my nape, not giving me any room to run. "You're so fucking beautiful."

I let go and did what I'd wanted to do but pretended I didn't. I became a full participant. I'd let him take me the first night, allowing first-time jitters to subdue me. The second time, I'd been swept away by chocolate memories.

Not now.

Not again.

My hands mimicked his, cupping his five o'clock shadow, digging my fingernails into his cheeks.

He jolted in my hold, his lips tearing at mine as if he could eat me, bite me, consume me.

We gave up our humanness and turned ferocious.

I loved the way he kissed me. I loved the way I kissed him back. I loved the noises and hardness and rocking and touching and clawing. I adored how muggy the limo became. I relished in how my dress clung to sweat-beaded skin.

I sucked on his tongue, holding it tight as he groaned and thrust up, his hands slamming onto my hips to push me down onto him.

His body rocked as if he was already inside me, already punishing me for things I didn't understand.

His eagerness and viciousness fed the well inside me that had been empty until he'd barged into my life. This was true lust, and I wanted to drown in the sensation of having this powerful, secretive man come apart beneath me.

His hand slid off my hip and up my skirt.

I gasped as he found my soaked underwear. He shoved it to the side with a simple flick. The moment I was bare, he thrust a finger inside me, causing my back to bend until I was sure I'd topple off his lap if he didn't wrap a long, strong arm around my back and clutch me hard.

"Fuck you, Elle," he panted, inserting a second finger, stretching me, stimulating the slight soreness from last night.

"Fuck me?" I blinked hurt and turned on. "Now, what did I do?"

"You're screwing me up, that's what." His mouth stopped his confessions by once again seeking mine. My skin burned from his barely-there beard, stinging from fresh bruises. With my knees hugging his hips, I deepened the kiss, taking control, licking his tongue with mine.

His words turned on a carousel inside my mind: *You're screwing me up. Screwing me up.'* I didn't know how, but I was glad. I was glad because I'd learned something terrible about myself thanks to him.

I might believe I was a woman with sinew, skeleton, and heartbeat, but in reality, my soul comprised of trust and my bones calcified with belief—I was a flimsy, trusting thing who could no longer tell if her instincts were true or masquerading as ridiculous desperation for hope.

Penn yanked away, digging his fingers into my hips. He shoved me back, teetering me on his knees, revealing his erection pushing up tight against the fly of his silver tuxedo.

I'd never seen a man dressed in silver before but, my God, it suited him.

It brought out the cinnamon in his eyes, the honey in his hair, the compassion hiding deep within.

"What the fuck are you doing to me?" His gaze couldn't hold mine, slipping over my body, locking onto my pushed aside panties and core. "It wasn't supposed to go on this long."

"What wasn't?"

"This." His groan was tortured as his thumb pressed into my wetness. "Whatever this is."

I quaked, fighting fluttering eyelids. "*You* chased *me*."

"Wrong." His teeth nipped my throat. "I hunted you."

Truth lay in that tiny paragraph, but I couldn't decipher it.

Finding courage in his undoing, I ran my hands down his chest, heading straight to his cock. He didn't stop me as I popped the fastener on his sleek trousers and undid the zipper.

I bit my lip as I inserted my hand into his tight boxer-briefs, never taking my eyes off his face. "I—I want you."

"Now?" His eyes narrowed then widened as I ran my thumb over his crown.

"Now."

He rocked up, grabbing my hand with his own and wrapping my fingers tighter, using me for his pleasure. "We do this...we do it my way." He glanced at the silver watch on his wrist—the same watch he'd noted when he'd told me my two minutes were up with the almost blowjob.

I swallowed. "Fine."

"Do you trust me?"

The car kept coasting. But my heart slammed to a stop.

That question.

Another man, another time—same four words, identical twelve letters.

My lips parted as I dove into his rich coffee eyes. I wanted to demand why he'd asked that at this exact moment—the same way another had asked before he kissed me.

But I couldn't. I couldn't shatter whatever existed in this limousine.

I nodded ever so slowly, pretending hesitation while my mind raced with possibility.

"Yes..."

"Good." He grunted, tearing my hands away and shoving me off his lap. "Get on all fours."

"What?" My eyebrows rose. My hair clung to my back, no doubt turning sweat-damp and curly.

"You heard me." Fisting his cock, he pulled a condom from his pocket, and with jerky control, rolled it down his length.

His throat contracted as every last bit of light disappeared from his face. "Fucking turn around, Elle. You started this. I'll finish it."

"I didn't start it. *You* kissed *me*."

"But then you straddled me and made me forget something very important."

"What's important?"

His jaw hardened. "None of your concern. Now, turn around." He slid off the seat, slamming to his knees. Shoving his trousers to mid-thigh, he twirled his finger in the air, waiting for me to obey and turn.

I didn't want to face away from him. I didn't feel safe not being able to see what he was about to do. But at the same time, the idea of being taken so rustic and pure made my breasts tingle and an orgasm already gather in my belly.

Without a word, I kneeled in the long runway of black carpeting with bench seats on either side. I had no support to hold onto as the limo turned corners. I had no way of preventing myself from soaring forward if we crashed.

I gave utter trust to Penn and his control of the situation.

My fingers dug into the rough carpet, already mourning the runs in my sheer pantyhose. No one in the outside world would know what we did even as we stopped at traffic lights and drove past pedestrians carrying their groceries.

I cried out as his hand clamped on my hip, tugging me backward. The tip of his cock found my entrance.

I tensed for him to take me. But he waited, tantalizingly close.

My body rocked back, forcing him inside a fraction.

He growled from behind me. "You have no idea, Elle. No

idea."

Then he thrust.

One fast, all-consuming, unapologetic thrust.

I fell forward onto my elbows. My wrists weak from typing all day, I was unable to brace against his power. His hands latched around my waist, keeping my ass high and driving into me.

I breathed hard, inhaling scents of leather and car freshener, but most of all *him*. His dark aftershave, his arousal, the rich indescribable scent of Penn.

"I need you," he snarled, thrusting faster. "I need you so fucking much."

"So take me then." My head hung between my shoulders, forgetting everything but where we were joined.

There was no soreness or tenderness. Only the righteous feel of him inside, bruising me in all the right ways. My body fisted around him, already banding with the beginning of a release.

He smacked my thigh. "No, you don't get to come until I do." He was breathless, same as me. He was possessed, same as me.

I wouldn't need to drink tonight.

I was already drunk.

On him.

"Goddammit, Elle." He pushed forward, driving into me as hard as he could. His torso fell over my back with such a heavy groan it pained and excited me. Everything he did was erotic and wicked.

Reaching between my legs, I grabbed the base of him as he withdrew to thrust back inside me. He was hard as granite; so hot and slippery.

He grunted as I squeezed his balls, rolling them in my fingers until he batted my hand away and entered me with cracking brutality.

My breath caught as I trembled beneath him.

"Lust makes us do the most terrible things." His teeth latched onto my neck, biting hard, his hips pistoning quick. "I'm going to come so fucking bad."

I didn't know if I'd been the one to seduce him, but he'd utterly decimated me.

I whimpered and moaned, feeling too full, too empty, too used, too protected. Polar opposites all at once. My craving increased until I bared my teeth and focused every nerve ending where he penetrated me.

I let go of decorum and placed my hand between my legs, rubbing my clit as I backed up hard into his next thrust. I played his game. I met him fighting. Lust tinged the humid air. Temptation cloaked us with every breath.

And that was the end for both of us.

His hands flexed over my waist.

I dared look back.

He was exquisite, his gorgeous body straining against the binds of his tuxedo. He didn't look human, just a man intending to mate until death.

His head fell back, his lips tight against secrets he refused to share.

A flare of pain from inside set the unbearable pleasure into a free fall. I rippled and squeezed, my legs locking against my hand as I rubbed my clit in time to his thrusting cock. Nothing else mattered but the incessant want to give in to this ravaging hunger.

It was too good.

It was too much.

He grabbed the back of my neck, rising onto his knees as he drove into me with short, deep jerks. My orgasm evolved into elastic boomerangs, bouncing down the walls of my pussy, tightening and splintering until I gave up and fell cheek first against the carpet.

The tip of his cock hit me too hard, too high. I squirmed to get way, but he yanked me back and joined me in the golden blissful glow. He quaked and quivered, coming deep inside me.

Epic aftershocks shook us as we stayed exactly where we were—a heap of finery joined in place.

The outside world slowly made an appearance as the limousine slowed and the driver's intercom crackled. "We're here, sir."

Penn slapped the button. "Give us a minute. We'll get our own doors. Under no circumstances open them, got it?"

"Got it."

I had carpet burn on my cheek and looseness in joints I couldn't even name, but as Penn slid out of me and disposed of the condom into a tissue, he gently helped me up and pressed a stinging kiss to my delicate face.

"Christ, look what I did to you."

With infinitesimal kindness, he grabbed another tissue, positioned me onto the seat and knelt between my legs. When I tried to close them, he opened my knees and kept them wide with a stern look. Never glancing away, he wiped me clean, slid my panties back into position, and pulled my dress down.

"You got away easy, Elle. So fucking easy."

Doing up his fly, he ran both hands through his hair then opened the door and stepped out.

# Chapter Thirty-Two

THOSE FIRST FEW steps into the night extravaganza were some of the hardest I'd ever walked.

Not only because I ached in places one should never ache in public but also because Penn shut down. He'd said things in the car I wanted to chase. He'd slipped, and I was anxious to encourage him to slip more.

All I wanted to do was find a quiet spot and demand him to open up to me, but he didn't give me a chance.

Grabbing my hand, he smiled and nodded at people milling around the entrance, tugging me inside the opulent hotel ballroom where the function took place.

Hundreds of people laughed and mingled, glittering like fallen stars all dressed in silver. The tables around the perimeter of the room looked like flying saucers adorned with lace and crystal candelabras.

"You have a choice, Elle," Penn murmured as he guided me through the thicket.

When he didn't give me the options to go with the choice, I frowned. "What options?"

"Two things are happening tonight that are non-negotiable."

My fingers tensed in his. "I don't agree to things I can't control."

He smirked. "Like you agreed to fuck me? That wasn't in your control."

I swallowed, hating he had a point. Then again, he'd asked me if I trusted him. He'd sought permission, passing me the power to deny.

*Which I didn't.*

I nursed that little conclusion, giving him the limelight.

"Two things." He smiled roguishly. "The only thing you can

control is the order in which they happen."

Pursing my lips, I accepted a glass of champagne he lifted off a silver platter carried by a white-uniformed waiter.

"Number one, you're going to drink. I want you tipsy—like you were that night you said yes. I want you loose and inhibited and open to doing whatever I want."

My swallow of champagne—already bitter and not wanted turned sour. "That was a one-time thing. I don't drink to excess."

"Tonight, you do." Unthreading his fingers from mine, he cupped my elbow, guiding me past a particularly big group of minglers. "I need you open."

"Why?"

"Because after this function, we're going to talk."

I tripped in my heels. "Talk?"

His forehead furrowed, his normally handsome face marked with frustration. "You want to know who I am, Elle?" He moved closer, whispering in my ear with seduction and chicanery. "I'll tell you. But for you to accept the truth, you have to have an open mind."

I took another sip of champagne—not because of his order but because my mouth shot dry with nerves. "Why do I need an open mind?" I pulled back, looking into his dark bronze eyes. "Who *are* you?"

"You'll find out soon enough." Rolling his shoulders, his voice clipped with tension. "You'll get your answers. But only if you do what you're told."

I bristled at the condescending remark.

"I'll tell you, Elle, but it won't change a thing." He caressed my cheek with sudden devotion. "You've been mine since the moment we met, and you'll stay mine until I let you go. Anything else—all your arguments, denials, and refusals—mean nothing to me." He leaned forward until our noses brushed. "Remember that when I tell you. You've already lost. Why? Because you are *mine*."

I jerked back, breathing hard and slightly scared.

He either didn't notice or didn't care. Looking over the crowd—his vision easily a few inches taller than most—he murmured as if he hadn't just ransacked my world, "Your choice. Either drink now…or…"

"Or?"

"Or I'll permit you to keep your wits until after you've met Larry again."

"Larry?"

*From the park?*

Deciding to annoy him, I said, "Ah, your fictional husband slash benefactor."

"That's starting to get old."

My courage sprang from nowhere, bolstered by monster-sized curiosity. "Who is he to you? What exactly is a benefactor anyway?"

His face blocked all answers. "Why do you care?"

"I care because I hate being in the dark."

"It's better than other alternatives."

My heart squeezed. "What do you mean?"

He sighed, rubbing his face with his hand. "Fine. I'll answer the basics if it'll stop your damn questions. Larry is family. He's the only family I have. Stewie will be his adopted son soon. Which will make him my brother, for all intents and purposes."

He took a breath, bracing himself to continue. "I used to…work…for Larry, until I branched off into my own expertise. He helped me when I had no one else, and I'll forever have his back so if he gets sick again and needs to move to Zimbabwe for treatment, I'll take him. If he suddenly told me he couldn't adopt Stewie, I'd do it in a fucking heartbeat. Larry is the reason I still have a life—even if it is messed up."

I clutched each answer before he could steal them back. So many questions to tug out more truth, but I focused on the easiest…for now. "And what is your expertise?"

"Stock market."

I didn't picture him as Wall Street guy. A lawyer perhaps with his sharp tongue and argumentative desire to turn every conversation into a debate. But not boring stocks and impersonal trades.

"Where are your mom and dad?" I drank him in, doing my best to read his body language as he stiffened.

"Dead. Have been since I was eleven."

I flinched. "I'm sorry."

"You didn't do it." He looked over my head, his patience fraying. I doubted he'd permit any more questions, but I asked another. "You say Larry gave you back your life. How? Where did you guys meet?"

Penn chuckled darkly, shaking his head.

I tacked on another before he could revoke me asking anymore. "What about Stewie? Where did you meet him?"

He grinned, slipping back into the cultured shell that was

utterly unreadable. "Enough." He cupped my chin with his finger and thumb, holding me tight. "Choose. Drink now or later. Your call."

I gulped as his gaze went to my lips. The room blurred with sexual tension. We'd just had sex but already the familiar ache began anew.

Deliberately placing the champagne on a table next to an identical empty flute, I straightened my back. "Later. I'd like to see what Larry will reveal before you scare me away and stop me from figuring out who you truly are."

He laughed softly. "He won't help with that, Elle. Only I can."

"Well, help me then. Tell me. I know nothing about you. Where did you go to school? What sort of stocks do you trade? What's your favorite hobby, drink, color, time of day?" My voice ran into one endless request. "It's uncomfortable for me spending time with a man I don't know, basing everything I do know off whatever chemistry our bodies decide to share."

His lips tilted. "So you're saying sleeping with me, while knowing nothing about me, isn't exciting but terrifying?"

I nodded. "If you want to use extremes, yes."

He removed his hold, letting my face go. "Careful what you wish for, Elle. Sometimes, secrets make things better not worse." Dropping his eyes, they lingered on my naked throat, almost as if he traced an invisible necklace then he looked away, once again taking control by guiding me forward with an elbow touch.

Music fell gently from speakers, light classical with a thread of contemporary. It was meant to be relaxing, but I found a hint of macabre hidden in the notes. The laughing crowd didn't notice and I didn't dwell. Whatever happened tonight, I'd meet headfirst. If it meant this was the last time I'd see Penn because of some disastrous divulgence, then I would still wake tomorrow. I would still have my company, my father, my world.

Sure, it wouldn't be as spicy without him in it, but I didn't need him to make me whole.

*Are you sure about that?*

My heart had been a stupid thing. My ears had heard his lies, but my heart didn't buy them. It didn't judge or interrogate. It blindly followed where affection lay—making my feelings toward Penn woefully complicated.

I let him lead me—staying quiet and obedient out of respect that this was his night. His night to either reveal something I could accept or run away with horror. I was ready for either as long as he gave me answers.

Stewie found us first.

A small hand appeared from the crowd followed by an arm dressed in gray with navy pinstripes. He grinned as he planted himself in our trajectory, his attention on Penn. "Whatcha think?"

Penn slammed to a halt, rubbing his chin with his fingers in mock-serious contemplation. "Hmm…"

Stewie bought into the pantomime while I watched as an outsider, witnessing once again how many facets Penn had. He was strict and unyielding, but with Stewie, he was a joker, friend, and protector all in one.

"Very nice." He looked at me. "What do you think, Elle? Your merchandise shrunk to Stew's size."

I reached forward, rubbing Stewie's lapel, playing into the role of judgment. "I think the tailors did an amazing job, but the suit wouldn't look good on just anyone." I smiled, standing upright. "You wear that suit, Stewie, the suit doesn't wear you."

Stewie's face scrunched up. "I don't get it."

Penn chuckled. "She likes it."

"Sweet!" Stewie spun in place. "Larry said I can wear it to my school interviews next month. Said it will help me open doors that may be locked thanks to my background."

Penn glanced at me quickly before nodding. "Wise man. But no doors will be locked; you have my word on that." His hands clenched before relaxing. "Now, speaking of Larry, mind showing us where he's hanging out?"

Stewie nodded, slipping into a quick jig-jog. "Sure, this way."

Penn raised his eyebrow at me, took my hand, and together, we navigated the room.

# Chapter Thirty-Three

"I WAS WONDERING when you'd show up." Larry grinned, shaking Penn's hand as we popped from the crowd thanks to Stewie guiding us.

We'd traversed the ballroom to a quieter meeting room off to the side. Here, men and women huddled in their array of silver splendor, their voices hushed in discussion, soft with business and not for other people's ears.

"Fashionably late." Penn smirked. "Isn't that what you taught me?"

"Not to your own event."

*Wait,* his *event?*

I frowned. I died with impatience to ask what the evening supported. Why Penn would be the figurehead for something that deserved such a turn-out. But Penn waved at Larry then to me. "You remember Elle?"

"Of course, I do. I'm not blind, you idiot." The name-calling carried heavy affection as Larry leaned forward to kiss me on the cheek. "Hello, Elle. You look ravishing."

I accepted his greeting, doing my best not to blush. "Thank you. You look dashing yourself." Just like Penn dressed in a silver tuxedo, Larry wore a darker version. His salt and pepper hair matched the silver theme perfectly. Stewie was the only one to break the metallic code with his gray pinstripe.

Champagne was once again handed out. Penn plucked a glass, handing it to me with another raised eyebrow. I accepted it but didn't take a sip—mainly in defiance.

Awkwardness fell.

I grasped for an appropriate subject. "So you said this was Penn's event?" I glanced at the men. "I must admit he hasn't given me any hints as to why I'm here or what the evening festivities are for."

Larry shot Penn a disapproving glare. "He didn't, did he?" He smiled. "Let me be the one to tell you then."

"Larry," Penn growled under his breath. "Remember our discussion."

Larry waved him off, taking my elbow and escorting me toward the bar and away from Penn. "This is a charity function. Every year Penn hosts it. He has since we started working together."

"Working together?"

Larry nodded as if it was perfect knowledge. "I'm a lawyer. My firm needed a helping hand, and Penn offered. He's smart with a quick tongue. He traveled with me to many cases—even helped provide the legwork on research when I got sick. However, while I was in recovery, he turned his hand to the stock market."

His eyes focused on a memory with pride. "He invested in a small penny stock. With his luck, it should've tanked. But it didn't. For the first time, he was rewarded for his risk and the stock took off overnight. He used the profits to inject into this charity and to day trade the same companies we took to court on behalf of some of its victims."

There were tangles and knots in his revelation that I couldn't work out. I needed a quiet room where I could write down what he'd revealed and mix them around on pieces of paper until I could rearrange them into comprehensible order.

"And what is the charity for?"

Larry beamed like any happy parent. "Homeless children, of course."

I slammed to a stop.

Homeless.

Nameless…

My strappy heels pinched my feet. "*What* did you just say?"

Larry noticed my sudden pallor. His face fell. "He hasn't told you yet. Has he?"

All I could manage was a shake of my head.

I felt sick.

I felt elated.

I felt *terrified*.

His face softened, looking over my shoulder as the electrical presence of the man I'd forever associate with heartache appeared. He'd lied and twisted my mind. He'd hidden honesty and made me crazy. He stopped me from learning anymore by interfering with our conversation.

Larry bent into me, murmuring, "I'll tell you this, then the rest is up to him. *He* was homeless himself. It's his way of giving back—to help other kids having a really hard time in life." Patting my arm, he said louder as Penn sidled close, "I need a refill. Anyone else?"

"No." Penn shook his head, wrapping his arm around my suddenly trembling body. "I think you've done more than enough."

Larry merely shrugged, unapologetic.

I glanced up, taking in Penn's profile. The way his jaw was sharp and strong and no longer covered in an unkempt beard. The way his eyes lightened and darkened depending on his mood but remained the same hue as the man in Central Park. How he'd asked me if I trusted him. How he had the same habit of jamming his hands into his pockets. How he'd kissed me with chocolate...

*Oh, my God.*

*It's true.*

My knees wobbled as Penn muttered under his breath, "We'll be right back."

I gave a weak smile to Larry, falling into Penn's fast stride as he guided me through the jostling ballroom.

I couldn't tear my eyes off him. Forcing my brain to overlap his appearance with that of Nameless. I started seeing things that weren't there. Or believing in things that had been there all along.

I couldn't decide.

Without facts or declarations or any confirmation at all, I tripped into the teenage crush I'd never escaped from. I was stupid. I was hopeful. I was blind.

A woman placed herself in our path, smiling coyly at Penn while ignoring me entirely. "Oh, Penn. Fancy seeing you here." She simpered. "Do you mind if I borrow you for a moment? I have a question about the Triple Segment Securities you recommended last week." She flicked her dark brown hair. "I want your *expert* opinion."

Rage and jealousy clawed me.

If Penn was Nameless, he was mine.

He'd been mine for three years.

I'd only just found him and now she wanted to take him away?

*No.*

*She can't.*

Disappointment and confusion followed as Penn sighed heavily and let me go.

Whispering in my ear, he commanded, "Leave the ballroom. Head to the first-floor restaurant. You'll see a family bathroom. Meet me there in five minutes. What I need to tell you should be done in private."

"But I'm not tipsy."

His gaze hardened then saddened. "It's too late. You need to know. I can't fucking lie anymore."

I shivered as he let me go.

He gave me one last eternally long stare then walked away with the woman, leaving me with fantasies and fears and a joy I never dared believe in.

# Chapter Thirty-Four

I MANAGED A few shaky steps toward the large archway that I assumed led toward the hotel foyer and a staircase or elevator.

I hated leaving him. But I wanted answers more. He'd promised he'd meet me. I had to trust he wouldn't forget or disappear without fulfilling that promise.

*Hopefully tonight, I'll finally know.*

The fear that he'd run and I'd never see him again escalated the further I traveled. I didn't see Larry or anyone else I recognized.

I reached the threshold of the ballroom.

A gray bullet collided into me.

My arms flew out for balance, steadying myself and the kamikaze who'd run into me. I blinked as recognition flowed. "Stewie. Are you okay?"

He smacked his lips, nodding distractedly. "Yeah, sorry for running into you."

"Don't worry about it. As long as you're good, it's fine."

He nodded, his face tight and not the usual happiness I'd grown used to. "Yep, all good." He pushed past me to join the throng but something sparkly fell from his pocket.

Something blue.

Something that didn't belong in a boy's possession.

He didn't notice, fighting his way past adults as I ducked and plucked the silver necklace from the ballroom floor.

My heart stopped.

The world closed in.

I couldn't breathe.

In my hands sat the very thing I'd lost the night Nameless had saved me. The sapphire star glimmered under the bright strobes of the hotel, the white gold chain snapped in half where one of the muggers had yanked it off my neck.

I stumbled, crashing into a man who cursed as a splash of his orange cocktail tipped onto his silver tuxedo. "Hey!"

I vaguely remembered how to apologize while my mind was no longer here but *there*.

Back in the alley.

Back where it all began.

In an awful twist of fate, Stewie looked back, his gaze latching onto the necklace dripping through my shocked fingers. He slammed to a halt, looking around feverishly as if searching for Penn. Hoping to undo this minor, inconsequential action that'd ruined all Penn's lies. Destroyed his stories. Revealed every fact.

I'd believed in a fantasy.

And it'd just crumbled into dust.

*I know the truth.*

*The awful, terrible, sickening truth.*

Coming toward me, Stewie sheepishly held out his hand. "Can I have it back?"

My fist curled tightly around the chain. "This is mine."

"No, it's not." His forehead crinkled. "My brother gave it to me."

My heels were no longer stable or capable of holding me up. I swayed. "Your brother?"

Penn's voice entered my head, sounding far away. *"Larry is family. Stewie will be his adopted son soon. Which will make him my brother."*

No.

If Penn gave Stewie my necklace…that meant he couldn't be my tragic hero.

He couldn't be my savior.

He couldn't be Nameless.

*It's not possible.*

*This can't be happening.*

Nameless had never retrieved my necklace.

I'd never asked for it back.

The last I'd seen it was in the alley, ripped off my neck, and pocketed by thugs.

My heart palpitated, threatening to faint.

*Don't let it be true…*

Only two scenarios existed as to who Penn could be.

The sapphire had shortlisted them.

My life had made a mockery of my heart.

The truth laughed in the face of my moronic trust.

My voice struggled to stay low so as not to attract attention when all I wanted to do was scream. "Why?"

"Why?" His face crunched.

I swallowed hard, pushing down my heart where it hyperventilated in my mouth. "*Why* did your brother give you this necklace? It's not something a boy would normally play with."

He scuffed his shoe on the ballroom floor. "I'm looking after it for him." His eyes blazed. "I would *never* play with it."

"You didn't answer me, Stewie." My panic made me sharp. "*Why* do you have this?"

His attitude prickled. He crossed his arms. "Because if he was caught with it, his sentence would've doubled."

My legs turned to liquid.

My knees to chocolate mousse.

"What sentence?"

His lips thinned. "I dunno if I should be telling you this."

"Yes, you should." I moved forward, towering over him, commanding my fingers to stay locked around my necklace and not reach for his throat to strangle the answers from him. "Tell me, Stewie. Tell me *right now.*"

He puffed out his cheeks, as if doing his best not to reply but unable to ignore the order from an elder. "His prison sentence, all right? He got done for robbery. He asked me to keep it, so they didn't have evidence." Fear turned his face red. "I know I should've hidden it somewhere, but I liked it, okay? I like blue, and I like stars." He kicked the floor. "I want to be an astronomer when I grow up. I know it's girly, but...I love stars." His hand came up. "Give it back."

My body obeyed before my mind caught up.

In a daze, my arm reached forward. My fingers opened, letting the sapphire slip from my grasp to his.

I was numb.

I was dead.

Two choices.

Two men I'd cursed their very existence.

Two men tried to rape me.

One man had succeeded.

But it wasn't rape.

It was consensual.

It was *wanted.*

He'd stolen more than just my necklace but my innocence and goodness too.

How could I move on from this?

How did I ever come to terms with what he'd done?

*Who is he?*

*Which one?*

Stewie clutched the evidence of Penn's heinous crime. He didn't wait for more questions. He didn't even thank me for returning what was rightfully mine.

Taking off, he vanished into the silver throng, leaving me destroyed and heartbroken.

Truth was a fickle thing. I'd believed I wanted it. I'd begged and cursed and demanded to receive it. And now that I had it...I wanted nothing more than for it to delete what it'd caused and choose a different ending to the one I'd been given.

I'd gone from euphoric joy believing Penn was Nameless to finding out my worst nightmare.

Penn wasn't Nameless—the boy who'd protected and kissed me in the park.

He was one of the muggers who'd tried to rape me.

They'd known my name from my I.D badge.

One of them had come after me.

*I'm going to throw up.*

# Chapter Thirty-Five

I RAN.

How could I not?

I didn't know what was worse.

The fact he'd lied so effortlessly. Or the fact I'd believed—that despite being so dishonest—he was a good person underneath.

I couldn't have been more wrong.

He was a thief, a rapist, a scam artist.

And he'd successfully used me for whatever mind games he wanted to play.

He'd lied from the moment he'd coerced me into saying yes at the Palm Politics. Any truth I thought I saw in the split seconds of tenderness were rust-covered and full of counterfeit honesty.

*Oh, my God.*

*How could I let this happen?*

Tears gathered like vinegar in my eyes, stinging with disbelief.

The taxi bumped through the arteries of the city, carting me away from Penn and his empire of fibs. I hadn't called David because I didn't want anyone who knew me to see me like this. See how far I'd fallen.

My cheeks still glowed from limousine sex. My dress rumpled. My hair tangled. My lips red from throwing up in the hotel bathroom before bolting to the street and hailing the first cab I saw.

I didn't wait for Penn to confirm the hideousness of Stewie's revelation. I didn't meet him at our rendezvous for yet more lies. I could *never* have sex with him again.

I clamped a hand over my mouth, holding back another wash of nausea.

*I slept with him.*

*I climaxed with him.*

*I have—had—feelings for him.*

The vinegar in my tears pickled my insides, fermenting my heart, marinating my blood until my entire body turned acidic.

I just wanted to get home, shower away his touch, and sleep so I could forget what I'd done and who I'd done it with.

I couldn't think about who Penn was.

I couldn't let my mind poke at such appalling conclusions.

*It's not real.*

*I can't let it be real.*

The drive took forever, but finally, the taxi dropped me outside my building. Climbing unsteadily from the cab, I refused to think about what explanation I'd give for breaking off the engagement. Why I'd inform security that Penn was no longer permitted to step foot inside Belle Elle. Why I would get a damn restraining order if he pursued me.

How would I tell Dad that the man he believed was suitable—the successful entrepreneur who pretended to be an old-world romantic—was truly just a clever deceiver?

Thank God, I never told him what happened that night in the alley. Thank heavens, I kept the robbery and almost rape a secret because he would hunt Penn down and kill him for being one of those men who'd tried to take me.

*A man who successfully got what he wanted in the end.*

I swallowed a sob.

I only had myself to blame. I should've dug deeper into his past. I should never have trusted him.

Entering the exclusive foyer of my building, I swatted at a tear that had the audacity to roll and marched to the elevators.

The doors opened immediately, and I climbed in. My heart plummeted, remembering Sage wouldn't be there to patch up my worries or lick away my hurts like normal. She was with Dad. Safe and secure.

*Not like me whose world has just imploded.*

My awaiting apartment was suddenly a cold, lifeless entity as the elevator zoomed me skyward. I wanted nothing more than to return home to the brownstone where Dad refused to decorate over Mom's last designs and constantly lived in the past with a broken heart.

Would that be me now? Had Penn ruined me for others? Had his lies destroyed whatever trust I had in men? How could I ever tell anyone I willingly slept with a man who'd tried to rape me three years prior in a dirty alley?

*Stop.*

*Just stop.*

*I can't...I can't think about it anymore.*

Unlocking my door, I kicked off my heels and headed straight for the sleek white kitchen. None of my lights were on, leaving the view to speak for itself as the skyscraper-filled horizon twinkled with bright orbs of light. The illuminated buildings seemed so happy, sheltering their chosen families. So sarcastic with their comforting glow.

I hated them.

Padding toward the pantry, I pulled out a bottle of wine I occasionally cooked with.

I never drank. But tonight was a night of firsts, and the liquor in my belly from a few champagne sips weren't enough.

I needed to drown every memory before they became long-term recollections. I needed to reset my life, so tomorrow I could be free.

Tipping the bottle, I swigged tart shiraz straight from the glass.

"Wow, I never thought I'd see the day."

The masculine voice terrified me.

Gulping my mouthful, I spun in the kitchen, facing the open plan living room. A figure sat on the leather couch.

He tutted, shaking his head. "Pity. I thought I'd be the one to drive you to drink." Greg chuckled then stood. His deliberate slowness reeked of mayhem and hazards.

He smiled coldly, his dark blond hair swiped back off his face. "Hello, Elle. Tough night?" He stalked toward me. "Should've gone out with me instead—like I said."

I froze; the wine bottle became more than just liquid friendship but a heavy weapon. "What are you doing in my apartment, Greg?"

This wasn't the first time. He'd been here for dinners and birthdays—even last Thanksgiving when I'd stupidly said I'd host it and burned the turkey. But he'd never been here alone, and he'd *definitely* never let himself in uninvited.

"How did you get in?"

He cocked his head. "The doorman. It's handy already having a relationship. It's allowed me to do things I wouldn't have been able to do if we were strangers."

*What things?*

---

My toes curled into the tiled floor, begging to run while I told them to stay put. I couldn't show weakness. This was my house. *Mine.*

"You're trespassing."

He sighed. "I was worried about you." He dragged a finger over the kitchen bench. "I wanted to make sure you got home safe and that prick didn't try something when he dropped you off." He grinned. "He doesn't deserve to fuck you, Elle." His face tightened. "I do."

I brandished the bottle. "You deserve to get your ass thrown out of my apartment or arrested. I'd prefer the latter. Now, get *out.*"

He shook his head, smiling. "Yeah, see? That's where you're wrong, Elle. I deserve what I've worked so hard to get."

"You haven't worked hard your entire life. You've coasted by on your father's goodwill and mine." I narrowed my eyes. "In fact, showing up here just gave me credible reason to fire you. Consider yourself unemployed."

I steeled myself for his retaliation.

I expected an outburst. A strike.

I shivered as he laughed, his eyes alight and face crinkled with mirth. "Aw, you're so cute when you're mad." He entered the kitchen, his gaze dropping to my legs as if judging how best to incapacitate me. "I'm not unemployed, Elle. I've just given myself a promotion."

I took a step back, trying to keep distance between us. Seconds turned to fractions, inching over a clock dial as his feet inched over my floor.

Closer.

*Closer.*

"Stop!" I cursed the wobble in my voice. "I don't want you here. It's time for you to go. Right now, Greg. I won't ask again." I fumbled for the silver bag I'd dumped by the pantry. My phone. The police.

Desperation for help pressurized inside me the closer Greg came.

He stopped, rubbing his jaw. "You're right, it *is* time to go."

I sighed in relief.

*He's all talk.*

*He won't hurt me.*

*He's smarter than that.*

He smiled a rapscallion smile. "But I'm not going alone."

# Chapter Thirty-Six

I'D CARRIED THAT day in the alley with me for three years.

It was my dirty secret.

My one major screw-up.

And most of the time, I was able to ignore how it had made me feel.

How scared I'd been. How god-awful it'd been to be trapped. How petrified I'd been while being molested. How I hated being a prisoner even for a few terrible minutes.

But sometimes, when I was tired or stressed or sleep deprived, I couldn't fight off the shadows of that night.

Baseball Cap and Adidas were there, ready to touch me, hurt me—make me forget I was safe and they could never touch me.

*I like the thought of you giving me a blowjob. Get her on her knees*

Those times, I was able to shove aside awful memories by remembering Nameless. Believing the world was good and bad but most of the time right won over wrong. He was there, fighting off nightmares, giving me candy and kisses.

He was my safe place.

He made me believe things were fine.

Tonight had proven me wrong.

Twice.

*If you scream, we'll beat you fucking bloody, and you'll wake up with nothing.*

My mind was full of useless snippets and three-year-old voices from that night. They became louder and stronger as Greg switched his stalking for attack.

A silent cry fell from my lips as he charged.

"No!" I twisted on the spot, my bare feet sticking to the tiles as I forgot about standing up to him and chose running instead.

Only, I didn't get far.

*First, we get what we want, and then you get what you want.*

"Gotcha." Greg's arms lashed around my waist, pulling me to him.

My fingers gripped the wine bottle as I hoisted it over my head, wildly aiming, blinding hoping. Blood-red shiraz chugged from the tip, splashing me, Greg, my kitchen.

"Give me that." He held me trapped with one arm, grabbing my wrist with his free hand.

"Stop!" I squirmed and wiggled. I swung and pummeled. "Let me go!"

I tried to defend myself.

But it was no use.

*You want to see my cock, bitch. Can't deny that shit.*

He twisted the bottle from my fingers and placed it carefully on the bench. He didn't smash it or cause any noise.

He kept his abduction as silent as possible.

*To keep it secret.*

*So make it* un*secret.*

I screamed as loud as I could. The back of my throat shredded, but I screamed and *screamed*—

He slapped a hand over my lips, silencing me. "Quit it." Breathing hard as I tried to kick his legs, he hissed, "Do you honestly think anyone will hear you? These apartments are triple walled. You're on the top floor. Save your breath."

Turning me in his embrace, he grabbed my wrists, trapped them behind my back, and kissed me quick and deep.

*Let's see what your tits are like.*

I tried to bite his tongue, but he was too fast. A swift claiming and then a retreat, knowing he'd won and I was his.

I fought harder, ignoring how strong he was and how weak he made me. "Stop this, Greg." My voice climbed a few octaves, making me beg even when I tried to command. "Let me go."

He merely laughed. "You're not the one in charge tonight." He strode over to the invisible drawer holding random pieces of junk. Unlike Penn, he knew how to press to open. Grabbing some twine I'd used to hold the turkey stuffing in place, he wrapped it around my wrists, tying tight.

*Before we show you ours, you have to show us yours.*

Once I was helpless, he marched me forward. "You and I are going for a little drive." Scooping up a pair of car keys I hadn't seen on my kitchen bench, he pushed me toward the door, opened it, and shoved me over the threshold.

Panic billowed faster.

I didn't want to leave with him.

*Please!*

"Where are we going?" My heart galloped as he punched the down button for the elevator and dragged me onto it.

He pressed the button for the garage below. "Somewhere no one will find us." He rocked his cock against my back as he kept me locked in front of him. "Somewhere we can get to know each other and finally agree that marriage between us is the best thing—for everyone."

I sneered. "I'm already engaged."

*To a liar—just like you.*

*To a criminal—just like you.*

I prodded the hurt inside that Penn had caused.

I asked the question I'd been avoiding.

Was Penn Baseball Cap or Adidas?

Was he the one who'd grabbed my breast or torn off my sapphire star?

Penn's promises echoed in my head.

*Say yes, and you're mine. You'll answer to me. Sometimes, you'll hate me. Most of the time, you'll probably want to kill me.*

He was right.

I *did* want to kill him.

Multiple times.

My chest ached as another of his truthless pledges rang in my ears.

*I will lie to others about us. I will paint a picture that isn't true. I will curse and hurt and do whatever I damn well want, but you have my word on one thing. I won't lie to you. What you see from me will be the honest fucking truth.*

Liar.

Liar.

*Liar.*

Greg chuckled. "That engagement is a sham." He kissed my throat, pushing aside my hair with his car keys, scraping me with the sharp-toothed metal. "I'm not a fucking idiot, Elle."

The elevator dinged, depositing us into the underground garage. He pressed his key fob, and a graphite Porsche beeped with welcome.

I'd seen his car before, hell, I'd been in his car when he drove me to a meeting across town when David suddenly came down with food poisoning. But I'd never been forced into his car or made to feel as if he would hurt me if I disobeyed.

I shot forward, taking him by surprise.

I managed a few steps before he looped his fingers around the twine on my wrists, slamming me to a stop.

"Where do you think you're going?"

My feet ached on the rough concrete thanks to mostly healed cuts and bruises from running barefoot a few nights ago.

If Penn was Adidas or Baseball Cap, why had he come to my rescue?

Why had he been my defender in my future when he'd been the offender in my past?

Nameless' voice was the third to enter my thoughts.

*You don't need to hide. I won't let them hurt you. You're safe with me.*

I fought harder, jumping in Greg's hold, kicking him as hard as I could.

He merely laughed, stripping me of strength with caustic ridicule.

*Do you trust me?*

Nameless and Penn had asked that.

I'd thought the link was enough to reveal his identity. Turned out, that question was common and far too flimsy to pin my hopes on.

Greg dragged me toward his Porsche, ignoring my attempts at fleeing.

I stopped fighting, choosing another alternative. "Greg…let's talk about this." I tried to appeal to the side of him I'd interacted with for years—the business side. The boy I'd grown up with surrounded by all things Belle Elle.

But that Greg was gone.

Compounded by jealousy and riddled with resentment, the man capturing me had a vendetta to earn what he believed was rightfully his, regardless if it was blasphemously wrong.

Opening the car door, he growled. "Get in."

"You don't have to do this."

He shoved his face in mine. "I know. I *want* to do this." He placed his hand on my skull, pushing me to duck so I could fit inside the Porsche. "Now, get in the fucking car."

I looked at the guard sitting in the distance by the exit ramp.

I made a stupid choice, one based on self-preservation.

I screamed. *"Heeeeeeelp!"*

He punched me.

The crack hit my cheekbone. The force threw me against the

car. The garage vanished. The ground disappeared. I came to with my knees buckled and my body sprawled like a ragdoll in the passenger seat.

The slam of the door vibrated my teeth.

The guard hadn't heard me.

My pain was for nothing.

My vision fogged with candyfloss as Greg yanked open the driver's side, leaped in, and gunned the engine.

I groaned against sickness and agony. "Stop." My head lolled on my neck, too heavy, totally useless.

Larry's voice entered the medley in my skull, bringing thoughts of Central Park, airplanes, and kisses on a baseball field. *Thieves can become saints. Saints can become thieves. Most of us deserve a second chance.*

My heart boycotted his misunderstood wisdom.

He'd known all along that Penn was more than just a homeless man who'd been arrested on my nineteenth birthday. The entire time we'd spoken, he'd known I slept with an immoral crook.

*He knows who Penn is.*

*And he didn't tell me.*

He let me develop feelings. He believed whatever connection Penn managed to cultivate would be enough to get past the alley.

To get past the threat, the taunt, the trauma.

My face throbbed as I tried to figure it out.

*I can never forgive him.*

Baseball Cap's threat filled my ears. The last thing he'd said to me as Nameless shielded me and kept me safe.

*You'll fucking pay. Both of you.*

They'd made me pay.

They'd kept their oath to rob me of everything I had, including my body.

But what about Nameless?

*What have they done?*

The Porsche shot forward, pinning my head against the seat as Greg drove fast. He slowed as we approached the guard.

I blinked, forcing my eyesight to work past the bruising on my cheek.

We stopped, barricaded by the red and white ramp.

The guard was too high in his little booth. He couldn't see inside the car. I kicked the floor, hoping to make a noise.

It was pitifully non-existent.

Greg reached over with one hand, planting his sour palm over my lips. He whispered, "No screaming." With his other hand, he fished out his Belle Elle pass and smiled. "Evening."

The guard did his job. He checked the credentials. He opened the exit. "Have a good night."

"Oh, I will. Believe me." Greg threw his I.D card at me as he stomped on the accelerator.

We sped into the night.

He removed his hand. "That went well." His face gleamed black with triumph. "The hard parts are over now." He patted my thigh with unwanted fingers. "A little road trip then you and I get to have a private *chat*." His hand slid up my thigh, probing the silver dress.

The same dress Penn had hooked over my hips as he fucked me in the limousine.

The same dress I'd worn when I'd found my sapphire star and learned the terrible truth.

I yanked my legs away. "Don't touch me."

Greg clutched the steering wheel with a chuckle. "I plan on doing more than that, Noelle. Much more."

As New York blurred with speed, Dad filled my mind.

Would he come for me?

Would he save me?

I had no one else.

Nameless was gone.

Penn was banished.

*I'm alone.*

But it didn't matter.

Greg wanted what he couldn't have.

Belle Elle was my empire and my body was mine.

Penn had taught me how to lie.

I would don a crown of them.

I would lie and cheat and steal and beg.

I wouldn't back down.

*I'll fight.*

# throne of truth

# Prologue

# Penn

LIES.

They have a life of their own. They multiply, divide, and conquer—not just the listener but the liar, too. They infiltrate the truth. They twist words until false is truer than reality.

I should know. I'd become a master at them.

For a while, lies had been my saving grace. They'd kept me warm on the coldest nights and kept me sheltered when only darkness remained, but now, I have wealth and family, and my lies aren't giving me power anymore...they're stripping me of it.

Stripping me of her.

She ran away from me.

She ran before I could tell her the truth.

It didn't matter the truth wasn't what she wanted to hear. It didn't matter I had so many confessions and only the guts to reveal a few.

She ran.

And then she vanished.

# Chapter One

# Elle

"GET OUT OF the fucking car, Elle."

I cocked my chin, glowering out the window.

*Get out of my life, Greg.*

The slur scalded my tongue, but I didn't have the balls to say it. My cheek still hurt. Fear still sliced my insides. The view outside the car was foreign and unwanted.

I was kidnapped, hurt, and pissed off.

*I hate you, Greg.*

*I'll make you pay, Greg.*

My lips pulled into a sneer of contempt.

*You won't win, Greg.*

"Elle!" He thumped the roof of his graphite Porsche for the third time. The rattle shook the interior, making me flinch. I'd done well for most of the journey.

He'd prattled on while miles slowly crept between me and my home. I'd remained stoic and deathly silent—I didn't wince when he shouted for a response and didn't cower when he raised his hand in threat.

I refused to let him affect me, even though I couldn't ignore my body's discomfort anymore. My bound hands were numb from the twine around my wrists. My shoulders screamed for mercy, and my butt was flat from the long drive.

For five hours, I'd tried to come up with a plan to either talk Greg out of whatever manic idea he'd concocted or figure out a way to incapacitate him.

My mind kept me entertained with images of knocking him out, leaving him tied to a tree, and stealing his car. I'd drive myself back to New York. It didn't matter I hadn't driven since I got my license—*all David's fault for driving me everywhere*. It didn't matter I barely knew how to operate a standard rather than an automatic gearshift. And it definitely didn't matter I had no idea how to knock out a full-grown male with my hands tied behind my back.

I would do whatever it took to get free from this lunatic who I'd been raised with.

*Starting with refusing to cooperate.*

"Elle…" Greg growled, thumping the car one last time before ducking to shove his face into mine. The night sky bled with shadows and gloomy clouds. Not one star; no sliver of moon. It was as if we existed in a dead end while the roads of the world were back at a U-turn somewhere.

"I won't ask again."

I forced every inch of authority I could into my glare. "I don't want to be here, Greg. Take me home."

He laughed, rolling his eyes. "Too fucking bad. We're here. *Now get.*"

I didn't let him undermine me. I didn't let him see my fear or frustration. "I'm not getting out of the car because you're driving me home. Right now."

"Oh, I am, am I?" He laughed harder, this time with a sinister echo. "That's what you think." He undid my seat belt and placed his fingers on my thigh. "I'm going to count to five." He squeezed. Hard. "I suggest you get out before I hit five.*"*

My heart coughed.

Greg dropped all pretenses and ripped off his mask. He was done masquerading as the boring son of my father's best friend and my employee. Out here (alone), he showed who he truly was, and I *hated* him.

I hated him more than I feared him.

But the longer he squeezed my thigh, the stronger my fear grew. I trembled with disobedience, cursing him, wishing the ground would grow teeth and chew him alive.

"One." He smiled, his fingers climbing up my leg toward my core.

I gritted my teeth. I didn't let him see how much my skin crawled to have his touch so close to where I vehemently didn't want him.

"Two." He crept the final distance, cupping me roughly with a harsh glint in his eyes.

I shivered as he let me go as quickly as he'd grabbed me. His touch slithered upward, stroking my belly, my hip, my waist. "Three."

I shifted despite myself.

My legs bunched to obey—to climb out on my own willpower to avoid whatever nastiness he had planned. But he wedged himself in the door, not giving me any room to exit.

He knew that.

He nodded slyly, knowing I'd figured out that he'd blocked me. That I didn't have a choice in what would happen next.

"Four." His touch switched from my waist to my breast, tweaking a nipple before climbing the rest of the way to my shoulder. His fingers dug into me like barbwire, sharp and steely—ready to rip me apart.

I braced for pain.

I sniffed in retaliation.

Not that it did any good.

"Five." The grasp he had on my shoulder became a throbbing anchor. Digging his fingernails into my flesh, he yanked with all his energy.

With nothing holding me in the car, I toppled sideways.

I had no way to fight or stop my sideways motion.

I fell out, landing painfully on my shoulder with my legs still in the Porsche and my arms tied behind my back. Sharp gravel dug into my cheek. Wind whooshed from my lungs.

With my face wedged against the ground, I had a perfect view of Greg's black loafers as he squatted over me. "Well, that's one success. You're out of the car." He nudged me with his toe. "Now, get up."

I squirmed, wincing as every joint and ligament squealed in pain. My spine hated the way my legs pretzeled above while my shoulders slam-dunked into the earth.

Terror sprouted like weeds in my veins as Greg took a step back. I tensed for a kick or reprimand, but he placed his hands on his hips, waiting.

If I'd climbed out like he'd asked ten minutes ago, I could've avoided the shrapnel to my cheek and the new contusions to my body.

*You were stupid, Elle.*

Was it wise to refuse everything out of principle or obey to save my strength?

I knew the answer even though I hated it.

Doing my best to stifle my moan, I slowly unhooked my ankles from the Porsche and wiggled forward to give my legs room to drop down. Slowly, achingly, I figured out how to slide sideways and push off the ground with my hands behind my back—granting just enough leverage to sit upright.

It took a while, but the moment I sat up, Greg clapped condescendingly. "Finally, you listen to the boss."

I spat out a mouthful of acrid dust. "You're not my boss."

"Wrong, Elle. I am. You've been in charge for far too fucking long. Things are gonna be different now."

I clamped my lips together. I wouldn't antagonize him further. He was delusional. There was nothing I could say to a crazy person. Let him think he was my commander. I'd correct him when he was in jail.

We held a staring war like children until I cocked my chin and ignored him.

He didn't speak as I navigated my sore body into movement.

It took a few minutes to figure out how to shuffle my legs beneath me and push off on numb tingling feet to trade driveway for standing, but I managed.

The second I succeeded, Greg captured my elbow. "About time you got up." Pulling me toward a large cabin resting on the boundary of a dense forest, he added, "Wasting my time, Elle. Gonna pay for that."

"You could've helped me. Better yet, you could take me home."

He chuckled. "Funny girl."

The cabin reeked of disappearing CEOs and illegal activity. In any other situation, the cute windows with yellow and brown trim would've made any guest feel welcome. In this situation—when I'd been stolen against my will—it was a coffin I had no desire to enter.

Every inch of me did not (with a thousand *did nots*) want to go into that place. But I was tired, hungry, and emotionally wrung dry. My head still throbbed from his punch at my apartment, and my heart still panged for the lies Penn had told. The glittery blue of my sapphire star dangled in my mind, destroying Penn's fibs over and over again.

Where had that necklace come from?

Was it true Penn was Baseball Cap or Adidas?

Regardless of the truth, I knew one thing for sure.

*All men are assholes.*

And unless my father or David could figure out where Greg had taken me, I was on my own.

I glanced out of the corner of my eye at Greg and his

pompous face. Everything about him irritated me to the point of sheer rage.

*He's a moron.*

*A moron who can kill me with no one here to stop him.*

Despite running from Penn and cursing him forever, I wouldn't be opposed to him hunting and freeing me. He was the lesser of the two evils tonight.

Climbing the porch steps, our footsteps echoed on a stained wooden deck, weathered with a stylish décor.

Greg let me go, fumbling in his pockets for a key.

I didn't run off or try to bolt into the forest.

My hands were still tied, and I had no idea where I was. I'd never been good at hikes in school and would rather deal with Greg than a bear in the wilderness while incapacitated.

I kept my voice icy. "Where are we?"

Greg grinned as he slotted a key into the antique looking lock. "My father's cabin."

I vaguely remembered Steve bragging about buying a vacation place before I took over Belle Elle. He and Dad had gone away for a weekend to do manly things.

I hadn't asked what those manly things had entailed.

*It's true. He* is *a moron.*

I blinked, forcing myself not to roll my eyes at Greg's stupidity.

He'd kidnapped me and taken me to a location that his father knew about.

I wanted to thank the nonexistent stars.

Bless him for his small brain. It would only be a matter of time before the cavalry came for me.

I kept my conclusions to myself, nodding respectfully as Greg opened the door and held it wide for me to enter. He followed, leaving me standing in the foyer as he turned on lights to reveal wooden walls, cathedral ceilings, and timber flooring.

It wasn't called a log cabin for nothing—every single inch, including the kitchen counter, was made out of sacrificed trees.

It was wood overload with a plaid couch, rustic dining room table, and a window seat that could fit ten children more inclined to read than explore the sinister forest waving its shadowy branches by the windows.

The place was big with hallways leading off to bedrooms and a second lounge down a few steps with a giant log fireplace.

Greg shrugged off his blazer, throwing it haphazardly on the back of the couch. He smiled. "Come here."

I wanted to kick him in the balls, but slowly, I inched closer.

Once I was standing in front of him, he spun his finger in the air. "Turn around."

I swallowed a retort and did as he asked. Instantly, my spine crawled. I didn't like having him behind me, unable to see.

His fingers latched around my wrists.

I tensed, then relaxed a little as the tight twine slowly loosened, sliding off one wrist altogether.

I looked over my shoulder, waiting to be freed completely, but he tied a new knot around one wrist, tugging it until I turned back around to face him.

His teeth flashed in the golden light bulbs. "Can't have you running now, can we?"

I glowered at the leash he'd formed, binding my arm into his control, tethering me to him while giving my other arm the relief of coming forward and working out the kinks in my shoulder.

"I won't run." I itched with the need to undo the knots imprisoning me.

"Don't take it personally, but I don't believe you." Pulling me forward, he grinned as my body pressed up against his, my arm forced around his waist with the aid of the rope.

Lowering his head, he nuzzled my neck.

I shuddered with repulsion.

"Now that I've got you, I'm not letting you go, Elle."

Doing my best to breathe slow and steady, rather than give into the overwhelming desire to scream, I said, "You don't have me, Greg. You'll *never* have me."

"Well, I don't see anyone else here claiming you." He kissed my cheek. "You're mine, and you're not going anywhere."

"I don't need someone to claim me. *I* claim me." The CEO in me came out. I looked down my nose with arrogant authority. "What do you hope to achieve here, Greg? You can't keep me prisoner for long. They'll find me. Whatever sick and twisted idea you have of marrying me to gain access to Belle Elle is riddled with flaws. Even married to me, I'd never give you part ownership of my company, and no judge would ever grant you my property if I said you forced me."

My mouth ran away with things I'd promised myself I wouldn't say. "And what about our fathers? Do you honestly think they'll let you get away with this? My dad will either have you murdered in your sleep or thrown in jail, and your dad will have to live with the shame of what you've done."

My free hand swooped up. I tapped him in the temple as if he were a simpleton and needed a good slap to wake up. "Think this through, Greg. Release me now, and I won't press charges. I'll tell our fathers to let it go. I'll inform everyone that you had to get whatever jealousy you felt about Penn out of your system and then everything can go back to normal."

His face didn't change from the cordial playboy I knew and tolerated. His dark blond hair cascaded over one eye, giving the illusion he was easy to play and manipulate. "Normal, huh?"

I nodded. "With no repercussions. Think about it." I tugged my wrist, jiggling his hand where he held the other end of the rope. "Release me, take me home, and we'll forget about all of this."

He pursed his lips as if contemplating my proposal. Then a dark veil fell over his eyes. "Too bad for you, I don't like normal."

Stomping forward, he jerked me through the kitchen and out the backdoor. Stumbling down the steps toward the forest edge, I swallowed my fear as his stride headed straight toward the looming forest.

*What the—*

*Where is he taking me?*

The cabin wasn't wanted, but it was a damn sight better than traipsing through a jungle late at night.

"Greg—"

"Shut up, Noelle. You've had your little speech; now, shut the fuck up." He yanked a small flashlight from his pocket and turned on the ray of illumination as we crunched through bracken, entering the world of looming leafy giants. "You think you have me all figured out, huh? Bet you thought I was a fucking moron for bringing you to my dad's cabin." He laughed coldly. "Bet David is already on his way here. Too bad for him."

He laughed harder as he broke into a jog, dragging me behind him. "I'm not a fuckwad, Elle. I've been planning this for months." Beelining toward an old shed tucked up against ancient trees, he skidded to a stop.

Looking back with victorious smugness, he wrenched the unlocked padlock off the rickety doors and slithered the chain from around the wooden handles.

The rope leash lashed tight around my wrist each time he moved, giving me no slack to run. Cracking open the doors, he pulled me through and shone the flashlight onto the one thing I didn't want to see.

Another car.

Clean and new—something that would guarantee to work and not break down in exhaustion.

A black Dodge Charger.

Pulling me around to the passenger entry, he opened the door and shoved me inside. "We're only half-way there, Elle. This was the decoy. The real destination is where no one will guess. A place only I know. A place where we'll finally get to know each other."

My heart switched from pissed off to manic.

Greg slammed the door in my face, locking me inside.

*Oh, God, what should I do?*

Jogging around to the driver's side, he hopped in as if we were honeymooners about to explore. Inserting a key into the ignition, the car woke up with a loud grumbling growl.

He placed his hand on my knee. "A place where we'll get to know each other *very* well." Throwing the car into gear, he shot forward and rammed the shed doors wide, not caring about marking the vehicle or ruining his father's retreat.

We fishtailed on the mulchy ground as the engine roared. He stomped on the accelerator and drove rocket-ship style through the small trail, past leering trees, over broken branches, and exploded onto a dirt track, leaving all phones, cars, and well-known cabins behind.

Penn wouldn't find me.

David and Dad wouldn't find me.

I truly was on my own.

# Chapter Two

# Penn

I THOUGHT THE night couldn't get any worse.

I was wrong.

Served me right, seeing as my entire life I'd had the shittiest luck of anyone. If I took a risk, it backfired. If I spied an opportunity, it was a con. If I saw hope, it was always false.

So why I thought tonight couldn't get any worse after Elle ran from the charity function, didn't answer her phone, and refused to come to the door when I drove over to her place, I didn't know.

This was my normal. I had to get used to it instead of being constantly surprised.

I'd returned home confused and fucked off with the entire world. I'd entered my building and climbed the steps to the renovated unit that I'd keep as my own while doing up the rest of the apartments for people transitioning from an existence on the streets back into the rat race we called life.

I had great plans for this place.

The chipped walls and leaky pipes didn't faze me. I had the funds to invest in its foundation and décor, and I couldn't fucking wait until the building crew had finished their current project in lower Manhattan and could work exclusively on mine.

My thoughts bounced between my past and Elle as I stalked into the kitchen and grabbed a glass of vodka on the rocks.

Carrying my drink to my bedroom, I didn't bother to undress. I merely kicked off my shoes, shrugged out of the silver blazer, and unbuckled my belt. The rest—a white shirt, silver tie, and metallic slacks remained on as I climbed onto the bed, sipped a sharp mouthful of liquor, and pulled the bag containing Elle's lingerie and sex toys from our first night together toward me.

I couldn't fucking wait to use the toys on her, but now, she'd run away. She'd run before I could tell her, then refused to have anything to do with me. Her door remained closed, her phone unanswered.

If I was honest, the anvil wedged where my heart should be made me ache. But I'd known we couldn't have a future. I'd banked on it. I'd hunted her knowing full well I would take what I wanted and then leave.

But that was before the chocolate mousse and the limo and the gala.

Each time I saw her, it got harder and harder to keep my emotions from spilling.

The fake engagement, the bullshit…all of it was gone. Just like Elle.

*Fuck.*

Exhaustion from all the years I'd been planning this finally caught up with me. I swigged the rest of my drink before my eyes could close.

I would rest tonight.

Tomorrow, I would apologize, accept her verbal lashing, and then walk out of her life for good.

The plan wasn't a good one but having it helped calm my messy thoughts.

I reclined against my pillows and vanished into sleep, just as Elle had vanished from my life for the second time.

* * * * *

Sleep began quickly and ended suddenly.

Just like I should've expected more shitty things to happen, I should've seen this coming.

But I hadn't because I was a fucking idiot.

I woke to a fist to my jaw, jarring me from chaotic dreams into manic reality.

Another fist landed on my solar plexus, stealing my oxygen, making me gasp.

Another fist to my jaw followed by a double jab to my stomach.

*What the fuck?*

Two men, four pummels, one of me.

I curled up on the mattress, protecting my head while they fucking beat me. Hip, chest, ribs, temple.

Wash and repeat.

I lost count how many blows they delivered or how many aches flared into being from new injuries and old. My past meant

I'd taken a beating a few times while others I'd done the nasty work.

Bones never forgot, though.

They heated some nights in remembrance. They ached on others in punishment.

I was a walking shambles of bones and lies, and these cunts had let themselves into my place to attack me while I was unconscious.

There was no way to retaliate without being knocked out. So I waited, grunting with agony, as they struck again and again.

Finally, when I didn't move or threaten to kill them, the bastards stopped their rain of pain, whispering to each other as I lay in my stupid little ball.

Spying an opportunity to fight back, I pushed aside the blazing discomfort and launched upright.

I always could move fast.

They didn't see it coming.

I landed an uppercut on one asshole's jaw and a side-kick to the other dickhead in the groin. "You fucking come into my place and hurt me?"

They stumbled backward, holding body parts.

I half-leapt, half-collapsed off my bed, fists raised. "Who the fuck are you and what are you doing in my apartment?"

The bigger guy of the two cracked his neck, rearranging his beefy body. He swiped at his lower lip where his teeth had sliced him from my uppercut. "You'll pay for that." He launched himself at me.

I met him head-on, fists to fists, kicks to kicks, but they'd already stripped my strength, and there were two of them.

His punches landed too often, whittling away my power.

"Hey, fucker," the smaller guy said with a balaclava over his face. "Lie down, or we'll knock you out."

The larger grunted something I couldn't hear, his face covered with acne scars and a chin strap. He decked me hard, ringing my skull with church bells, swiping my balance until the room spun.

I wobbled backward against the mattress.

I tried to blink it away—to keep fighting. But a solid punch to my chest sent me soaring into horizontal.

The smaller guy leapt on top of me, his knees pinning my chest to the bed. "Gonna stay down?"

I kicked, but the big thug grabbed my legs. "I wouldn't if I were you."

I glowered. "Get the hell off me."

"Say the magic words."

No fucking way was I being polite to these bastards.

"What do you want?" I spat. "Money? Too fucking bad, I don't have any here."

"Oh, we're not here to steal from you." The big guy chuckled. He motioned for his minion to get off my chest then planted a meaty hand on the same place he'd punched just a few seconds ago.

My ribs screamed as he pressed heavily, activating bruises. "Now that we have your attention, I'll give you the message."

"What message?"

He tapped my cheek in warning. "Ah, no talking back, got it?" He glanced at his buddy, rolling his eyes. "They never learn."

I bit my tongue with all the hate I wanted to spew. They broke into my place, beat me up, then had the motherfucking audacity to roll their eyes at me as if *I* were the idiot.

The second they left, I'd have them arrested, then ask Larry to ensure they never left the penitentiary system.

*Assholes.*

"Nope." The balaclava dude laughed. "I can hurt him more, if you want?"

"Nah, the orders were to rough him up not hospitalize him." The brute climbed off me, brandishing his fist in my face. "You have a message."

"From who?"

"Not gonna say who." He smirked. "Message is to stay away from her. She's mine. She's left you to marry me. So fuck off, and screw some other blonde." He cracked his knuckles. "Got it?"

Oh, hell yes, I got it.

That bastard Greg Hobson.

The guy I'd hated from the moment I first met him and not just because he was the competition. I despised the way he watched Elle. It bordered on obsessive.

"He hired you to scare me off." I laughed, hacking up a mouthful of crimson spit. "He's fucking delusional."

"Don't care what he is. Those are the terms."

I pressed my bloody nose, checking for a break. My eyes watered. "She'll never agree to be with him. He'd lost before I took her."

The big goon crossed his arms. "Don't care about the fine

print. We've done our job and delivered the message."

My mind raced, boycotting the image of Elle ever agreeing to be with Greg. She wouldn't. She couldn't.

Unless…

*Shit!*

I stood up. The room swam. My head pounded.

What if Greg hurt her? What if that was why she hadn't answered the door or picked up the damn phone?

*Elle.*

Shooting forward, I dodged the guys as they tried to hit me again.

"Hey!" They gave chase, but even bleeding and beaten, I had a lifetime of running on my side. Years of sprinting to save my skin. Decades of avoiding death.

I didn't look back.

Bolting from the bedroom, I skidded into the living room and slammed into the sideboard where I'd tossed my car keys.

My bare feet slapped on the hardwood, my trousers loose from no belt. But thank Christ I never undressed.

What I was about to do would've been severely inconvenient while naked.

My fingers hooked over the key chain as I propelled myself forward, ducked under a swinging fist, and bowled out the door before they could catch me.

I was gone before they managed to huff down the second flight of stairs.

# Chapter Three

# Elle

FROM ONE CABIN to another.

The décor and building materials were the same (pine everywhere), but this was smaller with a cozy living room, tiny kitchen, and narrow hallway to the bedrooms. However, judging by the car headlights that'd glinted off a body of water as we pulled down the long drive and stopped outside the quaint dwelling, we were now on a lake rather than buried in a forest.

The clock over the higgledy-piggledy stone fireplace said we'd been here an hour. A full hour since Greg tossed me onto the red and navy plaid couch, grabbed a bottle of gin from the fridge, and made us both a cocktail.

I'd accepted it and actually drank the sour liquid, doing my best to relax and let the liquor take away my fear so I could concentrate on the best way to get free.

My attention refused to leave the clock.

Four a.m. yet my eyes were wide and brain zapping with awareness rather than scratchy with sleep. We'd been traveling for hours. It felt like days since I'd seen Penn or Larry or Stewie. Months since I'd heard my dad or stroked Sage's soft fur.

Too damn long being Greg's little captive.

Greg groaned as he reclined on the single seat next to the couch; the twine from my wrist dangled over the arms of the chairs, forever joining me to him. "God, it's good to sit down."

"You've been sitting while driving."

He sipped his cocktail. "Driving is tiring."

"And kidnapping is wrong."

"Who said anything about kidnapping?" He smirked, bringing the glass to his lips again. "Last time I checked, you weren't a kid anymore." His gaze dragged up and down my body. "In fact, you're very grown up."

I fought the desire to slap him. My hands curled around my drink.

We stared for the longest minute, full of war and battle for authority.

Breaking the contest, I threw back the rest of the gin and planted the glass loudly on the wooden coffee table. "I need to go to the bathroom."

"So demanding." He stood, waiting for me to pull my aching body into standing. "But I can't have you being uncomfortable now, can I?"

"Just being in your company makes me uncomfortable."

His forehead furrowed. "Careful, Elle. That tongue of yours is going to get you into trouble."

Yanking on the rope, he marched forward, dragging me with him. He escorted me (for lack of a better kidnapping word) down the hallway to a single bathroom with a shower over the bath, an autumn leaf decorated shower curtain, and shell basin that had seen a few decades too many.

He sidestepped, letting me overtake him. "Don't try anything." Shoving me toward the toilet, he grinned and waved the string, pulling it with him. "I'll be right outside."

With his threat lingering, he shut the door.

If this had been a ploy to climb out the window or find a weapon in the medicine cabinet, the leash and my bladder would've made it impossible. The twine barely gave me enough room to fumble with my dress and back up onto the toilet to do my business.

My arm remained speared in front of me, doing my best to keep the rope from cutting off my circulation.

Once done, I washed my face in the basin. With droplets raining down my forehead, I glared at the whiteness of my cheeks from anxiety, the purple of my temple from his punch, and the redness in my left eye from his smack. My blonde hair mimicked a mini tornado with out of control curls, and my makeup had smeared beneath both eyes making me look like a haggard aging rock star.

I hated the reflection.

Turning away, I sucked in a deep breath, preparing to tolerate him again. But I paused, eyeing the mirror.

*I can't go.*

*Not without checking.*

Pulling open the medicine cabinet, I tried not to give into the despondency of finding nothing of use. No toe-nail clippers, no scissors, not even a Q-tip or floss.

The cupboard was bare, just like the water-swelled drawers beneath the sink.

Not one piece of human mess that I could use to saw at the rope or puncture Greg's jugular.

He smirked as I stepped into the corridor. "All done?"

I didn't reply.

He marched forward, tugging on the string. He didn't guide me back to the living room. "I think we've done enough for the night. I'm fucking wiped."

*So he's taking me to bed.*

*This is it.*

This was where my one-man experience became an unwanted two.

*At least, he won't steal my virginity.*

How would it feel to be taken against my control? Would I maintain my calm annoyance or break into pleading tears.

*I don't want to find out.*

He carted me into a bedroom, and turned on the bulb that hung in a sad tasseled shade above the queen-sized bed with a patchwork quilt, ancient wooden side tables, and wrought-iron bedside lights.

My skin crawled at the thought of sharing that mattress with him.

"Here, let me help you." His hands landed on my shoulders, spinning me around to undo the invisible zip of my silver dress.

"No, wait—" I darted forward, but he jerked the tiny zipper and yanked at the heavy satin on my shoulders.

"I've waited long enough." He tore the gorgeous garment off me, pushing it over my hips until gravity puddled it to the floor. Turning me around, he groaned.

The slinky silver and white lingerie I wore had been for Penn's benefit, not his.

Penn—the man who'd lied to me about everything. The man who didn't deserve me, just like Greg didn't deserve me.

I clamped my free arm over my breasts, hating that so much of me was exposed. I loathed the way his gaze latched onto my skin; how his hand came up to hover over my breast as if fighting his desire to touch me.

His eyes met mine as he licked his lips. "I was going to make us official tonight, but I've waited so fucking long to have you, Elle, I've become a bit of a sadist."

He leaned in, brushing his mouth over my bruised cheekbone from the driveway gravel. "I'm so hard for you, but the anticipation of what I'm going to do to you is almost as good as doing it."

Letting me go, he unbuttoned his shirt and tossed it on the floor, followed by his shoes, socks, and jeans. "For the next few hours, we'll rest. And then...we'll have some fun."

He wasn't lying that he wanted me. His cock stood proud in white boxers, mimicking a totem pole and flagstaff.

I tore my eyes away in disgust.

He chuckled under his breath. "Time to sleep, Elle. Tomorrow is a new day, and we have a shit-load of things to do." Pulling the twine around my wrist, he guided me to the bed and pulled back the sheets. "Get in."

My throat swelled with tears. The scream inside wanted to erupt and destroy—to summon help even though Greg had successfully laid a red herring and driven in a car I'd never seen before to a cabin he'd never mentioned.

We'd cut through forest and roads and small townships.

We were well and truly gone.

No one would come if I cried for help.

No one could save me but me.

When I didn't move, he pushed me onto the mattress. I fell forward, flopping angrily onto my side and curling my legs up to hide as much of my lingerie-clad body as possible.

Greg stared down like a doting lover, running his finger over my jawline, tucking in a curl. "I can't believe we're here. Together."

I arched away from his touch, trying to kill him with my stare. "We're not together. I don't want this. You're forcing me. Don't ever forget that I don't want you. I never have and I never will."

He stiffened. "You'll take that back. You'll see."

"Wrong. It will only become more and more real the longer you keep me. I liked you before, Greg. I thought you were a nice friend. But now...now, I *hate* you."

Clenching his jaw, he swiped the comforter from beneath my legs, making me roll a little. "Your lies are almost as bad as his were."

The painful barb wriggled inside me as he gently placed the linen over me. His footsteps fell heavy on the floorboards as he turned out the light and climbed into bed.

I remained stiff and unyielding, but he spooned me, gathering me tight in his arms.

His erection prodded my ass, making me sick.

The memories of sleeping with Penn and the chemistry between us tried to replace my current situation. But even that wasn't comforting. Penn had destroyed what I'd felt for him by being so terribly linked to my past.

He'd proven I couldn't trust anyone.

*Only my cat.*

Thank goodness, Dad had taken Sage home tonight; otherwise, she'd be unfed and unloved.

*God, Dad will panic when I don't show for work tomorrow.*

Fear about his heart pushed through me, ignoring my situation, tearing me into pieces about what this would do to him.

I swallowed my loathing, whispering in the dark. "Greg?"

He snuggled closer, his hips jamming forward. "Yes, baby?"

I shivered. "I'm not your baby."

"You are now."

I wouldn't let him distract me with an argument I couldn't win. "I need to call my father. You know he has heart issues. He needs to know I'm okay."

His nose tickled the back of my neck. "He'll survive."

I tried to wriggle away, but his arms looped tighter. The damn rope around my wrist kept me pinned. "He'll panic."

"Not my problem."

I shoved backward, rocking the bed. "It *is* your problem. And I'll tell you why. If he dies because of the stress of what you've done, I'll never stop trying to kill you. You have my undying promise that I will—"

He slapped a hand over my mouth, dragging my head backward until my skull wedged against his chin. "Hush. I'm trying to sleep." His cock thrust against my ass. "If you're a good girl, I might let you call him tomorrow. If you agree to our agreement."

I tensed.

No way in hell would I willingly sleep with him, but if he held my father's health as bribery, I would do what he wanted. I'd obey because I could never live with myself if Dad had another heart attack.

*I hate you, Greg.*

He kissed my cheek. "Now, no more talking." Wrapping the string from my wrist around his fingers, he stroked my hair with a threat disguised as tenderness. "Goodnight, Elle. Tomorrow is going to be so much fun."

# Chapter Four

# Penn

"SHE'S GONE, LARRY."

I fought every instinct to crush my phone with furious fingers.

My heart, my blood, my motherfucking breath raced with adrenaline from bolting from my place to Elle's and grabbing the security guard with the threat of a lawsuit if he didn't let me into her apartment to make sure she was safe in bed and not taken as I feared.

He'd done what I asked.

Her bed was empty.

And now, I stood in her kitchen where red wine stained the floor, her phone and silver bag from the party—the same bag I'd shoved off the limo seat to pull her into my lap—sat sadly on the counter.

A drawer hung open, the pantry unclosed.

Signs of an evident struggle made me fucking wild with rage and worry.

*I'll fucking kill him.*

He'd taken her.

He'd hurt her.

And I hadn't been there for her.

She'd run home because of me. She'd had to put up with that bastard for years because of me.

*I have to fix this.*

Larry cleared sleep from his throat, slipping into the authority figure I knew and respected. "Gone? Who's gone?"

"Elle," I snapped. "That idiot she works with has taken her."

Larry didn't ask how I knew or if I was sure. He'd never been suspicious of me because I only ever told him the truth.

He was the exception to my rule.

Mainly because he'd trusted me before I gave him reason to. After hearing my tale when we first met, I'd expected him to scoff and roll his eyes like all the others. But for the first time, someone believed me. He'd stayed by my side and done what he'd promised. He gave me a second chance when no one else would.

His voice lost its haze. "What are the details?"

"Greg came in and abducted her then sent his fucking goonies after me to scare me off."

"Time-frame?"

"Who the fuck knows." I paced the kitchen, ignoring the security guard who'd let me in and who was on his phone to the police. "Could've been the same time the assholes came to ensure I had bad dreams or could've been the moment she left the gala."

"Have you called her father yet?"

"No."

Rustling happened in the background as Larry no doubt clambered from bed. Waking him when he needed his rest was not a good thing, but I couldn't do this on my own. I'd tried to navigate life without leaning on anyone and look where that got me. The day Larry found me was the day I learned how to share and let good things happen to me and not just the bad.

"Hang up and call her father. Tell the police, get all the information you can, then come here. We'll go after him together."

*No, we won't.*

"Okay." I cut the call before I could tell him that I'd get Greg's whereabouts, but I wouldn't take him as reinforcements. His health had only just improved. I wouldn't risk him as well as Elle.

I'd go after her on my own. I'd chased her for my own selfish reasons. I hadn't cared about her mental state when she found out who I was.

Most of the time, I'd convinced myself that I would walk away before it got to that stage.

Shit, it had already gone on too long.

I'd tried to end it.

But each time, she revealed a little more of herself, gave a little more, and fucking stole everything of mine in the goddamn process.

And now, I'd get her back—even if it was stupid to go alone. I'd always done things the hard way.

I left the security guard to welcome the tardy police and stalked into her bedroom to call the brownstone where Elle used to live.

I knew the number by heart, just like I knew what window was hers, what her favorite food was (blueberry pancakes), how many times she'd snuggled with that damn cat (over six hundred since I'd starting watching), and how hard she worked for Belle Elle (every hour of her life), which was what made my guilt so much worse.

Guilt compounded on guilt for every awful thing I'd thought about her over the past three years.

The phone rang.

I paused with my fingertips tracing her pillow, noticing the pristine sheets with no feline ball indenting the mattress. Sage hadn't attacked me when I arrived, which made me suspect the cat was either with Elle's father or Greg had taken it when he'd taken Elle.

"Hello?" A groggy voice finally came on the line.

Thank Christ for landlines and the non-ability to silence them at night.

"Mr. Charlston? It's Penn Everett."

Joe Charlston cleared his throat. "What do you need at five o'clock in the morning that couldn't wait for normal hours, son?"

My heart did a weird flip at the endearment. He was nothing like I thought he'd be. I'd despised him almost every day for three years. I'd misjudged him just like I'd misjudged his daughter. "I need all the information you have on Steve Hobson's son, Greg. Any real estate purchases or favorite locations."

His voice whipped sharp. "Why? What's happened?"

I braced myself. "Greg has taken your daughter."

*"What?"*

I pinched the bridge of my nose, dislodging dried blood and activating bruises. I'd forgotten about my bare feet and bloody face when I'd shoved the security guard into the elevator. I must look fucking awful. "Elle has been taken by the cocksucker Greg Hobson. Her apartment is empty. There are signs of a fight. I need to find her. Immediately."

*Otherwise, who the fuck knows what he'll do to her.*

Joe barked, "Stay there, I'm coming over."

"No—just tell me—" The phone went dead.

I growled into the empty room.

*Goddammit.*

More time wasted. More people involved.

I had to leave. I'd call him from the road.

I wouldn't wait any longer than I had to.

Elle was mine.

I would bring her home on my own.

* * * * *

As planned, my cell-phone rang fifteen minutes later when Elle's father arrived at his daughter's apartment only to find me missing. "Where the hell are you?"

"Driving."

"You should be here helping me look for Elle."

My fingers tightened on the wheel. "I *am* helping look for Elle."

"By what? Driving in circles?"

I didn't bother telling him that Larry had contacts in the NYPD—that he could help me with phone records and credit card statements. I'd wanted a faster way, hoping Joe could provide, but if he was going to slow me down, then so be it.

He'd get left behind.

"Tell me everything you can about Steve and Greg."

Joe sniffed. "Greg lives with his father a few blocks over from me. However, he's not there. I called Steve, and he's as freaked as I am about all of this. He said Greg never came home last night—but that's nothing new. He has girlfriends who he stays with periodically."

I ignored the fact that the slime ball slept around all the while trying to get Elle into bed.

I'd kill him just for that.

"Any other property? Known addresses he'd go to on his own?" My car broke the speed limit as I weaved down Broadway.

"Steve bought a log cabin a few years ago out in Rochester. He said Greg might've—"

"The address. Now."

"It's off the beaten track. Look for a creek called Bearfoot Rapids. The house is tucked away with a carved lumberjack holding a mailbox at the start of the driveway."

"No street name or number?"

"No, that's what made it appealing. It can't be found easily."

*Fucking brilliant.*

Holding back my curse, I gritted, "Thanks. I'll call you when

I'm there."

I hung up and tossed the phone onto the seat beside me.

Rochester was a good five-hour drive away.

Christ, he could do anything to her in that time, and I'd be too late.

The Mercedes snarled as I stomped on the pedal, forcing gas to feed its greedy engine.

*Hold on, Elle.*

This time, I wouldn't let her down.

# Chapter Five

# Elle

SUNSHINE.
A new day.
No sleep.
No rest.
Only panic.

Greg shifted, his arm still locked around my middle, his skin against mine, his body sickeningly close.

Dawn had arrived, and I'd watched every painful minute of it as the sky switched from black to pink then pink to gold, basking the cabin, glittering on the lake through the windows.

It took all my willpower to stay calm and not give in to the panic gnawing at my bones.

How many more mornings would pass before I could get free?

Greg rolled over; the leash tethering me to him jerked my wrist. My skin was red and irritated from rope burn.

I grunted as he forced me to roll over, tucking me against his body. "Morning, beautiful."

I bit my tongue and didn't reply.

If I did, I'd spew curses and commands—neither of which would do me any good.

I had to hope that if I remained silent and obedient, he'd let me call Dad and ease his worry, so I remained parented and not an orphan.

The only good thing about Greg taking me was I didn't have time to stew about Penn and his deception. I only had the brain capacity to currently hate Greg.

*Penn will come later.*

"I don't care if you don't speak, Elle. I rather like quiet women." Unraveling the rope from his fist, he stood up and stretched. Morning wood once again speared his boxer-briefs.

He smirked, catching me looking. "That's all yours the moment you've had a shower." He bent over me, pressing his hands into the pillow on either side of my ears. "Can't fuck you without washing you first. Who the hell knows if that bastard touched you last night."

I fought the reply plastering itself over my face.

Penn *had* touched me.

He'd fucked me in the limo before I knew the truth. I'd believed he felt something for me while I felt something for him. I was excited, thinking he'd be honest and forthright and all the mistrust and lies would vanish like mist fading over the lake.

I'd begged for clarity.

Just not the clarity I'd been given.

My necklace had ruined those fantasies.

Grabbing my hand, Greg pulled me from the warm covers and into the crisp morning air. No heating meant goosebumps scattered over my flesh then layered with more as he leered at me. "All this time and we could've been waking up side by side, instead of working on different floors at Belle Elle." His fingers traced my belly button. "Isn't it nice?" He leaned forward, brushing his lips against mine.

I ripped my face away, not only because I had a phobia of morning breath but because he had no right, *none*, to kiss me.

"Let me go, Greg." The first words I'd spoken in hours.

He grinned. "You mean untie this?" He tugged the twine, making my arm bounce.

"You know what I mean. Everything. Cut me loose, drive me home. This has gone on long enough."

He shook his head. "You're not leaving until you understand your place is by my side."

"My place is running Belle Elle. With you in a prison cell."

He chuckled, mirth bright in his green eyes rather than retribution. "You'll change your mind the more you get to know me."

*I highly doubt it.*

Carting me from the bedroom, he guided me into the bathroom and undid the rope around my wrist. "Get in the shower."

I rubbed at my sore skin, backing up against the sink. "I'm

not washing with you in here."

"Oh yes, you fucking are." He grabbed the edges of his boxer-briefs, pulling them down his legs. His cock sprung free, heavy and hard with red veins bulging on the sides. He wasn't as big as Penn, but it looked angry.

Before I could move, he grabbed my shoulders and spun me around. With quick fingers, he unhooked my bra.

My arms slammed over my chest, covering myself.

It didn't do any good.

He snatched my arms away, making me teeter, bruising me as he ripped the straps down and tossed the bra into the hallway. He spun me back to face him. "Now the rest."

"Go to hell." I kept my arms over my chest, defending my modesty.

His gaze fell to my panties, a heated smirk on his lips. "Are you going to remove those or shall I?"

I backed up. "Greg...don't."

"Greg, don't," he mocked with a sneer. "Do you know how many years I've had to listen to you giving orders? Smiling at me over the dinner table with your holier-than-thou bitch face. Giving me commands at work when all I really wanted to do was fuck you." He loomed over me. "You thought you hid your true feelings, but every time you looked at me, I knew. I saw your disdain. I knew you believed you were better than me—"

I slapped him.

I didn't think it through. I just did it.

We both froze, equally shocked.

I hissed, "If that's the bullshit you're feeding yourself, then you're completely screwed up. I never looked down on you, Greg. For most of our childhood, I enjoyed playing with you. But then you went and let jealousy corrupt—"

He grabbed my jaw, squeezing my sentence to a stop. "*Jealousy?* You think this is about jealousy?" He laughed with utmost frustration. "I'm not jealous of you, Elle. I don't envy what you have."

He brushed my lips with his thumb. "I don't care that you're one of the richest women in the world. That doesn't intimidate me. What *does* intimidate me is some fucking loser thinking he can lie about being engaged to you just to get access to what you have."

I fought in his hold, lashing my fingers around his wrists to get free. "That wasn't why he lied."

*He did it to sleep with me after a three-year promise in an alley.*

"Don't care. He's gone now. I merely want to be with you, to share in what you have. Is that so wrong?" His voice lowered. "I don't want to take it away from you, Elle. I only want to enjoy it side by side. I'm willing to be a good husband, hard worker, and loyal father to any kids we have. This isn't about me stealing from you. It's about me giving you what you deserve."

I snorted. "What I deserve? Do I deserve to be kidnapped and held against my will?"

Please, he was moronic.

"Until you listen to me, yes." Shoving me away, Greg ripped at my silver and white panties and jerked them down my legs.

One arm stayed glued to my chest, and the other darted between my thighs to hide the trimmed curls and smoothness I'd taken to maintaining ever since I met Nameless and became a slave to my libido in an open park. I'd never wanted to be unprepared for a moment where sex could be a possibility—even when my life had been chained to work with no time for pleasure.

Until Penn.

My heart threw up then did an odd pirouette. Part of me was repulsed I'd slept with him knowing what I knew now, while the shallower, less cohesive part of me couldn't care less. He'd been a crook three years ago—could he have changed? Could he be a good person after being so bad?

*You're talking gibberish.*

I blamed it on Greg.

I only accepted Penn's lies and who he was hiding because even in that dark alley with his awful fingers shredding my clothes and stealing my money, he still wasn't as bad as Greg was. Sure, he would've scared me and stolen what he could. But Greg thought he could keep me in a lifetime of servitude, believing we were equals all while he suffocated me in a marriage I resented, revoked, and wanted to rip to shreds.

Grabbing me around the waist, he lifted me over the edge of the tub and held me until my feet gained traction on the slippery bath.

Climbing in behind me, I shivered with repulsion as he reached around my nakedness and turned the tap on.

I gasped as icy water spewed from the single showerhead directly onto my chest.

Greg wrapped his arms around me, keeping me under the glacial torrent, breathing hot breath into my ear. "See how cold you are on your own, Elle? How hard it is to get warm?"

Moving closer, his front pressed against my back, wedging unwanted but much-needed body heat against my back.

His cock thickened, pulsing against my lower spine as he cradled me. I hated that he offered shelter from the cold spray, twisting my mind as the protector when he'd been the one to turn on the water in the first place.

"Let me go." I reached behind to dig my fingernails into his hip. Shivering hijacked me until my teeth rattled. "Dammit, Greg. Stop!"

He flinched but only held tighter. Reaching with his left arm, he swiveled the tap to hot, and I waited with goosebumps and trembles as the liquid ice slowly switched to tepid waterfall to steamy stream to scalding tempest.

I winced as my skin turned lobster red. "Ouch!"

"Whoops. Can't have you burning up now, can we?" He twisted the tap again, finally finding the right hot to cold ratio.

My flesh no longer tried to turn into an ice-berg or melt with magma, but I didn't relax. Not one little bit.

Turning me around, he barely noticed my resistance. My feet slipped with no effort on the bath, my body stiff as a sword. When I stood facing him with my arms acting as my underwear, he grinned. "Back you go." He pushed until my head vanished under the shower, drenching my long hair.

The water offered a reprieve, filling my ears and eyes and senses with cleansing rushes rather than reveal the tiny bathroom in the tiny cabin with the madman I was currently with.

After I was sufficiently drowned, he pulled me forward and opened a bottle of shampoo on the ledge of the bath. "I'm going to show you how supportive and kind I can be, Elle."

He licked his lips, tipping synthetic berry bubbles into his palm. "I'm going to make sure you're squeaky clean, and then we're going to have a chat about our new life together."

I bit my tongue.

Words didn't work on him, and I refused to stoop to a level where I begged or pleaded for some rationality. There was no rationality left. I was in a shower naked with Greg while he promised to care for me after I'd promised I'd kill him if my disappearance hurt my father.

He either believed in his delusions or was so twisted, he honestly thought I wanted him and was merely playing hard to get.

His hands landed on my head, rubbing the unwanted bubbles

into my strands, coating me with a foreign smell.

I missed my bathroom and honeysuckle body-wash.

I missed Sage and her morning meow and head-butt.

I missed my father and his gentle smile.

Hell, I even missed Penn even while hating him.

"The silent treatment won't work on me forever, you know." Greg gathered my wet tresses, plopping them onto my head where he massaged more suds.

I refused to enjoy his fussing. My skin crawled rather than relaxed with the soft pressure.

I put my chin in the air, glowering.

*We'll see.*

"If you're going to be like that, turn around." He pushed my shoulder, swiveling me in place. I wobbled on the slippery surface, refusing to unlock my arms from protecting my decency to act as balancing rods.

His fingers trailed from my hair down my back, spreading more bubbles. My teeth chattered in horror as he hooked his hands under my arms, washing me intimately, cleansing me of my past life for whatever he meant to do to me in this twisted present.

"I can't wait until you're clean, Elle," he murmured as his fingers drifted to my ass. "Once he's washed away, I can replace every memory with me."

I swallowed a moan as his touch pressed into my crack.

I spun around, not caring anymore if he saw me naked as one arm swung up to punch him and the other gripped the white tiled wall for balance. "Don't fucking touch me!"

He caught my arm mid-swing, holding me steady. His gaze locked onto my breasts then to my core.

A blackness I instantly feared cloaked him. His cock grew harder as he captured my nipple, tugging hard. "Fuck, you're stunning."

"Let me go." I tried to fight, but he kept my wrist imprisoned and deliberately pushed me sideways against the wall to keep my other arm pinned.

"In another few days, you'll wonder why you fought this, Elle." His voice grew husky with desire. "I'll show you how good we can be together. You'll see." His hand dropped from my breast, trailed down my stomach, and cupped my core.

I fought harder, slipping and forcing him to take my weight to keep me standing. He balanced me but never let go where he held between my legs. His fingers remained on the outside, merely a dominating reminder that he believed I was his now and everything about me was his, too.

"This is the part of you that needs washing the most." He gathered more bubbles, pressing them into my short curls. "Fucking asshole needs to be deleted."

I tore my eyes from his, glaring at the ceiling while furious tears sprang. He washed me slowly, possessively, with so many threats and promises.

I couldn't stop the tears overflowing, mixing with the shower, rolling down my chest.

He caught one with his finger, bringing it to his lips. "Don't cry, Elle. You're clean now. What happened is in the past, we have a brand new future to look forward to." Pushing me under the spray, his hands trailed over every inch as he rinsed away the soap.

Cuddling me into him, his embrace reeked of contempt for Penn and lust for me.

A recipe that would end up ruining me.

"Are you hungry?" He kissed my wet scalp. "Come on, let's eat. And then…we'll get to know each other exactly the way we should've years ago."

# Chapter Six

# Penn

I PARKED AT the top of the long, sweeping driveway that disappeared into dense trees.

A stupid carved lumberjack with an axe and overalls decorated with peeling paint offered me a mailbox to place friendly correspondence, not deliver war on the inhabitants.

I wanted to hack it to pieces.

No lights glimmered apart from the fresh pink of dawn. No signs of habitation apart from recent tire tracks down the gravel.

But I knew.

*They're here.*

Leaving my Merc, I grabbed my phone and jogged down the driveway. I wanted to sneak up and surprise Greg, rather than drive and give him notice.

He'd already taken what was mine. I wouldn't give him the opportunity to hurt her, too.

My shoeless feet glided lightly as I ran, trying to make as little noise as possible. Pebbles bruised my soles, but I didn't stop.

*Goddammit, how long is this driveway?*

The gravel kept going, deeper into woodland. If this wasn't a rescue mission, it would've been a nice place to bring Elle. To get away from the city and relax together. And by relax, I meant fuck until we both couldn't walk.

There was something about her I couldn't fight. When I was around her—shit, all I could think about was touching, kissing, and being inside her.

Three years' worth of blue balls. Three years of waiting since the first time we met.

My gut clenched at the thought of her with Greg. I hadn't

been nice or even kind to her ever since I plotted the moment in the gin bar with her father. Everything about our 'convenient fate-designed' meetings had been meticulously planned.

I hadn't let my guard down once.

I'd taken what I wanted from her as I believed she owed me that after what had happened.

But now, I felt fucking sick that I could be such a bastard—especially since she'd been taken by someone she trusted, all while being lied to by me.

I was an asshole.

*I admit it.*

The sky slowly grew lighter as a cabin appeared in the forest. A small clearing with a homely retreat nestled in the foliage.

Greg's car sat out in front with the twinkling of dew on the gray paint.

My heart raced, preparing for a fight.

Keeping to the trees, I skirted the front porch, making my way to the side.

Ducking low, I charged toward the house and pressed against the timber siding. Twigs jammed into my bare feet but I ignored the pain. A bay window sat above me, taunting me to look.

My ears strained for noise. For footsteps or voices.

When nothing came—no creak of floorboards, no flush of water—I stood upright and peered into the dim cabin. Birds slowly woke up, their morning song the only sound apart from my shallow breathing.

The window looked into the kitchen, the kitchen opened out into a living room, the living room funneled traffic to the hallway.

Empty.

Every room.

No signs of life at all.

*Shit, where are you, Elle?*

Moving around the property, I peered into more windows, searching.

The bedroom with plaid blankets: nothing.

The office with overflowing bookshelves: no one.

The side living room with an ancient video cassette player and TV: empty.

Moving toward the front porch again, I forced myself to remain calm even while I fought panic.

Joe gave me this address.

Greg's car was here.

Yet him and Elle were gone.

*Fuck!*

Leaping off the stoop to continue my hunt, my eyes caught the displacement of gravel.

Footsteps.

One big with boot tracks.

One small with no tracks.

Was Elle barefoot?

*Like me?*

My feet had not appreciated the jog down gravel or looked forward to the pokes and pinches from more twigs in the forest. Knowing she'd felt the same discomfort didn't make me happy—it made me fucking furious.

Clutching my phone, I followed the prints into the trees, willing the sun to wake up completely and chase away the remaining shadows. I hadn't had quality sleep, I'd been beaten awake as my alarm clock, and twitched on an overload of adrenaline and rage, but my hands were steady (if not bloody), and my eyes were narrowed (if not blood-shot).

I was ready to attack.

No mercy.

Breaking into a jog, I followed the small path, hoping against fucking hope that Greg hadn't marched her into the undergrowth to shoot and bury her. Images of finding her corpse haunted me in ways I couldn't admit.

I thought I'd protected myself from her this past month. I thought I'd steeled myself against feeling anything.

I'd done a shitty job with the way my heart pounded with terror. I'd wasted so long, fantasizing about her being mine. And she'd been mine—for a brief moment. If I couldn't have her again…what the fuck would I do?

Leave?

Say goodbye?

How could I?

I forced my mind back to facts rather than idiotic matters of the heart. If Greg had wanted to kill her, why not just do it at Belle Elle—somewhere her father would see and destroy the company from the inside out?

*He's an asshole, but he's not mentally disturbed.*

Why would he kill her where he could be questioned? Much better to do it where no one would see, and he had a better chance of denying his involvement.

*Even if this is his father's cabin.*

Breaking through the tree line, my heart sank as a shed with open doors and an empty interior beckoned me closer.

Tire marks led from the gloomy cobwebbed shack, footprints in the dust showing Greg had been here with Elle.

And now, they were gone.

# Chapter Seven

# Elle

"YOU KNOW HOW to cook, right?" Greg asked, twirling the steak knife tip on the countertop.

For the thirtieth time, I tugged on the gold negligée he'd made me slip into. Where he'd gotten it from, I had no idea—it wasn't a Belle Elle brand, and the satin slipped over my nakedness in the most awful way—but he'd been extremely incessant I wear it.

*I hate you, Greg.*

The spaghetti straps barely held the material over my nipples while the hem skimmed my ass cheeks, leaving so much of me nude and available for his ogling attention.

I stood in the middle of the kitchen glaring at the knife, wanting so much to pluck it from his hand and plunge it into his leg.

I didn't want to kill him—just incapacitate him until I could get free, call David to come and break me out of here, and then press charges like a sane person would.

*Greg is not sane.*

*You have full reason to join him in that insanity and kill him.*

I didn't doubt I would if it came down to his life or mine. But call me old fashioned, I couldn't kill someone I'd known all my life. I couldn't switch off like that.

He slammed the knife down. "Better answer me, Elle. I've been kind and gentle, but if you don't start talking to me, I'll have to show a different side of me, got it?"

I planted my hands on the counter, bracing myself. "It's not a different side to you. I know that side better than you think. I've seen it in your eyes for years."

He grinned. "Great, so you know I'm telling the truth."

I swallowed as he moved toward me and stroked my cheek, his eyes dropping to my chest. "I showered you, dressed you, and now the least you can do is cook us a lovely meal to celebrate our new future together."

I cringed, stepping away from his touch.

His face shadowed. "I almost forgot." Clicking his fingers, he turned and disappeared into the living room where a duffel bag sat on the couch. Placing the knife on the coffee table—away from my eager fingers—he unzipped the bag and checked the contents.

Greg had many faults, but I'd never known him as so meticulous.

He'd planned my abduction flawlessly.

Clothes for me hung in the wardrobe right alongside clothes for him. The kitchen was stocked with delicacies and staple requirements, and hygiene products such as toothbrushes and toilet paper were in ample supply.

The bathroom had been bare when we'd arrived, but that was before he'd returned to the Dodge and emptied the trunk.

How long had he been concocting this?

*How long is he planning to keep me here?*

Greg returned with the bag, placing it with a loud clunk on the kitchen counter.

My hair was still damp from the shower, my skin still warm despite the lack of thermal properties of the skimpy negligée. Once he'd turned off the water, he'd dried me (despite my fight and refusal), then dragged me into the bedroom where he'd shoved the gold satin over my head.

He hadn't let me go until I stood in the middle of the kitchen and he'd grabbed the knife. The sharp blade didn't scare me, but the lack of warm clothes and shoes did. Even if I did spy an opportunity to run, I wouldn't get far unless I dressed appropriately.

Greg patted the duffel. A smirk spread his lips. "I brought these as a last resort, but after having the convenience of the rope around your wrist, I think they'll come in handy." Pulling out a leather cuff, the heavy clinking of chains sounded.

My mouth shot dry as his bicep bulged, hefting the weight from the bag to the counter.

He'd dressed in a white t-shirt with faded jeans, his dark blond hair swept back, drying from our joint shower, while the odd droplet turned his t-shirt translucent on the shoulders.

He looked innocent…familiar. The contents he'd just dumped into view were the exact opposite.

I backed away, bumping into the oven. "What the hell is that?"

He chuckled. "Gifts for you, of course."

"I don't want any gifts."

"Believe me, you'll change your mind soon enough." Unbuckling the leather cuff that attached to the glinting chain, he carried the metal across the living room to a sturdy looking hook. A fire poker and small shovel hung for cleaning out the ashes in the grate.

Removing the poker, he secured the chain and locked it with a small padlock before making his way back toward me, letting the links slip through his fingers to stain the floorboards with imprisonment.

The length kept going from the living room to where I stood petrified in the kitchen.

Dropping the remaining chain by my feet, he said, "Until you behave and stop looking at the door to run, I'm going to ensure you stay here with me, okay?"

"No, not okay. You've already squirreled me away where no one can find us." I darted backward, trapped by cabinets. "I don't like being tied up, Greg."

"Too bad." His eyes narrowed. "I didn't ask your opinion or permission." He held up the leather cuff. "Now, come here."

I shook my head, my eyes flickering to the knife on the coffee table over his shoulder.

If only I could reach it. "I won't run."

"I know you won't. This system will make sure of it." He advanced.

I pushed harder into the cabinetry but had nowhere else to go.

Only a foot separated us.

Greg smiled then dropped to one knee as if to propose. I held my breath, shock and horror crawling over my insides as he reached for my ankle and latched his heinous fingers around my leg.

The moment he caught me, he wrapped the leather cuff around my limb, pulling tight before running the chain through the small hook at the top and securing it with the aid of another padlock.

The second I was locked in place, he stood with a triumphant look on his face. "You should be able to go anywhere you need in the cabin but not outside." Returning to the bag, he pulled out another chain, this one shorter with two cuffs on either side instead of one. "Give me your hands."

"What?"

"Your hands, Elle."

"You can't be serious."

"I'm deadly fucking serious." He came forward, letting one cuff dangle while he reached for my wrist—the one with rope burns from the stupid twine he'd used.

*What the hell is he doing?*

"I'm not your prisoner, Greg."

"I beg to differ." His fingers bit into my arm as he wrapped the cuff around me and once again secured it with a tiny padlock. At least the leather was soft and supple rather than coarse and prickly. It looked expensive with gold stitching and faux fur trim. Not the cheap kink sold at wannabe sex shops.

*Not that I know what cheap or expensive sex toys look like.*

A memory of the Seahorse and other dildo samples from Loveline reminded me Penn still had my property.

*He has my underwear, too.*

At the time, it hadn't bothered me. I thought I'd be back for more sexcapades, and he would use the toys on me. But that was before he let me walk home and I was almost molested; before he scooped me up and washed my feet. Before his lies came crashing down and burst into fiery flames.

Capturing my other arm, Greg growled as I wriggled and tried to break free. "Stand still."

He grunted as he tucked my arm against his body and circled my other wrist with the last cuff. The soft snick of the fourth padlock shattered my thoughts of strangling him for my freedom.

"There, nice and secure." Greg kissed my forehead, pulling me forward thanks to the looping chain now permanently present.

I deliberated punching and kicking and screaming and *cursing* him, but what would that achieve? My leg was tethered to the fireplace, I was practically naked, and my arms were now joined like an inmate on death row.

He wouldn't let me run. He wouldn't let me go.

He'd only pay me back if I hurt him. And I already knew how painful his punches could be.

My temple throbbed in agreement.

Had it only been last night he'd hit me in my apartment

garage?

It had to have been centuries with how tired and stressed I was.

Even the thought of having sex in the limo with Penn didn't affect me the way it had before.

The tummy moths were dead, their paper wings dissolved in bile.

I'd gone from liking Penn to hating him, and it was *exhausting* hating two people at the same time for entirely different reasons.

Greg released me, inspecting his handiwork. "You look hot in chains."

"You'll look hot behind bars when the police catch you."

"There'll be no crime once you come around to my way of thinking."

"I'll never come around because I don't want what you do."

He chuckled under his breath. "So argumentative. I don't remember you being like that in the past."

I tried to plant my hands on my hips, but the chain wasn't quite long enough. I settled for threading my fingers together and holding tight with all the aggression I wished I could throw at him. "That's because you don't know me. You never knew me. You never *tried* to get to know me."

His brow settled angrily over green eyes. "I'm trying now. So give me a goddamn break and give me a chance."

I laughed, rattling the chain in his face. "This is not trying. This is kidnapping. Release me."

"Still used to barking orders, huh, Elle?" He padded barefoot from the kitchen. Hoisting himself onto a bar-stool, he added, "I'm hungry. Let's get back to the topic of food."

I moved to face him, glad that the counter now separated us even if he was demanding I cook for him like some slave. I moved my right leg, testing the weight of the chain locking me to the fireplace across the room.

*God, that's heavy.*

The metal loops weren't light nor were they easy to step over or kick away as I did a small circle, testing how fast I could move. The chain around my wrists was lighter, with just enough room to scoop and handle things but not enough to stab him with a knife or swing a skillet on his head.

My shoulders rolled, finally understanding that this wasn't just a game to him.

This was serious.

"What do you want, Greg?" My bravery faltered. "Tell the truth. I'm done playing."

He slid off the bar stool, came back into the kitchen, and hoisted himself onto the counter in front of me. "I'm glad you're finally ready to be sensible." His dangling legs thudded against the dishwasher as he pulled another knife from the butcher's block and twirled it tip first again. "But I've told you what I want. You just keep ignoring me."

"No, you haven't." I spread my hands, giving him the space to speak. "You haven't set your terms; you've merely demanded what you expect. They're different." I did my best to ignore the skimpy nightdress and leather cuffs, draping myself in an imaginary suit with bodyguards and personal assistants ready to do whatever I commanded. "Pretend we're in a business negotiation at Belle Elle. What would you say?"

He smirked. "I'd say this was a takeover."

"A hostile takeover, don't you mean?"

"No, Elle, a partnership. A new director of the board buying fifty-one percent of the stock but letting the old manager keep forty-nine."

*Oh, how generous of you.*

"That's not a partnership. It's a dictatorship."

"Wrong again. It *is* a partnership with the smallest amount of authority."

I would never sign Belle Elle over to him. Even if he killed me. The company wasn't mine to give. It was my family's—it belonged to my future children. The Charlston legacy would only go to a man worthy of serving by my side.

"If it's about the money, I'll give you some. What do you want? A million? Two?"

He threw his head back, laughing hard. "Oh, I knew your anger was cute, but you're just adorable when you try to bargain with chump change."

"A million isn't chump change."

"It is to you."

"Ten million." I pursed my lips. "Ten million and you walk away." I flung my hands in the air, hating the weight of the chain and the jingle of the links as I moved. "Walk away from this, from me, from Belle Elle, and I'll wire the money to you right now."

"We don't have reception out here. No Wi-Fi."

"Fine, take me back to the city, and I'll do it there."

*Where I can call the police, not the bank.*

"Nice try, Elle." He tapped his nose with the sharp blade. "I much prefer our current situation." Leaping off the counter, he inhaled my neck like a grizzly bear. "Ten million is still chump change. You can't buy me off. The only bribe I'd accept would be..."

He deliberately left me hanging.

I hated myself, but I took his bait. "Would be?"

"You." His eyes flashed. "Marry me, give me fifty-one percent of Belle Elle, fifty percent of the contents of your bank accounts, and then divorce me for all I care."

My eyes flared. "You're saying if I married you and gave you half of everything I own, that you'll walk away?"

He cocked his head. "Maybe."

"Maybe isn't an answer I can agree to."

"Guess you'll just have to make us dinner and stop trying to barter then, huh?" He ran the knife around my belly button, pressing the gold satin against my skin. "Cook me something, wife-to-be, then we can finally see if we're as compatible in the bedroom as we are in the boardroom."

"We were never compatible in the boardroom. You were never *allowed* in the boardroom."

"Precisely. You were boss there." His teeth glinted. "But here in my bed, in my cabin—I'm the boss.

"And I can't fucking wait to show you what I can do."

# Chapter Eight

# Penn

"HE'S NOT FUCKING here," I growled into the phone. "Does he have another property?"

Joe Charlston cleared his throat, the sound of an engine loud on the line. "No, that's the only one that Steve—"

"Everett? Is that you?" Steve Hobson's voice replaced Joe's. I envisioned him snatching the phone, either to stand up to me and beg me not to hurt his cocksucker of a son or help me find the woman who was like a daughter to him.

"Tell me where I can find him." I paced the woodland where the car tracks vanished onto a road. I had no clue what direction they'd gone in, no more hints or clues to chase.

Elle was still out there.

A new day had replaced the night, and I was fucking raging at the thought of her still with him.

"He's not at the cabin?"

I ground my teeth. "He was. His Porsche is here, but they're not. He had another car. They're still missing."

Steve cursed something I didn't catch. "I don't know what else to tell you."

"Tell me something helpful. Tell me you know your son. Hotels he prefers, locations he likes."

Steve paused then rushed, "I know he was thinking of buying a fishing lodge. I don't think he did, but then again, I had no clue he had another car up at the cabin." His voice turned despondent. "This entire fiasco is showing how little I know my own flesh and blood."

Another man came on the phone. A man I remembered vividly for multiple reasons. And he remembered me. "Everett,

David speaking. Elle's bodyguard."

"I know who you are."

*I remember the night we first met when your judgment stole all my joy at being with Elle and reminded me I was scum who doesn't deserve her.*

"I'm driving Mr. Charlston and Mr. Hobson to the cabin. Wait there, and we'll track them down together. I'll do some digging with my contacts and see if there are any other assets under his name."

Contacts.

Digging.

*Of course.*

I had someone better to call.

Urgency to hang up on such a pointless conversation made me snarl, "Come here, I can't stop you. But I won't be here when you arrive. I'll find her on my own."

I hung up, not caring I'd given Elle's father shit-loads of reasons why he should ban his daughter from ever seeing me again—if she ever let me in the same room as her, of course.

But I didn't care about family dynamics and winning favors.

All I cared about was finding Elle and making sure she was safe.

If she tried to kill me after I told her who I was, then I would accept that. At least she would be back home where she belonged.

My chest tightened at the future conversation we would have. The explanation about why I had her necklace, why I'd done what I had that night in the alley, and why I'd tracked her down (thanks to her I.D card) then taken things she wasn't ready to give.

But first, I had to find her.

My fingers shook as I punched a well-used number into my phone.

He answered on the first ring.

The man who I turned to for everything.

The man I called my father and friend.

"Larry speaking."

"You still have that Meerkat in your zoo?"

First thing Larry had taught me: people were always listening. The higher in society you climbed, the bigger your bank account grew, the more people eavesdropped on every part of your life.

Meerkat was code for cops and zoo was code for payroll. Larry was a lawyer. And a damn fine one. But it didn't mean he didn't use extra tools when it suited him—all in the name of defending the innocent, of course. The same method had helped free me, revealing what I'd sworn under oath to be true even when the jury didn't believe me.

Even when I'd been thrown away to rot in a cell for something I didn't do.

"Yes, my zoo is always full."

"Great, I need some apples."

*Stupid code for information. We need to change that one.*

"Name it."

"You know the animal in question. I need bucket monitoring for any large refills in the last few years. Track down his zookeeper and any cage cleaners. See if he's left his comfy pen and suddenly taken a liking to the wild or has any other nests tucked away. Got it?"

I hoped he did because my mind hurt remembering how to vaguely insinuate he look up Greg's credit card statements (bucket monitoring) for any out of place shopping sprees such as cars or rentals. And to research his mortgage documents (zookeepers) or line of credits (cage cleaners) for hotel statements or house purchases.

If Greg had planned this…something damning would appear.

*It always does.*

"Consider the report in progress." Larry cleared his throat. "He's still got her but—"

I knew he wanted to reassure me, but I didn't have time. "He might for now—" I crunched the phone tight in my hands "—but not for much longer."

"Give me twenty. I'll call you back."

I hung up.

Gritting my teeth against the cuts on my feet and the seizing of bruised joints from the beating, I jogged through the forest and up the driveway to my Merc.

The minute Larry called with new information, I would find her.

And this time, I wouldn't fail.

# Chapter Nine

# Elle

COOKING IN CHAINS wasn't something I was used to.

It was awkward, heavy, and I positively hated the clinking as I shuffled toward the pantry and grabbed ingredients for a simple tagliatelle with basil pesto and parmesan.

I had to hand it to my prison guard—he'd brought flavorful things that were easy to turn from separate food groups into a main course.

Normally, I wouldn't obey him out of principal—no matter he kept twirling the knife with a gleam in his eyes as if daring me to speak out. But normally, I wasn't starving. My stomach constantly grumbled, empty and ready to eat.

I told myself this meal was for me, and my unfortunate companion would have the leftovers.

Greg sat on the counter, occasionally kicking his leg out to prevent me from moving past, stroking my shoulder and tucking a blonde strand behind my ear.

"You ever think of giving up the corporate world and becoming a stay-at-home mom?" His touch dropped to my breast, squeezing it before I could swat him and continued to the sink to drop the cooked pasta into a colander to drain.

His touch made my heart quake, but I had to remind myself he was just a man. My flesh was just a body; it was repairable. Yes, he'd violate every commandment by taking me forcibly, but I couldn't focus on that yet.

*Only when it happens.*

I hated that my mind had accepted *when* not *if*.

"No. I've been too busy with Belle Elle." The hot water splashed from the pan down the drain.

*Besides, I'm still young. I want to see the world first. I want to explore and be reckless and fall in love.*

My insides knotted.

Penn.

Could I have fallen in love with him if he hadn't lied?

Could I have given up the idea of Nameless to find happiness?

Now, I would never know because I'd never see either Penn or Nameless again.

"You should. Domestic chores suit you."

"That's such a sexist thing to say."

"No, sexist would be that house chores suit all women." He smirked. "I just said you."

I rolled my eyes and returned the now drained pasta to the pot where I added sautéed mushrooms, parmesan, and pesto to stir through and warm.

I found comfort in cooking. The method hadn't changed even if my circumstances had. The recipe still worked even if I was chained in a nightgown waiting to be raped and my business stolen.

"Fuck, watching you cook for me makes me hard." Greg grabbed his erection. "See what you do to me?"

I had no desire to look. "It makes me sick."

"That's because you're still brain-washed by that bastard, Everett."

Goosebumps erupted on my skin.

I didn't know if it was Penn's domination over my body and the lust I still felt (no matter I wanted to murder him) or the belief that, in some strange way, he would save me even if he was a criminal.

*Don't be so ridiculous.*

I didn't reply, focusing intently on folding in the pesto sauce.

Greg huffed, pushing off from the counter to grab the chain around my wrists and pull me forward. "Come with me."

"What? But I'm not finished."

"Doesn't matter. Two minutes won't hurt it."

I had no choice as he pulled me from the kitchen and down the small hallway to the bedroom we'd shared. The bed clothes were tangled; my underwear still on the floor from where he'd kicked them from the bathroom.

He let me go, stepping over the chain wrapped around my ankle (that now snaked down the hallway back the way we'd traveled) to open the wardrobe door. Hanging inside were an array of lingerie and negligées—all completely impractical for making an escape. No shoes, only stockings. No jackets, only bras.

I sighed heavily, fighting depression and tiredness.

This strange role-play helped delete some of the immediate worry I had about my situation. Cooking in chains? It was odd, but at least I wasn't being hurt. Being washed and cuddled in bed? Awful on many levels but still not pushing the boundaries into horror.

*What is he doing?*

*Why is he dragging this out?*

Not knowing was the worst part. I didn't know when he'd pounce; when he'd demand me to open my legs and let him have me. I didn't know how much longer I could stay alert and constantly ready to fight.

Eventually, I would tire. I would sleep. And then I'd be at his mercy.

Greg pulled out a small turquoise bag with Tiffany's logo.

*Oh, no.*

My heart scrambled into my throat as he placed the bag into my hands. "Open it."

I backed away, tossing the offending gift onto the bed. I didn't need to open it to know what was in there. "I don't want it."

His jaw clenched as he scooped up the bag, tossed the ring box into his palm, and cracked it open. "Yes, you fucking do, Elle." Plucking the one carat diamond from the plush box, he grabbed my left hand and jammed the ring onto my engagement finger.

It fit perfectly.

Of course.

Instantly, I wanted to get it off. I'd cut off my own finger to be free of it.

"You're going to marry me, Elle. You're going to change your last name to Hobson. Belle Elle will be mine."

He slithered his arms around my waist, tucking me tight against him. "You're going to give me a daughter or son, so our families will forever be joined, and Belle Elle will always be mine by right, and then, once you've given me everything I want, I'll let you divorce me."

His teeth flashed as he chuckled. "But only with a hefty settlement for being the best husband ever. We'll spread a rumor that you cheated and the sympathy vote will ensure everyone will be on my side while you fade into obscurity."

He captured my chin, kissing me quick. "Or you could stay married and be my dutiful wife and share in everything I give you."

I wanted to disinfect my mouth, tear out my tongue, and zip up my lips so he could never kiss me again. But then I wouldn't be able to tell him what I thought about his ludicrous, monstrous plan.

I laughed in his face, shaking with rage. "Do you believe in fairies, Greg? Because you have to if you think that will ever come true." I shoved him away, swelling with pride as he stumbled. "Ten million is all you'll get out of me, and that offer is only valid for the next five minutes. I don't even know why I'm offering that." I shrugged, waving the damn chain between my arms. "Who knows? Perhaps, I still see the Greg who helped me pick the right bike when I was eight, or the Greg who helped me move into my apartment."

Stomping toward him, I stabbed my finger into his chest. "Ten million for the past we share and not a penny more. I'm not marrying you. I'm definitely not bearing your children. And no way in hell are you getting Belle Elle—"

I went to tear the ring off but he clamped his hand over mine. "You remove that diamond and I hurt you." His threat wasn't idle. It reeked with cold-hearted promise.

I gulped, letting him pull my fingers away, leaving the ring ensnaring me.

Then, as if he hadn't just petrified me, he cupped between my legs, his fingers bruising me. "Are you sure I won't get Belle Elle? Are you sure I won't get *exactly* what I want? That I won't get to fuck you, keep you, steal everything from you? Because it feels like I'm winning."

Hitting his arm, I scooted backward. My toes landed on the chain, making me wince. "Get away from me."

He walked with me, his fingers never loosening, curling tighter around my core beneath the stupid negligée. He didn't let go as I scratched his wrist, tugging for him to let me go.

I repelled backward so fast, I slammed into the wall, giving him the perfect purchase to slap his free hand onto the upright surface by my head and press a finger inside me.

I shuddered in grotesque denial.

I was dry. It hurt. It was brutal rather than blissful.

My mind shattered, begging for Penn and the wizardry of his touch. He made me wet even while he confused me with stories.

He made me come even while I denied how much I liked him.

Penn was a master manipulator.

Greg was just the devil.

I wanted him out of my life and far away from me.

*I want him dead.*

I shoved him, the chains around my wrists clinking loudly.

He grabbed the metal, hoisting it up, giving my arms no way to disobey before being yanked upright and pinned against the wall.

"This...Elle, your fucking pussy is mine." His voice became thick and cruel. "I'm going to have you. I'm going to fuck you. I've waited as long as I can. You wear my ring, you've slept in my bed, I've washed you in my shower. You no longer belong to him but me, get it?"

His finger hooked inside, his nail scraping delicate flesh. "I'm going to fuck you the minute lunch is finished."

Withdrawing his touch, he let me go and pointed at the kitchen. "Now, get in there and finish making me food like a good little wife."

# Chapter Ten

# Penn

THE MERC'S ENGINE snarled as I pressed the accelerator as far to the floor as possible.

Thirty-two minutes and Larry still hadn't called.

But I didn't care.

I had to stay on the move. Otherwise, I'd fucking take my rage out on an innocent tree and end up hurting myself in the process.

And I was hurt enough.

I didn't know if I was going in the right direction or wrong. I had no clue if Elle was still safe or if Greg had done something un-fucking-forgivable.

All I had was the hope I'd be on time.

Tearing down a country road, I jumped as my phone ring-tone split the air.

Answering with hands-free, I grunted, "Where am I going, Larry?"

"Cherry Cove, Medina."

"Hotel or private house?"

"Fishing chalet."

"His?"

"Not sure. Couldn't find any records of him buying another property."

"How do you know she's there then?"

"He bought another car—under a friend's name, but he helped secure the finance. The Dodge Charger is equipped with antitheft GPS. I had someone who owed me a favor switch it on. The car is outside the address I've sent to your inbox. I used Google maps to see what sort of abode it was."

"Your sleuthing never fails to impress me."

Larry's voice hid a smile. "You can tell me how great I am later. Get her back, Penn, and then you're fixing this. You're telling that poor girl everything. You're going to be honest."

I bared my teeth but nodded reluctantly, knowing she'd never want to see me again. "Fine."

I pressed end, downshifted, and grinned at the growling engine as I cannon-fired after Greg.

According to my GPS, I was just over an hour away.

A mere hour until Elle was mine again and then all my lies would be revealed.

But, at least, she would be safe.

I would be fucking heartbroken, but she would be back where she belonged.

Without me in her world.

# Chapter Eleven

# Elle

THE PASTA SAT like glue in my stomach.

I'd eaten because I was hungry, but the much-loathed company made nutrition unwanted by my body.

Greg slurped at the tagliatelle, swiping at globs of pesto sauce that splashed against his cheeks.

He grinned as he swirled more pasta onto his fork. "You really are a good cook, Elle."

"You're lucky I didn't poison you."

He chuckled. "There's nothing here to poison me with." He took another bite, eating with his mouth full. Steve would swat him if he saw—he'd been trying to break him of that habit since Greg was little. "No bleach, no cleaning products. Nothing that can harm."

I reached for my water glass, hating how the links clinked over the table and threatened to slide through my lunch. Hoisting my other wrist, I balanced the foot of chain above the plate and awkwardly took a drink.

Greg never took his eyes off me.

*Bastard.*

I glanced out the window at the sparkling lake and sunshine. If I were here with any other person, it would be the perfect vacation away from working so hard. A vacation I'd never had. I would walk around the lake, have a picnic, read a book beneath a tree, and then come back and make love to whoever had brought me here.

Penn.

*You would've made love to Penn.*

I shut down my thoughts.

I didn't want him in my head.

He wasn't allowed or permitted inside my mind anymore. Twenty-four hours ago, I would've given him the benefit of the doubt and listened to what he had to say.

That was before the necklace.

Now, I would tell him to go away—no matter what explanations he formed.

Greg finished his last mouthful, smacking his lips and pushing the plate away. He nodded in appreciation. "Best lunch I've had in a while."

"You obviously don't get out much then."

"I work for you." His eyes narrowed. "I normally work through my lunch break because you expect so much from your staff."

I couldn't let him get away with that bullshit. "Whatever, Greg, your executive assistant does her job and yours combined. You're never in your office; you're always off site."

His lips tightened.

"What? You think I don't notice? That I don't keep an eye on my *employees?*" I dragged out the word, enjoying the way he shifted full of annoyance in his chair. "It's my company. Of course, I'm aware of who's doing a good job and who isn't. And I hate to say it, but you've never done a good job. Even from the first day Steve asked Dad to give you that position. You've taken your salary and done nothing for it."

I wiped my mouth with my napkin, no longer hungry. "In fact, I've been claiming your salary as a charity donation on our tax returns because I have to pay your executive assistant twice her normal wage so she doesn't walk out and leave your department in shambles."

His mouth hung open. "You truly are a bitch."

"And you're just a bastard. Guess we're even."

He crossed his arms while I let the chain fall into my lap, the cuffs heavy around my wrists.

"What a way to ruin a nice lunch, Noelle." He stood, snatching his plate before storming to my side of the table and grabbing mine. "Does it make you feel good to think you're still so high and fucking mighty?"

I didn't let his shadow looming over me intimidate me. I straightened my back, glowering directly into his eyes. "First, it's Elle. I never have, and never will like Noelle. And second, yes it does make me feel good to point out your flaws and show you that whatever this is—" I flashed the engagement ring sparkling on my finger—the same ring I'd tried to pull off for the second time only to earn a slap so hard, I suspected his handprint still glowed on my cheek "—is a sham."

Furious tears and racing heartbeats wobbled my words. "You're just like him. You force an engagement on me and expect me to go along with it!" I laughed with disbelief. "I was an idiot where Penn was concerned. I should've stood up to him more. Should've dug into his background sooner, but I didn't because beneath his lies, I actually *liked* the glimpses of normalness."

I sneered at Greg. "But when I look at you, all I see is rotten greed. All I smell is hunger for things you haven't earned and never will."

My hands curled just before his fist connected.

It crunched against my cheekbone, layering upon the last punch, no doubt turning the faint grayness under my eye into a full-on black spot.

My head snapped to the side, my chin lolling on my chest as my arms shot out to grip the table. I teetered on the edge, only a fraction away from falling out of the chair and puddling at his feet.

I'd known it would come to this, yet I couldn't help myself. I had to tell him off like a silly little child because that was what he was.

A child.

An ignorant little boy who needed a good spanking.

"That's the last time you'll *ever* talk to me like that." His breath smacked my hair with fury. "Hear me?"

I blinked and dared to shake my head a little. The world righted itself. The pain dimmed. I sat firmer in the chair, planting my elbows on the table and cradling my head. The chain and cuffs hindered me as I hid behind a curtain of tangled hair and pressed exploratory fingers to my puffy, hot cheek.

*Ouch.*

God, it hurt.

My tears were from physical pain instead of emotional frustration this time. I didn't bother to stop them as they splashed sadly against the tabletop where my lunch had been.

Greg stomped into the kitchen and tossed the plates into the sink. China cracked with a loud splinter, but he didn't care. Marching back toward me, he hoisted me to my feet with biting fingers around my elbow. "You want to fight, Elle? Fucking fine, we'll fight." Dragging me into the living room, he pointed at the hallway. "Choose, right now. Bed or couch."

I squinted, doing my best to ignore the pain throbbing in my head. "What?"

"Bed or couch."

"I don't know what that means."

He pressed his nose against mine. "I'm going to fuck you. Would you prefer over the couch like a whore or in the bed like my fiancée?"

Everything went black and cold.

So, so cold.

I squirmed in his hold; stepping backward the cuff around my ankle jingled and I stepped on the chain looped behind me for the thirty-seventh time, hurting yet another piece of me. "Greg, stop. I don't want either."

"Too fucking bad. You need to learn your place. You're no longer my boss or the CEO, Elle." His voice lowered to a hiss. "I am."

Grabbing a handful of my hair, he threw me onto the plaid couch. The scratchy material stuck to my gold negligée like Velcro as I scooted sideways, trying to reach the other end and climb off.

He grabbed the chain around my ankle, hoisting me back.

The satin rose up my hips, exposing between my legs.

His eyes latched on greedily before I slammed a hand over myself with as much decency as I could muster. "Don't touch me."

"I'm going to do more than that."

"I'll scream."

He smirked. "No one to hear you."

"I'll kill you."

"I'd like to see you try."

My fury turned caustic, burning me up inside. I shook so hard my teeth chattered.

He leered over me, keeping his hold on the chain, giving me nowhere to go. Bending down, he grabbed me by the throat, pinning my body against the couch.

My legs stayed tight and crossed, hand wedged low.

"Kiss me. Show me that you can be nice, and I'll be gentle our first time."

I spat in his face.

Wrong move.

*Seriously* wrong move.

But it was the only move I had because I couldn't kiss him. I could never give anything of me willingly because the hate I had would transfer into hatred for myself.

Time slowed down.

His hand came up, rubbing at the bead of saliva I'd put there. Never looking away from me, he wiped his hand on his jeans, shaking his head. "You'll pay for that."

His face turned nasty, his fingers grabbing my elbows and plucking me from the couch as if I weighed nothing.

"No!" I pummeled his chest as he hauled me against him, marching me backward until my legs pressed against the couch end.

"Yes." Spinning me around, he pressed me over the rolled armrest, running his hands down my spine to my ass.

"Get ready to be nice to me, Elle. 'Cause I'm sure as shit not going to be nice to you."

# Chapter Twelve

# Penn

THIS CABIN HAD lake views, not forest.

This cabin had a Dodge, not a Porsche.

This cabin held Elle, not empty.

This place ricocheted with a scream, not silence.

*Fuck!*

I cursed that I'd left my Merc at the top of the driveway again, hoping for the element of surprise. I'd taken my time sneaking through the bushes and shadows, staying out of sight.

The occasional smell of cooking had carried on the breeze the closer I got.

The electrical tingle of being close to Elle revved me the nearer I sneaked.

But that was before the scream.

Forgetting stealth, I bolted forward from gloomy undergrowth to gleaming daylight. All instincts told me to barrel through the front door and tear Greg fucking apart.

But the sensible part of me—the part that'd kept me alive for decades on the streets—whispered patience.

What if he had a knife to her throat?

What if he had a gun ready to kill me?

I had to know where they were, what they were doing—then I could win.

Ducking, I snuck around the perimeter of the house. My ears strained for another scream, but nothing came. Ice water washed my spine. No scream could be good, could be bad.

I couldn't see inside the dim interior with the bright sunshine beating on my head.

I ran through the small garden with baby saplings swaying in the breeze and approached the side of the house where a bathroom window cracked to allow shower steam to dissipate.

No movement down the back of the cabin.

Pressing against the siding, I made my way back to the front where the living room and kitchen would be.

I kept my height beneath the window frames, listening for any hint of what room Elle was a prisoner in.

The sound of chains dragging on hardwood screeched in my ears from a cracked window.

*He's chained her up?*

That motherfucker.

He'd pay for this. Over and *over,* he'd pay.

He had his motherfucking hands on her.

Soon, I'd have mine on him.

Sounds of raised voices filtered through the afternoon, garbled and cut short as something thumped and then couch legs squeaked over floorboards.

I couldn't stop myself.

I stood upright, keeping my body low but my eyes above the trim. Peering through the glass, my heart fucking stopped.

Greg had Elle pinned over the edge of the couch. Chains on her wrists and ankle. A gold nightdress shoved over her hips, exposing her nakedness below.

I thought seeing her vulnerable with half-torn clothes in the alley three years ago was enough for me to turn rogue.

This...this was enough for me to commit fucking murder.

# Chapter Thirteen

# Elle

I SCREAMED.

How could I not?

When a man who you'd just eaten lunch with, grew up with, someone you watched turn from boy to grown-up suddenly takes away all control and prepares to rape you—all common sense, conversation skills, and bartering flies out of comprehension.

I gave up pain and precaution.

I felt nothing but wildness and terror.

"Stop!" I kicked. I wiggled. I clawed at the couch.

"All it takes is for you to be nice to me, Elle. And this can go so much better for you."

The promise whispered in my head to do something. To be generous with compliments if it meant he wouldn't hurt me. But I physically gagged on such blasphemy.

He stroked my back, running his fingers over my naked hips as he wedged his jeans-clad cock against me. He didn't move to unzip, but it didn't stop his hardness from sending disgust gushing through my blood.

A shadow fell over the floor for the briefest second, wrenching my eyes to the window where sun spilled upon my ruin.

Perhaps a fellow vacation-maker had come to borrow a cup of sugar. Maybe a fisherman needed to dig in the garden for some worm-bait. Hopefully, some good Samaritan was here to save me.

I opened my mouth to scream again, but Greg slammed his sweaty palm over my lips.

"Be nice, and we go into the bedroom." He fumbled with his belt with his other hand. "Don't, and you're mine right here."

My heart atrophied at the sounds of leather unbuckling.

*I'm running out of time.*
*Do something.*
*Think.*
*Kick. Fight. Bite. Scream.*
*Anything!*

The shadow came again, quick and fleeting, but I caught what made it this time. The barest glimpse of an angel come to free me.

I didn't believe it.

I *couldn't* believe it.

It wasn't a fisherman or a bird or even a confused bear out for a stroll.

It was so much better.

So much worse.

My heart grew wings even as heavy tar coated it. Greg undid his jeans. The sensation of denim switched to bare male flesh.

I moaned behind his palm, tossing my head.

The figure in the window appeared again, this time closer to the front door. His tussled dark hair scattered stencils on the floor.

Him.

The liar.

The alley abuser.

The man I had feelings for despite everything.

He ducked again.

Did he know I'd seen him?

Did he know I was grateful?

What would he do?

How had he found me and not David or Dad?

My questions evaporated as Greg's hard cock lined up with my ass. He shuddered, his hand clenching around my mouth while his other yanked my hips into him.

He was moments away from taking me.

So I did the only thing I could.

I chose survival over pride.

I decided to lie just like Penn.

Letting my body go loose, I forced my ass against him, rubbing his erection, deliberately arching my back as if being fucked by him was exactly what I wanted.

My body hated, *hated* me.

My heart cursed, *cursed* me.

And my lips didn't know how to form the falsehoods I was about to spill.

His hand tumbled from my mouth in shock, giving me

freedom to speak.

"Mmm, *Greg*." My sultry moan made my skin scratch itself with knives. "You're right...I'm so—" I rocked into him, making him groan and fingers spasm "—*so* sorry."

He froze, his thighs twitching against the back of mine. "What did you just say?"

I kept my voice slow and decadent—like chocolate and liquor and rich, rich coffee. "I said you're right. I should be *nicer* to you." I rolled my hips, dragging a revolting pant from him and a coil of nausea from me. "If you let me stand and face you, I'll show you how *nice* I can be."

My tongue burned with lies.

My throat slashed with fibs.

Was this how Penn felt every time he talked to me?

Greg nudged me with his hips, keeping me pinned against the couch. "Why should I trust you? You've been nothing but a bitch since we got here."

I jingled the chain around my wrists. "I'm yours, remember? I'm not going anywhere." I let my body go completely submissive. "It's time I listened to what you're offering rather than destroy what we could have together without giving it a chance."

Lies, lies, *lies.*

I wanted to vomit with lies.

I wanted to wash away the lies.

I wanted to bleach the lies.

Greg slowly relaxed. He stepped back, giving me room to stand.

I took one last look at the window. A slight shadow appeared closer to the door. Penn was many things, but I trusted him to help me. He'd come for me in his car that night. He'd fought for me in the club at the beginning. He would get me free, and then I'd politely thank him and walk away.

All I needed to do was keep Greg distracted enough, so it was an ambush rather than a full-on fight.

I didn't need more complications in my life by turning this abduction into death or bloodshed. Regardless of what Greg had done, the law would deal with him, not vigilante justice.

Standing upright, I pushed the negligée down my hips for coverage and turned to face him.

The only problem was he had a full view of the door where Penn would most likely come in.

*I have to change that.*

Placing my hand on Greg's chest, I disguised my shuddering fingers with a breathy laugh. "You know…I agree with something else you said, too."

His eyes widened then narrowed with suspicion. "Agree with me? That will be a first."

I nodded, licking my lips, taking a step to the left, doing my best to ignore the sound of the chain dragging on the floor behind me. "Belle Elle could be ours."

Another step, guiding his attention from the door. "You and me."

He followed, trying to sniff out my agenda. "What do you mean?"

"I mean if you'd work harder once Belle Elle was yours, then perhaps that's an option."

He smirked coldly. "And why should I believe this sudden change of heart?"

Another step, three-quarters turned from the door. He swiveled to follow me with every footfall I took.

"Can't I change my mind?"

"You can, but it's odd you change it now." His hand cupped my cheek, running his thumb over the bruise he'd given me. "Strange that you turn cooperative just before I show you how good we are together."

I swallowed bile as I stroked my finger down his chest, drawing a circle around his open belt buckle. "You scared me. But if you're nice to me—like you promised—I can be nice to you."

The sexual reference scalded my tongue, but Greg's eyes glowed. "Oh yeah? How *nice* are we talking?"

Another step and his back was toward the exit. Over his shoulder, I hid my victory smirk as the door cracked open with a sliver of warm sunshine.

Penn's livid gaze locked on mine.

I looked away, staying in character, and not giving in to the crazed patter of my heart.

He was bloody and broken. Smeared with rust and torn on the shoulder, he still wore his white shirt and silver trousers from the charity gala. He moved silently but with a stiffness that wasn't there before.

*What the hell happened to him?*
*Doesn't matter.*
*Keep going.*
*Keep Greg distracted.*

I moved closer to my enemy, tugging his belt, sliding it through his jean loops. "I can be very, *very* nice." I fluttered my eyelashes. "I've grown up a lot the past month. I know how to please."

Penn moved closer.

I daren't glance up. I couldn't afford to see how angry he was at my flirting or how angry I was at his fibs. We were furious with each other.

*Good, fury is better than lust.*

"That right?" Greg's hand landed on my shoulder, squeezing, adding downward pressure just like Penn did when he taught me a lesson and ordered me to suck him in my office.

I couldn't be on my knees. I had to watch Penn behind Greg's back, so I could get out of the way at the right time.

I giggled—I never giggled—but I amped up the flirt to terrible levels. "How about we discuss the terms first, and *then* I'm nice to you?"

"You already know the terms." He grabbed my hand, spinning the engagement ring on my finger. "This means you're mine. Everything you own is mine. That's the deal, Elle."

"And my body? Is that yours, too?"

He looked down at my breasts with a hungry glare. "Fuck yes, it is."

Nausea splashed my stomach as I stroked his chest, moving back up his body away from the hardness in his pants. "And your body? Is that mine in return?"

He licked his lips. "It is if you want it."

I dared look over his shoulder as Penn slowly slinked from the doorway into the living room. His eyes met mine again, narrowed and dark and full of murder. His fists clenched with no other weapon but his hate.

He was utterly sublime.

And totally terrifying.

My skin shivered with a mixture of frustration and appreciation. I'd felt something for him. I could've been happy with him. But the truth shattered that.

I was glad he was here, and this situation warranted gratitude, but after that…*I never want to see him again.*

Tearing my eyes back to Greg, I counted the seconds until I could stop this pantomime and let Penn incapacitate him.

Placing my hand over Greg's heart, the chain around my wrists dangled, nudging his erection with morbid jewelry. "Yes, I want it."

He wrapped his arms around my waist, wedging himself against me. "In that case, be a good girl and get in the bedroom. I'll make it good for you if you make it good for me. That's all I ever wanted, Elle."

I giggled again even though I wanted to strangle him. "Okay..."

Penn sneaked forward, his eyes darting between me in Greg's arms and his feet on the floorboards, searching for squeaky spots.

"Let's go." Greg moved forward, his head turned toward the kitchen. If his peripheral was any good, he'd see Penn and all my lying and touching would've been for nothing.

"Wait!" I grabbed his face, holding his gaze with mine. "Don't go, not yet."

His eyebrows knitted together, dark blond hair cascading over his forehead. "Why the fuck not?" Temper tightened his eyes. "If you're playing a game—"

"No game—" Panic made me blurt rather than hum with sexual intrigue.

Penn inched closer.

A floorboard creaked.

Greg's nostrils flared as he twitched to look over his shoulder.

I did the only thing I could.

The only thing I could think of.

Digging my nails into his cheeks, I wrenched his face to mine and kissed him.

The world screeched to a halt as my lips willingly found his and seduced him.

He tasted wrong.

He *felt* wrong.

He was *wrong*.

His body tensed.

For a second, I feared he'd slap me away and find Penn just a foot behind him. But then he relaxed, grabbing me close and spearing his tongue into my mouth.

I gagged as he kissed me deep, his hands tangling in my hair.

I hated every wet heat of it. I despised every swipe of his unwanted invasion.

Trying to stay in character, I did my hardest not to bite him. But I couldn't stop the moan of rejection or squirm of refusal.

He grunted, dragging me closer to him. The kiss turned brutal and basic. Teeth nipping at my lip, sharp and smooth.

And then…it was over.

Commotion, clamor, then Greg was torn from my arms and jerked backward. Instinct made him grab the chain around my wrists, yanking me with him.

A sharp gasp fell from me as we fell together, plummeting to the hardwood.

I landed with a bone-rattling jar half on him, half on the floor. I didn't have time to register pain as vicious hands wrapped around my waist, plucked me from Greg, and threw me to the side out of the way.

I rolled to my knees just in time to see Penn dive onto Greg as he pinned him to the floor and delivered two solid punches to his jaw. "You cock-sucking motherfucker!"

"What the—" Greg tried to protect his face, but Penn had the element of surprise.

"How dare you take her?" Penn rammed his knuckles into Greg's jaw.

"How *dare* you fucking touch her?" He hit his temple, his throat—his punches messy but swift.

"How dare you goddamn hurt her!" He turned diabolical, hitting every part he could reach.

Greg whimpered, his voice punctured by punches and pain.

Penn didn't let up.

He didn't stop the violence.

*He'll kill him.*

"Wait!" I scrambled upright. "Stop!"

Penn didn't listen.

Greg's nose popped in a gush of blood. He groaned something incomprehensible.

Penn pushed up, towering over him. His chest heaved with breath, his body covered in stains and injury. "You're an asshole." His foot kicked out, connecting with Greg's side. "A creep who ought to be exterminated—just like all the other fucking creeps who think they can take what isn't theirs."

Even in the midst of a fight, I couldn't help my inner voice from whispering, *hypocrite.*

Penn was one of those creeps. He'd tried to rape me in that alley. He'd stolen my necklace.

I backed away, holding my stomach in revulsion.

Two emotions tangled and braided. They knotted together trying to confuse me. I liked Penn. I hated Penn. I wanted Penn. I couldn't forgive Penn.

The flash of his bare foot brought me back as he buried it in Greg's soft belly. A sickening thud made nerves tangle into sickness.

I couldn't do a damn thing.

Penn was a ruthless machine, utterly unstoppable. He was no longer the surly liar who'd enchanted me but a cold, merciless killer.

Greg grunted, curling up, protecting every part he could. "Stop! Fucking stop!"

Hot tears came from nowhere, brimming with betrayal and exhaustion. They spilled over, distorting the room, tickling my cheeks as Greg spat red saliva on the hardwood.

Penn didn't move back, but he didn't strike either. Greg's blood covered his knuckles. His stance defensive and possessive. His intentions of winning blaring all around him.

He'd been in a fight before this one. He'd been hurt before he hurt Greg. Why? How? By who? Yet more questions landing on the unanswered hillside I already had.

I'd seen Penn in many moods over the past few weeks—sarcastic, protective, combative, and seducing. But I'd never seen him channel the wish of a murderer. He glowered at Greg with no compassion or belief he was even human.

Planting his foot on Greg's sternum, he pointed a finger in his face. "Go near Elle again, and you don't survive."

My chains jingled as I inched closer. I didn't know if I wanted to pull Penn away or check that Greg wasn't seriously hurt. I didn't want to be close to either of them.

Deciding they were both idiots and it was my turn to rule, I pushed Penn out of the way, yanked off the despicable engagement ring, and threw it on Greg's chest. "You can take that awful diamond back." The minute I was free from that shackle, I dangled the chain between my wrists over Greg's face. "Now, enough fighting. Where are the keys to the padlock?"

Penn blinked away his violent stupor, focusing on the cuffs around my wrist and ankle before focusing on the tossed away engagement ring.

His eyes turned black. "He fucking *chained* you." His fingers dug into my shoulder, holding me tight as he inspected me. His gaze flew over the gold negligée, down my chest, legs, and toes then spun me around and repeated.

His voice wobbled with fury. "He fucking tied you up, bruised you, forced his ring on you, and made you dress in whatever he damn well pleased?" He laughed with an iceberg in his throat. "He fucking *kissed* you? Oh, hell. Fucking. No."

Shoving me away, he launched himself on Greg for the second time.

Greg, to his credit, managed to land a decent head shot, rolling away and clambering to all fours. "Get off me, you son of a bitch."

Penn shook his head free from stars, dazed for a second. A second was all Greg needed to feed off adrenaline and stand.

"She's mine, asshole." He leapt on Penn.

Chaos erupted. Elbows. Knees. Fists and curses. They were no longer two men but one mass of punching arms and striking kicks. Their centrifugal force shoved furniture this way and that, their bodies crashing into a side table and sending a swan-shaped lamp smashing to the floor.

Greg tackled Penn into the couch.

Penn struck the back of Greg's head, getting free.

While Greg shook away the pain, Penn kicked him straight in his ribs then delivered a lightning-fast punch to his belly.

With fists up and biceps bulging, Greg attempted to strike again but Penn was too nimble. He landed a perfect uppercut to Greg's jaw all while quiet fury rippled off him.

His experience in fights was alarming. His past was the perfect training course for such systematical punishments, reminding me I knew nothing about him or how far into lawlessness he'd fallen.

He'd mentally disconnected. Focused entirely on winning.

"Stop! Both of you!" I screamed.

It didn't do any good.

They attacked with vigor born from survival.

The sound of a roaring vehicle outside wrenched my head up just in time to see the black Range Rover I knew so well hurtle down the driveway and slam to a stop. The windows revealed David leaping out with the engine still roaring, charging toward the cabin with his gun free from its holster.

"Quit it! Right now!" I darted to where Penn and Greg rolled. Someone's leg struck out, hitting my cuffed ankle.

I tumbled to my knees, a pained gasp falling.

Penn made eye contact with me just as his fist slammed into Greg's temple. "Shit."

Greg toppled sideways, his eyes rolling in the back of his head. Out cold.

A second later, the front door ricocheted open, and David stood braced with his weapon raised. "Everybody freeze."

I held up my hands, hating the chains so damn much. "It's okay, David. I'm fine."

"Ms. Charlston?" He stomped forward, his finger never pulling away from the trigger. His ex-Marine gaze swept the room, taking in the carnage, and understanding without being told the gist of what'd happened.

His attention latched onto my face where a black eye had formed and tear tracks painted me as exhausted and strung out. His gun pointed away as he came to my side. "Who did that to you?" He swung around as Penn stumbled away from Greg's unconscious form and stood on wobbly legs. He winced a little as he put weight on his right ankle.

David immediately trained the gun on Penn's chest.

Penn put his hands up in surrender, but his body still carried the remnants of battle.

David growled, "I knew you looked like a trouble-maker the first time I saw you."

Penn spat a mouthful of blood by Greg's prone body. "I don't care what you think of me." Stalking toward me, Penn grabbed my hand and wrenched me forward. "Come on, Elle. I'll take you home."

Home?

Was he insane?

He needed to go to a hospital. Greg, too. The police would be involved. Not to mention, I never wanted to be alone with him again.

"I'm not going anywhere with you." I tugged on his hold, looking down at Greg. "Do we need an ambulance?"

Penn chuckled coldly. "Doubt it. He's better off than he would've been if your fucking driver hadn't turned up."

David hoisted the gun higher. "Keep talking like that, and we'll have an issue. Let Ms. Charlston go."

Penn wrapped tight fingers around the chain joining my wrists. "No, she's coming with me."

My bare feet dug into the floor. "No, I'm not. I told you. I'm not going anywhere with you."

"Yes, you are. We need to talk about this." He swiped a swollen hand through dirty hair, letting me go. "Tell me where he put the keys and I'll free you. Then we're leaving."

I shook my head. I wouldn't go with him. I didn't trust him.

I didn't like him.

*I don't even know him.*

But answers…they were the only thing that made sense in this screwed-up reality.

*Maybe I should go…*

End this like adults.

David fought on my behalf, giving me time to weigh the pros and cons. "Don't move, either of you." Moving toward Greg, he ducked and put his finger on his pulse.

Greg didn't twitch. His legs splayed, arms spread, blood everywhere. It looked like a murder scene.

David muttered, "You're lucky he's still alive. Otherwise, I'd shoot you for killing him."

Penn snorted. "And I suppose that's fair justice to kill the man who rescued the head of Belle Elle?"

David stood, holstering his weapon with angry jerks. "I was about to rescue her."

"Yes, but I beat you." Staying close, Penn didn't touch me, but his eyes captured mine in a way that sent my tummy mimicking baby birds clumsily learning how to fly. He'd never looked so rough and dangerous but beneath the bloody smears was passion and desperation. "Elle, please. We need to talk."

I backed up. "Maybe in a few days. Once I'm home, and this is behind us."

"I don't have a few days."

My voice sharpened. "Why not?"

Penn shook his head, a sad smirk on his lips. "You'll find out soon enough."

*Is he leaving?*

*Why would he say that?*

Something about the way he shrugged tugged at me to know. He looked resigned. Pissed off and full of injustice but grudgingly accepting whatever he knew that I didn't.

*He knows many things you don't.*

He must've thought I was so stupid that day in Central Park when I'd asked where he was on the 19$^{th}$ of June three years ago. He would've known I'd refused him and his asshole friend in the alley but got it on with Nameless an hour later.

*Was that why he came after me?*

*Because he thought I was easy?*

I shivered, hugging myself. I wanted to know, but mostly, I just wanted this over with. For the first time, I missed the simplicity of my life before sex. I missed knowing what my day would entail: working, hugging my cat, and reading in bed.

There was comfort in blandness. I wanted that comfort back.

"No, Penn. I'm going home."

His eyebrow rose as if expecting an invitation.

My chin came up. "Without you."

I needed time to put aside this awful event with Greg and remember I was in charge, not these men in this tiny cabin.

*Me.*

"Let's go." I looked at David, seeing as Penn hadn't budged and his jaw worked as if chewing on things he didn't know if he should say.

David nodded. "Right away."

I held up my wrists. "Uncuff me and take me home. Please."

David immediately strode back to Greg, dropping to his haunches and rummaging in the unconscious man's pockets for keys.

Penn glowered at my bodyguard. "You're not taking her. Not until we've had a chance to talk."

"Another time, perhaps," David snapped. "We're leaving. Right now."

Penn's temper morphed into something calculating. Placing himself in my view, he scooped up the metal links between my wrists and tugged gently. "Do you trust me?"

That phrase again.

"No."

His voice softened. "You're safe. Just...come into the kitchen."

"The kitchen? Why?"

"Trust me." Pulling me forward, I swayed backward for a second, fighting him.

David looked up, unsuccessful on the key hunt, his eyes narrowed on Penn.

David was here. Penn couldn't hurt me.

*When did he ever hurt you? You were alone with him often.*

I punched common sense in the mouth.

Allowing Penn to guide me forward, our matching bare feet padded over the cabin's floor. I wanted to ask why he wasn't wearing shoes, but if I asked one question, I wouldn't be able to stop the avalanche.

Penn led me into the kitchen then let me go. He watched me warily as if unsure I'd stay or bolt away from him.

I gave him a slight nod, showing I was relaxed and had no intention of running. Yet.

His lips quirked at the corners, his gaze skating over my body, filling with desire. Clearing his throat, he pulled open a drawer and pushed aside a few utensils until he found what he was looking for.

A meat pulverizer.

I backed away. "What are you going to do with that?"

"Come here, and you'll see." Leaning over the bench, Penn pulled out a knife from the same butcher's block that Greg had taunted me with while I'd cooked lunch.

Dirty pans and plates sat in the sink, ready to be washed. What would Penn think of that? Would he think I'd played house with Greg? Get jealous that I'd cooked him lunch even though it was under duress?

Somehow, I got the feeling Penn wasn't petty or stupid. He held violence in his palm, ready to unleash it on his enemies but he also allowed kindness.

I took a step closer, warily.

"May I?" He pointed at the chain with the knife.

I swallowed, nodding.

Taking the links, he jammed the knife tip into the loops and placed it on the counter. Twisting the blade, he added pressure until the link refused to bend anymore. Picking up the meat pulverizer, he struck the metal with an awful *whack*. The noise vibrated through my limbs as well as my ears.

Tossing the pulverizer away, he pulled out the knife and with another twist, broke the link.

The chains fell apart, no longer together but still cuffed to my wrists by soft leather.

"That wasn't exactly worthwhile. I'm still—"

"Trapped, I know. You have a choice." He scowled. "Either come home with me where I have a lock picking kit and can undo the cuffs like I would with a key. Or..."

I ignored his comment about going home with him. "Or?"

"Or I use this." He held up the knife. "I can't exactly use the same method with the pounder, but the padlocks look flimsy enough to break with a blade."

David came forward. "The keys won't be far. Be patient and help me search."

Penn didn't look at him, keeping his eyes on me as he said, "By all means look, but she'll be free before you find them."

I quipped, "So arrogant."

He chuckled. "Only just noticed?" Pulling me forward by the dangling chain, I refused to let the shiver of lust infect me. The longer I was in his presence, the more I fought an unwinnable battle between my heart and body.

Penn wasn't good for me. He was a liar. But my body truly didn't care.

He stepped closer—closer than necessary—and hugged my arm close. "You have to stay still. I have a knife against your delicate skin. Don't move."

His voice licked down my spine. My nipples that had no right to be a part of this conversation tingled.

"I won't move." I couldn't really see as he hooked the knife into the small padlock and with a savage corkscrew, smiled triumphantly as the soft sound of something plopping against the floor came a second later.

"Free." Unwrapping the leather, his fingers feathered over my wrist with affection, protection, and most of all, a request to hear him out. To give him a chance.

The cabin vanished and all that remained was us.

The mystery.

The falsities.

David and Greg.

All gone.

Penn had a magical way of capturing my every sense and keeping me locked in whatever world he created.

Licking his bottom lip, he gently let one wrist go to manhandle the other.

I held my breath as his touch skimmed down my arm then a sharp tug and knife on metal freed me from the second cuff.

Not saying a word, Penn tossed the leather away, looped his fingers around my wrist and guided me from the kitchen, past David who didn't stop glaring, and toward the fireplace where the chain around my ankle locked to the hook.

His forehead furrowed, contemplating if he should break the chain or not bother and just undo the imprisonment around my ankle.

He chose the more streamlined option.

Ducking to one knee, he looked up as his touch landed on my calf.

I flinched as his breath fluttered the gold negligée and heat erupted between my legs. Black desire coated him as he glanced at my breasts then inserted the knife tip into the tiny padlock and jerked.

The final tether fell away, leaving me unbound by chains but unable to move from his hold. He massaged my ankle, rubbing me gently. "Elle, please. Let me take you home."

"I—"

David barged into our little moment. "You already know you're not taking her anywhere."

Penn ignored him, his chocolate gaze locked with mine. "I'm not taking no for an answer."

"Like hell you aren't. We're calling the police and getting this settled." David reached for his phone.

*Yes, the police.*

I had to report Greg. I had to ensure he didn't try something like this again.

But Penn turned cold, standing from his one knee pose. "Don't."

"Don't tell me what to do." David stalked away, already punching in the emergency number.

I wanted to ask him where Dad was, if he was okay, but Penn's stiffness and the way he inched subtly toward the door made me focus.

*He's nervous.*

As well he should be. He was a criminal who'd done time before.

He was right to be worried but not because of what he'd done to Greg. He'd gone a bit far, but he'd done it in my defense.

They can't arrest him for that. He was the hero in this scenario not the villain.

He rolled his shoulders as if it wasn't a big deal. "I'm not waiting around for paper pushing idiots. He's the one who needs to be arrested." He pointed his chin at Greg still passed out on the floor. "And he's not going anywhere."

David scowled. "You knocked him out. The police will want to talk to you, too."

"Well, I don't want to talk to them." Penn marched back toward me and took my hand. "Elle, please. Come with me."

My conviction wobbled. He looked so young, so pleading, so lost. But he was also the man from the alley.

"I—no, I don't think—"

Penn heard my uncertainty, my lack of absolution.

His fingers looped with mine, pulling me forward with a sudden burst of power. "Before you say goodbye, just hear me out.

That's all I'm asking."

The instinct to fight his unwanted coercion made me dig my heels into the floor. "No. Not today. Come to my office in a few days and we'll—"

"No. It has to be now." He stormed forward, dragging me behind him with no effort.

David leapt into action, abandoning the phone call where he'd been murmuring details to the police. He grabbed my other hand, using me as the rope in a tug of war. "You're not taking her, Everett."

"Goddammit!" Penn threw my arm away, severing all ties. For a second, it looked as if he'd run and never look back.

But then he spun around, seething with restraint, itching to leave. "Fine." Ever so slowly, he let his tension uncurl, holding his hand out to me like a lover asking me to go on a hot air balloon ride at sunset. "Elle, it would mean a lot to me if you came with me."

He lowered his head, watching me with hooded eyes. "One conversation. In private. And then you can leave. You have my word."

David relinquished me, so I stood on my own, no longer trapped by any of the three men currently surrounding me—even though one was still in la-la land.

"Ma'am?" David played with his gun holster, touching the handle of his weapon. He kept his gaze on Penn. "Let me take you home. Your father and Steve are on their way here. I dropped them off at a local establishment before finding you. I refused to let them come to the crime scene, in case—" He coughed. "Anyway, the important thing is to call him and say you'll meet him back at home. I'll arrange transportation for him to meet us there."

*Dad.*

I needed to check his heart was okay from this stressful night. I needed to do a great many things. I should nod and follow David to the Range Rover and never look back. I should file a police report, tell Steve as gently as I could that Greg was fired and if he ever got within a few hundred feet of me he'd be arrested, and spend the evening soothing my dad's nerves.

*And Sage—I need to feed Sage.*

But something about Penn bewitched me once again. He stood there with his hand shaking slightly, his invitation unanswered.

I tilted my chin, ignoring David and asking questions of my own for once. "Why should I go with you, Penn? You've done nothing but lie to me. I've been so stupid up until now not to dig into who you truly are. To force you to tell me what you're hiding."

He didn't move, merely cocked his head in agreement. "You're not stupid. You trusted me. There's a difference."

"I never trusted you."

"You did. Just like I trust you to come with me now and give me the courtesy of letting me explain myself."

"The courtesy? Where was your courtesy when you hid who you truly are?" I moved closer, rage replacing my fear from the past few hours. "Where was your courtesy when Stewie dropped my sapphire star necklace at the charity gala and told me he'd kept it for you to reduce your robbery sentence?" My voice rose. "Where was your courtesy when you hurt me in that alley?"

David stiffened, his weapon coming back out as my voice throbbed with unresolved hatred and pain.

Penn didn't move. His hand stayed up, waiting for me to accept him. His eyes remained unreadable, but his lips softened as he murmured, "My courtesy is now. I came for you, Elle. I didn't save you from Greg so I could leave and never see you again. I came for you so you could give me a second chance."

I huffed. "I've already given you a second chance. You blew it."

"Third chance then."

Shaking my head, I wrapped arms around myself, suddenly cold in the ridiculous negligée. "I'm done with lies."

"Good, so am I." Penn stepped closer. "I promise you on that alley three years ago that I won't touch you, I won't hurt you, and I'll drive you home the moment we've talked."

"So you admit you were there. On the 19th of June."

David glanced at us, watching our conversation with steely concentration.

Penn nodded. "I admit it. Just like I want to admit all of it. If you agree to come with me."

Answers were so close. I was desperate for them. Hungrier for closure and truth than I'd ever been. It didn't matter he was just as handsome as when he'd taken my virginity. It didn't matter he was just as silver-tongued as when he'd coerced me to say yes to his seduction.

All that mattered was ending this, finishing the clues, and

closing the story on this so-called romance.

David stepped closer, already knowing my decision before I did and ready to change my mind. "You can talk at a later date. Let me drive—"

I held up my hand, never looking away from Penn. "All right. I'll go with you, Mr. Everett, if that is even your real name." I stormed toward him, not caring he was dressed in blood and gore and so many unspeakable things from his past. A large bruise marked his cheek, his nose slightly swollen, his lip cut on the bottom. Despite all that, he was just as pretty as that night in the club when I'd said yes. "But the minute you've told me, I never want to see you again."

His jaw clenched. "Understood."

He moved toward the door. "Let's go. The sooner I tell you, the better."

I cringed at the bitter nastiness in his voice.

I couldn't help the sting.

He wanted to put this behind us, too. Whatever physical connection we shared wasn't enough to climb over the chasm of misdirection between us.

Good truth or bad.

Penn and I were over before we even began.

# Chapter Fourteen

# Penn

AN HOUR INTO the drive and we hadn't said a word.

I had so many of the bastards to say yet not a single sentence formed in my head.

Elle didn't help matters.

David had given her his blazer to sling over the gold thing she wore, and she sat with her arms and legs crossed, glaring at the road, the trees, the passing cars—anything but me.

Stopping for gas didn't make it any better.

While I pumped fuel into the hungry vehicle, she climbed out and entered the service station—not caring what she wore, making me fall even more with the aloof beauty she wielded.

Once I finished filling the Merc, I found her slipping into a pair of pink diamanté flip-flops and braiding her tangled hair with a rubber band. She stood in perfection, surrounded by chip packets, cold drinks, and smutty magazines.

Such a mundane store in a mundane world but Elle fucking took my breath away. She stood so strong, even after what that cunt had done to her. She still moved with authority even though I'd done my best to strip her of it.

She was older, wiser, and more supreme than she'd been that night in the alley but just as intoxicating.

I should probably buy some shoes too, but all I could think about was her.

Unable to tear my eyes off her, I walked into a display holding promotional chocolate bars, dislodging a sign and splattering it to the floor.

Her head jerked up, her lips pulling into half a smile as I spun around and marched to the counter to pay for the gas.

*Shit.*

The attendant swiped my card just as her electrical presence appeared by my side. My skin instantly rippled with chemistry, need, and heavy frustration that I'd been with this woman. That she'd let me into her body and started to open her heart, and now, I had no claim on her.

She wasn't mine standing in the middle of the gas station in a nightgown and bodyguard's blazer. She was free to be looked at, flirted with, and seduced.

I punched the credit card machine with fury.

"Can you pay for these, too? I don't have my purse with me." She dropped the price tag of the flip-flops and a bottle of water onto the counter, giving me a pointed look. "I'll pay you back."

I knew she'd pay me back. She was generous that way.

"I don't want your money. Call it a gift."

She shook her head. "No, it's fine."

How was she supposed to know buying her something—even something as simple as shoes and a drink—gave me more fucking pleasure than I'd had in years?

I wouldn't let her take that pleasure away from me.

I nodded, allowing her to think she'd won, not trusting my voice. Not trusting my body when she was around.

Every inch of me craved to grab her and just hold her. I didn't need to fuck her to feel close to her. I didn't need to kiss her to feel the supernova sensation I already drowned in.

Smiling at the attendant, Elle took her bottle of water and padded out of the station in her new shoes. I watched her go, drinking in the sight of her toned legs and the way the blazer skimmed beneath her ass.

The cashier cleared his throat. "You'll have to swipe your card again. I've put the new amount in."

It hurt to trade the vision of her with him, but I did and paid the eight dollars she'd cost me before pocketing the receipt and leaving the store.

Elle had already climbed into the passenger seat, sipping on her water.

The way her throat moved.

The way her hair fell over her shoulder.

Goddammit, I needed to get myself under control so I could have a civilized conversation with this woman. Knowing Greg had touched her—*kissed* her—caused a dominating urge to crawl through me. I had to replace the last man who'd had his hands on her with me.

But what was the point?

*She's going to leave the moment she knows anyway.*

Then there'd be other men. Men much better than me in every way.

Hiding my sigh, I yanked open the Merc's door and slid behind the wheel.

I needed to let her go once I'd found a pair of balls big enough to tell her who I was. But sitting with her in the small space, inhaling her smell, wishing I hadn't been such an asshole...it hurt.

She wasn't wearing perfume but her natural scent alone was enough to make me rock fucking hard and going out of my goddamn mind.

Turning the key and throwing the Merc into gear, I revved the engine and rejoined traffic.

Glancing at her, I said, "Are you going to be silent the rest of the drive or are you going to talk—"

She held up her hand, taking another sip of water before screwing the cap on. "Not a word, Penn. Not one word until you can give me your undivided concentration."

"I can talk and drive at the same time."

"But can you tell the truth and look me in the eye?" A droplet lingered on her lower lip, making me suffer with the desire to wrench her close and kiss her so fucking hard she only felt lust, not anger.

But I kept my hands to myself—just like I promised and fell silent.

She wanted to wait?

Fine.

I would wait.

The next few hours would give me time to formulate how best to tell her everything that'd happened to me, everything I was, and everything I would never be.

And I hoped to fucking God she didn't walk out the door the moment I'd finished and refused to see me again.

\* \* \* \* \*

The drive that'd taken me all night and most of the day to find Elle only took a few hours in the opposite direction. Mainly streamlined by knowing the address and direction and going a more direct route.

New York glittered on the horizon, welcoming me back with

hardship, promise, destitution, and wealth. I'd lived on two extremes. Poor and rich. Lost and found. Safe and scared. Most of the time, my new world was a thousand times better than my old one.

But that was before Elle.

Before I fucked everything up.

Pulling into the parking space attached to my apartment block, I turned off the engine and gripped the steering wheel with all the frustration and regret I couldn't show. Emotions I couldn't let her see if I was going to be honest tonight.

She had to think I had no shame. That I had accepted the consequences and wouldn't beg like a pussy for forgiveness.

The sun had gone down.

I couldn't remember the last time I'd slept, and I doubted Elle had managed any either.

She'd been kidnapped and mentally tortured. If she wasn't so damn strong, I would've expected her to cry and nap the entire journey home.

But she hadn't.

She'd watched the view but never relaxed. Not once. Then again, neither had I.

Fuck, I really should've driven to her apartment and allowed her to take a shower, have some painkillers for her black eye, and rest before I dumped this shit on her.

I wasn't any better than Greg was by holding her hostage at my place.

However, Elle didn't seem to care. Climbing out, her pink flip-flops smacked the pavement in the direction of the front entrance. She hadn't waited for me to hold her door. She didn't need my help in any way.

I followed, making sure to lock the Merc, glowering at the tire marks on the street from the night I'd peeled after her when that bastard jumped her.

I knew his situation was a shitty one. I understood his pain.

But that didn't give him the right to touch what was mine.

I'd thought sleeping with her wouldn't change my steadfast plan to taste her and then move on. That was why I'd kicked her from my place only moments after being inside her. I needed space to clear my head and school my stupid fucking heart.

But that was before I found out she was a virgin.

Before she trusted me enough to give me that first time.

In an odd way...she'd waited for me.

And fuck, that twisted me up inside.

I hadn't deserved that gift. Not in the slightest. If she knew what I'd done, who I truly was…she wouldn't have let me anywhere near her, let alone inside her.

*You didn't give her a choice. You stalked her. You infiltrated her life. You befriended her father. You're the worst kind of bastard.*

I jogged (painfully) in front of her before she got to the front door. Inserting the key, I didn't make eye contact, didn't reach out to touch her.

I couldn't.

My bones bellowed from Greg's henchmen beating me awake and the recent fight with Greg himself. I suspected a rib might be broken, and my nose had definitely earned a new bump.

I was sick of the crusty blood on my knuckles and the throbbing in my joints. I wanted to rip off my dirty clothes and have a long hot shower, a triple shot of expensive vodka, then pass out cold in my bed.

But I couldn't do that either.

Because Elle came first. Just like she always had and always fucking would. She didn't have a clue what she meant to me and how much I'd thought about her, cursed her, and bargained with my fate over her.

For years, I'd hated her. I'd planned ways to make her pay. But now that she'd been in my arms, now that I'd tasted her, listened to her, fucked her…that hate? Shit, that hate had turned into something so much worse.

Elle didn't look over her shoulder as she entered the building. Her footsteps were weary as she placed one on the flight of stairs, preparing to haul herself to the twelfth floor.

"Wait." I strode to the left where the foyer bent in a crescent, hiding the two elevators that served the building. I'd had them repaired and ready to use. "This way."

She huffed but followed. The slap of her flip-flops sounded like an accusation.

Pressing the button, an elevator opened, and I held the doors while she ducked under my arm and jumped in. She kept her gaze on the old-fashioned round buttons as I stood beside her and pressed my floor.

The only floor renovated so far, and the one I would move out of once the building was ready for inhabitants. I'd rent each apartment and buy another for myself.

The doors closed, and the clunking of mechanisms filled the

space.

Elle stiffened.

The atmosphere around us thickened. If there weren't so much unsaid shit between us, I'd shove her against the wall, haul up that ridiculous nightdress, and sink inside her. I'd force her to say hello to me, to see me, to truly listen.

But I'd lost that right.

I merely clenched my hands and counted the eternally long seconds in my head, so I didn't terrify her by slapping the emergency stop and forcing her to listen to me with no way out, nowhere to run, and no way to ignore me.

She shot out the second the elevator stopped and the doors slid open with rusty groans.

I followed, ducking around her to unlock the door. Stepping inside the art deco delight, I had no sense of comfort or relief at being back. My blood decorated the floor from the nosebleed I had as I barreled from the bed with thugs chasing me. The interior design company who'd modernized and styled the place had bought the furniture, so there was nothing of me in the walls or appliances. Nothing of me in anything because I'd been taught to be so transient in my world. To only covet that which I could carry. To only steal that which I could use. To only befriend those who wouldn't kill me.

The three cardinal rules.

Too bad, I broke all three the night I met Elle three years ago.

I'd coveted her when she wasn't mine to take. I'd stolen pieces I wanted because I had no choice. And I'd befriended her even when I should've kept my distance.

Elle kicked off her flip-flops by the door and padded barefoot to the black couch on chrome legs that made it look as if it hovered in the living room.

She sat demurely, her legs crossed, eyes narrowed with focus. She didn't ask to use the bathroom or beg to rest before we began.

She was all business.

"We're here. We're alone. Speak." Her chin came up. The loose braid she'd done in the gas station looped over her shoulder, begging me to fist it and drag her upright to kiss me. To take what I was desperate to take before she walked out the door and disappeared.

Not replying, I headed into the kitchen, grabbed two glasses, and filled them with water. Popping a few Advil—two for her, two for me—I took my haul to where she sat and waited until she held out her hand for the drugs then took the water.

We sipped silently, swallowing the painkillers as I sank into the chesterfield armchair at a right angle to where she sat on the couch.

She reached forward to put her half-empty glass on the coffee table, watching me carefully.

I didn't give up mine.

I kept it as physical support, tracing the droplets on the sides, smearing it with grime from my hands. I needed something to hold. Something to touch. I just wished it could be her.

"Are you going to spit it out, Penn, or do I need to leave?"

I brought the glass to my lips, buying another few seconds as I swallowed a cold mouthful.

She shifted impatiently, her thighs tight and fingers clutching the couch.

Wiping my lips with the back of my hand, I said quietly, "Where do you want me to start?"

She flinched as if I'd shouted. Her shoulders stayed around her ears as she snapped, "How about the beginning?"

"There are too many beginnings to know which one you mean."

She rolled her eyes. "Stop with the riddles and spit it out."

I inhaled hard. "You want to know about the alley."

She nodded, her tone sarcastic. "Obviously. If that's where you want to start."

I risked looking at her. Our eyes locked, heat and fire and brimstone. Passion and lust and denial. So much denial. She looked at me as if I wasn't worthy of being close to her even though I'd saved her life.

Twice.

"I was there."

"I know." She crossed her arms. "What part did you play?"

"Part?" I frowned.

"Were you the one to rip my clothes, steal my necklace, or try and force me to give a blowjob?"

I winced, gripping the glass too hard. Any harder, it would splinter. Placing it on the table, it wobbled in my haste to be free of it.

Elle flinched; her nostrils flared, waiting for my damning response.

Familiar anger toward her rose. Anger I was more acquainted with than whatever I felt now. Shoving myself off the chair, I slammed to my knees in front of her.

Grabbing her face, I held her firm as she shied backward, trying to get free.

My fingers dug into her cheeks, holding her even as she latched her fingers around my wrists and scratched me hard. "Let me go."

I didn't answer.

I couldn't answer.

My lips sought hers.

I dragged her forward, our mouths connecting in a vicious kiss.

She cried out as I held her close. My tongue licked her seam, begging for entry but not forcing, even though every cell in my body demanded to shove her back, climb on top, and show her in actions not words who I was.

It fucking hurt that she had to ask. That she looked at me and wasn't convinced. That she could think such awful things about me. That she couldn't *see*.

Her tiny fist connected with my sternum. If I hadn't been punched there a few times already, it wouldn't have registered over the sex haze in my brain. But she prodded a deep bruise, stealing my air, making me pull back.

"Stop touching me." Her voice was a hiss, a threat, a plea.

I didn't let her go, drinking in her rage, sinking into the vulnerability in her gaze. "How can you ask that question?"

She coughed in surprise. "What question?"

"Who I am?"

She bared her teeth. "Because I don't know."

"You do know. You've known all along."

"Wrong. You've lied to me from day one."

I shook my head sadly. "I never lied to you, Elle. Not once."

She swatted away my hands, sucking in a breath. "You lied about *everything*."

"Did I lie about how much I want you? Did I lie how much I—"

"You're going to sit there and claim whatever it was between us was purely physical?"

"*Is*. Not was. It's not past tense." I took her hand, my cock hardening against the intoxicating buzz between us.

"Answer the question, Penn." She tried to untangle her fingers from mine.

I didn't let her.

I wanted to nod with conviction. To say the connection linking and pinging and zapping like nuclear energy was nothing more than shallow lust. But we both knew emotions had crept their sneaky asses into our lives long before we'd acknowledged it.

They'd been there since that very first night.

They'd been there every day for three goddamn years.

I'd hunted her down, invaded her life, and befriended her father because of emotion. To deny that would be the worst kind of lie because it would mean I'd have to lie to myself.

"I won't say that because it's not true."

"Oh!" She rolled her eyes. "You're finally going with truth."

I scowled. "I promised, didn't I?"

She laughed, hard and brittle. "Sorry if I don't believe you. That I don't believe you're going to answer me honestly for the first time—"

"You dare lecture me on honesty?"

"You dare deny you've been anything but a liar?"

"Elle," I snarled. "Don't start an argument you can't win. You want the truth. I'm giving you the truth. You've known the fucking truth all along."

She stood up, knocking me sideways. My arm flew out, smashing her glass of water off the coffee table. Liquid spilled in a waterfall onto the brown and turquoise retro rug but I didn't care.

She charged for the door.

Launching upright, I chased after her. My body hurt, my head pounded, but I caught her arm, spinning her to face me. "Stop."

"Let me go." She kicked my knees, anger painting red spots on her cheeks. "I don't want to be here."

"You do. You have to listen."

"I don't have to do anything." Her chest puffed as she inhaled hard. "Let me go, Penn, or whoever you are." Her face turned nasty. "Or should I say Gio or Sean."

The world froze.

She remembered?

Christ, three years and she remembered.

Her father had said she was intelligent and I'd seen first-hand how capable and strong she was but to remember...fuck.

My heart raced. "My name is Penn."

"But what was it three years ago?"

Passion raged through me. I wanted nothing more than to hurt her the way she'd hurt me. To force her to be honest the way she was asking me to be. Couldn't she see she stabbed me with a blade each time she believed I wasn't who I said?

"It's always been Penn."

*Does that answer your question? See me. See who I am.*

It would be so easy to come out and tell her. To wrap my lips around the words and reveal my secret. But just as I hated her three years ago, I hated her now for doubting. If what'd happened that night was real she shouldn't have to ask.

She should know.

Just like I knew.

She should hurt as much as I did.

*I'll show her.*

The ridiculous idea popped into my head. Wrapping my fingers around her throat, I marched her backward toward the kitchen wall. She stumbled, her hand coming up to fight against my hold. "Let—let me go."

I didn't stop, not when she tripped and I had to pluck her feet from the floor and hoist her into my arms, not when she kicked my shins as I crashed her against the wall, and not when I grabbed her chin, held her firm, and kissed her like she ought to have been fucking kissed for the past three years.

She was a virgin.

She'd waited.

I liked to think she'd waited for me. That her body had always been mine just like her heart. But I was in the habit of lying to others, not to myself, so I wouldn't believe such fantasy.

Her tongue tangled with mine. Her breath feeding my lungs as I devoured her.

Her sharp moan made me pull back. Panting hard, I murmured, "I was there. I'll tell you even though you already know. I'm—"

A fist hammered on my door. "Police. Open up."

Elle froze in my arms.

My muscles atrophied in horror.

*Shit.*

*Shit.*

*Shit.*

I thought I'd have more time.

I thought I'd tell her. Explain why I'd acted the way I had, and then either win the lottery by having her forgive me or drive her home, so I knew she was safe.

*It's too soon.*

*I haven't finished.*

I knew they'd come for me. It was a risk I'd been willing to take. A chance I had to take to save her. But not so soon. Not before I could fix what I'd ruined.

"Elle, I'm—"

Her eyes flared wide as the pounding came again. "Penn Everett, open this door. Immediately."

"Fuck." I raked a hand through my hair, stepping away from Elle, seeing all my dreams and wishes evaporate into dust.

Elle slipped back onto her toes, smashing a hand over her mouth. "Oh, my God."

I didn't know if her sudden profanity was at our interruption or my roundabout confession. Her face shot white. Her eyes searching for something real, something she could latch onto and find—

"We know you're in there. Open up!" the police barked, destroying everything—just like they'd destroyed the first night we met. Just like they destroyed my entire fucking life before I ever found Elle in that alley.

My gaze danced around my apartment, looking for something, *anything*, that I could use against what was about to happen.

But I was at a loss.

All because I'd let the violence in my blood carry me away.

My shoulders sank with depression. There was no getting around this. Unfortunately, this time, I deserved what would happen.

*Larry is gonna be so pissed.*

Swallowing hard, I glanced one last time at Elle and stalked to the front door. I opened it just as an officer raised his hand to thump again. "It's open. Calm the fuck down."

One moment, I was a free man standing in my own apartment trying to repair the damage with a girl I would never admit to caring for.

The next, I was a prisoner held between two officers, brute force yanking my arms back even when I offered no retaliation.

"Penn Everett, you're under arrest."

I laughed.

It was the only fucking thing I could do.

That night.

That field.

That kiss.

Elle lost her shock, dashing forward and hanging on the arm

of the officer who snapped the metal restraints over my wrists. "Wait, you can't do this."

A female rookie with a fresh uniform, polished buttons, and a never-been-used weapon stepped forward and pulled her back. "Ma'am, don't touch the arresting officer."

Elle whirled on her. "Don't touch him? Well, tell *him* not to touch him." She pointed at me, her hand shaking. "We're not done. I need to talk to him."

"He's done." The officer who caught me grinned with smugness. His ginger hair prickled like a hedgehog with his buzz cut. "Guess you're going home, huh?"

I glowered.

Elle shook her head. "What's that supposed to mean?"

The officer replied, "It means I've followed his record, and it was only a matter of time until he slipped again. They always do." He chuckled, motioning to the rookie to grab an elbow and march me toward the door.

I went with them. I offered no resistance.

Things would only get worse if I did.

"Wait. You can't do this. Release him." Elle stayed by my side, fighting all over again for me.

*Does she remember that night?*

Did she remember the way she begged for my freedom in the park? The way she'd run as hard as she could and offered herself as a sacrifice when she couldn't run anymore? The way she'd kissed me breathless and frantic in the bushes while I waited for the police to take me because I didn't want her to hurt or fear anymore?

I'd fallen for her for that.

I'd fallen so fucking hard in only a heartbeat. She'd been the only good thing in my world. The only light after so much darkness. How could I control my free fall when she treated me with such kindness? When she'd kissed me. When she'd trusted me. When she'd given me half the chocolate bar I'd stolen from the convenience store only an hour before meeting her?

Christ, I'd fallen so damn hard, I hadn't recovered from the bruises even years later.

It was only till after I was freed from prison did my infatuation with the princess I'd met that night turn to malice. Such simple adoration twisted the more I learned about her. The more I researched and grasped at fragments of information widely available online and in newspapers.

She was rich.

She was powerful.

She could've helped free me.

But she hadn't.

She'd left me to rot.

She'd lied to me that night about feeling something. Because if she'd felt half of what I had, she wouldn't have left me behind bars without doing everything in her goddamn power to find me.

But I'd grown up since then.

Since Larry found me and did what I'd hoped she would.

I finally had someone on my side, and it wasn't her.

I wasn't proud, but I'd let the snowballing hate smash through whatever ground I'd stood on. I'd fallen harder for her but the wrong way this time. I'd allowed my stupid sleuthing to tarnish the only good thing in my world and turn it into the chalice of everything I despised.

I'd never felt like that before.

Never been so livid against injustice and frustration and anger. I'd known weakness and helplessness. I'd known destitution and abandonment. I'd known terror and shame and respect and confusion and every fucking emotion on the roulette called life.

But I'd never known love until her.

And I'd never known hate until her.

Never laid awake at night with my guts churning and heart burning and a paralysis that kept me stuck forever thinking about her.

Her out there. Free.

Her out there. Rich.

Her out there. While I was inside trapped and crippled by a system that'd failed me in every fucking way since I'd been born.

I had nothing to say as the officers led me from the apartment I'd paid for in cash—cash I'd earned the right way, not the wrong way—and crammed me into the hallway.

Elle chased us.

Her face alive. Her eyes disbelieving that once again, the law would tear us apart. She didn't even know. She didn't trust, even now. She believed I was Gio or Sean.

How fucking could she?

How could she kiss me and not trust in that?

How could she think I was a rapist when I had so much I wanted to fucking say to her but never would?

*You hurt me, Elle.*

---

*More than anyone.*

In a strange way, I was glad I wouldn't be allowed to see her again. It made this so much easier. I wouldn't have to deal with the betrayal or spill everything I'd done to make amends.

I wouldn't have to admit I was wrong.

That she was rich and powerful and above most rules, but she hadn't forgotten me. I knew better now. She would've come for me. If only I'd told her my goddamn name that night instead of keeping it secret—terrified she'd be embarrassed by me. That she'd go from thinking I was a down-on-his-luck passerby and know the truth. The truth that my bed consisted of cardboard and donated blankets. That my meals consisted of charity and theft.

It was my fault.

And hers.

We'd fucked up together.

All this time, I thought I would be begging for her forgiveness. That she would walk out of my life once she knew I'd lied to her and I admitted just how much my hate navigated my actions.

But in reality, I would leave her and the justice system would banish her from my world.

"Stop!" Elle stood to her full height in her ridiculous gold negligée, wrapping herself in authority not many excel at and few are born with. "Let him go. I won't ask again."

"Ms. Charlston?" David, her driver, bodyguard, and fucking nuisance, climbed the stairs with his arms loose by his sides. He seemed to have a knack for turning up at the wrong time.

Did he not trust me with his employer?

That made two of them.

His languid steps didn't fool me. He was packing and just itching to draw. He'd wanted this ever since he recognized me the night I picked Elle up at the Blue Rabbit and took her back to my place to fuck her the first time.

He'd glared into my eyes, and in that glimpse, we'd both relived that night in Central Park. The night when he'd come to claim sweet nineteen-year-old Elle and left me on my own. I'd expected him to say something. To say more than 'he looks familiar' but he hadn't. He'd zipped his lips and let Elle decide who to believe I was.

I had to give him credit for that, at least.

"David, tell them to let him go." Elle whirled toward him, looking to him to fix this. He might've stopped Elle from being arrested three years ago, but he hadn't done it for me then, and he wouldn't do it for me now.

His jaw tightened, his dark skin hiding stress and anger better than Elle's pale complexion as he moved to her side. He didn't touch her. Professional until the end. "Greg woke up and pressed charges. Mr. Everett hurt him. He'll have to suffer the consequences."

Elle growled, "Greg kidnapped me. He was seconds away from raping me. Penn stopped him."

The officer with red hair mumbled, "Greg will be taken in for questioning, too, once he's been cleared at the hospital."

"Hospital?" Elle threw her hands up. "Are you kidding me? He'll have a few bruises. He's over-acting the entire thing."

The office shook his head. "Reports of a bruised larynx and broken ribs have been confirmed by the doctors. It's a serious matter, Ms. Charlston, and both parties will be dealt with."

At least I'd hurt him.

He deserved to be in pain.

The rookie sidled up to Elle. My hackles rose as she said, "When you've returned home and eh, recuperated." She looked at the state of Elle's undress. "You're required to come to the station to submit your statement about how Greg Hobson took you, what his intentions were in the cabin, and any outstanding issues we need to be aware of."

Elle spasmed with anger. "I can tell you all that right now. In exchange for letting Mr. Everett go."

I chuckled. "Come on, Elle. You know from experience they won't do that. Just leave me like you did the first time."

Her hands wedged in her stomach as if I'd physically hit her. "Do you think I'm that heartless?" She moved closer, dragging my gaze to her perfect body and just how fucking much I suffered when it came to her. Love her. Hate her. Adore her. Abhor her. I could never win.

Because I wasn't telling the truth.

The truth was I'd never felt like this for anyone.

Ever.

*I'm in love with you, you chocolate-kissing, night time stealing, gorgeous girl. And I'm pissed as hell about it.*

My shoulders straightened. I would never tell her because she hadn't earned my truth. The only person who had was Larry.

*Fuck, Larry.*

I had to talk to him the moment I was allowed a phone call.

The ginger officer guided me toward the stairs. "Time to go."

"Penn, please!" Elle wrung her hands. "I believe you. Don't punish me for fearing the worst."

Was it wrong of me to want her to hurt just a little? To make her feel how awful it was not to have someone trust you.

Tears brimmed in her blue eyes, begging me to relieve that hurt.

I cursed her. But I couldn't let her suffer.

Tugging against the cop's pressure, I said, "Go into the kitchen. Above the fridge is a safe deposit box. Combination is 0619—19$^{th}$ of June."

Elle half-gasped, half-sobbed.

Before she could say anything, I added, "Inside, you'll find things that will answer some of your questions, but you'll also find my emergency details. Call Larry Barns."

"All right, enough chitchat." The officer pushed me.

My feet descended the stairs. "Tell him I need his services again. Tell him I know I fucked up but he better come."

Elle nodded, her hands grasping the banister as she stayed on my floor, and I slowly headed below. "Can you say it out loud? Admit what happened between us that night. Please…I need to hear that, Penn…"

Even now, she still had a splinter of doubt puncturing her trust.

*Fuck, that hurts.*

I smiled harshly. "The fact that you have to ask is all the answer I'll give you." I glanced down, judging how many steps to go. How many steps before I was trapped behind barbwire and bars again.

Tears welled in her gaze. "So you *are* Nameless?"

I shrugged. "I've never been called Nameless. But if you're asking who I am? How can I tell you? How can I make you see what you don't want to see?"

"But I *do* want to see. I've been dying to see for three years. I've been trying to find you, Penn. I—"

"Stop, Elle." I didn't want to hear her declarations of hardship. Of the occasional half-hearted search while she lived in her crystal tower and I rotted in a cell.

We reached the landing, ready to turn and vanish from Elle's line of sight. I gave her all I could. I finally admitted my truth. "I can't tell you who I am because I never told you my name. I could give you any name, and you would never know it was real because you never knew me."

The officers prodded me. "Get going."

I ignored them. "All you need to know is how I made you feel. What did you feel when I kissed you on that baseball field? How did you feel when I gave you the only food I'd had in days? How did you feel when you walked away from me and didn't look back?"

Her tears broke her disciplined wall, turning from sorrow to sob. "God, I felt something huge, something I'd never felt before. I fell for you when I didn't even know what that was." She whirled down a few steps, only for David to stop her from chasing me. "Penn, I'm sorry. So sorry."

Her apology didn't fade the pain I'd carried for so long.

I sighed sadly. "Glad to know it wasn't just one of us who fell that night."

The rookie shoved me forward.

I didn't look back.

Just like she hadn't three years ago.

# Chapter Fifteen

# Elle

APARTMENT HALLWAYS HAD a habit of causing damage to furniture edges and being scuffed by human traffic, but I never thought it had the power to hurt knees and palms.

Until I slammed to all fours under the colossal weight of despair.

*"I can't tell you who I am because I never told you my name."*

How many words in that single sentence? How heavy the truth in that string of confession? Enough to steal the remaining energy in my limbs and throw me headfirst into faintness.

I wasn't a woman anymore. I was sharp breaths, swirling thoughts, and lost bearings. Falling forward as if in prayer, begging the world for a better answer delivered in a kinder way, I pleaded for a do-over.

I'd dreamed of finding Nameless. I'd had fantasies of loving him, saving him, proving to myself that what I'd felt that night wasn't some silly teenage fling but the start of something raw and terrible and utterly undeniable.

But that was before he'd looked at me with pain so deep-seated, so long lived with, he couldn't stop the flash of disgust in his eyes.

He *blamed* me.

He blamed me for not finding him, for not doing exactly what I'd promised myself I'd do and didn't.

*Oh, God.*

I hugged my waist, ignoring the bruises from Greg and focusing on the bruises on my heart. I needed to touch him, promise him that I believed now. That I *trusted* now.

But how flimsy was that?

How awful of me to doubt and accuse, unable to see that my wishes had come true and I'd done nothing but fight against him since he came for me.

To finally find Nameless.

To come face-to-face with him and put aside the three years and pick up exactly where we left off—with passion and purity and no lies or worries.

*That* was the stupid teenage ideal, not the night we met. The belief that years later it would still be unsullied and ready to morph into something true.

*It's ruined.*

*It's over.*

My life had gone the exact opposite of everything I'd wanted.

Did young-hearted idealism make him my perfect other? Or fate?

Was he right to look at me as if I was a coward?

Penn had stared at me, not with happiness and satisfaction at finally reuniting, but with regret and disappointment. He acted as if he couldn't forgive me for not trusting the nudgings of my heart that his secret was one I'd wanted, not one I didn't.

How did I think he was Baseball Cap? How could I ever call him Adidas? Why was I so *weak*?

A soft gray blanket fell over my shoulders, smelling of Penn. David crouched beside me, rubbing my back with a warm, heavy hand. Slowly, he took my weight, plucking me from the dirty carpet of the hallway and onto my feet.

The minute I was standing, he guided me into Penn's apartment and motioned for me to sit.

To sit in the exact same place where Penn had sat just moments before. The place where my heart had started to unravel, already hearing Penn's truth but somehow unable to let go of my anger and finally believe.

He'd lied.

He'd been an asshole and covered up any sweetness that existed inside him.

*Why?*

Why be a jerk when I would've leapt into his arms the moment he'd told me the truth?

Why the make-believe?

Why didn't I recognize him?

Why couldn't I see the similarities between Penn and Nameless?

Why couldn't I see past the beard and dirty hoodie?

Why couldn't I see past the suits and wealth?

*Why?*

*Why?*

*Why?*

Ignoring David's request to sit, I stood and beelined for the cupboard above Penn's stainless steel fridge. Reaching on my tiptoes, I was able to touch but not grab the small safety deposit box.

*I can't—*

I tried to manhandle it, but my stupid fingers couldn't reach. I turned to spy a chair to stand on, but David reached for me and placed the metal navy box on the kitchen counter.

I didn't like him all that much currently. He'd prevented me from chasing after Penn. *Nameless.*

*All along, he's been Nameless.*

My heart stopped skipping a beat and settled for a jangled symphony instead.

I might not like David at the moment, but I kept my manners. "Thank you."

"You're welcome."

The box was heavy but not one to screw into a floor or wall. This was movable, only opened by the combination.

The combination Penn gave me.

The combination of the night we met.

Was that an unnecessary stab at my romantic ideals or had he felt something so strange that night?

*You know he did.*

He admitted it.

His voice echoed in my head with such delicious words. Words that clenched my tummy, suffocated my lungs, and restarted my heart. "*Glad to know it wasn't just one of us who fell that night.*"

And now, he'd been taken again. Locked up where I couldn't reach him.

Holding back more tears, I inputted the code and spun the dial. Holding my breath, I slouched in relief as the mechanism unlocked, beckoning me to lift the lid and learn its contents.

Cracking the top, I glanced at the treasure trove Penn had decided was valuable enough to keep safe.

Inside was his passport, a wad of one hundred dollar bills, an envelope marked stocks and bonds, and another one with the words: *'In an emergency.'* I opened that one, pulling out what I assumed was Larry's phone number.

David passed me his cell-phone before I could ask. His smile was knowing, his eyes obedient, even if he didn't necessarily agree with what I was about to do.

I took his phone but paused. "You knew. Didn't you?"

He clasped his hands in front of his belt buckle. "I had my suspicions when I recognized him outside the Blue Rabbit."

"Yet you didn't say anything?"

"It wasn't my place."

"Not your place to protect me?"

He smiled, chuckling softly. "My place is to protect your body. It was never in my contract to protect your heart." He motioned to the phone. "You already called me a meddler like your personal assistant. I wasn't about to risk my job by telling you who or who not to date."

Awkwardness fell between us. I'd spent years with David, yet we'd never had a truly frank conversation—especially about my love life.

"Just out of curiosity." I turned his phone on, typing in Larry's number. "Would you have protected my heart if I'd decided to date Greg like my father and Steve wanted?" My thumb hovered over the call button, waiting for David's answer.

He smiled, but it tinged with rage that Greg had taken me out of his custody and hurt. "I would've fired myself if you'd announced you were with him." His lips twitched. "Respectfully, of course, Ma'am."

Despite everything—the lies, the police, the fact that Penn was Nameless and he'd just been carted away for the second time—I smiled. "That's what I thought."

I pressed the call button as David said, "For what it's worth, I do believe he's a good guy. If you read between the lines, that is."

"I know." I held the phone to my ear. A ring tone sounded. "I saw it that first night."

*I just forgot to trust it and not let doubt and disbelief get in my way.*

I knew Penn was a good guy—despite his jackass ways the past few weeks.

In his mind, I deserved that treatment.

In my mind, I kind of agreed with him.

"Larry speaking."

My questions snapped away, leaving more important things. "Larry, this is Elle Charlston. Penn's been arrested."

He reacted straight away. "Ah, damn, I feared something like this would happen."

"Something like this?"

"Him getting mixed up with you. It's not exactly good for his temper."

I agreed Penn had a temper, but he could also control it. He'd unleashed it twice since I'd known him and both were to protect me.

He had my back. I hadn't had his.

God, I had to stop tormenting myself and fix what was broken, not focus on the reason for it. "It would've been a lot simpler if he'd told me the truth from the beginning."

"I did tell him that." Larry sighed. "Did he tell you the truth now?"

"As the police dragged him away, yes."

"And?" Larry prompted.

"And what?"

"How do you feel?" His tone cajoled.

"I...I don't know."

*Confused.*

*Annoyed.*

*Frightened.*

*Guilty.*

"What does that mean?" He sighed again, heavier this time. "Look, when I first helped him, he kept his feelings for you a secret. He didn't tell me about the girl in Central Park. But after a while, he confided in me. When I managed to revoke his sentence and free him, he said he would track you down and see if what you had was a one-night spark or real."

He didn't continue.

I blurted, desperate for more. "What else...what else did he talk about?"

"He, uh—he found you."

"Obviously."

"No, he found you the night he was released." He waited for that bomb to destroy me. "He found you and then refused to contact you."

Tears puddled inside, growing wetter with every breath. "Why?"

"I'm guessing that's his part to tell." He cleared his throat. "I'd better go. I'll get my ass down to the station and start the proceedings to free him. Again." Something clattered in the background. "I don't know how things ended with you tonight, but if you want, call me tomorrow, and I'll arrange a time for you to see him once he's been processed."

My heart lurched. "Wait, he won't be released tonight?"

Larry laughed as if I'd told a hilarious joke. "No, my dear. Where Penn is concerned, the NYPD have a thing against him. They'll keep him locked up for as long as they can. And they'll succeed."

"Why?"

"Because they have history."

# Chapter Sixteen

# Penn

I FUCKING HATED bars.

I hated metal sinks and hard-ass beds.

I hated the men who were as corrupt as everyone else, getting high off shiny badges and getting hard on screwing over innocence.

*Fair and just, my ass.*

The short journey down to the precinct irritated me. The cops and their radios irritated me. Pedestrians and traffic lights irritated me.

*Everything* fucking irritated me because I knew I wouldn't be treated fairly.

The moment I was on their turf, I had no power.

*None.*

I sat in fury, listening to my heartbeat pounding and splashing around in pools of regret. For once, the regret wasn't toward Elle but Larry. I'd let him down. I'd promised him I wouldn't be in this situation again because it was too fucking hard to get free last time when I'd done nothing wrong.

This time…I *had* done something wrong.

I'd beaten up Greg.

They had reason to detain me, and the man out for my blood would fucking wring his hands in glee when I showed up. He would ensure Greg would elaborate and collaborate; he'd document my victim's injuries with pride, and he would once again take great satisfaction in fucking over my life knowing he had me fair and square.

It wouldn't matter Greg had been the kidnapper and about-to-be rapist. It wouldn't matter his crimes far exceeded my own.

And it didn't matter I'd been taken shoeless, moneyless, and with dried blood and gore all over my body.

It would make an interesting mug shot.

It would only make his workday that much more enjoyable.

My head ached with the battle I was about to walk into. I wanted to rub my face, but the cuffs kept my hands tied. New York spat me out like a worm from the apple as the cop car slid through the reinforced gates and into Hell.

I didn't make eye contact or listen to the bastards who'd arrested me as they opened the vehicle, let me climb out with my motherfucking dignity, and didn't dare touch me as we stalked into the processing room.

And wouldn't you know? He was there already.

*Him.*

My nemesis.

His uniform, like always, was iron-creased with starched perfection. His salt and pepper hair cut short on the sides and balding on top. The paunch from too many years spent behind a desk and too much gluttony on the lost dreams of others thickened his middle.

His hands annoyed me.

His face annoyed me.

His entire fucking body pissed me the fuck off.

I stood tall, bracing my legs. "Hello, Arnold."

His chapped lips opened in undisguised joy. "Ah, hello again, Everett. Fancy seeing you here. This is my lucky day." He bared his teeth with bipolar emotions. "By the way, it's chief of police to you."

"Chief?" I cocked my head condescendingly. "Seems, I owe you congratulations. Last time you fucked me over, you were only a captain."

He buffed his nails on his shirt, gloating. "Yes, well, I've moved up the ranks since then."

*Not good.*

*Fucking so not good for me.*

"So it's Chief Twig now?" I wrinkled my nose. "No better than Captain Twig, is it? An unfortunate last name you've got there, Arnie."

His face reddened with anger. "You honestly want to piss me off? You know what happened last time, boy."

"I do remember last time. Quite clearly, in fact." I smirked. "And I have no doubt being polite or begging for mercy will get me the exact same conclusion as being a fucking bastard. So do your worst."

I shifted on the spot, spreading my stance. "Oh, and I'm no longer a boy. Then again, keep calling me that if it make's you feel better, seeing as I could kick your ass back when I was thirteen."

The other officers stepped forward, one on either side to teach me a lesson in respect.

But Arnold waved them off. He enjoyed breaking me too much to let others do it. "I'll take it from here, ladies and gentlemen. Good work bringing in this violent repeat offender. Coffee's on me."

"Not a problem, Chief." The officers left, closing the door behind them.

I wished they hadn't.

If they'd stay for the show, they'd finally learn what a twisted, immoral bastard their captain, now chief, was.

The room turned stagnant with history, slurs, and a past both of us would like to delete.

"Don't you mean the donuts are on you?" I glared at his waistline. "Put on a few pounds there, Arnie."

His hands clenched into balls, but he smiled tightly. "Keep being a dick and your rap sheet will just get longer and longer."

"I don't need to be a dick for that to happen. By the time I'm out of this place, the protection of a woman from an asshole about to rape her will have morphed into armed robbery, intent to kill, child molesting, and most likely a bank job and grannie murder." I smiled, even though I felt like tearing the room apart with rage. "Isn't that right, *Arnie?*"

He matched my smile, both of us using a normally kind human response to wield emotion filled with contempt and loathing. "You got it, my boy."

"If you're going to use a term of endearment, how about you choose a more appropriate one?"

Arnold grinned. "What would you prefer?"

"Oh, I dunno. How about the truth for once? Scapegoat? Fall Guy? Whipping Boy? Any of those work."

*I'm the one you blame and take the rap for others, you lying sack. Might as well own up to it.*

His face blackened. "Keep your voice down."

"Why? So your staff won't find out what a heartless cunt you are?"

He flinched.

I didn't stop.

"Five years of my life you stole on three different occasions—all for things I didn't do. And now, you're about to steal more. But this time, I'm not gonna be so silent. I have a family now. I'm rich. Charge me with whatever you goddamn like, but rest assured, I won't have some shitty state-appointed lawyer who's on your payroll to shuttle me off to the slammer and then be beaten by your men to keep me silent inside."

I took a step toward him.

It was a balancing act of pushing but not being an idiot. Any one of his officers could shoot me if they thought I was threatening him.

"I'm not afraid of you anymore." I lowered my voice. "Do your worst. Let's fucking dance, Arnie. Let's see who wins this time."

# Chapter Seventeen

# Elle

WAS IT WRONG of me that I'd taken Penn's box?

Was it immoral to sit on my bed after the longest bath in history, biggest dinner I could stomach, countless checks on my father and his heart, and endless cuddles from Sage to open his box of secrets?

For the past three hours, I'd assured Dad I was okay, made sure he was okay, answered his questions, dodged others, and then lamented with him while he directed his red-hot fury at Greg.

Steve called professing apologies, David stood guard at my door—even though I told him that wasn't necessary—and Sage wouldn't let me go even to use the bathroom on my own.

She curled up on a towel on the edge of the bath while I soaked away the aches and bruises Greg had given me.

Afterward, she swatted the belt of my Terry cloth robe as I padded warm, tired, and finally alone to my bedroom.

And there was Penn's box.

Begging me to read its contents.

To pry.

To sneak.

To steal everything I could about him.

I'd stared at it for the past hour while both angel and devil squatted on my shoulders, whispering to keep it closed, muttering to open it, murmuring to trust, nudging to search.

I'd failed him in the hallway when he was taken. I'd failed him when he'd kissed me, and I fought the knowledge my heart already knew.

Was I failing him again by picking apart his lies and seeking the truth without him here to fill in the blanks?

*He's Nameless.*

Wasn't that all that mattered?

I thought it would feel different to finally know.

To hear him admit that he was there, he was the chocolate kisser, he was the Central Park romance.

But his confession had split me. I couldn't add up the Penn I knew and the Nameless one I didn't. They didn't match. Why had he changed so much? *Had* he changed or was it all an act?

The stupid fantasy that I'd believed in of finding Nameless and picking up where we left off, faltered. What if that kismet attraction and instantaneous lust weren't enough to delete the mess between us and start afresh?

I'd slept with him. I'd lost my virginity to the man I'd been dreaming of for three long years.

I felt...ashamed.

*I'm confused.*

*I'm angry with him and myself.*

I didn't know how to make sense of anything anymore.

It made me doubt everything I'd felt that night and tarnished it because if I could be around Penn this long and not fall insanely in love with him, then what did that mean about that night in Central Park?

*Open the box.*

*Stop wasting time.*

Sage batted it with her paw, meowing softly as if she didn't approve of the foreign object taking up space on my lap. Her soft silver fur glowed warm like a tiny moonbeam, her tail flicking in impatience and curiosity.

"Don't look at me like that. Go. Fetch." I threw her purple mouse that was missing its tail and half of its whiskers.

She arched a kitty eyebrow as if pitying me that I thought she'd play catch like a dog. I merely held her stare until she scowled and leaped off the bed, hunting for the thrown toy.

While her back was turned and her judgy eyes were elsewhere, I cracked the lid and held my breath.

I held my breath until my head swam and my heart knocked on my ribs in a reminder that it needed oxygen to breathe.

I didn't want to breathe because beneath the emergency contact numbers was a driver's license of a man I wished I could forget; one I wished I could delete and pretend never existed.

Baseball Cap.

*Gio...I believe.*

I recalled the two men calling each other names but couldn't be entirely sure I'd remembered them correctly.

Then again, his name printed on the license told me I was right.

Why could I remember him so clearly when I'd struggled to place Penn?

My fingers shook as I plucked the laminated identification and stared into the heartless eyes of the man who'd tried to rape me. Without the cap, his hair was shaggy and unkempt, mousy brown with matching uneven stubble on his jaw.

He was nothing like Nameless.

Nothing connecting us enough to evoke the emotions Penn did.

How could I think Penn was him?

How could I have let the years erase the feeling of disgust and terror?

Penn wasn't Baseball Cap or Adidas.

He could *never* have been, and I must have known that all along.

*Oh, my God.*

Dropping the license, I clamped a hand over my mouth.

How insulting to him.

What a slap in the face for me to believe he could be as evil as those two bastards.

He was right to hate me.

Could he forgive me?

*But why does he have Gio's license?*

Gio Markus Steel according to his full address.

Steel…that name was familiar. It flopped around inside my head like a fish on a line, ready to reel in, but the string was too tangled to haul.

What was Larry keeping secret on Penn's behalf? Who *was* Penn? Where did he come from? His family? His past?

He'd given me a tiny part of himself, but I needed more.

So much more.

*Steel!*

I sat upright in bed, recalling the day Penn had ambushed me at work. The day I'd done my floor inspections and come upon a little boy having a suit made from a man's.

*Master Steel.*

Same last name as Gio.

Did that mean Stewie and Gio were related?

*Argh!*

How could I unravel this mayhem and make sense of it without Penn to guide me?

Penn had saved my life—multiple times—but now, I needed him to save me from my questions.

There was only one way for him to do that.

*I have to see him again.*

# Chapter Eighteen

# Penn

I KNEW THE process—I'd done it a few times before—but it didn't make it any easier.

The first time had been scary as fuck with a night in the station, arraignment with a useless public defender nodding to felonies I hadn't committed, and no cash to post bail. It took days to join gen pop before I settled in to serve time for a crime I hadn't done.

That night had also been the first time I'd had the joy of meeting Arnold Twig.

*Fucker.*

I'd served one year, one month of a three-year sentence—let off for good behavior.

The second time was unfortunate bad luck, but once again, Arnold was there to ensure I was the perfect scapegoat.

A night in the holding cells, another useless arraignment, another district attorney advising bail I couldn't afford, and then I was back in jail.

Once there, I enjoyed a two week stay in the infirmary after a vicious beating ensured my lips remained firmly shut about the secrets Arnold Twig had no intention of letting me spill.

I'd served three years, two months of a four-year sentence— let off once again for good behavior.

The third time had been the night I met Elle. The night when my heart was full and my head hurt, knowing if Arnold had his way, I'd be in prison for a lot longer.

He'd shuttled me back to Hell as fast as he could. The moment dawn arrived, he'd yanked me from the cell and sent me to the district attorney with yet another jaded public defender. By the afternoon, I was in a prison uniform and holding out a plastic tray for food.

Hey, at least I got to eat that day.

That night, though…fuck, that night I couldn't stop tormenting myself with memories of kissing the girl I'd rescued, imagining we'd been able to finish what we started—that in a better, kinder world, I would've asked to see her again and done my best to get off the streets so I could deserve her.

And now, while my bones still cried and my clothes hid a fight-sweaty body, Arnold once again expedited my case.

After our little chat, he personally escorted me to complete the sham of gathering my official information.

I refused to say a word apart from, "bite my ass."

Besides, I had no reason to give up my name, age, and entire autobiography. They had that information already.

My file listed exactly who I was and precisely what my past convictions entailed.

*What was it again? Oh, yeah.*

Incident number one—grand theft auto.

Two—aggravated assault and theft.

Three—aggravated assault and rape.

After that waste of time, he arranged for my transfer to central booking where they could keep me up to twenty-four hours in the cells affectionately called the tombs. The rank, filthy pens where homeless, drunks, and low-collar criminals were crammed together like livestock destined for the canning factory.

My statement consisted of, "Call my lawyer," and Arnold took great joy in repeating my Miranda rights as he slammed the bars closed.

Whatever evidence Greg had fed them while moaning and playing the victim at the hospital ensured my case was a special one. Not only did I have the chief of police ready to bury me in the system, but he also had the power to speed up or slow down my trial.

The meeting with the Criminal Justice Agency ensured a district attorney who bowed to Twig's every command, agreeing that I was too dangerous a flight risk to allow bond at any amount.

Unfortunately, my prior actions supported such a shitty denial because the last time I'd served in the great state's penitentiary, the moment I'd been released, I'd moved with Larry to LA to get my head on straight and the fuck away from New York.

Either Larry was too late to attend the hearing, or he was

busy putting together my defense. Whatever the reason, I trusted him because he knew what I was up against. If he thought it was worth staying away for now, then fine. I had no doubt he'd file an appeal and request an early trial to set this long-winded, beyond-aggravating system into motion.

*Greg had better get fucking arrested, too.*

I wouldn't be able to stomach going to jail while the real perpetrator got away with it.

Again.

At least this time around, I wasn't a penniless, homeless throwaway.

I had money.

I had friends.

And that made it even more imperative in Arnie's corrupted mind that he control my reinsertion back into prison with utmost perfection.

I had no intention of keeping his secrets this time. Give me a judge, a jury, a fucking court full of people and I'd tell them all about Arnold's precious son.

*Unless I get shanked, of course.*

Fuck, I missed Elle. I missed being free.

Hours had a tendency to blur together in this place. I had no idea how many had passed by the time I was collected in a minivan with bars on the windows and manacles on the floor.

Cuffed hands and ankles, I shuffled onto the vehicle and a clank of chains locked me into position. The noise of the links reminded me Greg had chained Elle.

That he'd hurt her.

Almost raped her.

My rage and desire to punch him all over again helped overshadow my fear at being trapped against my will. The incessant blistering fury fed me better than any food or liquor, and I didn't pay attention to the officer closing the door or the driver sliding the van into gear and taking me from police station to prison block.

At least, Arnold had retreated to his office like the scum he was.

\* \* \* \* \*

Arriving at the Department of Corrections, I was finally given a shower to wash away the blood, a quick check up by the in-house doctor, who kindly prescribed more painkillers, and searched for contraband—which was the single most degrading thing a man could go through.

Once clean and dressed in a dark green prison uniform, I was met with the usual welcome of a blanket, pillow, and toothbrush parcel then ferried into the prison population where remanded felons were kept just in time for the warning bell for lights out.

For now, I had a cell with two bunk beds pressed up against the wall to myself.

I had no doubt that would change, but tonight, I'd enjoy the fucking privacy.

Choosing the top bunk, I spread out my blanket, fluffed my pillow, and lay down to glower at the pockmarked ceiling.

Every inch of me hurt.

My head, my hands, my chest, my legs...*everything.*

But despite the heat and throbbing in my joints, I waited to feel something other than physical maladies.

To ache with unfairness and suffer discomfort at being somewhere foreign. To crave freedom and open spaces with the unsatisfied appetite of a drug addict.

And I did suffer.

But I couldn't fake myself into believing this place was foreign.

It wasn't foreign at all.

It was familiar.

A second home.

A well-known place I despised with every inch of my being.

Its welcome whispered over me, deleting the past few years where I'd been wealthy and cared for and obsessed with the girl who'd shared my chocolate bar, fell for me, and then looked at me as if I was scum even when she heard the truth.

Her apology echoed in my ears.

Her tears glistened in memory.

I'd hurt her, but she'd hurt me.

And now, I was here, and she was there, and there was no way to fix what was broken.

"Fuck." I punched my pillow, rolled over, and closed my eyes.

# Chapter Nineteen

# Elle

"I HAVE TO SEE him."

Another phone rang in the background, but Larry didn't make an excuse to end our call to answer it.

He sighed, but it wasn't cruel, more like lost as to what he could offer me. "I can arrange it but not for a few days. New prisoners are given a stand-down period before visitors are allowed."

"New prisoners?"

"He's being held without bail. I've already filed an appeal and fighting for a hearing date that isn't sometime in two years. We'll get him back, but the justice system is archaic. It'll take time."

"Time?" I sucked in a breath. "How much time?"

"Can't say. But it'll be as short as I can make it."

My heart plummeted, rolling in shame, coating in guilt until it sat tarred and feathered in my stomach. "But…he didn't do anything wrong."

"The previous times he was locked up, I would've agreed with you." His voice layered with tiredness, reminding me not so long ago, he was seriously sick, and Penn had been the one to look after him. Now, it was Larry's turn.

*How many times has it been his turn?*

"Previous times?" My voice was small, timid. My question hesitant.

Larry heard my uncertainty.

I hated myself for it. Here I was so close to the truth, and I wasn't sure I had the balls to learn any more.

The more I did, the more I cursed myself. Cursed myself for not trying harder to find Penn. For doubting him. For hurting him.

His arrogance and fine-edged cruelty had been the perfect mask to hide the loneliness and hardship of a life I could never imagine.

Fate had been so generous and kind to me. It had been an absolute bitch to Penn.

*How can I make it right?*

Once again, I had dreams of protecting him, cooking for him, caring for him the way I knew he would care for me if only he could forgive my doubting.

Sage waltzed over my desk, sprawling on her side on my notepad, unapologetically asking for cuddles while my mind whirled.

Automatically, my fingers sank into her soft fur. I blinked at my office in Belle Elle's tower, returning to the present rather than dwindling on awful, awful imaginings of what Penn was going through.

"Yes," Larry said. "The previous times he was arrested." Something banged as if he'd closed a desk drawer. "For example, the night in Central Park—when he was with you."

I froze. "What about it?"

"He was sentenced to eight years for aggravated robbery, armed assault, and attempted rape."

"But that's a lie!"

"Doesn't matter. He had no one to fight for him then. Neither did he have support when he was first arrested and held in an adult penitentiary, even though he was a minor. He didn't commit the crime, but he paid—purely because of bad luck and similar facial features to another."

My mind cartwheeled, growing dizzy. "I don't know what you mean."

"I mean, Elle, the first time he served thirteen months and was out early for good behavior. The state didn't ask him if he had a home to go to, family to see, or a job to earn a living. They just kicked him out with nothing—not even the lint from his pockets because he didn't *have* any lint when they'd arrested him."

"That's...awful." I didn't want to hear anymore.

Tears wobbled in my gaze, making my office dance and Sage turn into a gray blob. Belle Elle suddenly wasn't a tower of servitude but a pillar of strength. This was my core asset. This company had made me rich and powerful.

*It's time I used that wealth in other ways—freeing innocent men ways.*

Larry chuckled with pride. "He made do. He's a resourceful

lad. He stole—he's not innocent on that account—but he only did it to survive. The second charge was betrayal by a so-called friend and the result of bad luck, bad timing. He got time for theft and for knocking out the house owner and molesting his wife."

I gasped. "That can't be true. He would never—"

"Of course, he wouldn't," Larry snapped. "He was framed."

My fingers tightened on my phone, falling more into the tangled tale of Penn's past. "How?"

"Penn happened to be walking back to his current bed for the night when he saw his so-called friend entering the house in question. He followed. Tried to talk some sense into him, only for the wife to get confused and think it was Penn who'd touched her and the man to wake up groggy and brain-bruised and accuse him. The real perp had run before the police arrived. By the time Penn was processed, *he* had heard the news and personally oversaw Penn's arrest. By that point, it was too late."

Chills scattered down my spine. *"He?"*

Larry made a hate-thick noise in the back of his throat. "Arnold Twig."

The name alone made me shudder with anger and the need to scratch out his eyes for being the cause of Penn's misfortune. "And who is Arnold Twig?"

"Sean Twig's father. Penn's nightmare."

\* \* \* \* \*

I couldn't stop replaying the strange conversation over and over.

Larry had been forthcoming but cryptic at the same time.

How had this Arnold Twig got away with framing Penn?

Why had nothing been done about it?

Why hadn't Penn himself been a whistleblower and shouted to the world what had happened?

Why had I never been contacted to testify about the rape and assault charge the night he was stolen from me?

The man in the hoodie from the alley had honor and backbone. He didn't let me get raped because he morally had to help. That strong ethic code would stand up for himself, too, surely?

With my questions keeping me constant company, the day passed like all the others.

But it didn't feel like the others.

It was different.

Strange.

However, the calendar hadn't changed.

I had.

The second I'd wandered into Belle Elle after heading downtown with David and Dad to answer police questions and provide my statement about Greg, I'd had no mental capacity to work.

Even Fleur had frozen in shock and demanded to know what I was doing there.

I'd given her the socially acceptable response that I was head of this empire and I'd already had a few days away. I wouldn't miss more.

That was a lie.

The real reason was I couldn't sit at home on my own anymore. I couldn't raid Penn's safety deposit box and stare at the handsome passport photo of a slightly younger man with aged wisdom and persecution in his gaze.

The same prettiness that had beguiled me now broke my heart that I couldn't pick up a phone and call him or knock on his door and hug him.

He was untouchable, unreachable, and it hurt so damn much.

The only good thing was the knowledge that Greg had been questioned. He was under arrest pending discharge from the hospital. On the flip side, Greg had submitted his own statement about Penn's treatment and wanted him punished to the fullest extent possible.

*It's a damn racket.*

Greed had caused this and greed could kiss my ass.

My stomach never stopped roiling at how vindictive Greg had become. How a boy from my childhood could become such a conniving, jealous asshole.

I had no idea if he'd end up in the same prison as Penn or what it would mean for Steve's future at Belle Elle, knowing his best friend's daughter had sent his only son to jail.

But it wasn't my fault, and I was too tired to worry.

\* \* \* \* \*

Six p.m. rolled around, and instead of having a productive day, I couldn't remember where the time had gone.

My website browser had court processes and information on what happened to reoffenders. My history painted research on how unlikely a release was when the victim was pushing for full penalty.

Greg had not only tried to take Belle Elle away from me, but he also had the power to take away Penn.

The fermenting anger inside threatened to boil over. Nothing was simple all because of him. All because Greg thought he deserved something for nothing.

*He can't get away with it.*

I wished I had more knowledge on how to argue cases that weren't just black and white. But I was sheltered in that respect. I just had to hope Larry knew what he was doing—which drove me nuts, as I needed to do *something* to help.

Another kernel of loathing layered on top of my anger as I Googled Arnold Twig: chief of police, part-time volunteer at the soup kitchen, father to one son, and all-a-round good citizen. The scarce photos of him online depicted an older gentleman who preferred crisp ironed clothes and sensible shoes.

I couldn't see why he would be such a threat to Penn.

A knock raised my head.

I glanced at the door, yanked from my scattered thoughts. "Come in."

I expected Fleur. I smiled with kindness and welcome—grateful to see my helpful assistant and friend before she left for the night.

The true visitor turned my smile to marble. I hid my grimace behind it. "Steve…what a surprise."

I had no desire to see him. He'd done nothing wrong, he'd showered me in apologies, but I couldn't separate my fondness of him against the dislike of his son.

Steve lingered on the threshold. "Elle, I wondered…can I have a minute?"

My heart raced, noticing for the first time the similarities between Steve and Greg. Matching jawline, the way their mouth formed certain words, even their nose shared the same genetics.

It had never bothered me before, but that was before Greg punched me and drove me across the state to try to do what exactly? Rape me into falling in love with him? Arranging someone to marry us under duress and believing the marriage certificate would've held up against the lawyers I would've hired to bury Greg under litigation?

*Idiot.*

I stood, planting my hands on my desk. "I think you'll need more than just a minute to explain what the hell Greg was thinking, Steve." Nothing but swift authority was in my voice. No gratitude for his guidance over the years or friendship toward a father figure I'd grown up with.

I was his boss.

He was my employee.

He was also the father of the man I never wanted to see again.

He tugged on the bottom of his blue blazer, striding into my office. Wisely, he didn't close the door. Already I felt trapped, and the sounds of departing staff echoed in the hallway, inviting me to run with them.

"You have a point there." He stopped in front of my desk.

Sage, picking up on my vibes but not sure why, did what she always did and jumped to the carpet to wrap herself around his ankles in welcome.

He smiled sadly, his eyes welling with tears and more apologies. "Shit, Noelle. I'm so goddamn sorry." His gaze trailed over my bruises—the black eye of pain and memories of the short hostage situation I'd endured. "I never thought he'd do something so terrible. He's Greg." He shrugged. "He's never been violent. Greedy and spoiled, yes, but..." He spread his hands. "I don't know what to say."

"Tell me where he is."

"Still at the hospital. I think he's being discharged tomorrow." He looked at the floor. "Then he'll be transferred to the police station, I guess."

*Tomorrow.*

On the one hand, I was glad he would be dealt with so soon. On the other, it didn't give me much time to threaten him to drop the charges against Penn.

*Whoa...you're going to do what?*

The plan had come from nowhere, but...it made sense.

*It's ridiculous.*

But so what?

I had no other skill or way of helping Penn.

*I have to do something.*

*Even something moronic.*

Who better to help Penn than the woman who had power over the man accusing him? If I wanted to use that power, I had to be quick.

Steve didn't notice my hastily forming, crazily stupid plan, or the rush of heat over my skin at the thought of kicking Greg where it hurt and making *him* suffer for a change.

"I've arranged with human resources to create the necessary

severance packets. He won't be coming back to Belle Elle." He ducked to pet Sage before she wandered off with her tail high.

"Thank you."

I was glad he'd taken care of it but annoyed that we had to tiptoe around contract clauses and fulfill our end of the bargain with vacation pay and remaining sick leave.

I didn't want to give him a penny more than he'd already squeezed out of me. But I wouldn't give Greg any reason to come after me again—suing me for incorrect dismissal or otherwise.

"Do you know what time he'll be collected by the police tomorrow?" I delivered my question void of emotion. However, it held two sides. One innocent. One plotting.

I wanted Greg behind bars.

But not before I had a few moments alone with him.

*Don't do this...*

*It could backfire royally.*

I told myself to hush up.

For three years, I'd done nothing to help Penn. There was no way I could do that again. I could never live with myself.

I kept my body stiff; my secrets hidden. Ever since I'd found Gio's driver's license in Penn's box, a seed had been planted. I didn't know what that seed had been or what actions it would have me take, but now it had sprouts, straining for truth like a flower strains for sunlight, giving me a blueprint of a plan.

I knew what I had to do.

Penn was Nameless.

Nameless was Penn.

That put me in an uncomfortable situation.

Nameless, I owed a debt. That debt was still unfulfilled and never paid. Penn, I owed thanks for repeating history and saving me, but it didn't wipe his behavior clean. If we were to have any chance at fixing this, I had to know the *real* him...not the many faces he hid behind.

Nameless—I'd fallen for him in a lightning strike of adolescent stupidity. Penn—I'd fallen out of love with every lie he'd told.

It looked as though the same had happened to him with me.

We both had grudges.

Perhaps, a third chance would fix everything that went wrong.

"No idea. Probably early afternoon?" Steve said. "I think he has a final check up in the morning."

*It's now or never.*

I picked up my turquoise fountain pen, tapping it against my palm. "I want to see him."

"What?" Steve gripped the back of his neck. "I don't think that's wise."

"Too bad. I want to."

His face scrunched up. "Uh, okay. I'll come with you and act as a mediator to ensure you're safe."

"No. I want to be on my own."

"But—" His skin turned a sick pallor. "Elle, you have every right to hate him. I know you gave your statement this morning, which you have *every* right to do. But please...you're better than he is. You've always been so much gentler and smarter than all of us."

His tone switched to begging. "I'm outraged with him and don't know how to call him my son after what he did, but I'm begging you on our friendship, please don't send him to jail."

A cold smile slipped over my face. "Do you honestly think I have any power over that? He has to answer for what he did."

His head hung. "I know. I just...shit, it kills me that it ended this way."

"It kills me that the man who came to my rescue is now in jail because of Greg's statement." I cocked my head. "Would you say that's fair?"

He gulped. "No. That's not fair."

"If David had been the one to knock a little sense into Greg in order to save me, do you think he'd be rotting in prison right now with no bail?"

He sighed heavily, air expelling from his body, knowing that whatever pleading he'd come to do had backfired. "No. He'd be justified."

"Exactly."

My hands curled as my temper worked through me thick and fast. "Greg has to pay for locking up an innocent man—not to mention answer for what he did to me."

Steve flinched. "As you have every right to do."

"You keep saying I have a right to do these things, yet your voice says otherwise."

He looked away, unable to keep eye contact. "It's hard for me, Elle. I love you both. I hate everything about this. I hate Greg for what he did, but I still have the inherent need to protect him."

"Just like I have the need to protect Penn."

"I know."

"I'm going to talk to your son, Steve." I leaned forward, my wrists aching from hovering my weight over my desk. "But like you just said, I'm better than he is. He's a greedy little bastard who thought he could take from me. I won't stoop to his level. I want Penn's freedom, and Greg will give me what I want. He owes me, Steve. I'll get what I want, one way or another, so if you can't handle that, I can arrange human resources to give you a comfortable retirement package and sever our relationship right now."

He held up his hands. "No, I can keep this separate from work." He lowered his voice. "I love your father almost as much as I love Greg. If Greg gets taken away from me, I need to have someone to support. Your father's heart—I'll watch over him."

I twitched a little at his audacity saying I couldn't look after my own father, but I knew the bond the two older men shared. He wasn't answerable to his son's actions. I had to remember that just because blood made family, family didn't necessarily share the blame.

Penn didn't share Larry or Stewie's blood, but they were family, and they would stand by one another regardless.

*Just like I will.*

Tomorrow, I would give Greg a little visit.

And just like I'd told Steve, I would get my way—one way or another.

# Chapter Twenty

# Penn

"YOU HAVE A visitor."

I looked up from where I was reading. The Department of Correction's library had come a long way since the previous visits I'd enjoyed, but it still needed some TLC. The torn linoleum was ugly, and a lot of the books had missing pages from bastards not handling them with care. But at least, the government required certain books to be accessible to inmates.

For the past six months on my third stint here, I'd read most of the heavy volumes on law, company structure, and other mind-numbing jargon. Most of the time, they put me to sleep, making me wonder why I fucking bothered.

It wasn't as if I'd ever get out and have the money to either trade the same companies I'd researched or somehow build a community out of nothing for the homeless kids I'd met along the way.

But I never stopped reading because of that one chance in a million that somehow I'd win the lottery of life, and all of this would change.

It sucked 'cause a few months before I got locked up, I'd been introduced by accident to Gio's younger brother, Stewie. We'd met one night behind a pizzeria that donated their end-of-night waste to alley kids.

Gio and I didn't get along—mainly thanks to his friendship with the fuckwit Sean who used me as his 'get out of jail free' card, but Stewie was too young to get caught up in their world.

I had no idea how Sean and Gio became such idiotic friends. The son of a police captain and the orphaned, homeless kid. Just like most of us street rats, the young ones had no family to turn to.

Gio had successfully hidden Stewie and provided for him through crime. Sean was looking for kicks, and encouraged it.

I didn't approve, but I did approve of the love between the brothers and almost wished I had a sibling to care for like he did.

I liked Stewie. I enjoyed his juvenile naivety that life would get better.

But then I cursed myself for wishing such a shitty existence on anyone—even if it would mean I wasn't so damn lonely.

"Did you hear me?" The officer kicked the leg of my rickety chair. "Visitor."

I closed the book on truth and justice and what the court of law was *supposed* to do and not how it'd failed me, and looked up. "I don't have any visitors."

Any I wanted to see, anyway.

Sean I definitely didn't want to see. And Arnold Twig? Hell, fucking no. They were as bad as each other.

"Too bad. You have one, and they're not leaving."

I contemplated making a fuss, hitting this douche-bag over the head with the book to be reprimanded and not allowed visitors for a month. But I had eight years this time. I had nowhere else to be out there, but I was slowly fucking dying in here. I needed fresh air. I needed grass. I needed baseball fields and chocolate kisses with some girl who made my insides change owners and leap to belong to her.

Fuck...that girl.

She'd been a saving grace for me the past six months. I couldn't remember the last time I'd had something good to think about...but that kiss? Man, it warmed me on the nights I was coldest. The feel of her breast in my hand...wow, it gave me good dreams while I lived this fucking nightmare.

The officer rapped the table with his fist then walked away, pulling the proverbial leash that his uniform dictated over my prison overalls.

Reluctantly, I pushed the book away and followed.

Sean would be sorry if he ever showed up here again. Rules or not. I'd punch his motherfucking face in and screw it if it cost me an extra few years.

*Punch Sean, and you'll earn life.*

Punch Sean and Arnold would have exactly what he'd wanted

since the beginning.

A reason to crucify me.

No, as satisfying as it would be to waste my life on one measly face smash, I had bigger plans.

Someone had to pay.

Somehow, the law had to work.

Otherwise, what sort of fucked-up society did we live in?

\* \* \* \* \*

"Hello, Penn."

I scowled, shaking the hand of some old geezer with a canvas jacket slung over a shirt with a cravat and linen pants.

I'd never met him before in my life. "Who the hell are you?"

He grinned as we squeezed palms then separated. Motioning toward the metal table and chairs in a private room (not the welcome hall where normal inmates saw their loved ones), he sat first, waiting for me to join him.

"My name is Larry Barns. I'm your new attorney."

*What the fuck?*

"I hate to tell ya, but you're about six months too late." I waved around the space. "Look around."

Larry smirked as if he had a secret, pointing once again to the chair. "Please. Sit."

I paused for a second, weighing pros and cons, deliberating about being a dick or decent.

*Ah, whatever…I have nowhere else to be.*

The book would still be there. I was the only one who read them apart from Henry who got released last week.

The guy linked his fingers over a file with my name scribbled on the top.

Penn Michael Everett.

The only thing linking me to my dead father, Michael Everett. My mom died having me, and for twelve awesome years, Dad did his best to care for me, work, pretend to be normal, and hide the depression eating holes inside him.

In the end, the depression didn't kill him. It was the testicular cancer that he hadn't checked and never said a word about until I found him dead in bed one day.

Child Protective Services stepped in, and the same sob story that happened to most orphans began. I got shuttled around— different schools, different families—until one day, I never went back.

I vanished into the streets of New York and became an adult

rather than a burden on people who didn't want me.

"I've been doing a case study on inmates here. Studying how long between arrest to jury hearings and paroles." Mr. Barns opened my file. "I noticed you haven't been granted the same courtesies as other inmates. Do you want to talk about that?"

I crossed my arms. "Nope."

The beating I'd received still acted as super glue on Arnie's secrets. I hated that asshole with my entire being. But I hated his son even more—the son I conveniently looked like, who shared my height and build, so I was the perfect fall boy for his crimes.

Captain Daddy Dearest couldn't have a criminal for a son, now could he? So he'd used his power to shift that blame onto me and keep good ole' Sean squeaky clean.

"You know, I'm not like a normal lawyer." Larry slid me an icy can of Coke that he must've grabbed from a vending machine outside.

Part of me didn't want to take it as I didn't want to owe him a dime, but then again, it had been so long since I'd tasted pure sugar.

Snatching it, I cracked open the drink and swigged.

Tart bubbles hit my tongue.

*Christ, that tastes good.*

Wiping my mouth with the back of my hand, I muttered, "Don't care if you're not a normal lawyer or not. Not gonna change the facts."

His eyes narrowed. "Yeah, about that. It's the facts that interest me." He lowered his voice. "There are discrepancies in your file that I want to know more about."

My heart pounded as I glanced at the camera in the ceiling corner. Was this a trap? A test? Was Arnold watching me, waiting for me to slip up?

Wouldn't fucking happen.

I bared my teeth. "Don't know what you're talking about."

"I think you do."

I stood. "Back off. Leave me alone."

He reclined in his chair, holding up his hands. "I'm not trying to make this harder for you."

"Well, you are, so beat it."

Larry slowly closed the file and matched me standing. His eyes were soft, kind, but sharp with intelligence. "You know, I represent another man who refuses to say anything, too." His head tilted. "You wouldn't happen to know a boy named Stewart Steel, would you?"

My knees locked. Violence filtered through me to protect Gio's little brother.

What the fuck happened to Gio?

*Why is this guy representing Stewie?*

He was just a kid. He couldn't be charged with shit like this.

"Why?" I forced between gritted teeth. "What's that got to do with me? Or you, for that matter?"

He smiled, knowing he'd hooked me.

*Bastard.*

"I'm representing his older brother. Turns out, Gio Steel was picked up for arson while trying to cover up a robbery. Stewart helped start the fire. It's a shame really because that kid is impressionable, and I don't want him to end up where you are."

*You and me both.*

"Tell you what." He clapped his hands. "I'll tell you everything I know in return for you telling me everything *you* know. Off the record, of course. Complete confidentiality. Tell me why Gio told me to talk to you. Why he seems to think there's some conspiracy going on and why he's begging me to take care of Stewie until you're released, so you can take care of him yourself. Help me help you, Mr. Everett, and we'll see where this road takes us."

"Why should I trust you?"

His eyes turned sad, serious, utterly honest. "Who else do you have?"

He had a point.

I hated it, but I made a choice.

I sold my soul for the truth.

I nodded at the stranger and accepted whatever mayhem he'd bring into my life.

Either the truth would kill me or the lies would suffocate me.

I'd die and there wouldn't be any fucking difference.

# Chapter Twenty-One

# Elle

"MS. CHARLSTON IS here to see Greg Hobson." David eyed the police officer standing guard outside the hospital room we'd been advised to visit.

The entire drive here, I'd suffered David's disapproval. His posture said how stupid he thought I was being. My inner voice told me how stupid I was being. But all I could think about was wringing Greg's puny neck.

Parking and walking inside with me, David kept his mouth shut. Heading up in the elevator to the fourth floor, his opinions wafted full of frustration that he couldn't knock sense into me.

I'd watch what I said to Greg.

I'd be careful not to be overheard.

But if I didn't do this—after three years of not doing anything last time—I would literally have to smash every mirror in my apartment because I could never look at myself again.

As we stood in the linoleum-lifeless hallway, David pursed his lips, glancing at me quickly. That was the difference between a friend and employee. David was my friend, but he was ultimately my staff, and what I wanted...I got.

*Just like I'll get what I want from Greg.*

Because there was no other option. I couldn't fail.

I kept my hands folded in front of my black slacks and cream shirt, going for a somber uniform with my long hair curled in a knot at the base of my skull. It made me look older, stricter...cutthroat.

I wanted Greg to fear me.

I wanted him to quake knowing what he'd done and how hard I'd go after him to teach him a lesson.

The police officer stood from his plastic chair, hoisting up his utility belt. "I wasn't told—"

"You will. Expect a call any second." David smiled just as the officer's walkie-talkie crackled and a female voice alerted him to a visitor arriving at any moment and to clear access.

"That would be me." I nodded at the guard, moving to peer through the glass window of the door.

The officer stepped aside and then there he was.

The man I no longer understood or knew. The man who held the life of another in his rotten little paws.

"Five minutes," the officer said, dragging a hand through his short blond hair.

"Five minutes is all I need." Turning the doorknob, I looked back at David.

He ground his teeth, his head slightly cocked. "I'd ask if you wanted me to join you. But I think I already know the answer."

"You do." I patted his arm. "I want to be alone with him."

He scowled but accepted it. "Scream if you need me."

I laughed under my breath. "Got it."

Inhaling deep, I pushed the door and traded the sharp smell of disinfectant and giggles of nurses for the more subtle smell of a man I'd grown up with hidden beneath medicine and bleach.

Sudden gratefulness filled me. The last time I was in the hospital was to stay vigil at my father's bedside while he recovered from his heart attack. We'd walked out together, and I wouldn't be here today visiting Greg if it wasn't for him.

I'd called the police station and asked for a meeting but had been laughed off the phone.

I'd asked Larry to arrange it—believing he'd have contacts that would make it easy—but he had no jurisdiction over a felon who wasn't his client.

That left me near tears and furious when Dad walked in to bid me goodnight. I'd spilled my frustrations, and he'd mentioned he'd ask one of his friends to see if he could help.

Up until this morning, I had no hope that anything would come of it.

But the minute I walked wearily into my office, Dad had announced I had a meeting arranged thanks to Patrick Blake.

I hadn't managed to spend much time with Dad since my reassurance and the many hugs after my abduction, but I squeezed him so damn hard when he gave me the news.

Apparently, Patrick Blake—fishing buddy and fellow golf

enthusiast—was actually a judge.

Belle Elle hadn't been free of its own lawsuits and court appearances over the last few decades and thankfully, Dad had befriended a few people along the way.

He fished with a high judge. He played golf with a district attorney. He had friends who had held his hand while grabby people tried to sue for ridiculous things like incorrect sizes offending their snowflake personalities.

He hadn't once asked for favoritism or help fighting such claims. But for me, he'd requested approval and managed to give me the five minutes I needed to try and save Penn's life.

Not that I told him it was for Penn.

*He would've said no.*

He'd approved of Penn before this nightmare, and I hoped he'd stand by him while incorrectly incarcerated for something as noble as saving me. However, what he wouldn't approve of was Penn's prior convictions or his unsavory background.

He was a good man, my father, but a snob through and through. Only the best of the best could marry his daughter and run Belle Elle. Which was hypocritical when he put so much energy into getting me together with Greg, only for him to be the worst of all.

Greg opened his eyes as I shut the door with a harsh slap, getting his attention.

"Shit...Elle?" He sat higher in bed, shuffling against the mountain of white pillows, his skin rosy with health not white with sickness. "Came to visit. You love me after all, huh?"

His smirk made me rage.

I hated that he was here being pampered while Penn was in jail going through who knew what.

My hands curled, holding back my temper. "Shut up, Greg."

His forehead furrowed. For a moment, it looked like he'd retaliate and a small frisson of fear bolted into my legs remembering how it felt to be washed unwanted by him. To be naked in front of him. Cook for him. Such normal things but it left a terrible taste in my mouth that could never be washed away by mint toothpaste.

*He's a creep. Nothing more.*

Stalking toward the bed in my high black heels, I stopped close enough to glower but far enough not to touch.

My eyes fell on his wrist on top of the starched sheets. A silver handcuff attached him to the steel frame of the bed.

That was karma. A few days ago, I was the one in cuffs. Now, he had the joy.

I smiled before I could school myself to be cold and aloof. "I see it's your turn to be imprisoned."

He bared his teeth. "It won't stick. I'll get a good lawyer. I'll—"

I held up my hand. "Stop. I don't want to hear any more of your delusions, Greg." Before he could launch into another tirade, I said, "I'm here for one thing and one thing only."

His eyebrow rose, his body relaxing into a flirt. "Oh, yeah?" His gaze traveled over me. "Come to finish what we started?"

I hid my shudder. He wasn't worth my retaliation. "Withdraw your statement about Penn."

"What?" His green eyes flashed with surprise then darkened with anger. "No way. Look what that bastard did to me." He raised an arm, showing a few bruises. "He fucking broke me."

"I see nothing but a spoiled brat milking a stay in the hospital before he goes to jail."

He froze. "I'm not going to jail, Elle."

"I say otherwise."

The metal handcuff jingled on the bed frame as he shifted again—uncertain but still trying to dominate the situation. "He broke my ribs and bruised my throat. I've had a headache since—"

"Oh, spare me, Greg." I waved a hand at his prone body. "All I see is a boy who never grew up. You're an adult. You have to take responsibility for the things you've done and the people you've hurt."

Moving closer toward the bed, I growled, "I won't ask again. Revoke your statement about Penn. Drop the charges."

"Why the fuck would I?"

"Why?" I bared my teeth. "Because you kidnapped me, tried to rape me, and attempted to steal my company. Yet here I am being civil to you, asking you politely to be the bigger man and let Penn go."

His face turned nasty. "He's not going anywhere."

My skin crawled, fighting quicksand—a losing battle. Why did I think I could come here and negotiate with Greg like he was a sane, logical thinking adult?

He wasn't. He had a screw loose or ten.

*Fine, you leave me no choice.*

Looking over my shoulder at the door, I moved closer. Close enough that he could touch me if he wanted but close enough to hurt him if I did. "Drop the charges."

"Fuck off, Elle. If I can't have you, no one can—including that asshole."

I didn't respond, focusing on my task. "Drop the charges or *else*." My voice mimicked a general giving the orders on a firing line.

"Or else?" He laughed. "Who are you trying to be? A CEO who actually has the balls to threaten?"

"I'm being myself. And I *do* have the balls to threaten." I held up my finger. "I will *ruin* you—"

The door cracked open, followed by David's command, "Ms. Charlston, step back. You have two minutes remaining, according to our friend out here."

"Close the door, David." I didn't look away from Greg. "I know what I'm doing."

He knew better than to argue with me in public. The door clicked shut, leaving me alone once again.

I'd tried to do this kindly, but Greg was an asshole and left me no choice. "Drop the charges against Penn. Tell them you mistook everything that'd happened and no longer want to follow through with your statement."

"No way. They'll prosecute me for lying." His mouth twisted, knowing he'd just slipped into truth. The sticky substance had a way of coming to light beneath the slickness of lies. "Besides, I'm hurt. *He* hurt me. Bastard will get what's coming."

I breathed hard through my nose, doing my best to stay calm despite the overwhelming need to wrap the IV cord around his neck and strangle him. "Don't care. Be honest for once in your miserable life and accept whatever punishment is coming your way. Or…"

He still didn't look afraid, merely entertained—waiting to see what I would do. "Or?"

"Or I march back to the police station, and I tell them in *graphic* detail how you raped me. How you took advantage of me against my will. How after multiple times of hurting me, you planned to kill me."

He instantly froze, filling with doubt. "You wouldn't."

"I would."

"They'd prosecute you for filing a false report."

I shrugged. "If it's the price to pay to free a man who shouldn't be in jail, then consider it done. I would do it because he's right and you're wrong and I'm sick of not standing up for the truth."

"But that's a lie! You're insane. Why would you fucking do that?"

I shook my head, unable to believe he had no concept of loyalty or love. Did he even love his father like a normal son? Or was his selfishness a commanding passenger, making him only think of himself?

Time was running out.

Taking the final step toward the bed, I hissed, "So help me, Greg. I'll turn the kidnapping and Belle Elle takeover into a rape and attempted murder. I'll hire every lawyer I can and pay them to bury you in a life sentence. I'll do whatever it takes to make sure you're never a free man again." I glared with hooded eyes. "Who knows? Maybe I'll push for the death penalty."

He gulped. "You wouldn't."

"Wouldn't I?" I raised an eyebrow. "I tried to be nice to you, Greg. If you want me to play hardball, I will."

"You weren't even with that fucker." The handcuff screeched on the bed frame as he wriggled with anxiety. "It was a fake engagement. Why the hell are you—"

"Because he's worth it. He's decent."

"He's a liar."

"Not anymore."

Greg snarled, "You're completely batshit—"

The door opened; the police officer entered the room. "Ma'am, your time is up. I have to ask you to leave."

I looked over my shoulder, smiling demurely. "It's fine. I'm finished." My smile turned into a knife when I glanced back at Greg. "Yes or no. Tell me right now. Will you do what I asked?"

He pouted, yanking his arm, making the handcuff jangle once again. He wouldn't make eye contact, glowering at the drip, the heart rate monitor—everything but me.

I waited for some resemblance of contrition. That his money-hungry brain would put self-preservation first rather than screwing over another just because Penn had things he didn't.

For a second, I thought I'd won. His shoulders fell, his pout turned into questions.

But then he looked up, locked eyes with me, and something changed. Hard-edged contempt replaced his petty, childish greed. He snickered. "Oh, Elle."

It sent sharp claws down my back, shredding me.

He murmured soft and sultry as if we were in bed together.

"Guess you'll find out in court. Won't you?"

The world slowed down.

I'd come for a conclusion. To free Penn and finally uphold my side of the debt. But instead, all I got was uncertainty. The open-ended, unresolved fear that Greg wouldn't do what I demanded. That he would willingly gamble with his life if it meant destroying Penn's. That he would force me to lie under oath and join him in his manipulative game. That it might all backfire and I'd be the one behind bars for committing a crime.

This *was* stupid.

*I hate him.*

"How dare you—" I seethed.

The police touched my elbow, making me jump. "Ma'am, time to go."

"This isn't over, Greg." Fury stole the rest of my voice as the officer guided me from the room while Greg blew me a condescending kiss.

I'd come to save Penn.

I'd failed.

I'd screwed up.

Again.

# Chapter Twenty-Two

# Penn

FOUR DAYS IN hell.

I still had the cell to myself, which at least gave me some privacy. Recreational time and meals, I kept my head down and behavior impeccable. I didn't brown nose or try to make friends, but I didn't answer back or act like a dick if someone spoke to me.

I knew the rules. I stuck to them.

Larry told me to hang in there and stay focused on getting out. He pumped me with confidence only he could—thanks to the previous miracles he'd worked on my behalf.

I didn't let the thickening anxiety drown me because he was on my side.

He said he was working on my case when I'd been given a phone pass two days ago. Visitation rights were still pending and probably wouldn't be granted for a while. Remand prisoners sometimes got better rights than our convicted cousins, but most of the time, we got worse.

They liked to claim visits and phone calls were detrimental to remand prisoners because evidence hadn't been provided to the court yet and no verdict had been granted. Documents and information pertinent to particular crimes had a way of going missing, but at the same time, fact building and truth collaborating stalled because communication was denied.

An unwinnable situation.

But hopefully, my lawyer and benefactor of not just money but friendship and happiness would find a way.

*Like he always does.*

Besides, phone calls were better. At least, I didn't have to sit across from Larry and see the fucking disappointment in his eyes.

It would kill him to see me back here, and I'd already spent last year fearing he'd die. I didn't want to be the cause of his stress all over again.

Not to mention, I couldn't think about Elle in a place like this. I couldn't call her because it ripped my heart out knowing I couldn't touch her, kiss her, look her in the eye and tell her everything she wanted to know.

She knew who I was. She didn't know my past. Would she still apologize to me after I'd told her everything? Would she still trust me…or at least *learn* to trust me?

We were forced apart, and we would remain apart until I was a free man again.

*And if that never happens?*

I coughed with pain.

*Well, I guess it's over then.*

I wouldn't let her waste her life waiting for me while I festered in this hellhole.

Shuffling forward in the line for lunch, I handed over my tray as the men on kitchen duty slopped a runny taco with the barest amount of cheese. I pursed my lips in disgust then moved on to collect a bottle of water and a rosy apple.

Taking my food to the table squashed against the wall, I climbed over the bench and sat heavily. The prior times I'd been here, I didn't remember being so fucking down. Sure, I wasn't happy, but at least I still had a laugh with one or two of the guys I had become friends with.

I still had the motivation to go to the library or work hard on assigned tasks throughout the week.

This time? Fuck, I felt so *tired*. My body hadn't gotten over the beating. My joints were still hot and swollen, reluctant and stiff to move. I hadn't slept well with the occasional nap while glaring at the ceiling, and I had no desire to make friends, even while I knew it was safer to be liked than ostracized.

I just didn't fucking care about anything anymore.

Maybe it was because I'd tasted what true happiness should be? I'd been wealthy, working toward a good cause, and falling in fucking love with a girl I'd wanted for three very long years.

To have that stripped away…it hurt. A lot more than being told I had a bed and regular food after months of roughing it in a New York winter.

"Hey." A guy with black dreadlocks and a spider tattooed on his cheek sat opposite me. His long legs looked like a praying mantis as he clambered over the bench. "Name's Scoot."

I took a bite of my apple, extending my hand like civilized society demanded. "Penn."

We shook then released. Scoot dived into his taco while I worked my fruit.

"You in for long?" he asked.

I shrugged. "Could be."

"Me, I'm here for seventeen. Served three. Not even half-way there yet."

I nodded in commiseration, placing the apple core to the side.

As much as I should chat and get to know this new crew, I found my mind slipping backward to a few years ago.

To the day when Larry came for me and I was able to leave as a free man.

\* \* \* \* \*

## TWO YEARS, THREE MONTHS AGO

"We're leaving."

I did my best to control my heartbeat as it fucking leaped. However, I couldn't stop my mouth from hanging wide in utter fucking surprise. "Are you serious?"

For three months, Larry had been a regular visitor. Between representing Gio and me, I guessed he spent most of his life behind bars. The only difference was he got to go home at night, and we stayed inside.

I shook my head, not daring to believe. "How?"

"Lack of evidence and too much circumstantial hearsay. You're free to go." He grinned, waving with his briefcase to the door.

The door.

That was open.

The room where we always met had become a safe haven for me. I didn't know where in the prison it was located or how many steps I'd need to take before I traded locks for freedom but just the words *free to go* made my blood pump faster, feeding limbs speed and power, ready to bolt and never fucking stop.

"But—I have so much time left."

"Time that was never yours to serve." He leaned forward, whispering, "I wasn't able to point fingers at Sean Twig this time, but I'll continue to work on the case. I've had a few interesting leads pop up, so I'll follow those and see where they go."

I couldn't…

*How the fuck did he do this?*

Why had he helped me?

What made me so damn special?

Larry had achieved the impossible. Not only had he freed me but he'd also kept me away from Arnold Twig's hatred by not targeting his son. To this day, I had no idea why Twig hated me so much. Was it because I tried inherently to be good despite doing bad things? Because his son was a fucking idiot, who committed crimes because he was bored? Or had I mistakenly pissed him off at the beginning, and he'd had a grudge ever since?

Either way, it didn't matter anymore.

*Free.*

*I'm…free.*

I almost fucking came with how sexy that word sounded.

"What will you do with the information once you've got it?" I tried to keep my voice disinterested when really I panted for knowledge. Would he go after Sean? Would he give me an even greater enemy in Arnold?

He cleared his throat. "I guess that's up to you."

Most of me wanted them to pay. To do the time I'd been forced to and steal parts of their lives in return. But a part of me was still terrified of Arnold. He had the power to lock me up all over again.

I should run and disappear.

Leave New York.

So he could never touch me.

Larry followed my thoughts. "As far as I'm concerned, this is over unless you want vindication. You're free to do whatever you want." He grinned. "If in the future you want justice, and decide to go after Sean and his father, you'll have to promise me one thing."

After everything he'd done for me in the past few months? Everything he'd listened to? The judgment he didn't give? The kindness he delivered? The updates he gave on Gio in Fishkill? The visits he gave Stewie in Child Protective Services? The decision to apply for temporary custody of a kid who wasn't his just because he clicked with him and wanted to provide a better future than the one he had?

Fuck, I'd give him anything he asked for. "I promise."

"You don't even know what it is yet."

"Don't need to. You've done me a solid, Larry. Name it."

He smiled, and it was full of friendship and respect rather than demeaning and cruel. "Promise me you won't end up here again." His face shadowed. "If we do go after Sean and you end up back in here…God knows what Arnold Twig will do or how far he'll bury you."

Goosebumps spread under my prison uniform. That wasn't a hard promise to keep. I'd keep it for me, not just him. "I have no intention of ever ending up here again."

"Good. Keep it that way." Larry placed the paperwork I just signed, accepting my release and terms of my parole, back into his briefcase. "Let's go then. I think a burger and fries are the first points of business, don't you?"

My mouth watered to have junk food while surrounded by air and no bars in sight. "You're on."

Marching toward the door, I paused on the threshold, expecting a hand to clamp on my shoulder or an order to return to my cell.

Fear crashed over my thoughts of burgers, believing for a split second that this was a dream and I'd wake up in my cot with years left to serve.

But nothing happened.

No commands. No punishment. No opening my eyes and seeing the same gray cell.

"What are you waiting for?" Larry pushed past me into the hallway. "Come along, I'll have to leave you now while you're processed, but I'll meet you out front." He patted my back. "You okay, kid?"

I swallowed the nerves, excitement, terror, joy. "Yeah, I'm good."

\* \* \* \* \*

*This is all so surreal.*

Eating in a fancy-ass dining room; listening to the conversation between Larry, my lawyer turned guardian angel, and Stewie, Gio's baby brother—I couldn't get a grip on reality.

I liked Larry. I loved him for what he'd done for me. But we were still lawyer and client, not friends—we were on our way, but people like me didn't let their guard down easy.

For years, I'd lived alone on the streets. Scrapping for safe sleep spots, fighting over good quality dumpster food, arguing over the best corners to beg at.

Making friends in that situation wasn't easy, so I avoided everyone. If someone smiled, I took that as a threat. If someone followed me, I took that as war.

For Larry to open his house to me—a fucking thief—and make me welcome. Well, that made me feel like a real shitty person that I didn't have his class and trust.

It also made me ache inside with a heart that'd long since stopped looking for affection when he and Stewie grinned at each other.

Their relationship was totally different from ours.

Theirs was pure and uncomplicated.

Man and boy. Tutor and student. Father and son.

They laughed with each other. Joked. Stewie giggled with intelligence that I'd never seen him show on the streets, and Larry poked fun at him, throwing corn kernels, not caring if he got food on his expensive dining room rug.

I didn't say much that first night.

I couldn't.

I just soaked it in, waiting for life to interrupt this wonder and say *'you asshole, get back on the streets where you belong.'*

Instead, Larry offered me a place to stay until I got on my feet. He told me I could earn my keep by helping him with other cases. That I could go with him when I was ready to visit Gio and maybe let bygones be bygones and become friends, thanks to Stewie.

To him, the offers were so simple. But to me, they were the motherfucking world.

Before retiring to the guest room where a queen-sized bed and navy striped linen invited me so much better than scratchy single bunks, Larry called me into the drawing room where he and Stewie were playing a game of Chutes and Ladders.

I doubted Stewie had ever played games, let alone board games with no other purpose than social fun. His fun had been lighting fires with Gio to destroy evidence. Probably a pickpocket or two.

"Penn, before you crash, Stewie has something to give you." Larry looked pointedly at the kid with slightly protruding ears who stared at the game board as if he could magically make the dice roll so he could avoid all the chutes and climb all the ladders.

When he didn't look up, Larry prompted. "Stewie, remember what you wanted to give Penn? You spoke about it this afternoon when I said he was coming to stay with us for a while?"

Stewie's head suddenly sprang up. "Oh, yeah!" Pushing up from the coffee table where he sat on his knees on the thick carpet, he bounced over to me, pulling something small from his pocket. "Here." Handing it to me, I flinched as the cold slither of a necklace fell into my palm.

A sapphire star.

It might've been nine months since I'd seen her, but I remembered everything she said. How Gio and Sean had run off with her necklace. How her father had given it to her as a nineteenth birthday gift and how she'd forgotten to ask for it back. She'd also said it wouldn't have been hers anymore but mine for saving her.

I'd told her no fucking way would I accept her charity. And yet, somehow, the necklace had ended up in my possession anyway.

*It's not mine.*

*I'm not keeping it.*

*It has to go back.*

"How?" I cleared my throat. "Why do you have this?"

Stewie dug his foot into the carpet. "Gio gave it to me when he got snatched."

Larry came over, holding a glass of amber liquor, looking content and completely relaxed even though he had two thieves living under his roof. "He asked Stewie to keep it for him, so he didn't get charged for the robbery and attempted rape *you* were currently serving time for." He lowered his voice. "That would've been highly inconvenient to Arnold Twig if evidence came to light, and the girl in question testified that it wasn't you who'd accosted her in that alley."

My heart pounded. This one piece of evidence could clear my record of that misunderstanding. All I'd need would be for Elle to collaborate my story. I could have vindication.

But then I'd also have two vicious enemies.

Sean was still out there...who the fuck knew what he would do if he learned I was free and ready to start fighting rather than remain the easy scapegoat.

"You didn't return it to her?" I looked up, fingering the sapphire as if the jewelry could magically transport her to me.

"No."

Stewie reached for it. "It's mine. I gotta look after it. Keep it safe."

*It's not yours.*

I held it up, just out of reach. "Do you mind if I borrow it for the night?"

Larry met my eyes over Stewie's short height. He tilted his head, trying to understand why I wanted to keep something so unusual and unimportant to me.

But he was wrong. It was important. So fucking important.

I wouldn't say it out loud. I wouldn't admit that the plan to head to bed and sleep safely for the first time in forever had been put on hold for a few more hours.

But somehow, he knew.

He smiled, full of secrets as if he'd stolen mine and made them his own.

I'd told him a little about Elle. It'd been a mistake. I'd been down one day and didn't want to talk court cases and potential freedom, so he'd brought up girlfriends. I'd snorted and said, of course, I didn't have one, but then slipped as I mentioned the girl who'd kissed me in Central Park.

The entire story had come out.

Including the saga about the missing sapphire necklace.

"Uh, I dunno." Stewie chewed on his lip. "I'm not supposed to let it go."

I ducked to his height. "I know. And I won't do anything bad with it. I promise."

The lie burned my tongue, but I loved how easily it came. How swiftly I was able to bullshit. Was that my first real lie? The practice run for the torrent about to come?

Larry moved forward, placing his hand on Stewie's shoulder. "Let Penn borrow it. He's heading out, but he'll be back soon. Won't you, Penn?" His eyes were serious, intent on hearing my assurance.

*How does he know?*

"Upper East Side. Number twenty-two on Cherry Avenue."

I didn't need to ask who the address was for. Just like he didn't need to ask what I was about to do.

Not looking at Stewie—unable to see the unwillingness to part with the necklace—I nodded once at Larry. "I'm coming back. I promise."

"You'd better." He tipped his glass in a salute. "I'm counting on you to keep that promise."

"You can trust me, Larry."

With Elle's necklace clenched in my fist, I jogged to the front door and disappeared into the night.

* * * * *

*Fuck, she's even more beautiful than before.*

My heart hit a stop button and hung love-struck in my chest. Noelle Charlston.

The girl from the alley.

The name seared into my mind thanks to her identification card with the logo of Belle Elle—the largest retail chain in the US.

She thought I hadn't noticed. That I didn't believe her when she said she was an office worker at the one place I could never enter without a security guard throwing me out. My wardrobe told them all they needed to know and the fact that the last time I snuck inside I'd taken a nap in the houseware department didn't help my case.

I found it sexy that Elle worked there. I had fantasies of her working hard, renting a tiny studio, making something of her life while I looked up from squalor below.

I respected her for her tenacity to better herself. I was attracted to her for her lack of confidence or willingness to talk about her life when minimum wage made her so much richer than I was.

I'd become infatuated with her from the start. It turned to an obsessive need to know her the longer we walked back to her home. And when she mentioned it was her birthday, and she wasn't even out of her teens yet, I had the disgusting desire to be the first to welcome her to adulthood.

I'd taken her to the park to see how far her limits would go. A sheltered little girl out for a thrill. But then she'd agreed to follow me.

To break into the park with me.

To *trust* me.

Then she fucking kissed me. And I no longer wanted to test her but steal her to be mine forever. I'd lived in pure happiness for an hour out of so many years of loneliness.

That was before the night ended, and I never saw her again. Until now.

She sat in an overstuffed armchair with a gray cat on her lap, stroking it with languid pets while her shoulders remained tense. Her long blonde hair that I remembered filled with leaves and grass clippings from rolling around on the baseball field, draped over the back of the chair while her eyes locked on the three males in front of her.

Two older, one around her age.

Their lips moved, faces speaking with animation that I couldn't hear.

The closed windows were air tight; the occasional whir of traffic and murmur of dog walkers meant I couldn't distinguish any other noise but the city buzz.

The sapphire burned my hand, demanding I knock on the door and give it back. To say *'hi, do you remember me?'* To kiss her if she'd forgotten and remind her if she hadn't.

I wanted to give her the benefit of the doubt about why she hadn't come looking for me. Why I'd thought about her for nine long months, but she'd moved on and dismissed me.

But the longer I stood in the manicured bushes hiding me from the street and spied on her life, the more I understood why.

I thought we'd had a connection that night.

I thought she'd fallen down the same slippery slope that defied logic or reason as I had.

Turned out, it might've just been one-sided. Because there she was, smiling at the boy opposite with his sandy blond hair and a smirk that said he wanted to fuck her and she'd probably let him.

She wasn't surviving in a crappy apartment with annoying roommates and eating budget groceries to make ends meet. She wasn't dressed in cheap clothes and costume jewelry so common to girls her age.

Nope.

There she sat, leading a pampered life in a spoiled little world.

She was the daughter of a rich man.

She had a pampered kitten in a spoiled big house.

She was probably allergic to work and had servants for everything.

To prove my case, a woman in an apron trundled into the living room with a tray of baked goods and a teapot. Elle smiled at her but didn't get up to help pass out the sweets. She waited like the men until the woman had placed cupcakes onto glass dishes, accepting the food cordially but with the airs and graces of someone used to having things given to her.

This wasn't a recent climb up the monetary ladder. She wasn't poor and now suddenly rich.

She'd been born into wealth, and it *dripped* off her.

Why didn't I see it that night? Taste it? Smell it?

Fuck, I was so stupid.

For so long, I thought she was an employee. That she knew the value of hard work in a different capacity to me but still understood the cost of survival in a big city.

I gave her excuses about why she couldn't find or visit me in prison even if she didn't issue a statement saying I was innocent.

To her, I would've been an adventure, nothing more.

To me, she was untouchable, something I could never have.

Standing outside her castle, wrapped in the shadows I'd befriended, I gave up on my stupid fantasies. She was nothing more than an overindulged brat who ran away from her doting father to be something she wasn't for a night.

She wasn't who I thought she was.

She'd let me believe in a fairy-tale.

I had no time for brats.

The visions of returning her necklace faded.

She didn't need it.

She probably had thousands of replacements.

I wouldn't be lying to Stewie tonight.

He could have it back.

He was the rightful owner now, not her.

With a stupid heart that'd finally learned its lesson, I turned and walked away.

# Chapter Twenty-Three

# Elle

TWO WEEKS PASSED.

An insanely long two weeks where I went to work but didn't manage to do even the simplest of tasks.

I constantly hounded Larry for updates on visiting hours for Penn and promised him unlimited funds to gather whatever information he needed to submit for Penn's case.

Dad kept popping in to check on me, but for his benefit, I kept my stress hidden.

He didn't need to know I hadn't slept properly since the night Greg took me. He didn't need to understand I couldn't carry a normal thought without almost bursting into tears thinking about Penn locked up while I carried on my life as if nothing had happened.

I couldn't shift the guilt.

The awful compounding guilt that history had repeated itself, and instead of banging down police doors and ramming a bulldozer into the prison for a jailbreak, I was twiddling my thumbs bound by bureaucracy and tied up with paper pushing.

Even Fleur hadn't been able to get me out of my depressive funk.

Thanks to her heart of gold, she picked up my slack and kept Belle Elle running. She told me what to sign and when. She helped prepare my notes for business meetings and ensured my wardrobe screamed CEO when really all I wanted to do was cry in the corner with Sage.

*Enough with the pity.*

*You told Greg what would happen if he goes after Penn.*

Hopefully, in another few weeks when he went to trial or

Penn went to trial or whatever was supposed to happen next, Penn would walk free, and Greg would pay for what he'd done.

The last I'd heard, he'd been transferred from the hospital to some penitentiary system and processed. No mention of bail or whiff of him being released.

Would Penn and Greg see each other inside, or would they be kept apart, knowing the history and the reason for Penn's incarceration?

I had so many questions about the law and judicial system.

I hated being uneducated on topics I'd never had to know before.

Clicking open a new web browser, I typed in: *how to free someone framed for a crime they didn't commit.*

As the results loaded, my phone vibrated across my desk with an incoming call.

Sage tried to swat it before I scooped it up and looked at caller I.D.

Larry.

I couldn't answer it fast enough. "Yes? Larry. Any news?"

Poor guy called me every day and got the same panicked questions.

"I'm downstairs. They've allowed visitation. I'm heading over there if you want to come."

I stood up so fast my chair fell backward. "I'm on my way."

\* \* \* \* \*

Willingly walking into such a clinical, terrifying place tied my stomach into unfixable knots.

My heart lodged in my throat as Larry guided me through the process of signing in, being searched, and given a visitor badge. The forms we had to sign, the rules we had to abide by—it all made me believe I was the guilty party and I'd never be allowed to walk out of there again.

How did Larry do it so often with his clients?

How did loved ones visit their incarcerated family and not have panic attacks while trudging the hallways to see them?

David had followed in the Range Rover, even though I'd traveled with Larry in his Town Car. I'd refused to let David come in with us, and the last I'd seen of him, before entering this awful building, was his pissed off and frustrated expression where he sat in the parking lot.

"Why did it take so long to grant visitors?" I asked, handing over my gray cashmere jacket to go through the x-ray machine.

"Long?" Larry chuckled. "My dear, this is quick. I'll admit I leaned heavily on a few people to make this happen. But consider this super-sonic."

"It's been two weeks."

"Two weeks is nothing for a remand prisoner."

"Remand?"

Larry slowed his step, educating me on this terrifying new world. "Being held in remand is what Penn is currently facing. He hasn't been convicted or even given a trial date. He wasn't granted bail based on his prior record and could technically endure a long stint before we can show them the truth and get him freed."

I swallowed hard.

Two weeks had been awful. I didn't think I could wait much longer. It wasn't the fact I needed him with me or that I desperately needed to just *talk* to him to smooth out our crinkled edges—I just hated to think of him in here, locked up like a beast. "How long?"

Larry cleared his throat; his unwillingness to answer made his cheeks flush. "Well, I've already invoked the right for a speedy trial which technically means it should go before a judge within forty-five days. However, Penn is special. I wouldn't be surprised if paperwork goes missing or 'inevitable delays' occur."

My shoulders sunk as if he'd piled sand on top of me, burying me alive.

His voice shifted into caring. "We'll get him out, Elle, but I've had some cases that can take anywhere from one to three years for a verdict to be reached."

The floor wobbled as if it suddenly became a surfboard in high seas. *"What?"*

His hand landed on my forearm, features filling with pity. "That's why so many people take a plea bargain because it means they can skip the long wait time. But in Penn's case—he can't."

My brain throbbed. "Why?"

"Because any plea bargain would bury him—thanks to enemies in high places. His only chance now is to plead not-guilty and accept however long it takes to get that hearing and have evidence speak for itself."

I wedged a fist into my stomach, trying to hold in the acid threatening to wash away my heart. "Greg will testify against him."

Larry's face darkened, but he shrugged as if it wasn't a big deal.

He couldn't hide the fact that it was a *very* big deal.

"Well, I have a few game plans up my sleeve so that shouldn't matter too much."

I didn't want to ask but my lips formed words, and they traveled to Larry's ears. "What if they don't work? What if they—"

He shook his head, squeezing my arm kindly. "One thing this business has taught me is not to play the 'what-if' game. If there are any monsters in this word, Elle, it's those two inconsequential words. 'What-if'...well, if you invite that question into your life, you'll go insane, and nothing else will matter but the ever revolving answers and terrors that 'what-if' can provide."

I shivered. It wasn't the first time Larry had been so wise nor would it be the last I was sure.

"In here." The officer acting as our escort guided us down stark gray hallways where harsh lighting offered no comfort. My heels clacked as we passed through another locked door with bars on the glass window. "You have thirty minutes. No touching. No tampering with prison property. No giving the prisoner gifts or contraband. Break the rules, and you'll be asked to leave with a three week non-admittance. Got it?"

Larry rolled his eyes. "Frank, you know me. I'm here all the time. When have I ever broken the rules?"

Frank coughed, rubbing his prison guard uniform importantly. "It only takes one, Mr. Barns." He narrowed his eyes at me pointedly.

Larry rubbed his mouth. "You know, I had asked for a private room. Important lawyer stuff to talk over. You understand."

Frank scowled. "Not today. Fully booked. Take what you get. Next time, maybe."

Larry tapped his temple in farewell. "Next time, it is." Taking my elbow, he added, "Come along, Elle. Let's not keep Penn waiting."

We pushed into the room, and instantly, my eyes leaped over the couples and families gathered with their heads close over metal tables. The gray day outside offered no warmth to the gray misery inside. The only window showed gunmetal clouds with the odd speckle of rain on the barred glass.

Larry muttered under his breath. "He'd better not have refused his visitation rights again." He searched the room, looking for a handsome, arrogant prisoner and finding nothing.

"He can refuse?" My heart lurched. "Why would he refuse?"

"Because he has this stupid thing called pride." He lit up. "But it seems today, he's decided to join us, after all." Pressing my elbow again, he guided me toward the back of the room where a man in dark green overalls—same as all the other men in this place—appeared by the door escorted by a guard.

The instant his eyes met mine, the prison faded.

It was only him and me.

Me and him.

Larry didn't even factor.

My arms ached to hug him. To tell him I was here even if I wasn't there the first time he'd been arrested. I muttered under my breath, "I hate that stupid rule."

Larry raised an eyebrow. "What?"

"The no touching one."

He chuckled. "Ah, yes, I didn't factor in how hard that would be for you two. For me, touching clients isn't exactly normal procedure."

Penn was in hearing distance, striding forward to join us. "I stopped being your client the moment you gave me a bed for the night."

Larry grinned, relief coming off him in waves. "That's true. And you became the son I never had when you agreed to come back to New York with me for my treatment. I know how hard that was for you."

Penn flicked a quick glance at me. Hiding yet more things. Where had he been before Larry got sick? Did he hate New York because of the imprisonment or were there other factors, too?

*Factors like me?*

"Hello, Penn." I tucked my hands behind my back, mainly to stop myself from reaching for him but also to hide the shakes at seeing him again. It was the strangest date I'd ever been on with a lawyer as our chaperone and the state prison as our restaurant of choice.

"Elle." He crossed his arms, his biceps tight and arms ropy. Did he cross them for the same reason I kept mine behind my back? So he didn't reach for me?

"Are you—are you okay?" I glanced around the room as Larry took a seat at a free table.

"Fine." Penn motioned for me to sit too, pulling up a chair to face us. "You?"

"Good." I grabbed my hair, twisting it into a rope over my shoulder like I always did when I was nervous. Penn's gaze followed my hands, black hunger flashed with desire. His eyes stopped on the fading bruise on my face, his jaw clenching. "If he wasn't already in lock-up, I'd punch him all over again for what he did to you."

I had no reply.

Should I tell him I'd paid Greg a visit? That I'd been idiotic on his behalf? That I would never stop fighting for him?

The awkwardness between us reached an epic ten. My hands itched to grasp his. My lips ached to kiss away the pain of our last meeting and start anew.

Why couldn't we touch? How would we delete this strange tension?

I couldn't stop looking at him. His tussled hair, the thicker growth on his face. He hadn't shaved, and for the first time, he looked like Nameless from three years ago. His lips were the full kissable ones framed by a dark beard. Half of his prettiness masked by stubble.

My heart growled with possession and apologies. I couldn't stop reliving the awfulness of him walking down the stairs in police custody telling me he had no way to convince me he was who he said because he'd never told me his name.

How I could be so *blind*?

Tears tickled, welling from the constant pit I tried my best not to swim in. "Penn, I'm so sorry."

He stiffened. His jaw worked as his eyes filled with emotion so deep and tangled, I'd need a century to learn everything there was to know about him.

"I know." He lowered his face, his gaze hooded and dark. "Me, too. It's me who should apologize for—"

"No." I shook my head fiercely. "You have nothing to be sorry for. It's all my fault." A lonely tear escaped. "It's my fault you were taken the first time and now history has repeated itself. It seems whenever you're around me, I get you locked up."

He chuckled, his chest rising and falling, begging me to touch it. To smooth away the remaining faded yellow and green of his bruises. To reassure myself that he was still eating and drinking and staying alive even while caged up.

How did I ever believe I could walk away from him? How did one truth delete so many lies and make everything seem inconsequential now he was back in my life?

Technically, Penn was a stranger.

Realistically, we had two lifetimes to reveal and compatibility to test.

But something intrinsic and basic linked us together, ignoring timelines and date-numbers. I'd wanted him from the first moment I met him. I wanted him now I knew the truth.

There was so much to say but how could we with so many people watching and listening?

I wanted to spill how many sleepless nights I'd had while searching for him. How my need to find him wedged a small splinter between my father and me. How I'd never looked at another man because a part of me still believed he was the one.

*You* can *say all those things.*

*The other prisoners are here with their own families.*

They wouldn't listen to us when they had such a finite amount of time to listen to the people they loved.

I opened my mouth to blurt a billion things at once. To tell him just how desperate I was to fix everything I'd done wrong.

However, Larry saved me from tripping over myself with inappropriate nonsense. "I'm in the process of finding out when your hearing will be. I'll get it fast tracked as quickly as I can."

Penn nodded, keeping his thoughts about that hidden. "Thank you."

"Anything you need? Anything you think will benefit me in overthrowing this?" Larry pulled out a legal pad, ready to take notes.

Penn snorted. "Apart from getting Arnold Twig on the stand and interrogating him with hard evidence of his tampering with my life? Nope." He leaned back in the chair. "Talk to Gio. See if he's had enough and is ready to throw Sean under the bus. He was coming around to the idea the last time I visited him. He agrees it's fucking stupid to serve time for a crime that he only did on Sean's encouragement."

*That reminds me.*

Talking about Gio poked awake all my questions, making them buzz like angry bees. "Why do you have Gio's license in your safety deposit box?" The sentence splattered against the table with an offending command.

I hadn't meant to say it with no lead in or kind words.

*Whoops.*

Penn stilled, his eyes narrowing on mine. "You went through the box?"

I jumped, lies sprang to spill.

*No, of course not.*

*I would never.*

But I was sick of lies.

Truth only from now on. "Yes." I took ownership. "Every piece."

His lips ghosted a smile. "And?"

"And?"

"You want to know why I have Gio's license."

I nodded. "Yes."

"Anything else?"

I frowned.

Penn leaned forward, toying with me in his sexy, cocky way. Even trapped in here, he still captured me with every look and word. "You must have other questions, apart from Gio."

My heart turned into a hot piece of coal, desperate for the prison to vanish and a bed to miraculously appear so I could torture Penn with kisses to tell me the truth. Or let him torture me with them while telling me anything he wanted.

I licked my lips, my body heavy and wanting. "I have so many questions. We'd be here until next year if I asked them all."

His nostrils flared, hearing the sex in my voice. "I don't care if it took ten years." He switched to an intoxicating whisper. "But not in here. It fucking kills me to see you in here." Pain cloaked him as if remembering to cover his emotions from the harsh elements of incarceration. "If I'm being honest, I didn't want to see you today."

I flinched as if he'd slapped me. "What? Why?"

Larry sighed, understanding when I didn't, allowing Penn to enlighten me.

The intensity between us hummed as his gaze dropped to my lips then back to my eyes. He throbbed with frustration but most of all embarrassment.

His voice snapped, "Because I don't want you seeing me like this..." His sudden temper couldn't hide his anger. "It isn't a good place, Elle. Having you here? It fucks me off all while making me so damn grateful that you're willing to step foot inside just for me."

He scrubbed his forehead with both hands, hiding behind his palms for a second. Inhaling hard, he murmured, "I fucking hate all of this and most of me wants to tell you to leave and never come back, while the other part wants to beg you to stay so I don't have to be so goddamn alone. It fucking hurts that in a few minutes, I have to watch you walk away and I'm not allowed to go with you."

He shook his head, a slave to his own crippling rage. "Goddammit, I feel like I'm going to explode."

Larry looked around stealthily, vibrating calm. "Just keep it together for a little longer. You know the deal. Don't do anything to warrant longer sentencing." His face turned full of encouragement rather than pity. "Don't worry about Elle. She's here because she wants to be. Don't deny her the right to see you."

My throat swelled with so many things. I barely managed to breathe with the paralyzing need to touch him. To take away his pain, his loneliness, his entrapment. I would give anything to stay with him—regardless of where we were.

To realize that I would willingly trade my rich little life for a world of threadbare sheets and plastic furniture made me understand just how far I'd fallen with no comprehension of what I'd done.

He was hurting because of me. And I couldn't do a damn thing to help.

My hands balled as I said, "I don't care where you are, what you're dressed in, or what you say. I want to be here because *you're* here. Don't make it sound like I'm not strong enough to be here for you."

Temper I kept wound tight unspooled. "This isn't about you anymore, Penn. This is about you, me, Larry. *Us.*"

His back turned ramrod straight. "Us?"

"Us."

"Even after everything I've done?"

"What about everything I *haven't* done?"

We sat staring, breathing, understanding the weight of our own admissions. He'd made me pay. I'd given him a reason to. We both suffered for it.

Penn leaned forward, placing his hands on the table. His voice was dark and raspy, filled with fervor. "I like that word."

Almost unconsciously, I mimicked his position, placing my hands so close but not close enough to his. "What word?"

He glanced subtly left and right, checking where the guards were. Then, with his eyes capturing mine, he ran his pinky over my thumb, sending an electric fire bolt down my finger up my arm and directly into my heart. "Us. It gives me something to fight for."

That one simple touch made me wet in an instant.

I trembled, eyes hooding. "Please…"

Us was a word connected to love, companionship, and family. Please was a word belonging to a request, a plea—a blatant demand for connection.

I hadn't meant to moan it.

I didn't mean to press against his fingers as if he could take away the unbearable desire in my blood with a simple touch.

But he felt too good.

Too real.

Too warm.

Too Penn.

All my remaining questions evaporated as he stroked me again, breathing, "Fuck, I want to kiss you."

Larry cleared his throat in warning as a guard looked over at us. He didn't care how passionate or reckless this conversation had become. He allowed Penn to sweep me away and believe for just as second we weren't in a prison, we weren't facing separation, we had all the time in the world to talk and build a bridge over the whitewater of our past.

Penn licked his lips as I ran my finger along his.

I completely forgot Larry sat beside me as I moaned, "I'd give anything to kiss you."

That one piece of honesty allowed the rest to flow unhindered.

We tumbled over each other as I said, "I'm so sorry for not believing in you, Penn. There's no way you could've been anyone else. I hope you can forgive me."

While he said, "You hurt me, Elle, but fuck if I don't care anymore. The past few weeks with you...I want more. I want to tell you who I am. All of it."

Tears sprang to my eyes. "You go."

"No, you."

We laughed, our hands inching tighter, brushing pinky to thumb.

"Hey!" A guard pointed at us. "No touching."

I yanked my fingers back but couldn't swallow my smile. "We're going to get you out of here. And then we'll talk."

"Then we'll do a shitload more than just talk." He smirked a little; moving from intense connection to lighthearted joking, a genuine smile breaking his lips. "Going back to my safety deposit box. I always knew you were nosy."

I laughed softly. "Only where you're concerned. And only because you never tell me anything."

"He'll tell you now, though, won't you, Penn?" Larry asked, deadly serious, reinserting himself into the conversation. "Just like you'll tell her the reason why you have Gio's license is because you're listed as his next of kin and agreed to keep his possessions safe."

Larry turned his black-rimmed glasses onto me. "Gio and Penn have become friends thanks to me taking custody of Stewie. It was complicated for a while, but we're all on the same side now."

I liked how he barely knew me, but he was on *my* side as much as he was on Penn's. I'd never met anyone so unbiased and willing to trust than him.

Penn's forehead furrowed. "I know that must sound idiotic seeing as Gio hurt you that night and I roughed him up pretty good. But we've shared the same upbringing too long to turn away when the other needs help."

I blinked away the memories of my clothes being torn in the alley. "I agree. Enemies can become friends. Sometimes, they make better friends as you know the worst."

Penn shrugged. "I suppose." His features shadowed, thinking of things that left a strain around his eyes. "A couple of years ago, I was your enemy."

My heart skipped unhappily. I had no idea what he meant. "You were?"

His desire to talk faded. He reclined in his chair, hiding everything I needed to know. "Shit, I have so much to tell you but I can't do it here." He kicked the table leg, making it rattle.

A guard pointed at him in warning. "Quit it or you're back in your cell."

Larry rolled his eyes. "Plenty of time to talk later. Don't get yourself riled up."

Penn raked both hands through his hair. "This place makes me insane." Stark panic filled his brown gaze. "How long, Larry? How fucking long do I have to keep everything bottled up so I don't screw myself over even more?"

Larry consulted his notepad, void of scribbles but filled with whatever processes he'd already put in place. "You know I can't give you a time. I don't like dangling promises because they hurt like hell when they don't come true."

"I know." Penn sighed. "Fuck." His shoulders tightened, masking the truth that he was nervous and had no one else to trust but us. Trusting someone and then *trusting* someone were different things. He had no power over what we did on his behalf. He merely had to let Larry arrange dates and file paperwork while I went after Greg and fought for his assurances that he'd retract his statement and redeem himself by doing the right thing.

It was heartbreaking as well as chilling to play God with another's life.

Penn gave me a sad smile, wordlessly apologizing for ruining the remaining time we had left.

Larry took over, murmuring about strategy and evidence.

Penn and I never took our eyes off each other. Desperately aching, constantly seeking for a way to erase this mess and be together.

The thirty minutes went far too fast, and it physically killed me when a bell rang and the inmates said farewell.

No hug.

No kiss.

Nothing but a tear-filled grimace as Penn disappeared all over again.

* * * * *

"Ms. Charlston! Over here!"

Stepping out of the correctional facility, I found a sea of reporters, cameras, and microphones angled toward me instead of a clear path leading toward the black Range Rover and my trusty bodyguard.

*What the hell?*

Larry instantly covered my face with his briefcase, wrapping his arm around me as he guided me toward David who leaped out of the Range Rover, barreling through the reporters to get to me.

Wrapping me in his protective embrace, David glowered at the churning body parts in our way. "Leave!" he boomed, protecting my other side, marching with Larry as we bulldozed through the paparazzi.

They side-stepped to avoid being run over but it didn't stop their probing questions.

"Ms. Charlston. Are you in a romantic relationship with Penn Everett?" a young man shouted.

"Are you having an affair with Greg Hobson?" a middle-aged woman with blue-rinsed curls yelled.

"Do you think it's appropriate for the owner of such a prominent retail store to be dating two men at once? Both who are in jail, no less?" a male reporter with a squeaky voice asked.

Each question I cowered a little more.

*Oh, my God, how did they hear?*

Who leaked? Who tattled?

"No comment," Larry snapped, keeping his briefcase obscuring my face. "Go away."

I kept my head down as David opened the back door to the Range Rover, giving me shelter to hop into.

Larry jumped in too, not bothering to call his Town Car.

The questions kept plowing through the windows. Questions I had no answers to. Questions I should've been prepared for thanks to my high-society position, and how juicy my tale would be the moment the smell of controversy arose.

Right now, I was considered top news.

Penn's background would be dug up. Mine would be plastered beside his. Greg's actions would be known nationwide.

*Oh God, Dad is going to flip.*

The pandemonium of journalists brought everything home.

How deadly serious all of this had become.

How far we still had to go before it would be all over.

Exhaustion pressed me into the soft leather seats as David honked the horn and took off, barely giving the reporters time to jump out of the way.

# Chapter Twenty-Four

# Penn

DINNER WAS YET another sad affair of under-cooked potatoes and over-cooked beef.

At least this time, no one tried to talk to me. I'd earned a reputation over the past couple of weeks that I was a loner with history. I had respect because some old timers remembered me from my previous stints, but I had a mystery that newbies wanted to ruffle up and put me in my place.

I'd avoid all confrontation as long as I could, but eventually, something would snap, and I'd be in the middle of a war I didn't want.

Yard time after Elle and Larry left ensured I could run off some of the stress of seeing them. I'd fucking promised myself I'd deny visitation if they came. But that was before the temptation and overwhelming desire to see Elle overrode my common sense.

I'd braced myself for pity or loathing in her gaze, looking at me in my prison uniform. I waited for hesitation about her feelings for me, or the awful condemning admittance that she couldn't handle this.

But she hadn't done either of those things.

She'd watched me as she always did—as if she wanted me to jump on top of her and fuck her in terribly dirty ways. She listened to me as if I *meant* something. She spoke as if this was personal, and she'd have my back all the way. She touched me as if she cared for me despite everything I'd done.

It didn't escape me the way Larry looked at her. He was proud of her. Shit, *I* was proud of her. It made me wade through guilt that I could ever think she was a spoiled brat. Sure, I knew how hard she worked now. I understood that Belle Elle wasn't given to her or that she coasted through life on a trust fund. She worked her fingers to the bone. And she was strong—so fucking strong.

Why did I ever doubt she would fight for me if I'd given her the chance?

I'd had everything so wrong.

Assumptions had sure made an ass out of me and look how fucked I was. If I'd just knocked on her door that night, we might've avoided this whole disaster. Greg would never have thought he stood a chance with her because I would've claimed her.

I would've ensured she was mine just like the necklace I'd given back to Stewie was hers.

I was a moron back then, but I wouldn't be a moron now.

She wanted me? She had me. Because, Christ, I wanted her.

Tonight was TV night for the guys in my block. A lot mingled, not really listening, playing cards or placing bets on events they'd never be able to pay regardless of winning or losing—unless it was with things gained from inside.

Rubbing my face, I forced my body to let go of the lust Elle had created. Unsuccessfully reminding myself that Elle and I wouldn't be fucking for a long time to come. Celibacy was the new rule in our relationship. Which made it so goddamn hard as I wanted her so bad.

I needed her even worse.

I needed her to lie to me for a change and tell me this would all go away and I'd be free again. I needed her to touch me and tell me she'd wait for me no matter how long it took, even while I pushed her away so she didn't waste her life alone.

I scoffed at the thoughts, hearing the truth behind them.

She didn't need to touch me to assure me she'd wait for me— I saw her loyalty in every blink and heard it in every vowel.

And she didn't need to lie about my freedom.

I would get it back.

Eventually.

Larry was fighting for me. He'd win.

*He has to.*

There was no other scenario I could accept.

Stretching out my legs with ankles crossed, I did my best to unwind and watch the men around me—taking note of their weakness and strategies, cataloguing who to chat with versus those to stay away from.

I had to be smart and play a long game even if I hoped I'd only endure a short inning.

The sound of a car horn wrenched my head to the TV where local news was playing.

My chair legs screeched on the linoleum as I sat up and scooted forward.

Elle filled the screen.

A blurred photo of her climbing into the Range Rover with David and Larry doing their best to obscure her. They couldn't hide the tangle of pretty blonde hair or her sexy body, though.

I'd recognize her anywhere.

The news anchor in her bright red suit droned, "Today, a name that is normally reserved for retail news has been dragged into controversy with the recent love triangle. According to sources, Noelle Charlston, who is the head of the family's empire Belle Elle retail chain, has been dealing with a few unusual matters of late. Things haven't been smooth sailing for the young CEO ever since rumors began of her engagement to Penn Everett.

"After a string of unsuccessful romantic set-ups over the past few years, Ms. Charlston has somehow wound up dating two men—both who have ended up in jail for reasons not entirely known. What we do know is Greg Hobson, the son of Steve Hobson, who has worked for the Charlston family for four decades, is being held for kidnapping and attempted rape while Penn Everett, a well-known offender who struck it big with a penny stock a year ago, is being held for aggravated assault including attempted murder.

"We tried to get more facts from Ms. Charlston as she was leaving the correctional facility, but she declined to comment."

A prisoner turned to face me, his eyes glowing with violence. "Hey, you're Everett, aren't cha?"

*Shit.*

Another guy with tattoos all over his arms and a shaved head stood up, his posture screaming *'oh, it's on, buddy.'* He cocked his head. "Seems we have a celebrity in our midst, boys."

Christ, I didn't want to fight.

I smirked condescendingly, slipping back into the armor I'd perfected from the streets. "Nothing to get excited about. Typical news junkies don't know what they're saying."

The tatted inmate chuckled. "Oh yeah? Guess, we'll just have to find out for ourselves, won't we?" He cracked his knuckles. "Be prepared to spill, Everett. We'll plan a nice chat, you and me."

Goddammit.

I'd done my best to avoid this.

But the games had begun, all thanks to the fucking news.

A prisoner, who wasn't aware of the showdown about to start, bellowed at one of the guards. "Turn the news off, man. Who fucking cares about that shit."

*No one cares.*

*Apart from me.*

Never taking my eyes off the two men squaring me up, I stood and left the room. They'd let me go—they'd have no choice.

But tomorrow, they'd ambush.

I had to be ready.

I had to attack them before they attacked me.

I had tonight to prepare.

After that...*it's war.*

# Chapter Twenty-Five

# Elle

"YOU CAN'T GET mixed up in this, Elle."

I looked up as Dad appeared in my office, his fingers wrapped around the daily newspaper. He still wore his three-piece suits as fashion statements. The one of choice today demanded obedience in sharp midnight blue. His cheeks glowed warm; his eyes bright but disapproving. He'd lost the stress of my disappearance and bounced back healthier than ever.

I no longer leapt to my feet to hold his elbow in fear of his heart playing tricks. He was robust and old-fashioned, and my hackles rose as he marched to my desk, then perched on the side as he always did, looking down at me in my chair.

I'd expected this.

Ever since I'd turned the news on last night and seen myself being shuttled like a convict to the awaiting Range Rover, I'd waited for my father to railroad me.

To be told I couldn't be seen in such unflattering situations.

That all news was bad news, and it was up to me to keep controversy as far away from Belle Elle's shop shelves as possible.

"This will slander Belle Elle's name," Dad said.

Didn't he see it would slander me for the rest of my life if I did nothing? Belle Elle was decades old. It was more than just a company—it was a lifestyle: a part of so many people's lives. Our quality merchandise was in every adult's and child's wardrobe across the States and Canada.

Belle Elle didn't need me.

*Penn does.*

Meeting his eyes with confidence I didn't necessarily feel, I said, "Hello to you, too. Please, I'm not busy or anything."

"The passive-aggressive comments won't fly with me, Elle."
He scowled, his elderly face becoming even more wrinkled than
normal. "We need to talk about this." He waved the rolled up
newspaper, no doubt filled with more tabloids and finger pointing.

"There's nothing to talk about."

*Penn is mine and I'll stand by him.*

*I don't care what you say.*

I cleared my throat with impatience as Fleur came in. She
paused on the threshold, her arms full of paperwork that I'd
neglected. "Ah, just in time." I stood, waving her over eagerly. I
would use anything I could to postpone the inevitable fight with
my father.

I didn't want to have to yell at him. I didn't want to be
disrespectful, but I knew what he was about to say, and I wouldn't
let him stop me anymore.

"You sure it's a good time?" Fleur rocked back on her heels,
making her escape—knowing as well as I did what sort of
argument was about to explode.

"No, don't be silly." I patted my desk. "Just put those here."

"Okay…" Fleur clipped forward, smiling politely at Dad, not
giving me the usual broad grin of friendship. "Hello, Mr.
Charlston." Placing the folders on my desk, she gave me a quick
arched eyebrow. That eyebrow said: *are you okay? Want me to do
anything? Should I get the tranquilizer gun?* Her voice said, "Anything
else?"

I had no doubt she would do something crazy if I asked, but
this conversation was all on me.

I shook my head. "Thank you. That's all. It's getting late; you
should head home."

"Only if you're sure?"

"I'm sure."

"Thanks for your help." Dad smiled kindly at her. "You've
been a very loyal staff member to Belle Elle and my daughter."

Fleur wasn't the blushing sort, but her cheeks pinked. "You're
welcome." Turning for the door, she glanced back before
disappearing into the hallway.

Her interruption had been too short, but to Dad, it had been
too long.

His eyes glowed with irritation. "Elle, what the hell were you
doing at the prison yesterday?"

*And so it begins.*

I held my head high. "I went to see Penn. Or did you forget

we're engaged?"

It seemed like years ago since Penn had pulled that particular lie over my father and everyone at the office, but for the first time, I found it convenient rather than a nuisance.

He scrubbed his face. "Are you sure about that? I've been having doubts about you two. It happened too fast, Elle. After what just occurred with Greg and now court dates and testimonies—I don't want you getting stressed out."

"Me?" My voice rose with a perfectly curled question mark. "*Me* get stressed? What about you? Are you taking the meds your doctor prescribed? I don't think you should even be at the office. I have things under control."

*All right, that lie was obvious and entirely hollow.*

I wasn't coping. I didn't have things under control. Mainly because I couldn't stop my mind from drifting to Penn and Nameless and Penn and prison.

Penn, Penn, Penn.

It was a vicious circle and not one I could stop.

"Don't you worry about me." He took my hand, pulling me forward to pat it dotingly. "You were kidnapped by a man who's been a part of our family for years. You won't tell me what happened in the cabin. All you'll say on the matter is that Penn saved you, but then Greg filed charges." He scowled. "There's more to that story, Elle, and I don't like you keeping things from me. Why did you go see Greg in the hospital if he hurt you?"

I sighed heavily. "I'm not keeping things from you, but I am going to keep fighting for Penn. He didn't do anything wrong."

"Ah, yes, about that." His face fell even further, resembling an unhappy hound. "You can't be seen visiting inmates, Elle. You have a reputation to maintain. Our company as a whole has to do what it can to stay on the right side of the law with no controversy."

I laughed a little. "Don't you think Greg already caused controversy? No matter how we keep that under wraps, details will get elaborated and the story will snowball on its own. The best way to deal with the media is to grant an interview asking for understanding and give them the hard truth, so false rumors don't destroy everything we've created."

Dad blanched. "You can't be serious. The right thing to do is stay away from those vultures and just let it die a natural death." He paused before saying with fatherly authority. "Just like I don't want you seeing Penn again."

I gasped. "How can you say that? You liked him. You gave him your blessing to *marry* me even when I was telling you it was fake."

"So your engagement *is* fake?" His features lit up. "Well, in that case, I believe you now. That means you don't have to do anything reckless when it comes to—"

"Dad..." I shook my head with disappointment. "You don't get it. It started off fake, but it turns out he's—"

*The man from Central Park.*

The words dangled on my tongue, clinging with little claws to stay unsaid. I swayed between delivering them and swallowing them back.

For three years, Dad did everything he could to stop me from looking for Nameless (after he'd been cooperative at the start). When my hunt for him started to interfere with my work, Dad swiftly put a stop to it.

This time, I wouldn't give him any more reason to block my helping Penn.

Dad had an obsessive desire to keep Belle Elle and me away from less than satisfactory circumstances—including people.

Only, he didn't understand that no one was perfect. He wasn't. I wasn't. The world wasn't. Penn was no different, and he deserved every chance to prove he was more than just a liar and reveal the truth.

*He's special.*

To me. To my life. To my future.

I wouldn't jeopardize that for anyone.

Including my father.

"He's what?" He cocked an eyebrow. "Finish that sentence."

"He's on his own, Dad. Sure, he has Larry fighting for him, but I want to be there, too. I'm sorry if it upsets you, but I'm not going to stop."

He slid off my desk, crossing his arms. "It's not that I don't want you to be there for him, Elle. I'm not trying to be cruel by cutting him off from emotional support. But sometimes, other things take paramount. I'm thinking of the company. It's not good PR."

"Well, we'll hire a team to reinvent our image after it's over."

"Over?"

I nodded. "Yes, Penn will be given a court date soon, and we can finally get the truth out. Then he'll be released, and it will be over."

"How long do you think that will take?"

I shrugged. "It depends on the justice system."

I sounded so much more knowledgeable than I was.

The way he gnawed his bottom lip gave me an idea. "You know...you could help speed this process along, if you wanted."

"I can? How?" He narrowed his eyes warily.

"By calling your judge friend. Put in a good word. Get a court date, sooner rather than later, so we can all move on with our lives."

"You want me to tamper with courts and trials now, Elle?" He looked at the ceiling. "What's become of you?"

"The need to fix everything I did wrong."

His look was quizzical, but he didn't ask for a structured explanation of my cryptic reply.

Instead, he kissed the top of my head. "Oh, very well. If it means this will all blow over faster, I'll see what I can do."

# Chapter Twenty-Six

# Penn

THE AMBUSH HAPPENED four days later in the recreational yard.

Three men stopped me mid-jog.

After doing my best to come up with a counter attack, I gave up. I had no weapons, no friends to back me up.

I was on my own. And unless I wanted to die in retaliation, I had to let it happen.

So I did.

No matter how much it fucked me off.

Their fists gave me an unwanted 'welcome to the neighborhood' rough up. Their feet delivered a well-heard 'this is our turf, so don't get any fucking ideas' kick. Their growls told me exactly how to toe the line and behave.

They seemed to know where a dead zone existed in the security cameras on the jogging track. They didn't hesitate to gift a beating that activated old injuries, memories, and wounds from my past.

The punch-up only lasted a few seconds, but they knew how to deliver pain.

And I knew how to listen to their message.

I let them get in a few good strikes then exploded and delivered a few myself. I'd let them put me in my place because it meant I wouldn't be harassed further. But I wouldn't be a fucking pussy because that was just the start of a worse war.

The tightrope to walk was so damn narrow, but I'd walked it before. I could walk it now.

They were the shit in here. Not me. They thought they'd disciplined me. They hadn't. Everyone went away slightly happier and settled.

Even if I limped rather than stalked and their punches activated old injuries from Greg's morning wake-up call the day he took Elle.

I gave up running for the rest of the afternoon and sat on the bleachers tending to a busted lip and bloody nose.

No one commented on my state, and I nodded curtly at the assholes who'd given me the lesson when they walked back to their cells after the bell rang.

Just like school had bullies, prison had thugs. It was all a chessboard in the end. No one was king for long. And no one stayed a rook forever. We were all jumping over each other trying to win the queen.

Trudging back to my cell, I spat out a glob of blood. I'd never been soft or naïve in my life—I couldn't after seeing death and never having a home—but the awful fact was, I *had* begun to relax a little. I'd relaxed knowing Larry had my back, and Elle was mine after so many mistakes.

I'd relished in playing games with her because it soothed some of the pain. I'd become the bully, and with my belly bruised and face forming a nice black eye, I was reminded how much it fucking sucked to be the victim.

Yet here I was, held in remand with no way out on an attempted murder charge, buried up to my balls in shit.

At least, now I was in jail, Arnold wouldn't be able to fuck up my life as bad. Unless he was in the habit of bribing the warden or commissioner of corrections, I was out of his control.

For now.

I needed to see Larry.

And Elle.

Fuck, I needed to see Elle.

* * * * *

Another two weeks.

Fourteen measly days on top of all the rest.

A fucking lifetime.

I lived in sameness every day, tormenting myself with thoughts of a happier memory, spending whatever freedom I was given between working, eating, and yard work in the library.

The books hadn't changed.

The reading material was no better.

But at least the notepad and pen gave me an outlet to scribble my thoughts and see if there was any way around my mess.

I kept those notes with me safe, posting pages to Larry on mail days so he could have some idea of what I knew and suspected between our meetings.

Today was Wednesday, which meant the only thing to look forward to were spaghetti and meatballs for dinner and our turn in the media room for the allotted ninety minutes.

*My life is fucking riveting.*

As I made my bed, preparing for a new day in this walled city, a guard appeared. He had to be just out of his teens, filled with the need to be the best and most liked officer on staff. It made me hate him immediately.

"Everett, visitor."

I dropped my pillow onto the bed. "You sure?"

The guard rolled his eyes as if I was a simpleton. "Of course, I'm sure."

I had no response to that cocky attitude. I didn't feel like getting into a fight with a newbie. I'd been told that other personal visits would be strictly monitored and most likely denied because of the upcoming trial. Turned out, Larry got around it.

Then again, what trial?

I had no correspondence on when my case would be heard. If it was anything like last time, I'd end up serving more time waiting for the trial than I did after being convicted. The fact that the time served was subtracted from my sentence wasn't a relief. It was hollow—especially if you'd served six months and the offense only deserved a three-month term.

This entire process was screwed the fuck up.

*Innocent until proven guilty my ass.*

"Fine." I dragged my fingers through my hair. "Let's go then."

Following the officer through the usual riff-raff of prisoners, I kept my eyes forward, not lingering on anyone in particular. My prison-issued sneakers squeaked on the linoleum as the guard swiped his I.D and ushered me through to the small processing room then through another security point to the visitation areas.

I swayed to the left, following the hallway I knew led to the meeting hall where I'd last seen Elle and Larry.

"Not that way." The guard rubbed his nose, his dark hair dull and needing a haircut. "This one." He pointed at the right hallway.

I probably shouldn't but I asked, "Private?"

He nodded.

My heart did a strange skip cough. Private meant Larry had

come to talk—away from prying ears. Private meant Elle wouldn't be with him because only client-attorney relationships were deemed sacred enough to have privacy.

Conjugal visits in this place were like fucking gold nuggets—rare and hard to earn. There was no way to hug your lover or even touch to reassure both of you that this fucked-up place couldn't tear you apart forever.

*Goddammit, I hate it here.*

Swallowing back my frustrated anger, I followed silently.

Passing a few meeting rooms with matching metal doors, bars on viewing windows, and large locks, we stopped outside private room number six. The officer rapped on the door with his knuckles, giving me a quick glance.

I linked my fingers together in front of me. Remaining the perfect prisoner when all I wanted to do was handcuff the fresh-out-of-the-academy idiot and teach him what it was like to have your freedom stolen.

Larry opened the door, beaming. "Ah, great. Thanks for bringing my client."

The officer nodded. "Welcome. You have thirty minutes. Press the button if you require assistance before that. For your safety, we'll record visual but not audio."

Larry nodded, ever the professional. "Great. See you in thirty." Pulling my arm, he tugged me into the room and closed the door in the guard's face.

We couldn't lock it from the inside, but the illusion of having a door between them and us...fuck, it was the best goddamn thing in weeks.

"Hey." Larry slapped me on the back. "How you holding up?"

I shrugged. "Can't complain."

I could fucking complain, but Larry was already doing so much for me. I wouldn't turn him into my agony aunt, too.

"I'm glad." Pointing behind me, he added, "By the way, I brought you a gift."

"Better be a burger and fries." I smirked, turning on the spot.

Something light and sexy and so fucking addicting leaped into my arms. "Penn."

Instantly, my embrace wrapped around her, squeezing so tight I had to remind myself not to kill the girl I wanted more than anything.

I forgot about Larry.

I forgot about cameras and guards and court dates.

My body took over.

I did the only thing I could.

Her face tipped up.

Mine tipped down.

I groaned long and low as our lips connected, and she deepened the kiss the moment we met. I switched from expecting a friendly but purely platonic meeting with my benefactor to slamming Elle against the wall and kissing her until I couldn't goddamn breathe.

My hands no longer obeyed my brain; they tracked over her, my thumbs rubbing the beads of her nipples, barely hidden beneath whatever clothes she wore.

I was so drunk on her, I couldn't look away to see if she wore a convenient skirt to hoist up and delete the remaining space between us.

Larry cleared his throat.

It didn't register or stop me in the slightest.

But it did stop Elle.

She withdrew from the kiss, pushing my chest a little to give her some space.

I blinked, coming back to earth with a smash.

Fuck, what was I thinking? Touching wasn't permitted. I didn't want to layer yet more crimes to my long tally.

*I'll never fucking get out of here.*

And that was suddenly so important now I'd had a tiny taste of what I was missing.

Holding up my hands, I backed away from Elle, looking at the ceiling where a camera had recorded every passionate indiscretion.

"Shit." My cock throbbed, heavy and noticeable in my prison scrubs.

Elle rubbed her mouth. Her lips puffy and red from my overgrown stubble. Had it really been over a month since I'd kissed her? Fucked her in my limo? It felt like decades.

She smiled. "That was quite the hello."

I smirked. "You started it. You launched at me, not the other way around." And Christ that made me happy. To know she'd moved past the issues I'd caused, the lies I'd told. That she was willing to accept me as *me,* not as Penn or that phantom she called Nameless. Me. With no more bullshit between us.

I opened my arms, encompassing the room and jail behind.

"You're here."

"I am." Her gaze skated to Larry then back to me. Her fingers pulled the hem of her black blazer; smoothing it over the hip-hugging skirt that kissed her knees.

Black suit, white shirt, and silver heels. Her hair was twisted up on top of her head—showing off the expanse of her long neck where my canines watered to bite. A pair of black framed glasses stuck out of her blazer breast pocket.

She looked like a sexy librarian...or—

"Elle is my assistant for the day," Larry explained as he pulled out a chair and sat at the single table. "It was the only way she was allowed in."

My lips tilted, remembering other times when I'd been his assistant. He'd gotten me into Fishkill countless of times to see Gio—partly to be his helper and note taker but also to nurture the slowly developing friendship between the man I'd fought with on the streets and the man now begging for scraps of news about his brother.

We put aside our petty grievances and discussed Stewie's progress and intelligence at school.

We bonded over caring for his younger sibling.

We grew up.

Leaving Elle—even though it killed me—I marched to the table and sat. My skin tingled to touch hers. My mouth watered to kiss her again. But I'd already risked Larry's generosity by slamming her into the wall the second they arrived.

I twisted to look at the camera again. "They'll have that on tape." I licked my lips, tasting blueberry lip-gloss. "I shouldn't have done that."

Larry opened a folder holding the scribbled notes I'd sent him, along with a few computer typed ones from his own homework. "It'll be on record. There's no way for someone to alter the footage—not the lowly guy I have an understanding with anyway. But rest assured, they won't use it." He pulled his pen from his pocket, chuckling. "However, don't go thinking you can get away with sex. I'm not leaving and I can't go without my lovely assistant. Besides, screwing my staff would most likely end up on some dodgy prison porn site that would go viral and screw you over even more."

Dropping my hands below the table, I did some subtle rearranging of my hard-on. "I know you have a point but being in this room with Elle. Shit, you're asking a starving man not to eat the banquet."

Elle blushed, pulling out the last seat next to Larry. Her hand snuck across the table.

I snatched it, holding it sweetly as if we were first-time boyfriend and girlfriend rather than the reality that if I didn't hold on, I'd drown in this motherfucking place.

It took a lot to keep my cool and pretend nothing bothered me here. That I could handle whatever they threw at me. That I didn't give a shit about Arnold Twig and his lying sack of shit son, Sean.

But with Elle here...it made me softer somehow. Showed me how much I bottled up and how much I wished I could just run and be free.

Elle's gaze narrowed on my lower jaw where the fading bruise of the beating two weeks ago remained. "You're hurt."

I shrugged, down playing it as Larry narrowed his gaze. He knew full well what went on in places like this. Elle had no idea. I squeezed her fingers. "I'm fine."

Her blue eyes glossed with tears. "But someone hurt you."

"I'm okay, Elle. Don't. Don't torture yourself." My voice echoed with need for her to listen to me, obey me. She'd go mad if she didn't. "It's nothing that I can't handle."

And it was true.

Ever since the beating, I hadn't been touched. Sure, I'd endured a few curse words and stolen lunches, but overall, my strategy of staying low and alone was working. Half of the inmates couldn't be assed with me and the rest were slightly afraid, wondering why I was so quiet.

"Why did they hit you?" Her gaze danced over my face, latching onto a healing scratch on my neck. "Can we do something?"

My heart raced in fear of her making things worse. "Don't do a thing. It's my fight. Not yours."

Larry backed me up. "He's fine, Elle. Leave him be."

She sniffed, anger replacing her sadness. "I hate all of this."

"Me, too." My joints splintered to drag her over the table and into my lap. To kiss her and delete the awful cluttered space between us.

Larry caught my wistful expression. I wished he hadn't.

"It's going to be okay, Penn." He patted my arm, smiling at mine and Elle's joined hands. "You're doing great."

Once upon a time, I hadn't trusted him when he'd said the exact same thing. I'd laughed in his face. This time, I merely accepted his assurance with a grateful nod.

Elle brought my hand to her lips, kissing me quick. "I positively hate seeing you in here."

Her passion and affection electrocuted my heart.

She gave me the power to keep fighting.

Returning the favor, I ran my lips over her knuckles. "Same. Prison doesn't suit you."

She shuddered, sucking in a breath similar to what she did when I first entered her.

My body hardened, my voice softened, my promise beckoned to be believed. "Don't worry, I'll be out soon. And when I am, I'm never letting you go again."

# Chapter Twenty-Seven

# Elle

THE LOCUSTS FOUND me the moment I stepped out of jail.

"Ms. Charlston, can you confirm you're engaged to Penn Everett? Do you know he's served time for three other incidents?"

Larry gathered me in a hug as we walked swiftly to David and the Range Rover. David once again barreled through the journalists, his large mass shoving people out of the way with no apology. Once in front of us, he cleaved the crowd like a giant snow plow, giving us a clear path.

He couldn't stop the photos or recording devices from being shoved in my face, but he could at least get me to the vehicle a lot faster than before.

Penn's words echoed in my head. *"I'll be out soon."*

Would he?

The more time I spent with Larry, the more I understood his mannerisms. Just like Penn favored shoving his hands in his pockets, Larry favored scratching his jaw where salt and pepper stubble appeared at the end of a long day when he was either unsure or telling a white lie.

I said white because I doubted he'd ever truly lie. But he definitely wasn't showing his own nervousness about Penn's particular case.

He'd already been locked up for four weeks, four days. The fear that he could be held so long before a resolution or verdict was reached petrified me.

It couldn't be much longer.

*I can't leave him there.*

*I have to do something.*

If Greg wouldn't retract his statement and admit he lied under oath about the attempted murder, then I'd have to find other ways to free Penn.

I slammed to a stop in the midst of our rush from the paparazzi.

Larry glanced at me. "Are you okay? Did you trip?"

David looked back, his eyes darting to my feet. "Do you need me to carry you, ma'am?"

I scoffed. "No, I do not need to be carried." Peering at the reporters, losing count after seven of their eager faces and blinking cameras, I said, "I wish to make a statement."

"Of course, Ms. Charlston. We would be honored!" A female shoved her mic close.

Another said, "We offer great packages for exclusives if you'd like to come with me to the office!"

I ignored both, pushing Larry away to stand firm and on my own. I shouldn't do this. I shouldn't feed the vultures when they circled over carrion. But if I could start the campaign on Penn's innocence, perhaps it would help us get him home faster.

David's shoulders tensed, but he didn't try to grab me or interrupt what I was about to do. Thank God because the picture of a silly little CEO being bundled up by her security guard and driven away was not the look I wanted to portray.

*Dad will kill me.*

But I was past caring.

Inhaling hard, I said, "Penn Everett is innocent."

Questions landed around me like slingshot pebbles. I tuned them out, focusing on the short statement I wanted to make on his behalf. "Penn is innocent, and we will prove that."

"What do you mean by that, Ms. Charlston?" another reported asked.

I held my head higher. "I mean that Mr. Everett has been incarcerated unjustly and when he's freed, I won't stop from persecuting those who stole weeks of his life with lies."

The irony that lies had come back to bite the liar wasn't lost on me.

Penn wasn't innocent on that account. But I'd claimed him, and I wasn't an enemy people wanted.

I had funds.

I had power.

I had a grudge.

*I'll make those people pay.*

Smiling at the flashing cameras, I hoped my stand had finally shown New York (and my father) that I wouldn't run away from this; I strode confidently to the getaway vehicle and climbed inside.

"Let's go home, David. I have work to do."

# Chapter Twenty-Eight

# Penn

ANOTHER THREE WEEKS passed like soldiers marching me closer to battle.

Two months in this shitty place.

Two months of slop for breakfast, lunch, and dinner.

Two months of bad sleep, aching misery, and unbearable loneliness.

Two months that Elle and Larry went above and beyond for me.

Twice a week—which was my total allotted amount—regardless if I argued or begged for more—she and Larry would call. His conversations were upbeat and positive. Her chats were sex-loaded and frustrated. Talking to Elle made my cock ache and heart squeeze with need.

We never stepped over that line of turning a call into a pleasure fest, but it was hard. So fucking hard.

Especially when her innocent questions like if I was comfy in bed at night were answered by my libido admitting how hard and uncomfortable it was—just like every inch of me dying to sink inside her.

When visitations were permitted, she and Larry came as a pair. A new duo with a bond building by the day. They were no longer acquaintances brought together because of mutual affection for me. They were friends fighting the same battle.

Elle came with gifts such as freshly baked lemon squares from her kitchen. Prisoners weren't allowed to take such presents back to our cells, but we were allowed to eat as much as we could while in the common room, listening to tales of the outside world.

The world I should be a part of but had been stolen from.

Would I have gone after her if I'd known this would happen? Would I have beaten Greg up or merely waited until David arrived to do the dirty work?

I liked to think my answers would switch on those questions. But they never did.

I wouldn't change a thing. I wouldn't have waited for her father or bodyguard to do my job as her lover and protector. I wouldn't have been able to keep my hands to myself, knowing Greg had touched her.

He got what he deserved. And who knew? Maybe I got what I deserved, too.

I'd been an asshole to her. I'd lied and manipulated and cheated her feelings for me three years ago with the feelings she had for me now.

If this was my karma, I'd learned my fucking lesson.

I just wanted to go home with her and never let her out of my sight again.

I would never tell her, but her visits kept me breathing, yet they also stole my courage to keep going. She was so vibrant—so passionate in her fight to free me. So full of trust when before she'd been so riddled with doubt.

Two weeks ago, she broke the rules and hugged me in the common hall just because she couldn't be close and not touch. She risked a visitation ban when she kissed me last week to catcalls of other inmates. Promising me that we would find a way to get me free while being so goddamn sexy, I struggled not to come just from inhaling her perfume.

She gave me life, and she took my life. I hated that she was out there, working so fucking hard on my behalf when all I could do was sit on my ass and count the seconds as they evolved into minutes.

She didn't notice my slowly dwindling enthusiasm or my wavering belief that I'd be acquitted soon.

I smiled, I teased, I lusted.

But behind that, I slowly became lost. I reverted to the homeless kid who had nothing but a pillow and a blanket surrounded by thieves. I struggled to maintain my humanity when all I wanted to do was *kill* the motherfucker who put me here.

Arnold Twig shared my mind almost as much as Elle did.

My hate festered, making me snap at those I cared about when really I should grovel on my knees for all they'd done.

Larry kept pushing for a trial date and kept being told

everything was going as fast as it could. No matter who he called or threatened, nothing progressed.

And through it all, I slowly shut down. I packed away my need for Elle, my love for Stewie, my friendship with Gio, and my gratitude to Larry. Piece by piece, I systematically placed each person I cared about into boxes and sealed them tight.

I placed them in the basement below my heart and locked the door.

Because part of me believed the worst.

I was in here now.

And no matter what we tried, I wasn't getting out.

# Chapter Twenty-Nine

# Elle

"SOMETHING'S WRONG, LARRY. I can feel it."

I pressed my cell-phone hard against my ear as I paced my office. Sage trotted after me with every beeline from my desk to the door. The same door where Penn made me drop to my knees for him. Where he made me come just by pressing against me. Where he'd come the first time and showed me there wouldn't be any bullshit between us when it came to how much we wanted each other.

Those first weeks of our relationship seemed shallow now—all based on sex and no emotion. I'd allowed him to entrap me in orgasms and pleasure, keeping his truth hidden because I didn't have the courage to poke behind his lies.

But that was all over now.

Now, I only needed to look at Penn to know how he was feeling. His dark coffee eyes were so expressive; I doubted how I ever listened to his fibs in the first place. The way he held his stress like a boulder across his shoulders, how his jaw never fully relaxed, how his nostrils flared when he answered questions he didn't like, how his voice pitched into gravel whenever he told me how much he missed me.

His face was an encyclopedia into his heart. It had dictionary references and thesaurus connotations, revealing what an arched eyebrow meant compared to a tongue flicking over his bottom lip.

He'd never come out and said it, but I knew he loved me. I knew it in the way he whispered his thumb over my pinky when the guards weren't looking. I trusted it in the way he looked into my eyes, so deep, so pure. Whatever words he'd spoken were irrelevant because ultimately, all he'd been saying was *I love you*.

His face could even swear eloquently. A tip of his chin or scowl of his forehead was the perfect *fuck you* to the guards who broke us apart.

All this I knew now.

There was nothing shallow about falling head over heels for a man incarcerated where privacy was a none-given luxury, and physical intimacy was denied at all times.

Penn loved me. I loved him.

And that was why I knew something was terribly, terribly wrong.

Larry yawned, causing me to look at my watch. "What's up, Elle? What's wrong?"

It was almost midnight, and I still hadn't left the office. I couldn't. I was too wired, researching bits and pieces Larry had tasked me with, putting together a well-thought-out and correctly edited document to read in court if and when Penn was given a date.

I quit my pacing, forcing my heart rate to return to sane rather than crazy. "Penn isn't doing so well."

That was an understatement.

How could I expect him to be happy and thrive in a place where violence and misdemeanors were the only forms of conversation and habit?

He pretended otherwise, but each time I saw him, he seemed a little more...empty. As if he'd stuffed every feeling he'd had, every love and goodness, and buried it so deep, he was vacant inside.

"You noticed too, huh?" Larry cleared his throat, giving me his full attention. "He's losing hope."

"But he can't lose hope. He has to stay strong." Tears sprang to my eyes. My emotions these days were haywire—completely uncontrollable. Most likely from lack of sleep, too many things to juggle, the stress of Dad's frustration and Penn's distancing, and my own belief that I should be able to fix this and couldn't.

I'd tried calling the penitentiary where Greg was being held to ask again if he would revoke his statement—but he refused to take my calls. I requested visitation—he denied my name on his list of approved visitors. He blocked me from finding any relief or answers to 'will he or won't he' try to bury Penn alive?

"He's strong. He's been strong on his own for a long time before we came along, Elle. Don't take it to heart. He's only doing what's natural."

"Natural? Shutting down is natural?"

"It is to him." Larry sighed. "Think about it from his point of view. For years, he only had himself to rely on. He was hungry? He had to go steal or beg. He was cold? He had to find shelter or come up with a blanket. He was sick? He had to search for medicine or seek a place he could rest unmolested. He couldn't feel down and let another carry his troubles for a while. He couldn't hurt himself and expect someone else to feed and clothe him while he got better. It's a coping mechanism."

"I understand how it would've been imperative to keep his emotions in check when he was homeless, but he has us now. We'll get him medicine, we'll find him food, we'll give him shelter—"

"You don't get it, Elle," Larry said softly. "Even though he's placed his entire trust into our hands—his life and future, and he does believe we're doing everything we can—he can't help but expect to spend the rest of his life in there. Twig will try his hardest to make that come true. Greg will testify against him. His own past will throw away the key."

"But...he can't shut us out."

*He can't shut me out. Not now...*

"He can, Elle. If that's what he needs to do to keep himself alive and stay above the severe depression that prisoners succumb to, he can do whatever it takes. We'll stand by regardless if he's the confident, slightly egotistical man we've come to love or a cold-hearted, standoffish son-of-a-bitch. You can't give up on him."

I marched to my desk and threw myself on the chair. "I'm not giving up on him." My eyes fell onto the screen currently open on my laptop. A web browser I'd brought up this afternoon on a stupid whim.

I hadn't expected any results...only...

"Wait a minute..." I pulled myself forward, clicking on the link. Information spewed forth, giving me a different kind of hope. If Penn was shutting down, he needed reminding of why he needed to stay very much alive. He needed to be touched, kissed, given the age old cure of a hug.

Guards wouldn't allow that.

Visitation would only make it worse.

But there was one way.

A smile spread my lips. A sexy, sultry, entirely seductive smile, already imagining how incredible it would be if I could make it happen. "Larry, I have an idea."

* * * * *

"I can't believe you talked me into arranging this." Larry rolled his eyes, but beneath his over-puffed drama, excitement and relief glowed.

He knew as well as I did something had to happen to get Penn back. We needed him with us to continue fighting, and hopefully...I could be the one to remind him of that.

"Sign here." The prison guard pushed a form toward me. The fine print and pages of disclaimers were enough to put anyone off from signing.

But not me.

I grabbed his crappy pen and scrawled my name.

Honestly? I couldn't believe this had happened. I hadn't told Dad, Steve, or even Fleur. The only person who knew about my little quest and tonight's accommodation was Larry, and even discussing it with him had been nerve wracking.

It had taken two weeks.

Two very long weeks since Larry had given me the contact details of the person I needed to hound and then together, we didn't stop. Morning, afternoon, evening. Email, call, text, messenger, even tweet.

Over and over, we hounded and hounded until *finally*, we got an email giving us access with the firm instruction never to contact them again.

Never was a long time—especially if Penn's court date remained forever locked in the future. But I wouldn't worry about that now.

We'd won.

We were here.

At eight p.m. on a Wednesday, signing into the jail after visiting hours.

According to the prison roster, all inmates would've eaten, enjoyed rec time, and now be in their respective cells ready for lights out. Bedtime was early in this place. Morning alarm was even earlier.

Every man would be most likely stretched out on his cot, reading or passing the time in his imagination.

But not Penn.

Penn would be taken somewhere different. Somewhere he'd probably argue about and wonder why the hell he'd been separated and locked up in an unfamiliar place.

"Do you have all the necessary belongings?" The guard looked at my plastic see-through Hermes that held a change of clothes, my toothbrush, and other nighttime required accessories. The security processing had already x-rayed my things and cleared me.

"Yes, I'm all ready to go." My voice pitched slightly higher with nerves.

"You'll collect her first thing tomorrow?" The guard looked at Larry.

Larry gave my shoulder a squeeze as if I was about to go into a cage with a lion to tame it, instead of entering a cage with Penn to seduce him. "Yes, I will. Eight a.m. On the dot."

Knowing he knew what I'd be doing tonight made me blush, but the experience at having a night alone with Penn made me bounce on the spot.

Thanks to my online research, I'd learned that only four states allowed conjugal visits and one of those states was New York. I also learned that only medium and lesser security prisons permitted them, and were entirely dependent on prisoner behavior. The lesser infractions the inmate had, the better chance of being granted one of three conjugal options: six, twelve, or twenty-four hours.

I'd pushed for twenty-four. I'd been granted twelve.

I wouldn't argue because technically, in some states, you had to be legally married, and I didn't want that nuisance to stop me.

We were engaged. I had witnesses from the office stating as much. If it came down to that...I would no longer fight against it or call it fake. Technically, I wasn't even in a relationship with Penn. We'd never discussed exclusivity or rules. But just like I could tell he loved me, our hearts had decided that whatever this was—it was too deep to be labeled and too real to require laws to keep it alive.

Taking the form back, the guard checked I'd initialed each page and signed. I supposed the waiver was so in-depth because of prior incidents. The same website said an inmate murdered his girlfriend and committed suicide during one such visit in 2010.

The screening had tightened a lot since then.

"All right then, if you'll follow me, Ms. Charlston." The guard buzzed open a door, waiting for me to step through.

Larry gave me a wave, a chuckle escaping. "Well, Elle. Go give our boy one of the best nights of his life."

My cheeks burned, but I smiled. "That's my plan. See you in

the morning." As the door closed, absorbing me into the prison to have sex with my incarcerated fake fiancé, Larry blew me a kiss.

For a moment, my heart fluttered like any exciting date.

For a second…things were normal.

And then the door clanged shut, and my twelve short hours began.

# Chapter Thirty

# Penn

WHEN THE BELL rang to return to lock-up, a guard came for me.

All I earned was a barked command to grab my toothbrush and prison-issued pajamas and follow him.

To be honest, it freaked me the fuck out.

Why was I being picked on? Why had no one else been told to grab their shit and march to unknown territory?

He didn't give me any other instruction, and I didn't make small talk as I followed him out of general and through security. I was patted down as if I had an arsenal made from soap bars and candy wrappers stuffed in my pants, then directed down a series of hallways to a more modern, renovated side of the prison.

"In here." The guard pointed at an open door. Inside was a king-sized bed with black linen, tables, lamps, a dark red rug, two towels rolled on a chair, and a plastic basket with lube and condoms. A door ajar hinted at a private bathroom complete with shower.

*What the fuck is this place?*

Was I about to get ass raped by some dude I'd somehow pissed off? Had the warden suddenly taken a liking to me?

*Shit.*

When I didn't move, the guard pointed with a scowl. "Get in."

"I, eh—what's going on?"

"You'll see if you get in." He pointed again. "Now, Everett."

Not given a choice, I stepped into the love dungeon and spun around just as my roommate for the night appeared.

A fucking angel with debauchery on her mind and sex in her

smile.

*Elle.*

# Chapter Thirty-One

# Elle

I'D SURVIVED TWO and a half months without Penn in my day-to-day life.

I'd slept alone, I'd worked alone, I'd plotted his freedom every second I was awake.

Yet standing in that doorway, drinking him in while the guard reeled off the rules—

1. No BDSM
2. No anal
3. No toys
4. No role-play
5. No restraining
6. No airplay

—the minutes multiplied into years.

I wanted the officer gone. I'd never despised someone purely for talking before. Couldn't he see how unwanted he was? How Penn undressed me with his eyes and I made love to him with mine?

*God*, I'd missed him.

To be so close but then have to listen to this idiot pompously announce the rules as if we were about to be introduced to the president was too much.

Penn locked in place—a mirror image of me. His hands curled into fists, the dark green of his uniform bunched with power from his muscles. He looked ready to explode, like a track runner waiting for the starting gun.

I trembled with the desire to kiss him. I melted with the need to have *him* kiss *me*. And still, the guard stood in our rapidly growing sexual tension, utterly oblivious.

"At seven a.m., you'll be given breakfast and an hour to shower. Then at eight, you'll be escorted back to your cell while your guest returns home." The guard tapped his chin. "I think that's it...oh, almost forgot—"

Penn snapped. "Goddammit."

With bared teeth, he grabbed me by the hand, jerked me inside, and slammed the door in his face. "Fuck, we get it."

A giggle erupted from my lips—partly from lust, mostly from giddiness at how vicious he looked. How wild and untamed and already delirious with the temptation of me...alone.

I doubted an inmate had willingly locked himself up before. I opened my mouth to joke, to break the unbearable awareness between us, but Penn marched me backward, his eyes sharp with need, and his face black with lust.

"Fuck, Elle." His nose skimmed my throat, inhaling me, imprinting me, drowning in me. "What the fuck did you do?"

My spine slammed against the wall. His hands grabbed my wrists, pinning them brutally above my head; his body landed on mine, his hips drove forward, and his mouth...

God, his mouth sought mine with raunchy speed.

He didn't speak again. He didn't question or tease or ease into our physical reunion with soft licks or sweet caresses.

He exploded as if he'd ultimately die if he didn't have me that very moment.

We kissed until we were breathless. Until his voice returned and he mumbled incoherent thanks. Nuzzling my hair, he whispered, "Christ, Elle. Did you arrange this? Arrange a night to be together? *How?*"

Kissing my cheek, my chin, my jaw in his race to capture my lips, his groan unraveled the rest of my decorum. I'd come here to seduce him. I'd expected a moment or two of uncertainty before we attacked each other.

I hadn't expected him to turn rogue on me.

His lips found mine again.

He came utterly undone. His groan turned to a grunt, switching to a growl. He hummed, he purred, he sighed in utmost need.

His hips rocked forward, robbing me of breath as he pressed into me as hard as he could. His body tried to either consume mine or become one; regardless, we were still fully clothed.

I gasped, giving him access to my mouth as his hands formed tight cuffs around my wrists, his tongue diving deep, licking mine with impatience to join him in the frenzy.

He kissed and thrust as if he had twelve seconds to climb inside me not twelve hours.

There was no reprimand for touching. No bullhorns to separate. No knocks to keep our distance.

Just Penn and me.

Together.

Alone.

It didn't matter we were guests of the state or the bed wasn't our own.

All that mattered was our body heat as it exploded into sinful, the sweat slicking our skin in anticipation of joining, and the clenching in our bellies at just how good it would be to finally devour one another after so, so long.

Capturing both my wrists with one hand, he dropped his other to my neck. His fingers wrapped around my throat as he angled my head, taking me past the realms of sanity and into chaos with his kiss.

It hurt. It broke. It freed. It destroyed.

Teeth and tongue and wet and heat.

Our heads tilted and fought. Our breathing ragged and short. My lips burned from his as if we'd burst into flames.

His hand dropped from my throat, reacquainting itself with my breast. He pulled my nipple, rolled my weight, and squeezed the flesh until I cried out for more.

His touch moved again, this time dropping down my side to jerk my leg over his hip and angle my core, so his pants-clad erection pressed as perfect as ever, driving me crazy.

I'd deliberately worn a floaty daisy print skirt. Something he could gather and hoist up—which he did.

I'd purposely gone without underwear. So he could reach between my legs and find—which he did.

His mouth tore away from mine as his fingers found the slick heat that'd burned in me for months. Nothing could damper my need for him. No personal late-night ministrations. No celibacy. No tricks. Only he could help me because he was the one who ruined me.

"Fucking hell…" Pulling his fingers away, he brought them to his lips and licked. His eyes rolled back, his knees buckled. He stumbled away to slam onto the bed. "Christ, I missed you."

I expected him to command me to join him. To reach out and tug my wrist to strip me of everything and command me to my hands and knees. I didn't care what position he wanted. I just *wanted.*

But he leaned forward with his hands clutching his head, the slickness of my desire still coating his fingers. "As much as I want you. Shit, I can't—"

Ice water replaced the fire inside. I brushed my skirt down, wishing I had scaffolding for my knees to hold up the wreck he'd made of them. "Wh—what?"

He shook his head, bending over his legs. "I can't. We're in fucking prison. You came here for me. You're ruining your life for me just so I can get laid."

"Hey!" My temper burst. "You have it all wrong." Moving to stand in front of him, I snapped, "I'm here because I want to be here. I want you to do this." I stroked his hair, running my fingers through the overgrown strands. "I *need* you to do this."

He looked up, swatting my hand away with rage. "I'm not going to fuck you in jail, Elle." His eyes turned tortured as they skimmed over the beads of my nipples visible in the tight singlet I wore. "Even though I'm dying to be inside you."

I stepped back, searching his face.

In all my planning and hounding for this night to happen, I never envisioned him *refusing* me.

God, it hurt.

My chest squeezed as if my ribs had become an overzealous corset. My heart slunk away, reprehended with its tail between its legs. My breath caught when he looked up, glowering with unflinching morality. "You should go, Elle."

"Go?"

He nodded. "I can't do this with you."

I hated he was firm with commitment and convicted with certainty. The decision to deny what we desperately needed from each other all because of some stupid ideal.

He'd made that decision without me. He'd reached that conclusion without discussing it.

As we stared, I fought for calmness. An assurance that he couldn't just kick me out. That we had twelve hours. I'd paid ten dollars for this room. I'd signed the forms that promised no cameras would record our time, no recording devices, or guard supervision.

We were on prison property, but this room was neutral ground.

I crossed my arms. "Nope."

"Nope?"

"Just nope."

He frowned. "What?"

"I'm not going to let you ruin this."

Anger etched his face. "Let *me* ruin this?" He pointed at me. *"You're* the one ruining it."

I threw my hands up. "How exactly am I ruining this? We have an entire night together. We should be tangled almost at an orgasm by now, but you're the one who pulled away and complicated things."

He stood, raking fingers through his hair with a rage that sent my heart grabbing a white flag of surrender. "Don't, Elle. Don't start a fight you can't win."

"Oh, it's a fight now?"

How had this veered off course so badly?

But maybe...maybe that was what we needed?

We'd never had a fight. We'd started under false pretenses and then been torn apart before we could reconcile them. I still had unresolved frustration at being lied to. He still had issues from the past. Everything I knew about Penn was obscure and given to me by third parties.

The more I searched inside—past the guilt at being the reason why he was locked up, beyond the drive to get him free, was anger.

I thought I'd let it go. That I'd forgiven him for treating me as if I was nothing. That I understood why he'd been a jerk.

*But...I haven't.*

The anger still burned, bright and red and throbbing with explosives ready to spread shrapnel far and wide.

"It's not a fight if you just leave. Go home where I know you're safe." He sighed, pinching the bridge of his nose. "I don't want you here, Elle."

I understood his pride. His desire for me not to see him caged like an animal. But at the same time, he had to get over that. This was our life—for however long the gods in power wanted to play with us mere mortals.

He couldn't take the brief moments of happiness we might find and throw them in the gutter.

"What about what *I* want?"

His head whipped up. "What about it?"

My eyes burned with tears, but they were rage-filled tears. Tears I could hold back and swallow while I spoke the words clambering over one another to be spoken. "Don't I get a say in any of this?"

"Any of what?" His jaw clenched. "You're not the one locked up, so don't—"

"You're right. I'm not. But I *am* the one paying for what I failed to do three years ago."

All the oxygen evaporated.

I couldn't breathe.

Penn didn't breathe.

We stood in solid gravity, waiting for life to return.

When it did, it smashed into us, and everything we'd held back—all the truths we daren't speak and accusations we daren't think ricocheted like bullets.

Penn shouted, "You want to go there, Elle? Fine, we'll fucking go there."

I shouted, "You still blame me for not finding you. That I wasn't there when Larry helped earn your freedom."

Penn snarled. "You pretended to be poor. You broke into Central Park with me, you fucking kissed me—you lied to me the entire time I fell for you."

I snarled. "Larry told me you came to visit me the night you were released. That you left with my necklace and returned with my necklace. I never saw you that night. Where were you? What made you refuse to see me?"

Penn growled, "I did come find you, I admit. I wanted to return that damn sapphire you'd mentioned. I'd thought about you every day for nine months. You were my happy place, the reason I didn't let Twig get to me. I let myself fall in love with a lie, and when I went to your house, and you were there with Greg and your father and a maid providing everything your hearts desired, I saw everything I thought I knew about you was false."

I growled, "So you created my backstory on one voyeur through a window? You hated that I had money—"

"I hated that you were fucking rich and hadn't used that power to find me. I didn't expect you to. I never thought it would truly happen. But dreams are brutal friends, Elle. I lost count how many fucking times I dreamed of you in a tiny studio, cooking meals for one, pining for me like I was pining for you. Only to find out you were fucking loaded. A spoiled little brat."

*Oh, my God, he called me a brat!*

After years of toiling and sweat equity for that company.

I yelled, "Is that why you were a jerk to me? You thought I

was a spoiled rich bitch who deserved to be lied to? Deserved to have her virginity stolen by an egotistical, unfeeling bastard…to what? Teach me a lesson?"

He yelled, "Yes, all right? I wanted to hurt you. I wanted to take that privileged little ass and make it mine. I wanted to control you just like you'd controlled me for years without knowing."

My heart literally broke in two, blood rivered in despair.

I shook my head. "So from the very beginning, you chased me, not because of attraction or because you felt something for me, but because of hate? A damn vendetta?"

He shook his head. "It started that way, but the entire time I was lying to you, I was lying to myself more."

My anger spluttered; my heart grabbed a bandage. "What do you mean?"

He sighed. "I mean that I *wanted* to hurt you. I wanted to make you pay for things you didn't have any reason to pay for. I was angry. I was an idiot. I thought I could fuck you and then walk away." Coming toward me, he held out his hand. He knew better than to touch me, allowing me to make that choice to build a link.

I did so. Hesitantly.

The moment our fingers knotted together, he exhaled in a rush. "Dammit. I ruined this, didn't I?" He rubbed his forehead as if all the tension of our fight appeared as a headache.
"I'm…confused, Elle. I'm so fucking strung up over you, but at the same time, I'm just waiting for you to end it. You *should* end it. You should walk away, and a part of me *wants* you to walk away. I've been nothing but a bastard, and now, I'm locked in here. You can do so much better."

His stoic frame shook violently. "You don't see what I do, Elle. What I'm turning you into. You used to be so pure, and I'm…ruining you. I've trapped you in this life when really I should be cruel to you, so you'll leave me to my own fuck ups."

His honesty about hating me came full circle with his admission about why.

He was confused. I was confused. Just like every couple who ever had to climb over a few stumbling blocks was confused.

That was romance.

It wasn't paint-by-numbers or color within the lines. It was messy and scribbly and up to us to draw it how we wanted.

I'd forgiven him the moment he admitted he was hurting.

Taking the argument and turning it into confession, I said, "Despite what you think, I *did* try to find you. Every day for months, I called police stations. I asked David to hire private investigators to learn your name. I even hired a sketch artist to draw a likeness of you, so people didn't laugh me out of offices when I mentioned I had no idea who you were but had to help you."

Penn's face shattered. "You did?"

"Not a single day went by that I didn't have guilt on my thoughts. I fell for you, too. I think that's why I fought you so much when you came back. I couldn't stomach the thought that I could be attracted to another when I was still hung up on Nameless."

He swallowed, shaking his head slightly as if he wanted to take every nasty thing he'd done and destroy it.

I wished he could.

I wished we could go back to the night we'd met again at the Weeping Willow, and he'd pulled me into his arms to whisper about Central Park and chocolate kisses.

"You called me Nameless?"

I laughed under my breath. The angry tension snapped, leaving a calm rain-battered landscape in its wake. "What else could I call you?"

"I had no idea you tried to find me."

"Because you didn't ask."

He closed his eyes, tormented and full of regret. "Christ, I ruined everything."

"No, you didn't," I murmured, staring into his haunted gaze. "You just complicated it a little." Brushing my skirt with suddenly nerve-damp fingers, I added, "But you can't tell me what to do, Penn. Just like you couldn't pretend you were something you weren't."

I closed the distance between us. "I agree you screwed up. You should've given me a chance when you first came to find me. You should've trusted in what you felt that night and let me explain."

His throat worked as he swallowed. "I'm an idiot."

"You're not. You're just not used to trusting people."

"If I trust you, Elle, I give you everything I have. I don't—I don't know if I can."

I squeezed my fingers with his. He reluctantly squeezed me back, then almost crippled me with pressure-filled apology.

I brought our joined hands to my mouth and kissed his knuckles. "You have to. Because I've already given you everything

I have. Even if we end up killing each other, you have every piece of me."

Penn smiled sadly, utterly solitary and unreachable. "I don't deserve that."

He said it as if rejecting my gift.

I'd come here to be connected, yet at that moment, all I felt was loneliness. It wasn't just physical distance this time but emotional. Penn successfully tugged on all my self-doubt and made me wish things could've been different.

That we'd clung to each other that first night.

That I'd been honest and he'd been honest, and we'd fought for each other.

But things weren't different and could never be.

We had to fight for our future, not what went wrong in our past.

"I can't have that responsibility," he whispered. "I can't let you give me what I've always wanted when I don't fucking deserve it."

"But you do—"

His lips twisted into a snarl. "I don't. I was wrong, okay? You were never spoiled. I know how hard you work for your company. I see how much you dote on your father. I understand how Belle Elle and its staff wouldn't exist without you. You're so much better than any dream version I could've created of you, and that...well, it fucking terrifies me."

He looked at the floor, severing our connection. "That night in the limo...I was going to break it off. Hell, I was supposed to break it off with you the first time I let you walk out of my apartment without me and almost got hurt by that asshole on the street. I told myself I didn't care what happened to you. I'd got what I wanted. You'd gotten what you wanted. We were through. But that fucking night three years ago."

He squeezed my fingers. "I can't explain it. Maybe I was so lonely I would've fallen for anyone who treated me with kindness. Perhaps, I would've handed over my soul to the first girl who saw past my rags and lack of riches and kissed me. But I don't think that's true. It was you, Elle." His eyes shone with dark passion. "I fell for you the second I met you. I don't care if that's idiotic or improbable; it's true. The one piece of truth I could never hide with the countless lies I told. I just—"

His head hung. His fingers spasmed. "I'm sorry."

All my fight trickled away.

I walked into his embrace, slotting myself neatly into him as he rested his chin on my scalp. "I'm sorry, too. I'm sorry I didn't find you. I'm sorry I left you."

"You have nothing to apologize for."

"I do." I kissed his t-shirt over his heart, doing my best not to inhale the scent of imprisonment and cheap detergent. "And I might as well apologize for this, too."

He pulled away, searching my eyes. "For what?"

"For this." Standing on my tiptoes, I pulled his head down to mine.

My lips slotted over his, and I held on, linking my fingers tight around his nape as he tried to yank away. "Kiss me." I fed into his mouth. "Trust me." I poured down his throat.

We needed this now more than ever.

We'd ripped off scabs over old wounds. We needed to heal them rather than let them scar.

"Elle—" His hands landed on my hips, holding me firm. "Stop…" His voice said one thing, but his mouth said another. Slowly, he turned from stiff to pliant, unyielding to full participant.

His head tilted, angling me closer, kissing me deeper.

My anxiety quickened then lessened. My need thickened then loosened.

This was our night.

I wouldn't let him steal it.

"If we do this, there's no turning back…you understand?" He broke the kiss, whispering so soft my ears strained to catch it. "You let me have you, then you accept that I might never get out of here. That you'll forever be restricted to a lover who can't touch you, hug you, hang out and watch movies with you. If you stay, that's it…the sum future I can offer you."

He brushed his lips over mine. "I'm giving you a way out, Elle. Say the word, and I'll let you go. It will fucking kill me. You'll rip my heart out, and I'll die in here, but at least I'll be happy knowing you were free. Leave me, Elle. Don't let me get away with stealing yet more from you."

He was so open, so ardent.

He didn't have a clue he just glued me to him for the rest of my life.

My lips twitched. I hid my smile for as long as I could before it crept over me. "Tell me one thing. Then I'll make my choice."

He swallowed hard as if bracing himself for me to walk out of this room and take him up on his offer. But even in his terror, he nodded with shoulders braced. There stood Nameless, not Penn. The man in the hoodie who drove off two men to protect me. He'd drive himself off, too, if it meant protecting me from him.

*That's what he's trying to do by refusing to sleep with me tonight.*

Well, it wouldn't work.

He was mine. Simple.

"Tell me you don't love me." I placed both palms on his chest. His muscles beneath my fingertips rose and fell with rapid breath. "Look me in the eyes and tell me you don't love me and I'll go. I'll leave you alone."

He crumpled. The answer blared so loud and bright it filled the entire room. It didn't matter he'd said it already with admitting he'd fallen for me three years ago. I let him verbalize, so we both knew he could never take it back. That he willingly admitted that despite wanting to live in an ideal world with picnics and vacations and lazy Sundays in bed, we might never have that. This might be our world with precious conjugal visits and achingly hard visitation.

But love would overcome that.

It had to.

Because I didn't want, *couldn't* stomach the thought of loving anyone else.

Finally, his shoulders realigned into confident, not angry. His spine unlocked. His face shed its mask, and his voice said what his eyes had all along.

"I can't tell you that." His hand cupped my cheek, his thumb running along my bottom lip. "I can't tell you I don't love you because that's not true. It's never been true." He tipped forward, kissing me so, so soft. "I love you, Elle. I'm obsessed with you, consumed by you. You make me crazy and not necessarily in good ways. But I can't lie to you anymore. I love you. So fucking much it kills me."

My smile was sunshine and hot days as I kissed him back. "Then trust that. Trust that I love you, too. Trust that whatever happens, we'll fight it together. Turn off that voice inside you that's trying to screw everything up. Just trust like you've told me to do so many times before."

He nuzzled into my neck. "You're bossy as well as nosy."

I laughed softly. "You bring out the worst in me."

His eyes filled with intensity. "Yet you bring out the best in me."

"Guess that means we're perfect for each other." My lip trembled, happiness overflowing.

Penn frowned, kissing me gently. "Suddenly, you don't look convinced."

"I am convinced. Completely. I'm just—" More truth bubbled, and I blurted, "I'm so afraid of losing you. That I'm the reason why you're in here, and I don't know if I have the power to get you out."

"Hey..." He captured my cheeks with both hands, holding me tight. "You have power over me. That's all you ever need."

"Does that mean I can command you to spend the night with me, and you have to obey?"

A sly grin transformed him from serious to player. "Are you asking me to fuck you, Ms. Charlston?"

I nodded. "Again and again, Mr. Everett. Multiple times. Will you?"

# Chapter Thirty-Two

# Penn

I'D TRIED TO do the right thing.

I really fucking had.

The thought of having Elle in this place turned me right off, but kissing her blueberry-glossed lips and knowing she had nothing on underneath her skirt scrambled with my right and wrong.

My brain had had its chance at ending this.

Our fight had had its opportunity to push her away.

Our connection hadn't ended, and she hadn't gone.

That left only one thing to do.

"When it comes to you, Elle, I'll do whatever you damn well want." I kissed her softly, keeping my desires in check this time.

I couldn't believe how quickly I'd pounced on her before. I'd been a fucking animal. She'd arranged this for us. The least I could do was make it good for her rather than a three-second humping against the wall.

"How long do we have?" I murmured as her hands slid around my waist, gripping me close.

My tongue massaged hers. My heart thundered as she moaned. "Twelve hours."

"Really?" I could do so much to her in that amount of time. It would be the longest we'd ever spent together consecutively. Which, in the scheme of how many months we'd been 'dating,' was an embarrassment.

She pulled away, looking up. Eyes shining, lips bruised, skin flushed. The tank she wore showed the lacy indentations of her bra, revealing the pinpricks of her nipples, encasing her tiny waist in cotton just begging me to rip it off her.

My throat burned. "Christ, you're so beautiful."

She shook her head. "You're the beautiful one. Do you know that's what made me say yes that night? I thought you were so pretty. I couldn't say no."

"So you only agreed to sleep with me because of how *pretty* I am?" I kissed my way down her throat, adoring the way she shivered.

"I said yes because even then I think my heart knew. You reminded me of him. You put your hands in your pockets like him. You had demons like him."

I didn't doubt her. She could've cut off her long blonde hair, got piercings, indulged in tattoos, and put on weight, and I would still have recognized her.

It was one of those serendipitous things that couldn't be explained.

Our kiss turned into a conversation on its own, rolling like waves on a beach, sometimes deep, sometimes shallow, always rippling with power.

Pushing my fingers through her hair, I breathed, "Know what I want to do more than anything?"

"What?" Her head tipped back as I tugged the yellow-gold strands.

"For the next twelve hours, I want to be inside you for as long as possible. I really, really need to fuck you, Elle. Who knows? Perhaps for the entire twelve hours, I'll take you every way I can."

She shuddered, her arms tightening around my waist. "Do it. I miss having you inside me."

Electricity flowed from her to me, dragging me closer to the edge I'd almost fallen off before.

"If I let go...I don't know how controlled I'll be." My confession floated in the subspace we'd created, the soft protective bubble where no one could find us.

She smiled beneath my kiss. "I love the sound of that."

I clung tight to the rest of my self-control, desperate to ask a few more questions. Learn a bit more about her. Imprint her further on my soul. But all I could think about was sex. I'd study her body tonight...but it wouldn't be intellectual it would be entirely sexual.

"I'm going to take away all your control. I'll fuck you the way *I* want to fuck you. I'll look after you while I ruin you. I'll protect you while I hurt you—just like I promised that first night. I'll take everything you have to give. We play rough. We love hard. We live every fucking fantasy." I traced my hands up and down her spine, caressing her while forcing myself to stay gentle. "You came here tonight to sleep with me. Well, you're at my mercy. Locked in a room with a convict. Completely helpless."

Fuck, I was turning myself on. My balls drew upward, hard as marble. My cock twitched, dying to put what I'd said into practice.

"You're mine, Elle. No more secrets. No more lies. You fuck me knowing entirely what you're getting into."

She squirmed as if both aroused and scared, but her eyes glittered with lust so bright she incinerated me. "Penn..."

Cupping her breast, I squeezing her softness. Memories that she'd been a virgin before I'd taken her almost made me snap. Knowing she'd only had me inside her and only ever would turned me on so much I almost climaxed as her hand cupped my cock.

She moaned again as I pinched her nipple. "Do you want that?"

Her head rolled back. "Yes. Very much."

"Yes to me possessing you?"

"Yes."

"What do you say?" The precipice was there. I was about to fall. "Answer me."

"Please, Penn. Possess me. Do whatever you want. I'm yours."

"Fuck." My mouth sealed over hers, preventing any more talking and setting fire to the rocket fuel that'd replaced our blood.

She leaped into my arms. Her teeth nipped my lower lip; her tongue fought mine for dominance.

She tried to win. But she never would.

She was mine, and I'd spend all night teaching her that with fucking pleasure.

Fisting her hair, I yanked her head back. My message about who was in charge was undeniable as her throat arched.

She groaned long and low as I bit her neck, tossing her onto the bed. She bounced on the mattress, her legs parting and skirt hoisting up her thighs.

A flash of nakedness bewitched me. I couldn't control myself anymore.

Hunger surged.

I climbed over her, yanking at the tight tank. In one rip, I tore it over her head. Her pretty white bra stopped me from seeing what I wanted.

*It has to come off.*

Rolling her over, I undid the clasp and threw it across the room.

It landed on the basket full of lube and condoms.

Elle looked up as it crashed to the floor, spilling sex aids everywhere. She bit her bottom lip, hiding a smile. Slowly, like a sexy vixen, she opened her legs, pulling her skirt high.

I told her I'd be in charge but, goddammit, that one motion made me her slave for life.

I panted as she revealed her pussy, glistening with need. I became hypnotized with lust, barely able to register words as she said, "I don't think we'll need the lube."

"Christ." I slid off the bed, dragging her hips with me. The moment she was in licking distance, my mouth connected and my tongue speared inside her.

Hot. Wet. Elle.

She writhed on the bed, her fists grabbing at the sheets, her teeth biting at comforters. She whimpered as I inserted a finger then two, profanities hissing through clenched teeth.

I loved that I could make her come undone so easily. How ready she was for me. How greedy.

I could spend all night making her unravel, but there were other places to taste, touch, worship.

Crawling up her body, I locked my teeth around her nipple followed by the heat of my mouth. She bowed upward, her hands sinking in my hair, her fingernails unsheathed as she threw her head back. "Oh, my God."

While I sucked on her breasts, my hands shoved down her skirt, tossing it over my shoulder.

Naked.

Beautiful fucking Elle was naked.

*And I'm not.*

Moving to her other breast, I bit gently as I pushed at the elastic green pants and disengaged her hold on my hair to tear the t-shirt over my head.

The white boxer-briefs vanished next, leaving my cock bouncing with need and shining with pre-cum.

Elle scrambled to her knees, pushing me hard.

I fell backward in surprise, shocked at her aggression. She made a low sound of appreciation and hunger as her fingers latched around my cock, pumping me once.

I bowed upward, almost coming from how good her tiny

fingers were.

But it was nothing compared to her mouth.

I'd teased her in her office. I'd made her believe I'd force her to do something as intimate as blowing me. I would never have forced her to do something she didn't want.

But now...fuck, she wanted it.

She wanted me.

She had natural talent, sliding her tongue flat and long along my shaft, sucking hard until blood pressure throbbed in the tip. Her hands drifted low to cup my balls, rolling them gently— pressing at just the right spot to make stars twinkle in my eyes and my belly tighten, ready to explode.

"No. Fuck, I don't want to come in your mouth." I pushed her gently. "Not yet anyway."

Hooking my hands under her arms, I pulled her upward. We both groaned as our nakedness slid over one another. She spread her legs, straddling me, rubbing her wetness over my saliva-damp cock.

Having her so fucking close. Having the heat of her, the knowledge I could be inside her in one quick move made me lose all sense of what creature I was and turned wild.

I wanted to be inside her.

I would make it happen.

*Now.*

Palming her back, I pushed her forward as my hips rocked backward. The tip of me nudged inside her.

Elle sat up, pushing down, making my eyes snap shut, and my body turn into a weapon ready to fire.

"Fuck, fuck, fuck," I chanted at the moon, at chocolate, at kisses in the park. My fingers dug into her hips, holding her half way down me. "Wait...condom."

She arched again, hollowing her back until her breasts stood proudly and in grabbing distance. "I'm on the pill. I brought some condoms with me...just in case you wanted to use—"

I didn't let her finish. Sitting up, I clutched her nape, dragged her mouth to mine and thrust up.

I thrust so fucking hard, she cried inside my mouth. I embraced her with one arm while my other dropped to fist her breasts.

I impaled her on me, and it was the best thing in the world. My brain short-circuited. I forgot about breathing and prison and court dates. She made me go to battle, putting me under siege as our bodies strained to dominate and claim.

The bed rocked as I speared upward.

I groaned as she sank downward.

Our rhythm perfectly synced right from the start.

Her hips moved forward and back.

Mine shot upward and down.

The combined motion made this the best sexual experience of my entire goddamn life.

Flesh on flesh.

Body on body.

It was physical, but this time, it touched something spiritual, too. Opening my eyes, I latched onto hers. The blue turned black, full of rock pools and tidal waves, making me drown in her.

I hadn't been a monk while I'd been locked up. I'd serviced myself on regular occasions thanks to memories of that night at my place and the limo ride. But I was about to seriously embarrass myself.

After three months apart, the tremors rippling through me couldn't be denied any longer. Sexual deprivation only made my senses extra sharp. The scent of her lust. The taste of her kisses. The heat of her pussy.

*Fuck me...*

*I'm gonna come.*

Reaching between us, I stroked Elle's clit.

"Oh, God." Her entire body rippled with building pressure. Violent shivers hijacked her muscles. She tried to push my hand away, but I pressed harder.

"Oh, oh..." Her face pinched into a grimace, chasing her orgasm just like I fought against mine.

My legs burned with pleasure just waiting to shoot through me. My belly locked. My spine full of electricity.

Her legs wrapped tight around my hips as I continued thrusting faster, harder, deeper.

"Come, Elle. I need you to come."

A tortured moan trickled from her lips. Her hands landed on my shoulders, locking onto an anchor so I could take her deep into pleasure and know she could find her way back.

I felt her release in her back first.

She gasped as the first surge worked from her shoulder blades and down her spine. Her stomach tightened, her muscles trembling as the breaking orgasm fisted and milked me inside her. Her legs scissored, fighting the onslaught, but it was too late.

One wave, two waves, three, four, five. On and fucking on, she came, giving me no choice but to join her.

"Holy shit." My climax made my eyes water. It squeezed my balls until I groaned in pain mixed with pleasure. My quads cramped. My cock spurted everything it could into the girl I would never let go.

We jolted in each other's arms as the last dregs of our orgasms left us boneless and breathing hard.

With the softest smile, Elle curled into me, pressing kisses to my chest, wrapping her arms around my neck.

I thought I'd loved her before that. Before she showed such vulnerability, such trust, such affection.

I was wrong.

My heart swelled until it no longer fit inside me. All the mess, the lies, the uncertainty in our future couldn't steal how fucking happy I was with my body inside hers and her kisses forever imprinted on my soul.

Brushing my fingertips over her temples, cheeks, to her jaw, I tipped her head up so I could look at her. "I hate this. Being in here. Forced to stay away from you when I need you so damn much."

"I know. But you're innocent. They'll see that soon. And then you're coming home with me."

I kissed her puffy sex-swollen lips not agreeing or disagreeing because as much as I hoped she was right...

I had no idea if it would come true.

# Chapter Thirty-Three

# Elle

THREE TIMES FOR almost three months.

The second was in the shower with tepid water and threadbare towels, but my two toe-curling orgasms shattered the record for all other showers, making it the best I'd ever had.

The third was lazy and sleepy, under the covers half-awake, half-dreaming, my back wedged to Penn's front, his cock slipping between my legs and filling me effortlessly.

We'd fallen asleep with him still inside me.

And for the first time in years, I slept soundly in his arms. We didn't have time to talk or share things we needed to know. We'd depleted ourselves by showing our love in physical form before the beauty of touch could be stolen from us.

Our bodies reacquainted, our hearts pattered to the same rhythm, our minds synced into one frequency.

At seven a.m., our wake-up call came in the form of a prison guard carrying a tray of scrambled eggs and over-cooked bacon with a cup of chocolate-covered strawberries.

To have breakfast served in bed in jail would forever remain one of the most random experiences of my life.

We stayed where we were. Unapologetic and tangled together beneath black sheets.

The utensils were plastic, the crockery had seen better days, and the strawberries were slightly over-ripe, but it was the best breakfast we'd ever had.

Who knew the Department of Corrections would forever hold a fond place in my heart as well as the most hated?

We didn't dally over eating, our anxiety levels steadily increasing with every tick of the clock. Our twelve hours were almost over. I would be forced to leave. Penn would be forced to say goodbye.

Tears filled my eyes at the thought.

I couldn't do it.

I didn't have the capacity to walk away from him not knowing when we'd next be together.

"Elle, don't." His finger caught a tear, rubbing it into my cheeks as if it'd never existed. His fingers smelled of chocolate and berry, adding a flavor to the already familiar one associated with him. It reminded me of the night he brought chocolate mousse to my apartment and took me on the couch. It granted so many memories eternally tangled with him.

"You can't." His handsome face with soulful eyes and sharp jawline fractured with truth. "I won't be able to say goodbye if you cry."

Another tear escaped.

Tilting my chin, he licked it away then brought his mouth to mine.

We kissed long. We kissed slow. We kissed to last us however many months until the next time we could.

Pulling away, a mischievous smile spread his lips. "You know...we have time for one more."

"Lucky number four, huh?"

I was sore. I was achy. I didn't care in the slightest. I'd keep going forever if it meant I could keep him with me and not hand him back to the guards.

He nodded, springing from the bed and yanking me into a kneeling position. "I think four is a good number, don't you?" Grabbing me around the waist, he hoisted me from the mattress and planted me against the wall.

The cold concrete bit into my bare ass, but I didn't care at all as his lips found mine again and kissed me hungrily, violently—as if he could eat me for breakfast, lunch, and dinner, and I'd never have to leave him.

His cock pressed against my belly, grinding into me with unashamed sensual insanity. His hands slid down my body, cupping my ass as he lifted me up and I automatically wrapped my legs around his hips.

Any second, a guard would come to remove me. Any moment, this would all be a dream. But I couldn't think about that as Penn angled himself and sank inside me, inch by devouring, delightful inch.

One hand remained on my hip as he sank all the way inside, rocking harder when he filled me as if he could climb deeper. His other hand crept to my breast, tweaking my sore nipple from a nighttime of pleasure, then fisted my hair to hold my head exactly the way he wanted. He consumed my mouth with his. His hunger palatable—washing off him with droplets of needs.

The unabashed way he desired me made the upcoming separation so *incredibly* painful.

We'd wasted so much time when we could've been together. We'd lied and ruined, and who knew what the future held.

Now, we were together and committed, but we weren't permitted the freedom to consummate, grow, and find a home in this new relationship.

How cruel. How unfair. How unjust.

His thoughts must've been where mine were because he kissed me desperately. He kissed me savagely. We kissed as if we were starving. Our tongues fought, our teeth nipped, we became drunk on fucking with our bodies and our lips.

He pounded into me, slamming me repeatedly against the wall. There was nothing gentle. Nothing kind about the slapping of our skin against skin.

But my body ached and slicked, welcoming him to take me harder, faster.

His teeth captured my ear, breathing hard. "Fuck, I love you. I love fucking you. I'll never stop."

I trembled, undone by the circle of his hips and the frantic way we clawed at each other.

The ferocity unbound me. The fury at not being allowed to be together made us rebels in our desire to consume each other.

Perhaps, we *did* want to hurt each other. Perhaps, that was what our love was—forever tangled up with hate from past misconceptions. But *God*, it made for hot sex.

"You're going to make me come." He sucked on my throat, deliberately marking me, branding me for the entire world to see when he couldn't be there.

I sank deeper onto him, trusting him entirely to support my weight while he drove me off the cliff. "Good because I'm going to come. *God*, I'm going to come."

The tingles were back. The stars, the streamers, the candy floss and fairy wings. They all vortexed in my belly, spiraling outward, clenching my core as bliss I'd forever associate with Penn wiped me out completely.

I shuddered in his arms as I gave into the bands of pleasure.

"Christ, you'll be the death of me." He gripped my thigh, sinking fingernails into flesh. "Don't wash me away."

I wanted to ask what he meant, but his head fell back as his entire stomach sculpted into granite. His muscles seized as the pulsing of his orgasm deep inside me echoed with his groan of release.

His knees buckled as endorphins drenched his body, making him lethargic and sated.

Dropping my legs from around his hips, he gently placed me on my feet, withdrawing from me, watching the vision of his cock sliding free for the last time.

Tears wobbled over my retinas, but I sniffed them back.

He tipped my head up, kissing me. "Promise me you won't shower for the rest of the day. I need to know a part of me is still with you, even though I'll be locked up in here."

"Of course." I threw my arms around him, hugging him so damn hard. "God, I hate this so, so much."

He hugged me back, squeezing me until I couldn't breathe. "I love you."

And then the guard knocked on the door. "Ten minutes. Get ready to go."

Penn let me go.

We dressed in silence.

We kissed goodbye in pain.

We separated in agony.

# Letter from Penn

*I DON'T KNOW how you knew, but you did.*

*You knew I needed a reminder on how to fight. You knew I needed to taste and touch you, not just talk to you across a fucking table.*

*The fact you knew that—that you managed to find a way for us to be together—proved I was right to fall for you.*

*You're everything I want and everything I need.*

*Because of you, I feel strong again.*

*I won't give up.*

*I won't let those bastards win.*

*Tell Larry I'm ready to take him down. I'll testify if he gathers the evidence. I'll do whatever it damn well takes to get out of here and be with you.*

*Because one thing's for sure, Elle—that night in the alley, I wanted to keep you.*

*After last night, I want to fucking marry you.*

# Letter from Elle

*FROM FAKE ENGAGEMENT to prison letter proposal, your romance never fails to astound me.*

*I think you know I won't argue this time. In fact, if you tried to walk away, I'd use everything at my disposal to convince you otherwise.*

*Your letter took a week to be delivered.*

*A week where I couldn't stop thinking about you and how good it felt being together.*

*All my life, I've had privilege. I thought I never took it for granted, but I know now that I did. I'm grateful for the staff who do what I tell them. I'm thankful for the company that gives me power.*

*But none of that experience helps me help you.*

*I'm going out of my mind, needing to do something.*

*I spoke to Greg when I probably shouldn't have. I told the press you were innocent when I should probably have kept my mouth shut.*

*You're in there because of me, and I can't help.*

*Do you know how helpless that makes me feel? So pointless. So useless.*

*Knowing I was able to remind you to keep fighting helps me keep fighting because missing you is the most exhausting thing I've ever done.*

*But it's worth it.*

*Because that night in the alley, I needed you.*

*But after last week, I can't imagine life without you.*

# Chapter Thirty-Four

# Elle

I TOLD LARRY about Penn's readiness to go after Arnold Twig.

I'd never seen someone go from already working manically hard to increasing his energy until it reached chaotic proportions. He was a salt and pepper whirlwind with vengeance on his mind.

It didn't matter that he muttered about not being able to combine one trial with another—unless he could prove Arnold Twig's corruption affected this arrest and not just prior ones. It didn't matter that he mumbled about how tricky it would be to prove Penn's innocence on all accounts and expunge his prior convictions.

He threw himself into the task as if he'd been waiting for Penn to give the go-ahead for years. Which, according to another distracted reply, he had.

I asked why he hadn't gathered this evidence before so he'd be prepared for when Penn finally chose the right moment. He'd said evidence like this would poke the hornet's nest. He wouldn't be able to gather it without someone noticing, and when someone did, Arnold Twig would know.

It was risky to hunt for answers and prove Penn was innocent all while still in jail where Twig would bury him. But according to Larry, Twig had friends on the police force and a few corrupt district attorneys, but he hadn't been able to bribe the head warden yet, so technically, Penn was as safe as he could be.

We just had to hope that the judge who would preside over the case wasn't bought and paid for.

Life—as much as I hated it—had to continue without Penn.

Ever since our night together, it had become harder and

easier in equal measure. Harder because I missed him so much my bones ached with it. He'd injected himself into my veins with no promise of another hit. And easier because by giving him strength, it gave *me* strength. I didn't do anything reckless like try to have Greg murdered or go on some silly TV program with conspiracy theories.

I kept my eyes locked on the future—on a trial that would eventually have to move forward, despite lost paperwork, internal delays, and every other excuse they'd given us up until now about why Penn hadn't been granted a trial date.

Despite having no date to fight toward, Penn and I wrote often. We got to know each through ink and paper rather than voice and language. I found out he had a sense of humor hidden beneath his suspicious outlook on the world. That he could be self-deprecating behind his surly attitude.

That sickly feeling I'd had after his lies unraveled was gone now. With every note, every phone call, every snatched meeting with prison guards and escorts, my heart increased with shots of helium, slowly floating, becoming weightless until it bounced on a string tied to my ribs.

The three-year-old lust I had for him as Nameless and the four-month-old attraction I had for Penn finally merged. The infatuation I had with him irrevocably switched to love. That love (although new and fresh) morphed into a solid protector that would accept anything, tolerate everything, and care for him unconditionally. It made me grow up.

I was no longer a girl masquerading as a woman.

I was all woman, and if Penn was ready to take on the chief of police, I was ready to stand behind him and give him all my power, wealth, and notoriety to make that happen.

Four months to the day of my abduction and Penn's arrest, Larry called me—like he did most days with requests for help, updates on Penn from my point of view, or just catching up to see how I was. However, this phone call smashed through our limbo of waiting. Making everything we'd worked for become real.

"One month from now," Larry said, breathless with adrenaline. "Best I could do. Finally heard back."

Tears welled in my eyes. One month? Four more long weeks?

But what was four weeks compared to three years?

"That's wonderful."

*It's too far away.*

"I'm so happy."

*I'm gutted.*

"He'll be home soon."

*Just focus on that.*

"Your father really came through, Elle," Larry added gently, knowing I struggled with how my loving Dad could suddenly become so judgmental. "It's his friend who rearranged his time. Patrick Blake. I don't know if another case fell through or if he's taken on some extra hours, but he's granted us the hearing. God knows how he arranged for a twelve-seat jury to be ready in time, but he has."

Shaking travelled down my arm, making the phone thwack against my ear. "That's—I don't know what to say."

I wanted to run back to the brownstone and kiss my father stupid. I'd make him blueberry pancakes and apologize for being distant. I'd forgive the grudge I'd held for him for accepting Penn when he was an upstanding businessman and then shoving him into the shadows the moment he was arrested.

The fact that we hadn't been as close these past few weeks hurt.

"What happens now?" My voice wobbled. "What do you need me to do?"

Larry sighed heavily, sounding as exhausted as I was. "Well, I'll work extra hours on gathering the last few bits of evidence against Arnold Twig and his delightful son. In the trial, I'll use that to point direction at the true criminal and show the jury that Penn was innocent of those crimes, just as he's innocent of this one. With any luck, we'll be able to link it all into one, expunge Penn's prior convictions, and get the charges dropped."

"And if that's not entirely true?"

"What's not true?"

"Well, technically, he did hurt Greg. The hospital took photos, and Greg's moaning ensured a lot of people heard what happened. It's his word against Penn's."

"That only shows there was a fight." His tone turned sharp. "Penn didn't go to that cabin to kill Greg. The attempted murder charge will be easy to overthrow."

"How so?"

"There's no evidence whatsoever of intent or premeditation. No paper trail to link Penn to any prior thoughts of violence toward your employee."

There wasn't, but I didn't trust the law not to look into hearsay and find hard truth where there was none.

"They had a fight." Larry sniffed. "Two men in a fight over a woman. Shit, if the state locked up everyone for that misdemeanor, most of the male population would be behind bars."

Larry chuckled in frustration. "Greg was in the wrong for indecently assaulting you and holding you against your will. If he continues to say Penn went there to kill him, I'll personally go after him so hard, he'll be laughed out of court and be done for defamation and lying under oath. If there's anyone with premeditation and a paper trail, it's Greg. The packed supplies, the second vehicle—it all paints a picture of dishonorable intentions."

An icy gale blew down my spine like it always did when I thought about Greg.

I hated that he hadn't gotten in touch. The fact he'd gone from a patronizing presence—constantly popping into my office uninvited—to suddenly being completely elusive and silent...

It petrified me.

I'd told Larry what I'd done at the hospital—trying to bribe then blackmail him. He'd scolded me. Said how reckless I'd been. But after grilling me if there'd been anyone else in the room or any recording devices, he'd patted me on the back with pride.

The fact I'd put my neck on the line for Penn made his fondness for me triple. This entire stressful situation surrounding the man we both loved had brought us closer together than any normal situation.

Larry was the uncle I'd never had. My father-in-law, for all intents, if Penn ever did anything about our fake engagement.

"Okay." The word was woefully underwhelming, but I had nothing else. I thought I'd be able to save Penn months of lock-up when we'd first begun this journey. The fact he was still imprisoned irritated me to angry tears.

Being part of the family dealing with freeing innocence was the hardest thing I'd ever had to do. Turned out, I sucked at this hero stuff while Penn was such a natural.

"Tell me what I should do, Larry."

"I hoped you'd say that," he replied. "What are you doing tonight?"

"Nothing, why?" I looked up as Fleur came into my office. She carried a bottle of wine with two glasses. Ever since the afternoon I'd spoken to the reporters, she appeared at the end of our workday with alcohol of some description—ready-mixed watermelon vodka, Midori shots, even champagne.

I'd told her I didn't drink.

She'd told me I would have to start to survive the next few months.

I hadn't argued.

We'd gotten drunk that night, and for the first time in forever, I was able to laugh even though guilt slithered inside me. I despised that I had a good time with Fleur, that my job kept me busy, my cat kept me sane, and my self-control kept me rational enough not to become a serial killer and hunt Arnold Twig or his son.

It was wrong that I lived while Penn was caged.

She cocked an eyebrow as Larry spoke into my ear. "Come over. I'll be pulling an all-nighter. Need an assistant if you're interested."

The wine bottle in Fleur's hand would remain untouched. "Consider me there already."

A smile existed in his tone. "Excellent. Stewie will be relieved to see you. He wants to apologize."

"Apologize? Why?"

"He finally told me what happened with the necklace at the charity event after he acted so weird around you the last time you popped over. He's not coping well. Thinks he's the reason why Penn is in jail like his brother, Gio."

I rubbed at my heart. "Oh no, it's not his fault."

"Yep, all the more reason to come around. You can talk to him. I'll brew a pot of coffee. See you soon, Elle."

"Sure." I hung up, looking reluctantly at the alcohol in Fleur's grasp. "Can't. Have to go do lawyer stuff to break Penn out of jail."

"Oh, sounds fun." She waggled the bottle. "Any room for this bad boy and me to tag along?"

I stroked Sage as she padded over my desk and hooked her claws around the stem of one of the wine glasses. She tipped it over before I could catch it. Luckily, the glass bounced on the carpet and didn't shatter.

"Why would you want to come? It's just more work. More computer time. More fine print." I stood, slinging my black with pink-lace jacket on over the dark pink dress I wore. Pink didn't spring to mind as corporate, but once again, Fleur picked it out and was right.

"Well, my hubby-to-be is out on a bachelor night with friends. I don't want to sit at home wondering if he's motor boating some stripper's boobs." She pulled a face. "I'd much rather be sitting with you doing exciting things like researching how to break your lover out of jail. It's all very cloak and dagger." Her eyes twinkled as if spending a night bent over paperwork was as raunchy as watching the Chippendales.

"Well, if you're sure." I smiled. "You're more than welcome, and I'd love the company. I'm sure Larry would say we need all the eyes we can get." I took the wine from her and placed it in my large tote. "And for the record, your hubby won't have his face in some stripper's boobs."

"That's what everyone says." She rolled her eyes. "But bachelor parties are the Bermuda triangle of good decisions and decent men. They all get lost along the way, only to be spat back out the next day with no memory of it."

Looping my arm with hers, I patted my thigh for Sage to follow and prepared to work my ass off for Penn. "In that case, consider tonight as reckless as a motorcycle crack party."

"Oh, yay. I've always wanted to see what those two-wheeled outlaws do for fun."

# Letter from Elle

*TWO WEEKS, PENN.*
*Two weeks until this is all over and you walk free.*
*Larry has everything arranged.*
*I have duplicates of his research and evidence locked safe.*
*We're not backing down this time.*
*You're no longer on your own, and when you're free, I'm going to show you exactly how much I missed you.*
*With every part of me.*
*Lips.*
*Tongue.*
*Hands.*
*You get the idea.*
*I'll stop before this letter gets censored and not delivered.*
*Fourteen days.*
*I can't wait.*

# Letter from Penn

*ONE WEEK, ELLE.*

*I'd be lying if I said I wasn't freaking out. That the thought of facing everyone, of hearing that bastard testify against me in court when he was the one who stole you...fuck, just thinking about it makes me livid.*

*Seven days until I get to see you, smell you, feel you behind me in the gallery and know how much you mean to me.*

*Seven days until I'm hopefully free and I'm going to do so many dirty bad things to you I'll probably get locked up again.*

*And I'm fully aware that has probably just flagged me, and a guard is watching me extra close from now on. But I don't fucking care.*

*So close yet so far.*

*So easy yet so hard.*

*I've shared pieces of myself in these letters, but writing it down is different to pillow talk. I want to stroke your skin while I answer any question you wish to know. I want to hug you close while you tell me about your childhood.*

*We have a lifetime to get to know each other, Elle.*

*And soon, we can start living it.*

# Chapter Thirty-Five

# Penn

THE CALENDAR HAD crawled by.

Yet, as I was given a black suit rather than freshly laundered prison scrubs after an earlier than normal wake-up call, five months seemed like it'd been five minutes.

I was ready.

I wasn't ready.

I was prepared to fight.

I was terrified to fight.

I hated that half of me was unstoppable while the other was a fucking pussy.

I almost wished I didn't have Elle and Larry fighting for me, supporting me. Because if we lost today, losing them would rip out my heart and I wouldn't have the energy to keep going. If I was alone with only empty streets and long nights to look forward to, I might be more willing to play hard ass and point fingers at those who could destroy me.

I'd say goodbye to everything I ever wanted if this backfired.

But I'd told Larry I was done keeping Twig's secrets.

He'd spent months gathering what was needed.

I wouldn't let him down.

With my heart jumping like a heroin-cranked addict, I showered and shaved, hacking off the beard I'd grown, revealing some of the scars I'd earned thanks to my days on the streets.

Slipping into cotton instead of polyester somehow gave me a sense of power I'd been lacking while locked up like a dog. The too-big-for-me suit gave me courage that everything would go to plan and I wouldn't end up trapped in here for the rest of my life.

Once I was dressed, I hopped into a barred minivan and was driven to court where I ended up sitting in a holding cell for two hours. A kind-faced elderly guard took pity on my growling stomach—brought on by hunger but mostly stress—and delivered a sandwich complete with mayo, mustard, and roasted chicken.

Nothing had ever tasted so good.

I didn't have access to a clock, but noise slowly gathered as more prisoners arrived for their court time. I eavesdropped on the guard's discussions about who was next on the roll call.

The drone of conversation and the scuffing of feet above in the courtroom gave a perfect backdrop for my mind to drift and contemplate.

This was the first break from the monotony of jail in four weeks.

I hadn't been allowed visitors, and Larry and Elle hadn't been permitted to call.

Some stupid rule about preventing tampering of evidence now I'd been granted a court date. I hadn't had any other visitors, but I had enjoyed one phone call from a very pissed off chief of police. Not that the prison would ever know it was him. He'd called from an unknown number and given a fake name on a cell-phone handed to me by a guard on his payroll.

He'd pulled strings to talk to me, despite the risks.

He'd heard about Patrick Blake agreeing to preside over my case as the judge. He'd also noticed Larry digging for dirt—just like we expected.

The conversation hadn't lasted long and had been layered with cryptic connotations to get around anyone listening.

Those few sentences echoed in my head as a prisoner in a baby blue tuxedo was escorted from a cell for his turn at professing his innocence and begging for a second chance amongst the rest of corrupted civilization.

*"Everett. I hear you're about to head to the slaughter pen."*

*I gripped the phone tighter. "If you mean finally revealing the truth then yes, you heard right."*

*"Enjoy your last words before they throw away the key." He chuckled, but it layered with blackness. "Who knows? Perhaps, they'll put you out of your misery and grant the death penalty."*

*"Funny." I laughed back, matching his tone. "If I were you, I'd stay away from that party. I have no intention of keeping my mouth shut this time."*

*"You fucking—"*

*"Ah ah, language, Arnie." I grinned so hard it almost broke my face. Tormenting him like he'd tormented me for years felt so fucking good. "Thanks for calling to wish me luck, but the next time we talk, I'll be free, and you'll be ruined."*

The shot of pure energy at hanging up on him raced through me now.

I pictured him spitting red and throwing furniture around like a demented gorilla. Hopefully, the stress of what I might say in court and the anger at not being able to control me anymore would give him an aneurysm or heart attack.

"Everett?" A guard appeared in the hallway. Holding cages decorated either side—some filled, some empty with awaiting inmates.

I stood, moving toward the bars, waiting for him to let me out of this damn zoo. "That's me."

"You're up." Striding forward, he pulled out a keychain, inserted a key, and hollered to another guard to press unlock at the same time as he twisted the deadbolt. Everything was so minutely controlled, as if I'd commit murder right here beneath the courtroom surrounded by police.

The moment it was open, he held up silver handcuffs and waited until I pushed my arms forward for him to shackle me.

I cringed against the cold metal but kept my head fucking high.

Once pinioned, I stalked forward in my second-hand suit, walking beside the guard instead of behind him. Filled with conviction of truth, drowning in worry of failure, I told myself to stand tall and be ready to accept whatever happened.

I was innocent, not guilty.

And after today, I would be free for the rest of my goddamn life.

# Chapter Thirty-Six

# Elle

I WASN'T ON trial, but I'd never been so terribly nervous.

The jurors sat in their little tiered stands glowering at Larry as he sat proudly beside Penn. Dad had argued with me not to be seen at the trial. That it would be bad PR for Belle Elle.

I'd hugged him and told him I loved him then told him—in the nicest possible way—that he couldn't stop me from being there for Penn, and he might as well get over it.

I loved Penn.

I was here for Penn.

I loved my company too, but if he forced me to choose...well, it was probably best not to make me.

I stared at the back of Penn's head from where I sat in the rows designated for family. The courtroom was basic in its build with harsh wooden barricades and pews. The bench I sat on had already flattened my ass, and we hadn't even started yet.

Fleur crossed her legs beside me, reaching for my hand as a door banged loudly and hate filled my heart instead of love.

Greg.

He marched with playboy grace, dressed in a similar looking suit to Penn. He didn't make eye contact with anyone, keeping his nose high and arrogance wrapped tight around him.

He followed the guard escorting him until they stopped at an identical table next to Penn and Larry, holding out his hands to be uncuffed.

While the officer freed him, tucking the silver handcuffs back onto his belt, Greg's lawyer placed her satchel on the desk and pulled out documents relating to today.

I disliked her immediately.

Not because she represented my nemesis but because she was a hardnosed woman with hair tied so tight, her eyes turned cat-like with red lipstick smeared like blood across her mouth.

She looked like a weasel who wasn't afraid to fight dirty and tear off a few body parts to win.

Sharing a few whispered words with his lawyer, Greg took his seat, his gaze catching mine.

He flinched before straightening his shoulders and giving me a smirk. He waved a little, mouthing, "Hi, Elle," before his lawyer grabbed his shoulder and spun him to face the front.

I wanted to leap over the small wooden wall separating witnesses from accused and wring his damn neck. Not for what he'd done to me but for what he'd done to Penn.

Another door banged, and a judge arrived, climbing up to his podium in a regal robe. His black attire made my heart hammer.

"All rise for honorable Patrick Blake."

The court rose as one.

There weren't many people here—mainly court appointed reporters and the odd colleague from Belle Elle being nosy rather than supportive. I was glad and disappointed that the pews weren't full of people waiting to hear the truth. Glad because what if we all failed? What if the long nights of research and evidence gathering wouldn't be enough to save Penn from this bullshit charge? And disappointed because what if we did and he walked out of here a free man? No one would see honesty win over corruption or know how hard the battle had been.

The victory of winning over men who believed they were better than everyone would be so, so sweet but the failure would be so, so bitter.

"You may be seated."

The court sat in perfect synchronicity.

I stroked my somber suit, hoping the all black affair would grant me strength. I wished I had something of Penn's—a trinket or keepsake to clutch and give me hope.

Not for the first time, I thought about my sapphire star and how much was now tied to that silly piece of jewelry. It had my dad's love imbedded in it. It had Penn's rescue and then subsequently his lies swimming in the blue gemstone.

And now, even though it wasn't mine anymore, and Stewie had refused to part with it, it bore witness to this thanks to the kid himself sitting beside me, his tiny fists tight in his lap; a look of utmost concentration on his face.

He was my keepsake.

Over the past few months, I'd learned to truly like Stewie. He was rough around the edges thanks to his prior years of running wild with his reckless older brother, but there was a sweetness too. He adored Sage and couldn't stop petting her when I took her with me to help Larry research.

Unraveling my fear-sweaty locked-together fingers, I wiped them on my black skirt then took Stewie's small hand in mine.

He jumped, so focused on watching Penn and Larry as they bent to talk in hushed whispers in front of us.

I smiled, hiding my nerves, granting him some courage at the expense of my own. "It will be fine. You'll see."

His throat worked as he swallowed. He didn't nod, merely turned his gaze back to the two men who'd saved him from a life of homelessness and settled in for the longest day of our lives.

"Truth will prevail, Elle." Fleur leaned close. "That creep Greg can't get away with this—"

"Today, we have Penn Everett versus Greg Hobson," the court officer said loudly, narrowing his eyes at us lowly supporters. "Please remain silent. No outbursts will be permitted. No interruptions of any kind or you will be asked to leave."

When everyone hushed, the officer nodded at the judge. "Ready to begin."

The twelve jurors sat tall with importance with a rustle of clothing and murmurs of voices.

The rest of the court settled to watch, wound with tension, stiff with hope, wishing for a quick and fair verdict.

* * * * *

Recess.

How could there be such a thing?

I didn't want coffee and cake when the life of the man I loved hung in an uncertain balance.

For the past hour, opening statements had been delivered. Greg's lawyer went first, prancing around in knife-sharp stilettos, speaking to the jury as if they were dimwitted barn animals.

According to her, Greg had been mentally abused in his childhood. He'd been brainwashed by his father to believe he would end up marrying me and inheriting it all. When he wanted to travel the world after he finished college, he claimed his dad told him not to go. Otherwise, another man might steal our arrangement and my heart.

I burned through so many calories sitting through such filth.

Steve was a good man, and if he'd lied to his son about winning my hand, then I didn't know him as well as I thought I did. But I had a sneaking suspicion if he was here, he'd be as mortified as I was about the lies Greg spread.

Greg painted a picture of a tireless worker who would do anything for Belle Elle, but in the same breath, he came across as a brokenhearted lover who only wanted a second chance with me away from the influences of the company.

He claimed I went with him willingly.

That I wore chains and let him hit me all because I wanted what he had to offer. I wanted to be with him because that sort of thing turned me on.

*Please.*

Not for the first time, I wished Steve and Dad had come to bear witness—to finally see the games Greg loved to play, and they'd been so oblivious of. I understood why Steve wasn't here—he loved his son, but he couldn't stand by and watch two children he'd help raise battle in court. And I appreciated why Dad wouldn't step foot in the court because he fussed over Belle Elle as if it was his wife and needed mollycoddling while this nightmare carried on.

Greg pouted for the jury, saying how happy we'd been, only for our romance to be destroyed when Penn swooped in and claimed me for himself. He came across far too convincing.

I was glad I hadn't had anything to eat because I would've thrown up.

*Bastard.*

Larry's opening statement had been short and to the point. That the accusations were false. That Greg had kidnapped me and Penn had rescued me. The end.

The jury fazed out a little, hearing the same rebuttal most of us had heard on the news or TV once upon a time.

I squirmed in my seat, wanting to leap to my feet and beg the jury to listen to the girl who'd been there, lived it. Prove to them that I loved Penn, not Greg. It had *never* been Greg. Penn had ruined me for all other men even when I didn't know his name.

But Larry had sucked up their attention the moment he'd said, "What is on trial today isn't if Penn went to that cabin with the intention of murder but whether or not the chief of police, Arnold Twig, has been using Mr. Everett for his own son's misdemeanors for years."

The judge had come alive, rapping with his little hammer.

"Stick to the case at hand, Mr. Barns. We're here to discuss the aggravated assault and attempted murder charges—not some fictitious witch-hunt on a respected police officer."

Even though Dad was friends with Patrick Blake, we wouldn't earn any special treatment. Which was a good thing and a bad thing. I was glad it would be fair for both parties but was sick of evil managing to hoodwink good far too often.

Greg had snickered, pleased Larry had been told off.

Penn stiffened, his shoulders high, begging me to massage away his stress if only I was allowed to lean forward and put my hands on him.

I'd probably be arrested for touching the defendant.

I'd sat on my fingers, turning my attention from the man who turned my heart molten to Larry.

He'd merely smiled at the judge with his hands crossed politely. "It's all linked, sir. And I can prove it."

Goosebumps darted down my spine for the fiftieth time since he'd said that. My mind snapped out of the last few hours in court, slapping me back into the present.

Sitting on plastic seats outside the courtroom, holding a flimsy cup of coffee thanks to Fleur shoving it in my hands, I hoped and prayed that Greg would do the right thing.

I would've given anything to speak with him. To find out what his decision was and if Penn would be free or convicted.

*There must be a way.*

"Court resumes in five minutes." An employee stuck his head into the hallway where we gathered beneath monolithic arches and portraits of dead judges.

Minglers stood, gathering handbags and finishing coffee dregs.

"Ready?" I smiled bright as Stewie climbed to his feet, shuffling toward the double doors where we'd endure yet more torture while waiting for Penn to be freed.

He shrugged, his eyes large and worried. "I guess so."

Fleur and I exchanged looks.

My arm found its way over Stewie's shoulders, hugging him close. "It will all work out. You'll see."

He wriggled under my embrace but didn't push me away. He wore the suit Penn had bought from Belle Elle—a smart little man ready to battle for his friend. "I dunno. Shit happens."

I didn't reprimand him for his language.

Because he was right.

We might have every truth and honesty on our side, but at the end of the day…shit happened.

And there was nothing we could do about it.

# Chapter Thirty-Seven

# Penn

*SMUG FUCKING BASTARD.*

Greg sat next to his zombie of a lawyer, not even bothering to hide his arrogance.

Larry prowled in front, speaking to the court, blocking me from trying to kill Greg with my eyes.

My gaze met Larry's from the witness stand, remembering this was my time to be cordial and well-spoken, not fuming with fury at the bastard who'd stolen another five months of my life. Five months away from Elle. Five months away from happiness.

Larry interrupted my hate. "In your own words, can you describe that night in question?"

*That night.*

*What night?*

Oh yeah, he'd been talking about the charity gala. I sat up straight, glancing at the jury with a soft smile. "Ever since my success, I've given what I now have to those who don't have anything. I know what it's like to have nothing, and it's a driving force of mine to give them a chance like another gave one to me."

I gave Larry a look crammed full of gratitude. It might be years since he'd taken me in, but when I thought about what he'd given me, motherfucking tears almost came to my eyes.

"So the event was your charity?" Larry asked.

"Yes."

"What is it called?"

*Shit.*

I glanced at Elle. I hadn't told her this part. Would she think I was an idiot? I'd gone through so many names for many months. After the penny stock I'd invested in hit an all-time high—going from five cents a share to seventy-five dollars in a matter of months—a majority of the profits were reinvested into the stock, gradually buying more and more until I became the main shareholder of a company that recently got bought out by the CIA for an undisclosed, obscene figure.

After that success, I couldn't just let the money sit there.

I was set for life.

I might as well help others as well as myself.

I knew I wanted to help people but didn't have a clue what to call the charity.

I'd discounted the more generic names like *Homeless No More.* Or *Roof Over Your Head.* Things that would say what the charity entailed. But the charity wouldn't have existed without Larry's faith in me and Elle's ability to reach into my chest that night and start my heart beating for other things.

Things like her.

Things I could never deserve unless I got my shit together.

I cleared my throat. "It's called Chocolate Runaway."

Chocolate for that kiss.

Runaway because if she hadn't, we would never have met and my life would be so fucking different.

I might not be sitting here on trial, but then again, I might never have gotten free from the last arrest because I wouldn't have had the gumption to take Larry up on his offer.

I wouldn't have been ready to fight because I didn't have anything to fight for. And I definitely wouldn't have taken him up on his offer to stay in his house and obey his rules. I would've run back to the life I knew, not thinking I deserved anything better.

Larry hid his smile. He'd given me such a ribbing when I came home that day with the name registered and proud as fucking punch. I noticed some of the jurors smiling while others rolled their eyes.

My hands curled. "It's personal. I stand by the name just like I stand by the millions of donations the charity has been able to provide."

Larry nodded. "It's an honorable achievement."

"No, it's an ongoing dream. Even while I've been incorrectly imprisoned, the charity has still run and provided for countless of homeless kids."

A few jurors looked at each then glared at Greg.

*Score one for me.*

Larry marched in front of the witness box where I sat. "So

that night, you and Elle were happy?"

Goddammit, I wanted to skip over this part.

It wouldn't exactly paint me in a good light, but Larry had told me to trust him, so I did. "Not exactly." Inhaling, I said loudly, "I'd lied to her. I'd entered into a relationship with her all while letting her believe I was a businessman with no ties to her past. She didn't know I was the homeless man who'd rescued her from two attackers three years ago. I lied because I was hurt that she hadn't come for me. I was pissed off because I'd developed feelings for her and thought she didn't feel the same way."

"What way is that?"

"In love."

The jury shuffled.

I kept my eyes averted. Right now, I sounded like a fucking pussy. Greg chuckled while the judge hammered his gavel. "What link does this questioning have to the case in point, Mr. Barns?"

Larry stormed to the judge, craning his neck. "It's introducing the accused, so the jury can make a better informed decision, your honor."

For a second, I thought he'd overrule, but he reluctantly nodded. "Get on with it."

"Thank you." Larry returned to me. "So that night in question, Ms. Charlston thought she'd figured out who you were and left before you could explain she'd concluded wrong?"

"Yes."

"And you chased after her?"

"I did."

"Only she didn't answer her door or phone, correct?"

"That's correct."

"And you gave her some space as you believed she was upset with you?"

"It wasn't easy, but yes, that was my reasoning."

Larry nodded importantly. "However, you changed your opinions a little later that night, didn't you?"

"Yes." I glowered at Greg. "I woke to being beaten by two men Mr. Hobson had paid off to scare me away from Elle. They said she was with him now and to back off."

"And *was* she with him?" Larry asked.

"No. She'd confided in me that she didn't want anything to do with him."

Larry headed to his desk and collected photos of the day I was placed in custody. Sharing them with the jury, he said, "These are photos of Penn's condition received by Greg's courtesy."

"Incorrect evidence." Greg's lawyer stood up, planting her hands on the table. "Those injuries were given by Greg as he fought for his life while Penn tried to murder him."

The judge looked between the two lawyers. "Is that true?"

Larry shook his head. "No, your honor. I'm sure a few scratches were from the fight, but the majority were from being beaten awake hours earlier. I have doctors reports stating how long the contusions and bruises needed to form and discolor."

He picked up another piece of paper and handed it to the judge. "In his opinion, the discoloration on Penn's ribs, face, and other limbs were six to ten hours old before he had a chance to detain Mr. Hobson."

The judge accepted the evidence with a nod.

Larry turned to me. "In your own words, Mr. Everett, can you describe what happened when you found Mr. Hobson?"

"With pleasure." I bared my teeth. "Ms. Charlston was in chains. He had her bent over a couch about to rape her."

"Not true!" Greg blurted. "She'd just agreed to go to the bedroom with me."

"She knew I was sneaking up behind you, you fool!" I replied before the judge could yell for us to shut the hell up. "She used misdirection so I could incapacitate you."

"Silence!" Patrick Blake commanded. "Another outburst and you'll both be thrown back in the cells."

Greg crossed his arms, slouching like a pissed off child.

I sat taller, embracing fearlessness because I'd done the right thing. I wasn't the one lying.

*For a change.*

"So you don't deny you touched Mr. Hobson?" Larry waited patiently, his eyebrow rose.

I knew the answer he wanted. What we'd schooled over. *'Yes, I did. But only what was necessary to release Ms. Charlston and put Greg under citizen's arrest.'*

But I was done being polite. I wouldn't waste any more time. I'd tell the truth but in my own words, not his. "I didn't just touch him. I punched him. Multiple times."

The court gasped as one.

I turned my vision to the jury. "He hurt my girl. He was about to *rape* my girl. I wasn't going to have a conversation with him and ask politely if he'd stop abusing her. How many of you would have done that, instead of attacking the asshole who hurt your loved one?"

The jurors broke silence, muttering loudly amongst themselves. The reporters in the back pews started asking questions, adding to the mayhem.

Court propriety broke down.

The judge hammered his gavel. "Enough! Quiet down. All of you!"

Greg stood up, adding to the mix. "He's lying. She was mine. She loves me. Don't listen—"

"Enough!" the court officer bellowed.

A fight broke out between two jurors for reasons unknown but most likely had something to do with my question about what they would do and their mixed opinions on the matter.

"Quiet!" Judge Blake boomed.

The chaos only grew worse.

Desperate for order, he yelled, "Right, court adjourned. Reconvene tomorrow. Go home. All of you!"

And just like that, my time in the limelight was over.

*Back to prison I go.*

# Chapter Thirty-Eight

# Elle

LARRY AND I stood on the steps of the courthouse.

Fleur waited ahead with Stewie, bribing his attention with a stick of chewing gum.

I'd asked her to. I needed Larry on his own because I had a plan.

After the disaster in the courtroom, I couldn't leave things to chance anymore. I couldn't let my heart gallop and my stomach sizzle with fear that Greg would be utterly vindictive and testify against Penn with every viciousness he had in him.

I couldn't watch Penn be handcuffed and marched back to prison like this afternoon. I couldn't survive with one conjugal visit a year and weekly phone calls.

Penn was innocent.

Greg was wrong.

He had to be stopped.

Threats wouldn't work.

But I knew something that would.

"You have to get me a meeting with him, Larry. Tonight."

Larry slammed to a stop. "Penn? No can do. He'll be under lock-down now."

"No, not him. Greg."

His eyebrows disappeared into his salt and pepper hair. "What?"

"I want to speak to Greg."

"I don't—" He pursed his lips. "Why?"

"I need to try something. Before his turn to testify tomorrow."

Soon, it would be my turn to testify against Greg. I still had that trump card over him, but I doubted that would make him change. He was too naïve to understand what life in prison would do to him. He was too used to being the spoiled little rich boy and given everything he wanted.

He believed he was untouchable.

I didn't have the time or power to show him otherwise, but I could dangle a carrot he valued more than his own life to change his mind about Penn.

"What are you thinking?" Larry's eyes narrowed. "Don't tamper with things you don't understand, Elle."

In the past few months of working late and getting to know Larry, I had great affection for this man who had saved Penn. Who had given him money, a home, kindness, a family. A true benefactor in every sense of the word—offering security after a lifetime of none.

But he was also nosy, and I didn't have time to satisfy that curiosity.

"Can you do it or not?"

He shrugged. "I can't promise anything. He's probably been transferred back to corrections."

"Can you try?"

He frowned but nodded. "I'll do my best." Gripping my hand, he squeezed kindly then marched back into the courthouse.

\* \* \* \* \*

"Greg?"

I clutched the phone tight.

Larry hadn't been able to work his magic and get me a face-to-face meeting, but he had managed a two-minute phone call.

No more.

No less.

I had one hundred and twenty seconds to make Greg an offer he couldn't refuse. And do it in a way that didn't sound like bribery, blackmail, or any other illegal action that could end up with me taking his place in lock-up.

I didn't care it would be recorded.

I didn't care it could backfire if they decided to pull the records and use it against me.

Penn's life was on me. I would do anything I could to save it. Did that make me stupid? Most likely. Did that make me reckless? Most definitely.

But I was done playing nice, and Greg endangered everything I held as priceless.

"Elle?" Greg snapped. "What the hell do you want?"

I didn't waste time. "Tell the truth."

I wanted to barter with him. To say if he dropped his statement, I'd drop mine. That I wouldn't press charges because I didn't care about justice for me, just freedom for Penn.

But I couldn't—not on the phone.

Every word was a damn minefield. "Tell the truth, Greg, and I'll change your life."

A long pause then he finally bit. "How? How can you change my life?"

"I'll give you fifteen million. I'll put it into an account that will earn interest until you're released. You'll never have to work again."

"Is this some sort of joke?"

"No joke." My fingers turned white around the phone. "All you have to do is tell the truth."

*Retract that Penn was trying to kill you. Stop saying I loved you. Be a man for once in your damn life.*

"Be honest, Greg. And I'll send you the bank account number the moment court is adjourned."

My heart raced, bucking for his reply.

Finally, the words I feared I'd never hear came back.

"Twenty and you've got yourself a deal."

I didn't even hesitate. "Deal."

# Chapter Thirty-Nine

# Penn

GREG TOOK THE stand the next day, his gaze glaring into mine.

Freedom practically slapped me on the back and said *'see ya later, buddy.'*

The way he licked his lips—rubbing his jaw with deliberate poise as if he couldn't wait to get my ass thrown into jail where I'd never see Elle again.

His lawyer stalked in front of him like a rickety stick insect, her red lips barely moving as she asked him clipped questions.

"Did you love Ms. Charlston?"

"Did you have a happy childhood growing up together?"

"Did you get along with her father?"

"Did you kidnap and rape with the intention of forced marriage and company takeover?"

Such generic, everyday questions…apart from the last one.

Greg delivered his answers in fluid, concise ways.

I had to hand it to him. He sounded sane and came across as any hard working individual and not a greed-hungry psychopath.

"Yes, I did. Still do."

"Yes, we did many things together. Picnics, bike rides, you name it."

"Of course, Joe Charlston and I go way back."

"No, I did not. That wasn't my intention at all."

Time ticked onward. Jurors yawned a little.

Elle's eyes seared me from behind, and Larry didn't move in his chair.

The courtroom had turned from an explosive kettle yesterday to a stagnant pressure cooker today.

Tension gathered the longer Greg blah-blahed on the stand. I felt sick just waiting for that one question. That simple phrase guaranteed to launch him into a tirade destined to send me to hell. *'Did Penn Everett try to kill you?'*

I thought I wanted to get this farce over with. But being this close to a guilty verdict—again for something I didn't do—turned my heart to icy stone, trying to protect itself before the inevitable happened.

Already my ears rang with the jurors' conclusions.

Guilty.

Guilty.

*Guilty.*

I froze with visions of the judge bringing his fist down with a life sentence without parole.

Sweat trickled down my back the longer Greg and his lawyer enjoyed their question-answer dance.

And then, the question arrived, blaring like a freight train, smoking with authority ready to steal any happiness I might've earned.

His red-lipped lawyer muttered, "And do you, Greg Hobson, stand by your statement that Penn Everett went to that cabin to kill you? That you had reason to believe he'd plotted your murder and intended to carry it out?"

Greg glanced at me then Larry. His eyes flew behind me, no doubt looking at Elle.

The sound of fabric shifting on seats itched my ears. The entire courtroom didn't breathe.

I desperately wanted to turn around, to grab Elle's hand and thank her for everything she did and apologize that it wasn't enough. That my past had ruined everything anyway.

But I couldn't tear my eyes off Greg. Some masochist part of me needed to sear this moment into my brain forever. I'd use it as fuel in any prison brawls I had to win. I'd punch and punch and *punch* some asshole and pretend it was Greg.

I almost stood up and held my hands out for the cuffs, tasting the inevitable.

But something fucking miraculous happened.

Greg leaned back, shrugging like a toddler caught with his hand in the cookie jar. "You know what? I've had time to reflect on what happened that night, and I *think* I might have got it wrong."

*Fucking what?*

My chair legs screeched as I scooted forward. Did that really just happen? I needed a replay. To press rewind and see if my brain had fritzed or if this was real life.

Greg relaxed into his tale, bringing his leg up to cock over his knee as if he spoke to his brethren at a bar not a jury in court. "I didn't lie—I honestly thought he did want to kill me—but I'm a reformed man and recently been using the downtime to truly assess what I thought and what was real."

Christ, he had the jury eating out of his goddamn hand.

Everyone sat up, the jaded glaze fading from their eyes as if grateful he was about to tell them exactly what they should believe in so this sham could be over, and they could go back to their families.

Greg sighed heavily, acting the perfect grieving witness. "I won't deny that Penn Everett hurt me. Shit, I still have the bruises to prove it, and he did put me in the hospital—those are facts." He smiled at the jury. "My ribs were cracked and larynx bruised. The doctors said I was lucky to still have a voice box."

I rolled my eyes.

*Fucking, please.*

"But Everett had a point yesterday. I would've gone crazy over any dude touching my girl and thrown a few punches, too."

My mouth hung open.

*Did I just hear that correctly?*

*Wait, that can't have just happened?*

*I'm in an alternative universe.*

*I've stepped into the Twilight Zone.*

Elle's softest gasp sounded behind me, dotting my skin with goosebumps.

Larry sat ramrod straight, his fingernails scratching into the table.

I was glad I wasn't the only one fucking stupefied by this change of events.

*What the hell is going on here?*

"He got it wrong that I was raping her." Greg's face turned black with familiar greed then lightened to innocent once again. "We were role playing." He leaned into the jury as if it was a secret between them. "Ms. Charlston likes a bit of bondage, if you know what—"

"Stay on topic, Mr. Hobson," the judge muttered.

Greg held up his hands. "Hey, kink isn't on trial here, is it?"

A juror or two snickered.

Judge Blake scowled. "Continue without the sexual references that may or may not be true."

Greg nodded. "Yes, your honor." Sitting tall, he added, "Penn was jealous of Elle and me. Elle was going to break it off with him to be with me—"

Another noise came from behind me. A small keen like a broken kitten. The chemistry between Elle and I exploded as I felt her tension, endured her panic.

"Overruled." Larry stood. "We have multiple witness statements from Ms. Charlston's bodyguard, father, and other staff that state that is incorrect. Ms. Charlston and Mr. Everett were engaged to be married." Larry shot me a quick smile. "They still are."

"Sustained. Strike from the record," the judge commanded. Looming over Greg from his podium, Patrick Blake swiped his forehead as if this entire trial caused him a migraine. "I suggest you stick to the facts and not make-believe, Mr. Hobson."

Greg chuckled. "Fine. All I have to say then is Mr. Everett didn't try to kill me. I revoke my statement."

The judge's mouth fell open. "Are you sure?"

Greg looked at Elle again. Something passed over his face—half with loathing and half with utmost satisfaction. "I'm sure."

Larry stood up just as Greg's lawyer spluttered, "But—"

Larry clapped his hands. "In that case, I motion for my client to be freed from the incorrect charges immediately. As for the other evidence about corruption and unlawful imprisonment by Arnold Twig, I'd like to progress with pressing charges at a later date with intentions to expunge my client's record."

My head swam.

I felt fucking faint.

*Christ, don't faint like an idiot.*

I couldn't follow what had just happened.

I stood up on shaky legs only for the judge to bark at me to sit down.

I did, swiveling in my chair to face Elle.

She beamed with a happy smile.

"Did you do this?" I whispered.

She shook her head, tears glittering in her blue eyes.

*She's lying.*

All I wanted to do was kiss her stupid. She'd done something—regardless of her denial.

There was no way Greg would've retracted his desire to see

me rot unless he'd been given something he valued more than making me suffer.

Understanding suddenly filled me.

*Money.*

I pursed my lips, tilting my head for her to enlighten me.

She merely bit her bottom lip to prevent glowing like the damn sun.

The glint in her gaze told me all I needed to know.

*I'm right.*

She'd bribed him.

Fuck knew how much she'd promised to save my stupid ass, but she'd done it.

I was...free.

I spun around, facing the court.

Wait, *was* I free?

Nothing had been said.

Only scrambles of papers and impatient reporters to deliver a story to their editors. The jurors mumbled amongst themselves as if pissed that not only would they not get to contemplate a verdict but they'd also been robbed of delivering it.

With no accuser or statement and a thousand pieces of evidence about Arnold Twig, Sean Twig, and my past riddled with bad luck, nothing else could happen.

I was a good person—contrary to what most believed.

"Quiet!" The judge brought down his gavel. "In the case between Greg Hobson versus Penn Everett, I hereby dismiss all claims. The case is closed. Mr. Everett is innocent. You are free to go." In the same breath, he looked at Greg. "Mr. Hobson, you shall return and continue with the state as your host while awaiting trial for your own court case against Ms. Charlston. Until then, I hope everyone obeys the law and stops wasting public time and money." He stood in his robe then stomped down the podium.

There was no fanfare or clapping.

Only the surreal silence that it was over.

Greg threw me a sizzling stare full of contempt even while his fingers counted imaginary dollars. His lawyer stomped off with her satchel thrown over her shoulder. Larry grabbed me in a bear hug. Stewie wrapped himself around my legs. And Elle grabbed my face and kissed me.

She broke the spell.

She popped the bubble and proved it hadn't been a dream.

It was real.

It had happened.
I was *free*.

# Chapter Forty

# Elle

THE PRACTICAL THING after being released from jail would be to go for dinner with those who fought by your side. To answer the flocks of seagulls as news reporters begged for scraps of how I entered the court this morning with only Fleur and Stewie by my side and left in the afternoon wrapped in Penn's arms.

And we did do those things.

We stopped and kissed for the papers. We waved away questions and grabbed a quick celebratory drink with Stewie, Larry, and Fleur. We didn't think about the upcoming fight with Arnold Twig, and we didn't worry about my turn to testify at court against Greg.

He was back in prison, rolling in promised cash, waiting for his hearing.

I had no doubt he wouldn't care at all.

He wouldn't care because he had twenty million reasons to be happy.

And I didn't care because I had twenty million reasons to be grateful Penn was free. That he could stand beside me without shackles. That we could kiss whenever we wanted and whisper about a life we could claim rather than lament about the one we'd had stolen.

We allowed ourselves to celebrate the present without the future robbing us of our hard-earned joy.

My father called Penn to congratulate him, but he didn't join us for food due to indigestion brought on by stress of the trial.

I ordered him to bed, comforted to know Marnie, our

housekeeper, would be there to keep him happy.

Steve didn't join us for dinner either. Technically, today was not a happy day for him, as Greg would remain in prison without bail until his court date—and then who knew how long he'd serve.

But sitting at a table at a local bar with generic coasters, beer-soaked carpet, and red-leather booths in dim lighting, we toasted to Penn and grew drunk on the relief at having him back.

The celebration started off as a group endeavor. Penn accepted hugs from everyone. He chatted and joked, but he always had one hand touching me—my wrist, my hand, my hip.

After an hour, electricity laced those touches, zapping my belly, liquefying my insides. I couldn't prevent the way my heart imitated a bowling ball, knocking down my ribs as if they were skittle pins.

No one else noticed but my cheeks slowly glowed—and not from alcohol. Desire for him bubbled inside until the barest brush sent a lustful convulsion through me.

Need built and built until it was unbearable.

Half an hour later, Fleur whispered in my ear that she was taking off because she had a feeling Penn and I weren't going to be around much longer.

I playfully scolded her then kissed her goodbye.

I needed to be alone with Penn, but I wouldn't be rude and rob the others from sharing in this hard-earned party.

So, despite fireworks fizzing in my blood, we ordered French fries and prawn twisters. We downed more drinks. And when I excused myself to go to the bathroom, Penn found me like he had the night at the Palm Politics.

He didn't say a word.

He slammed me hard against a wall and kissed me so deep, I almost combusted. His tongue was totally sinful. His hands absolutely sexual. His cock throbbing as he wedged it firm against me with a glitter in his gaze. "I need to be alone with you. Now."

Words were hard to come by. He'd incinerated my insides. Burned my synapses. I merely nodded and allowed him to take my hand.

He dragged me back to the table of partiers where we said a guilty goodbye.

Then we caught the first taxi we saw back to his place.

* * * * *

"The blood's gone."

A random thing to notice the moment I stepped into Penn's

apartment, but my nerves jangled. I hadn't been in his place since the day he'd rescued me and started to tell me the truth, only for the police to rip him away for the second time.

"You're right." His calculating eyes, which once made me nervous, but now only revealed his keen intelligence, flickered from spotless kitchen to tidy living room. No bed sheets strewn across the floor, no blood, no signs of a fight. "Larry must've arranged a cleaning crew."

I hid a grin, kicking off my black heels and placing my handbag on the kitchen counter. "I'm glad. I don't exactly feel like doing housework." I hadn't meant it to come out so sexual, but it did. My voice was scratchy with desire, the need to touch him with no more rules or cages unbearable.

Only, he didn't attack me like he had on the night of our conjugal visit. He didn't pad barefoot toward me sensually. He merely stood in the center of his home and jammed his hands into his pockets the same way he did the very first time we met.

Knowing what I knew now, I understood why.

It was his form of protection against others and himself.

His arms bunched beneath the white shirt he'd rolled up to his elbows; black slacks hung off his hips too big, and his fists balled in pockets that made my heart sob with familiarity.

Despite the events keeping us apart, we'd grown to know each other. I knew enough to predict how he would react. And he knew enough to preempt my answer.

We stood staring at each other as if we couldn't believe this was real. That we were back here, alone, and unsupervised. Free to do whatever we damn well wanted.

I smiled, suddenly shy and overwhelmed by how simple but heavily charged the moment had become.

Penn's lips matched mine in a sweet smirk, the stress, worry, and panic of the trial finally slipping off his shoulders, down his arms, and into his pockets. Instead of loose change and old receipts, those slacks held five months of jail time, so Penn no longer had to.

It was me who moved first.

Undoing the buttons on my dark gray blazer, I stepped toward him. My pantyhosed feet slicked over the hardwood floor, making me shiver. Penn didn't move as I released the final button and allowed the jacket to puddle down my arms to the floor.

Never breaking eye contact, I reached behind me and undid the zipper on my skirt. Running my hands over my hips, I pushed the slinky lining down my body, wriggling slowly to ease the fabric off.

Penn clenched his jaw, his chest flexing as he forced himself to keep his hands in his pockets. "Elle…" He bit his bottom lip as his eyes glued to my fingers gliding up my body to undo the tiny buttons of my pale cream shirt.

I had no plan of seduction. I hadn't come here with the idea of stripping for him. But the way he watched me, drank me, breathed me.

God, it was the best aphrodisiac.

My stomach fluttered beneath the buttons as I undid them one by one. My core clenched as he let out a long ragged groan of pure male appreciation.

Yet he didn't touch me.

His lips parted to breathe heavier. His body swayed as if summoned by some invisible force to link with mine, but he permitted me to finish whatever striptease I wanted.

I had no urge to speak as I undid the last button and slid the shirt down my arms, letting it cascade on top of my jacket and skirt. Words were cheap when our stares said everything we ever needed to hear.

*I want you.*
*You're mine.*
*I need you.*
*I'm yours.*
*We're free.*
*We're together.*

Standing before him in my cream bra and panties decorated with black lace stars with garters and stockings, I felt stronger than I ever had before.

I'd worn a suit to court to borrow authority from cotton and silk but stripped of them now, left only in lace and pantyhose, I was more powerful, more invincible, more desirable than any outfit in the world.

Penn sucked in a gasp. His voice teasing a whisper. "You're so beautiful."

His words touched me, but his hands didn't. They remained in his pockets as if the moment he pulled them free, he'd reach for me, and this precious memory would shatter into passion.

I needed to see him. I wanted to run my fingers along his chest and assure myself he was here. That this wasn't some incredible fantasy.

Deleting the final step between us, I pressed my fingertips to his belly, relishing his sharp inhale.

Beneath my touch lived muscle and sinew—bone of the man I'd given my heart to and hoped he'd keep forever.

Tugging on his shirt, I slowly pulled it from his waistband, letting it hang roguishly undone and handsome, curling around his hands still wedged deep in his slacks.

He stopped breathing as I undid the bottom button then another, slowly working my way up his body, allowing the cotton to stay close together until I reached the top.

The courts didn't give him a tie, and the second the last button was undone, I invaded his warmth. Inserting my hands, I washed them over his smooth chest, his pecs, up his shoulders, and down his back until the shirt rippled down his arms to hang where his hands still remained wedged at his thighs.

The white against black looked as if I'd cut off angel wings. As if I'd corrupted a god and made him trade a celestial existent for lowly all because I wanted him.

My mouth watered to suck his skin.

So I did.

Leaning forward, I pressed the softest kisses over his breastbone, working my way to his nipple. As my mouth latched over him, he grunted, bowing backward, sacrificing himself to whatever pleasure I wanted to give him.

He trembled, his toes gripping the floor until they turned white as my tongue circled his nipple and my hands trailed down his belly.

His erection tented his slacks, but I didn't reach for it. Not yet.

Undoing the cheap synthetic belt, a ball of lust replaced my heart as he shuddered so hard—part from keeping himself in check and not reaching for me, but mostly, from what I did to him.

From my touch. My lips. My methodical way of stripping him of everything that'd happened.

I didn't just remove his clothes.

I removed his past.

I tore off the months of imprisonment.

I slipped off his lies and half-truths.

Piece by piece, I revealed the man I'd always known existed.

Someone kind but ruthless. Supportive but possessive. Intelligent but quick tempered.

He was an angel and monster in one.

Just human with perfections and imperfections.

"Elle…" he breathed as I undid the button of his slacks then slowly pulled his zipper down. With my bare feet, I moved my skirt and jacket to wedge in front of me then kneeled on the soft padding before him.

"Christ…" He sucked in a gasp as I left his slacks open, circling my fingers around his wrists. His hands remained locked tight in his pockets, but with a soft tug, he allowed me to lift his right one, giving me utmost control.

Never saying a word, I undid the cuff button so his shirt could fall then pressed a kiss onto his palm.

He shivered as I let go, moving toward his left hand.

Once again, he willingly gave me control as I pulled it gently from his pocket. His slacks fell around his ankles, leaving him in tight white boxer-briefs that only highlighted how hard and thick he was.

My mouth went dry as I undid his final button, undoing the cuff around his left hand. The moment it was free, the shirt fell, joining the rest of discarded clothing.

Only one piece left on him. It was a piece I savored as I pressed a kiss, blowing hot air on his shaft through the soft cotton.

He jerked, his hands (now with nothing to use as imprisonment) landed in my hair. "Shit, Elle…what are you doing to me?" His voice was faraway, in a land where nothing bad—no nights alone, no days unsafe, no cold or fear or hunger could find him.

He was mine now.

Tomorrow, I could cook him breakfast like I'd always wanted. I could keep him close, protect him for protecting me.

My hands wrapped around his hipbones, skating fingers over the tight elastic of his boxer-briefs. With my heart lodged in my throat at how turned on I was—how wet, how hot, how heavy and ready—I pulled his underwear down.

His quads clenched until delicious muscle rippled beneath perfect hair-sparse skin. His head fell back with a tattered groan as my hands stayed with his boxers, landing around his ankles but my mouth…that went on its own quest.

I opened and found his crown. I moaned at the taste, at how warm he was, how hard, how satin sheathed steel.

His legs buckled, his fingers digging harder onto my head—not to take control but to support himself, so he didn't collapse.

"Holy Christ," he groaned as I sat taller on my knees and swallowed him deep. My fingers came up, left hand cupping his balls, right hand gripping his girth.

I lapped over the thick veins coursing down his length. I sucked with long pulls, wanting to drive him to the pinnacle within seconds.

Penn turned mute, soundless. His fingernails scraped my scalp as he held himself back, his self-control fraying with every second.

Pumping his base, I licked with a feathering tongue. My tummy coiled tight, taking pleasure from giving pleasure.

His spine locked as a ripple of bliss worked up his shaft, coating my mouth with pre-cum. I wanted him to come. I wanted him to let go and relax.

But he captured my chin, bringing my eyes to his. His heartbreakingly gorgeous face was savage with self-control. "I'm not coming in your mouth, Elle."

I unsheathed my teeth and bit softly.

His hips jerked forward as I sucked him off.

I did what I'd been dreaming off since he made me get on my knees in my office then told me my two minutes were up.

It wasn't a competition to show him how well I'd learned my lesson, but if I could make him come undone in two minutes like this, I would gloat for life.

His eyes shadowed to coal black. "Fuck." He shuddered as I sucked him again, his throat working as he swallowed. "Answer me one question."

I flicked my tongue over his crown, nodding permission.

He swallowed again, croaking, "Are you wet?"

Was I wet? I was drenched. I was so turned on; I could come with the slightest whisper over my clit.

I nodded.

My tongue licked him, adored him, and that was the breaking point for Penn.

One second, I was in control on my knees. I had him by the balls—literally. The next, I was tossed over his shoulder with his hand spanking my ass and the floor moving fast beneath my eyes.

"You'll pay for that, Elle." Swatting me again, he stalked into his bedroom.

From my vantage point, I noticed the black bag still holding the dildo samples sitting on his dresser along with a freshly made bed full of white sheets and pillows.

Pristine, virginal, until he threw me onto the mattress and cupped my jaw in his hands. I sat on the edge while Penn slammed to his knees. The reversal of our roles sent my heart spinning wild like an out of control ballerina.

His dark, delicious eyes speared mine. "I've wanted you since the first moment I saw you. I want you so damn much it interferes with my head, my heart, my very fucking existence. Yet you fight for me, you bribe my enemies for me, you deliver my freedom, and then you get on your knees and pleasure me so fucking selflessly?"

He shook his head, anger dragging his brow over his eyes. "No. You deserve to be worshipped, Elle. You deserve pleasure and protection and everything your heart deserves."

His features flickered with nervousness. "I hope to God you want me as much as I want you. My shitty life has taught me that the things I want the most are the first to be taken away. I can't let that happen with you."

He kissed my lips, inhaling hard, his fingers shaking. "I've done things I wish I could undo. I'm not proud of who I've been, but, Elle, fuck, if you can stand by me in prison, if you can stand with me in court, then I will stand by you for the rest of your life."

I swayed forward, slinging my arms over his shoulders and grabbing a fistful of his hair. His obvious need to show me how he felt, his insatiable desire tainting the room—it all matched the depth of emotion I held for him.

It was endless. It was new. It was our future.

"Kiss me."

He froze as if to argue. But then his mouth smashed against mine. His teeth caught my bottom lip, his tongue plunging as if to bypass any more conversation and make me drink his vows.

I crab-walked backward on my elbows until I had enough mattress to lie down. Penn followed, stalking over me on his hands and knees, his mouth never ceasing in its dominance of mine.

His fingers traced my bra, then my naked belly, before teasing the topline of my panties.

His palm crept between my legs, grabbing me firm. "I'm going to fuck you for days, Elle. We're not leaving this bed until we're boneless and on death's door from orgasms."

I moaned as he ripped my panties down my legs then unhooked the garter belts to unroll my pantyhose.

I arched my back for him to undo my bra, and when I lay naked, same as him, his fingers found me again.

This time, there was no lace, no boundary.

Grinding his erection onto my hip, he sank a finger unapologetically deep.

My mouth popped wide. My body bucked in his control.

"Let go, Elle. Forget about rules and society. Ignore what civilization says we should be and how we should act." A second finger joined the first, filling me, stretching me as his cock throbbed hot and hard against my hip. "Let go and let me see you. Cry for me. Scream for me." His voice slipped into volcanic ash. "Beg for me."

My body rose to meet his thumb as he pressed my clit. "Penn..."

"Penn what?" he growled in my ear, his fingers fucking me, punishing me with pleasure.

My body surged to meet then bowed away. He pressed harder on the tiny bundle of nerves, making my eyes water, and a climax twist into a ravaging storm.

"I'm—I'm—"

I was so close to coming already. The sparkling transformation of my womb and spine warned me that it would happen.

I couldn't stop it.

Because that was what Penn did to me. The magic he held over me—the same magic he'd had from the start.

"You're?" He nipped my throat, his fingers driving faster. "Finish your sentence. Tell me." His thumb gave me no escape. I gave up trying to move away from pleasure and threw myself head first into it.

"I'm coming." I thought it would come out as a whisper.

It came out as a scream as I did exactly what he'd told me to do and let loose.

My body took control with the speed and power of a runaway train. The orgasm grabbed me, squeezed me, obliterated me.

Clenches and waves, I milked Penn's fingers until I moaned unintelligently.

He kissed me deep, soft, languid as I came down from the most piercing high.

"I knew you could come fast." His lips caressed my cheek, moving to my jaw. "That first night when you said yes—in the alley before I gave you back to David to take you home. Remember?"

I blinked, dragging myself back to human rather than liquid

bliss. "When you made me come against the wall?"

A smug glint filled his gaze. "Yes."

I shared a piece of me, giving him access to who I was. "I worried you'd take me that night. That I'd lose my virginity against a brick wall."

"Did you prefer losing it in this very bed?"

"I did." I smiled.

"You came that night too with my cock inside you." His eyes rolled as if reliving heaven. "Fuck, you were so receptive. Have you always been that way? That sensitive?"

I nodded. "It comes in handy when I'm on my own and need a quickie."

"You'll never be on your own again."

I arched up, seeking his lips. "You too."

I wasn't prepared for the way his arms latched around me with a vicious hold. He hugged me as if thanking me for becoming his. Telling me with actions that loneliness had been his cross to bear for so long, and now he no longer had to carry it.

His lips sought mine again.

And our conversation ended.

Just like that.

# Chapter Forty-One

# Penn

I'D WANTED TO make this last.

I wanted to memorize every inch of Elle so she wasn't just a girl in my past who I'd mistakenly despised or a woman in my present I was fucking.

She was my future.

She was my home, and I wanted to know every freckle and birthmark, every ticklish spot and turn-on zone.

But that was before she sucked me off then came in two seconds flat as if she couldn't stand having my hands on her and not reward me with every drop of her pleasure.

Slow would have to come later. Along with fun and toys and games and all the other exciting stuff we had to look forward to.

This was a hello after months of painful separation.

I wanted her heart thundering against mine, body to body, soul to motherfucking soul.

Without a word, I wedged my hips between her spread legs. My cock throbbed to come. My back locked as Elle grabbed the base of me, guiding me to her entrance.

Her eyes blazed blue as she rubbed my crown through her wetness, torturing both of us, coating me in her orgasm, begging me to do whatever I damn well wanted.

And I wanted.

So fucking much.

She was passionate, free, a lover and friend and partner. She was no longer a stranger or a spoiled brat I'd hated.

*She's mine.*

My lips locked together as I pressed the first inch inside her. A low, feminine moan echoed in her chest. Her legs opened wider, showing me everything, making me drunk and embarrassingly close to losing control.

Our gazes never unlocked; I looked at her with utmost awe. She bit her bottom lip, reading me better than I could read myself. Knowing I'd reached my limit on gentle and needed to be a beast.

She clenched around me, giving me permission to let go.

Slamming forward, I slid straight inside her. She spread wide and wet. A cry tumbled from her mouth and into mine as I kissed her fast and messy.

My arms went around her shoulders and nape, cuddling her close even while my hips attacked her.

The bed rocked, our breathing tore, her legs looped over my back, her ankles digging into my spine.

"Jesus," I bit out.

"Yes…God, yes…" Her fingers landed in my hair, twisting almost cruelly, adding fine-edged pain.

Christ, she shouldn't have done that.

I lost it.

Utterly fucking lost it.

My body was hard as stone, my stomach slapping against hers, my balls drawn up in preparation of shooting everything I had into this woman.

Her pussy clung to me every time I withdrew to slam inside her again. Her back arched until her breasts stuck to my chest, and I held her so close, gluing us together, slick with sweat and need.

The friction was too much. Every wet ridge of her, every hard inch of me. I pushed up, she pushed down; I thrust in, she welcomed. She rocked harder, her hips moving in delicious circles, rubbing her clit on the base of my cock.

I loved that she chased her own pleasure. That she wasn't afraid of letting go. Of learning me, revealing her, sharing what worked for us both.

"Christ, you feel good," I panted. "You feel so fucking good."

"You're mine, Penn. You always have been." Her lips found mine. We knotted ourselves into each other until I didn't know where my body ended and hers began.

The burn in my quads, spine, and cock smoldered until smoke and fire erupted. The irrefutable need to release came with agony laced with greed.

"Shit, I'm gonna come." I rode her harder, driving faster, turning sex into mania.

And Elle matched me.

The bed shifted, moving away from the wall with every thrust.

We had an agenda. An end goal. I arched my back, slamming into her soaked pussy, my muscles rigid with detonation.

She gasped, her fingernails scratching my spine. I loved the pinpricks of pain. The way her breath spurted in my ears, the seamless way my cock plunged into her body.

I fucked her with everything I had.

And when my release found me, it didn't fucking stop.

My thighs, ass, heart, every inch contracted with an all-consuming spurt. I sank deep, growling as euphoria shot from me and into this girl who'd given me my life back.

Elle let go too, her body quaking under mine, her pussy fisting me from root to tip as I filled her.

I chased the climax for as long as I could; shattering into tremors as the waves slowly grew weaker. I ceased holding my weight off Elle, slamming on top of her in a full-body embrace.

Her body was so hot. Radiating like an inferno.

Her pussy still rippled around me, sending delayed ricochets of bliss down my cock and into my legs.

"Damn, that felt good."

She giggled, kissing my cheek. "I agree."

She went to move away, but I grabbed her wrists, pinning them above her head. "Ah ah, you're not leaving."

"I'm not?" Her cute button nose wrinkled.

"Nope."

"Why?" Her gaze flickered to the bathroom. "A shower together would be nice...oh, we could take a bath. Spend hours relaxing."

Images of sliding my hands over Elle's nakedness definitely sounded like a great plan. But I couldn't admit I wasn't ready to let her go yet. I wasn't ready to withdraw and no longer feel her wet heat.

This wasn't about coming.

This was about connection, and hell, I needed it.

Her hips rolled in perfect circles, pressing her clit against me. "If you're going to restrain me, I might have to come again."

I raised an eyebrow. "Could you?"

"Not sure. Never gone for three before." Her smirk was the devil herself. "But I'm open to trying."

I nuzzled her hair, pumping slowly into her, already feeling myself grow hard again. "In that case, let's see what you're capable of. And then I'm washing you for hours, feeding you, and then we're taking a walk around Central Park."

"We are?"

"We are."

"But why Central Park? That's where you were stolen from me the first time."

"Because from now on, you're going to explore every inch of this city with me. I'm going to show you were I slept; I'll reveal my bolt holes, my food stashes, my emergency funds buried in people's gardens. This city has not been kind to me, Elle, and the itch to leave is building. Last time Larry freed me, I moved to LA to get away. It helped."

I kissed her nose as stress etched her eyes. "But—you can't leave. My work...it's here." Tears sparkled.

"I'm not leaving. That's why I need you to replace bad memories with good. With you, I can learn to love this city again, but only with you by my side."

A tear rolled down her cheek. "I'll go to every street corner, every park, every bench. I'll go wherever you want me to, Penn. You'll never be alone again."

# Chapter Forty-Two

# Elle

WE DID ALL those things.

After a second round when Penn flipped me onto my hands and knees, and a quickie turned into kinky playtime, we soaked in his bath before catching a taxi to Central Park and walking the same path we'd sprinted from the security guards.

We followed the chain link fence of the baseball field where we'd shared our first kiss and watched an evening game where men trampled the home diamond where Penn shared his chocolate bar.

We kissed in the same bushes where we were arrested and bought cinnamon-sugared churros from a street van as we strolled a few blocks of New York.

Penn didn't say much. His eyes turned more active, his entire body on high alert. The ruthless businessman I'd given my virginity to faded into the wild creature I'd met in the alley.

He sniffed the air as if he could smell a threat. He narrowed his gaze at a group of men coming toward us. He moved as a predator and prey all at once.

I took his hand.

He froze then relaxed. His eyes met mine. His lips turned from scowl to smile. And we made our way back to his apartment in harmony.

When we got back, I expected to climb into bed and either repeat what we'd done before or sleep. It'd been a long day and an even longer five months, but Penn ordered takeout from a local Thai place, and we snuggled on his couch while watching TV.

We laughed and snickered at jokes on the screen.

We licked our fingers free from curry puffs and slurped Pad

Thai.

> We shared normalcy and made it magic.
> Like any normal couple.
> Like a boy and girl in love.
> It was the best day of my life.

# Chapter Forty-Three

# Penn

*DEAR PENN,*
*I love many things in this world.*
*I love my company, my cat, my father, my financial security.*
*But I have to say, I love you more.*
*Watching you sleep this morning—you were soft for the first time. Your forehead wasn't creased; your eyes weren't narrowed in suspicion waiting for the next catastrophe. You trusted me to keep you safe while you dreamed.*
*My heart is so full because of that.*
*And I hope you can forgive me for not waking you.*
*Belle Elle needs me, and I have to go to work. However, I've left you a present. Call me when you're awake—sleep all afternoon if you want. You deserve it. Then come find me at the office and perhaps take me over my desk.*
*I'd like to put that particular fantasy into reality.*
*I love you.*
*See you soon,*
*Elle xx*

I flopped onto my back, a ridiculous grin on my face.

The gift she'd mentioned was her lingerie. She'd left it neatly folded on the covers, proof that she'd gone to work naked beneath her clothes, thinking of me as I thought about her.

I grew hard picturing her bare and waiting for me.

I shouldn't get so caught up over a note on my pillow and her underwear on my bed, but I did.

It gave me peace of mind that this wasn't a dream.

This was real.

The second I woke, I'd had a panic attack thinking I was back in lock-up and the soreness in my body and slight dehydration from so much sex was all make-believe.

Then I'd stretched, and the crinkle of paper brought my mind instantly back to Elle.

She knew more than I'd wanted to show her. She knew how my temper and sharp need to protect worked against me and filled me with fear. She understood that the world I was from was full of danger and enemies, while happiness and friends padded hers.

It would take a while for me to relax and not search for disasters, but with her in my life, I had no doubt I could find the one thing I'd never been able to afford—no matter how much I stole or earned on the stock market.

Love.

Unable to fall back to sleep with her on my mind and lust in my heart, I showered, dressed, and headed into the kitchen to enjoy some caffeine before heading uptown to Belle Elle.

While the coffee brewed, I collected my laptop from the locked drawer in the sideboard, and for the first time in five months, opened the internet.

Not having regular visitors or phone calls in jail was hard. Not having access to daily news, stock prices, and portfolio updates was torture.

Logging into my charity, I noticed the offsite staff I'd hired had been busy with a local food bank, lunch day, and a temporary tent city where the council had let us do a trial for homeless people.

I had no doubt Larry would've kept it running. I had so much to repay him for.

Perhaps, before I headed to Elle's, I'd take him to lunch and show him in a woefully understated way how much I valued his friendship and support.

Opening the local news, I grabbed a cup of freshly brewed coffee and prepared to spend the next fifteen minutes perusing the disarray the world had once again fallen into.

Only…my coffee cup slammed onto the table, spilling brown steaming liquid everywhere. My heart stopped. My fingers scrabbled at the screen to jerk the technology closer.

After the happiness of last night…this couldn't be happening.

*NOELLE CHARLSTON SHACKED UP WITH A HOMELESS CRIMINAL?*

*In terms of New York royalty, none come as close as the Charlston family—the owners and creators of the Belle Elle department stores. Not only have their clothes, toys, and household appliances graced our homes for decades, the Charlstons have regularly been noted for their impeccable social standing and unblemished record at avoiding scandal.*

*When Noelle's mother died, the country rallied in support and records showed florists in the New York area all had at least three deliveries a day to the Charlston family in condolences.*

*However, recent events have made the public doubt the Charlstons are as pure as they led us to believe.*

*Protesters were photographed yesterday outside their flagship store, boycotting their clothing line. Speaking to one protestor, they said they wouldn't dress in apparel provided by a company involved with criminals.*

*It brings up questions as to their own moral code and what they have been involved in over the years while painting the perfect family to the New York people.*

*Penn Everett is the man hiding in Belle Elle's shadow. Recently released from prison on an incorrect accusation, it's been said that his previous arrests are in discussion by local lawyer Larry Barns, pointing fingers at our very own chief of police, Arnold Twig.*

*Chief Twig states Penn is one of the most violent offenders out there, and it's a disaster to see the justice system fail the American people.*

*In a personal interview earlier today, Chief Twig also said he feared for his son, Sean, now that Everett was free. According to him, Everett has always been jealous of Sean Twig and there's history to show Everett places the blame for his crimes onto the innocent young man.*

*Neither Joseph Charlston or Noelle were prepared to make a statement.*

My elbows planted on the table either side of the damning article.

*Fuck.*

My legs jittered on the chair leg, my heart filling with snow.

I'd known this would happen. I'd heard rumors in prison and had updates from Larry that Belle Elle was regularly mentioned alongside my name.

But to see it in black and white?

To have a prominent newspaper tear Elle's family legacy apart all because of me?

Shit, it dug a dagger into my heart and twisted until I couldn't breathe.

I loved her. I would do anything for her.

But they were right.

This was all my fault.

I'd gone after Elle because of my hate. I'd dragged her into my chaos because of my love. I'd ruined her business because of my selfishness.

The longer I was with her, the worse the lynch mob would become.

It didn't matter what I wanted or how much I cared for her.

Elle had sacrificed far too much for me. I couldn't let her sacrifice anymore.

I loved her too much to let all she'd worked for be stolen.

Slamming the laptop closed, I grabbed my keys and left.

# Chapter Forty-Four

# Elle

"ELLE, CAN YOU come in here, please?" Dad's voice came from his office.

I'd arrived early—before most staff—to finally get stuck into my mountain of work that I hadn't mentally been able to cope with over the past five months.

I'd kept the company ticking along—mainly thanks to Dad taking on more responsibility and Fleur's help—but it was time I took the reins again now Penn was free.

I had finally settled my debt with him. I was unbelievably happy. And the rest of life would work itself out like it was supposed to.

Striding into my father's office, I smiled. He wore a simple black suit with a gray waistcoat and maroon shirt. He sat behind his desk where he'd given me Sage all those years ago.

He read a newspaper with a grimace. "Can you explain this?"

"Explain what?"

He tossed the article toward me, spinning it upside down so I could read it clearly. The blaring headline said: *BELLE ELLE MAY HAVE A NEW CEO AND HE COMES WITH A CRIMINAL RECORD.*

I warred with the need to burn the stupid thing and assure my father not to upset his heart.

"You know what reporters are like. They'll say anything to sell copies."

Dad scrubbed his face. "How much of it is true, though?"

"None of it."

"Most of it, you mean?" He sighed. "Greg retracted his statement. He wouldn't have done that if you hadn't have meddled."

My shoulders straightened. "I didn't do anything illegal, Dad."

"I'm not so sure about that. And now, you're dating someone who has done illegal things."

Standing primly, I refrained my temper from lashing back. "Penn is a good person. Or are you forgetting your approval when he first arrived?"

"A criminal record changes things, Elle." He slouched. "I want you to be happy, but I don't want Belle Elle to be dragged into this sort of scandal."

"The company can handle it. Why does the public opinion have so much sway over my personal relationships?"

Dad stood, patrolling around his office, bypassing awards for best retail experience, best merchandise, and best charity donations to organizations who supported fair wages. We followed the law and did our part for the world in all things business. Belle Elle ran my life. I wouldn't let it rule my love life, too.

"Because the public is our business, Elle. If you continue to drag the company's good will through the muck of prison and criminals, then I fear what sort of future you'll leave your heir."

"My what?"

"Your children. Come on. Be smart about this. I'm only trying to protect you, Elle."

I let him pace around me, holding my cool. Barely. "I'm not ending it with him. I'm in love with him."

"You barely know him."

"You were happy for me to marry him after four days. Now that I've been with him for five months, you say it's too soon?"

"Five months while he's been in jail."

"It doesn't matter. Not everyone is perfect. Those who make mistakes but learn from them are better than those who have made none. He makes me happy. That's all you need worry yourself with."

I didn't wait for his reply.

With my hands balled, I left his office and stalked into mine.

I loved my father, but I was done taking orders.

*Penn is mine.*

*And he's going to stay that way.*

\* \* \* \* \*

"Visitor, Elle." Fleur knocked gently on my office door after lunch.

I hadn't stopped to eat. In fact, I hadn't stopped since I'd sat down and fully looked at the financial statements and future dated campaigns. Fleur had done a great job, but a few areas had slipped through our fastidious control.

"If it's my father again, tell him I'll come over tonight, and we can discuss it like adults. But nothing will change, so he might as well get used to it."

Fleur took a few steps over the threshold. "It's not your father." Her mouth tipped up into the biggest smile. "It's your fiancé."

Instantly, I leaped from my chair and crossed the large space. Sage meowed from her basket, wondering if I was leaving or not.

Before I could assure her I wasn't going anywhere, Penn appeared, dressed in low-slung dark jeans and a black untucked shirt. He looked carefree and reckless and just as delicious.

The itch of having him last night wasn't sated, and my mouth watered to taste him again. To finish what he'd started last time he was here and be wicked together with orgasm-related fun.

"Hi." My cheeks pinked, picturing him inside me. How sexy he was. How lucky *I* was.

Only, he didn't wrap an arm around me and whisper hello in his raspy lustful voice.

He didn't smile.

In fact, he took a step back, holding up his hand. "Elle...don't."

Icebergs slithered down my spine. "Don't what? What is it?"

Fleur left, leaving us alone.

What the hell could've changed since I left him a few hours ago until now? His eyes tightened with pain. Pain matched inside me the longer he stared. "I—I have something to give you."

I rubbed my arms, my hands squeaking over the fabric of my wardrobe. The silver sundress with black panels over the chest that Fleur had picked out was a nod to the night we'd gone to his charity gala. My own way of telling him whatever happened that night was over because the lies were gone and we were together. "Give me what?"

A rap sounded on my door. Before I could snap for whoever it was to leave us alone, Dad popped his head in.

His gaze instantly latched onto Penn. "Ah, I thought I saw you." Moving into the room, he closed the door ominously behind him.

Goosebumps erupted full of fear.

I had no idea what was going on, but it hurt like hell already.

Dad held out his hand, trying to hide his thoughts (unsuccessfully) about the ridiculous news articles and slight inconvenience Penn's background was causing.

Penn swallowed back his own emotions, shaking Dad's hand. "Mr. Charlston."

Dad smiled. "Congratulations on being acquitted. I'm so glad." His voice lowered with sincerity. "I know I wasn't exactly supportive while you were locked up, but I want you to know, I never stopped being grateful to you for saving Elle." His soft gray eyes met mine. "She means everything to me. I get a little protective when anything tries to hurt her—reporters included."

Penn dropped his hand, shoving it into his pocket. "I understand."

Unlike last night when I got on my knees and sucked him, he wasn't doing it to hold himself back. He stood protective of himself—a safety thing to keep himself rigid and firm to do whatever it was he'd come to do.

*Don't let him.*

I had no idea what had changed, but every instinct screamed to stop him…before it was too late.

Striding to his side, I slinked an arm around his waist and kissed his cheek. "Do you want to grab some lunch? Maybe take a quick walk and get some fresh air?"

Penn shivered at my closeness then stiffened. Never looking at me, he clenched his jaw and sidestepped out of my embrace.

He didn't answer my question, sticking to his script, giving me no way to stop him. "There's something I came to do."

I trembled in terror, wishing I could grab the hands of a clock and shoot us back to last night when everything had been so rosy and bright.

Dad frowned. "What is it you came to do, Mr. Everett?"

My heart sank. It didn't escape my notice or Penn's that Dad had gone from calling him son back to his formal address. Just like Penn had called him Mr. Charlston.

*This is all so wrong.*

Penn needed to be welcomed—to feel as if he belonged because he did. Just because it would be rough for the next few months in the tabloids didn't mean Dad had to be cruel.

"Dad, Penn saved me. He deserves—"

"Don't, Elle." Penn pulled one hand out of his pocket and

pinched the bridge of his nose. "It's best if your father is here to hear this." His voice stayed calm and focused, but his muscles tensed, his back going overly straight.

"Hear what?" I locked my knees from sudden quaking.

"About our fake engagement." He looked at the carpet, his voice bitter and sharp, his body broken and sad. "I think it's time to call it off." He exhaled in a rush, the raw agony in his eyes a bleeding wound.

*"What?"*

Dad interrupted. "What do you mean?"

"I mean, I think it's best—for everyone involved—if we go our separate ways."

I stumbled. "You can't be serious."

Dad held up his hand. "What are you saying?"

Penn's face turned black. "I'm saying I have too much shit in my life to smear your perfection. I have a chief of police about to come after me, a criminal record, and a whole bunch of other issues. I saw how you being associated with me is already affecting your business. I never wanted that. I never wanted to make things worse for Elle, especially knowing how hard she works."

I gulped. "Penn, stop. It's over. You're free. The rumors will fade, and life will go back to normal."

"No." Dad held up his finger. "He's right. It won't. These sort of things last forever, Elle. Sure, it will fade in favor of other gossip, but the next time Belle Elle has a lawsuit or some nasty reporter has a grudge, they'll drag this story out all over again. We'll never be free of it."

"Exactly." Penn nodded curtly. "You'd never be free of me and the turmoil I'd cause."

Dad puffed his chest even as his confidence faded. His mood switched from corporate to apologetic. "Look, I'm sorry, Penn. I genuinely like you, and you make my daughter happy. You saved her, and you'll forever have my gratitude, but Elle isn't a normal girl. She comes with a company that has been a part of our family for generations. I can't let her jeopardize that."

Penn stood to his full height, hiding his wince. "Sometimes, love isn't enough. It doesn't conquer everything."

I flinched, holding my broken pieces together. "That's ridiculous. How can you say love isn't enough?" The dirty disbelief in my voice made me snarl. "You want me, Penn. I want you. Don't do something as stupid as—"

"I'm not being stupid, Elle. I'm being smart."

"No, you're being a raging moron." Stomping toward him, I placed my hand over his thumping heart. "Tell me you love me. Tell me what you told me last night. Tell my dad so he can hear what an idiot you are."

Penn gritted his teeth, moving away from my touch. "I'm not an idiot for trying to protect you, Elle. Why can you do so much for me and I can't do the same for you?"

"I didn't hurt you and call it helping!"

"You don't think I'm not hurting? That this isn't fucking killing me?"

My cheeks burned with terror that I wouldn't be able to talk him out of this. To stop this lunacy. "Then don't do it! It's a silly newspaper."

"It's in black and white!" He bared his teeth. "It's damaging. I know how awful the mob mentality can be, Elle. It can fucking ruin everything you love."

"Can you really stand there and talk about love even while breaking my heart?" I wrapped my arms around my waist, hugging hard. "I chose you, Penn. You're worth whatever silly stories they make up about us. Admit you love me and stop trying to be a martyr."

His lips remained stubbornly locked together.

He couldn't tell me that he loved me.

He wouldn't.

He believed he was doing the right thing.

*It's not.*

*It's not the right thing!*

"As much as I agree with you," Dad said. "Are you sure about this? You seem to care deeply—"

Penn tore at his hair. "Of course, I care deeply. I love your daughter—" His eyes flared, noticing his admittance. He waved it away as if it wasn't the point. As if it didn't matter. When it was the *only* thing that mattered.

His eyes met mine, but he spoke to my dad. "It's because I love her that I'm doing this. I can't stand by and be the reason for Elle's future to be at stake."

Dad crossed his arms. "That's a noble reason." His gaze turned calm, assessing Penn in a way he hadn't. Seeing him like I saw him—past the angry features and stuck-up confidence. Finally noticing the man who protected everyone he cared about by keeping them as far away from him as possible.

He was noble.

He was stupid.

He was so selfless, he was willing to cut out his heart and walk away as some misguided attempt to save me.

Couldn't he see I couldn't care less about reporters or phony tales?

Couldn't he understand I didn't want Belle Elle anymore if I couldn't have him?

Penn might not understand, but Dad did.

He shook his head, pinning his gaze on Penn, finally believing in the affection between us—recognizing its truth.

Not that it would help me win this fight with this stubborn ass determined on destroying me, all in the name of honor.

*Screw honor!*

"Penn…we'll fight this together. Just like we fought your sentence."

His body flinched with grief. "You've already done too much for me, Elle. I can't ask for anymore."

"Penn, perhaps you should sit down. Let's talk about this—" Dad pointed at the couch, his shoulders falling the longer he witnessed the life-splintering argument. "I'm sure we can work this out."

I waved my arms. "There, you see? Even Dad, who is adamant about protecting Belle Elle from controversy, is willing to discuss—"

"Just because he doesn't want to see you hurting doesn't mean he agrees that it's the right choice." Penn shook his head, his eyes black with agony. "I've already caused you more stress than you should ever have to live through. Don't ask me to make you live through more."

"I'm not asking you. I'm *telling* you." I stormed forward, desperate to touch him. "You don't have the right to walk away when I want you to stay, Penn. Don't punish me for loving you."

His jaw locked. He swallowed hard. He looked over my head. "I can't do this anymore."

"Anymore? We've been together one night!"

"And you were alone for five months to *earn* that one night. That's not a life you deserve, Elle." He suddenly exploded. "I've already taken far too much from you."

"No, you haven't."

He snorted. "Haven't I? What about the countless nights I gave you? The constant worry? The deliberating stress? I've cost you so much, and I refuse to take anymore."

"I paid that willingly. You're free. That's all in the past."

"Until the next fuck up."

Dad cleared his throat. "How about we all take a breather? It might be as simple as keeping your relationship quiet for now—until this all blows over."

Penn laughed coldly. "You know as well as I do that that won't happen. This is what has to happen. It's for the best."

"No!" My temper overflowed, but I battled it down. "Look, let's be rational. Did you forget everything we promised last night? All the love we shared?"

Turning to look at my father, I added, "Dad, you practically threw me together with Penn that night at the Weeping Willow. We're finally together. You can see what exists between us. Don't let him be ridiculous."

It was a low ball playing my father against Penn, but Dad was on my side now. If Penn needed fatherly approval—he had it.

Penn clenched his hands. "Not ridiculous, Elle. Smart." He smiled sadly. "I didn't come here to argue with you." His shoulders bunched as he pulled his other hand from his pocket. "Before I say goodbye, I need to do something."

"You don't get to say goodbye, Penn. Not after I waited for you in prison. Not after I fell in love—"

He planted a hand on my mouth, his eyes guarded and unreadable.

But I didn't need to read them. I knew how much he was breaking under his ironclad façade.

He howled just as much as I did.

*Why is he doing this then?*

He'd swiped away my foundations and made the world shake like an earthquake.

"This belongs to you." He held up his hand, and the necklace that'd started this catastrophe dangled from his fingers.

When I didn't move, he took my hand, turned it upright, and dribbled the chain into my palm.

With a harsh breath, he closed my fingers over it. "Stewie and Gio agree you should have it back. I should've given it to you years ago when I came to find you that night." He kissed me so soft, I barely tasted his lips. "I'm so sorry, Elle."

Dad coughed, but I ignored him, fighting my tears. My heart cracked open, dying, gasping. "Why are you doing this?"

Penn touched my cheekbone reverently. "Because for the first time in my life, I need to do the right thing. You helped me so much, Elle. Let me help you by not ruining your future."

I sniffed back a sob, hating the necklace locked in my hand. "I don't know what to say."

"Say you forgive me."

"Forgive you?" I cupped his cheek, mirroring his hold on me with the hand not holding the necklace. "The only thing to forgive is this. You're hurting me, Penn. I don't care about the newspapers or what the chief of police will do. All I care about is *you*." Tears rolled unbidden. "Don't do this."

He bent and brushed his lips once again over mine, licking away a tear at the corner of my mouth. "I'm sorry for dragging you into my mess, Elle. But your father is right. I'll never be free of my past, and you'll forever belong to Belle Elle. There is no place for us." He stepped backward, once again jamming his hands into his pockets. "I'm going away for a while. Let the scandal blow over." He shrugged. "Let me go, Elle."

Dad came to my side. "Look, Penn. Perhaps, I've been too hasty. Stay. Let's talk—"

Penn shuddered, squeezing his eyes before opening them again, full of wavering agony. "I can't."

My tears morphed into a shout. "You can. Who put you in charge about what is best for me or what I want? I know what's best, and I want *you*, Penn."

"And you'll always have me." He back stepped toward the door. "I'll never stop loving you, but we can't be together. I won't hurt you anymore. Goodbye, Elle." Hiding his pain behind a sharp cough, he opened the door and disappeared.

The moment he was gone, I fell to my knees.

"Elle!" Dad squatted beside me in horror. "Are you okay?"

I let loose, tears becoming sobs when before I'd been so damn happy. "Am I okay? No, I'm not okay."

Dad rubbed my back like he did when I was a child and I felt sick or had a nightmare. Before, his comfort would work. This time, it only made me miss another man more. "He can't do this, Dad. I love him."

Sage crawled into my lap, mewing sadly. I dropped the sapphire star onto the carpet and grabbed her, cuddling her close, using her as a tissue to wipe away my sadness. She let me. She purred in encouragement, letting me cry.

With tear-fogged vision, I noticed Dad pick up the necklace he'd bought me for my nineteenth birthday. He spun the star in his fingers, his forehead furrowing. Slowly, his spine straightened as he looked at the door where Penn had vanished and back to me in pieces on the floor.

"Right, that's it." Standing stiffly, he bent down and hauled me to my feet. "I've been a stupid old fool."

I sniffed, hugging Sage closer.

Patting my cheek, wiping away my tears, he said, "That boy loves you."

My heart squeezed all over again. A fresh wave of tears threatened.

"And you love him."

I bit my lip, doing my best to stop the torrent. "I do."

"I'm an idiot. He's an idiot. We're all stupid idiots." Pushing me toward the door, he scooped Sage from my arms and gave me the sapphire star instead. "Go after him."

I froze. "What?"

He laughed abruptly, rolling his eyes as if it was the most obvious thing after being dumped. "He's only breaking up with you because he thinks it's the right thing to do. I must admit I played my part in encouraging that. But that was before I saw how much he adores you. How much he put you first and himself second even though he's obviously going to pieces without you. I liked him before, Elle, but he just showed a noble, honorable side that is so damn rare."

He kissed my cheek as he opened the door. "Who cares about journalists and stories? We're solid. Our business is thriving. And even it if wasn't, it doesn't matter."

His eyes took on that whimsical glow he got whenever he thought of Mom. "I loved truly, and there wasn't a day that went by that I wished I didn't. Every morning, I was thankful. Every evening, I was grateful. No amount of money or good publicity can replace true love, Elle. And I'm a moron that I've fought for you to find that exact connection only to do whatever I could to break you apart when you found it."

His face fell. "I hope you can forgive your old fool of a father."

My tears dried.

Should I chase after him? What would I say?

But I had no choice.

Dad was right. I didn't care about Belle Elle's reputation. If we believed a few online articles could tear us down, then we didn't belong at the head of the chain. And if we sacrificed our own happiness for material things, then we didn't deserve to find love.

And I *had* found love.

I wouldn't let it walk away.

"I won't let him go." The oath landed by my feet before I noticed I'd spoken.

Dad hugged me with Sage scrambling between us. "That's my girl. Now go and knock some sense into that boy like he knocked sense into me. Tell him he's part of this family, whether he likes it or not."

With tear-slicked cheeks and racing heartbeat, I tore from my office.

Fleur asked where I was going.

Sage meowed.

Dad whooped.

And I flew on wings to claim Penn once and for all.

# Chapter Forty-Five

# Penn

I COULDN'T STAY in New York.

Not after this.

The moment I'd gone to Larry's to collect the sapphire star Stewie had been keeping for Gio, he'd known things were about to get sad.

He hadn't grilled me, but he had told me to call him when I got to whatever destination I would run to.

The reporters wanted to slander Elle and her company? Well, they couldn't fucking use me because I wouldn't be in town. By distancing myself, I was protecting Elle.

It hurt like hell.

But it was the best thing for everyone.

Arnold wouldn't be able to drag her into my chaos. Greg would remain locked up. My connection to the Charlstons would fade, and Elle could remain the perfect princess who so many people relied on for work and income.

Throwing a duffel bag onto my bed, I didn't pay much attention as I threw pants, shirts, and underwear into the general vicinity.

Everything fucking hurt.

My chest, my eyes, my motherfucking heart.

I hated myself for hurting Elle.

I despised myself for leaving her in tears.

But it was for the best.

The only way I could think of to protect her.

"You know, you should really lock your front door."

*What the—*

I spun from shoving socks into the side pockets of the duffel, my mouth falling wide. "What the hell are you doing here?"

Elle leaned against my doorframe, the sapphire necklace dangling from her finger as she cocked her hip. "Getting you back, of course."

My hands curled. "I told you. I won't put you through any more stress and ridicule."

She merely smiled. Her eyes bright and tear-free; her body poised and confident. "I want you to do something for me..." Her attention fell to my half-packed bag. "Before you go. Can you do that?"

I narrowed my eyes, searching for a trap, but she remained open and kind.

I nodded slowly. "Okay..."

"Great." Pushing from the doorframe, she came toward me with a sexy sway in her hips.

My cock instantly reacted against my will. I gulped as she planted herself in front of me.

"You did all the talking in my office. Here, it's my turn."

I didn't like it, but I nodded. "Fine."

"Good." She swung the necklace like a pendulum. "First, this no longer belongs to me. It belongs to the hooded hero who saved me. I told him that three years ago. I distinctly remember mentioning that if I *had* remembered to ask for it back, I would've given it to my rescuer in payment for saving me and walking me home."

I couldn't help myself. "And I distinctly remember telling you there was no way in hell I'd take it."

She smirked. "Yes, I remember that too." Tossing the necklace into my bag, she muttered, "Too bad, it's yours. I don't want it back. Know what else I don't want back?"

I stood frozen, not falling into her trap.

The longer she stood in my room, smelling so goddamn delicious and being so brave, the more I wanted to kiss her until I passed out from oxygen deprivation and took back everything I'd said.

I was an idiot.

Worse than an idiot.

I deserved to be lonely after throwing her away all because I didn't want to hurt her.

Eventually, I'd hurt her—either through my direct actions or indirect. It would happen. Could I afford to take that chance?

*She means too much to me.*

When I didn't answer, she beamed. "My heart, Penn. I don't want that back, either. It's yours. So you might else well carve it from my chest and stuff it into that bag of yours because you're not leaving without it."

"Elle," I growled. "Don't be so—"

"What? Dramatic? Immature? Literal?" She stabbed my sternum. "Listen here, Mr. Everett, and listen good. I didn't pick you. You didn't pick me. Fate picked us, and there's nothing we can do about it. The reporters can't change it. Life can't break it. And you most certainly cannot walk away from it."

I sucked in a breath to argue, but she planted a hand on my mouth just as I'd done to her.

"I don't care about anything else. I'm not going to worry about what may or may not happen. I've been fighting to deserve you ever since the night you were taken in Central Park. Do you know how much guilt I've carried since that night? How terrible I felt? The debt I endured to pay back?" Her bottom lip wobbled.

I crumpled inside for hurting her. I had no idea she suffered the way I had. Her with guilt, me with misplaced hate.

If only I'd told her my name from the very beginning.

But if I had, who knew if we would be here right now. About to do something stupid and reckless but so right. I couldn't breathe with the thought of not claiming her. Walking from her office showed me how much I adored her. How utterly real this was.

It wasn't a fling. It wasn't short-term.

It was forever.

And if I stood by and acted like a dick—thinking I could keep her safe while abandoning her to the wolves—then I didn't fucking deserve her.

It was my job to keep her safe.

I thought that meant from myself.

But I'd rather keep her safe from other assholes and screw my fears about not being the man she deserved.

She'd leashed me to her the moment she'd appeared in my doorway. Her cute little argument turned me on until I throbbed in my pants for her tirade to end so I could show her just how much I'd never let her go.

Today had started off blissful and slid into terrible, but now, it was exactly where it should be.

Acceptance.

This was real. So fucking real.

"So you listen here, Penn. I don't care what argument you try. I'm not—"

"Elle…" I put a finger over her lips, silencing her with my stare. "Okay."

"Okay?" Her lips brushed over my touch, making me shudder with desire.

"You win." I leaned forward, my self-control at its end. Capturing her mouth with mine, I kissed her with every yes and apology I could. "I'm a fucking idiot, but I'm yours. I'm not going anywhere."

It took a second for my vow to travel from her ears to her brain to her heart.

But when it did, she bounced into my arms as if she'd always belonged there.

"Truly?"

I chuckled. "Truly."

She peppered my jaw with kisses. "You're an ass. You know that, right?"

"I do know that. That was why I was trying to remove myself from your life."

"Well, you tried and failed. Don't you ever try again."

I nodded. "Yes, ma'am."

"And don't call me ma'am."

"What do you want me to call you?"

"Something dirty while you take off my clothes and have your wicked way with me."

My eyebrows rose. "In that case, turn around, Ms. Charlston. I suddenly have the overwhelming need to bend you over and stick my cock inside you."

She trembled. "I thought you'd never ask."

I swatted her ass, marching her to the bed. "Oh, I didn't ask. You've been a naughty girl, going against my wishes and making me keep you. You need to be punished."

Her laughter made my entire fucking galaxy blaze bright.

# Chapter Forty-Six

# Elle

"MARRY ME."

My eyes flew wide. "What?"

Penn spun me around, shoved his clothes-strewn bag off the bed, and tossed me onto the mattress. "Marry me. Make our fake engagement real."

"I—wow."

"Wow isn't the answer I want." His voice was a seductive rasp. "Try again. Marry me?"

A shiver darted down my spine, loving his authoritative kinky tone.

I knew my answer, but I bit my bottom lip. "Um, how long can I think about it?"

I gasped as he pressed me onto my back, then hoisted up the silver dress and revealed my nakedness. I'd left him the gift of my underwear this morning and hadn't replaced them.

He groaned. "God, you're going to kill me." He sank a finger inside me, burying his face into my hair. "Yes or no, Elle. Put me out of my misery." Hunger poured off him, infecting me until I squirmed with starvation. He was so much bigger than me, so much stronger, so damn beautiful, yet with one little word, I had the power to break him into smithereens.

Just like he'd broken me.

I toyed with the idea of saying no. To give him a taste of his own medicine, but he withdrew his touch and rolled onto his side.

"You're all I want, Elle. I was a jackass." He kissed me reverently then contradicted it with sudden aggression. "It fucking destroyed me to go over there. To tell you to leave me. Feeling that god-crushing emptiness of having everything I ever wanted then giving it all away again. It hurt so fucking much."

More tears sprang to my eyes at his confession and soul-bearing honesty. He cut me open, leaving me to bleed in his arms.

"I want you more than I've ever wanted anyone. More than I ever wanted a dry place to sleep. More than food even after two days of none." A cocky smirk twisted his lips. "That's the truth, but the one you truly need to know is I'm crazy in love with you, and you're not leaving my bed until you say yes."

"Is that a threat?"

"Do you want it to be?"

My eyes hooded. "Maybe."

"I don't mind spending decades convincing you." Undoing his belt and zipper, he pushed his jeans and boxer-briefs down to mid-thigh. His erection sprang thick and hard.

My legs spread in invitation. "Good because I think I need convincing."

Pressing over me, his body vibrated with tension. His arousal soaked from his skin to mine as he found my entrance.

His lips moved against mine, hot and wet. We devoured each other, turning wilder and more in lust every second. Bites and licks and the incessant urge to join, to mate.

His cock throbbed at my core, tormenting me, making me heavy and achy with need.

"I'll be miserable without you, Elle. Please don't make me be miserable."

"You're making me miserable." I rocked against him, begging him to fill me. My senses were drenched in him—his scent and taste. I needed him to finish what he started before I went completely out of my mind.

"You want me?" He angled himself, mounting me in every sense. "You have me." He plunged inside.

"Oh, God." My eyes blacked out. The room spun.

A groan splashed from both of us. I couldn't stop my hips grinding into him as he thrust inch by savage inch.

"Is this enough convincing?" He captured my mouth as his hips flexed into mine, driving me hard against the bed.

"Not...quite..." I patted myself on the back for even attempting to speak with him fucking me, drugging me.

"More?"

I moaned when he sucked on my tongue.

His kisses came wrapped in apologizes and screw-ups. His nips were loaded with passion and love.

He held nothing back. Giving me everything he had left to give.

But I was greedy.

"More, definitely more." I sank my fingernails into his ass, pulling him harder, making him fill me deeper. He completed me.

I wanted him. I wanted him inside me. I wanted him for all eternity.

His breath came out in a shudder as our rhythm picked up, going from teasing to committed.

His mouth locked on mine again. One hand in my hair and the other on my chin, his lips taught mine a violent dance. His tongue thrust into my mouth at the same tempo as his cock plunged into my pussy.

My teeth sank into his lower lip as I arched into his hold. I was pinned by him. Held hostage by sex while he waited for an answer to his unconventional marriage proposal.

"You said yes to the fake one," he growled, thrusting faster. "Say yes to a real one."

I drank air like liquid. "I never said yes to the first one. I remember saying no multiple times."

He flattened me into the bed. "I didn't let you say no then. And I won't let you say no now." His passion overflowed. His fist landed in my hair, tugging hard enough to remind me I was completely at his mercy.

I slept with him in utmost trust that he'd never use his strength to hurt me.

"You can't make me say yes by fucking me, Penn."

"I can't?" He surged into me, making the familiar fireworks grab a lighter and hold a flame to their fuses.

I glued my lips together, holding back my moan as my body prepared to spindle and shoot into euphoric abandon.

"Do you trust me?" he whispered, his tongue tracing my ear.

Even swept away, so close to coming, I nodded, grabbing his shoulders with my nails. "Unequivocally."

"In that case. Say yes."

His gaze searched mine, his features turning brittle and sharp with his desire to come. "You put me through hell because I love you so fucking much, and I put you through hell because I come with baggage. But I'm willing to fight together, Elle. Are you?"

His hands found my hair again, holding me in place as he undid me with desperate kisses. "Marry me. Goddammit, Elle."

He thrust into me, switching the spark for annihilation.

I threw my head back and screamed as my body waked around his. My pussy fisted his cock, and every orgasm bubble popped down my legs.

His black chuckle brought me back to earth where he chased me off the cliff.

His fingertips brushed across my cheek. "Fuck, I love watching you come." He drove deeper into me. "It makes me so hard." *Thrust.* "I can't fucking control myself." *Plunge.* "Christ, Elle." His wickedly sexy mouth brushed over mine, feeding me his growl as the splashes of his cum filled me.

His eyes snapped closed as his body jerked.

Holding him while he came down from his high, keeping him safe, threading our lives into one, I murmured, "Yes. Yes, I'll marry you, Nameless."

# Epilogue

# Penn

SIX MONTHS OF fucking heaven.

Six months of waking up with Elle in my arms.

Six months of being hissed at by Sage for crowding Elle on the couch at night after a long day at work.

Six months of working out of an office at Belle Elle, running my charity, and trading the penny stocks I'd become so fond of.

Six wonderfully happy months where Elle's father welcomed me wholeheartedly into the family, Larry finalized the adoption on Stewie, and life settled into a full, joyful world rather than an empty, lonely one.

A few months ago, I'd taken Elle to Fishkill to see Gio.

At the start, she'd been cold and standoffish—which I understood seeing as the last time she'd seen him he'd been yelling abuse and physically hurting her.

But just like Larry always said, *'Thieves can become saints. Saints can become thieves. Most of us deserve a second chance.'* Gio had changed. We'd celebrated with him over the phone when Stewie's adoption finally came through and he no longer carried hate caused by being in Sean's pocket.

He'd started a building course in prison, and in four years' time—when he was due to be released—he'd be a fully-fledged carpenter ready to trade a skill for money.

We'd already arranged he'd work for me building shelters and renovating apartments for those in need. He'd never be homeless again and had a readymade family who knew how to forgive and help rather than judge and ridicule.

The reporters never fully went away.

Arnold Twig ensured their tattletales and slander were given new details. Larry fought for me in another trial—this one with only judges presiding, not a jury. The evidence had three overseers, not just one.

I had the opportunity to stand and reveal everything that I'd endured. I looked Arnold Twig in the eye and buried him under details, evidence, and the long years I'd served incorrectly.

I was no longer a kid and afraid of him.

He was afraid of me.

And despite Arnold's rebuttal and lies, even marching Sean in front of the public as the perfect role model, the newspapers actually did a good turn for once and uncovered Sean's old juvie record for deliberately maiming a local dog.

That scrap of juicy detail encouraged more reporters to dig into the not-so-innocent world of Sean Twig.

Slowly, women came forward to issue statements that they'd been touched inappropriately at school and been sworn to secrecy by him. Even a female teacher swore under oath that Sean had raped her on the last day of senior year.

She hadn't reported it because she was afraid she'd be the one prosecuted for a teacher sleeping with a student.

The day Sean was officially arrested for more crimes than I could ever have done, Arnold Twig lost his position as chief of police and was detained, just like his son. His bail was set high enough that it would've hurt him in the wallet as well as his livelihood.

Despite knowing both would be sentenced for their crimes and would spend years paying for what they'd done to me, vengeance wasn't entirely sweet. It felt as if they got off too easy. That evil had won in some small way.

At least, I had one small victory. Sean had been sentenced last week. Due to the multiple charges and heinous felonies he'd committed, he earned twenty years with no chance of parole.

Hopefully, in another few months, Larry would have a verdict, Arnold Twig would be sentenced, and my records would be expunged forever.

That would be the day Elle and I would agree to an interview by the press constantly hounding us for our tale. That day I would be vindicated, and I'd tell the world everything. Finally proud enough and untainted by lies to stand beside Elle, not as a thieving shadow on her empire, but as her equal.

I couldn't wait.

All our loose ends were tying up neatly.

Greg finally went to trial, and Elle testified. However, our happiness meant she struggled to hold onto ill will, especially after seeing how changed Gio was. She hoped the same would happen to Greg.

She told the truth in court, the chains and cuffs that David had saved as evidence were revealed, the bank statements purchasing a second car, the diamond engagement ring he'd forced on her—every shred of premeditation Greg had done.

The jury oohed and aahed over her treatment. They glared at Greg and plotted his punishment even before the trial concluded.

Elle had full opportunity to push for a harsher sentence when the judge asked her what she wanted to see happen. However, she didn't get nasty. She didn't glower or beg for a harsh sentence.

She merely stated the facts and left—leaving the verdict up to the court.

It wasn't until a few weeks later, after he was sentenced to eight years, two months—which I thought was exceedingly short—a large donation in Greg's name appeared in my charity's bank account.

That night, Elle told me about the deal she'd made with Greg to give him twenty million for my freedom.

She'd paid him, as she was loyal to her bargains.

But the more she became involved with projects around town and traded Belle Elle's glitzy hallways for canvas tents and soup kitchens—helping those like me—she decided the bribery could be better used elsewhere.

Greg had done something unforgivable, and Elle took it into her own hands to make him redeemable. Fearing it would reflect badly on her character, she didn't take it all. But she did transfer seventeen million from his name into the charity's, leaving him with only three.

Only three.

It was a lot more than he fucking deserved.

The reporters noticed, as all charity donations had to be logged with the record service, and in the end, Elle's final zing at Greg turned out to paint his misdemeanors in a better light.

Who knew? Maybe she set him on a righteous path. He was interviewed and written about as the most generous criminal in history—not an idiot who was greedy.

At least, his father, Steve, had peace of mind. His son wasn't all bad. Belle Elle avoided more scandal about an attempted rapist who'd worked in their ranks for years. And I fell more in fucking love with the woman who was mine.

In a twist of fate, Sean was put into the same prison population as Greg and from rumors supplied to us thanks to Gio, Greg had earned his fair share of karma.

Unable to get to me, Sean took his frustration out on Greg. A broken arm and few other prison scuffles occurred. As much as I hated Sean for using me as his scape goat, I was kind of glad that Greg hadn't gotten off completely scot-free.

He'd suffered some bodily pain for what he'd done to Elle.

It was fitting.

Our fake engagement turned real engagement was celebrated only by the special people we invited. We kept it small, understated, but the ring I bought her was anything but.

The diamond glittered with rubies on either side, perfectly elegant and locked on her finger for eternity.

Her sapphire star necklace was fixed from Gio ripping the chain off her neck, and it hung in our walk-in wardrobe like a talisman, reminding us to keep fighting, because sometimes, even the bad guys turned out to be the good ones.

Without Gio and Sean, I might never have heard Elle scream and never have ventured into the alley to save the day. She would've walked around New York and returned to her tower, never knowing I existed.

The tragedy of that never failed to steal my breath at the thought of growing old without her by my side.

Her apartment had become my apartment when we moved into together two days after I was freed from jail. With me not living in my building, builders were free to move in, tear out stairs, rip out kitchens, and blitz the entire building in one go rather than piece by piece.

It was finished two months before I'd hoped, ready for new low-income renters who needed a break.

Everything we'd endured and survived had finally given us the benefit of the doubt.

We'd been tested to see if we deserved the greatest gift of all.

And luckily, we'd been found worthy.

Elle was my happily ever after.

And I was hers.

And who knew? Maybe in the future, we'd give her father and Larry what they wanted and deliver a new Belle Elle heir or heiress.

But for now...she was mine. I was hers, and we were having

far too much fun practicing.

*Speaking of which.*

Elle padded out of the bathroom with a towel on her head and another wrapped around her stunning body. Sage trotted by her heels as she always did when it was dinnertime.

I stayed where I was on the couch, flicking through a magazine on investment opportunities in Africa.

I waited until Elle gave the gray feline her ration of freshly cooked chicken then watched as she unwound her long blonde hair and tossed it over her shoulder.

Hoisting the towel higher around her breasts, she moved back toward the bedroom to continue dressing for the charity gala I was hosting with Larry.

I already wore the gold tux that was this evening's color of choice.

Elle had yet to dress.

Checking my watch, I cracked a smile.

I was the host. I shouldn't be late.

But I had a fiancée who was too delectable.

Tossing the magazine away, I followed her into the bedroom, grabbed her wrist, and spun her around. I yanked at the towel.

"Hey." She swatted me as the fabric tumbled to the floor. Her eyes glittered; her love that I'd never get used to or tired of seeing shone so damn bright. "If you kiss me, who knows how long we'll be."

I smirked. "I plan on doing a lot more than just kissing you, Elle." Biting her ear, I growled, "Get on the bed."

With a grin, she obeyed instantly, spreading her legs, acting coy and shy all at once.

The perfect woman.

My perfect woman.

Undoing my belt, I fell to my knees to worship her.

We'd get to the charity event.

Eventually.

In the meantime, we'd be together.

Just us.

We'd love. We'd argue. We'd protect. We'd evolve.

We were a family.

And that was all that fucking mattered.

# OTHER BOOKS AVAILABLE FROM PEPPER WINTERS

**Ribbon Duet**
*The Boy & His Ribbon*
*The Girl & Her Ren*

**Dollar Series**
*Pennies*
*Dollars*
*Hundreds*
*Thousands*
*Millions*

**Truth & Lies Duet**
*Crown of Lies*
*Throne of Truth*

**Pure Corruption Duet**
*Ruin & Rule*
*Sin & Suffer*

**Indebted Series**
*Debt Inheritance*
*First Debt*
*Second Debt*
*Third Debt*
*Fourth Debt*
*Final Debt*
*Indebted Epilogue*

**Monsters in the Dark Trilogy**
*Tears of Tess*
*Quintessentially Q*
*Twisted Together*
*Je Suis a Toi*

**Standalones**
*Destroyed*
*Unseen Messages*
*Can't Touch This*

---

Made in United States
Troutdale, OR
10/31/2024

24321795R00325